"You're a praying man, Bishop."

"Of course I am."

"And you believe in the resurrection, and the dead rising from their graves?"

The Bishop glanced at the pale men. "Yes I do."

Gideon grinned. "Then hosanna, brother, because this here's the rapture, and it's time for the righteous to be caught up and carried away." The pale men in the doorway lurched forward in a sudden rush, arms outstretched and mouths hanging open in a wordless hiss. The whole church erupted in chaos and screaming, and Gideon pulled out a pair of pistols. "That's what I love about Mormons!" he shouted. "Your church is full of virgins, and my church has need of some. Awful nice of you to gather 'em all up in one place." The people screamed louder, running from the pale men, but he smiled and shook his head. "No need to get all riled up, just five or six'll do me fine."

The pale men were reaching for women, and one of them already had Sophie Sutton in a grip like a vise.

other books from

PECULIAR PAGES

The Fob Bible

Out of the Mount: 19 from New Play Project

Fire in the Pasture: Twenty-first Century Mormon Poets

Dorian: A Peculiar Edition with Annotated Text & Scholarship

MONSTERS &
MORMONS

edited by
Wm Morris & Theric Jepson

PECULIAR
PAGES
EL CERRITO, CA

Monsters & Mormons
Edited by Wm Morris and Theric Jepson

Copyright 2011 Peculiar Pages
Preface copyright 2011 Terryl Givens
Introduction copyright 2011 Theric Jepson
All contributions copyright 2011 Individual contributors
Revised: May 2014

ISBN: 978-0-9827812-4-1 (paperback)
ISBN: 978-0-9827812-5-8 (ebook, all formats)
Library of Congress Control Number: 2011941727

Project concept and initiation: Wm Morris, motleyvision.org
Copyediting: Elizabeth Beeton
Book design and digitization: Elizabeth Beeton

Cover concept: Anneke Majors
Paint: Denise Gasser
Back illustration: Jake Parker
Monstropolis tag: Adam Greenwood
Layout: Lynsey Jepson
Image management: Adam K.K. Figueira

Publisher's Cataloging-In-Publication Data
(Prepared by The Donohue Group, Inc.)

    Morris, Wm (William Henry), 1972-
    Monsters & Mormons / edited by Wm Morris & Theric Jepson.

    p. : ill. ; cm.

    Issued also as an ebook.
    Summary: An anthology of science fiction, fantasy, and supernatural/occult pulp fiction, turning the 19th-century tradition of using Mormons as stock villains on its head by making the Mormons the monster slayers.
    ISBN: 978-0-9827812-4-1 (pbk.)

    1. Mormons--United States--Literary collection. 2. Monsters--United States--Literary collections. 3. Fantasy fiction, American. 4. Science fiction, American. I. Jepson, Theric. II. Title. III. Title: Monsters and Mormons

PN6071.M67 W66 2011
810.8/6/0921/289/3   2011941727

Peculiar Pages
115 Ramona Avenue | El Cerrito, CA 94530 | PeculiarPages.com

in collaboration with

B10 Mediaworx | 9754 N Ash Avenue, #204 | Kansas City, MO 64157 |
b10mediaworx.com

CONTENTS

ILLUSTRATIONS

PREFACE TO
MONSTERS & MORMONS

Terryl Givens

IN THE nineteenth century, Mormonism seemed grist for everybody's mill. Humorists like Artemus Ward and Mark Twain made hay out of polygamy; conspiracy theorists like Thomas deWitt Talmage imputed President Garfield's assassination to the Mormons; pseudo-memoirists like "Maria Ward" recounted their seduction, imprisonment, and torture at the hands of Mormon mesmerists; the Republicans jump-started their political party with a promise to expunge the Mormon "relic of barbarism"; and pulp fiction writers and serious novelists alike fueled sales with stories of bloodthirsty Danites, lecherous elders, and grief-maddened Mormon wives who murdered competitors.

Motives behind this array of representations ranged from the innocuous (audience twitters) to the malevolent (expulsion or eradication of the Mormon menace). What they all shared was the exploitation and manipulation of the Mormon identity for purposes of a self-serving agenda. Mormonism, in other words, was a pliable entity, largely fashioned according to cultural or ideological imperatives. The most remarkable evidence of the success of this enterprise is evident in an entry in the Harvard *Encyclopedia of Ethnic Groups*. Mormonism, suggests the entry under that

title, appears to be the only example in American history of an "indigenously de-
rived" ethnic community. The collective weight of generations of depictions of
Mormons as peculiar in their dress, their language, their customs – even their physiognomy – seems to have had its effect!

In the politics of representation, however, one's case is always stronger if identity
is presented as something that is revealed, rather than constructed. That is why
nineteenth-century (and some contemporary) treatments of Mormonism favor
words like "unveiling," in their titles ("exposed," "unmasked," and a dozen cognates
will also do). In doing so, authors like Eber Dudley Howe, who first employed that
term in his 1834 critique, were suggesting that the menace of Mormonism was in-
herent and objectively present in the religion, not a mere fancy of concerned Cas-
sandras. The ploy also kept Mormonism on the defensive. By insinuating that
concealment and subterfuge were Mormon strategies, their detractors dictated the
terms of the debate. And indeed, Mormons were initially willing enough to spend a
great deal of their time refuting charges and misinformation.

Parley P. Pratt was astute enough to recognize the implications buried in the language of the critics, which is why he refused to passively acquiesce to the status of clay
in the hands of rhetorical potters. When he found Mormonism unfairly depicted in
newspaperman La Roy Sunderland's 1838 series of articles, he responded quickly
and vigorously. Not hesitating to steal Howe's title, he published his own "Mormonism Unveiled: Zion's Watchman Unmasked." The turnabout was itself an important
statement. If Mormonism is to be unveiled, he was saying, we will do the unveiling
ourselves. His pamphlet was striking for its change of direction. Rather than retreat,
retrench, or correct most of Sunderland's allegations, he embraced them. Sunderland
objected to Mormons "placing themselves on a level with the Apostles." He replied
unapologetically, "This, we acknowledge, of course, for they were men of Adam's
fallen race, just like everybody else by nature ... I know of nothing but equality in the
Church of Christ."[1] Sunderland indignantly quoted the Saints as believing that they
"shall be filled with glory, and be equal with [Christ]," a paraphrase of Doctrine and
Covenants 7:33 (1835). Pratt ignored the safety of biblical precedent and instead
pushed possible metaphor into a literal reference to theosis. Indeed, he proclaimed,
"They [will] have the same knowledge that God has, [and] they will have the same
power ... Hence the propriety of calling them 'Gods, even the sons of God.'"[2] Why,
Pratt defiantly suggested, should he retreat from "this doctrine of *equality*"?

[1] PPP, *Mormonism Unveiled*, 9.

[2] PPP, *Mormonism Unveiled*, 27.

In the century and a half since Pratt's death, progress toward détente is not always easy to measure. Since the medals won by the Mormon Tabernacle Choir at the Columbian Exposition of 1893, Americans and Mormons have found a kind of peaceful accommodation. Mormon theology is still treated as largely outside the pale, but the faith group's cultural contributions are applauded and appreciated – on the stage, the dance floor, and the football field. When Mormons threaten to invade the White House, however, old fears and caricatures resurface, and the safe boundaries setting Mormonism-as-a-culture apart from Mormonism-as-a-religion threaten to disappear.

This collection could well serve as an ironic commentary on the contemporary situation, as much as it reveals a healthy coming-to-terms with the Mormon past. In a gesture reminiscent of Parley Pratt's, the contributors in this case are embracing the epithet. If there is anything monstrous or threatening about Mormonism, they seem to be saying, we will depict it – with all the silliness it deserves. "Cultural reappropriation," the editors call the device of exploiting rather than ignoring the historical associations of Mormon deviance, supernaturalism, and strangeness. Playful self-parody, I would call it. The selections range from the comic and lighthearted to the poignant and provocative. But taken together they should remind readers everywhere of a wonderful truth: humor can be the best revenge.

MONSTERS AND MORMONS AND THE DESERET BOOK

Theric Jepson

WHEN I served my mission in Korea, I learned from one of the other missionaries (whose father worked in the Church History Department) that Joseph Smith's seer stone (the one he used to translate the Book of Mormon) was in a drawer in the basement of one of the Church's museums. I've since read that seer stones became a rather popular item in early Utah – one girl even finding one to spy on her beloved as he served a mission to Hawaii. (It's true: I read it on the internet.)

"Magical objects" (if you will) have since fallen out of vogue. Aside from those Joseph dug up from the Hill Cumorah, we seem to have deliberately forgotten that part of our heritage. I guess maybe because we were constantly getting razzed for it. Still. It's in our genes.

As William Morris and I worked on *Monsters & Mormons*, reading about the holy bullets in Nathan Shumate's story or Joseph Smith's Jupiter medallion in Wilum Pugmire's chiller or the Brigham Young-blessed Bowie knife David J. West gives us, I realized I was long overdue on a family obligation.

You see, my family owns something that fits into this tradition.

My great-grandfather was a ditch digger in southern Utah. One time, while on a job, he uncovered a metal box, rather bookish in shape and dimensions. The metal is a dirty steel color, with holes along one side that my great-grandfather tied leather straps through, with the result that the box, book-like, now opens on leather hinges (which I've since replaced, but more on that later). On the "front cover" is an ovoid, the top half crosshatched and the other half plain, and two small circles on each side. If someone suggests it looks like a bee, it's hard to lose that image and, thus, once it got called the Deseret Book, the name stuck.

My grandfather (oldest son of my great-grandfather) tried to donate the Deseret Book to the Church before he passed away in the late 1970s but they didn't want it and so it stayed in his house in Nephi, Utah until my grandmother moved out about a dozen years ago. She didn't have room for it in her new apartment so I took it (along with the paper books I inherited during the move) to my BYU apartment.

I had three main criteria in picking the books I did from my grandmother's collection. First, books I thought I was likely to read myself or that related to my university studies. Second, books my grandfather had written notes in (which means I'm loaded with Milton – the man loved his *Paradise Lost* and I'm not sure he ever read the same copy twice). Third, books my grandfather had stashed papers in. For instance, I have a book about learning the abacus, in which is a newspaper clipping about a Salt Lake City accountant who had learned the abacus on his mission to Japan and who now used it in his daily work. Stuck between two other pages is a letter from this man to my grandfather, apparently in reply to a letter my grandfather had sent him regarding the article. I love that. The metal box qualified under the third criteria because when I shook it, it sounded like it was filled with paper.

I stashed it in a box with the other books and forgot about it until Lynsey and I were married two summers later and, given the teeniness of our new apartment, we started editing our things.

I came home one night to a pile of apparent junk on the kitchen table for me to go through. Mostly it was notes from classes I'd taken at Bakersfield College that I grudgingly admitted I didn't need anymore. Under those was the Deseret Book. I didn't dare open it because I was sure the leather straps would crack – maybe even turn to dust (though things don't always disappear so easily, as you'll learn later in this volume when you read "The Baby in the Bushes") – but I promised Lynsey I would pick up some fresh leather to tie it with the next day. And then I would finally open it.

As predicted, the straps practically crumbled when I opened the Deseret Book. Inside was what I had expected: papers. A small notebook, yes, but mostly loose papers.

The notebook is simply a list of names and sometimes dates – not even a long list – but striking in who's included. Apostles Anthony Ivins, Syvlester Canon [sic], and Charles Penrose. Utah governor William Spry. And none other than Joseph F. Smith, president of the Church. And then, circa 1920, it seems the notebook was closed forever.

The other papers are in several different sets of handwriting and stages of deterioration. Some are written in first person, some in third. Some I haven't been able to decipher at all because of the antiquated penmanship and/or the oxidation of the paper. I have them in archival folders now but still can't find a library or museum to take them (I should find out who has the "Mormon Golem" and ask them).

The gist of the papers is this: they borrow the Deseret Book from James Anthony Jepson, head into the wilderness, pray, open the book, and await the "Deseret Answer" – a recurring phrase.

I should pause to point out there is an alternate story to how the Deseret Book first came into our family (stories can be complicated as we'll learn later when we read Roberts and Gibson). In this version, the first wife of James Anthony Jepson, Louisa Cox Jepson (the story of how she died in my grandfather's first hours of life is filled with pathos, but now is not the time – read "The Living Wife" instead), received it from her father who had received it from his father-in-law who, in turn, received it from a "Misterios Stranger" as they left Nauvoo. In this version of the story, the "Deseret Answer" was used by said father-in-law in his capacity as head of law-and-order in Winter Quarters, where the Saints wintered before sending the first wagons to Salt Lake. (Saints are often called to bring order to the world as Birkhead, Nelson, and Stone will demonstrate.)

The journals of that man, Hosea Stout, have been published by the University of Utah and while one can "read between the lines" á la EC Buck's reworking of her ancestor's journals, I have a hard time reconciling the tales of the Deseret Book with my great-great-great-grandfather failing to mention them. Seems like he would have. Besides, everything in the box about the pre-James Anthony Jepson stories reads like hearsay. My theory is the Deseret Book only dates back to my great-grandfather's ditch-digging days, end of story.

(Speaking of digging, don't miss James Paul Crockett's story of a missionary sent to an area where the locals excel in such.)

Regardless. Whether the Deseret Book dates back to the pioneer era (as in "Pirate Gold for Brother Brigham" by Lee Allred) or is of more recent vintage, the stories in the box were compelling and I felt an obligation to try and renew the tradition.

In the stories dating to the mid-1800s (which, granted, I reject), the Deseret Book was used to protect the Saints from malevolent forces (as in Dan Wells's story). In those from the early 1900s, the Book was primarily used to promote agriculture and other food-production efforts (cf. Jaleta Clegg). Either way, the method was clear. While fasting, take the Book to a lone place, pray, and wait for the Deseret Answer to either afflict thine enemies or, I don't know, do something to the crops, I guess. Exactly *what* the Deseret Answer is and *why* the Deseret Book is required for it was never clear. I'll say this about our people: we know how to be circumspect (I think I'll plug Will Bishop here).

Anyway, last Saturday I got up before the sun (not easy, I assure you – I wasn't quite "Water Spots," but still) and drove up to Tildon Park, down onto San Pablo Dam Road, and wound my way through the East Bay hills until I found myself parked on a turnout off a small dirt road, surrounded on three sides by rusted barbed wire. I grabbed the Deseret Book and hopped over a downed fence pole and walked up a small rise where I paused to admire the view. By now the sun had crested and the first morning rays had set the Golden Gate Bridge on fire; behind me was an endless expanse of dead grass and noble oak trees and, unfortunately, Walnut Creek. Or maybe Martinez or Pleasant Hill – anyway, something less idyllic than what we see in Bailey's or Peterson's or Tuckfield's stories. Better to just face west.

I hadn't eaten since breakfast Friday morning, so my body was convinced I was plenty fasted. I opened the Book and thought about how to pray. I had decided to mix the enemies and agriculture aims and asked for a Deseret Answer to get the squirrels to leave my wife's sunflowers alone. Then I opened the Deseret Book and, for a moment, a wind rose up and rustled the papers inside and I thought I heard a soft rasping sound, and then all was silence. I sat and enjoyed the view a moment, lost in meditative pleasure regarding the beauty of the world (which reminds me now of Kate Woodbury's tale), then slowly walked back down the hill touching oaks as I went, got in the car and drove home, eating an old Starburst from my cup-holder on the way.

As I pulled into the driveway, Lynsey came running out of the house, followed by our kids. I stopped without driving down to the garage and climbed out.

"What's up?"

She just pointed down to the end of the driveway where the sunflowers' heavy heads leaned over the edge of the driveway. It took me a while to understand. Then I saw them: the bodies of three squirrels.

I walked up to them, and crouched down to inspect their bloated, misshapen bodies.

"What happened?"

What happened was, as the kids were eating cereal they heard a loud roaring buzz. They ran to the front room and looked out the window and started yelling, which got Lynsey out of bed.

A massive swarm of bees was crawling over the windows, blocking the view, and the roar of their collective buzz made it hard for Lynsey and the kids to even talk with each other.

Then, just as suddenly, the bees were gone. Lynsey kept everyone inside for ten minutes and then they went out and found the squirrels. An unpleasant discovery to be sure. Rather like what Graham Bradley's heroes find.

I sat on the cement and looked at the closest squirrel. His face was bloated, yet, somehow, his lips were drawn back into a grotesque smile. A viscous muck was slowly creeping down from one eye.

The kids' excited chatter ceased and Lynsey told me to come inside and finish the eggs, but I stayed sitting, looking.

I realized I was holding the Deseret Book, and I opened it, pulled out the note-books.

Recordkeeping – storytelling – is important to us Mormons. Consider the stories by Greenwood, Martindale, Jovan, Sampson, Peck. We keep our stories. We own our stories.

So I ripped a piece of paper from my Moleskine, wrote an abbreviated version of my tale, and added it to the others.

In short? I went fasting to a lone place with my great-grandfather's Book, I prayed, and I opened the Book.

And I received my Answer.

You know, it seems in our era most people of faith believe only in that which is fully ethereal. And even to Mormons, in everyday life, certain things are to stay in heaven and out of our everyday lives.

But sometimes the weird and the unexpected and the unexplainable can happen (ask Terrance V. McArthur) and faith breaks out of the box we try to keep it in. And that can make us uncomfortable. I don't want angels showing up in my bedroom. That would cramp my style.

But Mormons, ultimately, believe in a world that's more complicated than what we see every day as we drive down the road. And whether any story, from this introduction to the bios at the end, is fully true or fully fictional, stories allow us to take the idea of faith out of the box we keep it locked in. We can pull it out, play with it, read the stories, ask ourselves questions, and have a rollicking good time. Because while what is True mattereth much, what is possible must also matter. At least a bit.

These stories push the idea of the possible. Sometimes in silly ways, sometimes in frightening ways, sometimes in bewildering ways, sometimes in monstrous ways. But always in ways that are Mormon.

We're no longer the monsters we were in the early days of pulp.

But the world still has monsters. And who better to fight them than me and you and the wives of Erasmus?

So strap on your favorite six-shooter or particle annihilator or bullwhip and let's save the world.

Ole Port's waiting for us.

OTHER DUTIES

Nathan Shumate

THE VOICE on the other end of the telephone line overflowed with nervousness and apology. "Hi – Bishop Evenson? This is – My name is Steve Roundy, from the West Point Fourteenth Ward. I'm really sorry to bother you so late, but I heard that you're the agent bishop for stuff like this ... "

"I am." Norman Evenson rubbed the gummy stuff from the inside corners of his eyes with the thumb and forefinger of his other hand. He could see his wife Miriam up on one elbow watching him. Beyond her, the digital clock read "1:32 a.m." in glowing green. He gestured to her to go back to sleep and stood up, taking the phone with him as he walked out of the bedroom toward his home office.

"Tell me what the problem is," Norman said as he flipped on the light and squinted.

It took a little over ten minutes for Norman to get from Brother Roundy the salient details. After he hung up, he put on the white shirt, tie, and Dockers he kept in his office so he could get dressed at odd hours without waking Miriam. He avoided his two-piece suits for matters like this; not only were they all dry-clean only, but their crotches tended to split out if things got active. When the tie was knotted, he called his first counselor, Brant DeSalle.

"Sorry to wake you, Brant," Norman said, the phone cradled in his neck as he slipped on his shoes. "We've got a call to handle."

"Oh. Mercy." Norman could hear the lag as Brant's sleepy brain caught up to his words. "I don't need to shave, do I?"

"I'm not going to. Give Brother Wills a call and have him meet us ... Wait, he's still out of town, isn't he?"

"Baby blessing up in Idaho, back Thursday," Brant said.

"Right. Don't worry about it then. I'll see you at the church in fifteen minutes."

After he hung up and tied his shoes, Norman flipped back through his stake calendar. It was the first week of February; he had only been the agent bishop since the start of the year, and this was only their third real call. Maybe he could call the previous agent bishop to put together the needed quorum.

There was no answer at Bishop Stewart's home number, so he called his cell phone. It took three rings for him to pick up.

"Bishop Stewart, this is Bishop Evenson. Sorry to call at this hour, but we got an emergency call and my second counselor is out of town. I wonder if you can help us out."

"Yeah, I'm in Barbados on a cruise ship," said Bishop Stewart.

"Oh. Sorry to bother you."

"Best of luck, though."

Norman ended the call and paged again through the directory. The next person in the ward who held priesthood keys was Kyle McMullin, who had come back from his mission in May, gotten married in November, and been called as the elders quorum president in December. Norman doubted that the high councilor had even given Kyle's presidency any training yet on the full scope of the agent ward's duties. But that was the way the line of authority ran.

He dialed Kyle's number. "G'day," said a groggy voice. Norman smiled. Sometimes when caught off guard, Kyle slipped back into the accent he had picked up on his mission in Australia.

"President McMullin, this is the Bishop. Sorry to wake you, but I need your help."

NORMAN got to the bishop's office before Brother DeSalle or President McMullin. He had time to kneel and pray in silence; then he unlocked his desk and reached past the calling forms and welfare carbons in their hanging folders to the locked box at the bottom of the drawer. He had just set it on the top of his desk when Brother DeSalle entered, followed by the elders quorum president, who was still tying his tie.

"Thank you, brethren," Norman said. "I hope we can get this handled quickly." He looked at Kyle's sleepy, confused face. "President McMullin, I think I need to explain a few things to you ... "

Norman was right; Kyle hadn't been trained on any of this, and sat stunned as Norman sketched in their extra duties.

"So ... " Kyle said, trying to use his missionary *restate* skills to wrap his mind around the situation. " ... You're the agent bishop for supernatural stuff?"

Norman nodded. "'Paranormal and Occult.' Just since January. It's an annual rotation through the local stakes in northern Davis County. That makes our entire ward the agent ward, so in Brother Wills's absence, the duty falls to you."

"Wow." Kyle swallowed. "Should I have, like, brought my consecrated oil?"

"We have plenty." Norman inserted a key from his ring of church keys into the lock on the front of the box. "And some other things."

In the velvet-lined tray inside was a set of three gold-colored medallions on leather thongs. Norman took them out and handed one each to DeSalle and Kyle. DeSalle slipped his on over his head; Kyle watched him and followed suit. Norman put on his own and then removed from the same tray three spritzer bottles with short straps attached. He passed them around.

"As much oil as you'll need."

DeSalle leaned over to Kyle. "When you need to use it, put the strap around your wrist. Oil on your hands gets slippery. You don't want that. Trust me, I know."

"You guys have done this before?" Kyle asked.

"Yes, but don't ask us about it," Norman said. "It's confidential, just like a disciplinary council."

Norman pulled out the velvet-lined tray. Beneath it was another tray, this one containing a long-barreled six-shooter of burnished silvery steel, with cream-colored porcelain grips and accents. Kyle gaped at the gun but said nothing.

A small wooden box also nestled in the tray contained cartridges, and Norman began loading the gun. The bullets weren't metallic; they looked like clay, and on each there were inscribed tiny symbols. To Norman they looked like the "Book of Mormon Egyptian" characters on the souvenir bricks one bought in Nauvoo, but he was no expert; they could have been old-world Egyptian, or Hebrew, or even Adamic for all he knew.

"We forgot to replenish our supply of these after our last time out," Norman said. "Remind me to have one of the clerks order some more on Sunday."

"Will do," DeSalle said.

Norman snapped the revolver's cylinder shut. "Well, brethren," he said, "I think a prayer is in order." He lowered himself to his knees, and the other two men did likewise.

THEY TOOK Norman's Kia and drove in silence. The suburban regularity of Clinton faltered as they drove west, with clumped developments alternating with horse pastures and hay fields. The last snowfall had been a week before, but cold daytime temperatures had kept it powdery, and in spots it had drifted in half-hearted streaks across the blacktop.

A couple of miles after they passed the last streetlight, DeSalle in the passenger seat checked a reflective street sign on their right against the sticky note that Norman had given him. "Turn here," he said, "and then the second left, first house on the right."

Norman turned just after a sign that read, "CASTLEVIEW MEADOWS PHASE I COMING SOON – RESERVE YOUR LOT NOW!" Following DeSalle's directions, he pulled in by a thirty-year-old split-level that had been built on a large country lot. The night sky was punctuated with clouds, and once the headlights were off, Norman could see a long back yard separating the house from a horse barn, and fence posts beyond that marking a horse pasture.

They stepped out of the Kia in their parkas; Kyle also wore a cap with flaps down over his ears. As they started trudging toward the house, the front door popped open and out came a man with a camo hunting jacket thrown on over a sweatshirt and sweatpants.

"Oh, thank God!" he said. "I mean – I'm Steve Roundy. Bishop ... ?"

Norman waved to show which one he was. "I'm Bishop Evenson. When did this all start, again?"

Steve stuck his bare hands in his pocket. His tennis shoes were untied, and his feet shifted in the cold.

"Last night, I guess. I mean, Amy said there was something wrong – that's my daughter – she said for a couple of weeks that something was wrong, but, you know ... "

"Is your daughter here?"

"No. My wife took both kids into Ogden to her mother's house, right about when I called you."

Norman nodded. "So what have you seen?"

"Well, what I heard first was the horses ... Do you want to come inside?"

Kyle started moving toward the house, but Norman shook his head. "We ought to go right to work."

"Right." Steve led the way around the house, and they trudged in single file toward the horse barn. "Well, as I said on the phone, we heard something, Amy and I, we heard something from the barn last night. The horses were noisy, whinnying and dancing around. We went out after dinner, and we couldn't see anything wrong, so we just left them to settle down on their own. But they kept getting noisier. Finally, around midnight, we were worried and couldn't sleep, so I went out again. The horses were screaming by this point like there was a rattler in their stalls or something, so I went in, and before I reached the light switch I saw ... "

Steve stopped, and the other three stopped behind him. They were in the back yard now, closer to the barn than the house, on a well-worn path through the snow.

" ... eyes. I saw eyes, red and glowing. Like in the movies. I've never seen things like that for real, though. It wasn't like cat's eyes reflecting – these were glowing like hot coals. And a voice ... I don't know what it said, but it rumbled so low I could feel it in the soles of my feet, inside my boots. That's when I ran back to the house, Nicole bundled up the kids, and I called the bishop, and he gave me your number."

Norman looked at the barn, sturdy and unpainted. There were two glass windows on this side; nothing showed through them but darkness.

"Is that a new development going in over there, Brother Roundy?"

It took Steve a second to catch up to the change of subject. "Uh, yeah. They broke ground and started laying out lots in the fall. Used to be an alfalfa field. Why?"

Instead of answering the question, Norman asked, "How many horses do you have?"

"Two," Steve said. "Chaser and Star."

"They're quiet now."

"I know. They got quiet sometime after I got inside. After I called you, I stuck my head out to hear, and I couldn't hear anything."

Norman nodded.

"Well, let's get this started."

He raised his arm to the square.

"By the power of the Holy Melchi – "

He broke off as one barn window shattered and something sailed out, whirling end over end. Norman leaped to the side; it landed roughly where he had been. It was a horse's head, white with a black patch between the wide-open eyes. The steaming neck was severed messily, like it had been taken off with a chainsaw. Norman felt wet spots on his pants and looked down. Blood from the neck had splattered up his pant leg as it flew through the air. The hot blood immediately turned cold.

Behind him, Kyle breathed, "Oh, man ... "

Steve swallowed. "That's Star," he said. His voice sounded like he was trying to hold back a sneeze.

Norman unzipped his parka to give him clear access to the gun in his belt. "Brother Roundy, once we go in the door, where is the light switch?"

Steve was still staring at the horse's head on the snow. "To your left, when you go in. On the stud, about three feet in."

Norman looked back over his shoulder. DeSalle watched him, his lips together in a thin line. Kyle's eyes kept returning to the horse's head, but he didn't seem to be hyperventilating or trembling.

"Brother Roundy, you stay here and listen for us." He nodded to the other two. "Let's go."

They approached the barn quietly, but didn't bother trying to be sneaky; whatever was inside obviously knew they were here. A couple of times Norman thought he heard breaths or snorts. The other horse? It could still be alive; the head that was thrown out at them had obviously been alive recently enough for the blood to be fresh.

"Oil out," he murmured to the other two.

He heard DeSalle tell Kyle, "Put it in your left hand so you can raise your right arm to the square."

"Oh. Got it."

At the barn's double doors they stopped. Norman's nose had begun to run, and he wiped it quickly on the back of his sleeve. He noticed that Kyle had put his ear-flaps up.

Norman waved DeSalle to the left side of the double door. "Okay," he said. "One, two ... "

On "three," DeSalle yanked the door open, and Norman jumped inside, fumbling for the light switch. He heard a snuffling sound, and then drowning it out was a deep rumble, like an asthmatic whale. Then the bare lights bulbs came on.

At the far end of the barn, beside the horse stalls, was a monstrous humanoid figure, probably topping ten feet. At first glance, it was an articulated human skeleton. At second glance it wasn't terribly human, even allowing for the size; swept-back spines grew out of its skull and down its back, and the orbital sockets in its face were drawn triangular into a scowl instead of showing the round-eyed surprise of a human skull. On third glance, it was more than just a skeleton; its bones were held together by a thin layer of red meat and glistening tendons as if it had been recently and deeply flayed. Norman saw on the floor behind it a pile of moist, bloody bones, and understood: the skeleton hadn't recently lost flesh, it had recently gained it from the slaughtered horse.

Where was the other horse? The stall doors were open. One was empty; the other – yes, the horse was on its side on the straw, shuddering. Did horses faint? This one might have.

The skeletal thing watched Norman with its eyeless eyes, a glottal clicking or purring coming from its throat. Norman had seen the movie *Predator* once on TV; it sounded like that.

"Brethren," he whispered loudly, and DeSalle and Kyle edged into the barn, their eyes on the skeleton. Even without eyes in its sockets, Norman could sense its attention focusing on each of them in turn.

It spoke. Its voice vibrated like a passing freight train; the consonants were thick and grating. Norman couldn't understand the words, but he felt the menace in them. They were being warned.

"Okay," he said to the others, keeping his voice to a whisper. It probably couldn't understand them any better than they could understand it, but he didn't want to spur it to action. "We're going to try to corner it in the empty stall where I can get a good shot at it. Oil ready? Go!"

The three men spread out, advancing at the skeleton with their spray bottles held up. Norman could sense surprise from the thing as he spritzed out a fine mist of consecrated oil in its direction, surprise that turned into malice. It started backing up as the three advanced. Then it whirled and leaped into the stall, and from there it climbed up the wall, its long, partially fleshed limbs sure and spidery. Norman hadn't been expecting that.

It easily reached the top of the barn's space where beams and girders held up the peaked roof in shadows that the light bulbs barely reached. They craned their necks to keep it in sight as it clambered as fast as a man can run. Norman could tell it was bearing down on him specifically, for it had identified him as the leader. It leaned down suddenly and raked a clawed hand at him. Norman dove to the side to avoid the long fingers. He rolled over a hay bale awkwardly and landed hard on his left shoulder.

"Hey!" Kyle shouted, his voice breaking. He dashed forward and spritzed his oil on the still grasping arm. The thing shrieked like rusty metal being dragged across concrete and pulled back its limbs.

Kyle was still aiming his oil at the roof while DeSalle helped Norman to his feet. "Bishop?"

"I'm all right. Just clumsy."

The skeleton scrambled back and forth, glaring at them from its eyeless face, with an agility that Norman wouldn't have expected from an eleven-foot skeleton crawling through the crosspieces of a barn roof. There was no way he could get a clear shot at it. He glanced behind them; the barn door stood a few feet open as they had left it.

"Kyle," he said, "go close the door."

"Maybe we ought to call the hotline," said DeSalle.

"You know Salt Lake won't get any specialists here before dawn," Norman said. "Now that we've got it angry, who knows how much damage it'd do before then?"

Kyle got the door closed and he sprayed the handles with oil for good measure. The thing growled.

"All right, I have a plan," Norman said. "You two go back by the door."

DeSalle walked backwards to where Kyle was already standing. Norman side-walked to the opposite end of the barn by the stalls. The thing above them hissed and scratched at the beams.

Norman carefully stowed his bottle of oil in his pocket. Then he grasped the medallion around his neck and pulled it off over his head. He held it a moment so its golden glint could catch the light, then tossed it in the straw on the floor, only a few feet in front of him.

"Bishop!" shouted DeSalle. "What are you doing?!"

The skeletal thing watched Norman intently. Then, as if drawn by an urge it couldn't control, it started down from the roof like a spider examining something caught in its web.

Norman stood empty-handed with his arms well away from his body, feeling like a gunfighter in an old Western. There was a naked place around his neck where the medallion should be.

Closer, just a little closer ...

The thing paused, clinging to the wall and looking down at Norman. Then with a burst of speed it dropped to the floor in a crouch and launched itself in his direction on all fours.

"Arms to the square!" Norman yelled. He did so himself, drawing the gun from his belt with his left hand. His left shoulder ached where it had hit the floor, but the thing was close enough that his bad aim wouldn't matter.

"By the power of – " he started as he pulled the trigger. The rest of his words were lost in a sound like a pressurized airplane cabin being breached. There was no recoil from the gun; as far as Norman could tell, the clay bullets always vaporized into dust instead of going anywhere. But the thing shrieked and recoiled like it had been hit by a cannonball. It fell backward, folding at odd angles, and Norman could see its stolen flesh start to curl off before it even hit the floor. The bones that hit the floor were lifeless and inert.

He motioned to DeSalle and Kyle to come close and they did so, their oil held at the ready. Norman nudged the skull with his boot; it was now just a pile of gargantuan bones, surrounded by slivers of meat that sloughed off it and soaked the straw.

"It's a Gadianton," he said. "Brigham Young said that the Wasatch Front was thick with their spirits. I'm guessing that the heavy machinery for that subdivision disturbed it, and then once the winter solstice freed it, it started to wander."

"And the ... meat?" said Kyle.

"Gadiantons are robbers, always have been," said DeSalle. "This one stole flesh to clothe itself." DeSalle looked up at Norman, comprehension settling in his eyes. "And you knew that a robber would go for the gold. That's why you took off your medallion – as bait."

"Actually," said Norman, "I think it saw I was unguarded and decided to come for me. One way or another, though, it worked."

"That ... was ... *cool!*" Kyle exclaimed. "It was so awesome! Chew on *that* Priesthood, you Son of Perdition!"

Norman looked at DeSalle. "I guess that's better than the reaction Brother Wills had the first time."

WHEN they trudged back out of the barn, Steve was standing where they had left him on the path, his bare hands stuck under the arms of his coat for warmth, shifting from foot to foot.

"Is – did you – "

Norman nodded. "Taken care of. Your other horse is alive, but I don't know about injuries."

"Thank you. Thank you!" Steve grabbed Norman's hand and shook it ferociously.

"I can provide a letter for your insurance, but it'll have to be vague; it might not be helpful. Give me a call after you talk to your carrier."

"I will! I will – Thank you!"

Norman turned to DeSalle and Kyle, who was grinning from ear to ear. "If I get you both the paperwork tomorrow night – or tonight, I guess – can you have it finished by Sunday? We're supposed to turn it in to the Presiding Bishopric's Office within a week."

DeSalle nodded. Kyle said, "Can do!"

"And cleanup?" DeSalle said.

"The PBO will want the bones, too," Norman said. "I know just the person."

He pulled out his phone and scrolled through to a stored number. After two rings, he said, "Sister Cotter, this is Bishop Evenson. I'm sorry to bother you so late, but you're the agent Relief Society president in these cases ... "

THE LIVING WIFE

Emily Milner

I MARRIED Nathaniel Bitner in the Logan temple six days after I met him. I had no family present but Sister Hansen, who took me in after my parents died. "No crazy talking, now," Sister Hansen told me. "He doesn't know about you yet, and this might be my only, that is, your only chance."

"Don't worry," I told her. "I won't say a thing." The temple spirits floated around, following the patrons and workers. I stared at them. So many spirits, and so busy. I said nothing, though, because talk of spirits was the crazy speech Sister Hansen had warned me against. So I held my tongue and smiled at her.

"That's a good girl, Zina," she said. "I want you to be happy." And she did, in her own way. She witnessed our sealing and presented me with the tattered quilt I'd always slept under and a two-day-old loaf of bread. "You can keep them shoes I bought for you last spring, too," she said.

Nathaniel and I began the ten days' drive back to Star Valley, up through Montpelier and into Fairview, where he raised cattle. He brought back a winter's worth of supplies in his wagon. And a wife. Me. It was good to be alone with him, to have him and me and no ghosts around. Few spirits were bound to the road, and the ones that were ignored me. I felt an unfamiliar peace, the quiet of my own thoughts and Nathaniel's occasional conversation. I had spent my entire life listening to the spirits tied to Sister Hansen's home: Clarence Hansen, her dead husband. Sean Grady, a

traveling tinsmith who happened to die there. I had never known such calm in my life as the stillness of this road.

Nathaniel whispered to the horses as he rubbed them down at night. He cooked me breakfast in the mornings. He was kind with me, and gentle.

Our last day's journey, he drove the team one-handed, the other arm around my shoulders. The closer we drew to Star Valley, though, the more fidgety he became. "I should have told you this before," he said finally. "It won't make no difference, but I should have told you."

"What is it?" I said. I moved my hand down from his leg to the bench. A splinter stung my palm.

"I was married before. Two times."

I shrugged his arm away and stuck my splintered hand in my mouth. "You're supposed to tell the next wife you've got others before you go courting," I said.

"No, not like that," said Nathaniel. "I'm not trying to live the Principle. Some do, but that's not me. No, my wives both died. You're the only wife I've got alive."

"Where did they die?"

"At home. In Fairview."

I never had worked out how the living world tethered its ghosts in one spot. Clarence Hansen died while buying store merchandise in Salt Lake. I knew he'd died before Sister Hansen found out, because I saw his ghost in the store, behind the counter, trying to dicker with a customer. But the tinsmith's spirit stayed at the Hansens' where he had died instead of returning home. Perhaps Nathaniel's wives would be bound someplace else. I could hope.

I smiled, to make things seem right. "Well, they're gone now," I said. "So it's just us."

"That's right," he said. "Just us."

We arrived at the hill entering Star Valley. The fields spread out all yellow, dotted with haystacks. "It's beautiful," I said. There were bound to be some surprises in marrying a man I'd known only six days. I would not let the dead wives, whose ghosts I might never even meet, taint the moment right now.

"They were good women, both of them," Nathaniel continued. "Agnes and Grace. Agnes loved to cook, and everyone knew her by her bread and her pie crust. Grace saved every bit of fabric and sewed them all. She could make a stack of scraps into a perfect quilt top. They were both women to speak their minds."

"Well, I am one to speak up too," I said. "So it's a good thing you're used to that." I laughed a little. "Did you notice those clouds all pillowed up over there?"

"You would have liked them."

"I'm sure I would have," I said finally, since he would not be distracted by the sky. I was determined not to regret marrying Nathaniel, in spite of his previous wives. If I hadn't married him I would have been stuck another winter with the ghost of Clarence Hansen telling me every day I'd never be married. "Your ears stick out too much, your face is horsey, and you talk way too much for a woman," he always said. "No one wants that in a first wife, and since the Manifesto's done away with the Principle, no one will want you for a fifth wife either." Clarence Hansen's voice was the background to my day. No matter what lay ahead, how could I regret escaping that?

We arrived at the house. It was painted white, with a wide front porch, and settled at the base of a low hill. Two stories, with a front parlor and a piano, an iron cookstove in the kitchen, and three bedrooms upstairs. A big, empty house. I called "Hello?" when I entered, and the sound seemed to echo off the kitchen's stone floor.

Nathaniel tended the horses, and I unpacked the winter supplies. I stepped down the stairs into the cellar holding a fifty-pound bag of beans. It smelled like damp dirt, cold and musty. I had settled the beans into a corner when I saw Nathaniel's wives standing next to some onions.

"I saw them drive up," said the first one. "I think it's best if we stay down here for a while." She was pretty, her nose pert and smooth, her eyes big.

"Agnes," the other one said, "we don't need to hide like this. It's not like they know we're here." That must be Grace. They stood together. They talked as though they got along pretty well. That was a mercy. I hated listening to ghosts bicker.

I returned to the cellar with a bag of potatoes, settling it right through Agnes's legs. Spirits hate that. She shuddered and moved. I puttered around, adjusting things, so I could listen.

"See?" Grace said. "She doesn't even know we're alive."

"We're not alive," Agnes said. "But if we were, and Nathaniel went away and brought home a third wife, what would we do?"

"Not hide in the cellar."

"True. But neither would we go out to welcome her right off. We'd give her some space, let her get adjusted. Stay low for a couple of weeks first. Be polite."

"You do that. But I hate the cellar and I'm going where I please."

"Grace. Think of when you first married Nathaniel. Would you have liked to think I was there the whole time, watching you?"

"I'll stay down here tonight, but I'm coming up tomorrow, no matter what you say. I hate it down here. I can't stand watching the spiders skitter around and not being able to shoo them away. And he's been happy enough since I died. He doesn't need another woman."

I nearly shouted out, "Yes he does!" but held back just in time. So Grace would be snooping on me from the start, and Agnes would follow after a couple of weeks. I sighed. Both of them started, and then laughed. "Just as if she heard us," Agnes said.

In the dim light they saw mostly shadows, which saved me this time. I was used to ignoring Clarence Hansen's repetitious rants, and I ought to be able to ignore Agnes and Grace too. But I also wanted to listen to them, find out who they were, these pretty women Nathaniel had married before me. It was hard to listen well while feigning deafness.

Nathaniel returned from the barn and we finished unloading the wagon together. He walked down to the cellar and passed right by Agnes and Grace. He didn't shiver, or pause, or notice them at all. He had no idea they were close enough to breathe on. For all he knew, I was the only wife there.

We ate a late supper, bread and milk, in the kitchen by candlelight. The light flickered off the polished fittings on the cookstove. He kept the house clean, almost sterile.

"I like the house," I said. "I didn't know what to expect. It seems so spacious."

Nathaniel laughed. "What you mean is it's too big for a widower."

"Maybe it is. But I like it all the same."

"I meant to have a large family. I planned for a lot of children. There were supposed to be boys whittling by the firelight right now, and a little girl stitching on her first sampler. I came into an inheritance and I used it to build the house me and all my children would live in."

"Life doesn't always turn out the way you planned."

"It's big and empty. Just me and the voices in my head." The window above the kitchen table was open, exposed to the cold night air. I stood and shut it, and moved my chair next to Nathaniel's, so that we sat side by side.

"I'm here now," I said, holding his hand. "And I'm staying here. So we can rattle around in this big house together."

He smiled at me. "Welcome home, Zina," he said.

I SPENT several days going about chores. Grace followed me, keeping up a running commentary. "Did you make that dress yourself? It's a bit shabby. I'm surprised you don't have better wedding clothes."

I didn't speak the answer, which was yes, I made it; yes, it's shabby; and no, Sister Hansen didn't want me to have better wedding clothes, so I didn't. "Be grateful for what you've got," she always told me. "You're lucky I can afford to keep you."

I went outside to chop wood, and Grace followed.

"Why on earth did he propose to you?" she said. "I thought he still pined away for me. It's only been a year and a half since I died."

I don't know why he proposed, I thought. Why he'd single out a plain girl like me to marry. Bishop Fowler always said God knows our thoughts and hears our prayers, and maybe God looked down on me in mercy that day. Nothing I did or wore or said could have bewitched him. But I did have a little pride. I was about to turn him down, because it was too fast. Just six days from when he walked into the store till when he asked an astonished Sister Hansen for my hand. Then I heard a small voice tell me different. *Marry him*, the Holy Spirit whispered. *You deserve some joy.* So I did.

I had always heard the Holy Ghost clear enough, maybe a result of listening to spirits all my life. But the still small voice forgot to mention that if I married Nathaniel I'd only be trading one set of ghosts for another: Clarence Hansen for Grace and Agnes.

"You're clumsy too," Grace added, "you're about to trip on that branch."

I avoided the branch. But there was no way to avoid her. I spent several days listening to Grace's prattle. It always baffled me how no one could hear the dead but me, because they seemed so loud.

I wanted Nathaniel to talk about his wives a little more, but he said nothing. His forbearance as he tried to eat my cooking impressed me, though. Sister Hansen had never taught me to cook much beyond pancakes.

I made rocklike beans for dinner one night, crunchy and half-burned. I was just serving them when Agnes decided to emerge from the cellar for the first time. Ghosts can't smell, but there's nothing wrong with their vision.

"They're burned," Agnes said. She sounded shocked, wounded on Nathaniel's behalf.

"These beans, they have great flavor," Nathaniel said, crunching down.

I wanted to say, *You don't have to lie about it*, but I nodded instead. "Thanks."

"Why didn't he marry someone who knew how to cook?" Agnes said. "He's hungry after a long day, he needs to eat. She'll starve him!"

"Agnes, hush," said Grace. "You know not everyone can cook as well as you."

"I forgot to set them out to soak, and then I boiled them too hard," I said. "But I won't forget again." I nearly directed this last bit at Agnes, and then remembered that I wasn't supposed to be listening to her.

"Poor Nathaniel," Agnes said. "Really, he ought to have done better. Her ears stick out so far, and her chin is so weak that you'd think she would have developed some compensating skills."

"She doesn't sew well either," Grace said. "Look at the muddled job she did with that tear in his shirt."

I bit my tongue. Sister Hansen didn't like me in the kitchen. I had other jobs to do. I kept our woodpile stocked, and I kept the store running. As for compensating skills in my marriage, the best ones were not something Agnes would ever be privy to. But I stood up and said, "I need some air. Feels stuffy in here." I walked through Agnes on my way to the porch, and she yelped.

I sat on the porch swing holding my plate of beans. I picked at them with a fork. Worse than eating burned beans, and they were pretty bad, was knowing that both ghosts of my husband's dead wives despised me.

Nathaniel followed me. I wasn't sure I could bear his pity right now, and he didn't know the half of it.

"Don't cry," he said. "It's only beans. I'm not gonna die from some bad beans."

I sat there and cried for a minute anyway. He took out his handkerchief and wiped my face off.

"Your other wives," I said. "You said they knew how to cook well, especially that Agnes."

"Now listen, Zina. You can't go thinking about them every time this happens. I sure don't."

Agnes and Grace had followed him out. "Did you hear that?" Grace said. "He doesn't think about us!"

"He doesn't remember my cooking," Agnes said. "How can he not remember my cooking when he eats that slop?" She went up to his ear and yelled, "I NEVER IN MY LIFE WOULD SERVE YOU BEANS LIKE THAT. YOU ATE ONLY THE BEST WITH ME."

She kept yelling. I cried harder.

"Not that I didn't love them," Nathaniel went on, and Agnes hushed. "But you're you and they were who they were, and you'll learn. And maybe," he hesitated, then went on, "maybe you can channel their talents somehow. Maybe the spirit of Agnes's cooking lives on in the kitchen, and she'll teach you things, without you even knowing."

I didn't want to tell him that Agnes's ghost was already there and I would never ask her for cooking lessons. "I don't think I'll ever get it," I said. "We'll starve this winter."

"Come on," he said. "You're being silly. You're all tired out. I'll clean up, you go get ready for bed."

He pulled me up toward him and let me cry more all down his shirt. I saw Agnes and Grace over his shoulder. Both of them looked hungry, like they wanted to be me. I settled into his arms a little more and took one more glance at the longing ghost wives. They watched as Nathaniel kissed me. It felt good to be alive.

"Looks like they may need privacy," Grace said.

"Men," Agnes said.

"Don't blame Nathaniel. That hussy's got him wrapped around her little finger."

"I'll go clean the kitchen," Nathaniel said finally.

"Just soak the bean pan. I'll clean it tomorrow. There's no way that will come clean without a good hour of scrubbing."

I went upstairs to our room, which overlooked the back pasture. The moon peeked out from the hills. I washed my face, changed to my nightgown, and went for a hot brick to warm up the bed. When I returned I found Grace there.

"I know you can't hear me," she said. "But I wanted to tell you about this quilt. This piece, this green one here, that came from the dress I wore to Agnes's funeral. She was going to have a baby, you see, and then she lost the baby, and she died. But I met Nathaniel that day. He looked so sad. He really loved her. He needed someone to take care of him after she died, and that was me."

I sat down at the dressing table to ignore her, and let down my hair for brushing. A hundred strokes a night.

"And this piece is from one of Agnes's dresses. Nathaniel saved them. I couldn't bear to wear them, but I turned them into quilts. That was the dress she wore to the temple, when they drove to Logan and got sealed."

Thirty-one, thirty-two, thirty-three. Not listening, not paying any attention.

Nathaniel came up. "You ready?" he said. I was ready. Thirty-six strokes was enough for me. We climbed in bed and blew out the candle.

But Grace didn't leave. She stayed, still talking about the quilt. "This piece on the edge is from cloth I bought to make for my own baby clothes," she said. "I had almost finished the quilt top, and there was a bit of space left."

Nathaniel held me close and starting kissing my neck.

"You are sleeping," Grace whispered, "under a quilt I made. You're kissing him beneath scraps of the dress I wore on the day I met him. You might even be making babies right near the cloth of the baby blanket that I made. You are – "

There was no peace, even when I pretended not to see or hear. I could not abide it any longer.

"Nathaniel!" I said.

He started back. "What?"

"I am about to die of thirst. Could you go get me some water?"

"Water's on the dresser," he said, bending towards me again.

"But the cup's all dirty. I'll be right here when you return. Please?"

He sighed and went. As soon as I heard his footsteps creak on the last stair I turned to Grace.

"You leave right now," I said. "Out!"

"You do see me," she said. "I knew it. Agnes didn't believe me, but I could tell you were different, so she said I should test you and be sure."

"She put you up to this! I thought she was the one with more respect. Well, I see you and I want you out. If we were all three of us alive would you dare be in here? You leave and don't you ever come into this room again."

"How are you going to stop me? I could stay here all night, every night, if I chose."

"I'll tear this quilt," I said. "I will rip it and all your memories. I'll burn it if I have to. You leave me alone."

"You wouldn't dare," said Grace. She went to grab the quilt but her hands passed right through it.

"Be still, now, Grace," Agnes said, floating in. "Zina, I would have come and gotten her any second now."

"Oh really?"

"But you should have told us," Agnes said. "Weeks ago, when we first met." She eyed me, and I wondered if she was thinking about my walking right through her and setting potatoes down through her legs.

"What was I supposed to say?" I said. "Surely you haven't met anyone else who could see you all the time."

"No," Agnes said, as Nathaniel walked in, holding my glass of water. "But you should have let us know anyway." She looked over at Nathaniel. "I'll be going now," she said, floating out the door. "Come, Grace."

Grace followed. "Be careful with that quilt," she said. I stuck out my tongue at her.

Nathaniel handed me the water. "It's good water up here in Star Valley," he said. "Spring water, not well." The full moon shone through the window, and he looked bashful and maybe a little scared of me, this third wife who banished him from our bed to get her a glass of water.

I was grateful he wasn't angry. I took a sip of the water and set the glass down. I folded the quilt over itself to the foot of our bed. "The water's delicious," I said. "And I believe that quilt was a little too warm. In fact, I feel generally overheated." I loosened the tie around the neck of my nightgown. "Can you help me?" I asked.

He obliged.

"WE HAVEN'T been properly introduced," Agnes said the next morning. I scrubbed the burned beans out of the pot. She and Grace stood beside me. "Last night doesn't count. We're both sorry, we really are, but it was the best way to tell if you could see us. I'm Agnes Bitner, Nathaniel's first wife, and it's a pleasure to meet you, Zina. I hope we'll get on real well."

Last night counted for plenty. I said nothing. The beans stuck to the pot like they'd been forged a part of it. I could be scrubbing all day long, and it would make no difference. But if I focused on the beans enough, maybe the ghosts would go away.

"I can teach you to make great beans," Agnes tried again.

I scrubbed harder.

Grace said, "You can't pretend you don't see us anymore. You can't stand there scrubbing like we're not talking to you. It's bad enough us being here without Nathaniel knowing."

Still silent. I wished I'd never spoken up last night. Grace would have left eventually if I had stayed quiet a little longer.

Agnes gave up and went someplace else, but Grace followed me around the entire morning, while I tidied and fed the chickens and chopped rhubarb. "Talk to me, talk to me, talk to me," she said over and over until I had a headache. It was worse than the ghost of Clarence Hansen had ever been.

"Hush!" I told her, finally.

She smirked. "Knew I could get you to talk."

"Let me be clear," I said. "I hate ghosts, I hate seeing them when no one else does, I hate the way they try to interfere in my life. I don't want to talk to you again, now or ever."

Agnes overheard and floated over. "Are you sure about that, dearie?" she said. "We should get along. We can help you."

"Let me figure this out on my own. I'll learn how to cook eventually, I'll take care of Nathaniel eventually. I don't want you trying to relive your lives through me."

Agnes sighed. "You realize, don't you, that when you die you'll be with us in spirit. We've all been sealed to Nathaniel, and we're all going to be with him in the eternities."

"We'll learn then," I said. "Not now." I turned back to my rhubarb, letting the knife chop through the stems. The chopped bits fell all scattered, not the even lines I had hoped for. Behind me Agnes and Grace rustled. I waited longer. I did not turn around again until the kitchen felt empty and free.

I made a passable rhubarb pie for dinner that night. I had a hard time figuring out the trick of the stove, how hot to let the fire burn, when to move the pie around to the other side. But Nathaniel tasted it and praised me. "You make the best rhubarb pie I ever tasted," he said. "This is amazing."

I heard a ghostly sniff, and I didn't care if Agnes was rolling her eyes behind my back. Nathaniel exaggerated, but it was something I needed to hear after the disaster of the beans.

"Thank you," I said.

"Are you happy?" he said. "I want you to be happy here. I want to know you better, know all the things you're good at."

Bad at hiding my ghostsight from ghosts, I thought, but hoping to keep it from you. Good at jumping at offers of matrimony by kind random strangers. Good at keeping the woodpile stocked. "I don't cook well, and I don't sew well, but I work hard," I said. "And I'm happy doing it."

"Nothing else? No special talents, nothing you haven't told me about?"

"Oh, no," I said. "Except that rhubarb pie. That's about it." He smiled. Did he look disappointed? What else did he think I should do?

We spent three weeks in reasonable silence, Agnes, Grace, and I. I tried not to eavesdrop on their conversations. They seemed to leave me alone a good portion of the time, with the exception of meals, when they hovered over Nathaniel. "Nathaniel's not eating enough," Agnes said, glaring at me.

Grace inspected his clothes. "There's a tear on his collar here," she said loudly. I hated when they pretended to talk to each other but aimed all their comments at me.

"Does your shirt need mending?" I said to Nathaniel, pointing at the collar and the tiny tear.

He glanced down. "Hmm, maybe," he said. "Grace would say – that is, if you want to. It might grow larger."

Little slips like that reminded me that he hadn't forgotten Agnes and Grace. I wondered if he could feel their presence, even if he couldn't see them. Most irritating to me, they were still in love with him. They still wanted to care for him like a wife would.

Grace hovered around me one washday as I boiled water, grated lye soap, and scrubbed. Washday was a good day to be a ghost, I thought, watching other people rub their hands till they bled, knowing you'd never have to do it again yourself. I worked stains out of our clothes. She followed me into the yard, as far as her housebinding would allow, as if daring me to talk to her. Finally I said, "What?"

"You shouldn't be so rude. You ought to know what I've guessed already."

"What is it?"

"Haven't you noticed the laundry? Or have you not been counting the weeks? If I'm right, you're with child."

Ah.

She was right. And I had lost track of weeks. "You're the first person to know," I said. "I didn't realize." And then I scrubbed at the washboard and cried a little. She had stolen my good news from me.

Her glee at being right dissipated when she saw me crying. "I thought you'd be happy," she said.

"I wanted to know myself," I told her. "You should have guessed that. Or haven't you been pregnant before?"

"I was, once," she said. "But the baby came early, and died, and I died too. Didn't Nathaniel tell you?"

I shook my head. "But that's how Agnes died."

Grace nodded.

"I'm sorry."

"I had made all the clothes," Grace said. "The little gowns, and the cloth hemmed for diapers, and tiny booties. Quilts, too. I'll show you, if you want."

"Let me finish the wash," I said. She left me alone as I washed, wringing out the clothes in long twisted sticks, shaking the water out in a fine mist, hanging them on the line so the cold breeze would blow them dry. Sometimes I noticed the spirits watching me work, and I envied them their indolence, their clean, idle existence. *Don't wish away your work*, the Holy Spirit told me. *You don't want their pale half-life.*

Grace waited for me inside the door. "Upstairs," she said. "In the left bedroom, beneath the bed, there's a long flat box." She followed me as I went up the stairs and into the bedroom, and pulled the box from beneath the bed. I opened it and it was as she said, only more so. Stacks of diapers, rows of gowns, two baby quilts. Each little gown embroidered with flowers. Baby quilts dotted with tiny, even stitches.

"I didn't become pregnant for four years after we married," she told me. "I had time to work. I worried that Nathaniel would give my things away, but he didn't. He saved them."

"To remember you? Or to give to his next child?"

"I don't know." She reached for a white gown, but her hand passed through it. "I'll let you use them."

"You will?" I could use her baby things without asking, but I wanted permission. These were too beautiful to poach.

"I'll let you use them if you'll talk to Nathaniel for me. Give him a message from me."

Such a condition. "I can't," I said. "I can't do that."

"Of course you can. You can tell him that Grace loves him as much as she ever did. Or no, tell him this. Tell him that he's got the best darned socks in the world."

"What?"

"It was our joke, what he always used to say when I mended his things."

"And am I supposed to run messages between the two of you?"

"Not lots of messages. Just this one. Please."

I picked up a tiny bootie, knit out of white yarn. Five pairs of booties, each slightly larger than the one before. Careful anticipation for an arrival that came too early. "I'll think about it," I said.

I folded the baby clothes, stacking them in even rows, making them look as perfect and tidy as they had before. If Grace's baby had survived, she would have spent many hours scrubbing these clothes, removing yeasty yellow stains, doing wash more than once a week to keep up. A living, crying, messy baby, ruining and redeeming every stitch.

THERE was no sense putting it off. "I'm going to have a baby," I announced to Nathaniel the next morning at breakfast. I had grown proficient at boiling water and making mush, and this morning I even fried some sausage, in spite of the way its smell made me queasy.

"Congratulations!" Agnes said, and Grace managed a smile. "Grace told me, but I need to congratulate you myself. Don't you worry, we'll take good care of you." She fluttered around me, muttering to herself about baby food and how I needed to eat for two.

But Nathaniel's face went ashen. "Not yet," he said. "It's too soon."

"We've been married three months now. That's plenty of time."

"That's not what I meant."

"You mean you don't want me to die like Agnes and Grace." I guessed he would say that. It was hard for him to be risking his hopes for a family one more time.

"No, not before you – that is, no," he said. He cut his sausage into small bits, half again and half again, without eating anything.

"You're making a sausage mess." There must be something else bothering him beyond the thought of my dying.

"Sorry." He kept on with it, though, breaking all his food into pieces, not eating a thing. "Zina, can I ask you something?"

"Go ahead."

"Zina, have you ever seen a ghost?"

My turn to look pale. He knew. He'd think I was crazy like the folks in Logan did. Or worse, he'd ask me to talk to his wives. And should I lie, and be relieved of the messenger burden, or tell the truth, and be stuck talking to his prettier wives for him?

"I never have," I said.

"What?" Grace said. "Zina, you take that back right now. What am I?"

"Are you sure?" he said. "Because I married you after I heard talk about you speaking with spirits. And I, I could use some of that."

"You want me to talk to your wives?"

"Zina, I – "

"That's why you married me?" I said. "You heard about me and my crazy ghost talk, and you wanted to marry me because of it?" The news turned my fingers clumsy and my head dizzy. True, I married him for nothing more than being a man who wanted to marry me, but I had dreamed up all kinds of reasons why he asked. Maybe he had seen me working in the Hansen store and felt some kind of mystic pull. Maybe the Holy Ghost had whispered in his ear that I was the one for him, as it had whispered to me. I never dreamed he wanted to marry me for my ghostsight. *Did you think he married you for your looks?* said the voice of Clarence Hansen, with me still.

Nathaniel stared at his plate, picking the sausage into tinier pieces. "That's right. I got things I need to say to them. Sometimes it feels like they're still here, watching me, but I want to be sure."

"And if I miscarry like Agnes and Grace, and I die before you can talk to them ... "

"I'll have three dead wives instead of two. And I won't be able to talk to any of you."

And that was his biggest concern. Not my health, not even the baby. Just whether I would be talking to Agnes and Grace for him. But he was too wrapped up in his past wives to focus on me. "Ghost wives are ghosts," I said. "I'm real, I'm breathing in and out and growing a baby inside me. I'm here now, and you married me and brought me here to live."

"They matter to me too. I want to be able to talk to them, and I thought I had a little hope of that with you here." He stood up from his plate of sausage bits. "I can't finish this," he said. "I'm sorry."

He went out to the fields, and I cleaned up breakfast. "You lied to him," Grace said. "You told him you never saw a ghost when the truth is you've been seeing them your whole entire life."

"You hush," I said. "I'm the living wife, I'm the one he's got now. I'm the one who cooks and cleans and sews now, and I won't be a go-between for you. And besides, he lied to me too." I scraped the plates outside and washed them, but the sausage grease was too much for me, and I threw up breakfast.

"Oh, honey," said Agnes. "Honey, I am so sorry."

"Sorry for what?" Grace said.

"Sorry that he married her just because he thought she could see us," Agnes said. "That's not fair, and you know it."

"But we could talk to him again," Grace answered. "Don't you want to tell him things? Share old jokes? Hear what he has to say and have him know you heard?"

"I did," Agnes said. "But not anymore. It wouldn't be right. Zina, I'd bring you a cloth for your face and clean up the sausage if I could."

"It's all right," I said. "You go on." I almost let her pity me, she sounded so kind right then. But I did not want the ghost wives on my side. I wanted Nathaniel, and only him, and now I realized I'd never had him in the first place. He had only married me because of Grace and Agnes. He had only wanted me for the gift I resisted most.

NATHANIEL and I took care with each other after that. Polite. How are you feeling today, he would ask, and I'm a bit tired, I would say. Agnes and Grace kept their distance. Grace was still angry, and Agnes just felt sorry for me. I felt sorry for myself. Why had God told me to get married? Would it be so terrible to return to the Hansens? *Yes it would,* said the Holy Ghost. *You should stay.* But that was all the comfort I got.

I felt off the next few days, like I saw the world sideways and backwards. I went about my chores in slow motion, a weight sagging in my belly. One morning I scrubbed the kitchen floor on hands and knees, removing grease splatters and crumbs. Something sharp twisted inside me and I began to bleed.

"Nathaniel!" I called him, even knowing he was out working and too far away to hear me. Agnes and Grace came instead. Blood gushed out when I tried to stand, so I lay down again. And I cried, because I wanted to have this baby. I wanted to present him to Nathaniel and say, I grew this child, and isn't he beautiful. I did what your other wives couldn't. And now my baby dreams spilled out, in hot waves of red.

I heard Agnes yell "Nathaniel! Nathaniel, you come right now," and Grace joined her too. "Nathaniel! You get in here, you're going to have another ghost wife if you don't."

"He can't hear you," I said, between sobs. "And you're housebound, so you can't leave past the fenced yard."

"Sometimes if we both yell together, he hears a little echo," Agnes said. They called and called. I stayed on the floor in front of the stove. It was the warmest place, even though the floor felt hard beneath me, and I bled and listened to the ghost sister wives call our husband. I should get up, I thought, but when I tried again my head swam and Agnes stopped me.

"You stop right now," she said. "Don't you go anywhere until Nathaniel gets here. That's what I did when I died. I tried to clean myself up and keep moving and even make dinner, and instead I lost more and more blood."

"She's right," Grace said. "And breathe deep. Crying so hard makes you even more lightheaded. Breathe, and breathe."

For once I listened to both of them. I settled back to the ground, and I breathed.

"Nathaniel!" they called more, and their voices swirled around me and blood swirled out of me, and I fainted.

When I came to, Nathaniel was kneeling beside me.

"I lost you too," he kept saying. "I couldn't save Agnes, and I couldn't save Grace, and now you too." In his voice I heard fierce mourning for Agnes and Grace. He had a wide and strong heart, to love them both with so much grief.

"Zina, say something," Grace told me. "He thinks you're dead."

"But I'm alive."

"Zina?" Nathaniel said. "You're alive, you're alive?"

I nodded.

He looked at me as if he really saw me. Not Agnes, not Grace, but me, Zina. "Thank God."

"The baby's gone." Those were hard words to say, and they nearly stayed inside me. "But I'm still living, and we can try again."

"I know," he said. "Zina, if you had died I would have wanted to talk to you too, just like them, and tell you something."

"I'm listening," I said. Agnes left the room and waved Grace out too, to give us some privacy.

"I did want to marry you because I thought you could talk to ghosts, and speak to Agnes and Grace. And maybe that was wrong of me. I thought you might want to be married, because you hadn't had many offers, and maybe that was wrong too. And Zina, I am sorry."

"Sorry you married me?"

"No," he said. "Not at all sorry for that. I was selfish to bring you here, but even if you never see a ghost, I will not be sorry you're here."

He held me there on the kitchen floor, and if I cried more for my losses, and he cried more for his, it did not matter. We were together.

EVERYONE was kind to me as I recovered the next few weeks. I thought Agnes and Grace might be jealous of me, because I lived through what had killed them. But when Agnes warned me about my soup boiling too fast, and when Grace pointed out a tear on my dress, there was no triumph in their voices, only concern. Nathaniel did not ask about my ghostsight, but brought me bouquets of tiny spring crocuses. "Beautiful flowers for my beautiful wife," he said.

One evening, when I felt well enough to sit up and mend, I said to Nathaniel, "Do you have any socks that need darning?"

"I think so."

"Bring them down, and I'll work on those a while."

Nathaniel set down his whittling and went upstairs. "You're going to do it?" Grace said. "Tell him about the sock? Give him a message?"

"Can I give him a message, too?" Agnes said.

"Just wait," I said. "Be patient."

Nathaniel returned, bringing me socks and a few other torn things. I darned a sock, and handed it to him.

"I'll bet that's the best darned sock you ever had," I said.

Grace watched Nathaniel for a reaction.

He gave a little smile. "True," he said. "Best darned sock ever."

I darned on. I fixed all the holes in his socks, and moved on to a pair of britches.

"It's late," Nathaniel said. "You can't mend it all tonight."

"I can try," I said. "Nathaniel, if I could see ghosts, and I saw your wives, what would you want me to tell them?"

He thought for a moment. Agnes and Grace stood right beside him.

"I would tell Agnes that her pie crust was so light and flaky you could melt away on it. I would tell Grace that when she mended a shirt it looked better than new."

"Really, Nathaniel?" Grace said.

"I would tell them that I'm sorry I didn't get a midwife in time, that I'm sorry the babies died and they died." He was looking right at them, but through them and on into the kitchen. Even with all this talking, he still saw nothing. He was truly spirit blind.

The truth and power of my talent settled on me for the first time, gift instead of burden. *This is something you can give to this man,* said the Holy Ghost. *He's not perfect, but he is good.*

I took Nathaniel's hand. It was solid beneath mine. The calluses felt rough and he had dirt beneath his fingernails.

"I would tell them what I should tell you, too," Nathaniel said. "I love you."

"They know that, Nathaniel," I said. "They are always with you. And I, I know it too."

"But it's nice to hear him say it," Agnes whispered. Grace reached to touch his face and her fingers faded into his skin.

I held on tight to his hand. "Yes it is," I said.

BAPTISMS FOR THE DEAD

C. Douglas Birkhead

"**WHERE'S** your nametag, Elder Hansen?" Elder Ephraim Gardner eyed his junior companion as he chambered a round into his 40-caliber Glock. He slid the pistol into the shoulder holster he wore beneath his black suit coat.

"Who's going to know the difference? Everyone's dead."

"Maybe today will be different. We were spared for a reason."

Hansen dug into his pocket and fished out the nametag identifying him as a missionary of the LDS church and slapped it on his chest. "Happy now?" He flicked the safety off his own Beretta 9mm and glared at his companion. "Why do we still do this? You know just as well as I do the prophet's dead and we haven't seen a living member for over a year. When are you going to realize there's no Church anymore?"

"God's message never dies. Evil may rein on Earth now, but our calling hasn't changed."

"There's no one left to teach. Missionary work is pointless. All we do is kill."

"What about the baptisms?"

"What about them?"

"The scriptures teach us that in order to reach the Celestial Kingdom all souls must be baptized. The monsters deserve eternal salvation just like every other human."

"What makes you think they're human? God lost those souls the day the dead began to rise." Hansen jammed the Beretta into his hip holster.

"No. That's where you're wrong. I had a revelation after it started."

"Good for you, Gardner," he interrupted. "I've heard about your revelation a thousand times. I've prayed for months and haven't heard a peep from Heavenly Father."

Gardner placed a hand on Hansen's bony shoulder before continuing, "Have faith, Elder Hansen. I'm convinced that we were left behind to do God's work, to release these souls through the destruction of their corrupted bodies and to give them a path to salvation through baptism."

"Right, salvation." Hansen shook his head. "Whatever you say, Gardner." Hansen opened the door of their tiny one-bedroom apartment. He put on his coat and walked outside. Gardner followed him, closing the door as he stepped onto the small porch. The bright sunlight assaulted their eyes causing them both to squint for several seconds.

Gardner examined the tires on his bicycle before swinging a leg over the seat and pushing off into the street. The pair rode for a few minutes without saying anything. Finally the senior elder looked over his shoulder and said, "I thought we could work the Twin Oaks subdivision today. It's not too far and there were once a lot of families living there. Lots of souls to save."

Hansen rolled his eyes. "Lots of souls. Yeah. Lead the way."

The two missionaries pedaled on, weaving through abandoned cars and the decaying bodies of the undead they had dispatched in the eighteen months since the outbreak. In the early days, seeing corpses was a shock but now they barely noticed them.

As they rode farther from their own neighborhood, the bodies became less frequent until eventually they disappeared altogether and their surroundings looked more like the world before the evil came. Houses appeared more or less untouched and if not for the trash and overgrown lawns one could almost imagine nothing ever happened.

The elders coasted down a long hill. As they picked up speed, the breeze brought relief from the summer heat. Gardner blinked his eyes trying to fight through the wind raging against his face. He squinted when he looked toward the bottom and saw a blue minivan parked in the middle of the road. Next to the door on the driver's side, a mutilated and decaying man stood swaying. "I've got a dead one!"

Hansen and Gardner gripped the brakes on their bicycles skidding to a long stop about seventy-five yards from the bottom. The mindless creature hadn't noticed them and seemed preoccupied with its own reflection in the window of the vehicle. His left arm was broken and bent in the wrong direction. He was using the mauled fingers of his shattered right hand to tap the glass. His face was a sickly pale gray and his eyes were set in deep blackened sockets surrounded by dry flakey skin. The creature's midsection was an enormous cavity exposing coils of rotten intestines fighting a losing battle with gravity to stay inside.

Gardner dismounted, drew his Glock, and looked at his companion. "Be quiet. These things like to travel in packs."

"Really, Gardner?" Hansen mocked. "I hadn't noticed."

"Just get the scriptures." Gardner shook his head and smiled at his companion. "It's going to be a glorious day. I can feel the Spirit with us."

Hansen unzipped his backpack and pulled out the leatherbound Book of Mormon. He crept over and joined Gardner, who was crouching behind a row of overgrown bushes, surveying the street. After several minutes the senior elder nodded and said, "Looks like he's alone. Let's go."

Gardner stood up and walked toward the undead creature. Hansen followed him with his eyes and waited until he was about fifteen yards from the creature. A smile crept onto his face. Hansen cupped his hands over his mouth and yelled, "Come and get me, you flipping spawn of the devil! It's lunch time!"

The monster's head shot up. He had been wearing silk pajamas the day he turned. A tacky paisley pattern obscured the dried blood that had soaked into the material. His neck was shredded from a wound that had probably killed him months earlier.

"Quit messing around, Elder Hansen! If he bites me, I'll get infected." Gardner pointed the Glock and fired unsteadily into the monster's chest, causing it to stumble into the door of the van. The attack seemed to anger the monster, who lunged back at Gardner with startling speed.

Hansen laughed. "No good, Elder Gardner. Haven't you learned anything? Got to hit him in the head." He aimed his own weapon and pulled the trigger two times. The back of the monster's head exploded before the creature crumpled to the ground. "Like that."

Gardner looked over his shoulder with a terrified expression. Hansen's smile vanished. "I'm sorry. That wasn't cool." He held up the book and gestured toward the corpse. "Let's perform the baptism."

Gardner nodded and said nothing as Hansen opened his scriptures and knelt before the creature's body. Baptisms for the dead were usually performed in the temple and by immersion. In the beginning, this troubled Elder Gardner and he had prayed for some time for guidance. He finally concluded that under the circumstances, God would probably not mind a service tailored to the apocalypse. He liked to call it a "Battlefield Baptism."

The pair knelt before the body. Gardner seemed to come alive as he touched the creature's corpse. "Having been commissioned of Jesus Christ, I baptize you in the name of the Father, and of the Son, and of the Holy Ghost. Amen." He looked at Hansen. "Another soul saved. You might not see it now, Elder Hansen, but you were put here for a reason."

Hansen stood and brushed the dust off his suit. "I wish I shared your conviction, Elder Gardner." He returned the scriptures to his backpack and performed a tactical reload of his semi-automatic, replacing the partially used magazine with a fresh one.

Their position from the hill gave them an unobstructed view of the neighborhood and Gardner scanned the area with a pair of binoculars. "Why do you suppose there aren't any more? We've never been here before. I would expect to see at least a dozen by now, especially after the shooting."

"Yeah, that's weird. I can't say." Hansen zipped up the backpack and got on his bicycle. "Let's check it out."

The missionaries rode the rest of the way down the hill and into the heart of the gated subdivision. The large homes were extravagant and they marveled at the money it must have cost to build them. Neither of them had come from families with money and seeing such wealth made Hansen slightly envious. "A lot of good all that money did them." He pointed towards an opulent house on a corner lot.

"We're all blessed in different ways, Elder Hansen."

Gardner led the pair into a cul-de-sac and coasted to a stop. He looked over his shoulder and asked his companion, "How about some lunch?"

Hansen hopped the curb and jumped off his bike letting it crash into the porch of an enormous two-story house. "Sounds good. Let's eat."

Elder Gardner sighed as he dismounted. He shrugged his own backpack off his shoulders and unzipped the outer compartment, pulling out two military-style meals-ready-to-eat, tossing one to his companion. The rations were among the many surplus items – including their guns and ammunition – the two missionaries had scavenged from the military after they'd fallen to the undead army. Gardner groaned at the thought of more bland rations but Hansen tore into the prepackaged meal as if he hadn't eaten in days.

"Why don't you start us off with a blessing, Elder." Gardner's glare conveyed his disappointment and Hansen blushed slightly before bowing his head.

"Heavenly Father – " His words were cut short by a muffled scream.

The pair both looked at each other, not sure if what they had heard was real. They couldn't remember the last time they listened to another human voice and the sound seemed unnatural. Another scream, a woman's. Gardner cocked his head to the side trying to pinpoint the direction. Then a third, this one unmistakably a child's cry for help.

Gardner craned his neck and said nothing, trying to determine the source of the screams. Finally he pointed to the left and whispered, "Come on, it's coming from the next block over." Gardner sprinted between the pair of houses to their left. Hansen followed and by the time he caught up to his companion, they could both hear shouting.

They ran through the yard behind the house until they came to a wooden privacy fence at the back of the property. On the other side, they could hear the chilling moans of the undead. The missionaries scrambled to the top and before they could drop down on the other side, the pair froze in place, shocked by what they saw.

Shambling before them stood a mob of almost fifty of the creatures. They had surrounded a black Mercedes parked in the driveway of a Spanish-tiled rambler. Inside the car was a terrified family of three crouched behind their spider-webbed windows. The decaying monsters pounded their blood-stained fists on the vehicle in a frenzied hunger for human flesh.

The driver had his head down and was ignoring the attack, focused instead on starting the car. With each turn of the key, the sound of the engine grew weaker until there was only the sound of clicking from under the hood. The man pounded his fist on the steering wheel and started to cry.

The missionaries looked at each other and nodded. The idea of taking on a horde that size was crazy but the compulsion to help living human beings trumped rational thought.

Hansen closed his eyes and did something he hadn't done in months. He prayed with sincerity. He asked for strength, he asked for forgiveness. He called upon God to guide him in carrying out his will. Gardner smiled and said amen, then swung his legs over and pushed off the top of the fence.

Hansen followed, and as soon as he touched the ground, he rolled into a low crouch with his weapon drawn. A trio of the undead at the back of the group turned to investigate. A small woman wearing a bloodied apron bellowed out a loud moan upon seeing the missionaries. The rest of the creatures turned and, deciding the two elders were easier prey, began to shamble towards the pair with their arms outstretched.

The smell was overpowering and Hansen had to fight the impulse to gag. He raised his weapon and pointed it at the aproned woman. His hand was shaking and he tried to steady it with the other but it didn't help. He felt the sick sensation of paralyzing fear as he watched the woman's face dancing wildly in his gun's sight. He closed his eyes and pulled the trigger. The blast startled him and when his eyes opened, he saw that he had drilled a neat hole into her forehead, the gory contents of her head sprayed on the monster behind her.

He stood up and fired again, the second round delivering a fatal wound to the creature covered by deceased woman's brain matter. Something was happening to Hansen.

He felt an unnatural calm and sense of focus descending upon him. His fear had vanished. He fired again, knowing before the bullet left the barrel that the round would find its mark.

He didn't bother to check his aim before moving on to the next monster. He couldn't miss. Again and again he shot, each blast bringing down another creature.

The pair worked together in perfect unison, firing and reloading, moving in concert as a single entity. The undead continued their advance, slowly closing the gap. The pair continued firing, undeterred by the threat, possessed by something greater. The onslaught was relentless but the undeads' numbers gradually thinned as the last of the creatures stumbled over the growing pile of their fallen comrades. Elder Hansen never felt closer to the Holy Spirit than when he dropped the last one with a perfectly placed shot through the monster's left eye.

The smell of rot and cordite filled Hansen's senses and he looked around in awe at what they had done together. The family in the car sat stunned by the miracle they had witnessed. It wasn't until he reached down to help his companion up, that he realized Gardner had been bitten.

"Oh no." Hansen wrapped his fingers around his head and stared at the crescent shaped marks on his friend's arm.

Gardner looked down, not realizing something was wrong until he saw his companion's panicked expression. He stared at the wound for several seconds, not knowing what to say. Finally, he looked at Hansen and with an inexplicable sense of calm said, "I guess God has a different plan for me." He smiled. "If you think about it, I'm the lucky one. In a few hours I get to go home."

"It's not fair." The junior elder started to cry. "I can't do this alone."

"You're never alone if you don't want to be."

Hansen nodded slowly and put his hand on Gardner's shoulder. "Will you help me with the baptisms?"

"Of course I will."

Hansen pulled Gardner to his feet and the two missionaries walked to the car and gently rapped on the glass. "It's okay. Come on out."

The door opened and the family stepped out and embraced the elders. The father looked at them. He was shaken and struggled not to show emotion when he spoke. "Thank you so much. We were nearly out of food. We were trying to escape but that didn't work out so well. I can't believe this. We haven't seen anyone else alive in God knows how long. And that shooting. I don't know what to say."

"It is remarkable." Gardner shot a knowing glance at Hansen who pursed his lips. "Will you excuse us for a little while? There are some things we need to take care of."

The father nodded and led his family back into their house.

The missionaries spent the next few minutes reciting the prayer for the creatures they had dispatched. Gardner began to get sick after the first dozen. Around the time they had finished forty, his skin had turned pale and his coughing fits were becoming more frequent. Elder Gardner continued to work with a fierce determination and sense of purpose.

Finally Gardner collapsed. Hansen pulled his friend up and helped him rest against the fence. The senior elder coughed before speaking. "You know what comes next right?"

"Yes."

"I could do it myself, but I want you to do it for me."

"I understand."

"Elder Hansen. Don't be afraid to go this alone. I think you know there's a plan."

"I do. Thanks for helping me see it again."

"I didn't do much. I had some help." Gardner started coughing again and began to shake. "Goodbye, Elder Hansen."

"So long." Hansen pulled himself up and unholstered his semi-automatic. When he fired, he wasn't driven by the same force that had guided him during the day's battle, but by love for his friend.

Hansen performed a brief funeral service and when he was finished he walked to the house where the family was waiting on the porch. They had prepared a small meal with the last of their supplies and offered him a plate. He thanked them and sat down on the grass in front of the house to eat.

The father sat back down with his family and asked, "What have you been doing all of these months?"

"Missionary work." He looked at the family. "Are you members?"

"Mormons?" The father shook his head. "No, sir."

"If it's all right, I could take some time and tell you about the Church of Jesus Christ of Latter-day Saints."

"I suppose that would be just fine." The father put his arm around his wife.

"Great. Let me get my things." Hansen smiled to himself. He had one more thing to do that day. And he couldn't imagine a more important calling.

PIRATE GOLD
FOR BROTHER BRIGHAM

Lee Allred

UTAHNS have this really sick habit. It's called "fry sauce," a disgusting pinkish gray goopy mix of ketchup, mayonnaise, and pickle juice that they insist on dunking their French fries into. Thank goodness I grew up in Oregon, that's all I can say.

I mention fry sauce for two reasons: first, in order to believe the rest of my story you'll need to believe really strange things happen in Utah, fry sauce being only one of them; and second, it was because of fry sauce this whole chain of events started.

We were sitting, my friend George and I, in a booth at the Arctic Circle on State Street kitty-corner from University Mall in Orem. Arctic Circle is the drive-in hamburger chain that invented fry sauce. We've met for lunch on Saturdays at this Arctic Circle nearly every week since we were college roommates. George insists on eating there solely because of their fry sauce.

The thing about George is that he's an extreme Utahn; he puts fry sauce on *everything*. His burgers, his fries, his tossed salads. He hasn't tried putting fry sauce on Utah's other culinary masterpiece, green lime Jell-O, but it's only a matter of time.

So when he just sat there with his fry sauce still untouched, oh-so-lonesome in its little paper condiment cup, I knew something was wrong.

So I asked him what was wrong.

He didn't answer for a moment. Finally he asked, "Have you ever seen something you know you saw, but you also know you couldn't possibly have seen it because, well, because it's just plain crazy?"

I nodded. I opened my mouth to say "fry sauce," but I never got the chance. From behind, a voice boomed: "Yeah! My mother-in-law!"

Ralphy.

Ralphy was George's cousin – second or third cousin, I forget which. Utah families get rather complicated. Ralphy was the kind of pest who never gets the hint he's not wanted. That's why he slid into the booth next to me. "See, this one time my mother-in-law actually said she was glad to see me – "

I should mention here that Ralphy does not have a mother-in-law. He is not now nor has he ever been married. Probably never will be. As I said, a lot of strange things happen in Utah; Ralphy is three of them.

"No one's ever glad to see you, Ralphy," I said.

"That's not what you said last time you needed your Plymouth jump-started." My new 1997 Plymouth had a bit of a battery gremlin.

Ralphy stole one of George's fries and dunked it in that pink Utah goo. "Cut it out, Ralphy," George said. "I'm being serious here."

"You certainly are," he said. "Serious looking, that is." He popped the stolen fry into his mouth.

Ralphy had a point, much as I hate to admit it. George is the most serious-looking man I know. He even looks dour when he's rolling off a chair laughing. Comes a bit from his looking so much like old Brigham Young. Almost a dead ringer, now that George has grown out a Brigham-style beard. Of course, it's not too surprising that there's a resemblance. He's a direct descendant of Brother Brigham.

Then again, half the state is.

George sat quiet for a while, maybe hoping like I was that Ralphy would take the hint and leave, but Ralphy, as I said, never takes a hint.

Shrugging, George started up with his story again. "Promise me you won't laugh." We promised, although it took Ralphy a couple more lame jokes to get to that point.

George looked us dead in the eye. "I saw a pirate ship on the Great Salt Lake."

RALPHY put George's half-eaten Bounty Burger up on his shoulder like a parrot and in his best Long John Silver voice said: "Arrgh, Matey! 'Tis the scourge of the seven seas we be."

"You're a moron, do you know that?" George growled.

"*Brraa-waahhk!*" Ralphy's burger parrot squawked. "Mutiny on the Bounty Burger, me hearties. Walk the plank, walk the plank!"

George looked to me for moral support.

"Um, parrots aside," I said, "I think I'm with Ralphy on this one."

"I tell you I saw it!"

"You saw something, I'll grant you ... "

"Don't give me any 'weather balloon' guff. You're not the only one who went to college." Did I mention Utah's over-educated? More degrees per capita than any other state. Half the truck drivers in the state have at least a bachelor's degree. Half the auto mechanics, half the plumbers – even Ralphy has one. In what, he's never said.

"Look," George said, "I know what I saw. It was a pirate ship. It had sails. It had a pirate flag."

I tried to calm him down. "When did you, um, see this pirate ship?"

"Last night about midnight. I had a blowout on I-80 just off the Saltair exit." George drives a Pepsi truck for Birnelli's bottling plant in Salt Lake City. About three times a week he makes a run across the salt flats, past the Great Salt Lake, out to Wendover. "I got out of the cab and the moment I did, I saw it there on the lake."

I shrugged. "Must have been a sailboat from the marina sailing around." If you can believe it, they actually have a marina on the Great Salt Lake.

"At midnight? In this weather?" he asked.

I shrugged again. Myself, I couldn't imagine being crazy enough to get anywhere near that stinky lake, day or night, winter or summer – the stench of dead brine shrimp was enough to gag a maggot.

"And what about their pirate flag?" George persisted.

"A joke. Maybe a fraternity prank. You know the 'U.'"

Ralphy hissed at the mention of our archrival school, the University of Utah. Once a Cougar, always a Cougar. Just ask that greedy BYU Alumni Association. Did I mention Ralphy works for them? Now you know why your Alumni fund drive letters are so pushy.

"And what about all the men on deck, dressed like pirates and waving cutlasses?"

"I think the plural is 'cutlassi,'" Ralphy said, consulting his burger, which, in his so-called mind, was now a half-eaten dictionary.

"Maybe they had fishing poles and you just thought they were cutlasses?" I said.

"Yeah, right." George snorted. "Going fishing in the dead of winter on a dead lake with no fish. Not even tourists are *that* dumb."

Ralphy wiggled his burger, now a parrot again, vigorously. "Brine shrimp off the port bow, Cap'n! It's Moby Dick – Arrgh, Matey. From heck's heart, I stab at thee! Harpoons away!" Ralphy hit me right between the eyes with the end of the paper wrapper blown from his soda straw.

The people sitting three tables away got up and left, looking at us and muttering. I was about to follow them when George reached in his coat pocket and pulled out the Polaroid photo.

HE SLID it across the table. "Does this look like I'm crazy?"

You've all seen that old grainy photo of the Loch Ness monster. Compared to the photo George showed us, that Nessie portrait is crystal clear. George's photo was all out of focus. One of his fingers covered the upper third of the picture. Still, there was something there. Fuzzy, white, and vaguely pirate ship-shaped.

Of course, it was also vaguely Bounty Burger shaped. Truth is, it could have been almost anything.

"Um," I said. "Everybody knows ghosts don't exist."

"Everybody also knows you can't take pictures of them, either. Looks like everybody can be wrong."

Like everybody in Utah on fry sauce, I muttered to myself.

Ralphy grunted at the picture and popped the last of George's fries into his mouth. "So what do you want us to do about it, big guy?"

George leaned back in the booth. "I was thinking about going back out there tonight and getting a better picture. Maybe even take along some video equipment."

He paused and we both looked at Ralphy.

The Alumni Association has all that top-of-the-line video and camera equipment just sitting in their closet waiting for the next big BYU-U of U game. And Ralphy had the key.

"Why's everybody looking at me?" Ralphy asked. "Flip!"

Did I mention Utahns use "flip" and "fetch" for a certain other word used in the other forty-nine states? If really agitated, Utahns will add "you picker!"

"You pickers!" he added.

IT WAS about eleven p.m. when we pulled off I-80 and coasted into the deserted Saltair parking lot. Nobody in their right mind would be on the lake this time of year. Cold as a University of Utah football fan's heart and just as windy.

We unloaded the Suburban. We had more cameras and photography gear than that guy in *Bridges of Madison County*. I'd brought along that old beat-up telescope of mine, too. That was our cover story should the Utah Highway Patrol ask us what we three fools were doing out there on a cold winter's night. *Just looking at Jupiter, Officer.*

We hunched up like frozen penguins and waited. A quarter mile away, a constant stream of semi-trucks roared down the interstate, their drivers snug and warm inside their trucks. The pickers.

At least the night was bright. A full moon, of course. What was it about the supernatural and full moons, anyway? The moonlight reflected off the lake's calm, waveless surface. The light played across the white sandy beach.

Well, it's not exactly a sandy beach.

All that glinting white sand of Great Salt Lake beaches? Another weird Utah thing. Those smooth itty-bitty agate-looking sand grains aren't sand at all. They're what are called *oolite*. Layer upon layer of calcium carbonate formed around the chewy nougat of a brine shrimp fecal pellet.

That's right. We were standing on petrified shrimp poo.

It's a Utah thing.

George was munching on Doritos and fry sauce, and Ralphy was sipping at a Thermos of hot Postum. Ralphy asked if we could at least turn on the radio and listen to the last of the Jazz game. We promptly told him to shut up.

"Like ghosts are afraid of the radio," he muttered, but for once he actually sort of shut up.

Three minutes to midnight, we saw the pirate ship.

She was a Spanish galleon, one of those huge lumbering behemoths Sir Francis Drake so loved to sink. White and faint – you could almost see right through it – and slightly luminescent. As she approached the Saltair docks, she hauled down her Spanish Cross flag and hauled up a black pirate Jolly Roger in its place. We could see men on its deck. Some of them looked like pirates, and some of them had on Conquistador armor. The ship glided across the Lake right toward us, right toward the dock.

Right toward George.

The ship's captain stood on the poop deck. He held a captain's speaking trumpet. He put it to his mouth and called out something in Spanish. I only caught part of it – the name "Brigham."

He called once, twice, three times.

And then he, they, and the ship vanished.

"Oh my heck," said a shaken Ralphy. "I forgot to take any pictures."

WE ARGUED on the drive back.

George insisted we try again. "What for?" I snapped. "So we take the pictures. Then what? We say anything about this, people'll think we've cracked. Let's just forget all this happened."

Ralphy had been sitting in the back seat with all the photo gear, very quiet. Not like him at all.

"What do you think, Ralphy?" George asked. "Did you get any of that Spanish they were shouting?"

Like half the male population of the state, Ralphy had been a Mormon missionary. He'd gone to one of those Latin American countries – I can't keep them straight. Sometimes when I'm feeling charitable, I blame his irregularities on the endemic dysentery he had throughout his mission.

Sometimes.

Ralphy stared out the window, ashen-faced, watching the brine-crusted telephone poles flash by. It was the first time I'd ever seen him serious. "He was calling out for Brigham. Brigham Young." He turned to face us. "He said he'd brought gold for Brigham's temple."

"Flip!" I muttered. "Not another Lost Rhoades Mine ghost story."

Some weird Utah things are too weird even for Utahns to believe. The rumor about the Lost Rhoades Gold Mine providing the gold for the Salt Lake Temple's Angel Moroni statue is one of them. If you haven't heard the story, I'm not going to bother explaining it. Look it up. I'll add this: it was Utah-weird enough Hollywood made a Gregory Peck western about it: *MacKenna's Gold*. Sans Utah and Angel Moroni, of course. Hollywood isn't *that* weird.

Looks like ghost pirates are, though.

Ralphy pointed at George. "They think George is Brigham Young."

George almost swerved off the highway. "What?!"

"It's not the full moon at all. It's George. That's why they've shown up. They think they've finally found Brother Brigham after all these years."

A FIERCE argument erupted. It was me against George, George against Ralphy, and Ralphy against himself.

I whistled to get us all to shut up. "Quiet, you pickers!" I cleared my throat. "Now. It's obvious we need to know more before we decide *anything*. Like maybe find out who these pirates are and how in the heck they're showing up in Utah."

"I've never heard anything about pirates in Utah."

"It *is* a landlocked state, George," I said dryly. "There were plenty of Spanish running around here in the old days. Maybe we can find a connection that way."

"At least *one* of us can," they both said.

It was my turn to have everybody turn and look at me.

"You pickers!" I moaned.

"You have access to all sorts of old records at the 'Y,' don't you, professor?" Ralphy said.

In other parts of the country, when you say the 'Y', you mean the YMCA. In Utah, the 'Y' always means Brigham Young University. BYU. I'm not even sure they *have* YMCAs in Utah.

"Look, enough with the 'professor' stuff, already. I'm just a lowly adjunct instructor." The Y had another tenure cap going on. "Besides – "

"And what *you* can't find," George continued, ignoring me, "you can get from some of your historian friends up at the Church Office Building? Right?"

I offered dozens of perfectly valid excuses. They weren't having any.

"Flip!" I Utah-swore. "Flippity-fetch-fetch!"

IT TOOK me two weeks of digging, but I finally found the connection. I didn't find it at Church Headquarters or the 'Y' or even the YCMA. Instead, I found it over at the Utah Historical Society over in the old Rio Grande train station in downtown Salt Lake.

Seems back in 1540, the conquistador Francisco de Coronado's expedition reached all the way up to the Colorado River. In this account I found, Coronado expelled a handful of his men from the party. Coronado had discovered that the men had once been part of a galleon's crew who'd mutinied and turned pirate. They'd joined the expedition partly to slip out of sight from the Spanish authorities, partly to get their grubby little hands on the gold of El Dorado.

Juan Jose Avila, the captain of the mutineers, offered a bag of gold – booty from the pirated galleon – to Coronado if he'd only change his mind and let them back in the party. Coronado refused, swearing an oath at them, putting them under some sort of curse. Exiled into the wilderness, Avila and his men were never seen again.

At least not until George saw them.

"They must have made their way up through the desert, past the Indians and the crickets and the seagulls, to the Great Salt Lake," I told the rest of the guys. We were back at Arctic Circle, planning what to do next.

Ralphy had spent his time studying up on ghosts – watching umpteen cheesy cable TV shows and reading a stack of *Goosebumps*. "According to my sources," Ralphy said, "ghosts are just spirits who've got unfinished business on Earth. Once they get that done, they can go to their final rest."

I stirred my straw around in my Diet Pepsi (twice the sin with only half the calories). "So what you're saying is old Jose's trying to atone for all that gold he stole by giving it over to a holy cause."

"*I'm* not saying it," Ralphy said around a half-chewed French fry. "I'm just saying that that's what my sources would say, but that's only if you believe in that false Purgatory stuff, which we know if we read our good ol' Bruce R. that – "

I held up his hand. "Let's hold up on the McConkie for a bit." Any time a conversation turned Gospel-ish, Ralphy would drag out his battered copy of *Mormon Doctrine* and cite it like was the Fifth Standard Work. I just wish good ol' Bruce R. had proclaimed fry sauce to be against the Word of Wisdom.

"Yeah," George nodded. "What I want to know is how that pirate ship figures in, genius. Did they haul that thing around with them on Coronado's expedition?"

"Not to mention the Jolly Roger flag hadn't been invented yet in 1540," I added.

"Sometimes ghostly apparitions are symbolic rather than literal," Ralphy answered. I didn't even know he knew words that big, let alone could string them together in a sentence.

"So then, building on this R.L. Stine theory of yours," I said, "since the sin was piracy, they have to atone as pirates." I took a sip on my straw. "Seems simple enough. We just let them give their gold to Brigham – " I hooked a thumb at George. " – and they can go off and rest in peace."

"I am *not* Brigham Young!" George harrumphed.

"They think you are."

"Yeah," Ralphy chimed in. A calculating look came to his eyes. "We give them Brigham, and they give us the gold, and then we – "

"*I'm not Brigham!*"

"Uh, hold on a minute there, Ralphy," I said. "Rewind the tape. Just what do you mean by 'they give us the gold?'"

Ralphy, mouth full of fry sauce, looked at me like I was a simpleton. "They give us the gold. *Duh.* Now, I was thinking a forty-thirty-thirty split, since I'm the one who thought of it, but if you're going to get all sulky about it – "

"Oh, no!" shouted George. "I'm not keeping any haunted stolen pirate gold. I don't want blood on my hands!" George must have been reading some of Ralphy's *Goosebumps*, too. Or maybe he'd seen *The Mummy's Curse* last night on *Creature Feature*.

Ralphy glared at him. "Then I don't see any reason for us to stick our necks out for a bunch of goldy oldy moldy ghosts."

"We could always do it just for curiosity's sake," I offered. "'Discovery of the unknown' and all that."

"I get all of that I want at my singles ward," Ralphy sniffed.

I had one last arrow in my quiver. It wasn't very *Mormon Doctrine*-y, but desperate times and seasons called for desperate measures.

"Well, then," I asked, "how about the chance to save some poor lost souls suffering in Purgatory?"

Ralphy rose up in full Bruce R. high dudgeon. "There's no such thing as Purga*story* – "

I cut him off in mid-dudge. "Why, Ralphy!" I indignified. "I'm surprised at you!"

"*Huh?!*"

"You of all people! Don't you believe in the Eleventh Article of Faith? Or free agency?"

"*Double huh?!*"

"'We allow all men the same privilege, let them worship how, where, or what they may,'" I quoted. "Even pirate ghosts."

"But – "

"But, nothing! Doesn't Bruce R. himself speak of missionaries going forth to preach in the spirit world?"

"And during the Millennium," George added, not knowing where I was leading the discussion, but Georgishly crossing all the Ts and jotting all the tittles and threading all the camels through needles.

"Spirit missionaries means nonmember spirits, right?" I asked, not giving Ralphy time to answer. "Nonmember spirits with Eleventh Article of Faith free agency, right? Even good ol' Bruce couldn't begrudge some Catholic spirits trying to atone and get back to God's presence according to the measure of light they possess – "

"But – " Ralphy whimpered.

" – and didn't the Prophet George A. Smith say, 'Keep all the good that you have, and let us bring to you more good, in order that you may be happier and in order that you may be prepared to enter into the presence of our Heavenly Father?'"

Paper takes stone, stone takes scissors, and a Prophet takes a study aid, especially when that prophet is George's namesake forbear. George is a one-man walking DUP genealogy tree.

Ralphy agreed without another whimper. Live by the Bruce R., die by the Bruce R.

SO WE went back out to Saltair the next full moon. Yes, I know, the full moon business wasn't necessary, but we weren't taking any chances. Besides, the light was better.

George stood on the end of the pier. We'd borrowed a costume from James Arrington's one-man show. James is a friend of mine. I've done research for him from time to time.

George looked just like Brother Brigham, cane and all.

"C-couldn't you have g-gotten a warmer costume?" he said through chattering teeth. The costume was made of lightweight material. Stage lights get pretty hot.

"Just hold on, George. Only a few minutes to midnight," I said.

The pirate ship arrived right on schedule. It stopped short of the dock and the crew lowered a ship's boat. Avila and his men rowed up to the pier. They climbed up the rope ladder, hauling a large wooden chest with them.

George stepped up to meet them. He was a braver man than I, I'll give him that. My knees were knocking and not just from the cold.

George extended a hand toward the captain, but Avila declined to shake. Rather, he opened the chest to reveal a king's ransom. Precious jewels and Spanish doubloons glinted in the moonlight.

Avila whispered something lengthy in Spanish.

"*For the temple,*" Ralphy translated. His three-word translation seemed a bit truncated to me, but maybe Ralphy's Spanish was as rusty as my Thai.

George nodded at Avila's words like he knew what the ghost was saying and patted a hand on the open chest lid.

Avila and his men vanished, leaving only a smile. Cheshire Conquistadors. Who'd have thought?

Ralphy ran to the chest. "It's real!" he crowed, running his hands through the treasure.

I slammed the lid.

"Fer rude!" Ralphy muttered, rubbing his hands to check if he still had all his fingers.

George laid a hand on Ralphy's shoulder. "Now, Ralphy. Remember what we agreed?"

Ralphy looked down at the chest. "There goes my chance to be richer than Bill Gates. Jon Huntsman, even."

HERE'S another Utah geographic fact: the Beehive House, Brigham Young's old historic home, sits just half a block east of Temple Square. It sits there just as handy at two in the morning as it does in broad daylight. Even handier if you're leaving a pirate chest full of gold on its front steps without being seen.

A Volvo with California plates and an "RULDS" sticker sped past on South Temple, honking at us as it passed. Even at two in the morning, there was still traffic in the heart of downtown Salt Lake that night. The Jazz must have won. When they lose, Salt Lake's a ghost town, if you'll excuse the expression.

"Geez, we're in plain sight here. And we're parked in a no-parking zone. We're gonna get caught," Ralphy whimpered. Ralphy was huffing and puffing. We all were. That chest was *heavy*.

"Yeah," said George. He pointed up at the ugly slab-white modern skyscraper just to the north of the Beehive House. "I thought we were leaving this over at the Church Office Building."

"This is Brigham's house," I answered after I got my wind back. "It's Brigham's gold."

"Pirate gold for Brother Brigham." George shook his head as if he still didn't believe it.

We took one last look at the chest and drove off.

I CHECKED the newspapers the next day for any mention of the chest or the gold or anything, but there wasn't any. Not that day. Not the next day. Not ever. That week, though, the Church announced a slew of new temples, triggering yet another *Time* magazine cover story on how rich the Mormon Church was.

"Richer than they think," Ralphy said. We were back at Arctic Circle. This time George was slurping down fry sauce without a care in the world.

"What do you mean?" I asked Ralphy.

Ralphy cleared his throat. Always a bad sign.

"I didn't entirely translate everything Avila said at the time." He played with his straw. "Avila said something to the effect of, 'Here is a *second* chest of gold for your temple.'"

"*Second?*" George and I looked at each other. "You mean – ?"

"I think the real Brigham Young once met Avila at the shores of the Great Salt Lake. You're the historian, professor. Remember Church history? The Church was broke once. Flat broke. And suddenly we weren't."

George choked on his Sprite.

Ralphy's grasp on history was about as firm as his grip on reality, but even a broken clock is right twice a day. My digital watch chose that exact moment to chirp the top of the hour.

WE DIDN'T say any more the rest of that lunch about pirate ships or gold or anything else. In fact, we haven't ever been back to that Arctic Circle since.

George and I, however, did run up to Salt Lake and visit the Beehive House a few days later. The docent, an elderly lady who'd been there years and years and years, led us through the tour. In Brigham's bedroom, we saw an old wooden chest identical to the one Avila had given us. I asked the docent how long the chest had been on display.

She gave me a rather odd look. "As long as I've worked here. It sits right where Brigham left it."

Ralphy had said Avila had said *a* second chest. Not *the* second chest, just *a* second chest. I don't know about Spanish, but in English it can make a world of difference. Those old treasure galleons sometimes held dozens of treasure chests.

I looked at George and George looked at me.

The next full moon the Church announced another slew of new temples.

FIRST ESTATE

Katherine Woodbury

BEDET noticed the human woman during the lake's excavation. Over the past month, his people had worked everyday sunup to sundown – they must finish before the rains came – and his steward had hired extra help from Soldt. The human woman sat with the shifters where the diggers dumped the soil's detritus; the shifters set aside the best rocks to line the lake's bottom.

"Her name is Meg Olson," the steward said when Bedet asked. "She comes from Nativay. She lives in Soldt."

"She'll burn in the sun," Bedet said.

The steward nodded. The next day, he and the foreman erected a tarp over the shifters. Most of the workers, shaded by their gray- and brown-feathered wings, watched perplexed, but Meg moved under the shelter; Bedet saw her thank the steward and foreman.

He returned to his drawing board. The lake was Bedet's latest addition to his estate, Wyit. Wyit included one thousand acres on the agricultural side of the Griv world. It was surrounded by other estates as well as Soldt, a trading post, and Glefa, where the shuttles arrived daily from Griv's cities and off-world colonies, like Nativay. Meg would have arrived on Griv through Glefa – not a typical goal for an alien but perhaps she preferred the country; perhaps she couldn't afford city living.

His people completed the lake the next afternoon. Bedet released Thanksgivers, which flew amongst the workers scattering coins from their beaks. The gold flashed in the sunlight and the workers soared for the glitter. A few coins bounced into the lake where the workers let them stay. It was part of the ceremony: the adventurous would retrieve them after the lake filled.

Bedet snagged a coin. "Give it to Meg," he told the steward and watched the man weave through the crowd. Meg accepted the coin with a bow.

Bedet's cousin Pilf arrived. He strutted portentously through the workers, maroon wings curled tight to avoid contact. Bedet sighed and kept his own silvery wings furled. Pilf was a scavenger who wanted to feed off Bedet's wealth, appropriate Bedet's people. Pilf, or rather Pilf's eldest child, was Bedet's heir presumptive, should Bedet fail to produce an heir apparent. No one on Wyit wanted this to happen. Right now, behind Pilf's back, diggers rolled their eyes and flailed their wings. Bedet grimaced at them until they grinned, abashed, and flapped away.

"Excellent, excellent," Pilf said when he arrived at Bedet's drawing board. "They do good work."

"My people are dependable," Bedet said, and Pilf forced a smile. It wasn't polite to say, "My." Bedet said it constantly: *My* workers. *My* estate. *My creation.*

"Another two years," Pilf said, and now Bedet forced a smile. "Unless, of course, you marry," Pilf added with a smug glance.

"No revolutions today," Bedet said shortly, his eyes hooded.

Pilf looked over the drawing board, made several unworkable suggestions and took his leave. The workers also dispersed as gray clouds gathered. Bedet couldn't see Meg in the dimming light. He would have sent the steward to escort her home, but the steward had vanished into the departing crowd.

Bedet was finally alone. Wyit stretched about him, expansive and still. He flew down to the middle of the lake and settled on the wide-flat rocks nestled together to create a smooth bed. He would need to compliment both the shifters and masons again – this time, he would speak to Meg personally.

He brushed aside a few coins and lay back. His muscles twinged, loosened. He slept. Rain woke him, hard drops like thudding crystals. Masses of white fish eggs would follow; one storm would stock the lake for several years. Bedet held up his arms and raised his head.

Something huddled at his feet. Materials left over from the morning, he thought, but the heap moved, unwound. Meg gazed at Bedet through streams of water.

He spoke against the harsh slap of the rain: "Why are you here?"

Her lips quivered. With fear? He didn't dare touch her. She couldn't know what she was doing.

"Cover me," Meg said.

Or what those words meant.

"How – What do you mean?"

"Stretch your wings over me – "

He moved then, crouching beside her, a hand to her mouth. She could not possibly realize – "Who told you to speak those words?"

She stared at him through the slanting rain. Her eyes were flecked brown and green, disturbingly variable, unreadable. She was a pale creature of fluctuating color. She was utterly alien.

"Your mother," she said. "Norfa."

"My mother?" He gaped. "Why?"

"She wants protection in her old age." Meg shouted against the whip of the wind, and Bedet leaned forward to catch the fantastic words. "She said – she asked me to help her."

He shook his head. It wasn't like his mother to beg. Since abdicating Wyit, she'd kept all the proprieties.

"She doesn't have much." Meg was shaking, but Bedet couldn't touch her. "You could share."

"We don't."

She rocked backwards, and the rain spread harsh patterns across her face. Within minutes, the water would bury her. Bedet stood, hauling at her arms, and she stood with him.

"You have to get out," he said and pushed her toward the side of the lake.

She scrambled up the slope. Panting, she turned to sit on the edge, arms covered with gray mud. He hovered over her, his silver-blue wings steadying him in the air, his hands on the grass at the lake's lip.

She said, "You should be kinder to her."

Kind. He shook his head, bemused. He was kind. Meg was asking for something else – a reversal of inheritance. That wasn't kind; it was insane.

She tried to stand and slipped. He hauled at her arm, felt her hands against his chest, and his wings slid 'round her, covered her, kept the rain from her head.

Acceptance.

He carried Meg to the main house: several rooms around a sunken wood floor with stone inlays. A fire burned in a squat stove at the center of the circular hall. Meg sat beside it, curled inside the blanket Bedet found for her.

She said, "Your mother loves Wyit."

"I know, but she surrendered the estate to me, as was right and proper." A parent raised you, then left you. It was civilized: a reverse of working-class traditions that flung children out, leaving the parents in control of the house.

Meg's shaking subsided; she slept. Bedet watched her. He saw himself reflected in the hall's rain-streaked windows: a looming, shimmery winged figure, the pupils of its eyes so large they almost hid the greenish-yellow glint of the irises. Meg slept at the figure's feet, a blanketed mound of new and unusual life.

Bedet turned abruptly from his image, leaving the house. He returned to the lake and flew down to the foundation. He rose with the water, eyes narrowed against the streaming rain while fish eggs beaded his body.

He was now betrothed. To an alien. Marriage to an alien – a strange being unfamiliar with Griv customs – would not please the patriarchs. They were already suspicious of Bedet.

Not his mother's fault. There were estate-owning parents who could not leave their children, who wept and clung to the new-winged inheritors. There were parents who coddled their children in the early years, making separation at age ten harder than it should be. Norfa had done none of that. Bedet's father died when Bedet was nine; Norfa stayed three more years to make up for the loss. But she *had* left – suddenly, without warning, as was right – and Bedet had assumed the estate's management.

He would never leave.

Toward midnight, he flew back to the house. Meg woke as he entered. He sat on the divan nearest the stove, scattering drops from his hair, shedding pearly feathers. Meg picked one up, held it in her lap.

Bedet said, "You realize I've agreed to marry you."

"Yes."

"I'll have to speak to your patron." His mother, he meant, his mother who had never interfered in his adult life till now.

Meg said, "Norfa's been like a mother to me."

Bedet frowned. Meg's eyes were blue in the indoor light, the pupils small. They closed Bedet off, told him nothing.

She said, "Other boarding houses wouldn't take me. I owe her. I'm grateful to her like a child would be."

Bedet winced. Her words were barriers, hedges between them, worse than hedges, being tenuous, without weight.

He said softly, "A parent who expected gratitude would be ... uncivilized, a glutton or parasite. Even the workers give their children freedom."

"Husbands and wives stay together. Why not offspring?"

The hedges were dangerous, full of thorns. Bedet forced himself not to retreat though his hands curled. He watched those hands, avoiding Meg's unreadable eyes.

He said carefully, "Between parents and child – such a bond would be perverse."

Under the blanket, her limbs stiffened. She said, "We separate family intimacy from couple intimacy. The child-parent bond is different, strong in its way. Not the same."

He breathed that in, hands relaxing. He lowered his wings until they brushed her neck. She hunched away from the feathers, watching him warily. Bedet smiled. Wingless or not, she might be any pullet, ruffling against possible offense.

He conceded, "Norfa was a good mother."

Rain drummed against the roof. Bedet sat beside Meg, wings arched so the left one encircled her. She ran her hand along the radius; Bedet quivered, and his flight feathers rustled.

He was old to be unmarried, several years beyond the usual age, being twenty-six. He had refused Sarca, who lived with her elder brother on an estate in Laft. Eldest children inherited; Sarca's brother would provide Sarca with a good dowry. *And* she was the patriarchs' choice for Bedet.

But Sarca could still bear children, and Bedet didn't want an heir, didn't want to become a disinherited parent, living in town, exchanging daily courtesies with the patriarchs. *Useless.*

He rested his chin on his arm and contemplated Meg's short rumpled hair and sharp profile. She was greater danger to him than Sarca.

Toward dawn, the rain tapered off; the planet's suns crawled into a cloudless sky. Bedet stood with Meg on the veranda and gazed over Wyit's fields. Blue-tipped wahst covered the west field. The east field was a mass of dark, churned soil primed for alien crops: carrots and potatoes.

"You love it," Meg said, and Bedet scowled.

"I shouldn't," he said. "Pilf wants it for his offspring."

"He has an estate."

"He claims I'm irresponsible – " ever since Bedet refused Sarca. "He claims that by custom, Wyit must be passed within the next two years."

It wasn't enough time. Bedet had plans: not only the lake but expansion in the east field, improvements to the workers' cottages, the construction of a dye factory behind the house.

Perfecting an estate takes a lifetime.

Meg said abruptly, "My mother died."

He turned to study her. She said, almost unwillingly, "She was like Norfa. Full of common sense. You could tell her anything, no matter how outrageous, and she saw the purpose, the point, you know?" Meg effaced herself, grimacing, but Bedet did know. He recognized the woman she described. Norfa was intelligent, straightforward; she had helped him see Wyit in ways his father had missed.

"My mother died slowly," Meg said. "Her mind – She faded, but she never lost her amusement, amusement at herself. It broke my heart," Meg whispered, and Bedet's wings encircled her. "I want to help Norfa," Meg said.

For the sake of her dead mother. Bedet flinched from the image, whispering as it did of decay and stagnation. He flinched too from his own comprehension. Bedet's father was buried on Wyit – Norfa's decision, but Bedet could have disinterred the corpse any time in the past fourteen years and burned it as was customary. He preferred his father's remnants in Wyit's soil.

I have undermined too many traditions, avoided too many customs. If Pilf sues for control, the patriarchs may back him –

He said, "You asked me only for Norfa's sake?"

Meg smiled, eyes half-closed against the light. "You're a good master. The workers say you've brought wealth to Wyit."

Bedet breathed in that unexpected compliment and straightened tense shoulders.

"And you were kind," Meg said. "To me."

That particular definition of kindness he understood.

He walked her to Soldt. Early morning light stroked the graveled street. A few patriarchs congregated beneath the arched village gate.

"Good rain," they said to Bedet, but their eyes strayed to Meg. Bedet and Meg had reached the town's raised stone plaza when Odde, the oldest patriarch, called, "Bedet." Bedet returned, leaving Meg near the plaza fountain.

"That is Meg Olson," Odde said on a throaty cough. "She lives at Norfa's."

"Yes."

"What is your association?"

"She needs protection."

"You should think more about protecting Sarca."

"Sarca has many admirers. She doesn't need my attention."

Odde swayed forward, ragged quills scratching the ground. "Wyit does not belong to you, Bedet. You hold it for your heir."

I improved it. I complete it. But that would sound workish, low-caste. Bedet stared across the plaza at Meg, pale and wingless.

"Meg and I are betrothed," he said desperately. *Hold them off. Gain time.*

Odde's brow wrinkled. Pale green feathers, yellowed with age, wafted to his shoulders from distended wings. In a fight, Bedet could physically overpower

Odde. There was precedent: the workers sometimes fought over property.

"I do not support our world's open-door policy," Odde said.

"It brings in trade and investors."

"But can they give us heirs?" Odde coughed and wafted away.

Bedet went back to Meg, took her hand. People reported births of mixed children, some winged, on the colonies. But Meg with a child would leave Bedet no better off.

His mother, Norfa, waited for them outside her dwelling, a tall townhouse. She was a small, quick woman with golden wings that glittered in the morning sun. Meg broke from Bedet's side and hugged her. Bedet winced. It was a child's gesture. Meg seemed an adult, looked an adult, but he didn't know how humans aged.

"I asked him," Meg said, and Norfa smiled at Bedet over Meg's head.

"Good. Come in."

Bedet edged into the high parlor while Norfa fetched cups and saucers. Bedet could smell charcoaled wahst, and he grimaced at the implication. Roasted wahst kernels were used when boiling tea for nuptial negotiations. Norfa had anticipated his compliance or, at least, his curiosity.

He settled on the divan beside Meg while Norfa carried in a tray with teapot, cups, plus a bowl of charred grass. She positioned the tray on a cabinet, taking a cup of wahst tea for herself. She handed the bowl to Meg.

"This is for Bedet."

Bedet put up a hand. He said to Norfa, "You told Meg to approach me."

"She's a better choice for you than Sarca."

Bedet glanced at Meg. She stared at her knees, face shuttered.

He said, his voice neutral, "Sarca is traditional."

"Yes," Norfa said. "She would think nothing of abandoning – " Norfa looked at Meg; *abandon* was an alien word " – leaving the estate when your child was born."

"No," Bedet said.

"And she would expect you to go with her."

"Yes."

"Meg doesn't expect you to leave," Norfa said. "Do you, Meg? You would not push Bedet from his home? You would not expect a child to take what his parents created?"

"No," Meg said, "but neither would I push the child out. I was taught to honor bonds between family members."

Taught. By her religion, Bedet guessed. Human religion loved the quagmire of interpersonal relationships. Meg was encased by belief, an abstract vision of the future.

But wasn't Bedet? A long-term vision of Wyit held him in thrall. Every morning, he woke comforted, safe, enclosed by the thing he had nurtured and made. His mind would leap forward as he imagined how Wyit's fields, lake, and house might appear in some unknown, unrealized future.

While Meg imagined children who didn't leave, parents who remained in positions of honor. Meg, he realized, saw family as he saw Wyit: a made thing, only with people, not crops. The vision revolted and entranced him. He breathed out a long, halting sigh. He held Meg within the curve of one wing and gazed up into Norfa's shrewd eyes.

"Oh, Meg," he said, "my mother is not kind. She is entirely self-serving." And to Norfa, "You want the estate back."

"I left the place I loved in order to keep you strong. And you are strong, and I am tired of exile."

"I cannot return it – "

"I would not take it. I want only to live there again. I want – " Norfa's hands clenched; the cup of tea shook in her hands.

Bedet knew what she wanted: to reap what she'd sown. He grimaced, and Norfa's mouth twitched. She touched Meg's hand.

"I *am* self-serving," she said, "but I so much prefer you to Sarca. Do not *you* abandon *us*."

"I'm not so foolish," Meg said.

Bedet reached out and took a morsel of charred grass. Norfa watched. Meg watched. He put the grass in his mouth, chewed, leaned over and fed Meg with lips and tongue. When he pulled away, he found her flushed and out of breath.

"Ah," Norfa said. "Then you ratify the engagement."

"I do. You don't mind this," he said to Meg.

She shook her head. "No," she said faintly, and Bedet grinned. She moved to his knee and fed him the rest of the grass.

Out on the street, alone, he was less sanguine. The women's bargain seemed wild, unnatural, a plunge into a mad place where children lived parasitically on their elders, the elders demanded attention, and the whole family collapsed beneath its own stagnation.

He hardly noticed the filling streets, the shopkeepers laying out their sign mats, until he entered the plaza. Workers milled there. They turned to watch Bedet, to nod. He nodded back, bemused – *So many people visiting Soldt so early?* Nearing the gate, he saw Pilf's orange-winged wife. Beyond her, Pilf stood with the patriarchs, his maroon wings raised.

"You are betrothed," Pilf called as Bedet passed under the high arch. "To the alien." Bedet stopped, keeping his wings lowered. "Yes."

"An alien – with alien customs." Pilf addressed the patriarchs. "This unnatural master wants to keep an estate. A good master would give it up."

Bedet said, "A good master improves what he has. Ask my workers."

The patriarchs clucked, but the crowd in the plaza murmured approval. Pilf glared at them. He swiveled towards the patriarchs.

"Bedet's father never left."

"He left me," Bedet said tightly. "He died."

"You buried him on the estate. Your mother stayed till you were twelve. You are surrounded by dead things."

Bedet's wings rose above his shoulders like a shimmering summer rain cloud. Pilf paled. Bedet said, "My land flourishes. My workers are happy. Life is good on Wyit."

"Empty words," Pilf barked. "You – you abandon civilized behavior."

That word – *abandon*. Norfa could say it and mean something deeper than Bedet understood. Pilf said it to deride, condemn as if Bedet were perverse, wrong inside, wrong-headed. Bedet flung himself at Pilf, and their wings clashed as he struck a fist across Pilf's face.

Pilf surged upwards, wings beating furiously. Bedet followed. He grasped Pilf's arm, and Pilf whirled, teeth bared. "Your workers will revolt."

Their wings entangled. Bedet spit out feathers. "They respect me." Meg had told him that. "They are more flexible than the patriarchs. They want to survive."

Pilf twisted forward, so his jagged pollex sliced Bedet's forehead. Blood trickled into Bedet's eyes. He struck back with his free fist. He would have struck again, but a cry from the plaza caught his attention.

Meg – Bedet knew her voice. He pushed away from Pilf and scanned the ground below. Meg had entered the plaza with Norfa. She struggled now in a flare of orange feathers: Pilf's wife had attacked her.

Bedet let out a shrill, piercing scream, and launched himself towards Meg. Pilf blocked his way. "No," Bedet shouted. He gripped Pilf's neck, ignoring Pilf's fists and slapping wings. Pilf flailed, went limp. Bedet didn't drop him despite his rage. He swept low, released Pilf to the ground, and whirled towards Meg, wings twisting to bring him upright.

Norfa was already there. She stood over Meg, golden wings outspread to shoo away Pilf's wife. About the plaza, workers bounced into the air, exchanging squawks of information: "The human is safe." "Bedet flew like a shuttle." "Pilf is dead – " "No, unconscious."

"Well?" Bedet called to them. "Would you rather I controlled Wyit or would you prefer Pilf's squab?"

The workers murmured. "Bedet," they were saying. "Bedet."

The patriarchs hissed. Odde flapped forward. "Your request isn't natural," he said to Bedet, his voice low.

"It is natural to the workers."

"Your obligations go beyond Wyit."

Norfa spoke from Bedet's side. "Prosperous estates help everyone, including you, Odde."

"We have always avoided quarrels over land – "

"I am quarreling now," Bedet said.

"Love has corrupted you."

Yes.

"Better than Pilf's greed," said Norfa.

"The alien does not understand a mistress's duties."

Meg hunched on the plaza curb. She said, "Norfa could teach me how to run an estate."

Odde's eyes flickered, and Bedet suddenly wondered if Norfa was as strong-minded a force in Soldt as she'd been on Wyit. Odde might appreciate a decision that sent Norfa back to the estate.

He said, "Let the workers decide."

Odde's smile was thin. "We want no riots. Neither do you. If the estate should decline, the workers will remember what is right."

"I know the risk."

"Your life." Odde seemed to shrug. He turned to the square, lifted his hands: the image of orthodox approval. He raised his voice to a hoot: "Bedet will marry the alien. Norfa will be her attendant on Wyit."

Workers cheered and clapped. Wings fluttered as people launched upwards. Odde turned back to Bedet:

"Seven years. You have seven years to prove yourself."

It was more than two. Bedet squatted beside Meg, kissed the scraped fingers. He looked up into Norfa's cunning eyes.

"You'll have a voice on Wyit," he said and carried Meg into the air.

She turned against him as they rose, folding her arms around his neck, breathing against his cheek. The countryside – flushed with green growth – passed beneath them. Wyit slid into view. White eggs beaded the sparkling lake. Fields rippled around the main house. To the east, purple-black soil waited. To the west, blue-tipped wahst swayed like a mass of sky spread across the ground.

"It's beautiful," Meg said. "You should be proud."

"This isn't mere vanity?"

"I would not love that quality in you. Mere vanity could never create a world like this."

Bedet flew over the house, dipped down into the wahst fields. Meg tumbled out of his arms, laughing. She lay on her back, hands extended to brush the cerulean stalks. She curved her arm to stroke Bedet's face. Lowering his wings around her, Bedet saw the tattered tips.

They would heal by the marriage festival, appear full and feathered. It hardly mattered. He was strong, strong enough to beat Pilf, to win Meg, to hold the estate.

The land enclosed him and Meg like a firm shell.

Mine, mine to add upon, to magnify. Mine, perhaps, to keep.

Home.

FANGS OF THE DRAGON

David J. West

He who fights with monsters should take care to see that, in doing so, he doesn't turn into a monster himself. And when you take a long look into an abyss, the abyss looks back into you.

146., *Beyond Good and Evil*, Friedrich Wilhelm Nietzsche
(Trans. by Wm Morris)

1.

The water lapped hungrily at the shore. Waves rippled across shadowy liquid, pushed by something stronger than the moon's dominion. Something splashed far out in the lake as the mournful melody of a flute carried and abruptly went silent.

An eerie green ball of fire raced across the night sky on the far side of the lake. It shot chaotically from side to side down the mountain as if chasing down prey, then diving hard, it was gone.

A man driving his wagon approached the lake. "Look at that, Ahab. Who says there isn't even a lake monster to see around here?" said Phineas Cook to the dog that sat beside him. "I see lots of things." He cracked the reins and forced the ox, Petunia, down to the lake shore.

Bringing the wagon to the rim of the ebbing surf, he circled it around next to a massive gnarled stump.

Phineas didn't want to be on Bear Lake at night, but it couldn't be helped. Work at the mill had taken longer than expected and he still had to uphold the bargain with Brother Brigham. The rope was expensive and there wouldn't be a better time than now. Naysayers were asleep, as were curious onlookers.

Bleak stars hung overhead as Phineas removed a rowboat from the wagon and set it upon the lake shore while Ahab chased his tail.

The ox eyed the water, snorted, and threatened to depart.

He ran a hand across her flanks, "Easy, Petunia. I've work to do, nothing to be afraid of."

Ahab whined.

"Same for you. We capture this leviathan and we'll be able to take care of the Church's debts. Think of the good we can do."

Ahab buried his face with his paws.

Icy mist lingered over the lake as Phineas secured a thick hemp rope to the huge stump. He put a pair of buoys in the water, one larger than the other, next to the rowboat. From the buckboard he produced a flag, Old Glory, and attached it to the top of the larger buoy.

It was cold. Steam flared from his nostrils as Ahab whined again. "You coward," he said, loading the buffalo gun and setting it within easy reach.

A mournful sound carried across the waters and Phineas watched a moment, discerning nothing in the gloom. He waited a minute longer and whispered a prayer with eyes open. "Lord, walk beside me."

He lanced raw mutton upon a great triangular hook. Ahab whined so he tossed a small piece of meat to the dog, saying, "You wait here. Watch Petunia. I'll be back shortly." He then attached the hook to the smaller of the two buoys by a twenty-foot chain.

Phineas pushed the rowboat into the lake with the tethered buoys floating beside. He kept the baited hook in the boat with the buffalo gun. He waved to the pacing dog and rowed with soft sloshing sounds out into the lake. The rope slowly uncoiled from the stump into the frigid waters. It was fall but already frost danced across the valley.

Three hundred feet out and the larger, flagged buoy jerked, held fast by the great stump. Phineas had another three hundred feet for the second buoy but with as late and cold as it was, he decided he needn't row that far. He pushed the smaller buoy to let it drift away. The twenty-foot chain dragged from the boat. Phineas picked up the stout barbed hook and let it lightly into the water.

The smaller buoy shook as the weight of the chain pulled it taut. Phineas smiled. Nothing to do now but wait and let blessings come.

A tortured scream shot across the lake.

Phineas couldn't tell if it was human or animal nor from which direction it came. The boat rocked as he looked frantically in all directions. Picking up the buffalo gun, he was momentarily disoriented as the boat spun upon the dark mirrored water.

A horrifying roar echoed over the waters, terrible in its satanic majesty. Beastly divergent from the first cry, this was the sound of a bloodthirsty victor, not a victim.

If he had ever heard a monster, that was it. The sensation of that demonic call sickened him, inducing nausea worse than the time he fell into a swarm of pungent crickets. He'd never thought to feel that horrible again, but this enveloped him in thick dread.

Silhouetted against the hills, the greenish light of a fireball rose and floated across the lake some distance south, writhing worm-like in its flight. The color and speed were too strange for a lantern, the twisting trajectory maddening.

Phineas's eyes and rifle followed the thing as it moved away. He wondered briefly if he saw the eyes of a dragon, its colossal head lumbering back and forth as it swam the lake. If so, the brute would be far larger than he had anticipated, a behemoth for the ages.

The wicked firelight continued south, growing dim until it disappeared behind hills or sinking into the depths. Phineas couldn't be sure where it vanished in the dark. He pondered his predicament when a splash and knock against the rowboat made the blood in his veins turn as cold and thick as tree sap in winter.

Something was alive in the water beside him.

Heart thawed and racing, he paused and looked over the side.

A thick wet tongue caressed his hand.

Cursing, he leveled the gun at Ahab's wet black face. "Ahab, you fool, I nearly killed ya." He pulled the dog into the boat and was promptly rewarded with its shaking dry. "As if I'm not cold enough," he growled before rowing with all possible speed for land.

On shore, Phineas painstakingly loaded the rowboat into the wagon as the wind came down from the north. It whipped and gave him a chill as it cut sharply through his damp clothes.

"Let's go Ahab, we gotta get home."

The dog whined again as a loud creak caught Phineas attention. The rope to the first buoy was stretched rigid to the stump, water droplets catching moonlight before falling.

"The wind must be pulling her tight," said Phineas. "It's fine."

Creaking again, the stump lurched from the bank, exposing a few inches from the sandy shore. Phineas frowned and stepped up on the stump.

"Wind must really be pulling, but this is too heavy to go any further," he said, stamping his foot.

Shuddering, the stump heaved into the lake creating a white wake. Ahab whined as his master was pulled into the dark water.

2.

It had been a cold night on the mountain for Porter and he meant to stay indoors tonight if he could, but first he went looking for a drink. He was of medium size but broad shouldered and strong, a fighting man, a gunslinger. Dark hair beginning to salt erupted from beneath his slouch hat, and his beard was as long and wild as the north wind. But the most disconcerting thing to the townsfolk who watched him ride in, what made them turn away, was his piercing pale blue eyes. The eyes of a killer.

Riding the full length of the town and back again, he was disappointed. No saloon and no inn. He cursed the luck that broke two bottles of Valley-Tan whiskey on the ride through the mountains.

The most promising sanctuary looked to be a general store. He tied his stallion to the hitching post, knocked grime from his worn duster and went inside. His heavy boots pounded the floorboards as the spurs chimed in.

The air inside was stuffy; sunbeams swirling dust graced through narrow windowpanes. A thin clerk paused reading the latest edition of the *Utah Magazine* and smiled. "Morning, sir. What can I help you with today? Name is Thomas."

"Got any whiskey? Valley-Tan?" asked the rider, looking about the sparse room.

Frowning, Thomas put down the paper and grabbed a broom. "No, 'fraid not."

"How about a room then?"

Tightening the broomstick, Thomas said, "No, sir, we don't. You ought to keep moving along if you're looking for such things."

The rider gave a lopsided grin and ran a hand over his long peppered beard. "How's about you direct me to Brother Cook then," he said, staring through Thomas.

Thomas repeated, "Brother? You ... you're Porter Rockwell?"

Port grunted. "You sure you ain't got anything to drink?"

"Yes, sir."

Pounding the countertop, Port said, "I need a squar' drink!"

"Let me look again. Said you want to see Brother Cook? He's laid up in bed, had an accident last night, he did," said Thomas as he rummaged through crates behind the counter. "Seems he fell into the lake, near froze to death afore he got home. Heard he blamed it on the lake monster."

"What's that?" replied Port, only half-listening as he squinted at a suspect case in the corner.

Straightening, Thomas proclaimed, "The eighth wonder of the world, Brother Rich calls it. Right here in our own valley. You haven't heard of the Bear Lake Monster?"

"No," Port groaned, "What's in that case yonder?"

"It's for tinctures."

"Good enough, hand it over," he said, extending his broad palm.

Thomas paused.

Porter gestured with hands strong enough to break a bull's neck.

Reluctantly handing over a bottle, Thomas said, "You know the Good Lord doesn't want you to drink that."

Porter uncorked the bottle, sniffed it, and took a swig. "Well, has *He* ever tried it with raspberries?"

Thomas curled his lips at that. "After last night I imagine Brother Cook needs all the help he can get. Soon enough President Young will have to address things too." He held up the latest issue of the *Utah Magazine* to emphasize his point.

Porter looked at Thomas. "Don't know anything about that. I just need a place to sleep a couple nights. Give me four bottles."

"But you are here because of the monster?"

"Yup, a monster, sure," said Porter between gulps.

"You don't know much about it then, do you?"

"Nope. I understand there's been some killings. Brother Brigham asked me to come take care of it. *If* there was anything to it."

"There is," Thomas said with conviction. "We need true authority to take care of the problem. You can wait for Brother Cook to be ready to talk, but understand this: he had a hook and chain tied to buoys and then roped to a huge stump beside the lake."

"So?" said Port, quaffing another mouthful.

"This morning Brother Rich told me, he saw that stump in the lake heading north."

Port shrugged.

"Something pulled it up the lake, against the wind, the buoys were held down underwater. This thing may be too blessed big ... even for you."

"I got my own blessings," responded Port. "Where is Cook?"

"Fine house, above the mill, just up the hill. Talk to Brother Cook, but he'll be no help. If I was you, I'd talk to one of the Lamanites," he said, gesturing south.

Port's gaze hardened at that remark; it didn't seem that long ago he met the Shoshone on the Bear River. Images of frozen blood and thunder washed over him. "Which one?"

"You'll want to find Ligaii-Maiitsoh. We call him Lehi; he likes that. Knows everything about the monster."

"That's no Shoshone name," said Port.

Thomas shook his head, "He's not Shoshone. They avoid him. Don't know what tribe he is. But he's been good to us. He's nearly a convert."

"Where can I find him?"

3.

Stepping into the bright sunlight, Port stared eastward across the vast lake. He stretched his back, which in turn let his brace of pistols leer from his person.

A young mother and her son took one look at the long-haired gunfighter and wheeled around.

Port grinned. Watchdogs are rarely appreciated.

He went down the steps whistling an old tune, but a sixth sense that always rode shotgun with him whispered *Look around.*

Three men dogged his trail. They followed on his right with the rising sun at their backs.

"Hey, Rockwell! Need a word with you," shouted the foremost of the three.

Porter pretended he couldn't hear them while watching them in his peripheral vision. He crossed the muddy street in long strides, so that he was now on their right, with the sun and shimmering lake at his back.

"We're talking to you, Danite!"

Porter faced them where the alleyway between buildings flashed sunlight into their faces. He watched as townsfolk scurried off the street, all but a curious white-haired old Indian. He just stared.

"Hey, Porter!" called the foremost man. "Heard you can't be shot or cut."

Port spat, "You pukes need schoolin'?"

The first averted his eyes, pulling his revolver and saying, "Ain't you the funny man." A second with crooked teeth also drew a pistol, the third a shotgun. They kept their distance with guns trained on Port, who had yet to draw, but they respected the pistol handles sticking out of his coat.

"You want me to feed those to ya?" asked Port with a grin.

The three stood with guns pointed but still nervous. Crooked Teeth shook so that his pistol trembled.

"You boys think I've lasted this long to be gunned down by your sorry hides?"

The leader swaggered, "Maybe. You're getting old. Why not?"

Port prodded, "So why don't ya *try* already?"

Crooked teeth whined, "Boss said we could just run him out of town."

"Huh-uh. He ain't gonna run. Are you, Porter?"

Port shook his head.

The shotgunner chuckled. "We got him."

Port winked.

Crooked Teeth wiped his brow with his free hand, letting his aim go far afield.

Porter lunged sideways, drawing his two Navy Revolvers. Shots blazed and echoed. Bone shattered as Port's lead sowed scarlet upon dirty white fields.

Bullets whizzed like mercurial hornets past Port's ears, but he was untouched. He was always untouched, but he also respected how close death stood, always over his shoulder.

The three lay upon the ground, alive but wounded, mewling.

"Quit your caterwauling," Port ordered. He nudged their shattered elbows and forearms with his boot. "You pukes is lucky. I was aiming lower." Glancing about for onlookers, he said, "Where is the marshal?"

The only soul on the street was the old Indian.

"Chief, I need the marshal or deputy. Where're they?"

The Indian just stared.

The lead gunman stopped crying long enough to ask, "Arrrgh. Why don't ya just kill us?"

Grinding his boot heel into the bleeding arm, Port demanded, "Why'd you come gunning for me? Who put you up to it? How'd you know I'd be here?"

The man screamed as Port's heel pressed. The old Indian still watched, impassive as ever.

"Well?"

A new voice called out, "Rockwell! You can't do that. It isn't legal." A smartly dressed man approached, followed by two deputies.

"You the sheriff?" Port extended a handshake.

"I am." The man declined to shake, instead pointing at the three wounded men. "I respect your reputation, but you cannot torture these men."

The deputies picked up the wounded and led them down the road.

Grimacing, Port said, "I suppose it's right for them to threaten me on the street?"

"Of course not, but times have changed. You're not the judge, jury, and executioner. Not anymore," said the sheriff.

"I never was," answered Port.

The sheriff gave a sarcastic half-grin. "I could run you in for this."

Port glared.

"But I won't. I'll ask that you leave your guns with me while you're in town."

"Ha! *No.*"

Paling, the sheriff blustered, "Fine, but any more trouble and you'll be locked up."

"Someone put them up to this. I've a right to find out who."

"We'll find out. When it goes before Judge Jenson. Next week. They may counter-charge you, so if there were any witnesses, you may need their testimony."

"Got one saw the whole thing." Port looked for the Indian, but the old man had disappeared on the wide-open street. "He was just here."

"I didn't see anyone when I walked up. This may turn into a case of your word against theirs," said the sheriff. "Maybe you better leave town before any of that happens. Let Brigham protect you again."

Cocking an eyebrow, the old gunfighter spat on the sheriff's polished boots and walked away.

4.

Port rode to the house just up the hill. A black dog lounging on the porch watched him dismount. At the door it licked Port's hand.

"Hey, boy, what's your name?" asked Port, kneeling. He scratched its exposed neck before knocking.

A short blonde woman opened the door. "I'm so glad you're here. Come in," she said, beaming. "Ahab, stay outside."

Removing his hat, Port asked, "Really, ma'am?"

"Of course. I recognize you, Brother Rockwell. I'm Amanda Cook."

Realization dawned across his face. "Wheat! You're Dave Savage's papoose, ain't ya?" Port said with a laugh.

"Mary, see that the eggs are collected." Ushering her daughter out to the hen house, Amanda smiled. "No one has called me my father's papoose in years. Phineas is going to be so glad to see you and get your help."

"My help, ma'am?"

She turned her head. "With the monster," she said, raising her eyebrows. "That is why you're here isn't it?"

"I reckon so," said Port. "But everyone seems to know a trifle more than I do."

Amanda ushered Port into a side room where Phineas lay in bed. She then tossed a chunk of kindling into the fire.

Heat made Port uncomfortable. He longed for a cool breeze.

"Sorry if I don't get up," sniffed Phineas, "but I got a terrible chill last night."

"What happened? Heard you fell into the lake because of a monster," said Port.

"I didn't fall, was pulled in. Maybe twenty, thirty feet before I jumped off the stump and made it to shore. I was afraid the monster would get me," added Phineas.

"You think so?"

"Yeah, folks have been seeing the monster for a spell. Lately it's been killing livestock and Indians. Figured if we could capture it, it'd solve some of our local problems and make some money to boot." Phineas paused to blow his nose.

"It's been *killing*, you say?"

Phineas looked surprised. "Yeah, Porter. I thought that was why you were here. We all heard you were coming. I assumed Brother Brigham was sending you to help us deal. Have you throw down with it!"

Port scratched his beard. "Who told you?"

"That apostate writer Stenhouse. Been shooting his mouth off about how President Young is sending you, his avenging angel, up here to save face. Stenhouse has been up here the last few weeks writing up scandalous material for Godbe's rag. Keeps saying you'll fail, since Joseph's blessing for you weren't against tooth and claw. You read any of that trash?"

"Nope."

"You know how the Godbeites are, don't you? The *Utah Magazine*?"

"Nope. Don't read much."

Phineas wrinkled his brow and Amanda restrained a giggle. "Well, they keep pushing for mining rights, trade with gentiles and abandoning sacred law. They're upset with Church doctrine and are trying to change things. Think because they control the paper and wealth they have a right, I suppose. Things could get bad if they convince the government to seize Church property. We're at a crossroads."

Amanda broke in, "They believe they can steady the ark and dictate the Lord's commandments, telling the Prophet *he* is the one out of order. They are Spiritualists, communicating with either ghosts or charlatans through séances."

Phineas nodded, "Personally, I think it's all their high-falutin' British sensibilities, but I doubt any of that has to do with the monster itself."

Porter grinned. "Go on."

"This monster has been costing us livestock and even been killing folk on the south end. And Stenhouse is writing up articles, playing both sides, pressing for government regulation while also pleading sympathy from the Saints by saying if Brigham can't control a thing of the devil, how can he control Deseret?"

"Brother Brigham," Amanda corrected.

"That's what I said. Now Stenhouse writes if Brother Brigham can't control Deseret, if he's not in touch with the Spirit, how can he lead the Church and be right about everything else," said Phineas. "Monsters should be easy, he says."

"His fault?" Port wrinkled his brow in disbelief.

Phineas shook his head. "It's not. It's ammunition, a distraction for something else. I don't know what yet. But they're sowing seeds of doubt and discontent while something is murdering folks and livestock."

"Seems convenient," said Port.

Amanda nodded. "That's what I said."

Phineas pointed at the lake. "There is a connection somewhere, but one thing at a time. I already heard this morning from Brother Rich that bodies were found in the Shoshone area and I heard screams and saw weird fireballs last night. The monster got 'em."

"I'll go look around," said Port. "Is there anyone trustworthy who speaks Shoshone to go along with me? I heard about some old Indian named Lehi?"

Amanda shook her head. "You don't need him. I can go with you and translate. Soon as Sister Ann-Eliza arrives to look after Phineas."

Port raised his eyebrows and looked to Phineas. "This could be ugly," said Port. "I've already got somebody gunning for me."

Looking up at the old gunfighter, Amanda replied, "You need someone trustworthy to go along with you. I can help get to the bottom of this better than anyone, and take a crack shot at the monster too, if need be."

"Not a monster I'm worried about."

Amanda answered, "Have no doubts, Brother Rockwell, we do seek a monster. I've seen the slaughtered cattle and sheep. I don't think my Phineas realizes how lucky he is to still be alive."

Port raised his hands. "All right, little sister, we'll head out soon as the relief arrives. Now Phineas, why didn't your fishing tackle work?"

Phineas sighed. "It did work. I had stout chains and rope, but my anchor was too weak. Monster tore the stump out. If you find it, I need that rope back. It was Brigham's."

"Brother Brigham's," said Amanda.

"That's what I said. The point is, Porter, this thing is big. I'm not sure anymore what it'll take to rein the beast in."

Port tipped his hat and said, "I'll keep an eye out."

5.

A skin-drum throbbed as Port and Amanda rode into the Shoshone camp.

Port asked, "Why the drums?"

Amanda said, "They're letting everyone know we are here. Everyone is skittish after the Bear River massacre. The monster only increases the tension."

"I reckon so."

Crowds of people gathered, faces carved with somber expressions, hard and unfriendly. A tall young man approached Amanda and greeted her in silence. She turned to Porter saying, "This is Many-Buffalo. He is Chief of this clan, Chief Sagwitch's son." She then told Many-Buffalo of Porter.

The Chief glared at Porter and revealed a scar on his breast.

Port intervened. "It doesn't have to be like this. We don't have to be friends. I just want to know about the trouble."

Many-Buffalo gestured at his tribe and pointed at Porter.

"I'll get to that, but they aren't in a friendly mood," she said. "He says you were there. Why should he speak to you now?"

Rubbing a hand over his face, Port said, "I was there, but I've never killed an innocent man. Tell him that."

"I will in not so many words," said Amanda. She translated to Many-Buffalo and then pointed at the lake.

The talk from several of the tribe grew excited. Pointing at the lake, several made a ward against evil, but Many-Buffalo looked at the sky. He spoke quickly back and forth with Amanda, who pleaded Port's case.

Amanda finally revealed, "He wants proof that you are as good a man as I say you are before he will discuss the monsters with you."

"Monsters? There's more than one?"

"First things first," said Amanda. "He wants proof."

"Like what?" asked Port, extending his hand to shake.

Many-Buffalo hesitated, then extended his hand to Port's, but with only two fingers out, the rest clenched back.

Port questioned, "What's that?"

"He doesn't trust you."

"Wheat! I knew that. What do I need to do to get him to talk?"

A mountain of a man stepped forward, creating a hush among the tribe. Thick and strong, he looked down on Porter, scrutinizing him. "You are Mormonee?" he asked, bringing his bare chest to Port's nose.

Amanda said, "This is Big Bear."

"Yeah, I'm Mormonee," answered Port. "He is probably the second biggest Indian I've ever seen."

"Do you wear the sacred robes?" asked the grinning giant.

"Yes."

"Show me."

Port opened his shirt, revealing the garments. "Satisfied?"

"The woman is Mormonee too?"

"Yes."

"She will show me?" He smirked.

Port shoved Big Bear. "That's enough. Can we talk or not, Many-Buffalo? Or do I have to teach some manners to your boy?"

Amanda shook her head.

Big Bear knocked Port's hat off.

"Tell him I'm here to take care of things and if they don't help me, I can't help them!" shouted Port. "But I'm not here to play games."

Many-Buffalo stood impassive, then nodded to Big Bear.

The giant lunged, grasping Port in a bear hug, trapping his arms and lifting him off the ground. The gathering laughed as Many-Buffalo shouted in triumph.

Struggling to breathe, let alone move, Port asked, "What'd he say?"

"He said if you are the best the Brigham can offer, he doesn't need help," cried Amanda over the din.

Big Bear's laughter boomed into Port's face.

"Wheat! They ain't seen nothing yet."

Big Bear's hug cracked Port's back and grew tighter, forcing air from his lungs and still the big man laughed.

Looking Big Bear square in the eye, Port winked and then slammed his thick forehead into Big Bear's nose repeatedly. The huge man, blinded and bloodied, dropped Port, who landed on his feet. Porter slammed Big Bear an uppercut to the chin, dropping the man-mountain. Rounding on Many-Buffalo, Port snarled, "Was he the best you got?"

Amanda translated.

Many-Buffalo frowned, but motioned for Port and Amanda to follow.

Amanda picked up Port's hat, then handed it to him saying, "You know, might doesn't always make right."

"Didn't *I* just prove that?"

6.

Though it was still afternoon on a warm day, Many-Buffalo kindled the fire inside his tipi. He took a powder and scattered it about the perimeter of his dwelling, paying specific attention to the door flap.

Sitting on buffalo skins, Port and Amanda waited while Many-Buffalo sang a song of blessing and protection. Taking a seat opposite them, Many-Buffalo spoke quick, harsh-sounding words, staring deep at Port.

Amanda translated, "He said ... to speak of such things as we ask ... he must bless and purify his tipi. He will do it again ... after we've gone. They've had problems ... but he will not ask for help ... since he was already denied."

"Tell him this. A proud man won't ask, but a proud man can answer. Tell him I'm asking to know about these things so I can help his people."

Many-Buffalo looked at Port as Amanda spoke. He nodded and went into a lengthy round of back and forth with Amanda, as she gave Port snippets.

"He says the lake monster ... haunted the waters in the time of his ancestors. It has slept for many moons ... and only awoke when ... Mormons came. It eats sheep and cattle ... perhaps even men ... but it is not to be confused ... with other curses that have befallen his people. Murders have come ... the last few weeks ... only. Sorcery has tainted the people. They fear the witch and skinwalker ... more than they do ... the lake monster. The reason ... they have not moved yet ... because these evil things follow them."

"What's that?"

Amanda shook her head. "I'm not sure, but it has all of them afraid. He is reluctant to tell me more ... because it invites ... the evil thing into his tipi. They hoped

Brother Brigham could help ... but the ... drawing man ... told them Brigham ... would not help."

"What's a drawing man?"

Amanda shrugged. "There is no word for it, I translated as best I could."

"What can he say about the lake monster? How big is it? Is there a way to kill it?"

She asked Many-Buffalo and he pondered a moment, before going into a number of hand gestures and excited speaking with a final disgusted look before throwing holy powder into the fire that made it blaze brilliantly.

"He says they are related ... that Mormons ... brought the curse here ... the monsters are linked to each other ... yours and ours," said Amanda. "I'm not sure what yours and ours mean."

Port rubbed smoke from his eyes. "I thought we would get some answers here."

"I'm sorry. They're scared. This has touched them deeply," she said.

Many-Buffalo watched them and spoke again.

"He says their burial grounds ... have been violated. Something steals from the dead. As for your questions ... the lake monster ... is long as four wagons ... and its skin cannot be wounded ... by a gun or knife."

"Kinda like me," said Port.

"He says ... works of darkness ... fill this land. We walk ... the path of the ... skin-walker. May the Great Spirit ... protect us ... on our quest. He will say no more."

Murmuring drums outside beat again.

Amanda gasped. "Someone is here."

7.

A man on a rickety wagon pulled into the Shoshone camp. Bearded and slight, he glowered at Port and Amanda as they exited Many-Buffalo's tipi.

"What's the matter Stenhouse? Upset I wasn't chased outta town by your black-legs?" called Port, chuckling.

Stenhouse dropped off the wagon, tipped his hat to Amanda – "Mrs. Cook." – and extended a hand to Port. "My apologies. The uneducated rascals misunderstood my direction and inclination. I have not levied them out of jail and I directed the sheriff to let the lot of them stay a fortnight therein."

Port declined the handshake, as he tried not to smirk at Stenhouse's pretentious English accent.

Stenhouse continued, "Forgive my temper. I merely wished to meet with Chief

Sagwitch's son myself, and worried that he already had guests, you see."

"Yeah, 'I see,'" mocked Port. "You're upset we beat you here before you could spread more lies. How'd you know I was coming up to Bear Lake before I did?"

"Nothing of the sort. I came to speak with the Chief much the same as I imagine you did. As for knowing you would be here ... whom else would Brigham send? Understanding his mentality as I do, it was elementary, my dear Danite."

Port sniffed and spit.

"Regardless of what you may think of me, Porter, I am not the enemy. We may disagree fundamentally on authority, but our core is the same. The New Movement and I seek truth the same as you."

Amanda countered, "What was it Fanny wrote? To doubt one doctrine was to doubt all? Our core is not the same. You abandoned yours."

"Madam, I must protest."

But Amanda wasn't even close to being done. She reared up in the Englishman's face. Port stood back and smiled. This was gonna be good.

"You think we haven't all had hardships? You think we haven't all questioned the tests we have in life? Let me tell you something. You'll be caught in your own traps."

Stenhouse looked to Port for assistance from the feisty young woman, but the old gunfighter raised his hands, cocked his head, and smirked.

"Don't you and the other Godbeites fool yourselves. This life isn't where you will be successful. It's in the eternities. Just because Brother Brigham might have given you some bad business advice or won't let you mine our mountains to ruin doesn't mean you can become a law unto yourselves. If you lost faith in God, it's because you put your faith in the arm of flesh!" shouted Amanda. "Your lies and schemes will snap back upon you."

With that, she mounted her horse and cantered off.

Visibly disturbed at her words, Stenhouse slunk away.

Port followed after Amanda.

Big Bear, still cradling his broken nose, glared at Port.

Tipping his hat to the big man, Port gave his horse heels to catch up to Amanda. She turned in the saddle. "I'm sorry about that, but I'm so tired of his lies."

"No problem, little sister."

"I did give him what-for, didn't I?"

"Yes, you did." Port laughed, deep and loud.

8.

Dusk rode in with Port, lying red like a mantle across the valley. With no clouds, it would be a cold night.

In the Cook home, Phineas gave his wife a warm hug before grilling Port. "So what'd you find out?"

"Whole lot of nothing. Many-Buffalo didn't have anything I can use and wouldn't tell us much of what's happened to his tribe."

Mary, the Cooks' young daughter, offered Port a glass of water and hugged her mother's skirt.

"They're scared," said Amanda. "Something is happening. They feel powerless. And Stenhouse went out there after us."

"Really? What'd he want?" asked Phineas.

Port gulped down the glass of water and made a face. "Said he wanted to talk to Many-Buffalo. Don't know what for. Amanda gave him a good tongue lashing, though."

Amanda blushed. "I did, I suppose."

Phineas beamed.

Port took off his hat and slumped into a chair. "Now, I need to find out why Stenhouse tried to get me outta town. He should've known his thugs couldn't do it and why would he wanna talk to the Shoshone? Can't imagine him getting any farther than I did."

"Nothing to do now but get some rest for the morrow," said Phineas. "Way past your bedtime, Mary."

"Goodnight, Papa," said Mary, hurrying to bed.

9.

The little girl rushed up the steps to the loft. The moon shone in her window like a finger of ice. Nestling in the covers, she said her prayers, closing her eyes as the lamp downstairs dimmed. She slept restlessly with dreams of drowning.

She awoke with a start as a mystic green light passed her window. It wasn't the rising corn-yellow moon. Whatever it was lay outside her window. Sitting up, she gazed into the darkness and witnessed a pallid form shamble through the trees.

From behind the closest tree, a taloned hand gripped bark and then a white face leered. It was wolf-like, with red eyes glowing like embers that burrowed into Mary's.

Fear petrified her. She couldn't look away from the thing loping closer. She was so frightened, she couldn't speak, only shake. Did the monster smile at that? The hideous wolf-man looked at her and then the front door.

It would come inside.

She shivered, too terrified to warn her parents. She heard her father downstairs, talking with the strange long-haired man. Her lips trembled but no sound came.

The thing stood directly below her window. It seemed capable of leaping up and through the glass. Those eyes, so blood-red and evil. She couldn't look away. What horrors did it have planned for her? Her parents? Her sleeping siblings? It would come inside and devour them.

The monster, with white talons smeared scarlet, motioned for her to come.

Compelled beyond fear and reason, Mary released the latch on the window.

Saliva dripped as its tongue lolled.

Mary pushed the window open.

The monster beckoned her to jump, its eyes hypnotizing.

Too afraid to move, to scream or even look away, Mary did the only thing left her: she cried a prayer deep inside for deliverance.

The wolf-thing beckoned for her to jump into its waiting arms.

Tears streaming, Mary lifted herself to the sill and precariously balanced, half-way in and out.

Licking its lips, it beckoned again as the moon illuminated its awful red-matted fur.

Was there no relief? Did those who gave themselves to monsters deserve heaven?

Ahab bawled out loud in staccato.

The spell broken, Mary snapped back to herself and dropped to the floor, avoiding any possible eye contact. She heard Father and the long-haired stranger startle, each muttering as they stirred. The familiar cocking of guns told her they were prepared.

The wolf-thing snarled at Ahab, who cowered beneath the porch.

Praising the Lord for delivering her family from the evil of this thing, Mary shut the window latch.

Raging, the beast summoned a ball of green fire in its left hand and cast it through her window. Flames erupted all about the bedroom as Mary screamed.

10.

"What the devil was that horrible sound?" shouted Port, drawing his pistols. He threw back the front door and looked into the gloom.

Nothing.

Ghostly green-orange firelight blazed upstairs, licking the windowsill and rafters.

Phineas cried, "Porter, help! The house is on fire!"

Somewhere a child screamed in unholy fear.

Port replaced his pistols and stepped back through the doorway only to be grasped by the back of his coat and flung backward off the porch.

Stars reeled overhead as a black wind blew.

The breath knocked from his lungs, senses fled and only the fire above was visible. He struggled to sit up. Reaching for his pistols, his hands found empty holsters.

Someone forcibly lifted him and slammed him to the ground. The most disturbing part to the Danite was the low rumbling chuckle the attacker let out. He couldn't see his enemy, but he heard him all right.

Port kicked and connected to thick shin bone.

The midnight assailant didn't chuckle anymore.

Rolling to his feet, Port snatched his Bowie, ready for anything.

As the enemy grabbed him again, Port's blade slashed across its chest. Blood and tufts of white fur spiraled from the wound. Port trusted his honed senses to guide his hand. Listening intently, a twig snapped to his right. He barreled toward the sound, knife extended.

Port felt his steel bite flesh and ripped the blade across what he hoped were vitals.

Howling in pain, an inhumanly strong hand took Port's shoulder, tearing cloth, and threw him to the earth.

Roaring, "Wheat in the mill!" Port launched up, renewed to fight his foe with blood-maddening vigor. He spun about, waving the Bowie, expecting another attack.

None came.

Dark blood along with flecks of white fur trailed into the gulf of night. Port raced back to the house to fight the fire.

Inside Phineas and Amanda held their daughter. The fire was out. Mary was shivering, wiping the last of her tears away. "You did it."

"I've never seen the like," gasped Phineas. "The room blazed like a furnace. You must have slain the thing because the witch-fire up and disappeared. Thank you."

"Yes, thank you," repeated Amanda, her own tears falling. "It's over."

Shaking his head, Port growled, "No, 'tain't. I didn't kill it."

11.

A long night brought morning headaches and breakfast questions.

"So what do you reckon it was?" asked Phineas.

Port chewed his mouthful, saying, "Probably that Shoshone giant Big Bear. From what Mary said, sounds about the same size. Know I cut him bad, so he's probably gonna hole up in a sweat lodge for a while."

"What about the witch-fire?"

Stabbing another piece of venison, Port answered, "I've seen enough strange things in my time to say anything is possible. Tricks is key to the sorcerer type. Probably a wolf-skin mask and bear-paw war-club."

"That was no mask," broke in Mary. "That was a monster."

Shaking her head, Amanda said, "That wasn't natural."

"Darkness can play tricks on you."

The little girl shook her head. "No, this was real bad. That thing is of the devil."

"Men can be monsters too," said Port, finishing his last bite. "Much obliged, Brother Cook, Sister Cook." He looked to Mary and rubbed his broad hand over her head. "I'm gonna get to the bottom this, an' that's a promise."

Amanda threw down her dishrag. "And just what are you planning to do? Sounds like you're in denial of monsters."

Grinning, Port said, "No need to worry, ma'am. I think Stenhouse, the Godbeites, and some of the Shoshone are in cahoots. I need a few more answers and I'll get 'em."

Blocking the door, Amanda said, "None of that explains the lake monster. What we saw last night was something different, probably the same thing that has the Shoshone frightened. There has to be more to this than Stenhouse and a few bribed Indians."

"I'm sure there is, but I can't take care of it, jawin' 'bout it."

Amanda looked to Phineas, who nodded. "Then I'm coming with you. You need someone's help to translate and watch your back," she said.

Port shook his head, like a black-maned lion. "No, ma'am. I got an instinct about a few things I'd best check out on my own." Before she could protest, he added, "And I won't need a translator this time. Thanks for breakfast. Feel better, Phineas." Port tipped his hat, adjusted his gun belt, and went out into the cool morning.

As he made for the Cooks' stable, a hint of white moving in the trees caught his eye. It swayed with the light breeze at eye level. Port drew his trusty Navy Revolver and approached with grim determination.

It looked like a tangled bunch of pale sticks strung in the pines facing the Cook homestead, but closer inspection revealed it was a curious cobble of interlaced bones, calico twine and a couple of dark feathers, about the size of his hand. It was some type of Indian fetish or charm. Then again, it looked more like something a white man would make rather than a real Indian charm. The bones looked like chicken as opposed to eagle or crow. That and it smelt of coffee, not the succulent flowers of the field.

Port tore it down and put it in his pocket. He considered telling the Cooks what he found but decided against it. They were spooked enough.

12.

In town, a heated commotion carried over the streets. Men shouted at one another and Port could feel the contentious spirit waxing. There appeared to be two opposing camps, one backed by Stenhouse, the sheriff, and their full gang of thugs; the other fronted by tall Joseph Rich, the local newspaperman, who was supported by a good number of townsfolk.

Port couldn't tell what started the argument.

Rich's strong baritone proclaimed, "I lost a horse to the monster. But that doesn't mean it needs to be destroyed!"

Stenhouse countered, "You're the beast's greatest advocate. It clears you of the secret gambling debts you lost your mount to. It grants sensationalism and lurid stories for your amateur journalism, but you seem to forget the spiritual implications."

Men tried to shout him down, including Rich for the gambling crack, but Stenhouse persisted. "A duel is coming! The hour of struggle is at hand. If *infallible* Brigham," he said sarcastically, "can't cast out the devil, what good is he?"

A man swung at Stenhouse but was instead hit first across the mouth by one of the deputies.

Stenhouse continued, "If a man is to lead this people he has to be open to new revelation. We can change what doesn't belong. We can prosper with what the Lord grants us here in these mountains. There is gold and silver aplenty!"

Now Stenhouse had Port's full attention.

"My friends, Brigham is a good man, but he has lost his way. Don't you lose it alongside him. A new prophet will rise!"

"Yeah? Who?" squawked a man between Stenhouse and Rich.

"Why, the very blood of the great prophet himself, Joseph the third."

A number of boos and catcalls came with the mention of Joseph Smith's eldest son. Port just shook his head.

"What about the monster?" shouted a man.

Another cried, "It took my sheep."

"What can be done about it? It killed Big Bear and a half dozen braves last night."

Port's eyes grew. He struggled through the throng to get to the man who mentioned Big Bear. The rebuttal from Rich was lost to Port's ears as he pushed and grabbed the man's shoulder.

"You! Who told you Big Bear is dead?"

The man spun, trying to escape Port's grasp, then breathed a sigh of relief. "It's you. You'll take care of this."

"What about Big Bear?"

"He's dead. Seen him myself yonder. Chief Many-Buffalo brought what's left of his body and the others into town a half hour ago."

"Was he cut up with a Bowie?"

The man blanched. "No! The monster took bites outta him. It's gruesome. Go see."

Port let go of the man's shoulder and drifted out of the crowd.

Then a familiar voice spoke. "Porter, what do you make of this?" It was Thomas, the shopkeeper. "You ever go talk to Lehi?"

Port shook his head, then spotted Many-Buffalo.

"You should. I'll bet he could explain things."

"Much obliged," said Port abruptly, walking away.

13.

Many-Buffalo was surrounded by a dozen wailing women, the remains of his braves lying beneath a broad red blanket. He was speaking with local authority and Apostle Charles C. Rich.

"Brother Rich, can I take a look?" asked Port.

"Go ahead, Brother Rockwell. Chief Many-Buffalo has just asked my help in blessing them for their journey."

Port nodded and looked to Many-Buffalo who still gave the unfriendly glare he had from the day before. Lifting the blanket's edge, Port looked upon the terrible visage of Big Bear. He expected to see evidence of his Bowie, but not this – carnage to rival the worst horror he had ever witnessed. Claw and bite wounds from something huge. The same atrocities had been dealt to three more men.

There went Port's personal theory for last night's incident. Big Bear could not possibly have been the enemy he fought in the darkness.

"Many-Buffalo tells me that you and Sister Cook visited him yesterday," said Charles.

"We did. So did Stenhouse."

"He said Stenhouse came wanting to know what could be done about the monster, if there was anything he could do to help. He gave them some of the latest model of guns, repeating rifles and the like, and yet you see here what happened," said Charles.

Port squinted across the way at Stenhouse still fuming his 'New Movement' to the townsfolk. "Why try and get the Indians to deal with this thing, though? Why wouldn't he have that crooked sheriff and his blacklegs deal?"

"I couldn't begin to say."

Port threw back the blanket pointing at vicious wounds. "This gives more questions than answers. Seems worse than a bear attack."

Charles nodded. "These men could have handled a bear."

Narrowing his gaze, Port noticed Big Bear had a small bone fetish on his belt just like the one he found earlier. "Something is sending a message. But I can't read it yet."

"Some messages can't be read," said the Apostle. "And when words can't cut the evil, it's time to use a sword."

Port grinned as he drew, spun, and holstered his Navy Colts. "I find a six-gun is quicker."

14.

Port had a vague impression of where to find Lehi, the old Indian that supposedly knew so much about the monster. A whistle drew his attention.

It was Stenhouse, across the street. He beckoned for Port to come and speak with him in front of the sheriff's office.

Flexing his fingers, Port warily eyed the windows and hiding spots behind Stenhouse. He was ready to draw his Navy Colts like chain lightning if need be.

"What do you want?" he growled.

"Just to speak a moment without the self-righteous she-cat beside you."

Porter grabbed Stenhouse's tie, yanking him closer, "You'll speak kindly about the lady."

"Hey! You'll keep your hands of Mr. Stenhouse," called the sheriff from inside the office.

Port shoved the thin man away. "I've heard how you treat *your* women."

Stenhouse rankled at the insinuation. "I beg your pardon. We have had our differences, our run-ins, but I wanted to let you know that a new wind is blowing. Utah is changing. The railroad is here and new revelations come with it. You can be part of the old guard that is swept away and forgotten – or be a part of the reformation."

Port shook his head. "You really know nothing about me."

"I know this," said Stenhouse, his tone turning cruel and superior. "I spoke to Vice-President Colfax only a few short weeks ago. The government is tired of Brigham's unfriendly theocracy, his dictatorship of the territory, his dominion of Deseret."

"You always were too theatrical, Stenhouse."

"Oh no, not this time. This is real. They are going to invade. They are going to take our lands by force and destroy the Church if things aren't changed. We in the New Movement are working toward effecting that change before it's too late. We could use your help."

Port guffawed.

"Laugh," Stenhouse said coldly. "Evidence that Brigham is counterfeiting is being filed."

"That'll never stick," objected Port.

"Oh no? How about this. There are those who will testify that he ordered Mountain Meadows."

Port frowned. "That's a lie and you know it."

"Do I? Does it matter if the government gets hold of the evidence to destroy the Church? Our survival depends on change. Brigham is a fallen prophet. He has lost his way. He can't even repudiate a monster that threatens his own people – what about the monster that is the U.S. Army? The people must abandon Brigham and follow the New Movement."

Narrowing his steely gaze, Port rumbled, "What's your part in this? Who's gonna lose faith in the prophet over a monster?"

Stenhouse's tone changed again. "I'll tell you because I'm afraid. No one has put this together yet. Every night with a waxing moon, the body count doubles. The creature's blood lust cannot be sated. Brigham can't protect anyone. How many deaths have you prevented since you arrived? Yes, even the *Destroying Angel* is helpless against this monster."

"Then why doesn't the New Movement take care of it?"

"Things have to get worse before they can get better."

Port said, "Hogwash. You're all using this as an agenda. You make me sick."

"Say what you will, but shame is our only tool now. To shame President Young into acknowledging we who are his spiritual betters. Only then will we step forward and alleviate this threat."

Port shook his head. "So you will let men die to further your political ambitions? Out of my way. I got things to do."

"You think so small. Better for a few men to die than for a people to perish in ignorance. We will bring balance to the Church," said Stenhouse. "New revelation has been given; the spirits have granted us release and wisdom. They have given us solution to our predicament."

Port rubbed a hand across his beard as if pondering.

"I offer you a place. Reject us and it will not be offered again and you will be swept away as so much chaff! The field is ripe. Where will you stand?"

Putting his nose inches from Stenhouse's, Port whispered, "That's the name of the game." He lightly patted the Englishman's cheek twice, then strode down the street to fetch his horse.

"What does that mean?"

"Figure it out," Port called.

A few minutes later, Port rode down the hill from the Cooks' and came in behind the sheriff's office. He pulled the strange fetish of stick-like bones from his jacket pocket and tossed it upon the roof of the office. Chuckling, he rode on.

15.

Port rode with the wind at his back, watching the long lake and pondering. Why would the Lord allow these things to plague good people? What was the test? The lesson to be learned? What was his own part and responsibility?

All experiences are for our ultimate good, mused Port. Still ...

Sheep grazed in large swaths across the rounded landscape.

Most flocks were tended by young boys, so he trotted his stallion up to a tousle-headed boy and nodded. "Afternoon, son. You out here a lot?"

"Every day, mister."

"Ever see anything strange?"

The boy smiled. "Besides you?"

Port chuckled. "Yeah, besides me. A monster maybe."

The boy went serious. "I thought I saw it once."

Port folded his arms. Now he was getting somewhere.

"I was playing by the lake shore when I saw six or seven dark shapes out in the water. A big horse-like head with horns was coming out, right at me. I was so afraid. I couldn't hardly breathe, let alone move."

Port looked out at the lake again. "You saw it? Didn't it try to eat you?"

"No, it wasn't the monster," the boy smirked. "It was a herd of elk crossing the lake. The bull was in front, the cows behind. My fear made a monster."

"You don't believe in the monster?" questioned Port.

"I didn't say that. I'm just saying things aren't always what they seem."

"True," Port said. "Know where to find an old Indian called Lehi?"

The boy pointed southwest. "Over those hills somewhere. No one lives near him."

"Much obliged," said Port, galloping away.

"No one lives near him," called the boy.

"I heard ya," shouted Port over his shoulder.

16.

Over rolling hillocks and past a few stands of trees, Port saw a wisp of rising smoke, thin and gray, curling toward heaven through the light drizzle.

"Hello, the camp! Lehi?" Port called. Experience said you were better off letting folks know you were coming in.

Rounding the bend, a rotted tipi came into view. It looked smaller than the usual ten- to twelve-buffalo-hide tipis. It was made of perhaps eight skins.

Port's horse nickered at entering the clearing and tried to turn away. Glancing about for a possible predator, Port called again, "Lehi, you out here?"

"I am here," announced a ragged voice as the tipi flap peeled back and an elderly Indian peered out. "Go away! What you want? Blood?"

Laughing, he said, "You're the old man in town from yesterday!" Port dismounted the skittish horse. "You could've saved me the trip if you would've stuck around."

Exiting the tipi, Lehi frowned. "I have things to do."

"Take it easy. I just wanted to talk to you for a spell 'bout the monster. I'm Porter," he said, extending his hand.

Cocking his head, the old Indian stared with eyes hard and cold as the mountaintop.

MONSTERS & MORMONS

"I tell you as I told them. Monster comes to eat on clear night when moon grows like swelling belly." He stepped out of the tipi and stood uncomfortably close to Porter.

"They said you could tell me all about the monster."

Smirking, Lehi answered, "You want a story, you got to pay." He opened his hand, expecting.

The horse whinnied and backed away pulling the reins in Port's clenched fist. The ragged voice and unnerved horse put Port's guard up. He considered drawing his sawed-off Navy Colt.

Lehi grinned. "Forget it. I like you. We are the same, you and I."

Nerves calmed, Port said, "Anytime." He took one of the tincture bottles from his saddlebags and handed it to a pleased Lehi. "About last night: What do you know about the lake monster? What's it look like? Any weaknesses?"

Lehi nodded. "Trust in Great Spirit, but tie up your horse. Let us speak inside." He gestured to his faded buffalo-skin tipi.

A smell that Port attributed to the old man's lifestyle permeated the inside of the tipi. It was similar to wet dog but with a reptilian copper scent. Ratty old furs and skins made up the old man's bed. A handful of tools cluttered the far side of the tipi. A ring of stones held a few glowing coals in the center. Unexpected to Port was a worn copy of the Book of Mormon.

"You read?"

"I feel it is truth," said Lehi, "but my reading is not yet bountiful."

Port grinned. "Me too."

Lehi sat cross-legged opposite Porter and pushed back his beaded breastwork, revealing massive scars along his chest and shoulder. The trauma displayed was so extensive Port wondered how the old man survived.

Showing a missing finger and the stub next to it on his left hand, Lehi said, "This is where Great Serpent bit me, here and here." He pointed to his shoulder and chest, and upheld his disfigured hand.

"When was this?"

"To my life ... not long ago. Was first time I saw Great Serpent. I sang old songs calling for the Old Ones. But Great Serpent heard me and came. Him very angry with me," chuckled Lehi.

"Why is that?"

"Great Serpent not want to be wakened. He is lost and used."

Wrinkling his forehead Port asked, "Lost? Used? I don't follow you."

Wrapping himself in his cloak, Lehi said, "Great Serpent not meant to be here. He will not listen to me now. But there is purpose in all things."

"How big is he? Can he be killed?"

Lehi lit a pipe before answering and stared into the smoldering center a long while. "I will tell you, because you are like me, a hunter of men. No gun of white man can kill Great Serpent. It is long as four wagons. It is a thing from old times."

"But why is it here?"

Lehi shrugged, "Why does sun rise? Moon set? It is."

"Are you saying it can't be killed?"

Lehi smiled, revealing wicked teeth for an old man. "I say, do not even try. Monster will eat you."

Port didn't like his tone. "If it lives, it can be killed."

"You have brave heart. Perhaps is a way."

Port rubbed his chin. "Go on."

"Would be dangerous. We would be risking our lives."

"That's my business. I've got a charmed life."

Lehi nodded and beckoned Port to follow. He stepped out of his tipi, and trotted out of the glade and into the thick brush. The speed of the old man amazed Port.

Lehi gathered a handful of pale roots. "We poison Great Serpent, tonight."

Port looked skeptical. "How come no one has tried this before?"

Lehi chuckled, "Who stupid enough to face Great Serpent?"

"Good point."

17.

Lehi had a wide raft that would take them out into the lake. It was slow going, but, in Port's mind, allowed for more fighting space. The raft seemed safer than a canoe that could be capsized, leaving them at the mercy of the lake monster.

Port left his stallion on shore with a good bit of tether. Considering Joseph Rich had already lost a horse to the monster, Port left his farther uphill. He brought his blessed Bowie knife, his two sawed-off Navy Revolvers, and a 45-70 buffalo gun.

Lehi brought a deerskin sack full of the poisonous roots, Port's gift of a tincture bottle, his flute, a tomahawk pipe, and a bit of firewood that he would use to make a fire on the raft over the top of a stone and mud section he had pre-arranged. A small burnt scar upon the raft denoted where he had done this in the past.

"Tell me again how we're gonna get the monster to eat these roots," said Port, regretting not having another bottle of Valley-Tan.

Lehi watched the gunfighter's eyes and gestured to the bottle.

"Much obliged."

Lehi nodded and said, "I will call Great Serpent. When he comes, his mouth wide to eat, throw in roots. But not until he right beside us. Very close."

"Could it sink us?"

"Sure. But I will sing our death song and chant old ways. You can shoot if you like, but it do no good. Roots work fast."

Port wasn't familiar with that many plants, but he never heard of a poisonous root such as this before. Maybe it was Indian magic.

Dusk came quick, casting red twilight over the valley. Somewhere a wolf howled and Port watched the shore. With the sun down, cold wrapped its arms about them. The cold sapphire waters did not look inviting.

Lehi lit his fire with a bow drill. He was amazingly quick. He blew on the shards of spark and they leapt into action as if commanded by the breath of the divine. The orange glow fought and won against the encroaching night. The old man lit his pipe and inhaled deep breaths, puffing them toward the west, to which he bowed.

Port expected him to do something more, perhaps something to the east but he didn't.

"We will let darkness grow a little stronger," said Lehi. "Then I will call Great Serpent out."

"How about another pull on that raspberry tincture then?"

Lehi handed Port the bottle.

An hour or two later their kindling was almost gone and Port dreaded the idea of being on the lake in the dark. "Well, is it time yet?"

Flute in hand, Lehi stood and played a melancholy and disturbing tune. The notes rose and fell in a jarring dirge that Port theorized was never meant to be heard by a white man. It was primal and savage, a true song of the wilds, full of wonder and midnight.

Something splashed out in the waters, forbidden to Port's sight.

"It comes," said Lehi.

"You sure?"

Lehi didn't answer, but blew a long note from his flute and went silent.

Port dropped the sack of poison roots at his own feet and readied the buffalo gun. If anything could penetrate the monsters hide, he reasoned it would be his 45-70. Glancing about, Port was ready, but no more splashing came.

Lehi broke into song, a sad and painful chant.

Then Port heard a splash like an oar hitting the water. The bright moon was just coming over Black Mountain to the east and Port thought he could see a canoe heading toward them. "Someone's out there, Lehi. It ain't the monster."

The canoe glided closer and regardless of the dying fire, Lehi continued his chant. "Hey-yaw, taw hey-yaw. Zhoo' yea' Zhoo' yea'. Yana Glooshi, hey-yaw, taw hey yaw."

"Who's there?" asked Port of the darkness.

No answer came, or at least none he could hear above Lehi's chanting.

Port threw the last few chunks of fuel into the fire hoping to pierce the darkness a little better, absently wondering if whoever was about to meet them had seen anything up the lake.

The fire briefly flared and hid, perking up and down as it consumed its meager final meal.

Facing the incoming canoe, Port couldn't see anyone paddling it, just the form drifting closer. He strained to hear if anyone had fallen overboard or worse, if there was a struggle from someone becoming a monster's most recent meal.

"Hey-yaw, taw hey-yaw. Zhoo' yea' Zhoo' yea'. Yana Glooshi, hey-yaw, taw hey yaw. Oh yaw-hey! Oh yaw-hey! Yaw!" sang Lehi, powerful and deep.

The canoe was almost to the raft and Port puzzled over its missing pilot. Then he saw that the canoe was misshapen, strangely wider toward the rear. Was there a body slumped to the rear?

Gazing hard at the canoe, a wisp of flame from the firelight flared up for a fraction of a second and allowed Port to see two black eyes reflecting back the orange firelight. Two massive eyes each set in the wider portion of what was not a canoe but the monster's head. Like a crocodile it had cruised upon them, drawn by the shaman's song.

The huge multi-fanged mouth sprang open.

Port braced himself, too stunned to shoot or grab the sack of poisoned roots.

Ferocious jaws came down, splintering the raft into kindling, snuffing the weak fire and coals.

Pitched into the air, Port fell forward into the waiting jaws of the Bear Lake monster. He hit the giant tongue and was aware of a bright green light behind him as the cavernous mouth closed.

18.

Cold moonlight reached through the sheriff's office window, barely warded off by the wood stove. Eight men sat with greasy cards as the lamp guttered low. Stenhouse was the only man sitting out the card game, but his whiskey bottle was emptier than most as he wrote at a furious pace.

"Probably ought to call it a night," said the sheriff. "Just after midnight."

Stenhouse didn't bother looking at him from his crouched position over the desk. "I'm not yet done recording the events of today. I have more."

The sheriff laughed obscenely and dealt the next hand.

A thunder rolled off the lake and even against the hugely waxing moon, a green-hued light approached, casting wicked intentions on the office floor like a dueling gauntlet.

Stenhouse visibly shuddered, saying, "It will keep going, it will keep going."

"You know what that is or something?" asked one of his hired gunmen.

"No ... no, just unnerving is all."

Another hired gun added, "People been seeing 'em all week. Probably shootin' stars is all, boss."

From that remark the deputy told a crude joke, causing riotous laughter.

Stenhouse turned from the desk glaring, "Be quiet. I am trying to work!"

The chorus of laughter was interrupted by a loud thump upon the roof above their heads. Dust shook from the rafters, coating the men in pale gray hues.

The card players looked up in wonder, then terror, as steps bounded across the roof. Stenhouse was halfway under his desk by the first thud.

"What is it?"

"Wha' could be so big?"

Frantic, Stenhouse ordered, "It doesn't matter. Kill it! Shoot, shoot!"

The sheriff looked unconvinced. "Shoot what? Sounds like whoever it was jumped off the roof. Slim, Roger, check it out." He beckoned toward the door.

Slim and Roger went to the front door, Slim gingerly opening it as Roger covered him. With everything still as ice, they stepped out, pointing their guns in every which direction.

"Nothing out here, Boss," said Slim.

A massive white hand reached from the roof, picking Slim up by the head, yanking him out of sight.

A chorus of gunfire followed as Roger hit the deck. "Oh dear Lord, I saw it! Hideous!" As the shooting paused, he slammed the door shut and bolted it.

"Who was it?" demanded the sheriff. "Porter?"

"That was no man," wailed Roger.

A creaking across the roof was met with more lead, but no certainty. Then something slammed against the door hard and final. Silence reigned as the sheriff stepped lightly to the side window to look. "Whoever it was threw Slim against the door. That's a strong man."

"I'm telling you that was no man."

"Shuddup Roger. He'll eat lead like anyone else."

Stenhouse, beneath the desk, looked about fearfully.

The deputy coughed and was glared at for his mistake.

The men waited for another sound. None came for the space of eight heartbeats.

Bursting through the window, a savage white shape roared as it rendered men too slow to defend themselves. Shots echoed from several pistols but the bone-pale attacker cast aside the lamp, blinding the men.

The crunch and splinter of bone and wood tore through the room that lead could not hope to stop.

Brief retorts from the echoing firearms illuminated the room, letting the terrified men see what they faced before the end came on black talons.

Roger ran to the jail cell and shut himself in behind the bars.

Unimpressed, the thing loped to the man cage, gripped the bars, and tore the door from its hinges. Roger didn't last as long as the door.

Almost mad with panic, Stenhouse raced for the front door, clutching his notebooks to his chest. Three more shots rang out and the deputy squealed. Daring to look behind, Stenhouse saw green witch-fire engulf the office.

Stenhouse ran up the street in a panic and threw himself upon the threshold of what he prayed was refuge. He banged on the door crying.

Growling behind him, heavy loping steps drew near, but stopped cold.

Putting his arms over his face Stenhouse screamed.

The door opened.

Joseph Rich looked down at the gibbering mass of Stenhouse. "What the deuce?" Rich held his rifle at the ready and scanned the darkness as the hysterical crying man held fast to his knees.

"Bring him in," said Charles Rich, looking over his son's shoulder into the vacant gloom. "He needs a blessing."

19.

Porter had been baptized by water and by fire. Now he was sure where the twain should meet. Hot fetid breath whirled about him like a hurricane as a monstrous tongue lashed, attempting to force him down a bottomless black gullet.

Closed inside the leviathan's mouth, Port gripped the top two rear fangs in the monster's maw. Only they allowed purchase without shearing his hands off. The tongue, almost as long as he was tall, proved a formidable opponent. Kicking at the pink monstrosity, Port knew he could not hold out forever.

He despaired, thinking of his holy blessing. Not cutting his hair would not help against being digested. No bullets or knives were needed to end his existence here. What of his children, and Christine? What would they do without him?

Anger coiled up in him, like a serpent preparing to strike its deadly blow.

The tongue struck again, trying to fling him.

Roaring, Port launched himself at the tongue and grasped it as he would a greased pig. The air pressure changed and he knew they were at the surface. Twisting the tongue, the monster's mouth opened and Port let himself out, still grasping the end.

The monster wouldn't close its mouth for fear of severing itself.

Once out of the teeth's way, Port noticed something stuck on the inside of the lower left jawline: a crude contraption of tiny interwoven bones and rawhide, similar to the bizarre fetish he had seen earlier.

The monster struggled, but Port kept a firm grasp with one hand on the slimy tongue. Try as he might he couldn't free the fetish with one hand.

A deep bass inside the monster reverberated out.

He let go of the tongue and yanked the interwoven mess from the bleeding gums.

It let out a rumbling purr, and Port could swear that the great eye went from a dull black to blue. Whatever wicked spirit had held the monster in thrall was released.

Running a hand back and forth over the thick scaly hide, Port looked the monster in the eye. A thick eyelid closed in rhythm to his strokes.

It let out a rumbling purr yet again.

"What have I got to lose," he said to the monster as much as himself. "Lemme up, Blue."

Port slid over the head of the calmed beast. He found he could grasp the folds of skin where the jaw ended. Port lightly kicked at its neck with his waterlogged boots and the beast started forward. He could even guide the direction of the monster as they cruised over the lake by pulling one way or the other just like a horse and its reins.

"Wheat!" Port called aloud. He had broken the wildest stallion ever.

The Bear Lake monster swam quickly through the water in a way that reminded Port of the seals he had seen in California. It was quick and he had to pull upward a number of times to keep the creature from diving into the depths. It was exhilarating.

Piloting the monster to shore, Port finally realized how chilled he was. He needed warmth if he was to survive. Thinking of survivors ...

Glancing over the waters, there was no sign of Lehi. Old man must have drowned. Port bowed his head for some time.

The beast slumped its way onto shore using its shorter paddle-like feet just as a seal would.

Port ran his hand along the monster's snout and then ushered it away. He didn't want it getting any ideas about his horse nearby "Go on, Blue. Git. We'll be meeting up soon enough, I promise."

The monster seemed reluctant but finally went into the lake and disappeared beneath moon-stained waters.

It took some time to get a fire going, but once the blaze picked up, Port collapsed beside it. Who would believe it? Revenge could wait. He needed sleep after breaking Jonah's stallion.

Why had he named the monster Blue? He didn't know, but it made him laugh.

"Wheat," he chuckled as he fell asleep.

20.

After climbing off his horse, Port limped on account of his water-logged boots drying by the fire and shrinking to an uncomfortable size. He'd lost his 45-70 in the lake, one of his pistols, and all of his ammunition.

Shuffling into the general store, Port could only point at the ammunition.

"Morning, Brother Rockwell. You weren't part of that mess last night were you?" asked Thomas the shopkeep.

Port shrugged through bleary eyes.

"Did you drink all of those tinctures last night? No wonder you feel so terrible."

Port rubbed his face and responded, "No, just get me some cartridges."

"Anything else?"

"Cartridges!" hollered Port. "Wait, what mess last night? How'd you know?"

Thomas gave a patronizing smile. "Last night, right across the street. The sheriff's office burnt down. Everyone who was staying there is dead, burnt up, except for Brother Stenhouse."

"Stenhouse? Where is that polecat now?"

Sniffing, Thomas responded, "Brother Stenhouse is among the most respected men we have in the Church. He hardly deserves to be called a polecat."

"Cartridges and where is he?"

Thomas gulped. "I understand he is at Brother Rich's for the moment. He went there last night a-crying and a-hollering that something was out to get him. No doubt he was distressed about the fire that took so many lives."

Port paid for the ammunition and walked out, figuring he had almost all the pieces to the puzzle. Now to get the last one from the dog's own mouth.

21.

Stenhouse was shivering in the parlor, sipping warm milk. He started at Port's entrance, a dark avenging angel with the brilliance of the sun at his back. Charles Rich calmed him as Joseph shut the door and ushered the other family members out.

Joseph said, "He has been carrying on all night. Not a body in the house got a wink of sleep last night."

Stenhouse was still shaking, though the comfort of the Apostle had soothed him somewhat.

"Come and take a look at this," said Joseph, leading Port back outside.

On the ground in an obvious perimeter all about the Rich home, were big wolf-like tracks, as if a creature met an invisible barrier through which it could not pass.

"What do you make of that?" asked Port.

"What else? Father is here."

Port nodded and the two went back inside. Sitting across from Stenhouse, Port tipped his hat to Charles and said to Stenhouse, "All right, don't feed me any cow pies. What is that thing? What do you know about it?"

Stenhouse looked at Port and quivered again. "It will find me."

"Are you talking about the Bear Lake monster?" asked Joseph.

"We got bigger fish to fry," said Port.

Confused, Joseph shot back, "No, we don't."

"Hold on, Son," said Charles. "There is a deeper conspiracy afoot."

Stenhouse stared at the wall and looked far away, remembering. "It was Harrison and Godbe. They started it. Sure, I was right there with them, along with Shearman, Kelsey, Tullidge, and Lawrence, among others, but it was Harrison and Godbe that started it."

He took a sip of his warm milk. "I'm not mad. I have seen things. They discovered the answers when they went to New York and met the medium Charles Foster – he greeted them in Heber C. Kimball's voice! They knew it was Kimball communicating with them from beyond the grave. He told them our path was correct and Brigham was a fallen prophet, then others came and spoke the same: Joseph Smith, Alexander Humboldt, Solomon – even Christ spoke to them."

Joseph Rich snorted.

"Truly, they didn't see him, but he spoke to them and told us what we wanted to hear. Our reformation path is correct and Brigham is wrong. He is not infallible."

Charles quieted Joseph. "He is speaking what he believes to be true."

"Of course I am. They brought back their ideas and wisdom. We have communed with spirits. Then Colfax came. The government wants to destroy Brigham and the Church along with it. We couldn't let that happen. We had to do something, reform the Church from within, to save it. If we can show how we accept the world, then they will accept us."

"What's all this up here then?"

"We tried to talk to Brigham, to make him see, but he was obstinate and cruel. We knew we had to make a stand, but time was short. We met at the lodge, with the ferry on Bear River, Godbe's lodge. We held a séance. Harrison directed it. I remember it was cold no matter how we stoked the fire. A powerful force came to our room. It spoke from behind us, strong and vibrant. It surprised us. We all heard it but none of us could see it. It said to use an Indian shaman and the Bear Lake monster, to bring down Brigham. It said his master wanted to bring down Brigham and would use his earthly servants to do it. We were all so thrilled to know the Lord was on our side."

Port rolled his eyes but remained silent.

"We were validated. I thought it odd to use a heathen for the Lord's work, but we did as we were told. I found the shaman. He was staying just upriver from the lodge."

"What's his name?"

"Ligaii-Maiitsoh."

Joseph widened his eyes. "You mean Lehi? He's a friend."

Shaking his head, Stenhouse went on, "He is ancient as the mountains. He said he would call upon the Great Serpent to do our bidding. But something went wrong. Instead of just scaring people, the monster started killing people. I tried to help the Lamanites watch for the beast, but it only made things worse."

"Ever wonder if you're on the side of angels as much as you think you are?" asked Port.

Stenhouse looked sharply at the suggestion. "There have been setbacks, but no, we are right."

"Then what was last night?"

Shuddering again, Stenhouse said, "That wasn't right. I think it serves Ligaii-Maiitsoh. There has been a mistake. The fiend was supposed to be controllable, but it went blood-mad when it discovered the Shoshone were in the valley. It has surely slain old Lehi. It will come for me next. I will never see Fanny again."

"That's enough crying. What is it about the Shoshone?"

"The Shoshone used to capture Navajo and sell them into slavery. All sorts of horrible things happened. I learned of this from Chief Many-Buffalo. The Navajo retaliated by sending witches out to destroy the Shoshone. I believe Ligaii-Maiitsoh must be the last one."

Port rocked back in his chair. "I couldn't get him to tell me a darned thing and I even had a translator."

Stenhouse was surprised. "Why? He speaks perfectly good English. Oh yes, you were at the Bear River massacre. He was never going to tell you anything."

Port bristled as Stenhouse continued. "Many-Buffalo said his tribe was in the path of the skinwalker, and were under its doom. I wanted to help him but I knew there was nothing to be done when the crazy old man raved as he did over the Shoshone enemies."

"What about them fetish pieces I found? Collection of bones?"

"Some kind of curse is all I know. It lets the bloodthirsty creature focus where the shaman directs it," said Stenhouse trailing off as recognition washed over him. "You! You put the fiend upon me!" screamed Stenhouse, rising from his chair for the first time.

"Just like it was put upon the Cooks and I couldn't have that."

"It wasn't for the Cooks. It was for you," snarled Stenhouse.

"I didn't know what it would do. I just followed my gut," answered Port.

Stenhouse still fumed. "You black-hearted murderer." He stood ready to fight, bringing his fists up.

Port slammed him against the wall with ease. "This is what I do, boy," said Port before letting him go. "And I never killed anyone who didn't need killing."

Stenhouse collapsed to the floor and wept.

Joseph asked, "What about the Bear Lake monster?"

"Smoke and mirrors," answered Port. "It was a decoy for the old shaman. I don't believe it will give you any more problems."

"You didn't kill it, did you?"

"No, I made peace with it. It'll behave itself."

Charles Rich now asked a question, "What will you do now, Brother Rockwell?"

"We'll throw down with the shaman and his beast. I'll use 'em up."

22.

A posse was organized by mid-afternoon and rode out to old Lehi's camp. It was later than Port meant, but several of the men insisted on getting silver bullets cast. Fancy trays, silverware, and jewelry that had crossed the plains as priceless family heirlooms were smelted and molded into balls for precious family insurance.

Port didn't worry about any of that for himself. There were twenty guns riding with him to fire those sacramental rounds. He had his Bowie knife that Brigham had blessed and already knew that it could harm the creature. If he needed to, he would cut the beast asunder.

When they were close, Port had them come in from two directions to triangulate their fire and trap the old man and his creature. He kicked himself for not trusting his (or his horse's) instincts. The creature must have been nearby the whole time he visited with the old man. That would explain the wretched smell.

The tattered tipi was there in the glade but Lehi was nowhere to be found.

"There's nothing inside but this copy of the Book of Mormon that Father gave him," said Joseph. "I don't understand. He has been here, living amongst us for weeks. He seemed like a good man. He quoted scripture. He said he knew it was true."

Port gave a lopsided grin. "Don'tcha think the devil knows it's true?"

23.

Thundering into town as dusk closed in around them, Port knew something wasn't right. Something whispered on the wind, and the scent of wet dog hung heavy in the air.

Amanda Cook raced her horse up to Port. She had been crying. "I thought you'd never return," she sobbed.

"Calm down, Amanda. What is it?"

"We were in the garden, gathering the last of the harvest, just Mary and I. That witch-fire wolf-man came back. Phineas heard our screams. He tried to shoot it and fight. It hurt him real bad. Apostle Rich is looking after him, but it took Mary. It tore her from my grasp. It spoke, like a demon from hell, but it spoke. It said you, and you alone, had to come and get Mary at the lake shore past the camps. What do we do?"

Port held Amanda close and looked her in the eye. "I will get her back."

"How? It will kill her."

"No, I'll take care of it. Rich, you very good with that Sharps rifle?"

Joseph nodded. "Got a few silver slugs too."

"Keep to the tree line. If the right moment comes, take it. Everyone else stay put."

"I'm coming with you," broke in Amanda.

"No, you're not. Look after Phineas and trust me."

With that, Port turned his stallion about and made for the lake shore past the Shoshone camps, and the full moon glowed down like a dragon's face.

24.

The Shoshones had moved camp, but the markings of where tipis had sat, along with cookfire remnants, still dotted the ground. The loss of Big Bear and the others would be a hard tax on the small tribe. He remembered his own people's exodus in the dead of winter. *They'll be all right*, he told himself.

Fingers of ghostly clouds tried to shroud the moon, but still the cold light poked through, casting a long line across the lake. Where it ended up on the shore stood the white-haired old Indian, along with the little girl beside him. She was bound up tight as an old maid's bedroll, a rag stuffed in her mouth.

Lehi, or Ligaii-Maiitsoh, raised his hand in the common greeting, though the smirk on his face was mocking and cold. "I knew you would come, Long-hair."

"My motivations aren't hard to understand. What are yours, though?"

"I have blood of the Trickster in my veins. I am naked terror. I sow deceit and discord. I am your fatal error."

Port dismounted. "Well, I'm here. You gonna give me the girl?"

The tall old man smirked. "She dies, but only after you."

Port drew his gun. "Where's your creature? Nowhere to hide down here next to the lake."

Lehi cocked his head and laughed inaudibly. "I have no creature."

"You're blood of the trickster, a natural-born liar. I know you have some kind of beast."

"My name is Ligaii-Maiitsoh. It means 'White Wolf' in my people's tongue. If you knew anything about us, you would have known what kind of man wears skins of a predator."

"And I wear a dozen cow skins. Let the girl go."

Lehi didn't move.

Port sent a round nipping past the old man's ears, but he didn't flinch. "You got nerve, I'll give you that. Let the girl go or I'll shoot. I got no truck with kidnappers or rustlers."

"I know you. You don't know me," said Lehi. "A lifetime ago, I swore to serve the Trickster and his slave, the Master Mahan. They granted me powers beyond white man's gun."

"Enough! Let the girl go, or I scalp you from the inside out."

Lehi grinned, revealing terribly big teeth, a jaw that jutted and bristled with fangs. Port wasn't sure he was seeing correctly.

The old man's nose twitched and stretched. "You see what only the dead have seen."

Port sent a round through Lehi's chest. The old man flinched upon impact but no blood came, and his face stretched further. Port shot a second round and a third into the monster.

But the transformation wasn't complete. Fine white fur sprung from the old man's body, and beneath it muscles rippled. A howl came with the completion.

Port sent the fourth, fifth, and sixth rounds into the beast, none of which produced so much as a drop of blood.

Grinning devilishly, Lehi tossed the bound girl into the lake behind him.

Amanda Cook screamed from farther up into the tree line, then dashed downhill for her daughter.

"More to slay," growled Lehi, his transformation to skinwalker now complete.

Port dove for the girl in the lake but the swift hand of the monster batted him aside.

His pistol knocked from his hand, Port strained for his Bowie. But already the beast took him by the coat and threw him.

The thunderclap of a Sharps rifle boomed over the lake shore. A tuft of white fur flew, but still no blood came from the skinwalker's wound.

Amanda reached the water's edge and pulled Mary from the weak surf. The little girl took a deep breath, gasping from the cold water.

Then she was thrown back in the lake.

The skinwalker knocked Mary back into the waters while holding her mother like a rag doll. "Danite," it called, emphasizing the -ite. "Choose which to save, girl or woman."

Port had the Bowie out now despite how badly his body ached from the blow.

"Throw it away in the lake or I rip her apart, but choose," snarled the skinwalker.

Port knew Lehi was a liar, but he knew it could fulfill the threat. Even a silver slug from the Sharps did nothing against it. Only the Bowie knife Brigham had blessed in Nauvoo could harm it.

The girl was drowning. The choice must be made.

Amanda fumbled one-handed with something in her pocket.

The skinwalker stared cold-fire at Port, relishing the Danite's painful choice.

Somewhere above, Joseph Rich looked down the barrel of the Sharps, waiting to try another shot.

Mary sputtered in the cold lake water.

Port took the Bowie in hand. "Lord, guide my hand," he prayed. "Help me end this creature." He threw it true as he had ever thrown anything in his life, straight for the skinwalker's heart.

It caught the blade with the reflexes of diamondback's strike and sounded out in a cross between a dog's bark and a man laughing. It arched to throw the knife back.

Port thought it would throw the heavy blade at him. He ran for the girl and drew her from the water like baby Moses. She gasped again, her face turning blue.

Looking back, Port expected to be stabbed with his own knife, but the reveling skinwalker waited for Port to watch.

The blade went high and wide of Port, falling into the lake and disappearing in dark waters.

Port watched the trusty blade vanish into the inky darkness, then, glancing at the shivering girl, he had an idea. Facing the lake he called, "Blue! Blue! Blue!"

The skinwalker taunted, "Calling for your knife's return?"

Amanda found what she had fished for, a small glass vial. She smashed it against the only part of the monster she could reach, its shoulder.

Consecrated oil dripped down the white fur, surprising the beast. Amanda tore free, running to her daughter.

The monster puzzled at her choice of attack. "What is this?"

Granting a thin reflective line down the monster, Joseph Rich took his shot, nailing dead center the shoulder where the holy oil covered.

Now deep crimson flowed and the beast howled.

Barehanded, Port tackled the fiendish beast, punching, kicking, and clawing like the monster was the devil himself. The skinwalker resisted until Port jammed a finger in the wound. It let roll a string of wicked curses.

Though groaning, it prevailed and sent the avenging angel flying into the cold surf.

Joseph ran down the hill hoping for another shot to present itself, but Porter was too thick in the fray and he dared not take another shot. "Do you have any more oil? It works!"

"I don't," cried Amanda, desperately trying to untie her daughter and run away.

The skinwalker raked at Porter with its claws, but try as it might it couldn't pierce his skin. The sharp edges could not gain access. Yowling, it looked at the lake and dragged Port into the water.

Joseph took another shot, hitting the monster in the back, but missing the oil and nothing happened.

"If I cannot cut you, I will drown you," laughed the skinwalker, holding Port beneath the water.

Kicking, Port strained and fought but the monster was too strong, pushing him into the sandy bottom.

Underwater Port heard a strange set of clicks.

The shaggy white arms let go and Port straightened out of the water.

The skinwalker had stepped back away from the water. It beckoned angrily with its right arm, speaking a wolfish tongue.

Behind Port loomed the Bear Lake monster.

"Blue, I need some help. Get him!" Port shouted directing the lake dragon's gaze.

The skinwalker's chest began to turn a shade of pale green that was growing in intensity when Joseph shot it again, right where a stream of oil had touched along the ribs.

Wailing of pain and true terror, the skinwalker's glow faded.

"He won't bob off this time. Get 'im, Blue."

The Bear Lake monster lurched forward and swallowed the skinwalker, devouring the white horror entirely.

"Chew him up, Blue! Chew him up!" shouted Port. "Wheat!"

An infernal, hollow cry sounded from within the beast, dimming and fading to silence.

Blue opened its cavernous maw and let its tongue loll out between titanic fangs.

Port patted the tremendous beast's snout and examined its handiwork. "No coming back from that," he said, picking random clumps of white fur that stuck in the monster's teeth. "You did good, Blue. Now back to the lake with ya, old friend."

The monster rumbled a colossal purr and turned to slide back into deep waters.

25.

Amanda watched in amazement, holding Mary close. "He is good?"

"Yes, ma'am. He just needed some help and understanding," said Port.

Joseph ran down the hillside shouting, "What a story to tell. I'll get this posted in all the papers across the country. People will come from all over the world to be a part of our valley and see the monster."

"No!" Port stuck a thick finger in the tall man's chest. "You're gonna tell everyone you made it up. No good will come of this tale being told for true."

Confused, Joseph looked at Port and then the monster disappearing into the lake.

"You don't want what they'll bring to your valley. You don't want more trouble coming down on Brother Brigham. And you don't want 'em messing with the monster."

"I'll say I made it all up," said Joseph Rich, rubbing the sore spot where Porter had pushed. "It will be a wonderful first-class lie."

"Good. Some stories are better off that way."

BETWEEN HUSBAND AND WIFE AND THE LATE BRAM STOKER

Will Bishop

In my ignorance,
I guess I've always imagined the
so-called sacred, holy, and divinely ordained
act of love
as being embodied
in something like a vampire
or two vampires, rather,
two shadowy sets of sharpened incisors,
sucking the very strength, vim, and soul
from the full, flushed flesh of the other.
And perhaps this sounds problematic,
even pessimistic, all this sucking of souls, but remember
that eternal life is more than mere immortality
and in a world of pairs,
to be vampire is to be victim
and vice versa.

We drain and
we're drained and
we drain again. Besides,
I've seen those movies.
I've seen the lovely young ladies –
rouge-cheeked and rose-lipped innocents,
always curious virgins like me –
I've seen their long, white necks
and the way they look at The Count.
I've seen the way they give themselves to Bela Lugosi and his
irresistible raised eyebrow like he's the
last man on earth because
when it all comes down to it,
being cast as the victim
can be a pretty good role.
And surrendering that
last, warm, sticky drop of life
may be even better
than the ripe partaking itself. But anyway,
with lovers it always ends the same –
at least in my imagination –
with the two of them crash-landed and still smoldering,
slumbering close in their queen-sized, celestial coffin,
two more lucky members
of the blessed host of
undead.

I LIE IN BED READING FROM MOSIAH CHAPTER THREE AND THINK OF YOU, LON CHANEY, JR.

Will Bishop

What a drag it is
to be a reluctant monster,
to watch and pray for the sunrise,
only to heed the howling like a natural man
and go a-whoring after the moon
left to wonder what it would be like
to live an uncomplicated life
like those full-time blood-suckers –
zombies, mummies, or ghouls,
employed by pride, by lust, wrath, and greed –
creatures of the night,
or even to be like the opposite,
those bright-and-shiny saints,

unbitten,
immune,
with no more desire to do evil,
not even once a month.
How ridiculous the transformations look in retrospect –
all yak hair and faux fur and camera cut-aways –
but you should have been there back in forty-one,
when it was real and it was you,
alone in that darkened theater
knowing full well that
even a man who is pure at heart
and says his prayers by night
can still only grit his teeth and sit it out
like a true lukewarm lupine,
a part-time prodigal,
and brace himself
for the next full moon.

CHARITY NEVER FAILETH

Jaleta Clegg

"**SISTER** Thomas, thank you so much." Pam Jensen accepted the glass pan full of gently quivering green gelatin. Carrot shreds mocked her from the glistening depths.

Sister Thomas waved her hand. "I'd love to stay and help, Pam, but Jared and Omner have basketball practice and little Tiffany has her piano lessons and Sariah wants picked up at the high school in half an hour. You know how life is. Toodles!" Her designer sweats disappeared rapidly through the glass door of the church kitchen.

Pam sighed. Another lime gelatin salad. How many was that now? Twenty-three? She set the pan on the counter next to the fridge.

"Sister Jensen? I hate to bother you, but ... "

Pam stopped her eyes from rolling with a supreme effort of will. Charity suffereth long, and all that. "Yes, Sister Love?"

Nyra Love waddled to the cabinets, one hand spread across her extremely pregnant belly. "I just need a pitcher of water, you know, for the little ones, when they come." She smiled her vapid smile, like a brain-damaged hamster. Her breathless voice grated on Pam's already stretched nerves. "I hope you don't mind."

"No, no problem, Nyra. Are you sure you should be helping tonight? Wasn't your baby due Sunday?"

Nyra Love giggled. "Oh, no. I was due last Thursday but the doctor says all first babies are late. It's my responsibility to be here. It's my calling, to serve in the nursery at Relief Society weekly enrichment meetings." A frown crawled over her face. "What are we supposed to call them now?"

"Just call it a birthday dinner. Do you want help?" Pam wedged the latest gelatin offering into the fridge with the other green masses. All had carrots. A few sported pineapple tidbits or canned pears. Sour cream covered two on the bottom shelf of the fridge.

Nyra pressed her hand to her belly. "Oh, that was a strong one. Nothing to worry about, Sister Jensen. It's only Braxton-Hicks." She waddled from the room, a plastic pitcher clutched in her free hand.

Pam shook her head as she resumed arranging fresh fruit on trays. A faint gurgle caught her attention. She paused, glancing over the simmering Crock-Pots of ham. Must have been the lids rattling. She popped open a container of strawberries.

"You want real forks or them plastic atrocities?" Edith Merkel stumped through the door, her orthotically correct shoes squeaking on the linoleum floor.

"Just use the real ones, please."

Edith yanked the drawer open, extracting fistful of flatware. "Where's your committee at? Lazing around expecting those of us humble enough to serve to wait on them hand and foot?" Forks protruded from her fingers.

"I'm sure they had important things to do." Pam arranged a ring of strawberries on the tray. The other sisters had all made excuses when they saw Edith's name on the dinner committee list. Sister Merkel's tongue was legend in the Fifth Ward.

"More important than helping us set up this dinner they expect to eat?" The elderly woman shuffled from the kitchen muttering under her breath.

Pam ripped open a bag of marshmallows, dumping them into a serving bowl. She debated calling Sister Harris for help. No, Sister Harris made Nyra look intelligent by comparison. Another rattle sounded from the general direction of the refrigerator. Pam jumped, startled by the unexpected noise. She glanced at the fridge then gathered the strawberry tray and the marshmallows, carrying them down the hall to the gym. Nyra's off-key humming sounded from the nursery next door.

Edith stamped around each table, slamming forks on paper napkins. Her tightly permed white hair gleamed with blue highlights under the fluorescent fixtures. "I ironed each and every one of these cloths and they still have wrinkles. That's what comes of storing them in a cupboard. They don't make them like they used to, no, they certainly don't." She jabbed the last fork at the iron sitting on the edge of the main serving table. Steam curled from the vents.

"They look beautiful, Sister Merkel." Pam set her burden on the dessert table. She tweaked the position of the pineapple boats more to the center as she made a mental note to remove the hot iron before anyone else arrived.

"Where do you want these?" Edith pulled bunches of silk flowers from a laundry basket. "Can't even have decent flowers these days. Have to use these fake ones. In my day, we just plucked them from our yards. Everyone grew flowers then, not like these days."

Thumps sounded from the direction of the kitchen across the hall. Pam glanced over her shoulder at the open door. "It's March, Sister Merkel. The flowers are still buried under six inches of snow."

"Well, I can't be having these fake things dropping what-all into my drink."

High-pitched screams shattered the peace of the church building.

Nyra bolted inside the gym from the nursery across the hall. The pregnant woman yanked the doors shut, then leaned against them. Her eyes stretched wide in panic. "It ate the little ones' snacks! Every last box!"

"What did, Nyra?" Pam hurried to her side.

"It was hideous, all big and blobby looking!"

"I'd bet on the bishop, if I was a betting woman, which I'm not." Edith squinted and slapped silk daisies on a table.

"Not the bishop." Nyra's voice wavered. She tugged her blonde braid.

"Then what, Nyra?" Pam patted the younger woman's arm.

"That!" Nyra pointed at the far door.

Green gelatin oozed between the two sides, assembling into a wobbling mass. Carrot shreds and cheddar fish crackers danced in its middle.

Edith nodded. "Just like the summer of fifty-one. Back in Tooele, you know. We were setting up for a dinner just like this. Someone decided it would be tasty to put pears and pineapple in the same salad with the carrots. Some things should never be done."

The quivering mass of lime gelatin extended a pseudopod, inching across the wood floor. The sour cream toppings rolled together, extruding out the top of the blob. The three women inched backward.

"It's formed an eye." Edith dropped her armful of silk flowers on the nearest table. "This is a bad one."

"This happened before?" Pam asked, her attention fixed on the pulsing blob of gelatinous salad.

"It's an abomination, like Daniel said would come haunting us for our sinful ways." Edith plucked forks from the place settings, gathering them in her fist.

The women took refuge behind the dessert table. The blob oozed across the floor toward them.

"How did you stop it back then, Edith?"

MONSTERS & MORMONS

"We lured it out to the parking lot. Late July in Tooele. Thing melted."

Nyra pressed both hands to her belly. "My, that was a strong one."

"How far apart are the contractions?" Pam asked.

The eye quivered at the end of a long blob of green. It scanned the room, dripping shreds of carrot.

"About every five minutes for the last two hours," Nyra answered. "The doctor says this baby won't come until next week, though."

"Sweetheart, you're in labor. I birthed five of my own. Your doctor is an idiot." Edith thumped her fist on the table, stabbing holes in the tablecloth with her forks.

Nyra's lip trembled. "But I can't have the baby now. I'm supposed to be teaching the children's class. Ooo." Her eyes widened. Her fists clutched the table for support.

Pam patted her back. "Just breathe, honey."

The gelatin monster slid closer, leaving slimy trails of carrot on the floor. A fish cracker plopped from the eyestalk.

"Hahahee?" Nyra panted uncertainly.

"It's too cold to melt that thing," Pam said to Edith.

"We could try wrapping it in a tablecloth and stuffing it in the oven," Edith suggested.

"Hahahee!" Nyra grabbed Pam's hand, squeezing hard.

Pam winced. "I don't want to go near that thing."

"Try singing, honey. It helped me." Edith fingered the forks she still held.

"Tell me the stories of Jesus, I love to heehee HA!" Nyra wheezed, tears leaking from her eyes as she clutched her belly. "I don't want my baby to be born in a church gym."

Pam patted her pocket. Her cellphone was at home, where she usually left it for church activities. "I'll slip out and call your husband."

The main blob gave birth to at least a dozen smaller blobs that slithered under the tables, leaving trails of carrot shreds.

"They're flanking us." Edith hunched behind the chocolate fountain. "Did some idiot add marshmallows? No wonder they can think!" She flipped a fork at the largest blob. It hung, vibrating gently, among the pears.

Pam slipped the bowl of marshmallows she'd set out for the chocolate fountain farther down the table. No need for Edith to notice those now.

Nyra pulled away from Pam's support. She drew herself to her full five-foot-three height, chin set. "As sisters in Zion, we all work to – heeheeHA!" She grabbed a wedge of fresh pineapple, flinging it at the monstrous blob. Her quavering soprano carried on, pausing only for panting breaths. "The heeheeHA of his blessings we heeheeHA!" Her aim, aided by her faith, landed another wedge of pineapple on the monster.

The green gelatin stopped, wobbling in place. Burbling moans echoed through the room. The smaller blobs echoed the moans.

"I think you hurt it." Edith winced at a high note.

"You're a genius, Nyra!" Pam squeezed the younger woman's hand.

"I am?" Nyra smiled, like a ray of sunshine breaking through a storm. "We have been born as heeheeHA of old." She hurled a rain of pineapple at the blob.

Rivulets of green liquid dripped from the wounds inflicted by the fresh fruit.

Pam grinned at Edith. "Never put fresh or frozen pineapple, kiwi, or papaya in gelatin." She plucked a wedge of pineapple from the carefully carved serving boat made from the outside of the pineapple. "Take that!" Her wedge landed on the floor several feet in front of one of the smaller blobs.

"You need a bit more enthusiasm. Or better weaponry." Edith squatted behind the table, digging through her baggy pockets. "Ha! I thought those were in there." She waved three rubber bands.

The quivering mound of green gelatin retreated a few inches, oozing back until it encountered a table. The blob sucked the place settings and fake flowers inside. Green slime dripped across the tablecloth.

"That's going to leave a stain!" Nyra's eyes hardened. She pelted the monster with another handful of fruit.

Pam shifted another pineapple boat into Nyra's reach. The young mother-to-be snatched the empty pineapple shell, lobbing it across the gym.

"I belong to the heeheeheeeeHAAAAA!"

The quarter pineapple shell, carefully hollowed with its leaves still attached, struck the blob in its bobbing sour cream eye. The eyestalk retracted, dragging the pineapple inside. The thing pulsed, like a heartbeat. A warbling, burbling croak emerged from the interior.

"You've hurt it now, honey." Edith emerged from behind the table. She clutched a contraption of two forks and multiple rubber bands in one hand.

"What is that?" Pam nudged more pineapple in Nyra's direction.

Edith wedged a pineapple slice in the dangling rubber bands. "Wrist rocket. I spent twenty-seven years with the Cub Scouts. I can make anything into a weapon." She spun on the ball of her orthotically clad foot, letting the pineapple fly at one of the smaller blobs creeping along the wall. "Take that, foul fiend!"

The smaller blob dissolved into a puddle. Carrot shreds floated listlessly over the wood floor.

"Poor thing." Pam rose on tiptoes to peer at it.

Edith snorted as she reloaded. "That thing would have eaten you. Don't waste pity on that nasty salad."

"Onward Christian heeheeheeeee, marching as to war!" Pineapple rained down on the blob from both of Nyra's hands.

The burbling croak rose in pitch. All of the smaller blobs slithered to the main monster. It absorbed them, growing larger and taller with each addition. Streams of unset gelatin dripped from gaping holes left by the pineapple.

Nyra sent the last pineapple boat sailing across the gym. The creature howled when it hit. Goo splattered the nearby tables.

Nyra placed both hands on her belly. "We're out of pineapple. What are we going to do?"

"Do what the younger generation does. Ninja attack!" Edith grabbed the closest bowl of kiwi slices. Her shoes squeaked as she darted from behind the table, racing towards the blob.

"Oh, do be careful, Edith!" Pam clapped hands to her cheeks.

"Kill it!" Nyra shrieked.

Edith stumbled, clutching the bowl of kiwi to her bosom. "Dang my artificial knee!"

The far door of the gym opened. The bishop, a stout man who dearly loved his food and never missed a Relief Society dinner, peered inside. "Is everything all right, sisters?"

Nyra turned to Pam, her rabbity face creased with concern. "You have to stop it, Sister Jensen, or it's going to eat the bishop. Oh dear. Hee. Haaaa. Aaaaaaugh!" She bent double over the table, hands pressed to her belly.

"I don't know how! The fruit's gone." Pam dithered, eyes searching for anything that might help. She caught sight of the iron, still plugged in at one end of the table. Edith's iron was a massive old relic from the fifties, the kind that had been discontinued for safety reasons.

Pam yanked the plug from the wall, hefting the beast with both hands.

"Lovely centerpiece thing. What is it?" The bishop wandered closer to the undulating blob of green gelatin.

"Don't touch it! It's evil!" Edith limped closer.

The blob extended a pseudopod, reaching for the old woman's bobbing white head.

Pam closed her eyes, breathed a hasty prayer, then rushed at the blob, iron held before her like a weapon.

"Oh no, you don't, you abomination of desolation!" Edith thrust the bowl of kiwi at the tentacle, parrying the monster's attack.

The bishop reached one hand to the quivering backside of the monster. The sour cream eye, still leaking gelatin from the pineapple wedged in the center, rolled through the blob towards him.

"Stop, Bishop Alger! Oh, please stop!" Pam picked up her speed. She hadn't actually run for fifteen years. Her middle-aged body protested even while adrenaline spurred her on.

"Heee heeeeee heeeeee HAAAAAAAA!" Nyra's scream reached a new pitch.

The blob shivered, ripples cascading over its surface in time to Nyra's panting screeches. Vague recollections of resonant frequencies and shattering wine glasses surfaced in Pam's mind as she raced closer, the heat of the iron scorching her fingers.

The gelatin salad extruded a mass of carrot shavings onto the bishop's hand just as Edith sprayed the other side with kiwi.

Pam plunged the hot iron into the center of the blob as Nyra's scream reached maximum volume. The blob of gelatin exploded. Carrot shavings, cheddar fish, canned pears, and pineapple tidbits rained across the room in a sudden silence.

The bishop blinked, brushing his hand absently across the green splatters on his once-white shirt. "Dinner isn't quite ready yet? Carry on, sisters. I'll be in my office." He blinked again, then wandered from the gym.

Edith set the serving bowl on a table.

"Sister Jensen?" Nyra stumbled from behind the dessert table. "I think I should go to the hospital now. My doctor was wrong."

Pam hurried to the young woman's side, catching her arm. "I'll call your husband."

Nyra smiled her sweetly innocent smile, only now it had teeth and a backbone. "You tell him we're naming our little boy Lee. Brother Lee Love."

Pam patted Nyra's hand. "That's a sweet name."

Pam's gaze traveled over the scattered decorations, covered with gobbets of melting gelatin. She shook her head then straightened her shoulders.

Edith planted her hands on her hips. "You take Sister Nyra off to meet her husband. I'll get a mop. We'll still be able to serve by seven."

Pam led Nyra from the gym. They should have enough food without the gelatin. No one ever ate the green stuff anyway. And they had plenty of ham in the kitchen.

RECOMPENSE OF SORROW

W. H. Pugmire

I.

There is a place in Sesqua Valley where the hills rise high, far from the center of town. In this where the woods begin their dark descent there stands one small and solitary house; and when one walks along the woodland path adjacent to the back yard of the small yellow house, one can follow it to a place of legend. The circular clearing found there is home to a deep pool of dark water, around which, sporadically, stands a clutch of statuettes, five of which are not large, and one of which is life-size. This taller figure faces the pool, before which it lifts six wings. One large hand is held before its breast, the palm turned upward; the other hand holds an implement, with which the beast seems to be writing on the upturned palm. Strangest of all is the creature's proud countenance, which looks so queer that one imagines it to be a kind of impressionistic caricature. To look upon this statue is to be reminded of the biblical legends of fallen angels, proud and potent though exiled.

A scarecrow stood beside the angel and tried to study its outlandish face without falling into the dark pool. Her clothes were now too large for her desiccated frame, those limbs that had once been so robust, but were now withered by encroaching disease. Her skin, once so smooth and supple, had wrinkled and shrunken, especially around her throat and arms. Her voice, once so musical and strong, was now a strangled thing, croaked and hoarse. Her name was Theodora Oake, and she was a stranger to the supernatural place in which she stood. She steadied herself by clutching a graven wing with one frail hand, and with her other hand she touched the statue's granite cheek. "What a proud, disdainful beast you look," she whispered to it.

"'A proud look, a lying tongue, and hands that shed innocent blood, An heart that deviseth wicked imaginations, feet that be swift in running to mischief.'"

The speaker stood some distance from her, beneath dense trees. Theodora's first thought on seeing him was a passage from *Dracula*, wherein the vampire is introduced posing as a coachman. Before her was a figure in somber attire, tall and commanding, whose face was mostly hidden by a large round hat. Here, as in the novel, were the shining eyes, silver rather than crimson. "That's from Proverbs," the fellow spoke as he began to glide toward her. Theodora's initial impulse was to back away as he drew nearer; but this she could not do without slipping into the pool, and so she clung to the statue with both hands. The other creature stood quite near her. "This water is quite deep, my dear. Take my hand, and I will be your anchorage." She glanced at the large sallow hand he offered her, then at the twisted smile on his malformed mouth, and she knew that she wanted nothing whatsoever to do with him. Yet she was growing weak and dizzy, clinging to the statue so precariously above the pool; and thus, resigned, she reached out and took hold of the fellow's paw.

"Thank you," she murmured, not wanting to look at her rescuer. He continued to smile and momentarily doffed his hat.

"Simon Williams," he announced as his face was dimly illuminated by subdued light. Theodora could not restrain from gasping, for the fellow's fantastic physiognomy was a living mimic of the statue's countenance. "And you are ... ?"

"Theodora Oake," she rasped.

"Ah, young Oake's elder sister," he replied as he placed his wide hat again onto his dome. "Alas, your sibling is a slow student – so easily distracted, so he is. I've been instructing him from the terrible and forbidden Greek translation of *Al Azif*. Perhaps some evening you'll care to join us. We've seen little of you since your arrival to Sesqua Valley."

"My illness has made me a bit of a recluse." She straightened up and raised her face to the pale light that tried to peep into the place through the leafy limbs of spreading trees. "I ventured out today for a little walk and stumbled onto this place." She looked at the fellow again and then turned to observe the statue. "Forgive me, but did you pose for that?"

Simon Williams shrugged. "Not really. The artist was not fond of me, and it amused him to cast me as his mold. Initially I found it rather silly; but now I rather like that I stand here, in stony effigy, surrounded by my little ones." He swept his hand so as to indicate the more diminutive sculptures.

Theodora motioned to the tall statue. "What is it that you write upon your palm?"

Ah, his esoteric smile! "The names of those adopted unto my demesne." Something in the strange expression of his peculiar face perplexed the woman, and she stiffened as that face bent low so as to examine the medallion that hung from a length of cord just above her bosom. "How fascinating," he intoned.

She touched a nervous hand to the metal disc. "It's a replica of Joseph Smith's Jupiter Talisman."

"Smith? The lunatic Mormon magus?"

At this she could not help but laugh. "Even he. The original was found on his person following his murder. The legend is that he used the talisman to contact angelic beings."

His weird mouth curled in secret mirth. "And do you commune with the heavenly hosts, Miss Oake?"

Before she could answer, someone approached from within the woodland, and she was relieved to see her brother advance toward where they stood. "Burgess," she said, holding to him her hand.

"Ah, young Oake," Simon greeted. "I've just invited your charming sister to come study with us."

"Hello, Simon," the young man said in a dismissive tone. "Are you ready, Theo? I'm famished, and the corn chowder is nearly ready."

"Yes," she answered, moving away from the beast of Sesqua Valley. "It was pleasant meeting you, Mr. Williams."

Simon bowed to her. "Perhaps we shall see you tonight, with your moody sibling's permission, of course. You can tell me more about your angelic charm." He winked at Burgess, turned, and disappeared into the trees.

"You were rather unfriendly," the woman scolded.

"I'd rather you didn't have anything to do with Simon Gregory Williams. He's a bad influence. Where's your walking stick?"

"At home. It makes me feel too much an invalid." They departed the place and slowly followed the path that took them homeward. "Simon's a curious fellow. What's wrong with his face?"

"He's native to the valley – they all look like that. What were you two talking about?"

"Nothing. What do you mean, they all look like that? Is this valley a nest of inbreeding? Is that why you don't want me here? No, don't deny it. Your behavior has been so odd since my arrival."

"You suddenly showing up caught me off guard."

"Of what need you be on guard about? Are you frolicking in queer debauchery with the natives?"

"You have an unhealthy imagination, Theo." They reached the edge of the woods and walked onto the large lawn of his back yard.

"You're moody. I know that I should have been more straightforward about my condition, and my reason for coming here."

He let go of her arm. "You're coming here to die? Yes, it would have been nice to have prepared me for that." He turned to scowl at her, and then he saw the sorrow in her eyes. "Forgive me. I am moody. I'm no good at concealing my emotions."

She took his arm again. "You always try to hide what you're feeling, just as you've always liked to hide from the world. You're like a creature in Kafka, burrowing into the imagined safety of some hole. That's why you've come to this forsaken place."

He laughed. "That's an interesting word for the valley. Come, let me help you up these steps and into the kitchen. You look tired. We'll share a quiet meal and then I insist that you rest." She did feel fatigued, and so after their quiet meal she retired to the spacious bedroom on the lower floor. Burgess had transformed the room into his studio because of its large windows and luminous light. After undressing, Theodora sat at a table that was littered with sheets of discarded sketches, some of which quite disturbed her. One drawing showed a Sphinx with ponderous breasts, the face of which was an uncanny combination of her brother's facial features and her own. There was a weird drawing of the white twin-peaked mountain that loomed above the valley, and a sinister sketch of some faceless figure that wore a kind of triple crown. Most interesting of all was a smudged depiction of the statue by the pool, standing in a moonlit place and danced around by diminutive shadow-things. Finally she yawned and went to bed, and when she shut her eyes her mind conjured forth an image of the dark pool and its angelic beast. The seraph had exchanged its writing implement for a thin black flute.

From somewhere outside the bedroom window a melodious wind hummed as it pushed through trees. Surely it was the sound of wind, singing so eerily outside her window, so the weary woman assured herself as slumber claimed her.

II.

Burgess Oake walked the woodland path as a night-wind brushed his anxious face. When he reached the cyclopean round tower, he hesitated at the entranceway and listened to the sound that whistled from above – the piping that had lured him to this unhallowed place. There were many places of power within the valley, but this ancient stone tower held a kind of arcane potency that was almost overwhelming; it filled a human soul with a sense of fear and wonder. Sucking in air through clenched teeth, Burgess entered the edifice and climbed the winding stairs that led to the topmost platform. Simon Gregory Williams sat on his throne of gold with an old tome in his lap. His talons caressed the stops of his thin black flute. As he drew nearer, Burgess recognized the book by the smell that emanated from the wormy pages.

"I didn't know that the *Necronomicon* was a source of musical inspiration."

The beast ceased his piping. "There is much of which you are ignorant, Oake. What is music but a form of conjuration? These airy vibrations – how they slip between the realms and call."

"Stay away from my sister, Simon."

The other laughed. "You've come to command me? No, you've come pregnant with questions." Swiftly, Simon leaped out of his throne and flew to a large table that was littered with manuscripts and tomes. He placed the *Necronomicon* beside a slim folio edition. "But I have questions of my own. You never told me you were Mormon. Such a fascinating faith. You see here, this slim volume in folio – it's my own personal edition of your *Pearl of Great Price*, translated into Latin by mine own hand onto this parchment. Now, here we have that so interesting facsimile from which your Prophet Joseph culled what has been purported to be a translation of the ancient Egyptian text. Is it correct that an Angel of God told Joseph Smith that this was written by Abraham, and that it records the Patriarch's death? Yet how he could describe the events of his death is such a mystery."

"I don't know anything about it."

"You disappoint me, sirrah. For, you see," and he opened the edition of the *Necronomicon* that he had been studying on his throne. "Here, on page 333 – this sketch by, one assumes, Abdul Alhazred, describing an evocation of the Crawling Chaos. Look, Oake, it's almost identical to the facsimile from which Smith 'translated' his Book of Abraham. Look here – the figure of the Faceless God, which Smith absurdly 'completed' by giving the creature a human head. You see, in Alhazred's depiction, where Smith has drawn a dagger, the figure has its hand raised so as to form the Elder Sign, with which to evoke the Crawling Chaos. And here, so compelling – where the Smith thing interprets an alligator image as an 'idolatrous god of Pharaoh' – you see, in the *Necronomicon* the image lies on its back, which suggests the denizens of the Nameless City. We have such a denizen resting within a hillside crypt here in the valley. It holds an esoteric disc, rather similar to the charm your sister wears around her neck, in its upturned paw. Why are you making that obnoxious noise?"

"Sorry, Simon," the lad said, trying to control his laughter. "It's just – you're telling me that modern Mormon scripture is actually an evocation to the Great Old Ones! By god, what a rare joke if it's true!"

"I need to examine your sister's talisman, Oake."

"Just leave her alone, please. She's no concern of yours."

"Pah. Everything that happens within this valley is my concern. I can assist her moan of sorrow, and your own. Come closer, dear boy, and let me read your heart."

Burgess was overwhelmed with a sudden desire to flee, but he knew by the light in Simon's eyes that escape would be impossible. He stepped to the beast and looked away as Simon began to unbutton the lad's shirt. His fear became so palpable that he began involuntarily to moan, and Simon's large hand rose to him and covered his mouth as his own bestial lips moved near and pressed against the human's throat. Simon's kiss moved to the boy's ear, into which was whispered weird words that Burgess could feel slipping into him and tainting his mind. Talons pressed against the young man's breast, where his frantic heart trembled. Releasing him, Simon backed away slightly.

"She need not die, my mortal friend. Look," and he turned to another page of the *Necronomicon*. "Isn't that a delicious symbol? Can't your eyes feel its potency upon them?" Simon took the young man's hand and pressed a sharp talon's point into the flesh. "Can you feel it taint your blood as I etch it here on your hand? Ah – mortal man, you've come to me to learn the arcane way. I will teach you through word and action. You must have faith, but without works such faith is dormant." Simon brought the boy's wet hand to his mouth, and then he pressed his bloodstained lips against the young man's eye.

III.

Theodora awakened to the sound of voices in the living room outside her door. Pushing out of bed, she slipped into a robe and went to investigate. It was odd for Burgess, so non-social, to entertain guests. She was especially surprised to see Simon Gregory Williams sitting on the sofa, and she frowned at his innocent grin. Burgess stood at a window, his back to them as he gazed into night's big sky. "I hope we didn't wake you," Simon told her. "We've kept our voices low. Your brother has been telling me of your fascinating faith."

"I wonder that he has much to tell, being he hasn't been active in the church for many years. He was certainly never interested in doctrine."

"Ah – that explains why he knows nothing of your angelic charm, with which I am most interested."

Theodora hesitated one moment before removing the cord of leather from around her neck and handing the relic to the beast. "I found it in an odd little shop in Salt Lake City. Unlike others of my faith, I delight in digging into little-known aspects of Church history, which has some roots in folk magic. The church has a peculiar and fascinating history that isn't much discussed among members now. Our leaders seem to want to paint us as similar to other Christian sects. We were never that, nor shall we ever be, thank heaven."

Simon smoothed a paw over the Hebrew letters engraved onto the small metal disc. "And your original prophet wore this as a form of protection?"

"No. We have legends of being protected from harm by the wearing of temple garments, but that was never their sacred function. Nor was safeguarding the purpose of that talisman. Rather, I think it must have served in assisting the communing with angelic beings, through which the Eternal Father instructed Joseph in restoring the gospel of Christ."

The woman sat next to Simon and did not move as he slipped the leather cord over her head and around her neck. She avoided his mercury eyes as they peered upon the amulet that nestled just above her bosom. His voice, when again he spoke, sounded to her as she imagined the serpent's sounded to the ears of Eve. "And has your wearing of it initiated you into the angelic realm?" He had asked a similar question when they had first met; but now she turned to face him and noticed the way his outré eyes shimmered with queer light, how his wide nostrils quivered. He seemed to her, then, more beast than human, and she was suddenly afraid.

"My prayers do that, Mr. Williams," she quietly replied.

Leaning back, Simon smiled playfully. "You are stalwart in your faith, Miss Oake. Do you attend those bright temples that dot the globe? I visited one of them, in Nauvoo, just prior to its dedication. It's there that your comrades perform their curious rites for the dead."

"Oh, we're not supposed to talk about that," Burgess piped in as he suddenly turned to them. "It's all very hush-hush. Do you remember, Theo, when we went to the Oakland Temple as kids to do baptism for the dead? Oh, dear – what a scowl!" He laughed, perhaps expecting Simon to join him.

"Baptism for the dead – what an image that conjures," Simon whispered, completely serious. "It was a practice revealed to your Joseph Smith by an angel – perhaps one that he summoned with that curious charm?"

"He knew it by the spirit of prophecy," she answered.

"And do you believe that angels are living creatures?" the beast persisted.

"I do. But what do you believe in, Simon? Are you also a creature of faith?"

"I would say that I am a creature of secret ceremonies, who walks the hidden path and communes with arcane deity. This valley is my temple, wherein I work my rites."

Theodora suddenly looked tired, tilted her head and shut her eyes. Burgess went to her and smoothed her hair with his hand. "We are wearying you."

"No, not you. My disease needs no assistance in that." She smiled at Simon. "I shall soon be dancing in the angelic realm, I think. How lovely it will be, to dance again with no fear of falling. I was once quite agile, Mr. Williams."

"Still agile in mind, Miss Oake. I feel that there is much you may yet teach me." Simon's curious features had softened, as had his voice; she was puzzled and disturbed by his sincerity, this sudden tenderness. He took her hand and kissed it with his queer soft lips. Rising, he bowed to her, and then turned to wink at Burgess. "I shall expect you tomorrow at the tower. We need to discuss the Faceless God in connection to the Haunter of the Dark, as related in the Robert Blake diaries that I had stolen from the authorities in Providence. Good day."

"Well," sighed Theodora, now alone with her brother. "He is certainly occult." She tried to read the expression on her brother's face, seeing for the first time how utterly forlorn he seemed. With effort, she rose to her feet, went to him, and took his face into her brittle hands. "All that live must die, Burgess." How curiously he gazed at her. Gently, he covered her hands with his and kissed her, smiled, and went to the door, where he removed his jacket from the rack and walked outside.

The young man looked at the moonlit mountain for a long time, and then he hunched over and pushed back his elbows, impersonating the twin-peaked titan. Overwhelmed with a sudden sense of woe, he fell onto the chilly ground and crawled on hands and knees into the waiting woodland. He leaned for a little while against a solid tree, then used the trunk for support as he picked himself up. He staggered to the moonlit pool and removed a small ritual dagger from his jacket pocket. The implement was antique and had been used in nameless arcane ceremonies over the æons. He loved to hold the blade to starlight and let his eyesight swim over the symbols that had been etched onto its blade as he grasped the handle, a handle that was in fact some creature's hoof. Finally he knelt next to the winged statue, opened his free hand and peered at its smooth palm. The beast had instructed Burgess well, but the choice was his alone. As he pressed the knife's point into his flesh he could feel the pulse of Sesqua's magick beneath him, a force that seemed to echo in his heart. Simon had said that Burgess would be adopted by this supernatural vale, become kin with its shadow-children. He would bring his sister into the brood. He stood, and using the knife's point, he etched "Theo" into his palm. He kissed the bloodstained hand and then turned cautiously so as to press his wet red lips to the statue's mouth, against which he moaned his sister's name.

They came from the dark woods, the tiny creatures that gathered near him. They touched his legs and clutched his hands, the palms of which they licked as he dropped the dagger to the ground. He fell again to his knees and was embraced. Soft paws smoothed his hair; they dipped into the pool and brought cupped water with which to wash his hands and face. Their tongues moved against the tears that trickled down his face. And then, beguiled, they raised their unfathomable faces and blinked black eyes as from some secret place the beast of Sesqua Valley, a black flute at his mouth, filled the night with eerie song.

IV.

Despite her weakening condition, Theodora insisted on going for solitary walks. She had grown fond of the surrounding woodland, of the strangely sweet nectar that was the valley's air, of how the cool green shadows soothed her eyes and brain. She was charmed, when on her walks, to suddenly encounter, along the pathways or in less likely places, sculptured works of wood and stone. In one spot, one sunlit afternoon, she found a curious tree that she decided must be artificial, for the thing's bark was a very light green, an almost yellow hue. Here and there its soft bark was stained with squiggles of crimson moss, which upon further study proved to be words – or, more precisely, names. When Theodora touched these, her senses were so affected that she was assailed by sudden vertigo and had to struggle to keep her balance.

"Are you well?" She looked up and watched a blurred figure come slowly into focus. The beast of Sesqua Valley stood before her, to whom she frowned. "Ah – you grow weary of those words."

"I shall never be well again. What are these?"

"These?"

She touched the tree. "These names."

"Oh, they're some few of the mortals who, over the years, the valley has espoused."

"To what were they wed?"

He stepped nearer and fingered one of the glyphs, and then he took her hand in both of his and guiding her fingernail into the tree's tissue. How queerly her blood seemed to slow its flowing as he helped her to etch her name into the bark. "The surface is so soft, like flesh. This being is unique unto the region. You see how your name, sliced into the bark, pushes outward like some scar. And yet this dendroid knows no pain. Indeed, one almost senses that its lean and tender branches might reach down so as to enfold one's form – protectively, adoptively."

Theodora listened to Simon's peculiar language as, beneath her, the earth pulsed in time to the beating of her heart. Simon breathed her name into an ear. How warm his hands were as they held her own – and yet, how she shivered. Taking her hand from the tree, Simon brought it to his mouth and nuzzled it. She watched as his malformed mouth moved to the tree and kissed the place where she had written her name. His mercury eyes burned brightly when they turned to penetrate her own. "Come, follow me," he commanded.

How frantic she suddenly felt as he walked away, and like a child who hankered for a parent's hand she stumbled from the place. She walked quickly, despite her weakened state, following him to the dark pool and its stony seraph. Theodora was happy to see her brother waiting for them there, although she could not understand why he was dressed so queerly, in tight-fitting black clothes and a crimson robe as red as sunset flame. She looked at the box of sandalwood that Burgess held and wondered what it contained.

"Sit upon the ground," Simon ordered, and she did so, watching as he moved his fingers to the moon. When had it become evening? How mysterious a thing was Time. The beast stood behind her and massaged her shoulders, and she relaxed. He reached for the cord around her neck and removed her metal mascot. Holding the periapt to the lunar disc in heaven, Simon sighed some words of alchemy, the sound of which seemed to alter as the words sailed as mist from his mouth toward the moon. He then knelt beside her, smiled, and breathed the language into her mouth; and she gasped as her heartbeat echoed weirdly inside her head, a beating that faded until, at last, it ceased.

Burgess wept as he watched Simon place the amulet's cord around his head and pulled so that the metal disc rested against inhuman hide. He hated the look of mockery on Simon's face as the beast rose and advanced to him. Simon opened the sandalwood box and removed a weird mask of black cloth that wore no face. Tenderly, Simon fitted the mask into place over the boy's countenance of flesh. He reached again into the box and removed the triple crown of white gold, which was placed onto the boy's dome. Taking the box, Simon set it on the ground. He curtsied to Burgess and breathed a spell that together they had studied from the *Necronomicon*. Simon moved his hand so as to make the Elder Sign. Burgess raised his own hand and answered with similar motion. He watched as the beast removed all clothing and then went to tenderly lift Theodora's corpse and carry it into the dark pool. When the water was up to Simon's waist, he turned to gaze at the image of the Faceless God, to whom he raised the woman's body, as if as offering. Then Simon formed one arm into a square, called Theodora by name, and began to utter unholy language. Burgess watched as a thick mauve mist issued from the woodland and swirled around him. He listened to Simon's subdued chanting, and to that which answered from the hazy moonlit air. They sailed like spectral things, semi-incorporeal, denizens of Dreamland. Black, horned, slender, with membranous wings and barbed tails, three insubstantial night-gaunts floated to the pool and hovered over the beast and his baptism. Floating to the valley's child of shadow, they conjoined their essence with his, until nothing of them was visible except six phantom wings that protruded from Simon's torso. Burgess watched through the mesh of his mask as Simon buried Theodora's lifeless shell beneath the liquid surface. If the words that Simon now spoke had been in a language with which Burgess has been familiar the boy might have spoken an accompaniment of alchemy so as to assist the beast. All he could do was watch as the mist gathered more abundantly about him until it occluded sight. Frustrated and afraid, Burgess fell to his knees and prayed to whatever gods may heed him.

There came the sound of movement in water, to which the boy crawled. He could just see the figure of Simon sinking beneath the depths. A pale form then floated to the surface, one that waved its limbs with aching deliberation as it pushed through water, toward earth. White hands dug into the sod as the thing pulled itself out of the pool. Burgess shuddered at the sight of the soggy hair that clung to a familiar face, a face no longer withered with ailment. As that head lifted, Burgess saw the eyes beneath the wet strands of heavy hair – those silver orbs of the one now adopted by the place of crazy power. She dragged herself along the ground, to him, and he barely noticed the other things that emerged from the mist and pranced beside her, the black shapes whose chiseled kindred encircled the sacred pool, from which a cadaver, buried in water, had arisen to new life.

She knelt directly before him and tugged the black mask from his face, upsetting the white crown which fell to the ground. Her strong hands clamped her brother's shoulders, and he marveled at their force. Her hands moved to his throat, then lifted so as to weave into his hair. Her mouth, which all the while had stayed shut, curved with divine smiling as she bent to him. Burgess opened his own mouth in preparation for her kiss. But her lips did not press against his own. Rather, they touched his forehead; and when they parted, he felt the water of the enchanted pool that spilled from them, anointing him.

Far West. Missourri

Fall. 1838

A dark time for the Mormons...

All Joseph's thoughts and actions were devoted to the welfare of his suffering people...

Sleep evaded him as he prayed for inspiration to deliver them from evil...

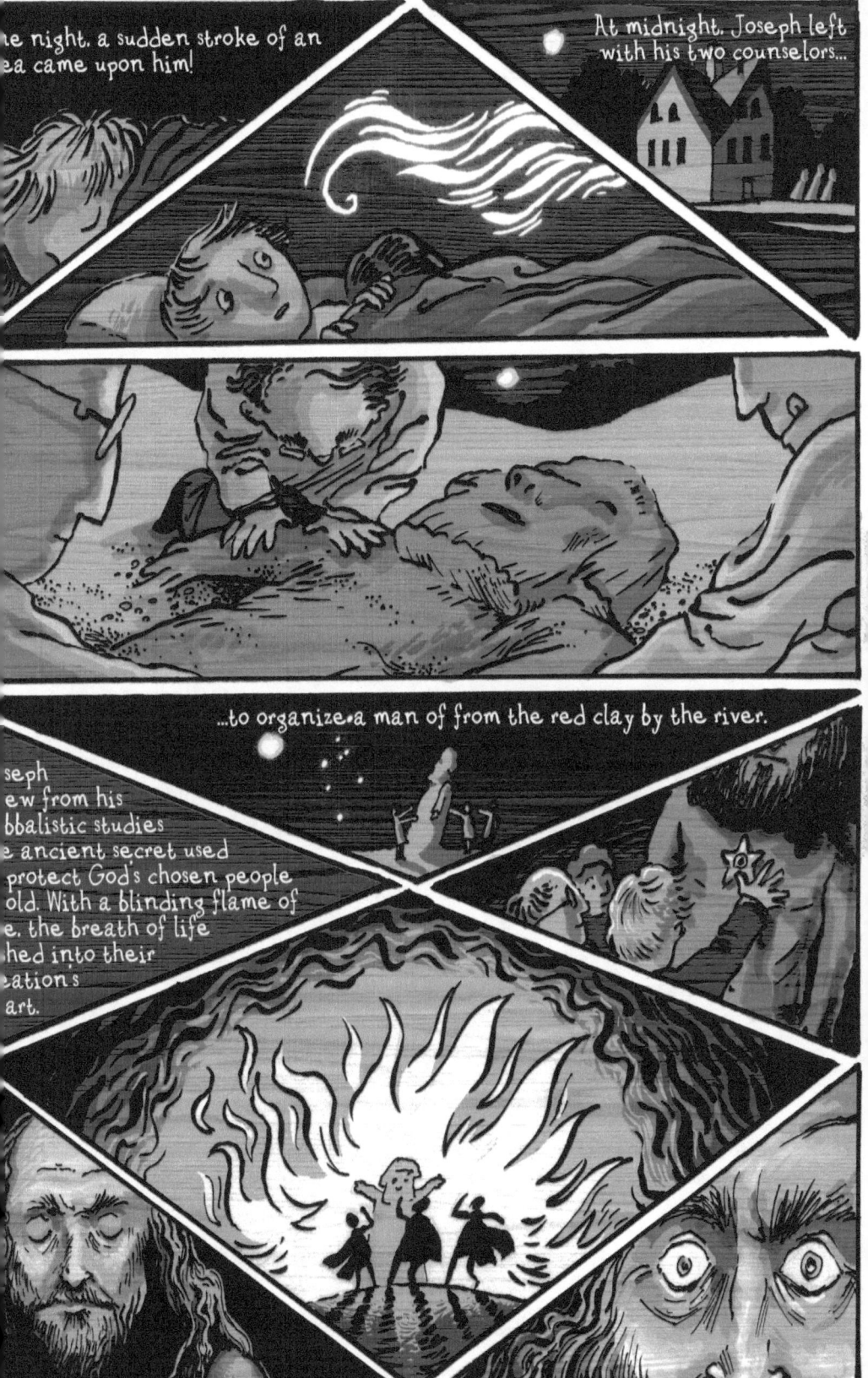

he Mormons must be treated
enemies--their outrages
e beyond all description.
you can increase your
rce, you are authorized
do so. They must be
iven from the
ate, or, if necessary--

exterminated.

Within days, innocent
Mormons were brutally
butchered at Haun's Mill.

The assassination of Governor Boggs was never solved by the authorities.

Rockwell stood trial ...

...but was not found guilty.

But despite his joy at the deliverance from persecution, Joseph was troubled by the whole episode.

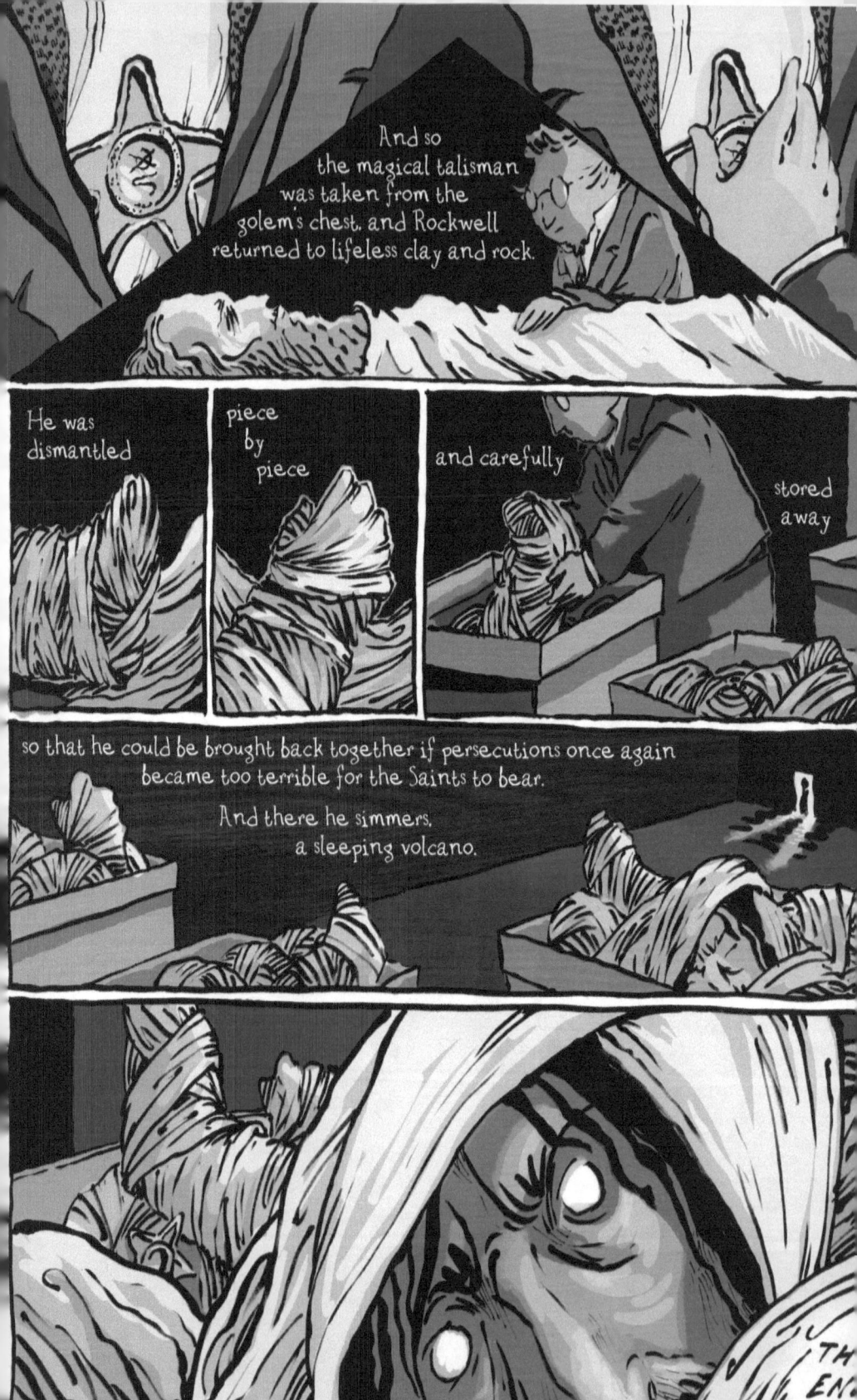

BICHOS

Erik Peterson

NOTHING in Aaron's life had prepared him for the way he felt when his wife dived over the side of the boat into the Amazon River. When she hit the water, his heart fell into his stomach, splashing his insides up into his chest.

The river swallowed her in a heartbeat.

He tried to call to her, but her name caught in his throat. His whole body rebelled, wouldn't let him acknowledge this was real.

Vanessa had dived in after the captain's son, Tiago, who'd leapt into the river from the top deck. Now there was no sign of either of them.

The khaki-colored river was remarkably smooth for such a fast moving mass of water. Aaron searched for motion. Bubbles. Anything.

"Ele não sabe nadar," the captain reminded God. *He doesn't know how to swim.*

And Vanessa didn't know what was down there.

He knew he should do something, move, save his wife, save the boy. But his body stood transfixed by the river.

At last she emerged from the water, brown hair drawn back, gasping for breath. She clutched the boy under her arm.

The captain cried out, pulled the boat around, wiped tears on his bare shoulders. Vanessa held the boy up to the boat as the captain cut the motor and rushed to grab him.

Aaron helped his wife out of the water and held her close.

"I'm sorry," he whispered.

It had only been three days since he'd learned what joy was, looking into her eyes, her face haloed by her veil, as they'd been married for eternity. He'd had all the seminary lessons on love and eternal marriage, but in that moment the reality of it had opened up an entire aspect of his existence so fulfilling he wondered how he'd ever felt alive without it.

But that beautiful realization had an ugly twin. The real meanings of a whole host of other ideas unfolded in his mind. Loss. Danger.

Death.

"I'm ... I'm sorry," he said again, forcing out the words.

She smiled up at him, the same smile she'd had in the temple. "Sorry for what?"

"I should have – you shouldn't go in the water. I should have gone in after you."

"What do you mean? I was – what is he doing?" She hurried across the deck. The captain turned his son, rubbed his arms and legs.

"He's checking for bites," said Aaron. "There are *bichos* in the water. Things. Creatures."

Blood smeared under the captain's hand and his inspection became more focused.

"Ele está machucado?" Aaron asked. *Is he hurt?*

"Parece que só se arranhou na madeira ao cair," the captain said.

"He says it looks like he just scraped himself falling into the water," Aaron told Vanessa.

"Did he catch any splinters?" Aaron asked, saying "little pieces of wood," instead of the unfamiliar "splinters."

"Sei lá," the captain said, brushing away the question, "Mas sua esposa tá cerando meu barco com o seu sangue."

Aaron looked down at his wife's feet, where she was, indeed, standing in puddle of blood. When she noticed what he was looking at, she screamed a little in spite of herself.

WHEN Vanessa's parents had offered to pay for their honeymoon, Aaron had seen it as the only chance for two starving college kids to make the trip to Manaus, Brazil, in the Amazon basin while he still remembered the language from his mission. Her mother hadn't seemed too keen on the idea, but her father had thought it would be good for his daughter – especially now that she wouldn't be serving a mission herself – and had cut the check. He wondered how her dad would feel if he saw his baby girl bleeding.

The bites hadn't been deep, though. Aaron figured it had probably been piranha or something smaller. She'd been lucky.

Aaron bandaged her leg with the first thing he'd grabbed, a lime green t-shirt. Her attention was drawn to the whitewashed cabin at the rear of the ship, where the captain was applying disinfectant to his son's scratches with what looked like a tiny flyswatter. The dark red liquid made the wound look bigger and bloodier than it already was. The boy was arguing loudly, and the captain handled him a little too firmly.

The captain normally only ran quick trips between Tefé and Coari, but had come into Manaus to get the hull repaired. Aaron had found him and Tiago soliciting passengers for the return trip to Tefé, and counted it as a blessing. He'd served almost a third of his mission there, and with only a few passengers on a boat that normally held dozens, they might get some privacy once in a while.

"There you go," Aaron said, giving the improvised bandage a final tug. "Not only practical, but stylish."

"Thanks, Aaron."

"If you like this, you should see my line of ascots that double as tourniquets."

She smiled a little.

"Não fui Eu, não, pai," Tiago said.

The captain's voice was low, but his body language was tense. The boy wrestled his arm away and shouted at his father.

"Foi o pererê! Ele me epurrou no Rio!"

"What's he saying?" Vanessa asked.

"That he didn't jump. He says he was pushed."

"By who? He's not blaming us, is he?" Aaron could tell she had a mild case of they-must-be-talking-about-me disease.

"He's not blaming us."

"Who then?"

"Sací-pererê." Another passenger cut in before Aaron could answer. Pedro Gonzales was a middle-aged naturalist from Peru, on his way to a research center just outside of Tefé. "It's a Brazilian folk tale. Sací-pererê is a little boy that goes around causing mischief – stealing things, making trouble. And, apparently, pushing little boys into rivers," he added with a wink.

Aaron nodded. "The kid might as well be blaming a leprechaun. Sací's this little black boy, wears a little red hat, smokes a pipe, and only has one leg. In the stories he causes all kinds of problems for people. Sometimes they stop him by stealing his hat, which can be used to control him. But usually they don't even need the hat for him to mess things up for himself. Like he'll try to steal a bicycle, but can't ride it with just the one leg. So he takes it up a hill, and tries to coast down, but biffs it at the bottom."

"That's a contemporary story by someone who didn't understand the myth," Pedro said. "Sací's problem isn't stupidity as much as pride."

"Right," Aaron said. "Like in the story of Sací and the woman."

"What's that legend?" Vanessa asked.

"Sací sees this beautiful Brazilian woman, whose husband is away, and he decides to seduce her."

"A little boy decides this?"

"Sort of. A little pererê. Anyway, he starts bragging to her about all of his abilities. 'I can get you riches,' he promises. 'I can make you jewels, give you palaces, whatever you can imagine.' He follows her everywhere, tempting her.

"Finally, the woman walks up to him, puts her hand on his chin, and says, in her best Greta Garbo voice, 'Oh, Sací, can you really do anything?'"

"This is all in the legend?"

"He's embellishing a little," Pedro said.

"Sací tells her he can do anything. And the woman says, 'Oh, Sací, could you fit yourself into this bottle?' and Sací jumps right in as quick as he can. And as soon as he does, Pop!, the cork goes in and Sací's trapped. Yet another victim of the real danger – woman."

Vanessa didn't even smile. "I don't get it," she said.

"Don't get what?"

"Why she didn't go with him," Vanessa said. "A boy who can make jewels, or a husband who's never around. Seems like an easy choice to me."

"Ah, but her husband was such a perfect picture of masculinity," Aaron said, showing off his less-than-well-developed physique, "that the mere thought of his chiseled body was enough to keep her faithful."

"Maybe," she said. "But she'd probably keep the bottle around, just in case."

From the table near the cabin, a passenger who'd been at a bottle of *cachaça* long enough to have become quite drunk, shouted at Aaron's wife in Portuguese to watch what she said about the legends of his homeland, and that just because she was a particular breed of American that he used choice expletives to categorize, didn't mean that a single one of the creatures would leave her out when the carnage started.

"What did he say?" she asked.

Aaron started to form an answer of sorts, but then it drifted through the clouds of alcohol in the drunk's brain that she hadn't understood him.

"Ela não fala Portuguese?" He rose from the table. Although he was wearing jeans and tennis shoes, his shirt was off, and his ebony body was as well built as it was dark. Aaron's stomach knotted, and he didn't answer.

The drunk half limped, half swayed to where they were sitting. "You no talk bad for the stories of Brazil," he said. His accent was so strong, Aaron wondered if she understood. *You no talk-y bad-y.*

"Mapinguari," the drunk man said, "he get you."

She shook her head. "Who will? Who?"

The drunk's head lolled a little. "Who? My name is Matinha Pereira da Silva. It is a pleasure to meet you." His words ran together. *Chisapleyzurchoo meecho.* "What is your name?"

"My name is Vanessa. Who's going to get me?"

"Vanessa Hoongontmi. Good afternoon." *Gude afanoon-y.*

"Good afternoon. Who will get me?"

"Who get you? Mapinguari. He get you. He get all world."

"Todo mundo," Aaron said. "He means he gets everybody."

"I still don't understand. What's he saying?"

Pedro jumped in again. "Mapinguari," he said. "Another legend of the region. Mah-ping-gwa-ree."

"Sort of like the Boogeyman, or Bigfoot," Aaron added, but Matinha had already reacted to Pedro's slow pronunciation, and decided to help.

"Olha," he said, tapping her on the shoulder, bending over close to her. "Maahpeengwaareee," he said, drawing out the syllables and enunciation. Vanessa didn't even wince at what must have been quite an olfactory experience. "Maaw-peeeng-gwaaaw-reeee." His eyes opened wide as he spoke, red lighting streaking across yellow clouds.

"Olha," he said. "He have un mouth, here." His hands arched around his belly, making a large circle. "Has teeth. Teeth afiados. How is afiados? Knife, faca. Has teeth is knives. One eye." He brought one hand up to his forehead, making an O. He paraded around the deck for a moment as Mapinguari, the hand at his belly opening as he roared.

Vanessa laughed at his antics, and Aaron forced himself to join in.

The drunk stopped prancing. "You laughing?" he said. "With Mapinguari, you no laugh. No. Tudo gritos. How is gritos?" He slapped Aaron hard across the chest. "Tell her how is gritos."

"Screams," said Aaron, resisting the urge to rub the spot where Matinha had hit him.

"Screams," repeated Matinha nasally, forcing the *r* sound. "With Mapinguari, all screams." He held his hands up near his ears and whispered screams, like they were surrounding him. "Where is Mapinguari is screams. You leg? Is red? Is nada. You scream, too."

"Yeah," Aaron said. "I scream, you scream, we all scream for ice cream."

"Sim. We all scream." The drunk didn't know he was being teased. Aaron felt a little vindicated for the slap.

The drunk pointed at the bloody shirt that bound Vanessa's wound. "He no do assim. He no bite. He arranca. He arranca. Say for her arranca."

"Rip. Tear off."

"Sim. He ripteroff you arm, you leg. Ripteroff all e you scream. Is much bad. Is much agonia. Tell her how is agonia."

"Thrill," Aaron lied. Vanessa shot him a glare.

"Sim. Is much thrill. Is thrill for all you body. Is much thrill. Thrill." Matinha struggled to pronounce the word. "Thrill."

He pointed at her leg again. The shirt wouldn't dry in the humidity, and moist blood pooled black. "You think is bad? É nada. Mapinguari no bite. Mapinguari is morte. Morte. Tell her how is morte."

This time Aaron was honest, to avoid the glare. "Death."

"Deaf," Matinha said. "Mapinguari is deaf. He is deaf to you."

Aaron still got the glare, as if he was somehow responsible for the drunk's mispronunciation. He shrugged.

Matinha tried to follow the exchange but gave up.

"I need a drink," he said, with near flawless pronunciation.

AARON found Vanessa on the bow of the upper deck, watching the sunset. Aaron handed her a guaraná soda. A slow reggae song bopped below, probably Cidade Negra.

Aaron had forgotten how beautiful the sunsets were here, an incredible mix of color splashed across the horizon around the deep orange of the sun. Light greens and purples even found their way into the mix, hinting around the edges of the heavy oranges and reds.

"Nice, isn't it?" asked Aaron. "Second most beautiful thing I've ever seen."

"Aaron, why did you lie to Matinha?"

He honestly couldn't remember what she was talking about.

"About the word. He obviously said 'torture' or something, but you lied to him. You said, oh, I don't even remember – " she took a swig from the bottle.

Aaron pulled it away from her. "You don't want to do that. Here." He handed her a metal cup and poured for her.

"Honey, if I have cooties, you've caught them already."

"No, it's the bottle. They don't guard them well in the factories. Rats." He wiggled his fingers over the mouth. "They climb across the top."

She set the cup down and gave him a look he was pretty sure didn't mean she was squicked out by the rats.

"Thrill. I said thrill. It's a hard word to pronounce here. The t-h sound, the r sound, even the English ells. It's funny to hear someone try. Didn't you think it was funny? I was trying to ease the tension."

"What tension? Because he was drunk?"

Aaron didn't reply. When Vanessa was eleven and her mother had been diagnosed with cancer, her parents had become inactive for a while. Her father had gone back to drinking like he had before he'd been baptized, so while Vanessa had kept going to church, she'd become reflexively defensive about comments she thought might be subtly directed at him.

"I'm not comparing him to your father," said Aaron.

"This isn't about my father."

"Then what?"

She turned back towards the sunset. "Did they ever figure out how Tiago fell in?"

"He's sticking to his story. You'd think he would know how to be careful on a boat, as many times as he's gone up and down this river."

"Yes, you would."

"You don't think he was pushed?"

"I don't know. I have a bad feeling. The way you reacted when I brought him out, talking about the creatures, then seeing this," she waved at her leg. "I just ... I don't know."

Aaron felt almost as helpless now as he had on the side of the boat that morning. What was he supposed to say? What was he supposed to do?

The river shimmered as the boat parted the water. This river, the Solimões, was one of the two rivers that joined in Manaus to form the large Rio Amazonas. The other river, the Negro, was somewhere north of them, out past the jungles that lined the shore, creeping towards Manaus, where the two would join, sort of. The two rivers actually ran side by side in the same riverbed for miles without mixing. It meant that for miles the Amazon River was two-toned, one light colored river and one dark colored river running together, sometimes even at different speeds.

That was exactly how Aaron felt, beside the woman he loved, but feeling like there was something he should be doing to get closer to her that he just didn't know how to do.

AARON was awakened that night by silence. The hum of the motor was constant as the boat crawled upriver, and it roused him when the engine died. There was no reason the captain would cut the engine on an upriver voyage. Something was wrong.

The curve of the hammock pressed his wife against him, and between them their clothes were soaked with sweat. Though the night had turned dark, the humidity was still sweltering.

Someone shouted at the back of the boat, an angry voice. He did his best to ease out of the hammock without waking Vanessa. The captain was looking for his son.

"What happened?" Aaron asked the captain in Portuguese.

"My boy. He has done something to the engine." He pointed a flashlight over the edge of the boat, but Aaron couldn't see anything through the murky brown water. "It won't start. I left him here to watch the motor and now I can't find him. He must have broken it, then run to hide, to keep from taking a hit."

"Oh, captain," Aaron said. "Tiago was trying to be the big captain like his father, wasn't he?" Aaron still couldn't believe how young the children were trusted with responsibility here, much less how severely they were punished when they failed at it.

"He has cost us so much time. We will have to get to the riverbank before the current carries us too far back. We can fix the motor on the shore. What a blessing that I awoke, or we would have been carried back to Manaus by morning."

"All right. You get the boat to shore and I'll go look for Tiago."

"No," the captain said. "I need your help." He handed Aaron a long wooden pole. "I have a small motor that can push us towards shore, but when we get close you'll need to steer in with that. I'll go get more help."

He came back with Pedro, the naturalist going to the jungle research center, and an outboard motor. Pedro grabbed a pole and joined Aaron.

"Vamos lá!" said the captain. *Let's go!*

Aaron struggled to get the long pole out of the boat. When the captain signaled, Aaron and Pedro dipped their poles into the river. Aaron's arms strained against the tugging current. When he found the river bottom, he pushed against it towards the shore.

"Looks like you'll be headed toward the jungle a little early," said Aaron in Portuguese.

Pedro smiled. "I miss the jungle. It is like exploring the big, beautiful house of a rich man. You want to see everything, but you're afraid of breaking the delicate, fragile treasures."

"And if the owner shows up, he'll bite your head off, right?"

"No, no. You are only afraid for the valuables. The terror is man, who barges in with big machines and loud rifles."

"Yes, and that is why the big terror always ends up as lunch for a panther." It was Matinha, who seemed much more in control of himself. Aaron hadn't heard him walk up. "This forest is not a playful harem for delicate little insects, my friend. There are things out there the size of your thumb that would love to kill you."

Aaron was shocked at how much more eloquent Matinha was in his native tongue.

"You say man is wild, pillages at random, upsetting the balance of nature. Do you want to see balance?" Matinha made a broad gesture that took in all of the twisted forest on the shores. "This is nature's balance. It is without form, chaotic. Man makes a place for himself, gives himself a chance to survive, and you call him vicious. You will see vicious, my environmentalist friend. It will find you."

"You completely misunderstand the entire ecological system," said Pedro.

Matinha turned to Aaron. "I'm sure that is what Vanessa was thinking when she saw her leg, isn't it?"

Aaron meant to tell Matinha to leave her alone. But the Portuguese expression he used was, "Leave her in peace." It sounded more like an epitaph than a threat.

Matinha smiled. "There is no peace here. The jungle is constantly at war. We drift through a battlefield. And so," he added, "does your wife."

"Don't torment the young man," said Pedro. "Can't you see he is already sick with worry for her? There is no reason to make things worse."

"On the contrary, my friend. There is no reason for him not to worry. But American," Matinha said, "if you feel that you cannot protect her, maybe we will help you. She will be very grateful to us, don't you think? Very grateful."

He walked off laughing at the look on Aaron's face.

THEY drifted under the foliage of the trees that hung over the edges of the river. The captain killed the engine. He dropped a few of the cement-filled Nestón cans that served as his anchor, then tied the railing of the boat to a tree close to shore.

Mosquitoes buzzed around Aaron, getting on his face and into his nose. He slapped at them, wondering how his wife was handling the onslaught. He hurried to the covered deck where their hammock was strung.

She wasn't in it.

Where had she gone? It wasn't easy to see, with the upper deck shadowing them from the moonlight. Some lantern light streaked across the boat from between the wooden slabs of the cabin walls.

"Vanessa?"

"Over here," she replied. "Just follow the sound of bugs chewing."

She rummaged through her bag. "If this is Tefé," she said, "I am going to kill you."

"Motor died. Captain thinks his boy must have done something to it. The boy's hiding now, so we're going to try to find him."

"He'll be lucky if the mosquitoes don't carry him off."

"Not mosquitoes. Carapaná," Aaron said, teasing her with the silly-sounding Indian word.

"Whatever."

Aaron winced. He had rushed to see if she was being attacked by mosquitoes, and she was. Why had he hurried if he was just going to stand around slack-jawed, watching her be eaten?

"I'm, uh," he stammered, trying to find something to say and deciding on "going to go help the captain."

"Don't you want some of this?" she asked, holding up the bug spray. He nodded and reached for it. "Here," she said, "lift your arms." She sprayed it on for him, like a mother tending a child, careful to get all the awkward spots.

He had come here to help her and she had ended up babying him. Doing him the favor. While he stood with his arms out like a dummy. Her helping him.

... maybe we will help you, and she will be very grateful ...

He excused himself with a good-bye kiss that tasted like Raid. He wanted to make a joke about it but couldn't think of one.

He shouldn't let that drunk spoil his honeymoon.

THE CAPTAIN wasn't at the back of the boat.

"Capitão?" he shouted. "Cadé você?" *What happened to you?*

The sounds of the jungle answered him. Loudest were the quick, high-pitched shrieks of frogs, like car alarms sounding in the trees. But there was something else, off in the distance.

His ears strained to hear it, as if something about the sound stirred him on the most primal level. It was difficult to make out over the din of the frogs, but it sounded like a wail. It sounded human.

Where is Mapinguari is screams.

"Americano! Come!" The captain darted along the edge of the jungle outside the boat. "Someone disembarked and came this way!"

Aaron hopped over the side of the boat and his feet sank deep in the mud. Cold muck oozed into his tennis shoes. He hurried for more solid ground.

"You can see where my boy has run." Some tall grasses among the trees were pushed back. The captain took the flashlight and led the way down the rough path.

"Do you want to call him?" Shouting might scare the boy away. Or it might attract animals. Like whatever he'd heard wailing.

"Yes, call him."

They cried Tiago's name as they trudged through the high grass. The flashlight beam bounced as the captain's hands trembled. The area it lit seemed so small. The greater darkness loomed around them. Every noise, every sound in the bushes left Aaron unsure whether to dart out and grab at it or run like a maniac.

They broke out of the grass and into a clearing several yards wide. A small black monkey looked up, eyes wide, as the light hit it, like a criminal caught in a police searchlight. It was eating something flat and round, like a small pancake. It squealed and scurried up a tree.

There were more of the round things scattered across the clearing. The captain crept up on one of them. Aaron waited at the end of the brush. Slowly, the captain reached down. As he did, the flashlight drifted, and Aaron couldn't see when the captain grabbed it.

"What is it?"

"It's lunch," the captain said.

Whatever it was, Aaron had the distinct feeling he wouldn't find it as appetizing as the captain did.

But when the captain brought it back and held it up, it really was lunch. A thin slice of meat, of bife. Pink and raw and moist, it shone a little as he held the light up to it.

The captain swept the light across the clearing. The meat was scattered everywhere. Aaron didn't know a whole lot about the fauna of the Amazon, but he was pretty sure bife wasn't found naturally.

"My boy must have brought it when he ran away. He thought he would need some food, didn't he? He dropped them by mistake."

Aaron nodded. But that was ridiculous. Tiago was a kid, but he wasn't stupid. If he was going to grab food, he'd have grabbed fruit. If he'd brought meat out here and scattered it, he'd done it intentionally.

But that was ridiculous, too. He'd know how dangerous that was.

"This meat's going to attract other animals," said Aaron. "Bigger than that monkey."

Every rustle in the grass felt like a pouncing creature. His heart beat faster and his imagination raced to catch up. What animals were in the bushes? What monsters?

He remembered the screams.

Mapinguari. He get you.

There's no Mapinguari, Aaron told himself. But the meat strewn around looked like excellent Mapinguari bait. Even better would be a screaming little boy, left tied up somewhere to call the monster.

The captain shouted Tiago's name as loud as he could. He was getting emotional, almost crying. "Son!"

"We'll find him," Aaron said. "But I think I should go back to the boat and get a gun."

The captain nodded. Aaron took off through the bushes. The foliage above was too thick to let much moonlight shine through, thick enough at his sides to make him claustrophobic. He stomped loudly and rustled bushes as he passed, trying to scare away anything that might be in the bush, and trying to be loud enough that he wouldn't have to hear whatever was out there.

His heavy running steps sank in mud up to his ankles as he came beside the boat, and he had to pull hard to get out and over the railing.

When he opened the cabin, he found Matinha there, holding a shotgun. "Olá, Americano," he said, through clenched teeth. He turned a little and Aaron saw he was smoking a pipe. The air reeked of it.

"The captain's boy is missing," Aaron said, in Portuguese. "He jumped ship. We need the gun to go after him."

"I don't think he really deserves that. He is just a boy."

Aaron didn't know how to respond.

Matinha laughed and slapped Aaron on the back. "I am joking, of course. The captain already told me. I thought you might come back for this." He handed Aaron the gun, smiling wide.

Aaron searched through the cabin for shells. Matinha had brought his things into the cabin with him. A bundled hammock lay at his feet.

It was when Aaron noticed the hammock that he noticed Matinha's leg. Matinha was only wearing a speedo, which was common enough in the hot Amazonian sun. Not so common was the prosthetic right leg.

The image reminded Aaron of dozens of paintings and drawings he had seen. Matinha had only one leg, and was smoking a pipe ...

Aaron grabbed the shells and ran out the door.

"Be careful!" the one-legged man shouted cheerfully.

A Brazilian folk song sang in Aaron's mind.

The Sací lives in the jungle. He hops on just one leg. Pó-ró-ró-pó-pó ...

Matinha must have been the one who'd pushed Tiago in the river. The boy had called Matinha "Sací" because he'd seen that he only had one leg.

But why would Matinha push the boy in the river?

Maybe for that reason. Tiago had seen him. He'd wanted to keep it a secret.

And why would he want to keep his leg a secret, unless –

Aaron tried to remember the legends. Could a pererê age? Would it abandon people to the other monsters of the jungle? The screaming in the forest had sounded like the screams that followed Mapinguari. Now the one-legged man –

He reminded himself that he was being stupid, that both creatures were legends, and that if the pererê aged it would be thousands of years old.

But a one-legged black man with a pipe had just handed him this gun. There was no way he could fire it, if it was given to him by the little prankster, all grown up.

He knew what he was thinking was fanciful, but in the cabin it had become real, from the smell of the smoke to the deep wrinkles in Matinha's face as he grinned.

It was the smoke, that's what it was. Matinha had some funny stuff in that pipe, and it was making Aaron delusional.

He rushed behind the cabin to find his wife. She wasn't there. "Vanessa!" he shouted. "Cadê você? Vanessa! Onde – " He stopped, realizing he was shouting in Portuguese.

He looked about for some sign of her. Even the hammock was gone, pulled from the hooks in the boards.

Then he remembered the hammock in the cabin, at Matinha's feet. What color had it been? What pattern?

He had pushed the boy in the river. Was Vanessa wrapped up in that hammock?

Aaron charged back to the cabin. "What are you doing in there?" He pulled on the door – it didn't give. Matinha had locked it from the inside. As Aaron pounded on the door, he could hear Matinha giggling.

Giggling like a child.

"You think this is funny, you one-legged freak?" Aaron raised the gun over his head and pounded the door with the butt. It came apart in his hands, the butt and firing mechanism separating.

The gun must have been doctored to explode in his face when he pulled the trigger. It could have killed him.

So much for doubts. This was Sací. And he wasn't just a harmless prankster anymore.

Aaron kicked at the door, pounding it with his heel. One of the slabs cracked and his leg went through to just above the knee. He tried to pull it out, but Sací grabbed his foot from the inside, pulling Aaron up against the door. His other leg folded up under him, between him and the door, keeping him from slamming into it. He tried to straighten his leg and push away, but Sací was too strong.

"Maybe the one-legged freak can use your leg," Sací said. "Not quite up to my standards, but it would serve better than this one."

Aaron turned himself over, reached for the pieces of the gun.

"I suppose I could let you have my leg. Want to trade?" Sací asked, giving a yank that shot bolts of pain up Aaron's side. "I stole this one from a little old man in Brasilia. But his woman wasn't half as good as yours. So I let him keep her."

He reassembled the pieces as best he could.

"She was disappointed, though. She spent the rest of her life regretting that I'd taken his leg, and not her. I suppose she got over it. When she died."

Aaron rolled back over and shoved the barrel through the hole above his trapped leg. Twisting his foot out of the line of fire and looking away, he pulled the trigger.

The shot rattled his entire body, but the gun held together. Sací's grip weakened, and Aaron slipped free, forced himself out of the hole with his other leg.

Aaron started to stand, but fell again as pain twisted his leg. Bits of shot had lodged in his shin and quad. Pools of black formed around the holes in his jeans.

He heard his wife scream from the cabin. "You've been shot!" She was hysterical. "Oh, I can't believe it! What am I going to do?"

He looked through the hole, trying to see how she could see him. The gun blocked his view, the butt resting on the door. He tried to speak, to let her know he was okay.

"Oh, you shot him! Oh, you poor thing! You shot my Sací!"

Aaron jerked upright in shock. It was too fast, though, and pain shot up his leg, into his abdomen.

"You're going to be fine. You're okay." They were comforting words from a comforting voice. Aaron couldn't believe they weren't for him. "You're the Pererê! You can do anything!"

Had his wife been seduced? How did the pererê get to her? The last line of the song he'd been hearing rang through his head: ... *he is my darling*. The Sací is my darling.

He reached out for the gun, but in his haste he knocked it into the cabin. He almost reached through to grab it, afraid Sací would use it, but he didn't want to put any other appendages through the door.

He heard splashing in the river.

"Captain, is that you?"

No one answered. He was alone. And he needed to find another weapon.

A dusty red crate of bottles of guaraná sat under the table. He pulled out one of the bottles without standing up. He braced himself with one hand, while he tried to break the bottle on the edge of the table with the other. With just one arm, he wasn't strong enough. But he tried again and again –

Water smacked the deck behind him.

A single dark green eye rose up between two scaly, clawed hands that clenched the railing at the edge of the boat. Staring into that eye was like staring into the blackest place in the deepest heart of the twisted jungle. In that eye, Aaron saw the same despair he'd felt that afternoon.

Only he saw it not just for his wife. Not just for him. In that eye, he saw the heart of nature itself.

It was exactly as Matinha had described. Without form. Chaotic.

Aaron saw that as sure as this world had given life, it was prepared to bring death.

As the creature lifted itself, its wide, round snout flared, the blood-red flesh of its nostrils glistening in the lantern light. There was no mouth in the face.

Rough, alligator-like skin showed through in places under tangled, mud-brown fur. Water poured off of it onto the deck as it cleared the side of the boat, as if it had brought all the danger of the river along with the jungle. The creature gave off a bitter, nauseating smell, a blend of rot and dung.

And there, set in the torso, was the mouth.

Teeth afiados. Has teeth is knives.

Rows of yellowed fangs lined its mouth like blades – if it could even be called a mouth. There was no jaw. The teeth sat in a mobile tissue that moved like the mouth of a worm. It gaped open impossibly large, somehow managing to seem wider than the creature's body. It seemed to Aaron it could devour them all. Staring into that hole, it seemed inevitable. It *would* devour them all.

Aaron hurled the bottle at it.

It felt so pathetic. He felt more useless, throwing that bottle, than he had when he hadn't moved an inch when Vanessa was in the river.

Mapinguari didn't even have to bite down to grind the bottle, shattering it to pieces. The guaraná fizzed and dribbled down its matted pelt.

And then it roared.

The sound of it drove Aaron to his knees.

It was every roar of every creature that had ever hunted in the Amazon. It was as if the earth itself was stalking prey.

A muffled shot sounded and Mapinguari barely flinched. A thick white dart stuck in its shoulder.

Pedro stood holding a rifle near the edge of the cabin. He fired two more darts in quick succession.

Mapinguari pulled one from its thick coat. Aaron wondered if the dart had even reached skin.

Pedro pulled a revolver out of his belt and began to fire. Once, then again, shots hammered the creature. Its eye widened at the provocation.

It moved away from Aaron and towards Pedro.

Pedro whimpered and leapt from the boat. The creature bounded after him, clearing the side of the boat with shocking agility.

"Wow, first me, now Pedro. I guess everyone else has to watch out for her, don't they? It is a good thing we were here."

The cabin door swung open, and Sací stood in its frame. In one arm, Vanessa clung to him, smiling, wearing a red felt hat that drooped over like a hat from one of Snow White's dwarves.

In the other arm, he held the shotgun.

Vanessa giggled.

Aaron scooted himself along the floor. Pedro screamed on the riverbank.

"Vanessa, what are you doing?"

"You were right about the hat, Aaron," said Vanessa, drawing a finger down Sací's bare chest. "It works great. Now, I have my very own pererê."

"You're controlling him?"

"Oh, yeah."

Matinha pumped the shotgun.

"Does it scare you, Aaron?" asked Vanessa. "Are you shaking in your sneakers like you were when I jumped in the river?"

"Vanessa, stop it. You're not yourself."

"Maybe not, Aaron, but you're still you, and that's bad enough that one of us has to start making up for it."

Sací laughed hard at that. "Do you see who is the true man here, and who is the foolish little boy? All the things you told your woman about me, which of us do they describe?"

Aaron reached out to grab Sací's leg. Sací kicked him in the face, knocking him onto his back.

"I have your woman, Americano." He shifted the pipe to one side of his mouth, and kissed her forehead roughly. "And I'm going to feed you to the Mapinguari. All that *bestera* you were saying came right back to you, didn't it?"

"You're the *besta*," Aaron said. *The beast.*

"I bester than you!" said Sací, in English. It took Aaron a second to understand it was a joke. It was Sací's pride again – his weakness, according to the legends. Aaron hoped he could exploit it now.

"That's not really Vanessa talking," said Aaron. "The hat works in reverse, doesn't it? The legends say you seduce women, and that wearing your hat lets people control you. But really you control the women who put your hat on."

"You want to believe that, don't you?" said Vanessa.

"Was it a misinformation campaign? Did you spread the stories yourself to get women to put the hat on? Or did other men just see their wives like this and think you'd wooed them away?"

"Aaron, seriously," said Vanessa. "You barely qualify as a man."

"It's so sad," said Aaron. "Because what that really means is no women actually want you at all."

"Your wife seems to want me."

"Then let her take the hat off."

"Oh, you want to take my hat off?" Vanessa let go of Sací and bent over towards Aaron. "Go ahead."

He reached for it.

She slapped his hand away, hard.

"Why would I give up my Sací?" She shouted the question. "He is the most powerful in all the jungle!"

Aaron replied to Sací, not Vanessa. "The most powerful? Right. That's why you hid in the cabin until Mapinguarí was gone."

"I am better than Mapinguari. He is only an animal, a *bicho*. I am the pererê, the cleverest in all of the jungle."

"And you're afraid you'll be clever right into the mouth of that monster."

"I can beat Mapinguari," Sací said.

"What do you think Vanessa? You're in control, right? Make him fight the monster, prove he's the best. What are you going to make her say, Sací? What's your cop out going to be? 'Oh, I don't want my Sací to get hurt fighting the monster.' Well, he wouldn't get hurt if he was really the best."

Aaron put all the emphasis he could muster on the word best.

The pererê's nose flared, his eyes wide, and his muscles tensed on his bare chest.

He pointed the gun at Aaron.

Aaron struggled not to show his panic. "Do you hear that?" Aaron pointed to the side of the boat, where they could still hear Pedro. "He is torturing him to mock you! He is taunting you with his strength! Mapinguari is mocking the great pererê!"

"You can't trick me into fighting the monster!"

"Trick you? You make it sound like he'd beat you."

"I'm going to beat you," said Sací.

"No, you won't," said Aaron. "I mean you can kill me, sure. But it's Mapinguari you'd have to kill to prove you're the strongest. To beat me, you'd have to prove Vanessa still wants you, even when she takes the hat off. You can't win."

Sací scooped Vanessa up in his arms and grinned. "Americano, I am the cleverest in all the jungle. I always find a way to win."

He carried her over to the side of the boat and surreptitiously dumped her over the side. When he turned around, he showed Aaron he was still holding the hat.

"Aaron!" screamed Vanessa.

"Now, woman," said Sací, speaking in stilted English again. "You have decision for make. See big monster?"

Aaron scooted towards the railing, but Sací leveled the shotgun at him.

"For big monster, you have big decision. Who can save you? Little boy who get scared of fishies? Or the great pererê?"

Aaron couldn't hear whatever Vanessa was telling him.

Sací pounded on the side of the boat. "Olha, big monster! You done eating nature boy? Look what I have for you! He comes, woman. Who do you want?"

Aaron spotted one of the long poles lying across the end of the deck. He grabbed it and swung it as hard as he could, knocking the shotgun out of Sací's hand.

He charged Sací in the instant the gun fell. It was awkward, with his hurt leg, but adrenaline and anger pushed him forward. He pounded Sací's chest, swung at his nose, his jaw.

Sací flung Aaron against the cabin wall.

Aaron charged him again. Sací punched him in the throat, and he flopped to the ground. Sací picked him up by his injured leg and held him upside down. Pain ran down his leg like claws dragging under his skin.

"Why did you think you could beat me?"

"I didn't," said Aaron. "I thought I could buy her time. Because I knew she wouldn't let you save her."

Sací dropped Aaron and looked over the side of the boat. He ran frantically along the railing, searching.

Vanessa had gotten away.

Aaron sat up, using the cabin to support himself. "It's close, isn't it? Mapinguari is coming. I think I can hear it."

Saci's eyes darted back and forth between the jungle and Aaron as he paced wildly back and forth across the deck. His shoulders and chest rose and fell as he fumed.

"So what happens now? Do you kill me and then run away from it with your tail between your legs? Or do you just run away with your tail between your legs and let it kill me?"

Saci scooped the shotgun up again and leveled it at Aaron. Aaron's heart thudded in his chest.

"Could you see what it was doing to Pedro? I couldn't see. It sounded so horrible. So horrible."

Aaron mustered every bit of energy to struggle to his feet. He limped four steps across the deck, and put his chest right in front of the shotgun barrel.

"Please, Saci, kill me now. I couldn't bear to die at the hands of such a powerful creature as that."

Saci gave a violent cry and threw down the shotgun. "I am the best!" he shouted, in English. It came out, "I emmy the besta!" He leapt over the side of the boat, pipe still clenched in his teeth.

Aaron grabbed the shotgun before dragging himself over to the side of the boat to look for Vanessa. Saci charged towards the jungle, bound-hopping on his real leg and his prosthetic leg.

There was a splash on the side of the boat that faced the river. Something else was coming up out of the water. He whirled around –

The captain pulled himself up onto the boat.

"Captain! Are you all right?"

The captain nodded. "We saw the monster. So we came around."

"We?"

He turned around and reached down, and his boy rose up to him, held up by two slender arms.

Aaron raced over. Vanessa was holding up the boy, like she had that morning.

After the captain pulled the boy on board, Aaron pulled in Vanessa. He held her close.

The captain tossed a frayed rope onto the deck of the boat. "This was in the blades of the motor. I think our one-legged friend wanted to stop us here, near the Mapinguari. We must leave now."

"Where did you find Tiago?" Vanessa asked, and Aaron translated.

"In the jungle. Unconscious. Matinha left him there. Come. We must go."

The captain started up the motor, and Aaron, still holding Vanessa's hand, took the shotgun over and perched himself on the railing by the jungle.

The battle was nauseating. Mapinguari had gutted Sací, and blood gushed down his torso. His prosthetic leg had come off, and he was forcing it down the throat of the monster to choke him, to give himself leverage to pull away from its mouth. That left him only one arm to defend himself with, and the monster attacked him on the other side, ripping away chunks of his flesh.

Vanessa wrapped her arms around Aaron.

"Vamos lá," Aaron said to the captain.

THE SHORELINE of Tefé spread lazily across the edge of the city. Tired men sat in the sand near their long fishing boats, waiting for trucks to pick up their catch. Teenagers frolicked on the beach, playing casual games of volleyball or lying and chatting with their friends. Tall brick buildings stood behind small wood houses that sat on wooden stilts, out of reach of rain and flood water.

Vanessa and Aaron watched from the bow of the boat as they drifted through the last of the voyage.

"Thank you," Aaron said.

"For what?"

"I realized something while that monster was controlling you. After seeing you dive into the river, I worried that I wasn't enough for you, that I could never protect you or be there for you like you needed. I worried there was something between us I could never cross."

"Aaron, I love you."

"I know. That's the crazy thing – I get it now. Whatever I was thinking was coming between us, it wasn't you. It was me. You're here, you picked me, you married me. Just like that creature couldn't accept that you would never want it, I have to accept that you do want me."

"Forever," she said.

"We can go home now," Aaron said. "Not by boat. And there are no roads out, but there's a small airport. We can fly back to Manaus and from there, book a flight back home."

But Vanessa took his hand. "No, let's go meet our friends. We could use some friendly faces."

"You're not worried about what might happen?"

"I think we've seen," she said, "that whatever it is, we can handle it."

Our friends. *We* can handle it. There was no wall for her. He knew he couldn't put one up either.

He looked back towards Manaus, back towards the "meeting of the waters," where the two rivers ran side by side in the same riverbed. And he remembered seeing them farther down the river, where they began to mix, churning together, though still distinct, their different colors swirling together like marble. Only time and distance blended them completely, made them flow together, feeding the forests, until at last, as one, they poured out into the sea.

THE BLUES DEVILS

Terrance V. McArthur

IF A drinking binge could be monumental, Gordon's bender was Mount Rushmore. For weeks, he'd played and drunk his way through bars and bottles of all types and sizes, from elegant to cheap, winding up in a room with some once-clean clothes and his guitar, the one thing of any value that he couldn't bring himself to pawn.

Gordon Collins had strummed and fingered the blues on that birch-bodied instrument since he was a kid of eleven – and silvery-gray spots now dotted his stubbled jaw. He was the only one who ever played Ella, which was why Gordon was surprised to hear sliding, strident notes in her familiar tones, when the bluesman knew he was face-down on the floor. He looked up and nearly spit out what was left of his guts.

Perched on the end of the fold-out bed, cradling Ella in a too-intimate manner, was a leering, smarmier-than-thou character, plucking indecent chords out of the steel strings. The fellow was thin as a husband's alibi, wore a battered fedora, dark glasses, and a too-large suit. And he was blue: not the blue of a five-o'clock shadow, or the blue of a sad song, but the blue of Paul Newman's eyes, with a touch of Frank Sinatra's, spread across his skin.

Gordon smiled enough to hurt his cracked lips, and he said, "I've heard of having the blue devils, but I never thought I'd ever see one."

"Wait a minute," said the stranger who looked like a working musician in a bright-blue wrapper, "I am not a hallucination, not the ordinary product of the delirium tremens, come to torment you. In fact, I am here to offer you salvation," he said, tipping his hat to reveal shiny, oily-black, slicked-back hair, and a pair of blue-white horns sprouting from his forehead.

Gordon said, "You're no angel. How can you give me salvation?"

"Now, it isn't a spiritual salvation, but it's a salvation for your career. I offer you ... a song."

A slow grin cautiously spread across Gordon's face. He said, "A long time ago, my momma warned me to never trust the devil. She said there's always a trick to it, somewhere."

"Nonsense, my friend," the devil said, "and you *are* my friend. You've raised enough Hell to make me happy as Death at a stock-car race. You've slipped so far from the faith of your fathers, you don't even qualify as a Jack Mormon. You're a Jack Daniels Mormon. After all you've done, I reckon I owe you. This one's for free."

He started strumming Ella, popping chords like popcorn, pulling out twisted, wailing sounds from the aged six-string.

He started to sing, but it wasn't a weary blues. His voice was cocky, wheedling, full of venom and guile. It was a prideful blues.

> *Been locked out of Heaven,*
> *There's no place there for me.*
> *Can't get into Heaven*
> *'Cos I done forgot the key.*
> *Looks like I'm bound for Hell.*
> *I could use some sympathy,*
> *Some sympathy.*

The devil tapped out the time, a sound like bones clacking in a graveyard.

> *It's you and me here, baby,*
> *I've got Heaven on my mind.*
> *You know it's just the two of us, sugar.*
> *What sort of Heaven can we find?*
> *We can make our own kind of Heaven,*
> *While we have one Hell of a time,*
> *One Hell of a real good time.*

He was stomping now, and the room shook around him. Spiders quivered in their webs, scared silkless as the devil came to the bridge in the music and burned his way across it.

> *Oh, we can shock the angels.*
> *And, we can shock the Lord.*
> *And we can go to both Heaven and Hell*
> *At once, in the back of my Ford.*

He was going instrumental, making that guitar talk, shout, and scream for mercy. Gordon felt the music all around his body, his fingers twitching out the chording and the picking against his will. He wanted that song, in more ways than he could possibly realize.

One more chorus poured out from the diabolic guitarist.

> *We're a pair of fallen angels,*
> *Falling fast with a broken wing.*
> *Yes, we're dropping like stones out of Heaven,*
> *Shedding feathers like the blossoms of spring.*
> *There's only one lifeline in sight;*
> *You better hold on to my guitar string,*
> *Hold on for dear life to that string.*

He stroked a few final licks out of Ella, and the devil was done. Gordon felt exhausted, wrung out, like he'd been run over by a high school football team ... and their bus.

A grin split the blue face, and all the tension and power vanished, leaving a benign little devil, who said, "What did you think?"

Gordon didn't say anything for a while. Finally, he said, "It's good. It's very good."

"It's yours."

Gordon shook his head and said, "I can't play that!"

"You can," the devil said, "and you will!" With that, the blue stranger held out Ella.

Gordon reached, nervously, almost expecting the guitar would take a swipe at him, but it didn't, so he closed his hand around the neck and supported the body of the instrument with the other hand. Tenderly, tentatively, he touched the strings, and instantly, he was playing those growling, insistent notes, every tone a match to the ones the blue devil had played. Gordon dropped Ella like he'd discovered she was made of human skin, and asked, over the wooden clatter on the floor, "Is it possessed?"

The blue one said, "I wouldn't call it possessed. I'd consider it more of a ... time-share," and he picked Ella up from the floor.

"It'll play like that ... every time?"

"With minor variations," the devil said. "Enough to sound like improvisation, experimentation, and style. Don't want people to think it's mechanical or something. That gets stale. Now ... sing it."

Gordon snorted, then said, "I have my own style, man. I don't sing like anybody else ... not even you."

"Don't worry. It'll sound like you ... with a little twist," the devil said, and he peered over the top of his shades, showing red eyes that glowed like the sign over a strip club, repellant and enticing at the same time. He offered the guitar and said, "Come on. Give it a try."

Gordon took Ella from him and started the opening riff once more. It felt good, easy, part of him, and Gordon hummed along in a countermelody for a few bars, then opened up into:

> *They locked me out of Heaven.*
> *Never been no place for me.*

"Good twist," the devil said. "Keep going."

> *See, I can't get back into Heaven.*
> *Where did I hide that extra key?*

The devil said, "Cook it until it's well done."

> *No place to go but Hell,*
> *I sure could use some sympathy,*
> *Some sympathy.*

Gordon stopped, held up his fingers, and looked at them like he expected claws to erupt from beneath the skin. They were still his fingers, still wiggled the way they always had, but, after what he'd seen and heard them do ...

Could he trust them?

The devil put a hand on Gordon's shoulder and said, "Easy, isn't it?"

"Too easy."

"Come on. They'll go for it. Chicks'll dig it, especially. Put it in your next show," the devil said with a wider grin.

"Next show? I've blown so many gigs, nobody will book me."

"Don't give up hope ... yet," the devil said with a little I-know-why-it's-funny-but-I-ain't-telling-you kind of chuckle. "I have some influence."

The blue one slowly closed his left hand, then opened it to reveal a business card. He gave the card to Gordon, telling him, "It's not fancy, but it's a start."

The rapidly sobering bluesman said, "I'm not too sure about this."

Those red eyes blazed over the dark lenses as the devil said, "Give it a try. Remember ... it's free."

"HELD OVER!"
"FOURTH WEEK!"
"SOLD OUT!"

Gordon still couldn't believe the signs as he turned the corner of the building, with Ella swinging from his hand in the cradle of a custom-made case, headed for the "STAGE ENTRANCE" door. From the cheesiest of dives, he'd played his way up to the classiest joint he'd ever been allowed into. Now, it was "GORDON COLLINS AND HIS BLUES DEVILS" screaming from electric-blue posters that were plastered over whole blocks when he came into a town. And it was all because of the "Falling Lucifer Blues."

That bothered him.

"Making it to the top on one song," he mumbled to himself as he entered his private dressing room.

"It's not right. It can't last," he said to the walls of the dressing-room shower.

"There has to be more," he grumbled as he toweled himself off.

"An artist needs to move, and expand," Gordon said, buttoning his shirt.

"I agree."

Gordon spun around.

The devil was as blue as ever, sitting on the hide-a-bed couch, his slouch hat on the love seat, oozing a slick of hair oil onto the upholstery. He was holding Ella.

Gordon said, "Why don't you knock?"

"Souls in torment, no matter how low-grade the torment may be, are too much fun for me to interrupt."

"Thank you so very much."

"You should thank me," the devil said, rising from his seat before he straightened his legs to reach the floor. "Without me, you'd still be drinking your way to my front door. Instead, you have everything you've always wanted: money, fame ... and the music."

Gordon said, "You can't stay on top with one song. I'm bound to fall."

"Aren't we all?" the devil asked with a conspiratorial smile. "It's a good thing I stopped by for a social call, because I do happen to have an answer to your problem."

He played Ella gently at first, like an aging Don Juan circling his next virgin. Soon, he was coaxing the pains and shrieks of the damned out of the strings, singing like all the knowledge nobody should ever have.

> *I've been bad,*
> *And I've tried to be good.*
> *My bad is better,*
> *Like I somehow knew it would.*
> *Warm up that lake of fire,*
> *Crank it up a notch or two,*
> *'Cos I'm damned if I don't,*
> *But you know ...*
> *You know I do.*

The song went on, taking on Goodness and nailing it to the mat in three straight falls.

Gordon retrieved Ella, lightly wiping his hands over her, as if it could cleanse her. "Same terms as last time, I suppose?"

"Not exactly."

"What?"

"Like my friends in recreational pharmaceuticals – you call them dealers, I call them my missionaries – would say, the first taste is free," the devil said, and lowered his blue face until he was nose-to-nose with Gordon, "but the second one is gonna cost you. I need your help on a project of mine ... "

GORDON stood outside the dressing room, hand on the doorknob, dreading what he would find, wondering, "How long has this circus been going on? How long will it last?"

He let out a sigh, took a deep breath, and turned the knob. The door swung open, and he entered his own personal Hell.

Fans, protégés, groupies, agents, publicists, critics, bodyguards, and all the worst trappings of fame covered the chairs, couches, and any available floor space. Clouds of several types of smoke – legal, questionable, and unquestionably illegal – swirled and intermingled.

Each person there was the price of a song, the cost of one more request for music from the blue devil. Each one was a "project" of the devil, someone that needed shepherding on the path of corruption.

Gordon snarled, "I'm a scoutmaster for Hell and a first lieutenant for Perdition," but he wasn't heard over the talking and the raucous laughter. He worked his way through the crowd, making small talk and giving strokes as needed. Finally, he reached the one sanctuary left in his life.

But the bathroom was not empty. One happy devil in blue sat on the toilet seat, smiling as he played a blues riff that seemed to come from somewhere beneath the skin.

The devil looked up with a smile, stopped playing, and said, "If it isn't my favorite partner. Hello, partner."

"This partner wants out," Gordon said.

"Sorry," the devil said with a negative shake of his head. "I wouldn't want to break up a team this good."

"I never signed a contract."

"No contract?" The devil snorted and said, "You don't have to sign a scroll with your blood for a binding agreement. Every song was a deal; every show was a promise. You sold your soul with every bottle you drained, with every one-night stand in another hotel. We are bound together, tighter than any lawyer could manage. It's you and me, Gordon ... for time and all eternity."

"We'll see about that," Gordon said, turning to leave the bathroom.

"Go ahead and try. I love watching 'em try. They wriggle this way and squirm that way, but they're stuck on that hook, and nothing they do can pull 'em off. They never get away, but they're so much fun to watch," the devil said with a smug chuckle.

"**I WANT** to thank all of you kind folks for coming here, tonight. I know what you want to hear, but you'll have to wait a while, because there's something new I need to try out," Gordon told his first crowd of the night.

A buzz of excited whispers swept the audience. Gordon faced a sea of pregnant expectation, a crowd of fans eager for a sneak look at his next hit. They were looking forward to that low-down blues that had made him a musical legend.

Gordon started strumming lightly, and the first clue that something was different was the major key, instead of the minor, atonal chords that filled his best-known songs.

Gordon sang, sweet and clear, *"We thank thee, O God, for a prophet ... "*

They were thunderstruck. Heads turned. People looked at one another. Whisperings popped up in many parts of the room, like bubbles in oatmeal, growing and popping out of existence, only to begin in another spot. His band watched in amazement, not sure what to do, but Gordon kept singing and playing.

"To guide us in these latter days ... "

It was simple, pure, and not what the people had come to hear. Talk was loud and open, full of angry tones and scattered arguments, with a twenty-percent chance of isolated fistfights. Gordon continued, with a delicate instrumental break that brought tears to a few eyes.

The song ended over a shimmer of applause, much lighter than the hand-pounding that usually greeted the end of one of his hits from *Songs in the Key of D'Evil.*

Gordon said, "Thanks for listening. If you liked that, you'll love this." Some folks were already headed for the exit by the time he started singing,

> *O my Father, thou that dwellest*
> *in the high and glorious place ...*

A group in the back started booing, and a voice hollered, "Play the good stuff!" Gordon played:

> *Praise to the man who communed with Jehovah ...*

The scraping of chairs made it hard to hear:

> *The Spirit of God like a fire is burning ...*

The back-up musicians started leaving when Gordon began:

> *Come, come ye saints ...*

THE BLUE devil was waiting for Gordon in the empty dressing room, a room cleared of all lowlife. The only remnants of the hangers-on, who were now looking for somewhere else to hang, were the bottles, the leftover food, and the lingering scent of burnt plant fibers.

"What do you think you're doing?" Waves of heat shimmered the air around the devil, who glowed with a positive purpleness. He shouted again, "What do you think you're doing?"

Gordon sat down, gave a serene smile, and said, "I'm just singing what's in my soul."

The devil said, "That's my soul you're singing with!"

"Hey," Gordon said, "it's the only soul I've got. If you don't like it, you can leave."

"If I leave, friend, I'm taking everything with me, everything I gave you: the fame, the women, the money, the good times, the music ... "

Gordon interrupted, saying, "You can't take the music."

"Yes, I can."

"No. You can't."

"Why not?"

"You can take everything you gave me. You gave me the songs, but *you* didn't give me the music."

IT WAS closing time in a little place no one ever heard of, and Gordon was playing sweet, sweet harmonies in a pool of light, amid chair-stacked tables, a bottle of water next to him.

A throat cleared in the darkness, followed by a hesitant, "Excuse me?"

"Hmmm?"

A slim young woman, a guitar slung over her back, stepped into the light. She leaned over, trying to see his face, and asked, "Are you Gordon Collins?"

"Yes, I am," he said, looking up into her shadowed face.

She didn't say anything for several seconds, then said, "I was told that you're the best."

He looked back down at his guitar, picking and strumming a quiet rhythm before saying, "I was, once. Not so sure that I am now."

"I was told," she said, "you could take me under your wing, teach me, lead me along."

"Depends," he said. He stopped playing. "Why'd you come here?"

"*They* sent me. I came here from ... Los Angeles."

"Los Angeles. The city of angels." He strummed, again, before he said, "Seems I have an opening in my schedule. Sit down, sling that guitar around to the front, and let's hear what you've got. What's your name?"

"Walker. Julie Walker."

"Pretty name," he said. He stopped, looked up at the instrument peeking out from behind Julie's back. Part of a painted rose showed next to her left shoulder. "Pretty guitar. Let me hear it."

Carefully, tentatively, the young woman started playing music.

Sweet music.

Music made in Heaven.

BROTHERS IN ARMS

Graham Bradley

SOUTHWEST UNITED STATES
OCTOBER 30, 2029
2100 HRS

My squad was hand-picked and told to get airborne with all of two minutes' notice. We'd be briefed in the air. All mission objectives would be announced on a need-to-know basis, and apparently I didn't need to know. Whatever. Marines don't complain.

Still, this didn't *feel* right. I'm not one to get worked up over feelings, but I couldn't ignore what nagged at me. I felt ... unprepared, like I'd forgotten something, and I felt a little ashamed about it. Couldn't put my finger on it, though.

Nine of us crowded into the dropship headed east out of Texas. Staff Sergeant Jack Maxwell watched the readouts from the artificial intelligence in the cockpit. He'd tell us what the heck we were doing once we'd reached a certain point on the map. I'd worked under him before on some training operations. I didn't know him personally, but I respected him.

The other two officers of rank were Corporal Rick Oswald and Lance Corporal Linda Claire. Oswald was kind of a character, the dude who laughed when nobody should. Claire was a cute Georgia peach from the Deep South, but she'd been known to bust heads on guys much bigger than her, so I didn't judge her by her looks. She's pretty accurate with a rifle, too.

The rest of us were privates, either First or Second Class. Unlike the officers, we all had nicknames written on digi-ink shoulder-screens attached to our armor, and some of the guys wore them proudly. I didn't, but you don't get to pick your nickname.

On my right sat Private "Compa" Gomez from El Paso. He was our tech guy, the one who fixed all our gear and knew how to use the little micro-functions and command-key shortcuts. He was sorting through some gadgets and gizmos to use when we landed.

Across from him was PFC "Ninja" Shinoda, and yes, the dude was an actual ninja. He kept those crazy-sharp swords in his footlocker and practiced martial arts during personal time. In his case I'm pretty sure that joining the Marines was easier than getting a girlfriend.

Next to Ninja was PSC Jenkins, the one guy I wish we would have left behind. His nickname was "Cannon," and he was a loose one. He never met a firearm he didn't want to discharge or a life he didn't want to endanger. He was just sane enough to keep his whack side off the officers' radar, but we knew what his true colors were. I pretended not to see him talking to his rifle under his breath as he checked it for the third time since takeoff.

To my right was PFC "Trex" Brennan. He spoke the least, and that said the most about him. He wasn't shy or wimpy or any of that – dude's a Marine – he just stuck to his job and that was it. He did it well, too. Ninja had explained to me how he got his nickname: "Back in Basic the other guys finagled it outta him that he doesn't watch pornos. Hates the stuff," Ninja said. "So they started calling him 'Triple-X.' Now they just say 'Trex.' I guess it works."

Trex was a by-the-book Marine. Lights-out and wake-up on time, clean shaven, and his equipment was always in working order. Yes sir, no sir, Semper Fi, all of it. Trex wasn't cleaning his gun like Cannon because he knew every single one of the moving parts was duty-ready.

As we flew, he held a well-worn book in his hands and was reading over the small words. It was a compact set of scriptures, but not the Bible.

I didn't want to tell him I recognized it.

As for me, I'm PFC Stone. The guys call me "Reverend." It's something that stuck from my own Basic days when my fellow recruits saw me praying over break-fast. It's a misnomer because my church doesn't have reverends, but explaining that only made the name hold harder. For my own reasons, I've since fallen out of the habit of praying – over breakfast, or anytime else.

"You about done there?" I asked Trex, nodding at his book.

"Just some light reading." His finger traced to the end of a verse and he closed the book. It fit perfectly in one of his waist compartments.

"Touchdown is in eight minutes," Staff Sergeant Maxwell said. "Helmets on, all of you." He kept his eyes on the flight map.

We all reached overhead for our helmets and pulled them on. Kevlar collars locked them onto our shoulder-armor, and the computerized masks linked to the hard drives in our suits.

On one side of my mask I got a readout of my vitals, the stock on my multi-munition rifle, and the functional parameters of my armor, all in real-time. I felt secure inside this suit, like wearing an impenetrable shell – fifty calibers couldn't break this blend of metal – and yet I couldn't silence the still, small nagging in the back of my mind. What was I missing?

"OUR TARGET is a small town in the mountains of the Santa Fe National Forest, here in New Mexico," Maxwell said. A small satellite image lit up on our face-masks, showing the town layout. "Officially this town does not exist. The officers on site have supply contracts with a few local businesses, and lately the delivery personnel who drive into the mountains have not returned."

"What's the town for?" Cannon asked.

"Shut your mouth, Jenkins. We're briefing," said Lance Corporal Claire. He'd interrupted the Staff Sergeant, and didn't address him as "Sir." Two strikes.

Cannon shut up, and Maxwell went on. "Doesn't matter why the town's there. Doesn't matter what happens inside it. All that matters is, four days ago it went completely silent. Nothing on radar, sonar, or anything else with an -ar. There's been a constant cloud cover, so satellite images are useless as well. The only things we've got are infrared and seismographs, and they're not painting a clear enough picture for the men at the top."

New pictures appeared, showing a circular cloud at different ranges, impenetrable by camera lens. Then there was an infrared scan showing dull buildings and a scattering of blurry humanoid shadows all over the place.

"Command has failed to contact the main office in town by any established method of communication. No cell phones, radio, internet, quantum-crypto waves, nothing. This morning at 0700 we sent in a trio of Pterohawk drones to take pictures. Before they penetrated the cloud, their cameras got scrambled by some sort of static burst, and we lost contact. What little data we gathered suggests a hypermagnetic field exists in the area, disrupting all outbound communication. Our job is to get eyes on the ground and find the cause of the anomaly. Any questions?" Maxwell made eye contact with all of us, one by one.

"Yeah, what's the town for?" Cannon asked again, adding "Sir" as an afterthought.

"It's full of the Americans you exist to protect. Stop asking, Jenkins."

"Sir, does Command expect us to find anything radical?" asked Compa. "Sounds like an EMP, if you ask me. Nothing works, nobody can get out 'cause anything with a motor is dead. Maybe something is casting off a constant pulse, or one that repeats often enough to keep screwing everything up."

"We're certain it's not an EMP. We know enough about the area to know that no EMP device could have gotten close enough to cause this," Maxwell said.

Yeah, we've got this area locked down so well, we're sending in fully armored Marines. I knew better than to say it.

If the others had questions, they didn't ask. "Two minutes to touchdown," said the Staff Sergeant. He switched off the map screen and slipped his own helmet on over his head, adding one final comment:

"Be aware: we have three hours to report back to Command."

He didn't say what would happen after three hours.

2:57:46

Our transport touched down next to the cloud. One look told me it was a definite abnormality. I'd never seen anything like it, like someone cut out a piece of the sky and dropped it right in front of us – perfectly flat, a hundred feet high, and from the looks of it, dense all the way through.

"Pair up by these assignments," Maxwell said into our helmet radios, and beamed us a portion of the mission data. A list of pairs appeared on my mask: the three ranking officers were matched up with Cannon, Ninja and Compa. Trex and I made the fourth pair, and we had to take point. We marched ahead twenty paces, putting us five yards inside the cloud. If we didn't hear from the squad after initial penetration, we had to walk back or wait for them to catch up with us.

"Sacrificial lambs," I thought aloud.

"Ain't no thing, Rev," said Trex with genuine calm. "Just a stroll is all."

As we drew nearer to the cloud wall, walking side by side, my suit informed me that my heartbeat was faster than it ought to be.

"You nervous?" Trex asked.

"Can you tell?"

"We're paired up. Your suit's telling me your vitals."

"Right." Sloppy mistake – I'd forgotten the suits did that. Ten steps from the cloud wall. "Does this just not feel right to you?" I asked.

"Yeah, it rubs the wrong way for sure. Still ... if you're prepared, you shouldn't fear."

"Odd choice of words," I said. I knew he was quoting a scripture, one I'd read a hundred times myself. "What if I said I'm not prepared?"

"Then you're just wussing out."

I laughed, despite the tension. Four steps. "No, not me. Just feels like I overlooked something."

"We're walking through the clouds. Gonna overlook a lotta things here in a second."

Who knew Trex had a sense of humor?

We reached the cloud. I extended my gauntlet and pressed on the grayish wall – no resistance. It went right through, like it was made of air.

Trex forged ahead without slowing pace. I hastily matched his speed again, counting our steps as we proceeded past the wall. A guard shack – the first indication of a town – stood about forty meters away.

"Staff Sergeant, we've reached the mark," Trex reported.

Maxwell's reply was scrambled. "Can – hear – us?"

"Uh, copy that, sir, but you're breaking up."

Static. Then, "How about now, Private?"

"Better, sir."

I heard footsteps at my six. The others came up behind us, and our communication improved.

"Looks like it's just the edge of the cloud cover, but we ought to test some other ranges to be sure, sir," said Compa.

We spread out under Compa's direction. Aside from normal buzzing, we had no other problems over our helmet channels. The Staff Sergeant urged us onward.

"I'm uploading a list of phone numbers to call in the area – start with the command center. Oswald, take Gomez and see if you can establish contact with any of them. The rest of us will scout the immediate vicinity," he said.

As we went about our business, Trex and I marked the guard shack on the maps in our helmets, locking down our position. Up ahead the gate stood open, and a delivery truck from a local bakery was parked right over the cattle guard.

"Staff Sergeant? Do we have a way to identify these markers?" I pointed to the gate's number, mounted on a post on the right. Maxwell uploaded a map from his hard drive – the commanding officer kept the mission data to himself, only doling it out as necessary. I didn't like the idea of being on a mission without full disclosure, but once again, it was part of the job. I located the gate on the map and sent the position back to the Staff Sergeant on his mask.

"Oswald? Gomez? Any luck?" he asked over the radio.

"No response yet, Staff Sergeant," Oswald replied. "Three contacts down, four to go."

Claire and Cannon brought up the rear. Cannon had his poor sense of muzzle discipline on display, keeping the nose of his rifle almost level with his hip, but just low enough that the sensor wouldn't alert Claire that he was aiming too high for the conditions. He was itching to shoot something.

Ninja shouldered his rifle and opened a compartment on his hip, removing a handful of small motion sensors. He stuck one on each gate post and another on either side of the bakery truck, marking the path as we went. If anyone came up behind us, we'd know. Ninja ventured deeper into the fog, and Trex and I brought up the rear.

The others came to our position a few minutes later. Compa said that the last contact – an encrypted wireless signal – was faint and they wanted to get closer before trying to connect to it. Cannon, Claire, Maxwell, and Oswald regrouped with us at the first intersection in the road past the gate.

Ninja came back and closed his hip compartment. "Got two dozen sensors out, so this area's covered," he said.

"We need to clear the cloud away," Maxwell grumbled to himself.

"What if we started a fire?" I wondered aloud.

"Hmm?" Trex asked.

"A bonfire. Wouldn't the heat dry out the air and force the cloud to break?"

"We'd just be filling the air with smoke."

Good point. I waited for Maxwell to give us our next order once Oswald and Compa made contact through the wireless signal.

"Hey, I got movement in that direction," Ninja said suddenly. He pointed toward our comrades, still visible about ten yards off.

"It's just Oswald and Compa," I said.

"Not it's not: the sensors ignore our suits," Ninja insisted.

A voice called out through the fog: Oswald. "Hey! We got a civilian! He looks sick."

"Everybody to Oswald," Maxwell ordered. Their outlines solidified as we approached, and beyond them we saw the staggering figure of a third person. Oswald moved closer to the newcomer, who definitely looked like he was having a hard time staying on his feet. He moaned as he shuffled forward, supporting himself on cars that had stalled on the side of the road.

"United States Marine Corps! Identify yourself," Oswald ordered.

The civilian coughed and groaned, but said nothing. A burning sensation ran up the back of my neck, making me tighten my grip.

"You feel that too?" Trex's eyes glued to the civilian. Our suit-computers registered twin reactions but didn't identify the cause.

Our helmet-cameras zoomed in on the civilian. He was armed with an automatic weapon in his right hand.

"Corporal, look out!" Trex shouted, snapping his rifle to his shoulder. Too late – even Oswald didn't see it in time. The civilian shifted to one side and fired point-blank into Oswald's mask. The "crack" of ammunition ruptured the eerie silence before the fog swallowed up the echo. Oswald staggered backward.

Trex didn't hesitate to open fire. He placed his shots well, hitting the guy once in the knee before shooting his gun hand. The civilian collapsed. Cannon pushed Trex aside, holding his rifle in one hand and pointing it at the civilian's stomach. Claire seized his muzzle in her gauntlet and jerked it skyward; bullets sprayed into the fog.

"Hold your fire, Jenkins! Target's down!" she snapped. Cannon huffed, obeying reluctantly.

Oswald rolled over and climbed to his feet. His face mask was cracked but not penetrated – the resin compound had held up well, but probably wouldn't survive another shot.

"Corporal, you okay?" Maxwell asked.

"A little shaken up, sir – didn't see his weapon."

"Gomez, check him out and see what we can do about his mask. Claire, Shinoda, examine that hostile," Maxwell said. Ninja and Claire advanced on the civilian. Ninja kicked the man's gun away.

"Nice shooting," I said, turning to Trex. He shrugged, always modest.

"Uh, sir?" Ninja said. "You should take a look at this."

Maxwell walked over to the civilian. Ninja kicked the guy's gun hand a few more times for good measure, showing us the problem: the gun *was* his hand.

"What the ... " Maxwell trailed off.

Claire hooked her toe under the civilian's side and flipped him over. We all gasped at what we saw next, what we'd failed to see in the fog.

His scalp was shaved but stubbly. He wore thin, flexible armor in lieu of clothing, and dark blood oozed from his wounds where Trex had plugged him. A mess of cables and wires ran from the base of his skull to a power pack on his side, and his armor connected to an array of mechanical parts like the ones in our suits – the ones that made us faster, stronger, and gave us greater staying power in combat.

But ours were removable. This was a permanent part of him, fused into his body somehow. On his right arm, the limb had been removed just below the elbow, and instead of a hand he had a MAC-10 firearm. The only thing he lacked was a serious suit of armor.

Ninja dropped to one knee and scanned the civilian with his suit's medical equipment. "Holy crap, this guy's been dead for two days."

"That's impossible," Maxwell said. "Check again."

"I just did, sir. Tissue decay matches that time frame. His eyes started to go, but he's had lenses implanted over them, like our motion sensors. The fiber-optics in his skull are computer wires, a direct jack between his brain and this thing." Ninja patted the computer box on the man's side, then ran a finger through the wound on the man's chest. A thick, dusty, black gunk piled up on Ninja's fingertip. "And this ... this is not blood."

"He's a good shot for a dead man," Oswald said.

"Reanimation," Ninja said. "I've heard of some experiments back when I was in medical training, but ... nothing this elaborate. Somebody crammed a bunch of tech in this corpse and started pulling puppet strings."

"A cyborg?" I asked.

"No, a zombie," Cannon snorted, like I'd missed something obvious.

"A zombie-cyborg," I amended.

"This is all wrong," Trex said, but not to us. He couldn't take his eyes off the corpse.

Just then, the dead-civilian-terminal-man thing sprang to life again, grabbing Claire by the ankle and yanking hard on her leg. But for the enhanced balance of her suit, she'd have fallen to the ground.

Ninja reacted first, punching Terminal Man hard in the head. His skull cracked, but that didn't stop him from firing indiscriminately into the thick of us. A bullet bounced off my shin armor. I kept my footing and leveled my rifle at the target. My helmet-computer lined up the shot and automatically selected a higher caliber bullet. I fired at the space right between his shoulders, blowing apart the junction with all of the cables running out of his head.

Claire tore free from his grip, and I shot the computer box on Terminal Man's side. Ninja got up and backed away, and I pointed my muzzle at the ground. Behind me, Cannon swore at having missed the action yet again.

"Everyone hold your fire!" Maxwell ordered.

"Uh, I think that did it, sir," Ninja said. He stood up, still examining the now-perforated zombie. Cyborg. Whatever.

None of us was sure what to do next. Maxwell consulted with Ninja on the condition of the body, trying to be sure about the time of death – the first time. I stepped away and cycled my rifle back to its standard caliber ammo, but Trex tapped my arm and gave me the "don't do that" signal with his hand.

"Keep it on the forty-four cal," he said, raising his voice so the others could hear.

"For what?"

"Them." He nodded past Maxwell and Ninja; the fog pushed away from us, clearing out in a wide radius. If not for my vital readouts on screen, I'd have sworn my heart stopped.

We were surrounded by at least two dozen of the zombie-cyborg things like the one we'd just shot to pieces. And they were all armed.

For the most part, they were uniform in composition. There was some slight variation in build, but they all had shaved heads, body armor, and mechanical exoskeletons fused to their outsides. Oh, and the lineup of firearms they employed was pretty diverse.

Silently they closed in on us, feet scraping across the pavement. Before any of us could say a word, the zombie-cyborgs opened fire.

"Take cover!" Maxwell shouted, moving behind a parked car on the curb. The rest of us followed suit and used other cars for concealment. Maxwell gave the order to fire back, and we happily obliged.

Cannon finally had his moment. He spun around and sprayed ammo into a line of targets even as their shots bounced off of him. When only two or three of the zombies hit the ground, Cannon instantly cycled to a higher-potency weapon and pumped a few RPGs into their ranks. Bits of Kevlar, endoskeletons and rotted flesh blasted into the air.

Trex spotted a crew of hostiles hauling some mortar equipment behind them, moving with greater haste and coordination than their counterparts. He sent me a signal from his helmet and marked targets for the two of us. In a fluid motion we brought our stocks to our shoulders and plucked off a half-dozen concentrated shots at the newcomers, aiming for the computer boxes and the cables in their brains. The mortar equipment clattered to the ground before they could get a volley off.

Behind us, the others had taken good care of the rest of the hostiles. Bullet casings littered the ground, and the parked cars were full of holes. Maxwell, Claire, and Ninja had a healthy amount of pockmarks in their armor from bullets, while Cannon had taken the most damage, fired the most shots, and made the fewest kills. Compa knelt down and tried to get Oswald's shattered mask to work.

"All hostiles are down, sir," Ninja reported.

"Good lord, what was all that?" I muttered, surveying the dead bodies everywhere.

"Fun," Cannon answered breathlessly.

"Jenkins, you will conserve your ammunition!" Maxwell growled. "Corporal Oswald, get back to the transport and replace your mask. Gomez, take one of these rotten puppet-corpses and follow Oswald. Throw it in the cargo hold – we need something to show to Command. The rest of you, keep your weapons primed. We're going to find out where these ugly mugs came from."

"Bet it's the same place as these guys!" Cannon dropped to one knee and pulled his rifle in tight, spewing bullets back into the fog.

Another round of hostiles surged forth from the haze, but these were not like the first wave: though their bodies bore similar technology, they moved with greater speed and agility, darting across the ground. Weapons at the ready, they let us have it.

Trex and I sought targets again, but quickly found a new problem: these hostiles didn't have junction boxes. Their skin looked healthier and we could see their eyes – they hadn't been dead as long.

But they were just as numerous.

Despite being fired upon by eight Marines, they overwhelmed us quickly. One of them jumped and tackled Cannon head-on, forcing him to drop his rifle. Cannon wrapped his huge arms around the hostile and squeezed until bones cracked and metal snapped, then tossed the body aside and scrambled for his weapon.

"No junction boxes on these ones!" I said.

"The head! Just go for the head!" Ninja screamed, peppering the swarm with fifty-cal ammo. I kept my finger on my trigger, trying to put every shot between a pair of deadened eyes. Trex never fired without aiming, and every one of his bullets hit home.

Someone cried out behind me and to my left. I jerked my head around in time to see Oswald get clobbered by three hostiles. Compa dropped the corpse he'd been carrying and picked up his rifle, covering himself and Oswald. He had his hands full.

"Somebody get to Oswald!" Maxwell said; he and Claire stood back-to-back with me and Trex. Cannon was prying his rifle from a hostile's hand and couldn't be bothered, so Ninja darted past us to help Oswald. While running, he unsheathed a massive Bowie knife from his hip and dived into the mêlée.

I could imagine what came next, though I was too busy shooting to watch it. Ninja hacked the limbs off of two zomborgs and then pushed Oswald toward the gate where we'd entered. Compa gathered up the sample corpse and followed.

The hostiles dwindled but held out longer than the first wave. One of them raised his arm – an RPG – and fired at my fleeing comrades. The explosion sent the armored Marines flying in three directions, and again Oswald found himself alone and confounded. Four hostiles were on him instantly, and he cried out for help.

"Oswald!" Maxwell shouted.

"Sir, we need to get out of here!" Claire said over the roar of gunfire. Trex and I never stopped firing. How many more of these guys could there be?

Never ask that question.

More hostiles arrived to replace the fallen ones, and things took an ugly turn: it dawned on me that the zombies were using strategy against us. Half a dozen of them provided cover fire for the quartet that swarmed Oswald, and every time I dropped one of them, another one took its place. They were bent on taking Oswald away. Maxwell told Claire to cover him, then took off bounding across the earth in long strides. Using his armor's enhanced strength, the Staff Sergeant swung his arms like overweight pendulums, cracking every zombie skull in his path.

Compa and Ninja got up and armed themselves. Ninja's rifle kept misfiring though, and Compa's targeting software caught a glitch. Just as Claire ordered Cannon to provide more cover for Maxwell, a new hostile arrived on the scene, almost seven feet tall and carrying a shoulder-mounted bazooka.

"*Staff Sergeant!*" Claire cried. Too late: Bazooka Man fired at a range too close to miss, striking Maxwell's chest. The explosion deafened us, the concussion throwing to the ground. Someone grabbed the tow-handle on the back of my suit and dragged me away.

2:12:16

When my vision cleared, we were in a dark cellar and there were two fewer of us. I couldn't see much – my mask was off – but everyone's name badges lit up in the dark, along with the rank emblems on their shoulders. Claire's insignia had upgraded to Corporal.

Which meant Maxwell and Oswald were both dead.

"PFC Stone, what's your status?" she asked in a quiet voice. I rubbed my eyes, glad that someone had had the foresight to pull my gauntlet off for me. I coughed but couldn't hear the sound over the ringing in my ears.

"I am fit for combat ... Corporal, ma'am," I said. "Orders?"

"Take a breather."

"What happened?" I asked.

"We had to leave Staff Sergeant Maxwell behind," she said, her voice grim. *That* was a hard pill to swallow. Marines don't leave their own behind.

"Where are we, ma'am?" I asked.

"Rock and a hard place. Shinoda pulled Gomez away from the main brunt of the explosion, and when Jenkins depleted his heavy ballistics, Brennan pulled you and him to safety. The town map showed an entrance to an underground service tunnel one block over. We should be able to hide down here for a few minutes before we start moving again." I didn't miss the venom in her tone when she mentioned Cannon wasting all of his big ammo. I wasn't surprised that Trex saved us both.

"Do we have any idea what those things were?" I asked.

"Yup: zomborgs," Cannon said, entering our dark room from an adjacent corridor.

"I thought I told you to secure the other entrances," Claire said.

"Did that. The one on the left goes about ten yards, then forks. One way leads to the waterworks, and the other has the controls to the gas main. I locked 'em both ... ma'am," Cannon said. He almost choked on that last word.

"And what about the other exit out of this room? The one on the right?" Claire said.

"Ninja and Compa are down there." Cannon left it at that.

"Jenkins, you're in enough trouble as it is. You will address your commanding officer in the proper fashion. Are we clear?" Claire snarled.

Cannon leered at her and grinned. "With you in charge, who says we'll live long enough for me to face formal punishment?"

I'd had it. I stood up. "That's enough, Cannon."

"Cram it, Reverend," he said.

Claire whirled and faced me. "Back off, Stone. I'm in charge here. I'll handle this."

"Yeah, sticking our heads in a hole in the ground. Doin' great, lady," Cannon said. Claire turned back and almost pulled her rifle. I could tell she wanted to – hell, *I* wanted her to.

"If you'd followed orders instead of spitting grenade-sized-solutions at bullet-sized problems, we might not be in this mess, Private!" she shouted.

"Whatever," Cannon muttered. He turned his back on Corporal Claire.

I don't know what made me do it; I'd never liked Cannon. He pissed me off a lot of times without getting a reaction. But his attitude right now – our Staff Sergeant just got blown away with a bazooka by a walking corpse, for crying out loud – pushed me over the edge. I shouldered Claire aside and tackled Cannon from behind. We hit the ground hard.

We started taking punches at each other, equally matched for strength by the enhanced properties of our suits. I managed to avoid taking any shots to the face, but that didn't mean it didn't hurt to be punched in the chest or stomach, armor be damned. Claire tried to pull us apart, but it wasn't until Compa came running back through the other tunnel that the fight got broken up.

"Attack me from behind, tough guy?" Cannon roared, even as Compa held him back by his tow handle. From five feet away, Cannon spat at me and hit me right in the eye. I wiped it off.

"You finally hit something!" I shot back, flicking the spittle off my fingertips. I tried to charge him again, but suddenly both our suits shut off.

Claire stepped between us. She wore her mask again, allowing her to access our suits by remote. With Maxwell and Oswald gone, all of the command files would've automatically uploaded to her computer, including the emergency kill switch for our armors. Without power, the armor significantly restricted our movement.

"I swear you'll both be spit-shining the brig when this is over," she seethed between clenched teeth. "Step out of line one more time and you get to take your chances outside, alone, unarmed, and in your skivvies. Are we clear?"

Cannon shot me a murderous glare, which I understood to mean that this was not over. Still, we acknowledged Claire's threat, and she powered up our suits again. Compa released Cannon, and I pulled my mask down into place.

"What've you got?" Claire asked Compa.

"We didn't want to call it in on the radio, but Private Shinoda and I found someone down the north tunnel, ma'am," Compa replied.

"Some*one*? Like another hostile?" she asked.

"No, ma'am: a doctor."

2:02:39

Compa led us down the other tunnel for a hundred yards before we emerged in the basement of the tech center.

"We found out that these service tunnels go all over the place, but there are only four entries into the whole network. This is where they transport all of the really sensitive materials," Compa said.

"What kind of materials, Private?" Claire asked.

Compa coughed. "Ma'am, I think that question is best left to the doctor. You, uh … you're gonna get a kick out of this one."

We stepped through a hatch and into a wide-open storage room, where Ninja stood next to a man in a tattered, dirty lab coat. The doctor nursed a bottle of water, keeping it at his lips like he might die if he stopped. Next to him was a vending machine with a boot-sized hole in the glass, and I put the pieces together: Ninja had given the dude a hand.

Sorry, a foot.

Ninja and Trex snapped to attention when Claire entered. "Ma'am, we found a survivor."

"Dare I ask what he survived?" Claire said, but we all knew.

"Oh good lord, I can't tell you people how glad I am that you're here," the doctor said, his voice raspy. He wiped his eyes – they were bloodshot and red, and had dark blue bags under them. He hadn't slept in a few days.

"I'm Lance Cor ... I mean, *Corporal* Claire, USMC. Sir, what's your name?"

"Evan Baxter." The doctor drained the last of his bottle.

"What happened here?" she asked.

"Take a seat. I'll tell you what I can," he said.

1:56:14

"This facility is for testing mechanical enhancement devices – like applications to augment performance in a wide range of areas. Recently we had a breakthrough with nervous connections – that is, making sure the brain is translating correctly between the mechanical parts and the organic ones." He stopped and pulled another bottle from Ninja's hole in the vending machine.

"How did that turn into what we saw up top?" Compa said.

"I don't know. I was just supposed to connect the meat to the hard drive. That's it," Baxter said.

"Let's talk about when it started. When did the cloud set in?" Claire asked.

"Four days ago. We were running our experiments like normal when all of a sudden, our communications shut down. Intranet, radio, phones, all of it. I did get a look at our surveillance, and I saw a man walking toward the base from the airfield side. He was doing this weird kind of dance, kicking his feet and waving his arms in the air. The closer he came, the foggier it got."

"What'd he look like?"

"Like bad news," Baxter muttered.

"Gonna need more than that, sir," Claire said. "What was he wearing?"

"Oh, hell ... he had some kind of dirty, red hide or pelt wrapped around his waist. His feet were bare but he had leather straps around his ankles and calves, I remember that much. Similar leather wrappings on the wrists and forearms, too. More red paint on his face, just across his eyes. Shaved head, dark tan skin – somebody said he looked like the Indians that live on the reservation not far from here. He walks in and disregards all orders to halt, so the guards open fire. It takes a second to notice that the bullets just … they just … "

"You couldn't hurt him," Trex said in a soft voice. "Nothing you could do to him ended up hurting him."

"Uh … yeah, actually," Doctor Baxter said. "How'd you know?"

All eyes were on Trex, and if he saw, he didn't show it. I noticed his left hand resting on his belt – right over the compartment holding his scriptures.

"Did he say what his name was?" Trex asked.

Baxter snorted and shook his head. "There was no time for that. Once he stepped over the boundary of the base, our power cut out. The fog jammed up our remaining tech. He kept advancing, nobody could hold him back, and then … he started tearing apart the soldiers. Going straight through them, killing them with his bare hands. I've been running ever since, trying to hide."

"How do the zomborgs fit into all that?" Cannon asked.

"The what?"

"Zombie cyborgs. Zomborgs. The guys outside."

"Oh, *now* they're cyborgs," I said under my breath.

"Jenkins, I'll do the talking here," Claire snapped. "Keep your dumb mouth shut."

I almost wished Cannon would push the envelope, but he held his tongue.

"The hostiles, Doctor. We need to know about them," Claire said.

"I can't tell you about that. It's classified," Doctor Baxter said.

"Let's pretend it's really important – like it might decide whether we all live or die," Claire said in a carefully controlled tone. I'd served with her long enough to know that she was a storm on the inside right now. I'm sure she was still seeing the Staff Sergeant getting capped by a bazooka. The memory was less than thirty minutes old.

Baxter ran a hand down his face and moaned, staring at the patch of ground between his feet. He slumped against the wall, sighed, and gave in.

"The main project we've been working on here, it deals with reanimation of dead tissue. Been at it for years, mostly with small subjects – plant life, then simple animals – but a week ago we got clearance to begin testing on voluntary human subjects. A number of soldiers from the war in China signed up for the program, and when their bodies came home, they arrived here.

"The animal tests were such a success that we didn't have much trouble adapting the program to human subjects. Seven days ago we had our first successful human trial. I saw it with my own eyes ... we brought a deceased soldier back from the dead," Baxter said.

"*Madre mía*," Compa whispered.

Claire cleared her throat. Her voice trembled, but she urged him on. "What happened next?"

"Well, we started to reanimate them in batches. Three days after the first success, we had twelve more. That's when the Indian arrived and took over. That's all I know. He made a beeline for the tech center, and I came down here to hide. I was able to tap into the mainframe on one of the peripheral computers and track his movement for a while. Two days ago he left the tech center and I think he went to the command center. Now the only movement I see is from the resuscitated soldiers. The, eh, zomborgs," Baxter said, trying out Cannon's name for them.

"Where's that peripheral computer?" Compa asked. Baxter pointed at the wall.

"How many dead servicemen do you keep in this place?" asked Ninja.

"We had twenty-eight in cryogenic preservation when the base fell."

"There were a lot more than twenty-eight of these zomborgs up there," I said to Claire.

"Hold up and I can get you a count," Compa said. He plugged his facemask screen into the peripheral computer and ran the footage from the firefight. "Yo Doc, do you have facial-recognition software on this thing?"

Ninja helped Baxter to his feet. He went over to Compa and brought up the FRS program on the computer. Compa interfaced it with the battle footage, and soon the computer started counting the unique faces in the crowd: thirty-nine.

"Oh, hell," Baxter moaned.

"What?" Claire asked.

"The only way there could be that many is if they finished with the frozen soldiers and started reanimating the people the Indian killed." Baxter moved Compa aside and opened a registry of the town's residents. Out of sixty-eight full-time residents, the FRS isolated eleven and matched them with faces in the second wave of attackers.

"I've got twenty-three of the dead soldiers in the first wave, five more in the second wave, plus eleven of the more advanced models," Compa said, finishing with the FRS.

Baxter hung his head. "I knew those people. That monster ... he killed them all."

1:50:02

I felt bad for the doctor, but we were in a time crunch so we couldn't let him mourn. He got his bad news, and then we were grilling him again.

"How many times can these guys come back from the dead?" Claire asked.

"As long as they can get replacements for their failed body parts, in theory they could go on forever. Realistically, I'd say a few more days. Nobody knows – this is the first trial run."

"And when you reanimated the first subject, was he aware of what had happened to him?"

"Er, no. Not really. He retained basic motor skills but had trouble understanding our speech. Didn't remember anything else either, from the looks of it. He needed to be dressed, cleaned, fed – he was a fully-grown newborn," Baxter said.

"His soul was gone," Trex muttered to himself. The thought made the back of my neck burn.

"Why all the cables and computer boxes?" Ninja asked.

"The successful subjects were the ones who'd been frozen for the shortest amount of time. We worked on them first. Later we tried with the older ones, but they had the lowest cerebral potential. Some of them had to be bypassed with compact computers that would send the necessary impulses to their limbs." Baxter pointed to one of the zomborgs and zoomed in on the computer box on his side. Not all of the zomborgs had one.

"The ones with those boxes, they don't move very easily," Compa said.

Baxter nodded. "It wasn't perfect. We built in a remote control prototype – eventually the generals wanted it so that if a soldier was killed in the line of duty, his commanding officer could use the tech to walk his body out of hostile territory. No man left behind, and all that. If we couldn't reanimate them, we still want to save them."

Claire perked up. "Wait a minute – the ones with the boxes can be controlled?"

Baxter shrugged. "There's no reason why not. The remote controls worked. It's just that the ones with the boxes are *only* good for that. Without them, they're complete vegetables."

"Where are the controls? We gotta shut 'em down," Compa said.

"Good luck," Baxter huffed. "The only active control node is in the command center. And I'd bet you'll all be dead before you get within fifty feet of the door."

A red light suddenly lit up on my helmet screen. By the way my comrades jerked to attention, I knew they'd seen it too.

"The motion sensors!" Ninja said.

Claire brought up her rifle. "We've got trouble, people!"

1:44:59

"Doctor Baxter, you're with us. Whatever we need to know, tell us – we're just as interested in living as you are," Claire said. "Gomez and Shinoda, you take point. Jenkins and I will flank the doctor, Brennan and Stone, bring up the rear. Move!"

Trex and I fell into place behind Cannon. Ninja and Compa led us out of the basement through a new tunnel, which I ambushed behind us with a claymore. Our heavy footsteps thudded down the tunnel and drowned out any verbal orders, so Claire kept a tight grip on Baxter and had us block all external audio.

"Just focus on getting out of here," she told us through our radios. "I have a plan. Gomez, work your computer magic and find out what's parked on the airfield."

"Aye, ma'am," Compa said.

We took a right at the next bend and kept moving. The tunnels had very few exits, and based on the airfield's location, I could see on the map where we'd be getting out.

"Motion sensors have gone quiet, but that just means they're out of the zone. The most current readout has them headed for the break room," Ninja said.

"We're getting outside ASAP," Claire said. "Nobody fires until we're out of these tunnels – can't have a ricochet hit the Doc."

"Airfield computer says there are two Chinooks, four Longbows, and a pair of Harriers. Fully fueled the day before the attack," said Compa.

"You planning on flying out of here, ma'am?" I asked.

She checked the clock. "Not yet – we have a little under two hours to wrap up here. If we can get the vehicles started and throttle the engines in neutral, we'll create enough turbulence to punch an opening in the cloud. That'll let the eye in the sky get a good look at what's happening down here."

"That'll draw the zomborgs, ma'am," said Compa.

"Then Command will have something to look at, won't they?"

Far behind us, my claymore went off with a loud boom, and Baxter covered his ears. I grabbed his shoulders and helped him keep pace. We reached the exit and climbed up a ladder – the hole almost wasn't big enough for us to get out in our armor. Compa and Ninja popped out first to check the area: a narrow street between a row of portable buildings. Ninja gave us the green light to come up.

He shouldn't have.

A German shepherd – make that five – sprinted out of the fog. I caught a glimpse of fast-moving legs, shaved patches of fur, sharp teeth, and more cybernetic upgrades. *Great. Zomborg dogs.*

"Hold your fire!" Claire ordered. Her hand instinctively grabbed Cannon's barrel and pushed it up high. "Take them out quietly!"

The dogs didn't bark, which worked to our advantage. Ninja and Compa dropped their rifles and pulled their Bowie knives, meeting the dogs head-on. One dog lunged for Compa's throat. He socked it hard in the jaw with his free hand before crushing its skull with the butt of his knife, then thrust the dagger straight into the open jaws of a second dog.

Ninja was even faster. He caught one dog under the throat with his knife, where the junction box was strapped to its collar. Something gave, and the dog hit the ground unceremoniously. The remaining two Shepherds pounced, and Ninja's dagger flashed too fast for me to follow with my eyes. I guess all his off-duty swordplay paid off: the dogs bit the dust.

"Take notes," Claire said to Cannon, and released his gun.

"Behind us!" Trex said.

All eyes went to Trex, and then to the wave of a dozen zomborgs coming at us from the other direction, weapons armed. Cannon whirled around and – as usual – fired first. Trex and I were right beside him. Ninja and Compa gathered up their rifles as Claire dragged Baxter away from the fight.

"The dogs were a diversion!" I said. Nobody heard me over the rapid discharge of weaponry.

These zomborgs were like the second wave – advanced, with no junction boxes. The software in my facemask scanned them from every angle as we traded shots, but I couldn't identify any weak spots in their design. I was about to aim for the chest when Trex got into position, targeted a zomborg's forehead and shot twice. Twin red holes appeared on the zomborg's face, and he fell to the ground, dead for the second time.

Looks like it's still the head then, I thought, and followed his lead. Six seconds later we dropped them all. Or at least those twelve. Naturally, more came up behind them.

"Stone, Brennan, Jenkins, fall back!" Claire ordered. We retreated and followed her between two portables to the next row over. Ninja and Compa joined us.

"Ma'am, I think we'd have better luck going across the rooftops," Trex offered.

"Agreed," Claire said. She shouldered her rifle and grabbed Baxter with both hands. "Hold your breath, Doc." She picked him up, trotted up to the side of the nearest portable and bent her knees.

Another wave of zomborgs shambled out of the mist. One of them fired a gas canister from a shoulder-mounted launcher. The canister whistled through the air and struck Doctor Baxter in his ribs, cracking several of them. The doctor screamed.

Claire pointed at the gas-launcher zomborg. "Jenkins, take him out!"

Cannon was two steps ahead of her, deploying his last grenade into the zomborg's chest. The result was a fine mist of ... well, you can guess what it was. Ninja, Trex, and I joined Cannon, while Compa ran to Baxter's aid.

The three of them were behind us when the next surprise attack struck: a manhole cover in the street flipped open and out poured more zomborgs, rushing up like man-sized cockroaches, too many for us to handle. As for the wave in front of us, each one that fell was replaced instantly by another. High-quantity ammo made up for their poor aim, and I constantly felt bullets ricochet off my armor.

The wave to our rear overwhelmed Compa and Claire before any of us could help them. They both fell to the ground, and an unarmed zomborg grabbed Baxter's arm. A syringe shot out of the zomborg's wrist into Baxter's neck, and the doctor went limp.

I trained my rifle on another zomborg that was headed for Claire with a similar syringe at the ready. Three more ganged up on Compa ... I couldn't get rid of them all. These ones had even more armor, and after they got the needle into Compa's throat – where our collars didn't cover – he was helpless. The dragged him into the depths of their throng, making retrieval impossible – and I still had to save Claire. There were just too many zomborgs in the street now.

"Guys! Rooftop!" I said. Claire scrambled to her feet, dazed and unsettled. I grabbed her tow handle and told her to jump with me. We crouched and sprang with a hydraulic *whoosh*, and soared fourteen feet into the air. I kept my grip on Claire as we landed on top of the portable. Ninja, Cannon, and Trex touched down next to us a second later.

Fortunately, the zomborgs couldn't follow or didn't want to. They dispersed, retreating into whatever hellhole they'd crawled out of. I tried to spot Compa, but no matter where we went the fog still only gave us about five yards of visibility in any direction, and he was nowhere to be seen.

1:32:17

"Shinoda ... I'm putting you in charge of the tech," Claire said in an even tone. Her posture betrayed the sick feeling she had over losing Compa and the doctor. None of us could blame her.

To my surprise, Ninja put his rifle down, rested his hands on his hips and hung his head in thought, his posture oddly relaxed.

"Ninja, you okay?" I asked.

"Gimme a sec," he said. "Gotta wrap my head around this."

"Now's not the time for a breakdown, man," I said.

Ninja snorted. "We've got the best gear, the best armor and guns and tactical forecast equipment. Based on what we know is in this compound, in the worst-case scenario we should still out-gun everything. And instead, *four* of us have fallen behind, including the doctor." He looked up at Claire. "Tech won't save us, Corporal ma'am. This isn't right, how they're beating us. There's something else at work here."

"On your feet, Private," Claire growled, leaving no room for argument.

Trex spoke up, his words soothing. "We can do this, Ninja. They can be stopped."

"They're learning, Trex," Ninja said with a scowl. "Half an hour ago they were no better than a street gang with high-powered guns. Now they've whittled away three Marines."

"We're learning, too. They're monsters, but that's all they are." Trex looked almost peaceful, the way he stood perfectly still as he spoke.

Cannon snorted at Trex. "Monsters? What is this, a bedtime story? They're stiffs with wires shooting out of their butts. They go down if you shoot 'em right."

"Yeah," I said, "but you don't shoot right, Cannon. You just shoot."

"Stuff it, Reverend," Cannon said.

"Both of you, cram it," Claire ordered.

"Or what?" Cannon snapped.

My face flushed with rage. I shoved Cannon hard and knocked him off-balance. He roared and took a swing at me; Trex jumped between us and absorbed the hit on his shoulder as he tripped Cannon and took him down. The three of us collapsed and the roof shuddered under us.

Claire shut our suits off. "As God is my witness, I will see all three of you discharged without honors after this mission. This is no way for Marines to behave. *On your feet!*"

Our suits powered up. Ninja grabbed me and Trex by the tow handles and pulled us upright. Cannon was left to fend for himself. I saw Trex patting at one of the compartments on his belt that had fallen open.

On the ground in front of his foot was the book he'd been reading on the flight over. The scriptures that weren't a Bible.

He leaned down to grab it, but Claire was faster. She picked up the book, read the title and narrowed her eyes.

"You're Mormon, Brennan?" she asked.

"Yes, ma'am." He extended a hand. "May I have it back, please?"

She tossed him the book. "We're out here in a blind firefight with the worst kind of hostiles I've ever seen, and you're toting around fairy tales. Good lord, but I had you pegged for smarter than that."

To my surprise, I was the one to shudder at her sharp words, but Trex didn't seem bothered. He just held up his hands and said, "For what it's worth, Private Shinoda is on to something. I think the source of this problem is beyond technological. We should be mowing through these guys, even with their numbers. Instead they've got some deeper power setting its will against us, something we can't see or measure with our equipment, and it ... "

Claire cut him off. "Save it, Brennan. You've got an imagination, I'll give you that, but what you've got there is a fantasy and it's not helping us."

"Oh great, now the fundies are going at it," Cannon huffed and rolled his eyes.

Trex pocketed the book. "What we're up against isn't just physical, it's spiritual. Stuff like this goes all the way back to the Bible times. Moses performed miracles for Pharaoh, and Pharaoh's sorcerers had tricks of their own. Com scrambling? Unnatural clouds? Unbeatable undead? What would you call that, ma'am?"

"I'd call it a great time for us to keep shooting," Claire said. "Unless of course the book has a better idea."

Trex took up his rifle and gave a noncommittal nod with a degree of self-control that I will never have. He left it at that.

"For now, everybody stays together. We're going to jump rooftops wherever possible and keep making our way toward the airfield. On my mark," Claire said.

1:25:29

It would be easy to gain a Superman complex from these suits: strong, mostly bulletproof, and able to leap tall buildings in a single bound. Claire took the first jump to the next portable thirty feet away. The roofs held up surprisingly well, considering our luck. Cannon went next, then me, then Trex and Ninja. As we chose jump sites, we kept jumping in that order until we got within range of the airfield. Then we had our next problem.

The nearest building to the airfield was out of our jump range. Between us and the next building we saw eight zomborgs mulling about, patrolling the area.

"Terrific," Claire said.

"We could snipe 'em." That was Cannon.

"Really?" I said. "That's a great idea. I bet the moment we dropped one of them, the rest totally wouldn't get pissed and come after us."

"No sniping. We're going to be smart about this. And, Jenkins: I'm shutting off your weapon – however the hell you made it into the Corps, this will be your last tour of duty," Claire said. Then she took a deep breath before saying, "Men, set your armor to stealth mode."

A sudden tension filled the air. Stealth mode was something used for recon, *before* you're surrounded by enemies. You basically run your armor's special capabilities at a hundred percent; it'll drain your battery, but it allows the reflective properties of the metal to change colors and blend in with the background. You have to move slower to silence your mechanical components, so you're basically a sitting duck if a fight picks up. It takes a second to revert back to normal, and that can be too long in battle – especially since some of these guys had RPGs.

But Claire didn't give us time to object. "We're going to scale the side of this building down to the ground as quietly as possible. Get off the sidewalk and get onto the pavement. Don't step on anything, don't leave any footprints. Nobody fires unless I say so. Are we clear?"

"Yes ma'am," said three voices at once. Cannon's came fourth, with much less enthusiasm.

We proceeded to scale the building and entered the streets a moment later. Claire took the lead. We followed in single file, slowly approaching the band of zomborgs between us and the gate to the airfield. These were the crude kind, with the junction boxes on their necks.

Slowly, slowly, I put one foot in front of the other, staying right behind Cannon, right in front of Trex. I realized after a minute that I was holding my breath; I let it out, my eyes darting back and forth between the inanimate faces of the zomborgs. Claire beamed a readout of everyone's vitals to our facemasks, along with a whisper telling us to keep our heart rates down.

"Especially you, Jenkins," she said.

Cannon's pulse went erratic – the guy was running on pure adrenaline. Was he afraid, or did he just get a rush from this? I couldn't tell, but the way he carried his rifle made me glad that Claire had disarmed him.

The zomborgs continued to amble about without much direction, pacing back and forth, walking in circles. They left enough space between them for us to walk on through to the airfield gate, just another ten or twelve yards beyond. Nine yards. Eight.

Cannon moved his rifle to his left hand and reached for his Bowie knife with his right. I gnashed my teeth. How stupid could he be? He grabbed the knife's handle, waiting for the right moment to pull it out – it couldn't go invisible like his rifle. One of the zomborgs came within swinging range. Knowing Cannon was stupid enough to take a swing at it, I reached up with my left hand and grabbed his tow handle.

I tugged it to the left twice, signaling him to let it be. He tried to shrug me off but I held my grip. He kicked at me to get me off his back, and the noise alone made everyone freeze in fear.

This would end badly.

If I held on, he'd start thrashing about like a two-year-old and draw the zomborgs' attention. If I let go, he'd use the knife and we were equally screwed. I hated this guy.

I released his tow handle and he spun around to face me.

"Keep your hands off," he snarled loud enough to wake the dead. Or at least in the quiet of our march, that's how it sounded.

"Cannon, you *idiot*," I growled. I didn't have to look to know that the zomborgs had all eyes on us now.

The nearest one attacked. Cannon slashed at it and missed. Another one came from the opposite direction. Shedding my stealth mode so I could move faster, I shoved Cannon aside and shot the thing straight between the eyes.

The others also shut off their stealth and joined the fight. Claire snapped at us, but I couldn't make out her words; we were all too busy shooting for our lives. Trex and Ninja went back-to-back, and Claire and I got in on it with them. Our shoulders formed a square behind us, allowing us to fire in all directions.

"Jenkins, get in here!" Claire ordered. Cannon ignored her. He actually threw his rifle aside and charged at one of the zomborgs with his knife, chopping right through the junction box at its neck. Three more swarmed him, and he knocked them all down with a wide swing of the arm.

Claire called a cease-fire. Ninja, Trex, and I kept our rifles trained at the ground and scanned the area for any more active hostiles. Cannon dropped the last one, having brutalized it far more than was necessary. Black ichor clung to his blade.

"Airfield. Now," Claire said. It wasn't a request.

None of us got the chance to comply. Another wave of zomborgs emerged from the haze in the road, armed with newer weapons.

Three more dogs appeared and charged Cannon at full speed. He defended himself with his Bowie knife, but the distraction made him fair game for the zomborgs. One of them fired a bola at his chest. A high-strength cable wrapped around him and pinned his arms to his sides.

"Reverend, on your ten!" Ninja said. I spotted a zomborg at my ten o'clock, sporting another bola-launcher attached to his arm. I locked onto his head and neck and fired three rounds in half a second. Trex dropped two more, and Ninja switched to grenades so as to break up a dense band of incoming hostiles. The air popped and roared with high-powered explosions.

"Switch to triangle formation!" Claire ordered. She broke away from our band and ran for Cannon, who couldn't free himself from the bola. When I got a chance to scan him out of the corner of my eye, I only caught a glimpse of a zomborg coming at him with a pickaxe in hand, aiming straight for his power pack. The sharpened tip buried in the pack, and Cannon went down.

I had a fleeting image of Trex and Ninja on the roof, talking about how the zomborgs were learning. They were targeting our power packs now. That alone would drop us faster than anything.

I covered for Claire. Bullets rained down on us from all directions. None of them were of a high-enough caliber to break our armor; even so, the impacts had a tendency to disrupt our aim, and the noise just drew more zomborgs out of the fog.

Claire drew her knife and shanked the pickaxe-zomborg straight in the neck, severing his spinal cord. He collapsed without any more fight. She knelt down and tried to cut Cannon's bola off.

"Bazooka Joe, incoming!" Ninja said. We all knew what he meant. I patched my facemask camera to his and got a glimpse at the seven-foot cyborg that had done Maxwell in.

"Shinoda and Brennan, kill him at all costs!" Claire said. She made no progress with Cannon, who remained immobile.

For the first time, Trex switched to grenades and set them to explode on impact. Ninja matched ammo and they took turns blowing the rocket-man to bits. While he drew their fire, even more zomborgs arrived and closed in on us from the sides.

Two more went for Claire. I raised my rifle and fired.

Click-click-click.

Of all the rotten luck ... I was out of forty-four cal. I switched to steel-tipped .746 rounds, and by the time the ammo cycled in, the newest wave of hostiles was upon Claire. I blew away one of them and had just set the second one in my crosshairs when he thrust a thin blade into the edge of Claire's power-pack. Her suit instantly slumped over, all illuminated insignia shutting off.

"Corporal's down!" I shouted. Trex and Ninja went back-to-back again as I ran for Claire and Cannon, dropping zomborgs with my rifle to clear a path. I reached both my comrades and grabbed their tow handles in either hand ...

Where would I drag them? Back to the center of the road with Trex and Ninja? There was no path to safety in any direction.

It didn't matter what I chose, because it turned out we hadn't completely taken down Bazooka Joe – his semi-functional upper body, which only had one good arm left, unstrapped the bazooka from his dismembered torso and aimed it at me.

"*NO!*" Ninja screamed. Trex popped a grenade at Bazooka Joe. It struck his collarbone on the right side, separating both his arm and his head from his shoulder.

The bazooka dropped to ground, pouring smoke from the rocket it had just fired.

The rocket went wide and hit the ground to my right. Dirt and rocks spewed into the air, and the shockwave knocked me over. Instantly I scrambled to get on my feet, grabbed Claire and Cannon, and looked for my other comrades.

Lying on his belly, Ninja pointed at Trex, then at me. He said something that I couldn't make out through the ringing in my ears. Trex nodded, got up, and threw his knife to Ninja. Then he came after me. Ninja took both knives and flipped them around in a blur before diving into the thick of the incoming wave of zomborgs.

"You take Cannon, I'll take Claire!" Trex said. "Ninja will cover our retreat!"

I clenched Cannon's handle hard in both hands and ran to the nearest building. Zomborg parts littered the road. Many of the still-intact guys dragged their comrades aside and immediately set about putting them back together so they could keep fighting.

We were five people – two of us injured – and the zomborgs still numbered in dozens. I crouched, ready to jump with Cannon's weight, when Trex suddenly tackled me from behind and we all hit the ground. I knew what he'd saved me from when I heard the *whoosh* of a bola overhead.

"They're everywhere!" he shouted.

"Trex! Reverend! Go!" Ninja bellowed, coming up for air in between bursts of Bowie-fueled slaughter. I gazed in awe at the pile of zomborg parts that rose up around him in all directions, severed by clean strikes from his knives. He was doing it – he was really doing it.

"Reverend, we won't make it out of here with Cannon or Claire – we've gotta get up high!" Trex said. We both stood up and then ducked again when another wave of bolas came at us from the entry of a building across the street.

"We can't leave them!" I cried. Trex grabbed my helmet and forced me to look at his shoulder emblem. In the haze and confusion, all I could see was that it was no longer the emblem of a Private First Class. With the shutdown of Claire's suit, the burden of command fell to the highest-ranking soldier that remained – by seniority, that was Trex.

"Please, Stone ... don't make me order you," he said.

"I got this!" Ninja said behind us. "Stick to the plan, Trex!"

Plan? What plan?

"Reverend, let's go! Rooftop, now!" Trex said. Following my training, I obeyed my commanding officer. I vaulted myself up onto the nearest roof. As bullets echoed up and down the street, and bolas failed to hit their mark, I heard Trex leap up right behind me.

1:12:42

The moment we touched down, everything quieted on ground level. Trex dropped to his belly and crawled to the edge of the roof so he could see the road.

"Ninja had an idea: the zomborgs are targeting our power-packs this time. He could tell we wouldn't all make it out, so he gave us the all-clear to get away. Then, he shut off his suit," he whispered. "They're trying to capture us, not kill us. They only bring out heavy artillery when we put up a fight."

"That's reassuring," I whispered back, taking a vantage point next to him. Down on the ground, the zomborgs cleared out fast. They collected the pieces of their fallen comrades and scurried away into the fog down the road. No sign of Ninja, Cannon, or Claire. "Explain to me why this was a good idea?" I said.

"Ninja's suit isn't completely shut down, so his emergency transponder is still broadcasting on an ultra-low frequency. If we stay close, we can track him even through the fog." Trex patched a live feed over to my facemask. I saw the map of the town with a blip moving near the airfield. That would be Ninja. I shuddered at the thought of him being dragged away helplessly by the zomborgs, all as part of a plan to ... to what?

"So what are we tracking him for? Just to get him back? Was all that a tactic to end the firefight?" I asked.

"No. The zomborgs will take Ninja back to their home base. The command center, the one Baxter was talking about."

"He also said we'd be dead before we opened the front door."

"Yup. Switch to stealth mode. Let's go," Trex said. His armor rippled and blended in with the background. I could barely make out his silhouette as he lowered himself down from the roof. I took a deep breath, concealed my own armor and went after him.

The command center was attached to a factory with a loading dock on the east side. We closed on the zomborgs and arrived in time to see them carry our three comrades in through the bay doors. Trex urged me onward; we got right behind the very last zomborg in line and walked without making a single sound. The procession entered the loading dock, and the roll-up doors closed behind us.

"We're in the hive now," Trex whispered.

I almost shuddered at the word "hive." It was a good description, though. The way the zomborgs shuffled around in here, walking in lines everywhere they went ... yeah, it felt like a hive.

The zomborgs kept moving deeper into the loading dock, which opened up into the zomborg factory.

If the crude layout was any indication, they'd thrown this area together pretty quick in the last few days. On the north end I recognized a bunch of transfer cases – metal caskets from the China War.

Next to the caskets was a pile of clothing – male and female, all sizes and styles, including military uniforms. Probably belonged to the town residents, who were now half-human, half-machine. I stayed close to Trex and as far as possible from the zomborgs.

"We need Claire's hard drive," Trex said. "I got promoted to Lance Corporal but it didn't give me her clearance code, and I'll need it to get the engines started on those vehicles at the airfield."

"I still have explosives," I offered. "If we can blow something up on our way out of here, it might buy us time at the airfield."

"Hard drive first and, if at all possible, a silent escape. For now, let's split up. Holler on channel 3 when you find Claire," Trex said. He loped into the factory, and for a moment I felt alone and exposed. I hadn't realized it, but Trex's companionship lent me a kind of strength that I'd been missing. Without him covering my back, I felt ... unprepared again.

I really hated that.

Most of the factory was open, like a warehouse. Long workbenches filled the open space, and zomborg parts covered most of the flat surfaces in sight. The zomborgs moved wordlessly along the workbenches, bolting and welding things like machines on an assembly line, and I realized they were reconstructing their comrades – the ones that had been blown to bits by a certain band of Marines.

It wasn't enough to make these things dead for the second time; we'd have to kill them three, four, maybe five times. I resisted the urge to shed my stealth mode and drop my explosives right here, and level the place. I had to find Claire.

I made my way past the zomborgs and moved deeper into the factory. With two minutes to go, I found a station that made my heart stop in my chest: inside, stretched out on operating tables, were four bodies: Maxwell, Oswald, Compa, and Baxter. Restraints held them around their wrists and ankles, and they had identical junction boxes affixed to their necks at the backs of their heads. Cords and fiber-optic cables ran from their skulls to nearby computers with flickering monitors.

I took a closer look at the computer, and my blood ran cold: it was a necro-cerebral extraction interface, a very rare machine that the higher-ups used on dead Spec-Ops warriors. It could extract information from dead brain tissue within a certain time period.

The zomborgs ... no wonder they took over the base so quickly. Once they got Doctor Baxter's colleagues, it was game over. They knew everything they needed in order to make a zombie army.

1:00:26

I hailed Trex and tried to patch a live feed through to him. The moment I gave the "send" order, an ear-splitting alarm screeched overhead, sounding an intruder alert. A factory full of zomborgs dropped what they were doing and rushed directly at me, regardless of my stealth mode.

Idiot! They had all of my frequencies!

"Reverend, I found Claire – what's happening?" Trex said over the radio.

"I found Maxwell and the others, but we gotta bail!" I shed my stealth, shot the interface computer, then turned and fled, vaulting over a conveyor belt.

A zomborg leaped at me. My armored boot shattered his neck with a satisfying *crack*. I pushed past him and ran back to where Trex and I had split up.

"Trex! It's go time!" I shouted.

"I'm coming, just hang on." I heard simultaneous gunshots, both through the radio and in the factory. He was close, I just couldn't see him.

Then, even louder than the echo of a gunshot came a booming voice that reverberated through the factory, venom dripping from every word.

"Seal the exits! Shut everything down! Find these intruders!"

Just the sound of the voice crippled me with paralyzing fear. I grunted and fell to my knees, my rifle clattering to the floor a few feet away. I pressed a hand to my chest. No good. I could barely breathe. I was only able to lift my neck enough to spot the source of the voice.

And I wished I hadn't.

Baxter had described the Indian pretty accurately: dark markings over his eyes, a shaved head, and a pelt around his waist colored red and brown, with rusty layers of dried blood. He had almost feline features – eyes black but glowing, teeth and fingers sharp, every inch of muscle coiled and ready to pounce. I couldn't avert my gaze, no matter how hard I tried.

The Indian appeared at a balcony high against the far wall, where the factory met the command center. Effortlessly he jumped over the railing and fell no less than twenty feet, landing lightly on his toes. The whole time he never took his eyes off mine as he advanced. With a bored motion he flicked his finger and I felt my legs and arms move against my will. They pulled me into a standing position, and he walked right up to me.

"Your name is ... Zachary Stone," he hissed. I swallowed hard; he'd read Maxwell's hard drive. He smiled and nodded, as if hearing my thoughts. "You are afraid of me, PFC Stone. You reek of fear. I enjoy it."

"Put ... me down ... " I forced the words from my throat. He leered and shook his head.

"You're quite the specimen: you actually have the means to *force* me to release you. You have authority against which I am bound, and yet you have not maintained your power within it. You are lax, Zachary Stone. It is your undoing," he said.

My insides burned at his words. Much as I tried to ignore it, I knew what he meant, what he was talking about. In an instant I felt hot tears in my eyes, tears born of regret and sadness. The Indian spoke the truth. Then he shrieked and lunged forward, grabbing my helmet in both hands.

"Would you like to know how you will die, Zachary Stone?" His words stabbed my heart. His eyes bored directly into my mind, and a wicked power took over me, filling me with visions of darkness and despair.

I saw the town overrun by zomborgs, hidden in an unnatural cloud. The smothering cloud spread and expanded, consuming other towns, converting the population, expelling peoples' souls from their bodies and leaving empty shells behind. Dark spirits arose and inhabited the shells, multiplying everywhere they went. Before long they covered the whole earth and their evil devoured every living thing.

And when they all died out, as mortal things inevitably do, there would be nothing left but ashes and sorrow.

"Your ashes," the demon hissed. "Your sorrow."

"Let him go!"

Ninja's familiar voice snapped me out of the Indian's trance. Seething, the Indian turned to see Ninja on his feet – part of his armor was removed, having been stripped away manually by a team of zomborgs who now lay at his feet in several pieces. Ninja brandished his Bowie in one hand and his rifle in the other. He fired.

In a flash the Indian released me and jumped straight up to the ceiling – four stories, I kid you not – where he grabbed the rafters with adept hands. Ninja adjusted his aim, but not before the Indian spouted a stream of foul-sounding words in a dead language, cursing Ninja with a supernatural power. In response, four more zomborgs appeared and tackled Ninja from all sides.

"*NO!*" I screamed, slowly gathering my wits about me. My hands still wouldn't respond to any orders from my brain. My rifle waited uselessly out of reach.

One of the zomborgs injected Ninja with a sedative. He collapsed and his weapons fell from his hands. The catlike Indian dropped back down to ground level as the zomborgs carried Ninja away to their integration areas.

"Your turn," he said to me, locking our eyes once again. Any control I'd regained disappeared in seconds. I was separated from my body, losing the freedom to move. I couldn't even scream, and heaven knows I wanted to.

And then ...

CRUNCH!

Trex appeared out of nowhere, shedding his stealth as he cocked back his fist to clobber the man with a pile-driver punch to the spine. Several of the Indian's ribs splintered out through his chest under the force of the blow. Trex wasted no time before driving his elbow down onto his collarbone with crushing force. More bones cracked and he went down hard.

The Indian tucked and rolled to his feet between us, bleeding profusely. I heard more bones popping as his body re-formed and healed itself in less than a second. He spat and snarled at Trex, seeking to meet his gaze like he'd done to me.

I tried to warn Trex, but couldn't speak yet. I wished for something, anything, a miracle ...

Trex met the man's eyes, and he did something impossible: he charged.

Such was the Indian's shock that he didn't completely avoid Trex's swinging hand, and consequently ended up with eight inches of Bowie knife in his throat. Choking and gagging, the demon fell aside and Trex pushed past him.

"Let's bail!" he said, grabbing me by the arm and jerking me toward the bay doors. The movement freed me from the demon's trance, and I grabbed my rifle. Trex selected a grenade and blasted the door to pieces. We made our escape with about two dozen zomborgs on our tails. I looked back in time to see the Indian pull the knife free, and his wound closed up right away.

"We need to get to the airfield," Trex said. "Claire's plan is still our best shot."

"Left, up ahead," I replied. Our suits got us there in under a minute. The whole way there I struggled to focus on running – I wouldn't soon forget the demon's dark power.

Later. Right now I had to make it to the airfield.

00:54:32

"Hostiles!" Trex said the moment the airfield came into view. Six high-tech zomborgs waited for us at the gate, weapons at the ready. The demon was pulling all the puppet strings and making sure we didn't go back to any familiar ground.

"They got Maxwell's computer. They can use his main uplink to track us," I said.

Trex brought up the map on our facemasks as we changed course and sprinted in the other direction. "We gotta find a place where we can reboot our suits or we'll never lose them," he said. "Any ideas?"

"Yeah. Follow me," I said. I didn't want to tell him while the suits were still on – with Maxwell's uplink he could even hear our speech.

And by the time he figured out where we were headed, I wanted him to know it was too late.

I led Trex to the Major's quarters, one of the few buildings that would have a bomb shelter with a panic door. Nobody could open it from the outside unless it was empty.

We found the house even as the newer zomborgs dashed after us, closing the gap with freakish speed. Their weapons buzzed and crackled, and I didn't want to guess what they could do. I bounded up the steps of the Major's house, busted the door to splinters with my shoulder and kicked the coffee table aside in the front room. Trex was right on my heels. We burst through the next wall and into the bedroom, but all I saw was a full-sized bed.

"Where's the door?" I asked in a panic. Trex kicked a quick-release handle at the foot of the bed, and it swung up into the wall to reveal a trapdoor in the floor.

"Get in!" he said. I dropped down into the shelter and Trex came in behind me just as a zomborg appeared in the front doorway and fired something at us. It was a can of knockout gas – I recognized the smell. It bounced into the shelter. By some miracle it ricocheted off Trex's armor, though not before a good amount of it got stuck in what would soon be an airtight space. Trex threw a grenade back and closed the trapdoor. From within the security of the shelter, we barely felt the explosion.

"Kill your suit, now," Trex said. He sagged and coughed, shaking his head vigorously.

"The filters," I began, tapping my mask. I couldn't say anything else; my throat was on fire. The room spun and I couldn't force my fingers to stay tight around the handle of my rifle.

"No good ... need air ... " Trex said. The rest came out in mumbles, and we both blacked out.

00:48:19

I lay in a casket, my body held fast by something impossibly heavy. The more I strained, the worse it got, and I couldn't move. My mouth was full of cotton and breathing proved to be a chore. The bitter taste of the knockout gas clung to the roof of my mouth, and dark memories replayed before my eyes. Among them I saw a swarm of zomborgs kill my comrades one after another. As they spread out to consume the world, they made a beeline for my home in Colorado. They burst into the living room where my wife was waiting for me on the couch. Waiting for me to come home.

I was home. But I wasn't me. With horror I realized that *I* was a zomborg.

The demon appeared, leering with his beady eyes and cackling like a madman. *"You could have stopped me ... "*

"NO!"

I bolted up into a sitting position and swatted the dream away, coughing and spitting to clear the taste of the gas from my mouth. With my suit deactivated, it weighed me down. I reached up and hit the emergency release, sliding my finger into the concealed catch between my neck and shoulder. My helmet popped off and I sighed in relief when the armor around my chest slipped open.

"Reverend?" Trex asked in the darkness of the shelter.

"Here," I called back. "I'm ... okay." I coughed again. "Any idea how long we were out?"

"Too long – it took the gas a while to lose potency."

The unspoken danger hung in the air. We still didn't know what would happen if we didn't make it out in time.

"You were having a bad dream," Trex went on.

"Ain't that the truth." I felt my arms tremble at the thought. Seeing Marie's face in that vision was so real, it stuck with me.

"Did you see the man from the factory in your dream?" Trex asked.

"Yeah. How'd you know?"

"He came to mine too. He's not natural – he has a dark power, an evil gift. We can stop him, Reverend. I know how to bring him down."

I paused. "Trex, I saw Ninja shoot him close enough that he couldn't miss, and the guy *still* dodged the bullets. He moves faster than we can hit him with these," I said and patted my rifle. "You even force-fed him your Bowie and he walked it off."

Trex was silent for a while. Then: "What if I told you that I really *knew* we could beat him? What if I saw it in my dream?"

"What?"

"I had a vision, Reverend – a revelation. I know what he is and what he's doing here. I know how to stop him." He groped around in the dark until his fingers caught his belt compartment with the scriptures. "You ever see this before?" He held it up.

Time for the moment of truth. A welcome calm settled over me, and I sensed that maybe Trex really did have a solution to this. But that sense of calm brought guilt with it, because I knew that this wasn't a coincidence. I knew what the demon meant when he said I could have stopped him, that I carried the power, but hadn't maintained it.

"Yeah, Trex. I know what it is. I'm a member too," I said, my voice barely a whisper.

Trex put the small Book of Mormon on his knee, tapping the worn cover with one finger. "Something on your mind, Reverend?" he asked. Funny that he would ask that instead of getting into the important things, like stopping the Indian. Funny that I would answer him instead of worrying about other things, like our time frame.

But I'd spent too much time worrying about other things.

"Lotta things on my mind, Trex. I felt something was wrong the moment we touched down for this mission, and after going eye-to-eye with that ... thing in the factory ... I know why.

"I've been a member my whole life. I grew up in West Jordan. Baptized at eight, didn't date till sixteen, mission at nineteen, married at twenty-one. Everything the way it was supposed to be. I just ... I hit a wall, man. I got to a point where I ... I stopped caring. I didn't want to do it anymore.

"So I quit. My wife kept going at first, but after a while she didn't want to do it without me. I kept finding stupid excuses not to go. And lately, she ... " I stopped because I felt tears coming. Why? Why now, of all times? I'd been indifferent for all these years ...

The answer came to me with shocking clarity, in words I knew well: because I was faced with the truth of my own mortality.

Trex was silent but I felt his eyes on me. I cleared my throat and drew in a deep breath. "She's been asking me to go back with her and I always BS my way out of it. I've gotten comfortable where I am. Now it's too late for me to fix that."

"Are you dead yet, Reverend?" Trex asked quietly.

"What?"

"It's not over. We're still alive, we're still kicking. Do you believe you'll survive this?"

My vision blurred and I had to wipe away my tears. "I want to believe. It's just ... with those zomborgs outside, I – "

"Water that seed, brother. Believe. Whatever you need to sort out with the Man Upstairs, you can do it. But we have to finish this mission. Your wife needs you – and right now, I need you. Are you with me?" he asked. He held out his hand for me to shake it. I hesitated.

"Trex, I looked that demon in the eye. He has a power over me that I can't ignore, and there's no bedside repentance that'll cure that."

"Doesn't matter. Holy men go two by two. Now is the time to act. Are you with me?" he asked again, still offering his hand.

I marveled at how easily this came to him. He didn't doubt, didn't even waver. In a hundred years I would never have his faith ... but to know that, I'd have to live another hundred years.

Hey, why not?

I took his hand and shook it hard. "I'm with you, Brother Brennan. What's our next move?"

00:19:28

Trex opened the small Book of Mormon to a chapter in Third Nephi. "While we were knocked out, I had a revelation about that guy, Kumenihah. I remembered reading an account of his physical description before: it matches the Gadianton robbers," he said.

I knew about the Gadiantons: the Chicago Mafia of the Book of Mormon.

Trex went on, quoting from the book. "'They had a lamb-skin about their loins, and they were dyed in blood, and their heads were shorn, and they had headplates upon them ... ' People were really scared of them. Their appearance alone could probably numb you with fear. At least Kumenihah didn't have any Lamanite armor just lying around."

"Kume-who? You keep saying that name."

"Yeah, that's the Indian's name. It came to me in my dream. Anyway, lambskin in blood with shaved heads and a really evil disposition: that's our guy. He's a Gadianton robber, one of the last of their bloodline. Here, there's something else." Trex flipped back through the book again. "Helaman 6 says that Gadianton's ideas weren't his own. 'They were put into the heart of Gadianton by that same being who did entice our first parents to partake of the forbidden fruit – that same being who did plot with Cain ... '"

"You think this Kumenihah is speaking with the devil?" I asked.

"I know he is. That's how it was put into his mind to come take over this base, this *specific* base. Come in, hijack the tech, and turn everyone into empty shells that can be controlled. He had access to the necessary power because of ... well, he's got an evil gift."

"You lost me there."

"Moroni, chapter 10. 'Touch not the evil gift.' Kumenihah has evil gifts. They allowed him to call in the cloud, block out surveillance ... "

"Dodge bullets, break into the factory ... "

"Build up the zomborgs, you get the idea."

"But why the zomborgs? Why not just kill everyone?" I asked. "If he's got all this power, he could easily take over a tactical nuclear site and end humanity."

"He doesn't want us flat-out dead: he wants our bodies. A third of the host of heaven will never have bodies. He wants to take them and redistribute them to that one-third," Trex said.

I whistled, long and low. "Sheesh, I hope you didn't get into doctrine this deep with your investigators."

"Say what?"

"On your mission."

"Didn't serve. I'm a convert," Trex said. He slipped the book back into his belt. "Anyway, we have to get back and kill Kumenihah. I know how – we've got to do it barehanded. Problem is, he knows just about everything we know. When I pulled this out from Claire's suit, they already had a USB cable extracting data off it." He held up Claire's hard drive. "They'll know that Claire wanted us to go to the airfield."

"Then they'll have set a trap. We can't go there now," I said.

"Yes to the first, no to the second. We can't go because there's a trap, but for that same reason, we have to go there. He's expecting us to try something else now. Springing the trap is the only way to catch him off guard," Trex said.

"Right. He'll be really surprised once we're in his trap. 'Cause it's a *trap*."

"You're not watering your seed, Reverend. Have a little faith." Trex pulled himself to his feet. "In a minute we're going to power our suits up so I can tap this drive – we need the startup codes for the vehicles on the airfield. Once we open the door, the zomborgs will be ready for us."

"I bet they've got more knockout gas up top," I pointed out.

"Bet you're right. Filters on, don't breathe too deep. We'll punch through and run to the airfield. You ready?" he asked.

"As I'll ever be," I said, and climbed to a standing position. In unison we booted up.

00:13:02

When we shoved the trapdoor open we found three zomborgs standing patiently outside. Another can of knockout gas immediately popped into the shelter, and then they tried to force the hatch closed on us. We were ready for them.

Trex and I used the full power of our suits to push back on the door. We exerted so much force that the zomborgs lost their grip and the door swung up with shocking force. It caught the nearest one on his jaw and snapped his neck. He went down, and Trex and I vaulted out of the shelter.

I plugged the second guy with two shots from my rifle. Trex grabbed the third guy in a one-armed headlock and snapped his neck before tossing him out of the way. We ran.

I didn't know how far we'd gotten, but I ran until I couldn't hold it in any longer. I took a breath and was relieved to taste fresh air for once.

"Got some bad news, Reverend," Trex said. "We were asleep for a while down there."

"How long is a while?"

"Well, according to the countdown ... we have twelve minutes until Command blankets this place with napalm." He said it like a weather report. *Cloudy with a chance of fire from heaven.*

"Guess we better call them then, eh?" I suggested. "Right?"

"Still can't broadcast past the cloud. It's Kumenihah or nothing. Here!" Trex pointed to the airfield's entrance. Our night-vision guided us through the fog and darkness.

The taste of fresh air disappeared, replaced with the acrid fumes of jet fuel. I coughed and held my breath again as my boots suddenly splashed through oily mud on the airfield's pavement.

"Trex, what is this?"

He groaned. "It's the trap: they drained the fuel from all the aircraft."

Gunfire erupted behind us. A wave of zomborgs appeared, cutting off our exit. The fog pushed back and our night-vision gave us a clear view of some thirty hostiles surrounding us in a circle, tightening at pace with their shuffling walk.

I laid eyes on the nearest armored helicopter. The choppers didn't have vertical fuel drains, so there would still be some left in the tank. "Trex, this way!"

We ran for the open side door and jumped in. The zomborgs trained their weapons on us; bullets ricocheted off the inside, but we got the doors closed and locked them tight.

"There might be enough gas left for one short flight," I said. "Say, from here to the command center?"

He got my meaning. "Here's the startup code," he said, and beamed it to my computer. "I'm going to see if I can't get these weapons operational. Should have some mini-guns on the sides."

"Yeah, I'll man those."

Trex paused. "I can't fly."

"Me neither."

This was a problem, but Trex was not deterred. "Okay then, we improvise. Wing it, Reverend."

"Bad pun, Trex." My fingers flew across the keyboard to get all the automated stuff out of the way. The controls looked simple, except I couldn't make sense of the pedals. Hopefully the autopilot would make up for it.

The turbine whirred and the propeller engaged up top. The sound was punctuated by the click of an ammo magazine: Trex had one of the mini-guns up and running.

Fists pounded on the outside of the chopper. Bullets still echoed off our armor with no result – the weapons were too low-caliber to do any damage. Using the chopper's external cameras, Trex manipulated the controls to spray high-speed firepower into the starboard wave of zomborgs.

"Why aren't we flying yet, Private?!" he shouted over the turbine.

"One minute to liftoff! Autopilot takes time, but it's faster than I am!" I shouted back. I returned to the middle of the chopper and loaded up the portside mini-gun, clearing out the zomborgs opposite Trex. I didn't realize a minute had passed until the chopper lurched awkwardly into the air, veering for the command center.

"Open the door!" Trex ordered.

"What?"

"Do it!"

I unlatched my door and slid it open. A zomborg was clinging to our belly, but a few kicks to the face solved that problem. He fell ten feet to the ground, and the darkness swallowed him up with a splash. As the chopper turned and flew to the command center, Trex fired an RPG into the lake of fuel that had accumulated.

"You can close the door now!" he shouted.

A deafening roar of fire and chemicals ballooned out all around us; the flames shone through the cockpit windows, and the concussion threw us hard to starboard. Trex and I lost our balance, and the autopilot screamed to compensate. When we got back up we saw the top observation deck of the command center swelling in our window.

"Why aren't we turning?" Trex asked, steadying himself on the back of the captain's chair as collision warnings echoed in the cabin.

"Damage from the explosion. Brace yourself!" I said.

00:06:30

The chopper buried itself nose-first in the window, hacking and slashing its way through solid brick and metal. I grabbed Trex by his tow-handle and pulled him upright.

"Door!" he said. I opened it again and we jumped out, rifles at the ready. The helicopter crashed to a halt. Red lights danced off the walls – emergency sirens. We ignored them. Trex uploaded a blueprint of the command center to his helmet and patched it over to mine.

"There," I said and indicated the factory wall. "That's where he was last time."

"Follow!" Trex took off and led me down a maze of corridors to the second level. We saw labs, offices, filing rooms, a cafeteria ... he found the next turn and we ran into it blindly.

Mistake.

Simple mines protected the hallway. Our radar-detectors didn't pick up any motion sensors or invisible eyes in the vicinity. Just good old-fashioned proximity mines that go boom when you get too close.

Instantly a set of decibel-suppressors plugged my ears, protecting me from the noise. Being older-model ordnance, the payload didn't bust through our armor. That's not to say it didn't hurt like stepping in ten bear traps that are all on fire. The floor blew to pieces beneath us, and if the chopper crash hadn't alerted every zomborg in the building, the explosions did.

Somewhere close, I could sense Kumenihah's dark gaze on me.

Trex and I dropped through the wreckage. Debris buried me instantly. After thrashing around like a fish on land, I broke free of the metal and plaster and called Trex on the helmet radio. No answer.

I signaled my helmet to unstop my ears. I needed all my faculties right now.

A procession of footsteps echoed off the walls on this floor, punctuated by mechanical whirs and clicks. *Zomborgs.* I'd lost my rifle in the fall and couldn't find it in the knee-deep pile of wreckage around me. When the first zomborgs open fire on me from behind, I drew my Bowie and attacked. I hacked and slashed through limbs and armor to keep them away, to protect my suit – the one thing that would keep me going in this fight. A fired raged inside me, and I burned with a primal determination to survive.

I thought of Trex and his faith.

Hack. Slash. Stab.

I thought of Marie, how she needed me and how I'd failed her.

Hack. Slash. Stab.

I needed to get home to her.

Hack. Slash. Stab.

I needed to make this right ...

Zomborgs fell on all sides, their mechanized bodies blending with the debris from the caved hallway floor. With three of them to go, my knife lodged in one man's neck, and when he fell back he deprived me of my weapon.

Whatever. I still have fists.

That brave thought crossed my mind and stayed there right up to the point where Kumenihah got the drop on me. Literally.

The Gadianton tackled me from behind. Before I could stand up, he rolled me over and locked his paralyzing gaze on me.

"Private Stone, welcome back," he hissed. "Thinking about the wife, are we? We'll get you to her soon."

00:01:29

I screamed internally and lunged at him. All I managed was a weak twitch, but the movement surprised him. It was more than I could do just a few hours earlier.

"Interesting ... finding your strength, Zachary? It's a little late for that. You three!" he said to the nearest zomborgs. "Take him to the factory. Make it hurt. Make me laugh."

As the zomborgs pulled me up, the wreckage surged behind Kumenihah, bursting like a depth charge. Trex emerged from a pile of detritus and grabbed the Gadianton by the arm, whirling him around to face him.

"Keep laughing. Joke's on you," Trex said, and he drew back his fist. Kumenihah shrieked and dodged to one side; all of his supernatural speed abandoned him as Trex's bare knuckles crushed his jaw. That's when I noticed Trex wasn't wearing his armor: he'd hit the release switch while he was buried. He wore just his neoprene uniform now, a tight covering that regulated his body temperature.

"What? How? *NO!*" Kumenihah screamed. He swung and missed; Trex ducked and put an elbow into his throat, crushing Kumenihah's windpipe. As he stumbled, Trex grabbed him and lifted him into the air like he weighed nothing.

"Here's a little laying-on-of-hands for you, chump!" he roared. Where Trex's bare hands touched Kumenihah's flesh, white-hot flames erupted and the Gadianton screamed in agony. But Trex, seemingly unharmed by the fire, threw Kumenihah down and drove a knee up into his spine, snapping it like a piece of chalk.

A shock wave blasted out from Kumenihah's body, and I literally felt his power break its hold on me, like I had crawled out from under a pile of rocks. The zomborgs staggered backward and collapsed as the shock wave rippled outward. Through a window at the far end of the corridor, I saw the black wall of fog fade away to nothing, the desert landscape glowing under clear moonlight.

Trex had done it.

"Please tell me your phone's working," he said, not taking his eyes off Kumenihah's corpse.

I tried the satellite phone in my helmet. "PFC Stone to Command, come in Command! Do you copy?" I checked the time – thirty seconds. Was that thirty seconds to liftoff, or thirty seconds to napalm?

My earpiece clicked. "PFC Stone, this is Command. Where is Staff Sergeant Maxwell?"

"Injured, like most of us. We've isolated and neutralized the source of the anomaly, sir," I said. "Mission accomplished, call off the storm!"

00:00:12
END COUNTDOWN

It took a few more minutes to relay a head count to Command; I was ordered not to go into particulars over the phone, but they had re-established satellite and all other surveillance, and would be sending in teams to extract us and assess the damage to the town. Trex and I were to stand by until the teams arrived.

I helped Trex dig out his armor. He suited up, and we headed into the factory to look for our fellow Marines; I led him to the place where I'd found Staff Sergeant Maxwell and the others earlier that evening. Good thing, too – Maxwell and Oswald had got it into their heads that it would be a good idea to pull their cables out, but we convinced them to wait until someone else could take a look at them. We gave them mild sedatives from our med-kits and told them to take it easy.

Some of the zomborg bodies twitched, even moaned a little. I surveyed the darkened factory with my night vision and tapped Trex's shoulder.

"You think Command knew about this when they sent us in?" I asked, indicating the downed zomborgs.

"Maybe," he replied. "The debrief is gonna be interesting."

I nodded. "Guess we'll see. I'm going to keep searching, see if I can't find Claire and Ninja." As I turned, Trex grabbed my arm and shook his head at me.

"I'll take care of that, Private; you've got a personal call to make," he said. My throat tightened with emotion, and I smiled.

"Thank you, Trex."

He smiled back. "Godspeed, brother."

And as I punched up my home phone number, Trex walked off in search of other people to help.

GEORGE WASHINGTON HILL AND THE CYBERNETIC BEAR

George Washington Hill and EC Buck

Historian's Note: The terrible Cyborg War of 1874 remains an indelible part of American history. With the United States reeling from the Civil War and in the throes of reconstruction, Dr. Gregor Schnurrbart and his army of cybernetic minions rampaged through the Southern United States and up the East Coast. Today, nearly 140 years later, the major port cities of America – Atlanta, Boston, New York City – lie nearly vacant, mere remnants of the thriving metropolises they once were. The remains of cybernetic life forms litter the wilds of the United States, and any hiker with keen eyes can easily find a souvenir.

Due to the lack of primary source material from this troubled era, little is known about Dr. Schnurrbart's early history and work. Because there are so few extant records, the world has little choice but to succumb to speculation or open conjecture. There exist in academia those who pass the time perpetuating rumors as to Dr. Schnurrbart's origins (he crash-landed on Earth from another planet, he was a time traveler, etc.); however, conventional academic methods have yet to substantiate these claims.

While we may never know Dr. Schnurrbart's true origins, recently discovered documents suggest that Dr. Schnurrbart may have been experimenting on wild animals as early as the late 1840s. The following account details an encounter between a company of Mormon pioneers and a small group of what appear to be some of Schnurrbart's early creations. This account gives new insight into our ancestors' struggle against the cybernetic menace; if these early prototypes were so difficult to kill, how much more challenging must it have been to defend our nation against an entire army of far more advanced creatures?

This new evidence also suggests that the author of these words, George Washington Hill, may have gotten a look at Dr. Schnurrbart himself. The description of a white, wolf-like animal is very similar to later accounts of the insane biologist, who was widely known to have been afflicted with a severe hair-growth disorder and terrible posture.

George Washington Hill was born in 1822 in Athens, Ohio. Following his arrival in the Great Salt Lake Basin, he devoted much of his time to serving as a missionary among various indigenous Indian tribes. The Nez Perce people affectionately called him "Inka-pompy," meaning "Red Beard."

SOMEWHERE ALONG THE PLATTE RIVER
SUMMER 1847

As we were coming along one evening just before camping time, we saw three bears on the other side of the river near a thicket. Abraham Smoot, the Captain, called to me to get ready and go with him and kill them, as other game was scarce and it had been several weeks since our families had tasted fresh meat. Accordingly, I got my gun and loaded it with a double charge, as I knew the bear would not be brought down by less than that. I also took my pistol, a single barrel, in case I got into a close fight, and went with him. By the time we got started, there were three more boys who had got ready, and also went with us. Their names were Charles Chipman, George Peacock, and Lorin Roundy.

By the time we got across the river, the bears had gone into the brush, so that we could not see them. We had three large dogs with us which we put on their tracks, and into the bracken they ran. However, when they got to the bears they were so astonished they would not even bark at them. As we could not see the bears, we were puzzled as to why this could be. Were they not, after all, only bears? When we got pretty well up to the brush, Smoot charged right up, thinking, I suppose, to get the first shot, but when he saw the largest bear he was almost like the dogs. He was so excited he forgot he had a gun but hollered, "Here she is boys, come and

shoot her quick! There is some Spirit of Devilry in them!" I heard them growl in unison, a noise that reminded me of the grinding wheels in a saw mill.

Accordingly we ran as fast as we could right to the brush, but when we got there the undergrowth was high enough that we still could not see them on foot. I placed a few spare bullets in my mouth so I could be sure of a quick reload. Just at this time the old bear noticed Smoot on his horse and she paid no attention to the dogs, but came for us with a vengeance. This excited Smoot the more, and he hollered, "Take care boys, here she comes, she is a fifteen hundreder!" Turning his horse, he laid whip and away he went with due speed.

This so alarmed the boys that they all turned and ran as fast as they could, leaving the bear and me to settle our little differences as best we could. In the moment of running by me and leaving me to fight it out alone, I thought of Daniel Boone's companions running and leaving him alone in like circumstances when attacked by a panther. But I thought I was equal to the emergency. Knowing my gun and myself also, I brought my gun to my face and ran backwards from the brush to try and get enough way from the dense foliage to give me a chance to shoot. The old bear, in the meantime, was not fooling away her time. I had not got more than twenty feet from the brush until she made her appearance. She was indeed a formidable beast, and unlike any bear I had ever before seen. She had not a left eye but a ruby or red piece of glass, which glowed with a sinister light. Her claws flashed in the sunlight, as if they were made of steel. A series of small pipes or cables wove in and out of her thick hide all down her left side. I could easily see why she had so unsettled Brother Smoot and the dogs also.

When she saw me she was filled with rage and she came for me with all the fury that she had in her, blowing and whistling with noise like a train so that you might have heard her a half mile at least. But there was no time to lose; quick as thought I brought my gun on her and fired. The bullet struck her in the chest and came out through her kidney, knocking her into a backward somersault. To my great astonishment, sparks as if from gunpowder spewed forth from the bullet's striking place. Lightning of an uncanny blue color coursed over her body as she lay dead.

I immediately reloaded, turning the powder out of the powder horn and into my gun while I was getting a bullet out of my mouth for I expected a fight from the smaller bears.

After I had killed this one I looked to see what had become of my companions. They were just turning around some large trees about fifty yards from me. When they saw the bear down and that I was master of the field, they came running back as fast as they had run away, but I was reloaded and ready for another before they got back to me.

We then got the dogs after the young ones. The dogs would fight these. They all three turned loose on one but they could not stop him. He would travel along as fast as a man could walk with all three dogs doing their best on him. Though he looked the same as any other bear, a grinding mechanical sound could be heard when he moved his joints. I went up to him while the dogs and he were fighting and ran my knife through him, killing him instantly. However, I was much dismayed by the shock I received to my whole arm, as if I had been smitten from On High by the Lord himself. I cried out and immediately dropped my knife, so strongly was I afflicted by the unseen power that was in the bear.

The other one fled and got across the river and almost the whole company went after him. Of all the dogs in camp there was but one that would fight the bear cub and he couldn't do much with him. Then a man by the name of Armstrong came close, put his gun close to the bear's head and fired, missing him. He then turned the butt of his gun and struck the bear over the head, breaking the gun in two places, but not hurting the bear any. There was another fellow that ran up to the bear and also put his gun right to the bear and missed him. Not taking time to bring any ammunition with them, and not having any more guns, they had no other resource but to throw rocks at him. Finally Mayor Russell, the captain of the fifty, hit him on the nose with a rock and knocked him down and he laid there until I ran up and cut his throat. Thus ended the first bear fight I was ever in.

The first bear which I shot proved to be an old she-grizzly, with her teeth all worn off. Yet when we cut her open, we saw not the usual guts of an animal. Interspersed in the internal organs were pieces of metal of cunning shapes and lengths of gold and silver wire. No sooner had we made this discovery when a most foul odor greeted our noses, much like molten lead. The smell so overcame Brother Smoot that he had to retreat to empty the contents of his stomach. Many of the she-grizzly's bones, including the left portion of her skull and her front paws, were constructed wholly of steel. The younger bears were likewise afflicted. We found in the skull of the last bear a layer of curious flexible material. Lodged within this substance were two bullets – Brother Armstrong had not missed after all! We could not guess how such creatures had come to be. We knew not if they had been transformed by artifice or if they were the offspring of nature. We dragged the carcasses back into the brush and left them as they were, for no one in our camp could stomach them.

That night, as we were making ready our camp for sleep, there came the most singular looking animal what we had seen. He looked like a wolf with long shaggy hair and was white. Brother Smoot, fearful that this animal was in some way related to the other strange creatures we had seen that day, requested me to kill it. I took my gun and just as it came to the river and commenced to drink, I shot him. When he dropped dead into the river he sank like a rock, and with all the hunting we could do we could not find him. But what he was we never knew.

We now proceeded slowly. Our teams were getting worn out with heavy loads and no roads. We traveled at a reduced pace until we got to the Pacific Springs. Here we met the First Presidency returning from Salt Lake Valley. We rehearsed to them our account of the strange creatures we had encountered. This made them seem very grim, and they exchanged dark looks one with another. And yet, here our hearts were also made glad by their telling us that they had found a good country at Salt Lake Valley. They counseled us on our arrival in Salt Lake Valley, to weigh, put our provisions, and ration ourselves so as to make it hold out until time for harvest.

THE BABY IN THE BUSHES

S.P. Bailey

1.

"What is in the boxes?"

"Knives."

"Yeah?"

"Those are knife boxes," he says.

"You haven't opened them?"

"Not yet. I'm saving them for later."

"You like that part."

"What part?"

"Anticipation. Possibility."

"As in, 'It could be anything in those boxes'?"

"Sure."

"It's probably just knives."

We don't talk for a minute. I watch him sort through ceramics. Each piece is packed in layers of yellow newsprint. He unwraps a green and gold teapot in the shape of a frog. Snow White and three of the dwarves: Sleepy, Dopey, and Bashful. A wedding cake bride and groom. Tiny. Art deco style. He looks them over one by one. Weighs them in his hand. Taps at them with a fingernail. Wipes dust from their eyes.

"Anything valuable?" I say.

He looks up at me. Squints. The sun is big and orange at my back. It bathes the storage unit in dusk-light. Howard sits in my shadow, and he looks at me like he can't make out my face. He wipes his forehead. "No," he finally says. "No. Look – there is a lot of stuff in here – "

"This isn't the unit, right?"

"Where I found it?"

"Him?"

"Him. That's what I meant."

"Is it?"

"No."

"Where?"

"Unit 1883."

"Where is that?"

"Two rows over." He nods.

"That way?" I point.

"Yeah."

Jets roar, taking off and landing. I can't see them from here. This is the Salt City Self Store. Storage units between Redwood Road and the airport. I stand outside Unit 1926 on asphalt weathered to the color of cool ashes. There are seven buildings total. Long parallel cinderblock fingers. The countless overhead metal doors are also gray – the color of low clouds heavy with rain. There are flies and moths' feet up here and there on the tops of boxes. And dust. And furniture shapes – sofas, tables, chairs – under blue plastic tarps. It smells like old people and their things.

"Can you get me in there?" I say.

"No."

"Can you get in there?"

"Not yet."

"When? What about your stuff?"

"They said they would let me know."

Howard is shutting down on me. I need to pry him back open. "Interesting," I say. "How did you get into this in the first place?"

"I don't know. I've always got something cooking."

"Yeah?"

"Before this, I sold juice squeezed out of some tropical berry at $58 a bottle."

"Must be good stuff."

"It tastes like cough syrup and it makes your teeth feel like you've got a mouth full of little pieces of chalk. I used to say that's how you know it's working."

"Working?"

His eyes light up. "You know – it's like '*Let me tell you what it cures. First, I need to know what you've got.*'"

"Oh."

"Snake oil, man!"

"You move a lot of juice?"

"Yeah."

"What happened?"

"Some people get wise. Most just move on to the next thing. The next tonic so powerful you can't even get it with a prescription."

"Huh."

"Before that – " he says. He points at the boxes.

"Knives?" I say.

"You got it. I sold them to everybody. Relatives. Neighbors. Girls on blind dates. My aunt's book group. Parents of old mission companions. Community college teachers. On and on. I sold the hell out of those stupid knives."

"They cost, don't they?"

"Hundreds of dollars."

"It dried up at some point too?"

"I got excited about the berry juice. That and just about everybody I knew had a block of wood on their countertop with my knives in it."

I smile and nod to tell him that I am into his story.

"There were a few other things between the knives and my mission," he sighs. "Nothing worth talking about. Pest control. Magazines. On and on."

"Those are all direct sales jobs."

"I know!" he says. Like I just got a glimpse into his soul, and he liked it.

"Nothing like this – nothing quite so *entrepreneurial* – "

"I never planned to sell forever. I was a good little squirrel. I made me a pile of nuts. Now I am investing."

"You got some nuts in the market?"

"*This.* I mean *this.*"

"Of course," I say. "How do you know what units to bid on?"

"There are tricks. You look at the lock. Is it expensive? Old? Rusty? People don't use cheap locks to protect nice things. And vice versa. You look at the door. Has it been opened recently? Are there cobwebs? How thick are they? Stuff like that."

"Are cobwebs good or bad?"

"It's more of an art than a science."

"Do these tricks work?"

"About half the time."

"Is there money in it?"

He gives me skeptical look. "I don't know! You looking to cut in or something?"

"Relax. You've got nothing to worry about."

"No offense, man. It's just that things get bid up and then nobody makes out but the storage unit people. But sure, sometimes people find jewelry. Or stashes of comic books in acid-free sleeves. Big units can have cars in them. Boats even."

"Unit 1883," I say. "What can you tell me about it?"

"The lock looked old. Big and chunky. I had a good feeling about it."

"How much did you pay?"

"$485."

"So you win. They cut the lock off and open it up. What do you see?"

"It was packed tight. Organized. Boxes stacked to the ceiling. Furniture. A motorcycle."

"What kind of bike?"

"Dirt bike. Yamaha. You interested?"

"Not really."

"It's a nice bike."

"Did you find him right away?"

"No. I was in there for a few days shifting things around before all that – "

"Find any good stuff?"

"Other than the dirt bike?"

"Yes."

He gives me another glare.

"You don't want to tell me," I say. "That's fine – "

"I will think about it," he says. "I already talked with the cops, all right?"

"When you did find him – can you tell me about that?"

"There was a barrel sitting there in front. Plastic. Blue. I couldn't budge it. And it had a definite smell. Turned my stomach. I pried the lid off, and there he was."

"You knew what you were looking at right away?"

"A guy."

"Dead?"

"Definitely."

"And?"

"And what?"

"The guy. Tell me what you saw."

"I don't know! He had no clothes on or anything. He's kind of crammed in there, and he's completely submerged. And – like I said – it smelled horrible."

"I'm sorry you had to see that."

"Yeah."

"What did you do?"

"I puked. I didn't even fight it. Just boom everywhere right there on the floor."

"After that?"

"I went to the office. I told the guy there. He got all freaked out because he said it's bad for business. The guy called the owner, who yelled at him for not calling the cops first, because apparently that is even worse for business."

"You had a phone on you?"

"Yes."

"Why didn't *you* call the cops?"

"I don't know. I was freaked out, and I guess it seemed like the management there should know. I wanted to get myself cleaned up too. The puke – "

"Did you take anything out of there before you found him?"

"No." Howard says. "They give you a week to get things out. I wasn't in a hurry. Then all of the sudden it's a crime scene." He gets up. He tears open a box and peers inside. I can't see inside the box, and I can't read his face in the shadows.

"Well?" I say.

"Knives," he says.

2.

My old pickup truck shakes vigorously when I bring her up to freeway speed. The vibration radiates up the steering column and through the wheel into my hands, which always tingle for a while after I get off the freeway. At least the storage units are not too far from my next stop – a mansion north of the city just below Ensign Peak. It's about six miles. I am going there to talk to Sandy Burton, the widow of the man they found decomposing in my client's storage unit.

My name is Alma Knox. I am a student at the U, but what really matters here is how I pay for the luxuries – ramen noodles and everything – of student life. I work for a private investigator. The State of Utah says I need 2,000 hours of investigation experience before I can take out my own license. As of yesterday, I was at 1,223 hours. For the next 777 hours or so, I will operate under the license of LeGrand McCauley, a gentleman whose recent investigation work is limited to the fairways and greens of St. George, Hurricane, Mesquite, and environs.

I had been out serving papers yesterday afternoon. I had a stack of Complaints and Summonses sitting on the passenger seat. A few divorces and personal injuries. The usual thick stack of debt collections. And a single breach of contract.

I was compounding my boredom by reading through them while waiting for a guy who had been dodging me for weeks. At that moment, he had been in a guitar store for a good hour test-driving every Fender and Ibanez and Gibson in sight.

He finally gave up and went for the door. I grabbed my papers and got out of the pickup. Then my phone rang. It was Zack Burton – a guy from my home ward growing up. Zack is a family friend. He was my Young Men's leader before my mission. I haven't seen him or talked to him since my homecoming.

I took the call.

"Zack," I said. "Hey man!"

"Alma!"

"Great to hear from you, brother. How long has it been?"

"I know."

"Give me one minute, Zack."

"Sure."

"Bill?" I said to the guy. I looked him square in the eyes.

"Yeah?" he said. His eyes lit up. That was the recognition I was looking for. Then he understood. I saw it come over him. He was crestfallen. Game over. I win.

I gave him my customary *You've been served*. I shrugged and put the papers in his stomach. He took them. Everybody takes the papers if you put them right there in the bread basket. Some guys like to throw papers at people. It's a flourish. A punctuation mark. I just touch them with the papers – gently – where most people are soft. The papers pull at their hands like magnets. I don't know why.

I watched Bill walk away with his Complaint and Summons in hand. "Zack? You there?" I went back to my truck.

"Alma. Do you have a minute?"

"Sure."

"What's up? Did you say *Bill* something?"

"An old friend. He's gone now."

"Your mom told me you are basically Magnum, P.I. now."

"She said that?"

"Maybe not in those exact words."

"It's not all that glamorous. For example, I don't have a butler. Or a mustache."

"So it's true."

"It's a part-time job. I'm still at the U. Zack, I am trying not to take this personally. *Magnum, P.I.?*"

"The ladies can't resist Tom Selleck."

"I remember that poster in your wife's craft room."

"Of course you do – "

"Still there?"

"I am not answering that."

"Anyway – how are things with you, Zack?"

"It's actually been a tough week, Alma. That's why I'm calling."

"What's up?"

"Can we meet? I just left the police station."

"Cops, huh?"

"Alma, I spent the last six hours being interrogated. I don't know how else to say it – " His voice cracks. "I'm scared, man."

"Did they charge you with something?"

"No. But they called me a *person of interest*. And they strongly encouraged me not to leave the state. Can they do that?"

"What is this about?"

"Let's talk in person. Can you come to my office?"

"Sure, Zack."

"This afternoon work for you?"

"Yes. Sure. Same place? It's been a few years."

"Yes. Thank you, Alma. I'll be here waiting."

I gave up on service of process for the day. I went to Zack's office, which occupies a corner on the 21st floor of an office building downtown. Zack had his back to the open door when I got there. He was standing at the window – gazing south and west across the valley at the Oquirrh Mountains. It was May, and all the northern exposures were still white and gray and blue with snow. I joined him. He didn't seem to notice me.

"Zack," I finally said. "Hey – "

"Did you ever meet my uncle Rex?" His voice was soft.

"No."

"Well it's too late now. He's dead."

"I'm sorry."

"They found him in a barrel of acid. Can you believe that? In a storage unit. It was my – let me clarify this point – *my* storage unit. Leased in *my* name. I was supposed to have the only key."

"Zack," I put a hand on his shoulder. "That's awful. What can I do?"

"It's humiliating," he said. "People – people in my family – went there to drop things off. I don't think anything ever left that place once it when in!"

"I'm sorry, Zack."

"Except Rex, I guess. Oh *hell* – " He blurts out a bitter, anguished laugh. It becomes a sob that trails off into silence.

I pat him on the shoulder. "I'm sorry. For your loss – and for – six hours? That's rough – "

"Nobody wanted to look at all that stuff packed away in there. Of course, nobody had the heart to throw it away either – "

"There's no shame in that."

"Yeah? Well, I missed some payments on the unit. You see any shame in that?"

"Zack – "

"I didn't have to miss the payments. Money is not *that* tight. I am employed," he nods over his shoulder at his office. "Alma, I keep asking myself – maybe I wanted to lose that unit. I managed to throw it all away in the end."

"Don't overthink it, Zack. Don't beat yourself up."

"It's probably a good thing that I lost the unit when I did. We wouldn't have known otherwise. I still feel terrible about losing personal things. Family pictures – "

"What happened to your stuff?"

"They auctioned off the contents of our unit sight unseen to the highest bidder. Some guy is in there digging for stuff to sell on eBay, and he pulls the lid off this barrel."

"Surprise."

"A freaking tub of acid! What kind of sicko does that?"

"That's where I come in?"

"I am not even capable – I mean – acid? These cops have me spooked. What can you do for me, Alma? I can't go to *jail!* I saw it in their faces. They already had me on trial for Uncle Rex's *murder!*"

"I don't know. I can't promise anything, but I can look into it – "

"How much? It's got to be fair to you."

"Come on, Zack."

"This is your job – "

"Forget it."

"Tell me your hourly rate. Tell me or I am calling somebody else. I need to be your first priority, Alma."

"Are you kidding? You will be. No question."

"I want to pay to be your first priority."

"Zack – if it makes *you* feel better – I will do a flat fee. You can pay me a grand."

"That's ridiculous – "

"Take it or leave it. You can call whoever you want. I even have a guy I recommend when I can't take a job. Let me know."

"Thank you." He gets out a checkbook.

"Put that away. Pay me when you are out of the woods."

"Fine."

"Two things, Zack. First, this looks like a family mess."

"Fair enough."

"I don't represent your family. Understand?"

"I guess."

"I believe you when you say you didn't do it. I've known you all my life, and I will do everything I can to clear you. And, of course, I don't want to hurt your family. But – I just want you to understand – I don't represent them. Only you. Follow the distinction?"

"This is awkward. Does it have to be that way?"

"Yes."

"I understand then."

"Who else had a key to the storage unit?"

"I've been over this a few times already today. I thought I had the only key. But it was a big unit, and I was glad to have people put it to use. My wife and kids have taken things out there. My mom has been out there a few times. I have loaned the key out to Rex himself, his wife, and a few of their kids. The same goes for my aunts and their husbands and kids. My wife's sisters and their families have borrowed the key a few times each. Pretty much the whole clan."

"Can you think of a reason why somebody would want to hurt Rex?"

"No."

"Can you think of a person who would – "

"No."

"How long had Rex been missing when they found him? Where was he last seen? What was he doing? Who was he with?"

"Rex had some convention he was attending. We thought he was in North Carolina – he flew out days earlier for all we knew. Looks like he never got on that plane."

"Tell me about your dad's family."

"Grandpa Burton – his dad – is long gone. Grandma Tillie is still hanging on. My dad has a brother and three sisters. The oldest is Deanna. She lives in Texas. Next is my dad, Lane. Then Rex. Then the twins – Cindy and Marianne. Except for my dad and Deanna, they are all nearby – between Provo and Ogden."

"They get along?"

"Well enough."

"All of them? Always?"

"There is a lot of water under the bridge. And a lot of bridges. We're talking about decades. The usual stuff that happens in a family – "

"Anything in particular?"

"It probably has nothing to do with this, but my parents got divorced when I was fifteen. My dad – he just – I don't even know how to explain it. Something changed in him, and he had to get away. He withdrew from everything. He moved to Boulder. Said he needed the space."

"Boulder, Utah?"

"You know it?"

"Escalante area, right?"

"Yeah."

"I spent a week last fall hiking down there. Calf Creek Falls. Peek-a-Boo and Spooky. Coyote Gulch – "

"Yeah – I stayed with my mom after the divorce. But I spent a few summers down there with my dad. We did a lot of hiking and climbing and shooting. Not much talking though. That's just my dad."

"Huh."

"Anyway, the entire family took it hard. Rex and Sandy – they took it hard. Of course, my mom – I guess that goes without saying. Nobody talks about it even today. I think my mom still loves him."

"Do you have any brothers or sisters?"

"Only child," he said. "My parents wanted more – "

I ask him about all the others. His wife and kids. In-laws and nieces and nephews. Even neighbors and friends. Everybody who might have copied the key to the storage unit. It added up to a long list of nice, normal people. I filled half a notebook with names, addresses, cell phone numbers, and other details. Finally, I got up to go.

"Alma?"

"Yeah."

"What was the other thing? You said *two things*."

"Right. Who were the cops you talked to?"

"Detectives," he said. He grimaced, racking his brain for their names. "Smith and something Greek-sounding. Fotopoulos, I think."

"Did they arrest you?"

"I'm not sure."

"Did they just ask you to come in? Were you free to leave if you wanted to?"

"Maybe, but it didn't feel like it. They came here to my office. Gave me the bad news about Rex. We talked for a while. Then they said I needed to come with them to the police station. Maybe I said something that bothered them – "

"Did you sign anything?"

"No."

"They read you your rights?"

"I don't think so."

"They tell you a time of death?"

"They kept asking about Monday night."

"Have they talked to anybody else in your family?"

"I don't think so."

"They going to?"

"I don't know."

"You need a lawyer. That's the second thing."

3.

That is how I got to the Salt City Self Store. That is how I got here – I look small under the grand arch over Rex and Sandy Burton's front porch. I ring the doorbell. I ring it again. A woman finally appears.

"Sandra Burton?"

"I don't know you," she says.

"I am sorry for your loss, Ms. Burton. My name is Alma Knox. Unfortunately, this is about Rex. I am investigating the circumstances of his death. Can we talk?"

"Come in, please," she says. "Call me Sandy." She leads me through the formal entryway into a large living room. She is probably fifty-five. Still very pretty. Blonde hair and lots of it. Black sunglasses that cover half of her face. And a form-fitting black sweatsuit that would be appropriately somber if there weren't big white letters across her ass.

The entire far wall is glass – a single, continuous window from floor to ceiling and wall to wall. The state capitol building, the temple, and the rest of the valley are to the south. Lights come on here and there. The lake and Antelope Island are to the west. Only I-15 and the oil refineries – countless steel pipes and towers and tanks expelling smoke and flames – mar the scene.

"Sit," she says. "Please."

I sit. She crosses the room and stops at a console table backing a sofa. She picks up an expensive-looking patent-leather purse heavily adorned in buckles and straps.

"Pretty sunset," I say.

"The smog from the refineries makes it red like that."

"I don't want to be insensitive. Can we talk about Rex?"

"I will do all that I can to help," she says with a flat affect. "I am a mess right now, but I do want justice for whoever did this to my Rex."

"When did Rex go missing?"

"I didn't know he was missing until they found him. I thought he was in North Carolina. He was supposed to fly out Monday morning. That was the last time I saw him. They found him on Thursday."

"When did you speak with him last?"

She gives me an appraising look. "Monday," she says. "Before he left."

"He didn't call you when his plane landed in North Carolina?"

"Of course not. He wasn't on that plane."

"Did you try to call him?"

"I can't remember."

"Any calls or texts between the two of you – anything like that – between Monday and Thursday?"

"Again – I – I just can't remember."

"How do you explain that?"

"What?"

"My dad traveled for business. He always called my mom just as soon as his plane landed. They talked every day while he was on the road."

"I guess we have never been much for cellphones."

"Who would do this to Rex?"

"That's the weird thing. I don't *know*!"

"Was Rex involved in anything potentially dangerous?"

"I don't think so."

"Drugs? Gambling? Other women?"

"No, no, no."

"What did Rex do for work?"

"He was in real estate – a broker." She is crying now.

"Again, I am sorry for your loss. I can stop. Give you time to grieve. We can talk later. Is there anything I should know right now?"

"I don't think so. I don't know what might help you. I guess I am *useless*."

"It's all right."

"I just miss Rex so much."

"I understand. Thanks again." I get up to go. She stops me at the door.

"You're right," she says. "I didn't call Rex, and he didn't call me. I'm sure you can get my phone records. Maybe you already have them." She is getting this out between sobs. "We fought Sunday. We weren't speaking. Usually he would have called. We would have called each other – it sounds terrible now that he's gone."

"What did you fight about?"

"Nothing. It sounds very petty now. I just wish I could go back and apologize and just say I love you. That's all I want now. Just a proper goodbye."

"Thank you again, Sandy."

"Let me know if I can help you in any way," she says as I go.

TILLIE Burton – Rex's mother – is frail but sharp. I put her somewhere in the neighborhood of eighty. She interlaces her fingers into a bony knot on her lap. Her pale blue eyes cut right through me as I finish a chocolate chip cookie. It is soft and strong on the baking soda. The thermostat in her home – an old Sugarhouse brick bungalow – is set somewhere north of her age. I am sweating in a tee shirt and jeans. Despite the tropical air, she wears a heavy cable-knit sweater. It is gold and coarse. Her hair is silver, thin, and neat. I think they call it a pixie cut. Think Tinkerbell in a nursing home.

"You say Zack sent you?"

"Yes, Ma'am. I am sorry about your son."

"That's a call no mother wants to get. Did you know Rex?"

"No."

"He was a good son. How do you know Zack?"

"I grew up down the street from Zack. He was my Young Men's leader."

"Zack got a lot of boys out on missions."

"I know."

"Did you serve?"

"Brazil."

"How long have you been home?"

"Years now."

"How old are you, Mr. Knox?"

"How much do you weigh?"

She glares at me.

"A little joke."

"Jokes are funny."

"Not always – not mine anyway – "

"You are still very young. And you have a sweet face. Almost cherubic. Do you even carry a gun?"

"Yes."

"Right now?"

I just smile at her.

"Well really. I do not appreciate that."

"I can't win."

She does not disagree.

"Mrs. Burton, thank you for sitting down with me despite your reservations. I am grateful for your hospitality. Your cookies are delicious. Zack is obviously worried. I am just trying to help him out. The police questioned him for hours yesterday about Rex. Zack suggested that I talk to you. You don't have to, of course."

"Do you have something that you want to ask me?"

"I want to talk to you about Rex."

"I see."

"Have you already spoken with the police about – in the last couple of days – have you spoken with the police?"

"No."

"No?"

"Perhaps they didn't approach me out of sensitivity. You should look into it."

"Who would want to harm Rex?"

"I don't know."

"Did Rex have any bad habits?"

"Bad habits? Such as – "

"Drugs."

She laughs. "I suppose he took something for his allergies," she deadpans.

"Gambling?"

"No."

"You sure?"

"He owned a few mutual funds. He might have been better off playing craps."

"Did he have an ex-wife?"

"No."

"He was loyal to number one?"

"Yes." Her voice goes stiff all of a sudden. She stares me down. She didn't like that one for some reason. "Of course he was. Why would you ask me that?"

"When did you last see Rex?"

"Sunday dinner about ten days ago. Here."

"He was in good spirits?"

"Yes." She expels a deep sigh. "I'm sorry," she says. "I am afraid I am not going to be much more help to you. Apologize to Zack for me, Mr. Knox." She starts to get up. I get the distinct feeling that I am being dismissed.

I get up. "What was Rex's relationship with Lane like?" I say.

"What does that have to do with anything?"

"Please – "

"Zack could tell you that. Ask him."

"I will. I wanted to ask you too. As their mother – I value your insight."

"Things between Zack and Rex have been very cold."

"How so?"

"I mean recently. You couldn't possibly understand. Zack and Rex loved each other. They were very close when they were younger. I just say they grew apart."

"Lane moved away at a certain point?"

"Yes."

"Why?"

"He got divorced. He needed space."

"Is there some reason why Lane had to get away from the whole family?"

"Leave Lane alone. He has suffered enough."

"Again – I just want to help. Zack felt like the police were accusing him of something. Falsely accusing him. Lane wouldn't want that."

"Of course not."

"When was the last time you saw Lane?"

"It's been a while. Last year. I visited him."

"And Rex – when was the last time he and Lane saw each other?"

"I don't know." She stands, eyeing the front door. "It was certainly a pleasure to meet you, Mr. Knox."

"The feeling is mutual," I say.

"I hope you will visit again sometime."

I POINT my truck in the direction of the Salt City Self Store. I call Howard's cell phone. He doesn't pick up. I try him two more times before I get there. No answer.

Unit 1926 gapes wide open just like yesterday. Howard doesn't notice my profile darkening the door. He is examining a chess set. Counting jade pawns.

"I tried to call you," I say.

"I'm busy. I was going to call you back. Eventually."

"Sure."

"What did you take out of Unit 1883 before you found the body?"

"What?"

"Before the cops shut it down. What did you take?"

"Nothing."

"Come on, man!"

"I don't have anything else to say."

"So let's say the cops get an anonymous tip – are you telling me they won't find Burton family things back at your apartment?"

"That's what I am telling you."

"In your car maybe? Listed for sale in your eBay store? Your mom's house? Maybe you already moved the stuff, in which case you would have some cash to explain."

He closes his eyes. He rubs his face with both hands. "What do you want?" he says.

"Tell me what you took for starters."

"I have a routine. I sort things out. Some stuff goes straight to the trash. Some things I move quickly. I have a guy who buys old books, for example. Personal things I set aside. You know – photo albums and scrapbooks – that kind of stuff. If I can track the family down, I let them have their stuff back."

"You give it to them? Free of charge?"

"This is a business."

"I see. So the more sentimental or personal their stuff is, the more it costs them to buy it back. Am I right?"

"That had never crossed my mind."

"Of course not. You are a humanitarian."

"Very righteous, aren't you?"

"What do you have, Howard?"

"The usual. I filled a box. Pictures. Scrapbooks. Home movies. Family history stuff. A silk wedding dress. Some hand-knit baby-blessing gowns. Stuff like that – "

"How much will you extract from these poor people for things that have no value to anyone else in the world?"

"We'll see what the market will bear."

"Where is this box?"

"I can't tell you that!"

"You told the cops that you hadn't taken anything out of Unit 1883. Yes? That's obstruction of justice, Howard!"

"Relax, all right! I have a unit here. It's close – "

"Let's go," I say.

He takes me there. I look at the pictures. Rex and Lane appear together in countless shots – both as boys and as men with their families. They were happy. Tillie was pretty as a young mother – and prim and imperious like she still is today. I flip through the scrapbooks. Countless photographs, birthday cards, drawings, report cards, certificates, little hand and footprints – there are about twenty books in all.

4.

Boulder is about 250 miles south of Salt Lake City. You take I-15 to Scipio. That part goes fast. At Scipio, you head southeast on two-lane highways through Aurora, Sigurd, Loa, Lyman, Bicknell, and Torrey before you hit Boulder. The last stretch winds through sandstone mesas and hoodoos and cliffs every shade of red, yellow, and white. There are high mountain forests on the plateaus above the sandstone and neat rectangles of crops in the valleys below, a backdrop out of some heroic old western.

Lane Burton's place is a small cabin outside of town. The word "shack" probably also applies. It is a white box of siding with a small square window on either side of the front door, a real-life version of the standard four-year-old child's rendering of a house. There is nothing resembling landscaping in front – just rock, hardpan, and hearty desert plants – yucca and thistle and sagebrush. A lizard runs across my path as I approach the front door.

I knock. Nothing. I push the button. It buzzes loud inside the house. Still nothing. I can't see anything in the windows – the white, lacy curtains are drawn. I back away from the door. Something hard jabs me about halfway down my spine. My head jerks around. I see arms (sunburned, strong) and a shotgun (black barrel, walnut stock). I don't get a look at his face. The end of the barrel jabs me again.

"Stay right there," he says. "No need to turn around. Who the hell are you?"

"Lane?" I say.

"I said *who the hell are you?*"

"I work for your son. Put the gun down, please? You are not going to shoot me in the back, are you Lane?"

He grunts.

"My name is Alma Knox. I just want to talk. Then I will be on my way."

"You can turn around."

The shotgun hangs barrel-up from a strap on his shoulder now. I recognize his face from the photo albums and scrapbooks. I reach out my hand. He looks at it for a long second before he gives it a firm shake.

"Good to meet you," I say. "Nice shotgun."

"Thanks."

"How did you come up behind me like that without me hearing you?"

"Never mind," he says. "I don't get a lot of guests. The guests that do come around are invited."

"I see."

"I figure for some people getting a gun in the back is a good learning experience. You will call first next time, won't you Mr. Knox?"

"Yes."

"What can I do for you?"

"You know about Rex."

"Of course – "

"I am sorry for your loss. Some cops up north think Zack has something to do with Rex's death. They are wrong. I am trying to prove it."

"You are wasting your time down here. I don't know a thing about Rex's passing apart from what they had in the papers."

"Can we talk for a minute?"

"Do you have any water on you?" He starts to walk away.

"No." I follow him.

"That's all right. We won't go far. Step into my office." We walk around the house and into some ragged desert brush. We come out of the stunted, spiny trees into the full sun. It is a hot, bright day. The sky is brilliant blue – a color I never see anywhere but the desert. We make our way down into a bowl. There is no trail. Just otherworldly basins and folds and pockets of sandstone. The rock is sun-bleached pink. Almost white.

Lane moves fast down the steep grade, his boots clinging to the sandstone in a way that seems to defy gravity. I follow him. More lizards scatter in front of us.

"Who would want to hurt Rex?" I say.

"Most people loved Rex."

"Where were you last Monday night?"

"I haven't left Boulder for a few years now. Everybody in town will tell you that. The papers didn't mention a time of death. So that's when it happened? Monday?"

"Not sure. The cops were focused on Monday night for some reason – when they questioned Zack."

"Anyway – I couldn't hurt Rex. He was my brother."

"So you were his keeper or you weren't?"

"Cute."

"When was the last time you saw him?"

There is a long pause. "Couple of years," he finally says.

"It's been longer than that, hasn't it?"

"I don't know."

"Have you seen him since you moved down here?"

"No."

"Have you two talked since then?"

"No."

"What happened?"

"Does it matter?"

"You tell me."

He doesn't say anything. He just keeps walking.

"You keep in touch with Zack?"

He glances back at me over his shoulder. I think I see something in his eyes. "I try," he says. "I used to have a World's Greatest Dad mug back at my house. I threw it away because it made me feel like crap."

"Yeah?"

"How is Zack anyway?" he says. "How is he taking this Rex thing?"

"You love him."

"Yes," he says. "Of course I do."

This is where I go out on a limb. "You love him like he is your son," I say, watching Lane closely for any kind of reaction.

"He is my son."

"I know that," I say. "That will never change."

He stops. He turns around. His eyes are no longer sullen or stubborn or self-assured. He is afraid. He fights back tears.

"I looked through some family photo albums yesterday. Judging by the pictures, I couldn't tell whether you or Rex was more proud of Zack."

"I was."

"And I thought I noticed a resemblance between Rex and Zack."

"You have a point?"

"I borrowed some lockets of hair I found in the scrapbooks. Yours. Your brother's." This part is not strictly true. "I got a sample from Zack too. I am having a DNA test done.

I should get the results back in a week or so. You know how it will come out, don't you?"

"Rex was – you don't understand. You can't."

"What don't I understand?"

"All we wanted was a baby – Jessica and I – we had tried everything. Technology was limited back then. We were poor anyway. We had lost hope. We were studying the Old Testament in church. Before that time – there is not a nice way to say it – I thought the Old Testament was – I thought it was *barbaric* and *creepy*. You know – Lot offering his daughters to the mob. Lot's daughters getting him drunk and – you know – and David had a harem and he still sent Uriah to his death so he could get his hands on Bathsheba. And Solomon had what – hundreds of wives and concubines?

"Anyway – we started noticing these stories about infertility. Isaac and Rebekah. And Abraham and Sarah and Hagar. And it was like we were reading them for the first time! We found comfort in them. We knew God understood. I realized for the first time that he is more flexible than it seems. We talked about it constantly. We prayed about it.

"And then I came across something more recent. In 1857, Brigham Young gave a sister permission to choose an elder of the church to act as a proxy to father her children. She already had a husband at the time. Like me – he couldn't – so Brother Brigham married this sister and the elder she chose – her proxy husband – for time. She had two sons. The woman and her husband – her real husband – raised these two boys.

"It came up with Rex one day. He and I were shooting baskets in his driveway. I told him what I had been thinking about. And he offered – he *offered*. Like I said, the technology was unproven and expensive. Jessica and I decided – he was only with her once. *Once!* It was a miracle."

Lane stops fighting it. He lets the tears come.

"Zack doesn't know, does he?"

"No."

"He didn't hurt Rex."

"I know that. Why would he?"

"What about Rex's wife?"

"Sandy."

"I assume she was on board too?"

"Rex told us that she was all for it. Then – after Jessica started to show – he admitted that he never even told her. He didn't think she could handle it. I said he had to tell her. I never wanted it to be a big secret. It wasn't dirty! There was no shame! Why act like it? He refused. Zack brought so much joy to our home. The price I paid for that joy was my brother Rex. We fought about it. We were both so angry. We didn't talk for years. Then one day he called me on the phone to tell me that Zack was *his* son. He said the time had come for him to take his rightful place as Zack's father."

"And I lost it. I'm not blaming anybody but myself. Starting on that day – I made a series of bad decisions. Decisions that ended my marriage. That took me away from Zack. That led me here – completely alone."

"Does Sandy know? Did she ever find out?"

"*I* didn't tell her."

5.

I have three tickets – two signed by Wayne County sheriff's deputies – that say I was anxious to get back to Salt Lake City. I am on Sandy's porch again – small under the grand arch. She opens the door, but only a crack.

"You," she says.

"We need to talk."

"You are not a cop."

"Can I come in?"

She steps back. I follow her into the room with the great views. The temple. The capitol. The lake off to the west. Another red-orange sunset. I sit.

"I have already told the police everything." She produces an SLPD detective's card from her purse. "I thought you were a cop. Then the real thing came by."

"*Everything,* huh?"

"Yes," she says, surprise in her voice.

"I work for your nephew."

"I see."

"Zack."

She nods.

"Zack is very troubled about Rex's death."

"We all are."

"Before he left, did Rex tell you anything about Zack?"

"No."

"Rex didn't tell you that he was Zack's biological father?"

She pulls a gun out of her purse. It is a little Kahr .45. She shows me the end of the barrel.

"Sandy," I say. "You are making me feel very unwelcome."

She lunges at me.

"Hands up," she says.

"Seriously? *Hands up?*"

"Now."

I comply. She pats me down. Up close, I can see her shaking. She finds my gun – a Beretta M9. She throws it across the room.

"Careful," I say. "That's not how my scoutmaster taught me to treat firearms."

"Shut up."

"You don't want my blood on your hands. Aren't things bad enough already?"

"What am I going to do?" she says to nobody.

"Did you study chemistry in school, Sandy?"

"I said *shut up!*"

"I am trying to make sense of the acid."

"I have a master's degree in zoology," she says. Her voice is far away. Wistful. "I wanted to be a large animal vet."

"The acid – where did you get it?"

"South Salt Lake. Some industrial chemical place."

"How did you get it to the storage unit?"

"The barrel fit in the back of my Escalade. The acid came in five-gallon buckets. It took a few trips."

"How did you pay?"

"Cash."

"Give me the gun?" I slowly reach for the gun. She jerks it out of my reach.

"It was an accident!" she screams. "That pig slept with his own brother's wife! I am the victim here!" Her sobs are getting increasingly hysterical. I am extremely uncomfortable with the way the gun shakes in her hand.

"Give me the gun, Sandy. If it was an accident – maybe you can explain one death. Two in a week is more difficult."

"He told me about Zack on Sunday. He was going to tell Zack. He was so damned proud of himself, and he was going to tear this family apart. We fought. He *hit* me. He had never laid a hand on me in all these years. I grabbed a picture off the wall – a family portrait – and I threw it at him. It hit him hard on the forehead. He fell. I was so scared! I shouldn't have – I shouldn't have – "

I reach for the gun again. I get my hand on it. She tries to jerk it away. She screams. I push her hands down with everything I've got. She tries to the squeeze the trigger. It doesn't matter. The gun is pointed at her feet now. She lets go before she can get a shot off.

"I'm sorry," she says.

I raise her gun to my nose. "Fired recently," I say. "I suppose it will be educational to see how much a few days of acid can hide."

She is silent. I call the police.

"Sandy, I don't plan to tell the police what you and Rex were fighting about. It's up to you or Lane or Jessica. If you decide to tell Zack – one of you should do it. And not like this. There will statements to the police. There will be reporters."

I DRIVE down Capitol Hill toward my apartment. I call Zack.

"Alma," he says. "Any news?"

"Your aunt Sandy has been arrested. I am sorry. She told me that it was an accident. I think she shot him, Zack. I will spare you the details for now. It will all be in the police report. If it isn't – whatever they leave out – I will fill you in later."

He does not speak. He sobs violently under his breath.

"You are clear. That's the good news. I don't know – maybe she pleads self-defense. At worst, she is probably looking at manslaughter."

"If it was an accident, why not call for help? I mean – did she say anything about the acid?"

"Not much. Not *why* anyway. Of course – she was destroying evidence."

"I can't make heads or tails of any of this – "

"She never considered the possibility that you would lose the storage unit. In time, Rex's body would have disappeared completely. Longer still, and the acid turns into water. That barrel sits there long enough, and even the water evaporates."

"Incredible."

"I am sorry about your loss. Your losses – "

"Yeah – Rex was kind of like a father figure to me. After my dad left – "

"I went to Boulder today," I say. "Your dad is a good man."

"How is he taking all of this?"

"I don't know. He didn't open up to me much."

"That's my dad."

"I hope you can be there for him. For all of your family, of course. Things will not get any easier as far as the cops and reporters go. For now anyway. But especially your dad. Drive down and see him, Zack. You two need to stick together."

BOKEV MOMEN

D. Michael Martindale

ANOTHER dead heaven carriage. Primewife Eteaki had seen too many of them during the routine interstellar patrols they did as part of the family business. Through the cups of the tendrils she'd attached to both her eyes, Eteaki studied the image of the heaven carriage floating lifelessly in the vacuum of space. The carriage's four eyes, two on either side of its face, stared vacantly with the glassy aspect of death. But its belly still glowed, so it couldn't have died more than a few octals ago.

Pulling on the fleshy ropes she held in her hands, Primewife Eteaki reined Glaittli, their own heaven carriage, toward the derelict. She found the identifying tattoos she was looking for. "It's a Murdzak carriage," she said, scowling at the thought of that race of barely humanoids. "Great Lords, I dislike those people."

"Do you think they had any captives?" Thirdwife Pezeli said. "And quit swearing."

Eteaki ignored her rebuke and sang a command to Glaittli through the transmission tendril attached to her neck. "It's a definite possibility," she said as Glaittli's auditory tendril sang a response into her ear. "The only inhabitable planet nearby is part of an unallied system that's classified *no contact*." She requested more information about the planet. "Standard electronic technology based on artificial mechanisms. Barely becoming spacefaring." She tittered. "It's another one of those planets that some people think is the birthplace of the Anointed."

Pezeli scowled. "What's so funny? *Some* planet has to be his birthplace."

She steered Glaittli alongside the Murdzak carriage and brought it to a relative stop. "And out of the hundreds of planets that people claim is his birthplace, do you think anyone will ever figure out which one? If he ever existed?"

"It's possible," Pezeli said obstinately.

A hand touched the nape of Eteaki's neck and began to fondle the strands of her hair. "What's happening?" Husband Orbanek said. He had been back in the bowels of Glaittli and must have just crawled through its gullet into the rear mouth chamber. With the tendril cups covering her eyes, Eteaki couldn't see him, but she knew him well enough to know that his other hand would be fondling Pezeli's hair as well.

"We ran across a dead Murdzak carriage," Pezeli said.

"Sphincter scum!" Orbanek muttered at the mention of the Murdzak.

"Language," Pezeli growled.

"There's scorching on the hide," said Eteaki as she studied the image that the tendrils transferred from two of Glaittli's eyes. "And some flesh hanging loose."

"Probably a blood feud with some other Murdzak clan." Orbanek's hand lifted from Eteaki's neck, and she assumed that he now sat on the Husband's fleshmound that protruded from the floor of Glaittli's mouth chamber. "Any indications of life?"

"No, but the belly is still glowing," Eteaki said.

"Well ... " Eteaki could picture Orbanek stroking his wispy beard as he thought. "I suppose we should check, just in case. Primewife, kiss the derelict."

"Yes, Husband."

Eteaki sang the docking command to Glaittli. As their heaven carriage drifted forward, she gazed at the dead Murdzak vessel. No glow in its four eyes, no rippling colorations along its hide. Lots of scorching and damage. The mouth hung limply open. Only the glow of the graviton emitters on its belly showed it had ever been alive. Probably the whole crew died instantly from vacuum exposure. Any survivors would have to be in the gut past the esophageal valve. Assuming that hadn't been damaged also.

"Thirdwife," Orbanek said, "do you see any indications of other carriages in the vicinity?"

After a pause, Pezeli said, "No sign of anything. Whoever did this to the Murdzak must be gone."

Eteaki completed the kiss maneuver by moving Glaittli face-to-face with the Murdzak carriage and pressing its open lips against the other's mouth, first extending, then constricting them to form a tight seal. When the connection was secure, Eteaki dropped the steering ropes to the side and removed the tendril cups from her eyes, blinking against the bright illumination from the phosphorescent strips along the membranes of the mouth chamber.

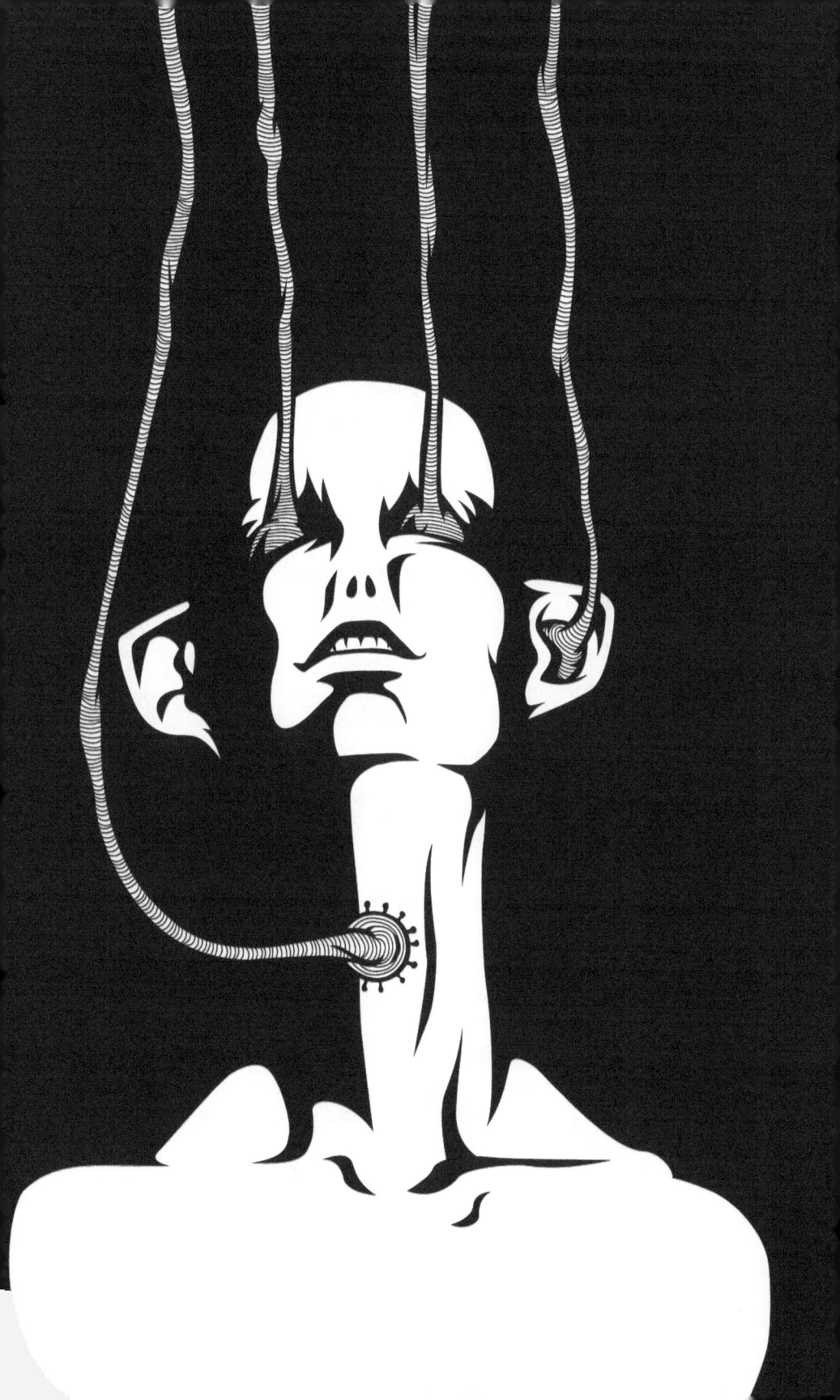

"Let's investigate," Orbanek said. The three of them stood up from their fleshmounds. Their heaven legs – the advanced balancing skills they'd developed through years of walking on soft, uneven flesh – helped them maintain their balance. The three stepped their way onto Glaittli's quiescent tongue, grabbed a fang two-thirds their height, and carefully stepped through the gap between two of the front teeth. Eteaki as Primewife led the way, with Orbanek next and Pezeli in the rear.

As they entered the dead carriage's mouth, Eteaki could already smell the faint odor of putrefaction diffusing into the air. They stepped past the fangs and across its tongue. The only illumination was the phosphorescence filtering over from Glaittli's mouth, since the Murdzak carriage's strips were dark. Its oral sphincter ahead hung limply open, and blackness filled the void beyond.

Each of them pulled a lightstem from their sleeve pouches and caressed them until they purred and glowed a bluish white. Past the oral sphincter, dangling tendrils corkscrewed from the roof of the rear mouth chamber. Some of them were attached to crewmembers who lay still with death, tiny mouths gaping, eyes bulging from their sockets. Eteaki shuddered at the sight of those eyes: huge, deep black, oval-shaped with severely pointed corners, housed within pale white faces that seemed too small in comparison. Six individuals; how could they stand the cramped living conditions? Utterly naked, their frames seemed emaciated by the standards of her species, the Tetzl. They were all male.

"Disgusting creatures," Orbanek said. "Can you imagine, living so long in space together with people you have no familial relationship with?"

"Maybe they're brothers," Pezeli said.

Orbanek humphed in dismissal.

"What is the usual size of a Murdzak crew?" Eteaki asked, stepping between the fleshmounds and kicking the steering ropes out of her way.

"I think anywhere from four to twelve," Pezeli said.

Orbanek sighed. "Then we still need to check down the gullet for survivors. We may not have accounted for the whole crew."

"Plus there may be captives," Pezeli added.

"Yes," said Orbanek. "We *are* dealing with Murdzak."

Eteaki crept toward the gullet until she came to the closed esophageal valve. The carriage's reflexive response of closing that valve with any severe stress had saved crews on many occasions when a carriage died. It kept the air within from escaping when the mouth and oral sphincter relaxed at death. Unfortunately, it was worthless if the crew was caught within the mouth chamber. If the carriage's death was slow, they'd have time to crawl back. But if its death was sudden ...

Genetic engineers had been trying to develop a strain of heaven carriages that would reflexively close the oral sphincter in the same way, but so far they had not succeeded. The seal was never tight enough without the conscious control of the living carriage, and the air seeped out within moments.

As Eteaki stowed her lightstem in its pouch and slipped on a nonconductive glove, she traced out the three tightly closed flaps of the esophageal valve with her eyes. Retrieving the lightstem and holding it in her gloved hand, she touched its glowing tip to the center of one of the flaps and gave the little creature a squeeze in the belly. Its defense reflex discharged a burst of electricity which caused the muscles in the flap to contract. An equalizing rush of air from behind the valve hit Eteaki in the face, and she balked at the stench. The phosphorescence of the lightstem dimmed with the discharge. Her double shadow from the other two lightstems fell across the flaps in front of her.

"Great Lords!" Orbanek said. "We should have told Glaittli to close its sphincter after us. Our air will smell like this for octals."

"Stop swearing," Pezeli murmured. It was no more than a ritual these days, since no one ever heeded her.

Eteaki waited for her lightstem's energy to rejuvenate before opening another flap. Using only one lightstem to open all three flaps left the other two glowing adequately. She touched it to the second flap and squeezed, then the third. By the time the flaps had all opened, her olfactory nerves had become accustomed to the stench.

"See anyone back there?" Pezeli said quietly, as if she didn't want the "anyone" to hear.

Eteaki peered into the gloom down the carriage's gullet, but her lightstem's weakened glow offered too little illumination. "Hello?" she said. "Is someone there?"

Her words fell dully into the air. She caressed the lightstem to excite its metabolism. It purred weakly as the glow increased to normal. She stretched her arm through the open valve and waved the lightstem slowly back and forth. It illuminated the gullet, but the gut beyond remained in darkness.

"Can you see anything?" Orbanek asked.

"No. I guess we'll have to crawl through." She stepped past the valve, then crawled on hands and knees through the gullet. The bluish light wavered back and forth with the movement of her hand. When she reached the end of the gullet, she held the lightstem up and gazed into the gut. "Great Lords!" she whispered.

"What is it?" Orbanek said. He was right behind her.

"Look at this chamber." She noted depressions in the artificial wall below her that would allow her to climb back up, so she swung her legs forward and dropped slowly to the surface in the weak gravity. There was a gentle tap when her feet hit the floor – because it *was* a floor, hard and planar. No curving, fleshy membrane.

Orbanek crawled forward and gasped. "What did those sphincter scum do to this poor creature?"

Eteaki scanned the chamber. It was a box-shaped artificial enclosure – a room – that had been embedded in the carriage's gut. And it was big: the lightstem illumination couldn't reach the far wall no matter how much Eteaki caressed it. This room was built to maximum capacity, which meant its sharp ninety-degree corners must cut into the creature's membranes as they stretched around the structure.

"How did they get it in here?" Orbanek said from the opening above.

"What's going on?" Pezeli's faint voice wafted in from behind him.

"They must have surgically installed it." Eteaki noticed square openings partway up the side walls, exactly like the one she had just dropped from, which had to be entrances to the living bladders that extended from the gut. Did the Murdzak equip each of these with an artificial room too?

Pezeli protested again, and Orbanek slipped down to the floor so she could crawl forward. "How does the carriage eat when they dock with this thing in here?" he asked.

"They must remove it each time," Eteaki said.

Pezeli's eyes widened as she saw what they were talking about.

"Surgery every time they dock?" Orbanek said, and shook his head.

Pezeli dropped through the opening that led to the gullet and peered around, her mouth gaping. Almost in a whisper she said, "I've heard rumors that the Murdzak take each carriage on one journey, then kill it. This must be why."

Pezeli – always up on the latest galactic folklore. "That would be such a waste," Eteaki said. "Why would they do that?"

"They must feed them before the journey," Orbanek said, "then install this Divinity-cursed thing. Rather than carefully removing it after docking so the carriage can eat, they just kill the poor creature and tear this out to use in the next one."

Eteaki shuddered. "Do you think they'd really do that?"

"I could believe it," Orbanek said grimly.

No wonder the Murdzak had not been admitted into the Alliance. Eteaki had always wondered how many of the ugly rumors about them were true. Now she was beginning to think they all might be.

"The poor animal probably ends up with too much internal damage from the box anyway," Pezeli said. "Killing it may be merciful."

The room was featureless as far as their illumination reached, except for some markings on the floor. The surfaces were probably white, because they had the same bluish tint as the lightstem glow. The floor markings were enclosed by a square outline that covered about half of the visible portion of the room. Orbanek peered at the markings, his eyes tracing the lines and curves. "You know what I think this is?" he finally said. "Some kind of game court."

Pezeli gazed at the markings with a new intensity. "It's a smashsphere court, I think. The markings are similar. A little larger than usual."

"I think you're right, Thirdwife," Orbanek said. "Probably some Murdzak variation."

"Is this how they stand living together with non-relations?" Eteaki asked. "A playroom for diversion?"

"I wonder where the sphere is," said Orbanek. "I'd like to see if theirs is the same as ours."

Eteaki studied the living bladder openings. "I suppose we should search every bladder, just to make sure."

"Yes," Orbanek said without enthusiasm. "After all, we're Tetzl, not Murdzak."

Eteaki advanced first, with Orbanek and Pezeli following close behind. The vague sphere of illumination advanced with them, showing more of the same stark room. The floor beyond the smashsphere court was featureless again. After several steps, a shape emerged directly ahead of them, something broad and about waist-high. Eteaki studied it as she took slow steps toward it. Straight edges and sharp corners – artificial, like the room. A table, and with some shadowy figure stretched out upon it. A few more steps and the first glimmering reflections from the far wall appeared, along with more edges and corners – cabinets against the wall.

As the figure took on definition, Pezeli gasped. "They did!"

Eteaki understood her at once. The Murdzak *had* taken a captive. The figure was humanoid shape, the same general design of nearly all intelligent life in the galaxy. Taller and more stocky than the Murdzak, but not quite as tall as the Tetzl. Eteaki rushed forward, followed immediately by the others, and quickly felt around on its chest. In the upper center she discovered a steady thumping that had to be a heartbeat. "It's alive."

"He," said Pezeli as she stared at its groin. "It's a he."

Orbanek chuckled.

Eteaki gazed at the figure. Light-colored hair covered the scalp, cropped fairly short. No beard. Two closed eyes, two ears, a nose, and a mouth arranged on the head in the usual way. Strapped to the table at the chest, thighs, ankles, and wrists. Naked, with skin almost as pale as the Murdzak, and as Pezeli had noticed, male.

And five fingers on each hand.

Eteaki gazed at her own four-fingered hand, dark with brown pigmentation, and wondered what it would be like to calculate in a ten-digit number system. How clumsy that must be compared to octal!

"Another species in the image of the Great Lords," Pezeli said with reverence.

Yes, Pezeli, Eteaki thought. Another humanoid species. Just like the thousands everywhere else.

"Seems most like the Kiryluk," Orbanek murmured.

"No ... " Pezeli brushed the chin of the figure. "He's got the stubble of a beard growing."

Eteaki could see them now – faint, light-colored bristles.

"Not like the Kiryluk, then," Orbanek said. He turned to Eteaki. "Did you get any more details on the culture of that no-contact planet?"

"Not much is known about it."

Pezeli ran her hand around the face. "The beard covers from below the nose down to the throat, and along the sides of the face, merging with the scalp hair."

The stranger's eyelids fluttered, and his head rolled sideways.

"Looks like he's regaining consciousness," Orbanek said.

A soft moan escaped his lips.

"Let's get him loose," Orbanek said as he worked on the nearest wrist strap with his free hand.

"What if he's dangerous?" Pezeli asked, starting on the chest.

Eteaki freed both ankles as Orbanek released the thighs. "Not likely," he said. "He's probably coming out of some drug-induced coma, knowing the cowardice of the Murdzak."

A faint, obnoxious odor reached Eteaki's nostrils. The smell of this species. Every species had a distinctive smell, and most of them were unpleasant. At least he didn't reek as strongly as the Murdzak.

The last strap was flung aside as the stranger moaned again, louder this time, and lifted his arm to his forehead. His eyes opened, blinking against the glow of the lightstems. He saw the three of them and jerked with a loud cry.

"Calm down, friend," Orbanek said soothingly, holding out his hand palm up and waggling it. "We won't hurt you. The ones who did this to you are dead."

The stranger's eyes glistened as they darted back and forth, looking at each of them. His pupils were round, and the irises probably green. Eteaki wondered what he thought of their sulfur-yellow irises with slitted pupils. Members of the Tetzl species shouldn't look as dreadful to him as the Murdzak. But strange eyes *were* disturbing, no matter how normal the rest of the body looked. And this poor creature had probably never seen strange eyes in his life until the Murdzak captured him.

The fellow slid off the far side of the table, putting it between him and them, never taking his eyes off them. He stood staring with some intense emotion tightening his face, then looked down at himself. His face flushed with color, and those five-fingered hands shot down to his genitals, covering them.

The stranger looked around desperately. Was he trying to find clothing? This was an extreme attitude toward nudity! In the midst of what must be a shocking, probably terrifying experience for him, was he really more concerned about being seen naked? The Tetzl didn't walk around nude like the Murdzak, but they didn't get overly excited if someone happened to see them naked either.

"I think he wants something to wear," Eteaki said.

"Perhaps," Orbanek said. "Maybe those cabinets?"

Eteaki moved slowly around the table to the cabinets. The stranger fastened his gaze on her, matching her moves to keep a distance from her. His face was sleek with perspiration.

"Everything's fine," Orbanek said, waggling his hand palm up.

The stranger stared at it, maybe counting fingers. His lower lip began to tremble.

"I don't think I'm calming him down at all," Orbanek said. "Find something quick."

Eteaki held her lightstem out as she opened cabinet doors and scrounged with one hand. Most of them contained instruments that looked like they had medical functions. Medical experiments on captive aliens from a no-contact planet!

"Here's something," she cried as she pulled out a wad of shimmering material. The wad fell apart into three articles of clothing, two on the floor, and one in Eteaki's hand. She held it up; it was a flowing Murdzak robe, the only kind of clothing anyone had ever seen them wear. No one had figured out what motivated the Murdzak to wear clothes those rare times that they did. Some thought they might have a ceremonial significance.

"Here," Eteaki said, extending her arm to present the robe to the stranger. "For you."

He shrank back, eyes wide and jaw open.

Pezeli sucked in a breath. "I don't think he wants to wear Murdzak clothes."

"Look some more," Orbanek said to Eteaki. "His own clothes must be here somewhere."

Eteaki dropped the robe and searched more cabinets. "Look at this!" she said with a titter as she pulled an object out. "The smashsphere!"

"Great!" Orbanek cried. "Let me see it."

She tossed the smashsphere to Orbanek, who caught it one-handed and tossed it up and down, examining it.

The Tetzl version of a smashsphere was a spherical creature with a thick, elastic hide and no skeleton or loose organs. All its bodily cavities were stuffed with impact-absorbing fat. The sensory nerves just under its surface connected directly to the pleasure center of its small brain. Genetic engineers said that a smashsphere creature felt something like an orgasm every time it bounced into a floor or wall or against a player to score. Both players and smashsphere received their own kind of pleasure from playing.

But the Murdzak smashsphere was artificial, with a hide almost as hard as a tree trunk, and with stubby hexagonal bumps emanating all around it. The only purpose Eteaki could see for the bumps was to cause pain and bruising on impact. Was there anything the Murdzak would not corrupt?

Orbanek dropped the smashsphere and it bounced away leisurely in the low gravity. Eteaki continued to rummage. She discovered more clothing – black and white material wadded up. She brushed the wad onto the floor and separated out multiple pieces, then held up one black article of clothing with two tubular extensions joined at one end. The stranger marched over to her, yanked it from her hand, and held it in front of his crotch, glaring. She stooped and gathered up the rest of the clothing into one bundle. There was another black article, two white ones, and a long strip of material, probably bright red or violet. She offered the bundle to the stranger. His glare softened and he accepted it, carefully keeping his genitals covered.

"Perhaps this would be a good time to search the living bladders, while our friend here gets dressed." Orbanek pulled out a spare lightstem, rubbed it, and handed it to the stranger. He accepted it slowly, staring at the creature as it purred. Orbanek turned and headed for the nearest bladder. Pezeli and Eteaki started searching others.

Each bladder opening had depressions in the wall leading up to it that could be used for climbing. Eteaki found more boxy rooms ensconced in each bladder, with a comfortable bed and desk and various personal effects. What a strange race! Comfort in their regular lifestyle, while turning smashsphere into a game that inflicted pain and injury. But she didn't dwell on that thought long. If the Murdzak wanted to inflict pain on themselves, that was their affair. But the pain they inflicted on others – this captured stranger and their heaven carriages – disturbed her. She wished, for the sake of all Murdzak heaven carriages, that someone could figure out how the creatures hyperphased, so they could design the ability into a machine. Then the Murdzak could make their carriages entirely artificial.

When the three of them had searched all the bladders, they returned to the stranger, fully dressed now and searching through the cabinets himself. He found something, grabbed it, and stood. His face looked relaxed. Feeling more comfortable with the Orbanek family?

His clothing was strange, but no more so than thousands of other species. Black outer coverings and a white inner one over the torso. The other white pieces must have been underclothing because they were out of sight. From his neck hung the red or violet strip doubled up with a knot at his throat. He must have found foot coverings on his own, because his feet were black with shiny surfaces. Attached to one side of his chest was a black, square object with curious writing on it.

In his overly fingered hands was a large, deep blue pouch with two looping straps attached on one side. He handed the lightstem back to Orbanek, then slid an arm into one of the loops and let the pouch hang from his shoulder as he hooked a thumb through the strap.

Orbanek placed his hand on his chest and said, "My name is Orbanek. Orb-an-ek."

The stranger studied him, then bobbed his head slowly up and down. "Or-ba-nek," he said with a slurred accent.

Orbanek gestured for his wives to come close on either side. "This is Eteaki, my Primewife. Et-e-ak-i."

The stranger repeated it as best he could.

"And this is my Thirdwife, Pezeli. Pez-el-i."

He repeated it.

"My Secondwife is back on Tetz with the children," Orbanek said, then grinned sheepishly. "As if you could understand me. So what's your name?" He pointed to the stranger. "Your name?"

"Al-da-kirsh-tan-sin," he said carefully, holding his free hand against his chest.

"What a mouthful!" Orbanek said with a grin. The stranger smiled back. Most intelligent species had smiles and laughter ingrained in their genetics. "Please say your name again."

The stranger swung his head back and forth and said something in a rushed language.

"Orb-an-ek," Orbanek repeated, hand on his chest, then pointed. "Your name?"

"Al-da-kirsh-tan-sin," he said with exaggerated slowness.

"Ald-ak-irsht-ans-in?" Orbanek tried.

The stranger laughed. It sounded coarse compared to the tittering laugh of the Tetzl.

"How about if I call you Alda?" Orbanek said. "Ald-a?"

He smiled and bobbed his head up and down. Head gestures for no and yes?

Orbanek pointed at the pouch. "What do you have in there?"

Alda looked at it, opened a flap, and pulled out a dark – almost black – rectangular object. He held it up and used his extra finger to point at the writing on its surface as he spoke. "Bo-kev-mo-men."

Orbanek stared at it and said, "Whatever."

Alda's eyebrows tightened together, and he put the object back in his pouch. He took a deep breath, then placed his hand to his mouth and uttered something. He moved his jaw up and down.

"He must be hungry," Pezeli said.

"Sorry, Alda, our food probably won't be nourishing to you," Eteaki said. "We need to get you back to your planet."

"Yes," said Orbanek. "And we need to get back to Glaittli. The air in here is getting stale. The generator lobes in this carriage are probably about dead by now."

Eteaki held her hand out, palm up, and said, "Let's go, Alda." After eyeing it suspiciously, he placed his hand in hers and gripped. It surprised her, but she smiled back. His grip was pleasantly strong.

The others had already started for the gullet. Before releasing the grip, she pulled on his hand to indicate for him to follow.

They approached the depression in the wall below the gullet opening and climbed. Pezeli went first, followed by Orbanek. As the room darkened with the disappearance of two lightstems, Eteaki gestured for Alda to go first. He climbed until he reached the opening, placed a hand through it, then recoiled with a grunt. He looked down at Eteaki, pointing into the gullet, and jabbered something. What was the problem?

"Everything is fine," she soothed, holding her palm up. "Go ahead." She waved him on.

With a solemn face, he crept into the gullet. Eteaki climbed up and followed him in. Alda's breathing became heavy. When he emerged into the mouth chamber, he let out a sigh. Eteaki was glad herself to be out of the gullet. The confined space concentrated the pervasive stench of death mingled with Alda's odor.

Alda looked around with squinting eyes. The muscles in his jaw and mouth looked tense.

"I don't think he's ever seen organic technology," Pezeli said. "Didn't you say theirs was all artificial?"

Eteaki waggled her head yes. Species unaccustomed to organic technology often disliked being surrounded by flesh.

Alda stared at the walls, the floor, the roof of the mouth chamber, at the fleshmounds protruding from the floor. *And* at the dead Murdzak. What emotion registered on his face? Fear? Disgust? Loathing? Satisfaction at the death of his captors? It was precarious to try to read the expressions of an unfamiliar species. Most of his body language seemed to fit reasonable patterns, but one could never be sure. His nose twitched a little – that one was easy to guess at. The assault of unfamiliar stenches – decaying Murdzak bodies, dead carriage flesh – probably bothered him as much as her. And her own odor? She wondered how she smelled to him.

Alda carefully avoided the dangling tendrils as he picked his way through the mouth chamber. The heaven carriage's teeth definitely upset him, and he seemed to dislike treading on the tongue. The poor fellow had to navigate two mouths. He wouldn't touch the fangs; it was slow going to get past them.

At last they arrived in the mouth chamber of Glaittli. The three of them stowed their lightstems away. In Glaittli's white light, the strip tied to Alda's neck was clearly red.

Pezeli sat on her fleshmound and began hooking up tendrils. Cup over her eye, bulb in her ear, adhesive pad on her throat – each tendril designed with the appropriate connector on its tip. Alda watched her as he moistened his lips with his tongue. Orbanek sat down, gestured to the empty mound next to him, and told Alda to sit. Eteaki also sat, but waited before connecting her tendrils. She was having too much fun watching Alda react to everything.

It took a few more gestures from Orbanek before Alda seemed to understand what he meant. Alda swung his head fiercely back and forth with lips pursed hard together, then pointed toward the gullet with enthusiasm.

"He wants to go back into the gut," Eteaki said. "He probably thinks we have an artificial room back there, too."

Orbanek jiggled his head no. "No room, Alda, just flesh. You won't like it there any more than here, and you'll be all alone."

Eteaki said, "Let me try." She stood and walked up to him, swung her head back and forth in the gesture she thought meant *no* to him, and pointed toward Glaittli's gullet. She patted the wall of flesh he stood next to and pointed again. "Flesh, just like here. No room."

He looked at her without a response, so she did it again and again. Finally he touched the flesh briefly and pointed down the gullet. Eteaki bobbed an Alda-style yes. He seemed reluctantly satisfied and moved to the empty fleshmound, touching it and rubbing his fingers together.

"It's dry," Orbanek said testily. "You don't think we'd allow scum in our carriage, do you?"

Alda sat with a dismal look on his face.

"Thirdwife," Orbanek said all of a sudden, "trade places with me."

"What?" Pezeli said.

Eteaki felt like saying the same thing. A Wife on the Husband's mound? It wasn't illegal or anything, but it violated time-honored custom.

"You're more sensitive than me. Sit next to Alda and try to make him feel comfortable."

Pezeli stripped the ocular tendril from her eye, but stopped there and peered at Alda.

"Do it, Thirdwife," Eteaki said in her command tone. Pezeli's sensitivity also made her more timid. But she was the one interested in other cultures, other species. If she warmed up to Alda, she might actually start enjoying this.

Pezeli removed the rest of the tendrils and switched with Orbanek.

Eteaki smiled to herself, then attached tendrils to her eyes, her throat, and one ear, and sang the initializing command to Glaittli.

"Primewife, head for that no-contact planet. By the way, what's its name?"

Eteaki sang the request. Husbands didn't learn carriagesong, so Orbanek couldn't ask for the information himself. Glaittli sang a response after it had accessed its information organs. "Just a catalog number," Eteaki announced. "We don't know its name."

"Well, what's the catalog number?"

"Raviza Kirkil 752116."

"Planet Raviza," Orbanek announced, "here we come. Primewife, begin the phase sequence."

Eteaki ordered Glaittli to close the mouth sphincter and release itself from the dead carriage, then ordered its generator lobes to step up production to replace the air they had lost to the Murdzak carriage and clear out the lingering stench.

"We could discover what that planet's name is," Pezeli said. "We'd get a bonus."

"I don't know," Orbanek said. "It's *no contact*. We might be fined instead."

Eteaki gave Glaittli the command to hyperphase.

"We can ask Alda," said Pezeli. "Our contact with him has been legal."

"Go ahead," Orbanek said.

Hyperphase began. Alda cried out as his body, along with every other particle within Glaittli, stretched through hyperdimensional space to exist at two real points at the same time. His cry died down when a sudden quantum shift collapsed the stretch. A glorious view of his planet filled Eteaki's eyes.

The Orbanek family had long ago gotten used to the sensation of hyperphasing, but Alda probably hadn't even experienced it before. Most likely he was unconscious when his Murdzak captors had phased. It wasn't painful, just disconcerting, like the relaxing of muscles as one dozed off that caused the sensation of falling. Perhaps they should have warned him. But how do you say "We're going to hyperphase now" in sign language?

Alda chattered heatedly. Pezeli said, "Everything's fine, everything's fine. It was just a hyperphase. Now we're near your home."

The planet loomed in the view that Eteaki had through her tendril cups. She always loved approaching planets teeming with life – they were so beautiful. This one was no exception. "We should let him see his planet," Eteaki said. "Then maybe he'll feel better."

"Okay," Pezeli murmured.

It was fun to see the shapes of strange continents. Each world was unique, and Alda's planet had a huge expanse of oceans, larger than most. There were two continents before her, one above and one below, connected in the middle by a narrow strip of land. The right edge of both continents had crossed the meridian into night.

Alda cried out again.

"What now?" Orbanek said.

"He doesn't like the tendril," Pezeli answered. "He won't let it near his eye."

"Then don't bother."

"No," Eteaki said, "you should get him to look. I think he'll be glad he did."

"Alda, it doesn't hurt. Look." Pezeli must have demonstrated on her own eye. "Doesn't hurt. There's excretions in the cup that soothe your eye." Moments of silence passed, then Pezeli said, "That's right."

Alda exclaimed a single syllable with an impossible sound at the end – impossible for Tetzl mouths, anyway. No such sound existed in any Tetzl language Eteaki was aware of.

"That must be his planet's name!" Pezeli cried joyfully.

"What was it again?" Orbanek asked.

"Irf," Pezeli repeated, getting as close to the impossible sound as she could.

"Planet Irf," Orbanek tried. "Hmm, I like Raviza better."

"Irf," Alda said, but with the proper pronunciation, then spoke a torrent of strange words. Eteaki wished she could see him. She wondered if he had one or two tendrils on. Two, she hoped, so he could see his own planet as a globe floating in space instead of a circle against a flat backdrop. It wasn't likely he'd ever see his planet from this vantage point again with his species' level of technology. He ought to make the best of it.

In fact, she became so obsessed with the idea that she removed a tendril and looked back. He was pointing straight ahead as he talked with one tendril on and one eye shut.

"Attach a second tendril, Thirdwife," Eteaki commanded. "He has to see this in three dimensions."

Pezeli was holding Alda's blue pouch in one arm, and an object in her free hand. It was an elongated rectangle and very thin. She peered at it with her eyes wide and intense. "The Anointed!" she gasped.

"Pezeli, you're picking up our bad habits," Orbanek said.

"No, I mean the Anointed!" She held the object up so they could both see it. Eteaki squinted with her one available eye. On it was an image of a humanoid, much like Alda, but with a full beard and long hair, standing in the air with his arms outstretched and his head bowed. No, he wasn't in the air; he was attached to a pair of milled logs formed into a cross. He was nearly naked, but for some material wrapped around his loins, and blood oozed from several points – from a headpiece with sharp protrusions, from his palms and wrists, from his feet, and from one side of his torso.

The same wounds as the Anointed Savior!

This supposedly uncontacted planet had the belief of the Anointed Savior. And not only that, but they had an explanation for the wounds included in descriptions of the Anointed.

"What makes you think that's the Anointed?" Orbanek asked.

"Look at the wounds!" Eteaki cried.

"Let me see that, Thirdwife," Orbanek said. He took the object and peered at it.

Believers claimed that knowledge of the Anointed had been revealed independently to each planet, but the Alliance had intermixed the cultures of the galaxy for so long that no one could prove such a thing, any more than they could prove which planet the Anointed might have lived on. In Eteaki's lifetime and for generations before that, no new planets had joined the Alliance: all the eligible ones had done so already, and none of the no-contact planets had become eligible. No one could remember what it was like to be an isolated planet. Even renegade species like the Murdzak had enough contact with the Alliance that its influence had permeated their culture long ago.

So where had this planet gained its knowledge of the Anointed? Had the Murdzak contaminated their culture? No, they were too opportunistic. They wouldn't take the time to introduce a religious system into a primitive culture.

Could it be possible that this planet really was the birthplace of the Anointed? The information on this planet indicated some people had made that claim, although so little was known about it, hardly anyone took the claim seriously.

Alda had opened his available eye and was studying Orbanek. "Jy-eh-ziz-kir-ast," he said distinctly, pointing at the image.

Orbanek looked at him. "What?"

"Kir-ast-seh-av-yur." Alda closed his eye and pointed straight ahead. "Irf."

A thrill shot through Eteaki. "Great Divinity, does he mean what I think he means?"

Orbanek frowned at the picture. "No, it couldn't be."

"Why not?" Pezeli said defensively. "Some planet has to be. Why not this one?"

Eteaki got an idea. She sang to Glaittli, then removed all her tendrils and approached Alda. Gently she removed his tendril and led him to the side wall. Glaittli had prepared its flesh to change pigmentation at a touch. She pointed to the wall and said, "Draw a map of Irf. Draw Irf." Off to the side she touched her finger to the flesh and drew a circle. The wall's pigmentation darkened where she touched. As best as she could remember, she drew within that circle the two continents she had seen through the tendrils. "Draw Irf," she said one more time. She spread her fingers and held her palms up near the blank part of the wall, thumbs and forefingers touching, then swept her hands apart to indicate a wide expanse of surface. "Irf." She made the gesture again.

He got it. He drew the two familiar continents out flat, then added several more land masses to the right that must have been on the other side of the planet. These he drew more hesitantly, and carelessly rushed through the last few strokes of the rightmost shoreline with an odd expression on his face. He pointed to each continent and named it, but it was too much for Eteaki to follow.

"Alda," she said, touching his chest with her palm, then pointing to the map he'd just drawn. "Where do you live?" He swung his head back and forth. "Where Alda?" she said, pointing to the map.

He touched the upper of the first two continents, near the right shore above a peninsula that protruded down into the ocean. A spot of color formed. "Joh-jah," he said.

Eteaki pointed at the image still in Orbanek's hand. "The Anointed. Uh, Jyez ... uh ... "

"Jyez-iz-kirast," he said, bobbing his head."Jyez-iz-kirast," she repeated, then pointed to the map. "Irf?"

He bobbed yes and touched the map on a spot that connected the largest continent with another, right at the end of a sea that extended deep into the land.

Eteaki stared at the spot of color his finger had formed. The homeland of the Anointed. This planet, that location. That tiny point in the universe. She jiggled her head in denial. No, it couldn't be possible.

"Iz-reh-il," Alda said, pointing at the spot. His eyes were alight with some kind of emotion.

Pezeli wept silently. Orbanek gazed at the map, then at the image in his hand. "Izrehil on planet Irf," he said with half a smile. "Add one more claim to the pile."

Pezeli scowled at him. "It's a no-contact planet! Where did the belief come from?"

"The Murdzak could have introduced it," Eteaki said, ignoring her own doubts about that theory.

Pezeli's expression darkened even more as she turned her gaze on Eteaki. She wasn't buying the theory either.

"Return to your mound, Thirdwife," Orbanek commanded. "It's time to bring Alda home." He stood, his mouth twitching a little. Eteaki felt sure he was holding back the cynical retort he wanted to express. But with he, a confirmed agnostic, Pezeli a latent believer, and Eteaki ambivalently somewhere in between, family harmony had been maintained by strict respect for one another's opinions.

"Alda, we're taking you home," Eteaki said, "to Johjah."

He bobbed his head enthusiastically. "Johjah."

She gestured to his mound and he sat. She took her own place and attached the tendrils. Pezeli dabbed at her eyes. Orbanek returned to the Husband's mound and handed the image back to Alda just as Eteaki covered her second eye.

Through Glaittli's eyes, Eteaki could see the glow from its belly intensify as it generated massive amounts of gravitons to interact with the gravity of planet Irf, controlling their trajectory through its atmosphere. Johjah languished in night, punctuated with glittering illumination from the cities of Irf. Glaittli indicated that it had detected some surveillance energy coming from the planet, and had compensated for it – a legal requirement when visiting a no-contact planet.

Eteaki searched for an isolated region to land. Alda would have to find his own way back to the exact location where he wanted to go – it would require more communicative ability than they shared to determine where that might be. As they settled gently to the surface and Glaittli opened its mouth wide, Alda pulled the dark rectangular object out of his pouch that he had shown them light years away in the artificial room of the Murdzak carriage. With a smile, he set it on the mound he had vacated, patted it, and said, "Bokev momen." Then he laid the alleged image of the Anointed on top.

Eteaki's last sight of him before Glaittli closed its mouth was as he stood on the ground of planet Irf smiling. He raised his hand palm forward and said, "Gud-boh-e."

When the Orbanek family completed their patrol and returned to their home planet Tetz, Secondwife and the children greeted them warmly. The next day Eteaki reported to Cultural Studies to deliver the items Alda had left – the object called "bokev momen" and the image. Her family should earn a hefty bonus for delivering artifacts from an unknown culture.

As she waited to be called in for her report, she thumbed through the "bokev momen." It was a lengthy writing in Alda's language with a few images of individuals from his species doing inscrutable things. Perhaps it was her imagination, or the way Alda had treated the object, but Eteaki could feel a sense of significance about the writing. She hoped they'd be able to translate it – a tricky thing for an unknown language from an unknown culture.

Eteaki gazed at the image. Could it really be the Anointed One? Had there ever been an Anointed One? She was embarrassed to realize she felt an urge to accompany Pezeli to the next veneration gathering. Perhaps Orbanek wouldn't tease her too unmercifully, since she was Primewife.

THE WORLD

Danny Nelson

And the world passeth away, and the lust thereof:
but he that doeth the will of God abideth forever.

– I JOHN 2:17

"IT'S THE World," said Sister Ma.

They were standing on the sidewalk, Sister Ma and Sister Schuester, halfway between the chapel building and Sister Ma's quiet, clean-smelling house on Leona Drive. Sister Ma was a short, steel-haired woman in a light purple blouse, sensible brown shoes, and a white crocheted sweater buttoned at the third button despite the July heat. She had the high cheekbones and thin mouth of her Japanese-Hawaiian ancestry, and she pursed her lips as she said it again. "It's the World. Like in Lehi's dream. I *never* thought I'd see it here."

Sister Schuester was bigger than Sister Ma in every way. She was a tall, solidly build blonde of Scandinavian stock. She wore an off-white dress with a pastel flower pattern, and clutched a large fabric handbag. There were three flaking paint-prints of her children's hands on the bag. Sister Schuester's mouth, which was used to smiling, was now trembling slightly.

"It's so *awful*," she said. "Just – really terrible."

They were friends. They had been called as first and second counselor in the Primary presidency in their ward, now more than five years ago: Sister Ma, childless, terrified, and reliant on prayer for the smallest participation; and Sister Schuester, her children already entering adolescence, tired, and worried about fulfilling her calling by rote. Their strengths balanced, and each found the other's conversation pleasant. When they were released their friendship only strengthened, because they chose it. So, when faced with the challenge that now lay before them, it was natural for Sister Ma, though she was the elder of Sister Schuester by fifteen years, to ask in a clear, girlish voice, "What should we do about it?"

Splayed on the sidewalk in front of them, its spine forming an off-center pyramid, was a pornographic magazine, bleached and frayed with age and buried slightly in the gritty gravel that strayed from the road's embankment onto the cement. On the cover, where exposure to the sun tinted everything green, a dark-skinned woman drew two fingers heavily across her lips over the forced perspective of one enormous breast, her teeth out, her eyes heavily painted. It was the nipple of that ridiculous breast that accosted the viewer, more than the lidded eyes of its owner: it was what Sister Ma and Sister Schuester could not bring themselves to look away from.

"We should just – leave it alone," said Sister Schuester. "It wouldn't be right to pick it up."

"But we can't just leave it," said Sister Ma. "Someone might come by. Some child, maybe."

They stared at the magazine, as if their joint gazes alone could banish it from existence. The magazine's corner seemed to incline toward them, and for a moment the two women, each in her own way, saw it not as a cheaply printed bit of filth, but as the corner of a buried artifact from some powerful and loathsome civilization, a Pandora's box left over from an ancient evil from before the Restoration. The impression faded almost as quickly as it manifested, but it had occurred, and it guided what happened next.

Sister Ma said, hesitantly, "What if it's a test? What if it was put here to see what we would do?"

Sister Schuester wrinkled her nose. "You mean – Heavenly Father?" The name felt blasphemous in her mouth in this situation, the concept absurd. Sister Schuester had strong if vague feelings about God: He made sick people well, made sure that food was safe to eat, and from time to time helped you find your keys when they were lost. He did not, she was sure, drop pornographic magazines in front of his Saints on their way home from church.

Sister Ma was wringing her fingers slightly. "Or – *you* know. The other one."

Sister Schuester's feelings about the devil were less powerful and less defined than her feelings about God. The suggestion was enough to reorient the situation slightly, however. She grew less befuddled and became more pragmatic. "I think we should probably throw it away."

There was no garbage can in sight. It was Sunday, post-church, and the suburban Idaho street was drawn in on itself as families made dinner and guiltily watched TV.

"I suppose – we could – take it home and – throw it away – there," said Sister Ma. The gaps in her speech were caused by frantic thinking: what garbage can would she use? What would the garbage man think if he noticed the magazine under the ends of greens and pristine white eggshells? And a deeper, barely articulated thought – could even her garbage become infected with this vileness, so that she would never again feel the simple satisfaction of cleaning the house, and taking out the trash?

"It wouldn't be right, to leave it where some young man could find it," said Sister Schuester.

"No, it wouldn't be right at all," said Sister Ma. "Still, I wish we could – just kick it to the side, or something. Or bury it."

"There's no place to kick it to," said Sister Schuester. "We'll have to pick it up."

"Okay," said Sister Ma, taking a deep breath.

"And then – throw it away," Sister Schuester said – hesitantly, because Sister Ma's house was closest, but also because Sister Schuester had three teenage boys at home, who always seemed on the cusp of breaking out in carnality. Test or no test, she would not bring the magazine within five blocks of her home.

"We can throw it away at my house," said Sister Ma, bravely. "But – don't you think – I mean, wouldn't it be better to burn it?"

This suggestion was an enormous relief to both of them; looking back on it, Sister Ma would consider it divine inspiration. It changed the situation from a problem to a crusade. Eradication was a different matter than transference: their souls would stay clean if the magazine no longer existed.

"Well, then, we better pick it up," said Sister Schuester. There was no question that she would be the one who did, now that Sister Ma had given her a way to escape bringing the magazine near to her home. She crouched down and grasped the spine of the magazine between her finger and thumb. "It's *awful*," she said, almost in a whisper. "It feels like it's moving." She straightened, still holding the magazine in front of her. "It's just so filthy." After a moment of deep breathing, she put the magazine into her tote bag, wincing as she did so. "There, now, at least we won't have to answer any awkward questions. If anyone asks."

Kindly, Sister Ma took her arm, and that made the awful moment better, because they were sharing it. Arm in arm, they walked to Sister Ma's house, silent except for the one moment when Sister Ma suddenly said, without prompt, "The World is everywhere. It's so sad." Sister Schuester nodded.

There was a hesitant moment at Sister Ma's doorstep: Sister Schuester had the vague idea that the burning would take place in the back yard, forgetting in the moment that Sister Ma's back yard was a tiny square of grass and overgrown cinderblock paving, visible from the road. If carrying a pornographic magazine would invite judgment from the neighbors, burning one in the back yard might even bring the police.

Sister Ma had already worked through the difficulty. "We'll have to use the kitchen sink. It's the only place, really."

Sister Ma's house had the slightly overwarm, sun-drenched Sunday feeling widows' homes often build up over the years, and the thick white carpeting and heavy porcelain decorations invited visitors to speak more loudly than normal. Sister Ma always felt slightly ashamed of the dampening quality of her home when Sister Schuester visited, not realizing that Sister Schuester, coming from a home filled with the hormonal rumble of teenage boys, viewed Sister Ma's swaddled existence as an enviable luxury.

They put the magazine face down in Sister Ma's gleaming stainless steel sink. The back of the magazine was just as obscene as the front, but the obscenity – other than a red-tinted picture of a blonde in a black lace bra – was written rather than visual, an ad for some service neither cared to comprehend, and that made it less objectionable, somehow. Still, after Sister Ma lit a match and dropped it into the sink, she threw away the rest of the packet, even though it was more than half full. The match burned on its own for a full second, and then in a swirl of yellow the magazine caught fire.

"That does it, then," said Sister Schuester, feeling deeply satisfied.

The two women would forever wonder if what happened next was pure coincidence. For, just as Sister Ma was opening her mouth to wonder, belatedly, whether the fire would leave a mark on the sink, the phone on the kitchen wall let off a short burst of noise, as someone dialed Sister Ma's number only to hang up the phone again. The strangled, abortive noise startled them both; it awoke in both a feeling of being caught at something illegal.

Sister Ma laughed apologetically, placing her hand on Sister Schuester's forearm. "Oh, that spooked me," she said."

But when they looked back at the sink they were horrified to see that not only had the fire gone out, but the magazine had disappeared, and in its place a small, furry creature was clambering weakly out of the sink, its small translucent claws scraping against the steel as it did.

Sister Ma shrieked and closed her eyes. Sister Schuester backed away from the sink, pulling Sister Ma with her, staring wide-eyed at the creature. The beast, now clear of the sink, stared back at them with unnaturally large, lantern-like eyes.

It was about the size of a large cat, and had a long sloping head with a rounded nose, a little like a rabbit's. Its ears were pointed and lay flat along the side of its head. The large eyes were trapezoidal, their pupils indigo. Most disturbingly, its front legs were built backwards, so that they arched out in front of the beast, giving it an ungainly, spider-like appearance. Its feet were round pads, terminated in a complicated snarl of clawed toes. It sat down on the counter, next to a brightly colored statue of a mother reading to her child, and began to lick itself.

"What – what is it?" asked Sister Ma, trembling.

"I don't know," said Sister Schuester. For a moment suspicion and common sense battled within her. Finally, she said the thing that seemed most true to her. "I think – I think it came from the magazine."

From their vantage point, they could see the sink. It was perfectly empty, perfectly clean, except for the twisted and blackened twig of the spent match.

"Changed – transformed – " Sister Ma was mentally reviewing the stories of the Bible for an analogue. Finally, she decided. "It could happen. I think it really could happen."

"It couldn't," said Sister Schuester, sounding as if she were going to cry. "Oh, Charlotte, I don't think it could happen. But – where did the magazine go?"

They drew closer to the sink, to get a better view. The creature stopped licking itself and snarled at them, showing needle teeth. The sink remained empty, clear even of soot.

"What happened?" said Sister Schuester in a small voice.

"It wasn't a miracle," said Sister Ma. "That – that *thing* is not a miracle. So it must be – well, it must be the other thing."

They peered at the beast, which seemed to be gaining strength the longer it rested. Now it was sniffing the statue, brushing the amorphous faces of the knickknack with its short whiskers.

"Is it a devil?" asked Sister Schuester.

"I don't think so," said Sister Ma. "Wouldn't it have tried to shake our hands?"

The beast did not look like it was likely to shake hands any time soon. It was now exploring the rest of the countertop. It had the upright, leaf-shaped tail of a deer.

"What is it, then?" asked Sister Schuester, her voice trembling.

The phone rang again, a long ring this time. Instantly, the creature leaped off the countertop and skittered across the linoleum – not away from the sudden noise, but toward it, gleefully, as if it were a dog and its master had just come home.

The two women screamed as the monster raced under their skirts, and fled to the den to avoid coming near. From the den they watched as the beast pawed at the wallpaper below the phone, making short, anxious leaps toward the sound, as if it wished to answer the call.

Sister Ma had a sudden, heart-wrenching certainty settle upon her.

"Beth, Beth, it's the World," she said. "Think of what they said in Relief Society today, about the many ways the World can gain access to our homes. Think of how we found it – how it found us – and look how much it likes the phone." The beast was now tugging intently at the phone's white cord. "It's the World, I'm sure of it. It wants to get back out – out there."

"What are you talking about?" said Sister Schuester.

"It's – " Sister Schuester put her fingers to her lips. "It's a symbol. It's what the World would look like, does look like. In its true form, I mean, not in the guise of the media or something. That's why it's a monster, that's why it came out of the magazine. Oh, Beth, what are we going to do?"

The phone was still ringing. The World, for that was how both women now thought of the creature, was indeed now acting as if it were caged: it whimpered and spun around in small circles underneath the jangling phone.

"Could it – do that?" asked Sister Schuester. "Escape through the phone?"

"The World can come to us any way through the outside," said Sister Ma. "Anything from the outside – anything at all; the media our neighbors, even phone calls. And if it can get in, I suppose it can get out too."

"Should we let it out?" said Sister Schuester. "We could knock the handset off, see what happens.

"We shouldn't let it out, though. Think of it, Beth – it's trapped here. It can't do any damage to anyone. We were going to destroy the magazine; this is ten times worse than any magazine could ever be. We can't let it escape. We have to destroy it, keep it from hurting anyone."

"Destroy it?" Sister Schuester swallowed. "I – I don't think I could."

"I could," said Sister Ma. "My father showed me how to kill a rabbit. This is probably the reason why he did. This could possibly be the reason for a lot of things in our life. Oh, Beth, this must be a test – what else could it be? We can't let it get away!"

The phone stopped ringing. The World cocked its head, as if listening, and then suddenly scuttled toward the den and the two women. Sister Ma and Sister Schuester screamed again and fled before it, eventually jumping to stand on the low-slung couch while the World snuffled about the edges of the furniture, searching the carpet with the sweeping focus of a dog following a scent.

"It's looking for a way out," said Sister Ma. "Look, there, it's found the TV!" The World seemed especially interested in Sister Ma's boxy television set: it pushed its pink nose against the slate-blue screen and hissed sharply. For Sister Ma, this was confirmation; she was certain, had the TV been on, the World would have vanished in a blaze of sparks and escaped their grasp.

"Beth," she said, taking Sister Schuester's arm, "we can't just run away from it. We need to catch it. At the very least, we need to make sure that it can't get out. What is it Sister West said today about keeping our homes safe? 'We need to face up to the World.' If we don't back down, it's the world that will be afraid of us."

"But what if it bites us?" said Sister Schuester. "You saw its teeth."

"We'll have to be brave," said Sister Ma. "I can do it, if you'll help me."

Never before had their friendship been defined in such clear and vulnerable terms, and it is a mark of how genuine their attachment was that Sister Schuester did nothing but turn pale, nod, and squeeze Sister Ma's hand where it rested on her arm.

They stepped down from the couch. The World, as if catching some hint of their intent, turned and snarled at them. Sister Ma stepped slightly back; Sister Schuester stepped slightly forward. Connected as they were the action unbalanced them somewhat, and the World took that moment of uncertainty to skitter away back into the kitchen.

"The computer!" said Sister Ma, and the two women broke apart, to chase after the World.

The World was indeed sniffing around the computer, a white rectangle of modernity looking out of place on Sister Ma's ancient cherry credenza. "Shoo!" said Sister Ma shrilly, shaking her hands at the World a good six feet away from it: to both her and Sister Schuester's surprise the World *did* shoo, and leapt to a nearby bookshelf, where it ran down the length of a free-standing shelf, scattering church books as it did so.

"It's afraid of us!" said Sister Ma triumphantly as she got on hands and knees to yank the power cord of the computer from the wall. The computer died in a staticky moan. "We can catch it, Beth – look at it run!"

The World was now tearing through the house like an insane thing, thundering from room to room and leaping to any surface large enough to support it: countertops, window ledges, the top of the refrigerator. Things tumbled to the ground as it passed, thudding dully into the thick white carpet like rotten fruit.

Sister Schuester followed it, her instincts honed after years of chasing children in spaces that, for her, were claustrophobic. At last she cornered it in the living room, where the World darted from behind couches and chairs, and once made a quick but failed attempt to scale the curtains.

Sister Ma came up behind Sister Schuster, a large knife in her hand. "Can you pin it down?" she asked.

Sister Schuester thought she had just seen the World disappear behind the couch; gathering her breath, she crouched down between the chair and the couch and peered carefully around the edge of the sofa's back.

The World, however, was in fact on the other side of the chair, and as Sister Schuester leaned to look behind the couch it burst from the other side of the chair, just inches from Sister Schuester's face. Sister Schuester pounced, knocking the World over, and, in the next second, pinning it with her weight.

Sister Schuester held the struggling beast down, her large pink hands securing its odd legs and its twitching, clawed toes. She could not help noticing that the monster was warm-blooded, and that its fur was wiry with the slightest curl, like a setter's.

Sister Ma kneeled next to her, set the point of the knife in the carpet next to the World's neck. The World looked up at them both with large, terrified eyes.

"It's for the best," said Sister Ma, and drove the knife down through the World's neck with a heavy crunch, leaning with her whole weight.

For a moment, the two women sat kneeling next to each other, their heads nearly touching, their hands still on the World, the dark blood from the severed head staining the white carpet in a pool about their knees. And then Sister Schuester began to laugh, a low laugh shaking with relief. Sister Ma joined in. For nearly five minutes, they clutched each other, their foreheads pressed together, laughing helplessly. Their souls had never felt so pristine.

The next morning, an unusually rosy Sister Schuester rang Sister Ma's doorbell, balancing a plate of lemon cookies, a bucket, and a newspaper clipping on the best way to remove bloodstains from white carpeting.

WATER SPOTS

Terresa Wellborn

In my bathroom sink
there are faces
in the water spots
between toothpaste and spit.

Today it is a two-headed woman

bleeding water.

Hair dripping in wet needles,
retracting lips,

her jaw unhinges,
a splintered door;
she eats her own,
shared heart.

I watch her,
transfixed,
an avalanche of tears,
a celestial scream,
slipping down the mouth of the drain.

A LETTER FROM THE FIELD

James Paul Crockett

DEAR Mom and Dad,

I can't believe it's been only a week since I left the MTC. So much has happened. It's P-Day, and my companion is snoring on his cot, so I thought I'd take a minute to write home and let you know how I'm doing.

After eight weeks learning Troll, we were finally on our way! The trip out here wasn't as bad as I expected, although I started to think the tunnel would never end. A couple of office missionaries were waiting for us at the station, and they drove us to the burrow of the mission president. We took a nap, and then ate dinner with the mission president, his wife, and their family. The dinner was pretty good – although it took me a few minutes to work up my nerve to try wild ground sloth, the native food. Elder Johannsen, my companion from the MTC, said that he wasn't used to meat quite that rare. At least the president's wife didn't make us catch and skin the dinner ourselves.

After that, we met our new companions, said our goodbyes, and went off to our respective burrows. Ours more resembles a pit than the warm and cozy burrows described in cultural orientation. My companion told me that it used to be a lot bigger before two of the rooms caved in. The elder who was here before me started missing the sky – some people go a bit loopy after a few months – so he poked at the ceiling with a stick until it all came down on him. Fortunately, the locals are used to cave-ins, and they had him out in just a few minutes. It's good that our burrow is right underneath a fairly busy tunnel, otherwise it might have taken a while before anyone noticed.

In any case, the zone leader has asked the other missionaries to help us excavate our other two rooms this Saturday. That should give us a bit more room. I guess the folding shovel on my list will come in handy after all.

We went out the next day to meet the members. I learned several words and phrases in the MTC, but since the members can't understand me yet, my companion does almost all the talking. We spent some time with an inactive sister, Sister Beglg. She's struggling with her testimony, and asks a lot of really hard questions. They might seem like easy questions to you or me, but not to trolls. For example, she has a problem with the brass plates. There are twenty-seven different words in Troll for 'brass,' and I guess the early translators picked the wrong one. Sister Beglg says that the plates couldn't possibly have been made out of 'fluggten.' Any child knows that you can't hammer 'fluggten' flat enough to make plates. So my companion had to explain that that's not really the point of the story, and besides, the up-dated translation should be out in a year or two. Until then, he told her to just have faith.

Sister Beglg also has issues with Laman and Lemuel. Why did they have to be so rebellious? Why couldn't they just obey Nephi? After all, he was the youngest, wasn't he? The word for 'oldest child' in Troll is the same as the word for 'proto-type.' It's kind of shameful, in my opinion, seeing little kids bossing around their older siblings, but my companion says that I'll get used to it. He says he plans to raise his kids that way.

Sister Beglg said that one part of the book really moved her, though. She said that it was such a blessing that the Lord sent those robbers so that Nephi would stop cooking the women's food. She says it's bad enough that they had to lose all their money without having to eat burnt food too.

Well, my companion's waking up, and I'm supposed to go catch dinner. I'll write again soon.

Your son,
"Elder" Jake

LET THE MOUNTAINS TREMBLE FOR ADONIHA HAS FALLEN

Steven L. Peck

EARTH, azure in brightly lit Leo, was setting in the West on the remembrance day of this, The Prophet's 1900th birthday. From highlands on the flanks of Albor Tholus, Sir Santos scanned his holdings. A light breeze brought the scent of lush grasses and wildflowers, imbuing the air with a sense of home and familiarity, a strange contrast to the burden now oppressing him. He scowled dismally as he dismounted his black war cor to seek solace from his Heavenly Father. The light from Phobos and Deimos softly disclosed his well-tended lands stretching into the distance – a patchwork of crops, windbreaks, and pasture. To the Northeast, Elysium Mons rose to dominate the horizon. To the east he could clearly make out his white frame house, which even at this distance radiated a warm glow that he knew masked the bustling preparations for tomorrow's Christmas Eve celebrations. Underlying the radiance of the lanterns illuminating the windows, joyous activities were underway – presents were being wrapped, decorations were being made and put up on the tree by the children, and, best of all, a delicious meal of salmon ludfisk and new red potatoes was likely being just pulled from the oven. Further in the distance, kilometers past his house, the Temple of Salt Lake Mons soared above the plains awash in bright white lights, each

situated such that the holy edifice seemed to rise above the grassy plains like a vision of heaven itself. Although it was over twenty kilometers away it seemed so present he could discern the hovering spirit that animated the sacred edifice. Holiness seemed to dance through the air around it. Could all this soon be lost?

He turned his gaze a little higher where Earth readied to follow the sun below the horizon. Not long ago, Saturn had risen bright and cold in the East, but it was toward the blue planet, where Joseph Smith had been born nineteen hundred years ago this very day, that the knight directed his gaze. As the blue planet prepared to touch the western horizon, he pulled his worn copy of the Book of Mormon from the saddlebag. The celebrations of the next two days of Christmas would necessitate his presence and here, alone in his pastures, at this awful day's end, would likely be his only chance to pay his devotions properly. Lady Santos would expect him to help with the dodo, his children would demand that he attend at the opening of the presents, and at the end of the day he would be expected to pass out gifts to those he held in stewardship. Phobos shined high in the sky, and he smiled sadly as the Earth finally touched the horizon. He loosed his large broad sword and placed it on the ground in front of him as he kneeled uncomfortably on the grassy ground. It was a bit old fashioned perhaps, but like his father, he would never pray while wearing a weapon. His cor gave a stamp and began pulling on the sweet grass growing on the mountain's flanks, its muzzle glowing white in the dancing light of the virgin's lamp he had carefully placed on the ground. As the knight positioned himself on the ground, he caught the twist of the cor's head as it turned curiously to see what his master was about, but then just as quickly returned to its business with the forage.

He opened the book to Helaman, where it described the visit of the preexistent spirit of the Lord Jesus to Nephi, the ancient American prophet, on the night before the Savior was born in Bethlehem on Earth. Strangely, here Lord Santos was, nearly thirty-seven hundred years after that event. The auspicious signs brought him a deep feeling of meaning. The portends were immense: Earth setting in Leo – his own sign; it was exactly nineteen hundred years since the birth of The Prophet; and it was one hundred and twenty years since his own birth; again on this very night.

The sky was cloudless and a soft breeze whispered in the grass as Earth slipped beneath the horizon. As Sir Joseph Kimball Santos began to pray, he discovered for the first time since his marriage he was deeply frightened. It was not for himself, he knew, that fear crept into his stout heart, but for all that he saw below him, for all that he had given his life, and all that he loved – for Earth had awakened from her long sleep.

The message had come that morning.

"Lord Santos, greetings." The messenger was dressed in the bright red and yellow

LET THE MOUNTAINS TREMBLE FOR ADONIHA HAS FALLEN
STEVEN L. PECK

livery of New Zion and was obviously from the Brethren. He was riding a skittish pony that kept turning impatient circles as he spoke and despite the man's official demeanor he betrayed a panicky nervousness. "I come from Elder Whitehead. He bids you come at once to council." The harried man seemed breathless and made as if to spur on after delivering his message.

"Hold, good fellow. Why are the Twelve Apostles calling a council on The Prophet Joseph's Remembrance Day? Tomorrow is Christmas Eve!" However, the anxious man only stopped his retiring pony long enough to turn and call back. "I don't know. But they bid me gather all the Seventy in a day's ride. Excuse me, I must be on my way."

Sir Santos grumbled. He was about to dispatch a dodo for the Christmas dinner and he knew Lady Santos would not want a servant to kill a bird for the feast of the Lord's birth. She was a woman with strong ideas about tradition.

"Thomas!" A man stepped out from an outbuilding and the knight called him over. "Kill this bird and tell your mistress that it was I that done it proper. There will be an extra Brigham in your pocket if you do it right."

"Yes, Sir." The man could not hide his smile. Lord Santos, considering the man more closely, fished a blueglass coin out of this purse as he mounted his cor to ride to the city, and tossed it to the servant. "Here. Take it now, buy your lady something nice for Christmas." The man doffed his hat and the knight spurred his mount into motion.

THE CITY was not far, but the traffic was terrible. Carriages and hansoms were all over the muddy, rutted road. Merchants' wagons were clogging every path into the city and a fair number of arguments were to be heard among the teeming holiday throng despite the demands of the season for kindness and tolerance. When he reached the Church Palace Building he found the place abuzz with activity. Other knights, mostly of lesser houses but nevertheless members of the Council of the Seventy, were arriving and hurrying inside, exchanging confused glances as if to ask, "What's this about?"

He handed the reins to a groom and marched up the red sandstone steps to the large building that housed the rulers of the planet: The First Presidency and the Council of the Twelve Apostles of the Church of Jesus Christ of Martian Saints.

Sir Santos was surprised to see Elder Whitehead waiting at the top of the steps. This Apostle was known for his no-nonsense tendency to keep others waiting and to offer no apology for making himself the most important item on the agenda. To find him waiting ashen-faced at the steps was unsettling in the least.

"Sir Santos! Good. Good. Come with me. I need to speak with you before the council is gathered.

"Your Grace. What is going on? Has another apostate risen? If so, we'll have him buried head first in ... "

Elder Whitehead mopped his face with a bright green handkerchief and held up his other hand to silence him. "Come with me. It may be that the last days are upon us."

The tightness in the apostle's voice disturbed the knight even more than his pale face and labored breathing. This was a man who, Sir Santos would have bet, feared no one but the Lord Jesus himself or maybe the Angel Moroni, but his palpable worry was so unsettling that he followed the Apostle in silence.

They began descending steps into a part of Holy Palace that Sir Santos did not even know existed. Three times, they passed palace guards dressed in white tunics and green kilts who let them pass without question upon recognizing the apostle, but scowled suspiciously at Sir Santos. These guards were large and well-muscled, to the point they might rightly be called giants. Sir Santos eyed them suspiciously. There was something odd about these guards.

As they descended into deeper layers of the ancient structure, the rough-hewn red rock gave way to ... could it be? Metal? Sir Santos shook off the thought. It certainly had a metal-like texture, but it could not be metal. The sound of their footsteps switched from dull thuds to a strange hollow ringing. Soon, there could be no doubt, metal doors lined the passageways. They stopped at one.

Sir Santos stared in wonder. Iron? Tin? So much in one place! And to make a door of it seemed an obscene waste. A window glazed with frosted glass disclosed a bright light within. The knight looked down in wonder at the apostle who stood catching his breath from the long climb down the stairs. What was this about?

"Sir Santos," the Elder began. "What I'm about to show you, you must make an oath never to reveal. I place you under a most sacred vow, as binding as any you have made in the House of the Lord. Do you understand?"

The knight nodded, bowed his head, and said, "I understand."

"The Church Palace was built upon the great structures that our forefathers constructed upon coming to this world. Their knowledge was great, and to our regret the knowledge of their craft is long gone. However, there is one charge we have not neglected."

He opened the door. The room was enormous. Its walls were banked with strange metallic devices. Rare plastic artifacts were everywhere, and strange box-like structures arrayed carefully on tables. The objects scattered about the room were so foreign and otherworldly that for a second the knight thought he might have entered into God's realm itself. The lamps were not so much lit as they were brightly aglow – not a flicker of flame to be seen in their iridescence.

His heart was racing and it took a moment before he realized that they were not alone. Seated at a desk was a mousy man dressed in the white tunic, tie, and black trousers that made up the uniform of the Palace: one of the Church servants.

"Brother Sen, have the voices continued?" The despair in the Elder Whitehead's voice was palpable.

The man looked up, startled, as if he had not noticed the noisy entrance of the two men. "Yes, my Lord. I have discovered other voices. As I spin the 'knob of searching' I find even more.

"Come, let us hear it."

The man nodded and pulled from the box the smooth black cord that ran from the box to a set of earmuffs on his head. A strange voice filled the room, a voice clear as if someone had just joined the conversation. Yet the words were incomprehensible and demon-like. A voice from Hell, it seemed to Sir Santos, filled with harsh consonants and breathy vowels. Sir Santos had never been afraid of anything in his life, but he felt the hairs on the back of his head rise as a chill spread across his shoulders.

"Dear Heavenly Mother. What is that?" he squeaked.

The apostle grabbed him by the arm. "Swear not in this place! Do you want to bring down the wrath of the Almighty?"

"My apologies, Your Grace. It's just ... "

The awful voice continued.

"I understand, but watch your language in these halls, and anywhere. You understand?" The knight nodded and the apostle softened and continued but with the disapproving frown that never seemed far from his face.

"What you hear is a voice we have listened for, for generations on generations. For over three hundred years we have listened to the still silence of this box as commanded by the Prophet President Dunlich in the 729th year of our Prophet's birth, the 1900th of which we celebrate this very day. It is a voice that portends our greatest fears. May the Lord truly bless us in our hour of need."

The aged apostle turned to the seated man, "You say there are other voices as well? Let us hear them."

The small man turned a small knob, like one might find on the lid of a cooking pot and the voice changed. This one seemed as strange, but no less harsh. Then another, with another turn of the knob, this time clearly a woman's voice, although it sounded less demonic and more sing-songy. Its foreignness seemed unnerving and wrong. The more he turned the knob, the more voices that presented themselves. The apostle had slumped into a nearby chair and placed his head in his hands.

The Church servant settled on a voice chanting something with a low cadence and a regular, almost hypnotizing rhythm. The men listened to it for a few minutes before the apostle gave a shudder and signaled for the man to reinsert the cord attached to the earmuffs back into the box.

Sir Santos stared at the apostle, "What does it mean? What are we listening to?"

The apostle did not answer quickly. "They are fiends and monsters, sir. Demons of terrifying mien. I brought you here because what you've heard signals war ... "

"War, Your Grace! Who are these men that threaten such! Let them bring it. They will face ... "

The apostle held up his hand. "Good. Good, Sir Santos. That's the spirit. That is why I argued before the Twelve this morning that you were the man for this. I am asking you to command the armies."

"Your Grace? What armies?"

"For the first time in three hundred years we must form a planetary army united from all the provinces. You will be the commander. Now, come to council, there is much to discuss and preparations must begin immediately. We battle Hell itself."

THE BLUE planet twinkled intensely as it neared the horizon. His cor gave another toss of his head, its single silver horn catching the dim light of the two moons as it stepped forward to find another patch of uncropped grass. That distant sparkle shining brightly in the night sky had always been his favorite star. The birthplace of The Prophet in a place called New York. How peacefully it shined. How did this happen? War?

The knight, looking over his holdings, smiled slowly, turning into a laugh when he thought about what he had said in council. The President of the Church, the Prophet himself, President Sanders, stood up and told them that war with demons from Earth was imminent. In the silence that followed, Sir Santos had stood and drawn his sword and cried out,

"If it's to be war then let them come! I have over four thousand war cor and trained retainers ready now. I will mount such a force that they shall rue the day that they ever left their hot blue world to trouble our peace!"

LET THE MOUNTAINS TREMBLE FOR ADONIHA HAS FALLEN
STEVEN L. PECK

The chamber had erupted in applause and shouts of "Hear, hear!" and "Let it be so!" But the Prophet had silenced everyone, and told them to hold their peace until they heard the whole story. But there was little to tell. No one knew how they would come from that distant planet. Old tales of great flying cor that could soar though the air held sway in the numerous conversations that wove their way through the great chamber, until the Church Historian had stood on trembling legs and took the ancient red podium that had been made from a tree felled from the Prophet President Hinckley's own yard many hundreds of years ago on Earth. As the aged scholar began to read his prepared statement, the Prophet himself, no young man he, stood to support the older gentleman. But his voice was clear as the historian yanked all the supports from under Sir Santos's well-ordered world.

> *My Brothers of the Priesthood. The Prophet himself has asked me to tell you these things. I remember as a young historian being confronted with these things and found them so troubling and unbelievable that for many months I could not sleep at night, nor eat a proper meal during the day. The documents I have read and examined myself, and all bear the proper signature of many former prophets and apostles and I have no reason to doubt their authenticity despite the strangeness and unbelievably of their contents.*
>
> *When I was a boy my mother told me that long ago God prepared this world after Earth had become polluted both physically and spiritually, as prophesied in Mormon 8:31 from the* Book of Mormon. *And that we had been brought here by the Lord much like the great city of Enoch had been taken from the Earth as we read in* The Pearl of Great Price. *I somehow imagined that the City of New Zion had been scooped from the surface of the Earth and brought here by the hand of the Lord himself.*

There were many nods and expressions of assent.

> *However the truth is stranger, and again, I have little reason to doubt the tale, as it is attested in our most ancient documents. Long ago our ancestors made machines. Machines of such wonder that we can scarcely now imagine them. They apparently were common on Earth. They were made of metals such that are rare here, but on Earth it is recorded that buildings were made of steel!*

Murmurs of astonishment rose from the chamber, but Sir Santos remained silent. He had seen such possibilities just hours ago. His hand went instinctively to the sword at his side, the only steel he had ever owned.

Indeed, so clever were the men of Earth that they built great machines that could fly from place to place as easily as a hawk glides among the rushes of the Ort sea. But these cunning men honored not their priesthood. They allowed women to work at their side as equals and impregnated them with more children than they themselves could feed and the Earth was filled with unbelievers and heretics. They cut the forests and threw their refuse into the sea. They had smelted metals with abandon, fouling their air. They thought themselves gods. They could take the bones, fur, and feathers of the animals that the Lord had made during the creation and make new unheard-of creatures of their own design, or bring creatures back that had vanished in the great flood of Noah. They made monsters and demons and filled their lands with abominations. Then they became demons and ogres themselves, tampering with the seeds of life. But their abomination did not cease there. Oh, no. The oath breakers filled the earth with evil to the point that the air itself tried to choke them. They came to Mars and with their power and in gross arrogance made this planet into the garden we know today, yet bringing filth and contagion with them.

However, the men and women of that blighted world were in constant war and when this world was made anew, it was sold to the highest bidder one small piece at a time. But the Lord's will be done, and it was the Church of the Firstborn, the one true Church on the face of the Earth that had the means and power to buy it up, slowly, under the noses of the Earthers, until the Kingdom of God owned it all. In great metal ships that sailed through the skies our fathers came to make a new heaven and a new earth where the old one had been destroyed by sin. After many years greedy Earthers decided to take away our home by force, but our fathers had prepared for that day and under the Prophet President Mikel K. Clark, they struck against the evildoers. First here, then on Earth. Our father's fathers wielded awesome fiery blasts structured by the Lord's light itself, such that we cannot now comprehend or reproduce – called the Wrath of God. They rained down blazing fire on the Earth from the heavens in ways that I cannot now read about without marveling at the power of the good Lord. To

LET THE MOUNTAINS TREMBLE FOR ADONIHA HAS FALLEN
STEVEN L. PECK

keep the Earth demons on their won world, our grandfathers filled the heavens around the Earth with balls of solid steel, painted as flat-black as the night sky, each the size of a cor's hoof, to the number of, if the records speak true [and I have no reason to believe they do not] *one hundred billion to ensure that no flying machine could leave the Earth again and trouble our peace. Until now. The voices of which you've been told, tell us that Earth has left the confines of their planet as the Prophets foretold they would. They have again entered the sky. And the Prophets of old divined that their first act would be to seek their revenge. War is upon us.*

There was silence when the Church Historian finished reading. What could they say? Metal ships? Fire rained from heaven? One hundred billion steel balls? One such sphere would have been traded for a tenth-hectare of prime pastureland. Steel was for weapons, not for daily use where glass, wood, weaving, or even leather could be used in its stead! How much air had been fouled to make such an abundance of steel?

The Prophet rose from his chair and stood at the podium. An expectant silence sliced the room.

"I don't know what to do," he said.

LORD Santos walked into his manor house and hung his coat on the oaken peg and removed his green leather boots in the entryway.

"So what was so important that the brethren had to have another meeting on the day before Christmas Eve? If you are not meeting to decide where to build the servants a new chapel, then you're meeting on who gets water when, and if you don't have anything to meet about then you have a meeting to decide when to have more meetings." His good wife Sarahmit shook her head and checked the rice pudding boiling on the stove. "Now wash up. The kids have been dying to show you what they are planning for the Christmas Eve program and the pork-pie has been done for an hour! If you don't ... " She realized that he had slumped in his chair and was holding his head in his hands.

"Oh come. I didn't mean to scold. Are the burdens of the Priesthood so weighing you down? Have the Twelve got some new task for the greatest cor breeder on this side of Olympus Mons?"

He looked at this wife. They'd met at the Church's university. She was studying midwifery and medicine, and he animal husbandry. They had now been man and wife for twenty-seven years. She had borne him their two allotted children and a third, having won a petition from the Children and Families Committee under a farm and ranch exemption. Their life had been exciting, meaningful, and full of surprises. They owned over ten thousand hectares of pastureland. They ranched and bred nearly five thousand cor, including over a hundred midnight black war cor – a line that Sir Santos had created himself.

His wife had seen him lead retainers in four wars and in twenty-six battles. In the War against Nephi Blick, the Heretic, he had commanded an army of eleven thousand, including a cavalry of six thousand war cor against twenty thousand foot soldiers and eight thousand mounted ponies. He had won a decisive victory, bringing the lands of Sir Kim back into the Church and killing the Heretic himself with his sword: *Monson's Hammer*. How could he tell her that for the first time in his life he was genuinely afraid?

CHRISTMAS had not been what he had hoped. Even his little daughter Emmers could sense that something was wrong. The Hymn for the Dodo seemed somber and forced, with the meal itself rather silent and hurried. His wife had been prone to wiping her eyes too frequently or laughing too loudly at inappropriate times. But this morning he awoke feeling resolute and fierce. The day after Christmas, he called together the seven presidents of the Seventy, his most trusted advisors (and friends), to meet in a council of war a fortnight hence.

As he rode to the meeting place he was not disappointed to find several cor already tied outside of the chapel. He stepped in and Sirs Tong and Baglet were already there – arguing, of course; not about the war, but football, and Port Taylor's new goalie. Sir Sansei was sitting morosely by himself, studying his shoes and muttering to himself, no doubt about some injustice or other. He had been sour ever since he had been bypassed as president of the Seventy. The Bishop was bustling in and out of the attached kitchen, directing his staff in preparing lunch of duck dark-quarter sandwiches, cormare cheese, bean curd and noodles, pickled turnips, and the Bishop's own boiled barley malt chill. Sir Santos loved conducting meetings here because the Bishop was a chef worthy of Pilipino Hill in the Provo Temple.

He called the Knights to order. For the opening prayer, he called on Sir Tong, viewed by the others as the most spiritual man in the group; he could call up as heartfelt expression of faith as any man alive. With the Bishop acting as scribe, Sir Santos began.

"Sirs and Bishop," Sir Santos began, "war is upon us, a war such as has not been fought in living memory, for it is between planets. We cannot imagine what this means. As newly appointed head of the war council, I have spent a good part of this last week in consultation with the Prophet and the Twelve. The records of the previous war are incomplete and sketchy at best. We know that it was fought over the Church's possession of Mars, but how it was fought is unknown. We are not sure how the travel between the planets was achieved. The nature of the weapons used is obscure. There are references to "bombs," "destructions," and "holocausts." There were things called spaceships and shuttles, but accurate descriptions of these things are not to be had in the archives of the Church. Sirs, we face an unknown enemy, with unknown weapons. The Prophet (God Bless Him) says he has nothing to offer us but the Lord's good blessing."

Suddenly, Sir Tembean leaped to his feet and Sir Santos nodded to him, yielding the floor and taking his seat.

"I must contend with Sir Santos." The tall, stately knight cried passionately, "He said that the Prophet offers 'nothing' but the 'Lord's Blessing' but what more could we ask for? If we have that then shall we want for anything else? While we do not know the weapons and countenance of our enemies, surely the Lord God does. If we have His blessing, then we cannot fail."

Tembean sat down and there were several claps and a cry of "Hear, hear" from the Bishop.

Sir Ita stood with the help of his son. "Good Sirs. I do not fear what lies ahead. I have lived now on this good land for two hundred thirteen years. We know it was given us of the Lord and that His plans and blessings will support us. Sir Santos, how stand we? And where are the soft spots in our armaments?"

Sir Santos gave a grateful smile to his old friend and mentor. "Thank you, good Sir. We have many assets. From the Northern provinces we have promised thirty thousand footmen, twelve thousand ponies, and twenty-five hundred war cor. Here in the plains, we have the pleasure of offering eighty-five thousand, nine hundred seven footmen, thirty-two thousand ponies, and twenty-three thousand war cor. The Southern have been less than forthcoming, as is their habit, but I estimate that they can mount a force about half that of the North. The Navies of Port Ortfell have promised the Prophet all their resources for the movement of men and beasts to wherever they are needed. And there is something else that you might find most surprising ... " He paused for dramatic effect and smiled inwardly as the gathered Knights leaned forward to hear the mystery his voice employed.

"The Church has offered twelve hundred transgen warriors."

There was a collective gasp. Lord Ita found his voice first.

"Transgens! Then they exist?! They have been rumored for as long as I remember, but the Church has denied their existence. Have the brethren lied to us?"

"Watch your tongue!" Lord Tong cried as he jumped to his feet.

"Knights!" Sir Santos's voice sliced through the air. "We have enemies enough. Now sit down and act like brethren of the Church. There is no time for this bickering."

Lord Tong stood and bowed to Lord Ita and his son. "My apologies."

Lord Ita, too, rose from his chair. "And I meant no offense to the officers of the Church. I was taken by surprise by the news of living transgens." He turned to Lord Santos. "And truly I am surprised by this news. These were long rumored, and, I thought, the stuff of legends. Can you tell us more?"

"I can. These are the giants and men of renown spoken of in scripture. By the Apostles they are called the Adoni. Like Nimrod of old, they are men standing as tall as a war cor's head. I have seen them and they are fearsome. Their arms in girth are akin to my legs, and they move with an uncanny swiftness. They make a most formidable foe. They have been raised in secret in the forbidden mountains of Phiegra, not far from the lake of the same name, in a citadel called Adoniha. To arrive there, I sailed north from the port at Palmyra with Elder Domkin the day after Christmas. I have now seen first-hand their prowess. They are fiercely loyal and have sworn their lives to the protection of the Church. From the time of their youth they are trained in the arts of battle. I do not envy the man that would face them. I myself matched swords with a youth of sixteen and I was disarmed in moments. I then grappled with him and found myself pinned to the mat so quickly, I felt like I was a wispy girl wrestling a seasoned warrior. And gentlemen, if I, a married man, might make the observation, their woman are of such beauty and grace as to make a man long for the days of Brigham Young when a man might take more than one lady to wife. These precious maidens are warriors like the men, and they are as deft with a sword as any of you standing. Nevertheless, in form they are like the Mother in Heaven Herself." He paused as his focus passed from the present table to his visit to Adoniha.

"Brethren, they will make a fine force in our war with Earth. Their promised help from the Prophet, however, comes at the request that we do not reveal their existence to even our wives and children. Knights, arise. And mount your swords toward Heaven and the Celestial Kingdom above."

LET THE MOUNTAINS TREMBLE FOR ADONIHA HAS FALLEN
STEVEN L. PECK

The men arose and pointed their blades to the sky.

"I do swear as a Knight of the Kingdom of God, that I will never tell another about the transgens, or as they are called, Adoni, if it is within my power. Bow your heads and so swear."

The men took their seats again. Sir Ita spoke as he maneuvered his chair back under the table. "These are good and strange tidings, indeed. But there is the other side of the coin to consider. What are we facing? To know our strength requires not only that we know our own strength, but the strength of our enemies, that we might ascertain our chances of victory. If we have a million men, it brokers no advantage if our enemies field one hundred million."

Sir Baglet joined in. "'Tis true enough. What do we know of Earth? What size their army? When come they to attack? How will they mount an attack from one world to another? Have they flying cor as rumored? We must know these things if we are to strategically order our companies and arrange our battalions."

Sir Santos looked troubled and did not immediately answer the query. He looked at the faces of these great knights. In them flowed the blood of generations upon generations of the Church's greatest knights and warriors. They reflected courage and fearlessness, wisdom and ken. These were the brethren of the Priesthood of Melchizedek, the knights of the Kingdom of God. If any could face the terrors that lie ahead, it was these, but nevertheless a cold spasm flowed through his spine.

"We know little. For twelve hundred years the Earth has been a bright blue star spinning in the heavens, whose beauty has inspired poets and enchanted our evenings. We know it is our original home, and from where we are sired. We are clear that the events of the *Book of Mormon* and the Bible, and the teachings from the *Doctrine and Covenants* took place on that distant world. We know that they have become corrupted and demon-like. We know that we went to war when they attacked and destroyed the temple and library of Mies. We know also that we obliterated them so completely that we thought they would never return, but took precautions to listen in case they did. And now they have. We also know that we are not of our former strength or learning. We can no longer master the heavens as we once did. However, we have reason to hope. The Prophet believes that they will come on flying cor. If so, they are vulnerable to our arrows. He thinks the machines and metal ships mentioned are nothing more than wagons and carriages, pulled by these beasts."

There was a long silence as the gathered knights considered the weight of these tidings. The thoughts of each spun through oceans of doubt and bewilderment. At last Sir Ita rose.

"Good Sirs. We can yet prepare. Let us assume that the attack will come from above and so we will hide in the deep below. We will make a home in the lava tubes of volcanoes and the caves of mountains. But gentlemen, we will force them to the ground in the end, and when they step out upon the Martian surface they will meet such warriors that the tales they bring back to their wives and children will leave them shaking in fear for a thousand years!"

SIR SANTOS swayed in his cor's saddle staring at nothing, lost in thought. He considered the growing fear among his people as the arrival of the strange red star sent shockwaves of wonder through the villages of the Saints. The new heavenly ember circled the planet with a rapidity that matched no celestial object ever seen. In a single night it would pass overhead seventeen times. Because it passed in front of Phoebes, it was clear that it was close. How long could they mask the fact that conflict with the Earth loomed?

Even his wife scoffed as the Church astrologers at first tried to pass it off as an unusual comet, and Sir Santos noted that sleep for the Saints was becoming a precious commodity. Even among his servants few could resist the temptation of watching the star throughout the night, most taking it as a sign from God, perhaps of the Second Coming itself.

Sir Santos wished the Saints could be made aware of what they faced, but as of yet, the attack from the blue planet was known only to the knights and general Church leadership. The populous and the ordinary soldiers were told only that the Prophet had commanded a series of large-scale battle drills. Among the commanding nobles, however, there was little doubt that the "star" was from Earth.

Sir Santos reined his cor to a stop and dismounted, signaling the others to do so as well. Only the fierce transgen commander Hyrum Wilks stayed mounted. While he acknowledged Sir Santos's leadership, he was surly and ill-tempered; when asked to do anything, he did so with an air of condescension bordering on insubordination but never quite crossing the line. One of Sir Santos's servants set up a table, and on it a map was placed. Not until all the rest of the commanders were gathered around did Wilks dismount and join the gathering at the table.

"We have surrounded New Zion with armies here ... here and here," Sir Santos said, pointing to the map. The supplies have been placed underground at these locations, which will allow for a speedy retreat to the caves. I have asked the Prophet's astrologer to auger the best time to alert the brothers and sisters of the Church and move them to the cave. He has been less than forthcoming ... "

LET THE MOUNTAINS TREMBLE FOR ADONIHA HAS FALLEN
STEVEN L. PECK

"Do you criticize the Prophet's choice of astrologer?" Wilks's eyes seared under the narrowed slits that graced his face. "If you do not trust him to provide for the needs of the Church in his choices, what loyalty can we expect when the Earth creatures attack? At Adoniha you would have been whipped with wet leather thongs for such disloyalty to our beloved Prophet."

The Knight looked with exasperation at the transgen warrior assigned to be his "assistant." He could not open his mouth without the man (if he could be called such, given his gigantic size) interpreting it as somehow expressing a lack of faith.

"Look, Transman," Lord Santos spat at him. "Do you question the Prophet's choice of me as commander of this army?"

The look of horror and momentary confusion on the oversized warrior's face disclosed that the Knight had struck the nerve he was aiming at.

"No my Lord! Forgive me. It's just that ... "

"Speak it now and let's get the air clear. You have sulked around here for the last week and I've had my fill. Say what's on your mind!"

The transgen lowered his head. "I have been raised all my life in holy places. There I rose to the rank of High Priest. There, every thought was given to honoring the Prophet. When we were not training for battle, we were studying the scriptures or were about our prayers. When we spoke of the Prophet it was with respect and awe. We knew the names of the Twelve by heart and at night we would ponder their lives and accomplishments. But here?"

"Go on."

"But here, I've not seen one of your command crack the scriptures. The nights are filled with endless chatter. You speak more of football and cor fights than you do of the sacred scriptures ... "

"Enough." Lord Santos looked at the man, not unkindly, but with a grim look on his face. "Your battles have all been pretend and fashioned of straw. You have not placed your fingers in the dirt of this planet or had the need to raise a crop to feed your family. Behind walls you have imagined a world without complexity or entanglements. When you have walked in the world a bit, then you may judge us. We honor the Prophet here." He said sharply striking his breast with his sword. "And just because it is not on our lips, doesn't mean it is not in our hearts. I will have no more of your whitewashed clarity. If you serve the Prophet, then I am his hand and I expect you to act accordingly."

THE MESSENGER breathlessly burst into the commander's tent.

"Commander!"

Lord Santos rose from his cot and blinked at the man, trying to get his bearings. "A moment." A servant leapt up and helped the Knight into a tunic.

"What news?"

The messenger spoke urgently, salted heavily with fear.

"Commander Newels sends greetings and bids you know that the Earthlings have landed. They came this evening. The new red star split in two just before dawn and one of the pieces burned bright enough to cause an early dawn. It came right at us. Then it ceased to burn, and great bellowing clouds trailed from the black meteor like sheets on a line, only larger than the Church Palace in New Zion. It has landed north of Hecates Tholus on the planes near the Ort Sea."

"Take a fresh mount and ride now to your commander and bid him meet me with his army on the northeast side of Hecates Tholus, near Seaview." The man did not hesitate but was gone.

"Telamon!" A captain rushed into the tent, fully clothed and ready for battle. "Sound assembly. We ride to war."

It took his army, about a thousand cor riders and five thousand footmen including archers and spearman, longer than it should have to get ready to ride. He cursed that they had not drilled more. He was a little chagrined to see that the Transman commander had his two hundred or so men ready almost instantly, but he was glad they would be part of his army. He wondered, not for the first time, if the Earthers had transgens.

By the time they rode, the sun was well up. The ride was not far, but he kept the pace restrained. The Knight did not want to take his cavalry into an unknown battle with exhausted mounts. The transgens unnerved him a bit. Only Wilks rode (upon one of Sir Santos's own Midnight Blacks, he was proud to note). The rest of the transgens ran on foot, but were managing to keep up with the riding cormen.

By Moroni's beard, thought Sir Santos, they even look like they are holding back. The striding warriors' mouths were closed and they did not seem to be breathing hard at all. He had told his men that they were warriors from a far-off village where they drink from a special spring that made them large. At some point, Sir Santos realized, they would have to know the truth, but to reveal the Church had been less than forthcoming about the existence of the transgens would not be wise on the eve of war when men needed their faith unsullied by messy complexities.

Even Sir Santos wondered how the Church could have hidden such a force for many hundreds of years. Secreted in the mountain forests of Phlegra, it would have certainly been hard to find, and the Church had long ago declared the mountains sacred and restricted travel to all but General Authorities. Now the knight knew why. But how had they managed the logistics of feeding the population of transgens? There must be wagon masters who knew the secrets and who carried supplies. He had seen no evidence that they grew their own food. There was nothing to suggest that they did anything other than train for war.

Sir Santos looked over and shook his head. He could have used such men as these in his battles with heretics. It certainly would have made anyone pause before trying to leave the Church. Why had the Church never let their existence be known before this?

What else were they holding back? He thought of the words Isaiah the Traitor's brother had said to him as he prepared to turn the captured man over to the Church for execution: "The Church is not what it seems. It is nothing but a dog with a horn tied to its head, passing itself off as a great war cor, but one day it will turn and bite you and you will see the fairy tale you've given your life to."

Sir Santos shook his head. *No. I won't go there.*

At that moment the transmen burst into an eerie song, a hymn that was almost a chant that kept time with their jogging feet. Sir Santos found the hymn rather odd. He couldn't put his finger on it, but he found the rhythm a little too stiff and ... angry? It seemed more shouted than sung, and it was a little too fervent, he thought. He wasn't sure, but it was not the kind of hymn he thought he would enjoy singing in church.

He rode forward to his second.

"Sir Dondon, at this pace we will be engaged in battle too soon. I don't want to come upon the Earthers at dusk, so we will make camp here. It is a good ten miles before the landing site. We will meet them at dawn fresh, and on our terms."

Wilks was livid when he learned that they would not engage the Earthers that night. He did not say anything to suggest that Sir Santos was leading the force poorly, but his every action, huff, and puff let the Knight know that he was very displeased.

He listened as Wilks let his warriors know they would be bivouacking tonight. "It appears that in this *army* we do not fight at night. So we will idle away another day after our slow trot through this pleasant land."

Sir Santos decided to send off some trusted scouts to spy out what the situation was with the landing of the Earthers. He then retired to his bed after a bit of beef, maize, and beans. Through the long night he listened to the ringing of the transgens' steel swords as they continued training exercises and mock battles until the hours before dawn when assembly sounded.

THE SCOUTS returned just as the army was ready to depart. Their report was strange and unexpected.

"We found the billowing tents of the Earthers blowing in the wind. They have erected a large metal hexagonal altar but we could not see any of them about. We crawled within a few hundred yards, but there were no Earthers in sight. Only a wondrous wagon stands guard a few feet from the altar with thick black wheels, and a great medallion mounted above turning in slow circles. But other than this we could find no trail – we circled the altar twice – hinting at where the Earthers went. They have disappeared."

"Fools!" Wilks looked angrily at Sir Santos. "Clearly they have flown off on their great flying cors. If they do not have demon wings themselves. If we had engaged them last night we could have taken them in their sleep, but now how can we catch them?"

He suddenly reached into his saddlebag and pulled from it a scroll. "I am to blame. May the Lord forgive me. I felt the Spirit prompting me to do this last night, but I hesitated. The Prophet told me to use this only in an emergency, and clearly, last night your idiocy warranted immediate action. I have failed. I will not make such a mistake again." He handed Sir Santos the scroll. It read,

Dear Sir Santos,

You have served faithfully as commander of this army and we extend to you an honorable release from your calling. The Church of Jesus Christ of Martian Saints thanks you for your service. Please turn over all command decisions to Adoni Commander Wilks of the Prophet's Arm. We look forward to your continuing obedience and loyalty.

President Sanders and The First Presidency
of the Church of Jesus Christ of Martian Saints

Sir Santos looked at the scroll and then looked at Wilks who was staring sternly back.

"But had we ridden," Sir Santos stammered, "we would have arrived at nearly the same time as the scouts did last night. We would have found what they found – an abandoned site. There is no reason ... "

"You have been relieved. Do not try and confuse me with your 'what ifs' and excuses," Wilks said, cutting the knight off. "Read the letter to your men."

Sir Santos read it humbly then, turning to Wilks, said: "The army is yours. How may I serve you?"

Wilks seemed taken aback by Sir Santos's humility. His countenance un-grimmed itself, moved into perplexity, and finally became a full smile.

"Sir Santos, you are a true servant of the Lord." He held out his hand and Sir Santos took it without hesitation.

"Well done," Wilks said. "I will make you my second. I reserve only the command of the Adoni to myself. Come, we ride now with a will to the altar the scouts found. We will track these Earthers to the gates of Hell if we must."

Wilks shouted orders and the company took off at a gallop. Sir Santos was angry and confused. Why did Wilks have that letter from the Prophet? His Grace clearly had provided for Wilks's takeover. Did not the Church President trust him? Who were these odd strangers that they were given leadership over Knights of the Church?

They rode swiftly now. The knight was disturbed to see that the transgens were keeping up with the cor – at a full gallop. These giants are clearly different from the rest of us, he thought darkly.

"WHAT DO you make of it, Knight?" Wilks turned a doubtful eye to the slowly moving wagon. Sir Santos did not know what to make of it. He'd never seen anything of its like before. It was about the size of one of his wife's larger trunks, with six pitch-black wheels as thick as a loaf of bread is long. It was covered with devices, blocks, points, strange tubes, thin metallic cords, and other mysteries, the purpose of which seemed as inscrutable as the braying of an ass. It was moving slowly, almost imperceptibly so, but it had moved about twenty yards from the hexagonal altar of which the scouts had spoken. Atop the strange wagon was a large bowl that turned slowly. Near what he deemed was the front of the wagon a tube with a smooth round crystal or glass imbedded in the end seemed to swivel with a mind of its own.

"It's not from this world, that's clear," Sir Santos said, removing his helm and scratching his head.

"Obviously it's from Earth," Wilks said derisively. "What I want to know is, is this a weapon? Is it a warning?"

When they had arrived everyone had searched for evidence of the Earther force, but it was clear there had never been an Earth demon force. There were no tracks, no hint of anything but the platform that had fallen from the sky. The wagon had rolled off the metal contraption, as evidenced by the great wheel tracks leading from the altar to the wagon. A great load of a silky cloth had gotten hung up on a scrub oak and a few empty canisters looked like they had fallen off the platform.

"I cannot even guess its purpose." Sir Santos finally said quietly.

Wilks seemed very disturbed. "I will go and pray about this. My mind is dark." Just as he was turning away, the thing spoke. The power of its voice was terrifyingly loud. It clearly spoke something, but, like the voices on the box Sir Santos had heard on Christmas Eve, it made no sense. Everyone froze. The great tube was pointing its crystal at Sir Santos and a red light was blinking below it. The glow from the light was like nothing he had ever seen, like a red star fixed in dark green metal.

Wilks seemed shocked and even frightened. "It is from Satan, not Earth!" he cried. "This is the work of Demons." He pulled out his sword and raised it threateningly.

The thing spoke again. Then silence. Wilks hesitated.

Then again. Then silence.

Then suddenly it said, "People of Mars. You seem to be speaking a kind of English. Is that right?" A woman's voice, clearly.

Wilks seemed too stunned to answer. Sir Santos had never met a demon before and was less inclined to see Satan in the souring of cormare milk as easily as some of his neighbors. That this machine was the work of demons was certainly less clear than Wilks seemed tempted to embrace. He took it upon himself to answer the wagon.

"We speak the language of Adam. Why are you here?"

There was another long silence. Sir Santos looked at Wilks to see if he wanted to take over, but Wilks nodded to him. It took a few minutes for the thing to finally speak again.

> *Good people of Mars. Greetings. I am Sasha Borges, the President of Unified South America. We come to broker a peace. We know your power to destroy is great. We have long sought a chance to plead our case and beg you to remove the blockade you have placed above our upper atmosphere. Please do not take our sending you a satellite as an aggressive act of defiance against your measures. It was launched from Antarctica under a joint effort of Greater Estonia and ourselves to contact you and sue for peace. For long we have been apart and we wish to once again send into orbit those things our ancestors once flew to allow us to become truly one world. We do not seek domination. We only want peace.*

LET THE MOUNTAINS TREMBLE FOR ADONIHA HAS FALLEN
STEVEN L. PECK

Wilks listened with a scowl. "The thing is from Earth. We must consult the Prophet on this." He said it mostly to himself. He then turned to the wagon and spoke.

"Earthers. We do not fear you. If you could see the mighty force arrayed against you, you would tremble in fear. The God of Abraham, Isaac, and Jacob stands at our side. Nonetheless we will bring the Prophet of the Lord God, the President of the Church of Jesus Christ of Martian Saints to consider your words."

With that, he commanded all to ride away from the wagon. The scouts rode out about a mile to where the armies waited before Wilks commanded a halt.

"That thing has ears," he whispered darkly. "Sir Santos, I'm going to fetch the Prophet. You camp here and ensure that thing does not go far and does no mischief. I fear a trap. These Earth demons are shrewd and not to be trusted. They speak of things we don't understand to confuse us and frighten us. They call a woman president to mock the Priesthood. We will not be intimidated. I and my Adoni will travel swiftly to New Zion, but our beloved Prophet is old and it will take many days to reach here. You remain until I return. In the meantime, tell the armies we fight with Earth. It is time they understood the nature of the evil we fight."

THE NEXT several days were wondrous. Sir Santos and his commanders spent every moment they could talking with the Earthers. He had a feeling that if Wilks had thought about it, he would have forbidden the communication, but since he did not, they started a long conversation. Their conversation was awkward because of the time required between speaking and being spoken to. He learned that Earth was so far away it took his words several minutes to fly there and theirs to return. It made the conversation stilted and slow, but of great worth. He was no fool, so he did not talk of military matters nor did he give away their strength. But there was much to learn. And much he found strange.

He learned that many bred cors there as well, but they called them Unicorns. He was disappointed to learn that black cor were abundant on Earth and of no special achievement. He learned that there were striking differences between the people of South America and Greater Estonia. The first worshiped a strange invisible three-part god, and the latter worshiped no god at all. He found, to his surprise, that the Earthers had a wonderful sense of humor and told a few jokes that left him chuckling for days after the hearing.

But he learned some disturbing things. He learned that between the planets was an expanse of airlessness, where travel required mighty ships that carried their own air. He learned that the Earthers had vast stores of metal, and that steel was so abundant they could make buildings out of it, as rumored. He learned they had self-propelled vehicles and immense airships that could fly from one end of the planet to the other. He also learned that they hated and feared Mars, for Mars had done terrible things to their ancestors and put in place something that did not allow them out of their "atmosphere," which he took to mean something above their planet. He thought silently about the millions of steel balls.

There was much he did not understand about them and it was clear they did not understand the things that he said. They seemed especially interested in things called "computers," which seemed to be men of great learning who could handle complex tasks and had prodigious memories. He assured them that their computers were very good at what they did and that their memory was unsurpassed. They tried several times to get him to talk about military, but he would not be drawn in.

Sadly, one thing was absolutely clear: They had capabilities far beyond his own people's. The wagon itself was evidence of that, but more than that, they could talk of these remarkable feats such as flying between planets or flying across their planet in great "planes." These were people with powers found only in fairy tales. Whenever they asked about how things were done on Mars, Sir Santos always answered cryptically, "Much like you do. Much like you do."

But it was clear to him that the people of Mars were nothing compared to these Earthers with their command of metal and air. At one point in the conversation, they had asked, "How do you power your cities?"

Carefully, he asked, "How do you power yours?"

They had answered, "Solar and nuclear mostly."

He had answered, "The same," but he did not know what they meant. He feared if he had said, "We do not power our cities, but rather power the people in them," they might have realized their advantage. What did it mean to power a city? A strange fear was growing in Sir Santos.

AFTER fifteen days the Prophet arrived. He came in a large black carriage trimmed in gold and silver. Thick red curtains were thrown back revealing his brightly smiling face. Cheers erupted from Sir Santos's army and he too joined in the cries of welcome. Many of his army were from the outer reaches of lands around the Ort Sea and did not often have the opportunity to see the Prophet in person. The carriage halted in the grass before the army, and as the Prophet was helped down the stairs placed there to assist him, the army broke into the hymn *Blessed, Holy, Prophet Dear*. The transgens who had escorted the Prophet joined in. The President of the Church was clearly touched and, with water framing his eyes, he waved his bowler hat into the air and danced a jig.

"Sir Santos. It is good to see you. It may be that the Last Days are upon us. I will join you and Commander Wilks in your tent. I want to get your counsel before I talk with the so-called Earthers' President."

The Prophet was clearly exhausted.

Sir Santos offered the aged man his elbow and escorted him slowly toward his nearby tent. The Prophet's steps were slow, but steady. He was two hundred fifty-seven years old this year and had been a prophet for nearly fifty. He was beloved by all and had had a long and productive reign. Sir Santos felt deep honor supporting this eminent man as they walked silently to his tent.

The Prophet bid him bring together his war council, and in a few minutes all seven of the war Lords were assembled – along with Wilks. "Brethren of the Priesthood, we gather here on the eve of war." The Prophet spoke with confidence. "The Earth demons will taste the resolve and determination of the Martian Church and I fear not that the Lord will stand at our side and bring us a swift and certain victory. There is no reason to fear and great reason to hope. May the Lord's blessings be upon you individually as you lead your army to war and upon you collectively in this great undertaking."

Lord Santos was somewhat confused by the Prophet's words. He could tell his war council was similarly confused. Many of them had been present during Sir Santos's conversations with the Earthers, and nothing had indicated that war was as inevitable as the Prophet seemed to suggest.

Commander Wilks joined in. "President, I will assure you that our forces will never be overcome. This war will end the creature's confidence in the arm of flesh."

Sir Santos slowly raised his arm to the square, seeking recognition. The Prophet nodded to him.

"My beloved Prophet. We rejoice in your presence here with us today. I speak on behalf of all the men of these armies. We are your humble servants." There was some cheering by the commanders, after which Sir Santos continued.

"My Lord, I assure you that, like your commander of the Adoni, we are ready to do battle with the Earthers – should it come to that. But Your Grace, I humbly submit that we think that the Earthers are here to sue for peace and want nothing more than to establish assurances that we have no intentions on their planet. I am convinced – "

Wilks jumped to his feet and shouted at the knight. "Are you a coward? Do we make peace with Satan? Do we deal with the Devil? You dare stand before the Prophet and suggest we compromise on truth and righteousness?"

The Prophet reached out and patted the leg of the fierce transgen. "Come, come, Commander. Let the man say his piece. I have come here to consider all counsel. Would you be surprised that sometimes even Elder Whitehead and I disagree?"

Wilks sat down almost sulkily and Sir Santos continued to lay his case before the Prophet. He told him about the conversations he had had with the Earthers, of the things he had learned about them, that they were likely children of Adam and not demons, and of their power over metal.

When he confessed to having talked with the Earthers, Wilks looked as if he wanted ed slay the knight. Sir Santos openly expressed his concerns that they may have the technological advantage. Several of his war commanders chimed in and gave support to the things he was saying. A few, he hoped, would have said something they did not, likely intimidated by the rage on the giant Adoni's face. But the Prophet listened attentively and when all had finished, he rose up from his chair and spoke.

"I have heard interesting things this day. But it is clear to me that the Earthers are lying. Weak minds are easily influenced and deceived. Wilks has assured me of the intent of these devils, which our grandfathers so easily defeated, and I have received the sweet, still prompting within that tells me that Wilks knows whereof he speaks. My councilors and Elder Whitehead are in full agreement. I will speak to them by and by, but first I would like to speak to the armies to strengthen and embolden their courage for the battle ahead. Sir Santos, call the armies together."

Wilks supported him as he walked out of the tent and into the open air. Sir Santos called assembly, which was accomplished quickly and easily, as most of the army was near the tent trying to get a glimpse of the Prophet. He then set up a stage upon which the Prophet could stand, supported by Wilks who had not taken his eyes off him except to scowl at Sir Santos. The Prophet hobbled forward and with a trumpet held to his lips addressed the assembled army.

"Brethren of the Priesthood, we gather here on the eve of war. The Earth demons will taste the resolve and determination of the Martian Church and I fear not that the Lord will stand at our side and bring us a swift and certain victory. There is no reason to fear and great reason to hope. May the Lord's blessings be upon you individual captains as you lead your army to war, and upon you collectively in this great undertaking. In addition, I would like to add some instruction.

LET THE MOUNTAINS TREMBLE FOR ADONIHA HAS FALLEN
STEVEN L. PECK

"All of you wear the blue feather in your helm as a symbol of the Church. It has become stylish in some of the outlining areas to wear this feather at a tilt. I have seen this trend spread throughout much of the land, and I find it disturbing to say the least, as do many of the Twelve Apostles. When I was a young warrior in the cavalry, we were always proud to wear our blue feather standing straight and tall upon our helms. We took great pride in ensuring that the blue feather symbolized what was in our hearts. We would no more put a tilt in the wearing of a blue feather than we would break one of the basic commandments. This tilt is not becoming of the way that servants of the Lord should wear their feathers, especially a feather representing the Church and Kingdom of the Living God. A tilt in the feather speaks of slackness and slovenliness. It speaks of weak-mindedness and debauchery. It is my hope that there will be no man found within the ranks of these great armies with the feather not standing up tall and straight. I hope that we will also teach our children to wear the blue feather standing, as it should with not a hint of a tilt. I think this is what the Apostle Paul was referring to when he said that 'to be carnally minded is death.' I encourage all of you to look to your feather and see that it is straight, true, and bright. May the Lord bless you in all your endeavors."

Wilks helped him off the stage to the wild cheering of the men, many of whom had removed their helms to straighten their feathers. He signaled Sir Santos over.

"Let us now go speak to the demons. And let me add, Sir Santos, that I have always admired the way you always wore your blue feather straight and true, just like your father did. Come. Let us see to these devils. Sir Santos, I would like you and your seven to accompany me and Commander Wilks as we speak to these Earth demons."

The Prophet continued to be supported by Wilks, but Sir Santos was deeply troubled. What had Wilks done to convince the Prophet that these Earthers were so nefarious? The transgen had only heard the woman from the other world once and knew nothing about the Earthers. Sir Santos had heard them many times and was convinced not only of their sincerity and desire for peace, but that they had vastly superior machines, which likely implied vastly superior weapons.

They arrived at the wagon and without ceremony, Wilks shouted at it, "Earthers. I bring before you the Prophet of the Living God. The President of the Church of Jesus Christ of Martian Saints. The High Priest of Mars. His Grace President Sanders."

The Prophet was about to speak, but Sir Santos spoke quickly, "Your Grace, the voices travel slowly across the void between Earth and Mars. It will take a few minutes to receive a reply."

The Prophet nodded and Wilks scowled menacingly at the Knight. After a time the wagon came alive.

Welcome President Sanders. It is an honor for me to speak to you across the miles between our planets. As I said to your able commanders, we seek to establish peaceful relationships between our worlds. For too long we have been separated by an immense distance, and for too long have held unnecessary fears and suspicions. We believe that we have much to offer your people. We have made great advances in medicine, philosophy, genetic engineering, nanotechnology, literature, and in computer technology. Now at last we have even stretched our reach to offer you our hand across the vastness of space. We have seen from afar your fair fields, and the breathtaking way your terraforming efforts have unfolded into a beautiful and ecologically stable world. However, we have been through a great period of darkness and war due to our last conflict with your planet. Only in the last hundred years have our abilities reached that of our ancestors. We are unsure of what brought about that terrible and ruinous war between our worlds, but we know that we are one people and we humbly extend our hand in friendship and fellowship. We would like to discuss ways to remove the blockade placed in our upper atmosphere. We would like to resume trade. I, President Borges, hope that you will join me in forging a strong alliance of mutual benefit and lasting peace.

Sir Santos could not help but mark the distasteful scowl that had set upon the Prophet's face the moment the message began coming through. The beloved man fidgeted and kept glancing up at Wilks, whose stern face was a mask of disgust. When the message stopped, Wilks whispered to the Prophet's ear. The Prophet nodded repeatedly and then looked at Wilks and patted his cheek affectionately. He then turned to Sir Santos and asked, "How do I speak to them?"

Sir Santos thought he might have just a moment. "You just begin speaking in a normal tone of voice, my Lord, but before you begin, may I respectfully offer my opinion that these Earthers are sincere ... "

"Silence, dog!" Wilks spat at him in a harsh whisper, then turned earnestly to the Prophet. "My Grace, he has done enough damage. Now is not the time to listen to Satan's lies."

The Prophet turned to Sir Santos and placed his finger over his pursed lips signaling silence. He then smoothed his suit and cleared his throat.

LET THE MOUNTAINS TREMBLE FOR ADONIHA HAS FALLEN
STEVEN L. PECK

"Earthers, you speak whereof you do not understand. We come here on the eve of war. You will taste the resolve and determination of the Church and I fear not that the Lord will stand at our side and bring us a swift and certain victory. There is great reason for you to fear and great reason for us to hope. May the Lord's blessings be upon us in this great undertaking, for you will find yourself again smitten in such a manner that you will not rise from the dust for another many hundreds of years. By the power of the Priesthood you will be smitten. Send your flying war cor. We will cut them down. We do not fear you. Know you not that we have over a thousand Adoni standing ready to smite you bone and marrow? Do you think you can stand against us? The prophets of old warned you. You were never to contact us again. You have awakened the sleeping boxes to which we have listened since your defeat; we listened to ensure your compliance. And now, against all that you were warned, you have started your Satanic chatter once again.

"Then, in an affront to all the dignity of Mars, you send this abomination, this ungodly wagon from your demon-filled Earth. You will feel the wrath of the Lord as proclaimed by His servants. We will cut you off, root and branch. As the Lord said unto Joshua as they entered the Promised Land, we will destroy you, man, woman, and child. I am the President of the Church of Jesus Christ of Martian Saints and, like the Gadianton Robbers of old as is spoken of in the Book of Mormon, you will be cut down."

Sir Santos was horrified. He stared at the Prophet with as much disbelief written on his face as smug satisfaction was written on Wilks's. He did not know what to do. He looked at his commanders and saw only confusion written on their faces. Was it to be war than? Against what kind of enemy? No one spoke as they waited for a reply. When it came it sent chills through the knight and his commanders:

So be it.

THAT NIGHT a feast was held for the Prophet. Several wagon masters had arrived with the Prophet's carriage and his personal staff. In swift order they conjured abundant courses of dodo, water buffalo, maize cakes, watercress, pickled beets, salmon, Ort Sea perch, turkey and duck eggs pickled in white wine vinegar, rice casserole, seven cheeses, and green pony-hoof gelatin with carrots.

Sir Santos was in no mood for the festivities. He walked alone into the grasslands. A soft breeze was blowing off the sea and Earth was just starting to set. How could such a beautiful star harbor such nemeses? Or did it? Was it his people or (dare he think it?) their prophet who was the monster? He found himself meandering down to the Earth wagon where it had not moved for the weeks they had camped there. He walked up and sat down before it, looking at the red blinking light shining even more brightly in the darkness. Had the Father in Heaven really told the Prophet to start a conflict with these people? Surely the God's mouthpiece here on Mars was above reproach, or so he had always believed. Yet now the Prophet's actions had not only seemed unwise, they seemed misdirected. He was asking them to risk their existence on his insistence that the Earthers could be defeated by a handful of arrogant transgen giants.

He looked at the Earth wagon. The subtlety by which it had been crafted was far beyond anything that could be done on this planet. He knelt where he was and tried to pray but he could not find the words, or was it the humility he lacked? Why not trust the Prophet? That was what he had spent his life teaching his children. That was why he had fought three wars with heretics. But now? Something seemed wrong.

Sir Santos. It is good to see you tonight.

Sir Santos jumped at the voice, but quickly settled down as he recognized the familiar voice of his distant friend, the President of the southern continent.

"Hello, President Borges. Things did not go well, did they?"

The long pauses between replies left him more and more convinced that war with a people that could traverse such distances with a self-propelled wagon was a fool's quest. Tonight their conversation seemed awkward and unanimated. Times had indeed changed. By the time the short and stilted conversation was over, the knight had learned some things that frightened him, but also gave him a new resolve.

"President. Give me a month or so. I am determined not to let this come to war. Will you give me that? I will convince the Prophet that this is not in our or your interest. Will you grant me a month?"

The reply in its time came.

Of course. But we will be watching the skies. If you launch an attack we will be ready.

When Sir Santos returned to his tent, he told his servant to contact the seven commanders and to meet him on the hillock north of the camp. As he found his mount, he stroked the sides of his magnificent black war cor. The feasting had ended and the tent of the Prophet was dark and silent. In the distance, he could hear the singing of the transgens camped on the flat to the north. Their hymn might have once provoked a feeling of reverence, as they voiced the sacred hymns of his youth, but now it seemed a hollow foreboding that portended ignorance and poverty of thought.

The seven commanders came as requested. No one spoke as they gathered, and their mood was black. For a moment Sir Santos thought it might have been the lateness of the hour, but he soon learned that none of them had been sleeping.

Sir Santos began. "It seems that our beloved Prophet has chosen war, and my sense is that it will soon be upon us. We have much to do to get ready. I do not share His Grace's optimism that the transgens will make a difference. I need your thoughts and I need them honestly. What is our course of action? Sir Ita? What was meant by your grunt?"

Sir Ita set his jaw, but turned away. "I meant nothing."

Sir Santos considered him a moment. "You meant something. You meant what I think all of us are thinking. Is any man here eager to fight this war with the Earthers?"

Sir Ita spoke up, slowly at first, but picking up heat as he spoke. "I am old and have been in many battles. I know war like I know my own household. But how do we fight an enemy of which we know not their strength? We don't even know what weapons they use, but I suspect they may be terrible. The headmaster at the school at New Moab told me that the crater that now is Lake Kimball was made by a house-size piece of rock that fell from the sky. If these Earthers can toss things from the sky, as we know they can, as we can see from the wagon they sent, we may not even see them coming as they toss things upon our cities at their leisure. In the end we will be wasted without even bloodying a sword."

There were nods of assent. Another added, "We don't know their numbers. We don't know their weapons. And lastly, we cannot bring the war to their world. It must be fought here."

Sir Tembean seemed to be talking to himself as he spoke, "The fabric they sent with the wagon from the sky. I've never seen its like. It is stronger than canvas, yet lighter than the strand of spider web. It is not made of flax, hemp, cotton, or wool. If they can make such use of fabric, what else can they do?"

Sir Tong frowned. "But the Lord knows what they can do. And if he told the Prophet to fight, then we will prosper in the end. Many times what seems like it cannot succeed can if we rely on the strength of the Lord. Remember when Nephi's brothers Laman and Lemuel complained that the Lord could not deliver Laban into their hands because he was a mighty man and could command fifty?" Sir Tong then looked into the sky and repeated the words from First Nephi, "As the scripture says, 'Let us go up again into Jerusalem, and let us be faithful in keeping the commandments of the Lord; for behold he is mightier than all the earth, then why not mightier than Laban and his fifty, yea, or even than his tens of thousands?' Should our faith be any less?"

There were nods of agreement, but Sir Alma spoke. "Something is wrong here. The Prophet spoke to us about our feather today. Do you believe that the Lord cares how we wear our feather on the verge of perhaps the greatest war we have ever fought? Besides, his faith in these transgens is misplaced. They are mighty. But they are few, and again what is to say that the Earthers don't have transgens?"

Sir Santos bowed his head. "The Earthers *are* transgens."

Those gathered looked up in surprise. "I teased from President Borges something about themselves. They have had many years of darkness, but during that time they bred freely with transgens, or as they call them, transgenic humans. But her description was clear."

Sir Santos rubbed his face with this hand. "As you all know, I have bred cor for many years seeking the best characteristics. I suspect that the breeding stock of our own Martian transgens has been of limited stock, as it were. To breed the finest cor, I travel the world bringing together the best stock to create the features I want. These transgen, while mighty, seem lacking in some ways. They seem too focused, too limited in expression – quite humorless and quick to anger. They seem inbred, if you'll forgive me for saying so, and made to follow orders, not give them. This is not true of the Earthers. They are curious, articulate, and have a wry sense of humor. If it is to be war, then it will be against humans who might have the strength and quickness of the transgens, and our own level of intelligence."

Sir Santos took a breath, "But there's more."

The gathered knights stared silently, waiting.

"The Church, Joseph's original, The Church of Jesus Christ of Latter-day Saints, exists on the Earth."

"What!" Sir Ita staggered back.

"It's true. President Borges said it was one of the larger churches on Earth."

"But that can't be," Sir Tong said. "That would imply there are two prophets. Impossible."

"It is what she said."

There was a long silence, until Sir Tong said, "I move that we take these concerns to the Prophet. Surely he will listen to reason about this new information and if this is from the Lord then he can tell us how the revelation came and why our lives and that of our families should be placed at such risk. And what we should do if we risk fighting brethren in the gospel. This is stunning news."

THE NEXT morning after breakfast the Prophet agreed to see Sir Santos. It took some effort to see him alone and Wilks was angry with Sir Santos's insistence that he visit with His Grace alone.

Once alone with the Prophet, he laid out the concerns raised the other night. He explained that there might be lost brethren on Earth. The Prophet listened attentively, even asking some clarifying questions, but in the end he shook his white-haired head.

"Sir Santos. Who am I?"

"You are the President of the Church of Jesus Christ of Martian Saints. You are the Prophet."

"And yet you doubt me?"

"No, my Lord. I just have concerns."

"And who are you to have concerns?"

"I am a Knight of the Kingdom. I am one of your generals."

"No." The aged man paused, then continued, "No. No longer. I cannot have you leading men when you will not be led yourself. I do not need to justify my revelations to you. The Lord speaks through me. That the demons claim to have the true church is a lie – a cheap tactic to trick weaker spirits. I saw in my mind the arrival of their armies arrayed for battle riding on great white flying war cor. I saw them come in a dream, and I saw them face our armies. The Earthers were dead within a day. So I saw. So it will be. Go sit in your house while we fight the Earthers."

"But Your Grace. They don't have flying war cor. I asked. They will come in great flying wagons ... "

"You may go. Send in Wilks and get me Sir Ita. He will lead my armies under Commander Wilks. I will not have a doubter lead my armies to glory and honor in our war with the Earth demons."

WILKS WAS waiting by the door. There was little doubt he had been listening. He smirked as Sir Santos passed, but Sir Santos did not even look up at him.

Sir Santos walked slowly back to his tent. The morning sun was just burning the haze from the grass and the smell of the alfalfa flowers was strong on the breeze. He met Sir Ita on the way and told him that the Prophet had chosen him as the new leader and was now in charge and that Sir Santos was leaving that morning.

"Sir Santos. Hold. We will meet again tonight." Ita looked troubled.

Sir Santos nodded.

LATER that night, Sir Santos laid out his talk with the Prophet. Even Sir Tong seemed disturbed by the news. Sir Santos was well loved and known as a warrior of excellence. To be stripped of rank and told to go home was not only an insult, it was unprecedented and strange. There was a long silence. Then suddenly, Sir Ita stepped forward and upon one knee, offered his sword.

"Sir Santos. I will be led by you."

Sir Santos stepped back. "You speak heresy."

"Yes. I fear it is. But for a long time perhaps the heretics have seen something that I have been slow to see. We went to war with Sir Kendell when he dissented from the Church because the Church had taken his lands for their own pasture. We went to war with Sir Kim because the Church demanded that we wear only the shifts made by the Church workhouses in New Zion, when, for as long as we have memory, the shifts were made in New Moab by Sir Talon's people from the wool grown of sheep raised on the slopes of Olympus Mons. But the Church needed money for its coffers, and took over those folks' livelihood. In each case, was there any one of us that thought the Church's cause was just? We went for loyalty's sake. Blind obedience was the only reason we can give for our actions, but the actions of the Church were wrong! No more. I am a heretic."

The silence that followed this declaration was stunning.

Suddenly at his side was his son, Sir Alma. "I too will stand by your side."

"Knights! How can you do this thing? Have we not all sworn fealty to the Prophet? Do we not owe him our lives?" Sir Santos said quietly to the kneeling men.

"What of our obligations to our wives? To our children? To those we hold stewardship over? What weight does our fealty carry to the Prophet when these things are added to the scales? We have sat in council with the Prophet. He is a man as we are. He has claimed no vision from heaven. No angel has appeared. As far as I can tell, his words are coming from what you have called an inbred transgen!" So saying, Sir Ita pushed the hilt of his sword toward Sir Santos.

LET THE MOUNTAINS TREMBLE FOR ADONIHA HAS FALLEN
STEVEN L. PECK

Suddenly Sir Tong arose. All eyes in the tent turned to him. He was quick to defend any offense made to the leaders of the Church. He stood and surveyed the men assembled and slowly began to speak:

"My fellow knights. You know me. You know my heart. What you now propose to do goes against all that I have believed, all I have fought for, and all I have stood for since my baptism at age eight by the hand of my father. If the Prophet were to ask me to fall upon my sword, I would do so without hesitation ... or so I would have. But I have sat with Sir Santos by the wagon for many hours and am convinced that if we go to war with Earth, we will all die with our families. But death is not my concern. Should the good Lord wish to send us all to his Kingdom at this time, I would gladly go there. But I will not go there under a man's best guess.

"My obligation is not to the Prophet, but to Him that he represents. In this matter, I feel nothing in my heart that bids me follow him into this madness. If the Spirit whispered that I should follow him in this war, I would follow the Prophet into the depths of insanity. In this, however, I am convinced he speaks as a man.

"Alas, these are not the days of Joseph, Brigham, Hinckley, or Nather and it has been long indeed since our prophets claimed to speak directly to the physical Lord. Opinion seems to rule over revelation and to the extent that he does give his opinion he is open to a man's frailties and errors. It is our individual obligation to seek a higher confirmation that the Prophet speaks as such. In this, I believe he does not.

"Sir Santos, in this I, too, am your man. But be warned. Should you use this opportunity to enter open war with the Church or its leaders I will be the first to cut you down. But in stopping this war with Earth, I am with you. I am your servant."

One by one, they were joined by the others until at last even the aged Sir Baglet knelt at his side holding their swords out to him. And one by one he laid his hand upon their hilt and head and raised them up.

He stood before them and scratched his beard, deep in thought. Venus was just rising and the night would soon be over.

"Our action must stay in this circle. Many of our men would not understand our reasons, nor should they need to. Our dissent from the Church's head must be subtle. Like the scriptures say, we must be 'as wise as serpents' and as 'harmless as doves.'" He looked out over his captains and gave a sorrowful sigh. "Sir Alma. How many men wait for you at Dimple Downs, and have they seen the transgens?"

"They have not seen the transgens, nor heard any word of them. I have about twelve thousand in my cavalry and twenty thousand footmen."

"As I thought. I give to you the greatest challenge then. Ride to the transgen citadel in the Phlegras and sack the city. Tell your captains that the Earthers have established a city there. Do not underestimate their abilities. They will have nearly a thousand men left there and you face a long and bloody battle. Even worse, women and children may fight, but spare them as you can."

"And if they surrender?"

"Honor them if they do, but do not expect it. They have been trained from their youth to seek a glorious death in battle. We have here about nine hundred war cor and a thousand spearmen. How many archers?"

"Less than seven score, my Lord," Sir Ita answered.

"It will have to do. Are the transgens still singing?"

"Yes," said Sir Tong. They all knew what his next command would be.

"Sir Ita. Lead your men against the transgens here. Start by using the archers and be quick. The armies must believe that they are in league with the Earthers."

Sir Santos suddenly bit his lower lip. "What have we become if we kill mercilessly those we have no quarrel with?"

Sir Ita, put his arm around him, "Truth and war do not go well together. What is the alternative? This war cannot come to pass. It simply cannot."

Sir Tong added, "And as the angel said to Nephi, 'It is better that one man should perish than a whole nation perish in unbelief.' Better the transgens now, and here. The Prophet is under their influence. What can we do?"

Sir Santos nodded. "Then it is better to put the transgens to the sword than our planet pass away."

"What of the Prophet?" Sir Baglet looked deeply troubled.

"I will take care of the Prophet," said Sir Santos firmly. "Not a hair of his head will be harmed, brethren. That, I promise you. He maybe misguided, but he is still the Prophet."

Sir Santos was near tears. "Gather your army swiftly and silently. When you see the lamp in the Prophet's tent alight, attack."

"YOUR GRACE, the Earth demons have attacked!"

Sir Santos burst into the Prophet's tent holding aloft his lantern. His transgen guards jumped to their feet, their steel swords drawn and ready.

"Wilks asks for you! I will guard the Prophet. Go!"

The Prophet, too, had leapt up surprisingly swiftly. The Church president nodded to the two guards, who rushed to join the sudden sound of battle.

LET THE MOUNTAINS TREMBLE FOR ADONIHA HAS FALLEN
STEVEN L. PECK

"Where?"

"On the plain below."

The Prophet rushed to the door, but Sir Santos intercepted him. "No, Your Grace. The Earth monsters are searching for you high and low. You must not let your face be shown. Let me be your eyes and ears."

"Yes. Yes you are right of course. But why are not you in the battle?"

"You have relieved me, Your Grace. Remember?"

"Oh yes. Well then, what is happening?"

Sir Santos moved to the door and peered out. "President Sanders, it is a terrible battle! Great white flying war cor are descending from the sky."

"I knew it!"

"They are landing upon the ground, but the Adoni are upon them. They are fighting like the very angels of heaven."

The sounds of battle permeated the tent. The screams of men and cor rent the air. Steel on steel. Steel on flesh. The twang of arrows being sent into flight and the sickening thud when they found their mark.

"What's happening?" the Prophet yelled impatiently as Sir Santos had gone silent. The battle below him was like nothing he had ever seen. The transgens *were* fighting like dragons, men of renown. Their swords sang in the air as if animated by a fire of their own. For every one of the Adoni slain, fifteen of Sir Santos's force lay torn asunder by the wrath of these ill-bred demons. Great war cor lay scattered about the battlefield, with wounded and dead men flung all around.

"Sir Santos, what is happening?"

Sir Santos looked at the Prophet, afraid the old man could see the fear etched on his own face. "The Adoni are fighting like nothing I've seen. Their speed is like that of a popmaize kernel exploding."

The Prophet laughed "Are they winning?"

"Yes."

But what the transgens had in strength, they lacked in numbers. When the transgen were engaged with four of Sir Santos's men, a spearman would slip behind and thrust a spear deep into his spine, cutting off his legs, and allowing the others to slip in and kill him. One by one, the transgens were dying. The tide had turned, but at what cost?

"What devilry is this?" Lord Santos said, as if to himself.

"What is it?" The Prophet said breathlessly.

"Whenever an Earther or its flying cor dies the others cast a powder upon it and it disappears," Sir Santos said.

"No! They are sorcerers as well!" cried the Prophet.

"So it would seem."

"The devils!" The Prophet scowled.

"They are focusing on the Adoni. They recognize their strength. Sir, the slaughter is great."

The Battle seemed to go on for hours, but in reality it was less than one. The transgens were slain, but the battle was terrible. So many had been killed. Sir Santos sobbed as the Prophet put his arm around him.

"It was as I foresaw. The Earthers have been defeated. Who could stand against my army of Adoni?"

"Yes, Your Grace. Who could stand?"

THE PROPHET bowed in sorrow. "They slew them all? How is that possible?"

Sir Santos looked deep into the Prophet's eyes and found emptiness.

"A great loss." Was all that Sir Santos could muster.

They walked through the field of the dead. The Prophet seemed worn and fragile and took no notice of the Martian regulars that lay scattered about the field in droves. He commented occasionally at the loss of a cor, but of the others he said nothing, only his precious Adoni currently occupied his grief.

After the battle, Sir Santos had contacted Sir Tembean who had an army of thirteen thousand waiting less than one hundred fifty kilometers away, and sent them to join Sir Alma in their conquest of Adoniha. They were going to need every man. He also sent with them Sir Ita, who had been in the battle with the transgens, in order to prepare the army heading for Adoniha for the kind of fighting that would be necessary. Archery and spears were what turned the battle against the transgens. The importance of these units could not be overestimated in the coming battle; in close hand-to-hand combat, the transgens were indomitable.

"The Earth demons will pay for this," the Prophet said quietly. "The fact that the ordinary men were able to drive them off after the dogs had been nearly destroyed by the Adoni says to me that we will prevail. They will face the Adoni again and in greater numbers next time. We will see how brave they are then."

Sir Santos did not say anything. Heaviness weighed upon him despite the victory of his armies. He was convinced he had saved his beloved planet, yet at the cost of betraying everything he had ever believed.

"Sir Santos," the Prophet said kindly, "in the meantime, I feel impressed by the

Holy Spirit to reinstate you as the commander of my armies. You have been a strength to me in this and I will reward it. With Wilks dead – " And here his voice choked. " – I will need strong leadership until another Adoni commander can be chosen." The Prophet suddenly began to sob. "We will build a temple in this spot to commemorate the death of these mighty men. So terrible a loss. So terrible a loss."

Sir Santos knelt, as he was expected to, and pointed the hilt of his sword toward the Prophet. The holy man placed his hands upon the hilt and Sir Santos's head and lifted him to his feet.

"I, for one, am glad you are here." The Prophet said, smiling sadly at Sir Santos.

"I am glad, also," the knight responded, casting his eyes toward the ground.

IT WAS nearly two weeks before the news came. Sir Santos was impressed that the Prophet had stayed at the battle site and personally dedicated the grave of every man slain, both the regular brethren and the Adoni. The action seemed strange to many in the army who had been told that the Adoni had been in league with the Earthers, but Sir Santos's commanders portrayed it as an example of Christlike forgiveness – an act of unrestrained mercy.

The rider reported to Sir Santos first, who nodded sadly when told that while the Adoni had been slain, it had been at the cost the lives of nearly ten thousand men. The report of the battle sent shivers of sorrow through the knight as he listened.

Because Sir Santos's armies carried the Prophet's banner, they had been welcomed into the city. Were it not for that, there is little doubt the city could have maintained a siege indefinitely. The fighting had been monstrous. Both the male and female transgens had fought tirelessly. It was again only by dint of sheer numbers that had allowed Sir Santos's army to prevail. The transgens had never given up. Surrender would not be accepted even when only ten of them remained alive and the battle all but over. Sadly, even children had joined the battle and the only transgens to remain alive were a few of the babies and very young children. Even many of those had died at the hands of battle-maddened soldiers drunk with blood, believing they were Earth demons who deserved to die.

Sir Santos found the Prophet in his tent. The old man was in a somber mood after having come from dedicating the last of the graves of the men in battle.

"Your Grace. I fear I bring sorrow upon sorrow. The Earthers have attacked the city of Adoniha. None have survived."

The Prophet staggered back. "It cannot be! Who said this? It is a lie. The city is full of our finest Adoni. They are invincible. The Lord has whispered to me that they would prevail. This can't ... This is ... This ... " Suddenly the Prophet fell forward, his eyes rolling back into his head as a seizure rippled through his aged body. Sir Santos carried him respectfully to his bed, laid him down, and covered his shaking body with a warm wool blanket.

The knight called for the Prophet's medical attendants, who quickly rushed to his side and began to wipe his sweating brow. They frantically tried to administer healing spirits from their colored bottles, but Sir Santos had little hope in their skill. Whose heart could survive such loss?

Sir Santos staggered out of the tent and vomited violently. The deed was done. The betrayal complete. He staggered to his own tent and lay upon his bed and stared coldly at the ceiling. A numbness seemed to spread over his soul. The depth of his betrayal seemed to choke his emotions. He lay stunned.

What have I done? What have I done? What have I done?

THE WAGON clicked at last and the voice returned.

> *While we are saddened at your reluctance to come to know us better, we will agree that for one hundred years we will have a silence of peace between our people. As you said, this will give our people time to adjust to the idea of our contact and perhaps learn to forget old hatreds and long-standing disagreements. We thank Sir Santos for negotiating this peace and congratulate him on his call to the apostolic office. And most heartily we thank you, President Whitehead, for agreeing to these accords. We hope that in the intervening time we may teach our children to not think of each other as enemies, but rather long-separated brothers and sisters. With this communication we bid you adieu.*

The new Prophet President Whitehead sighed as Sir Santos helped him to his feet. They walked away as the remaining guard covered the wagon with sticks and prepared to immolate it as agreed in the treaty that Sir Santos had negotiated.

"One hundred years." The Prophet sighed.

"Yes." Sir Santos said quietly.

"We must spend that time in preparing for their contact. We have only a handful of Adoni, mostly children, who remain after the attack. We must start a breeding program as soon as possible, as President Sanders had planned."

"With respect, President, as the newest member of the Council of the Twelve Apostles and as your new first counselor, I think we must first learn how to fly."

The two men continued in conversation as they walked over the windblown prairie toward the carriages that had brought them here. One man was God's new spokesman for an entire planet; the other, a man who believed himself damned, but who loved Mars more than his own soul.

ALLOW ME TO INTRODUCE MYSELF

Moriah Jovan

I SIT IN Relief Society picking lint off my new denim skirt – "new" meaning I scavenged it from the '80s sales rack at the vintage consignment shop below my apartment. It's a cute skirt. I don't know why the '80s are so maligned.

The lesson today (the law of chastity) has devolved into the temptations and dangers facing the singles of the church, of which I am one – not by circumstance, you see, but by calling. I am a nun.

It's not an official calling in the church; in fact, the Metairie Louisiana Singles Branch President doesn't even know about it.

This calling comes straight from the top.

There are others. We have no title but for what we call ourselves: nuns and monks.

We draw our strength from celibacy. If we should marry, our bodies' enhancements and talents will vanish.

Like cutting off Samson's hair.

Spouses, families – they would hamper us. After all, they don't sell life insurance for what we do (Acts-of-God clauses are pesky things) and there is simply no way to multiply and replenish the earth if it's possible you'll die the next evening in the line of duty. There is an extra layer of protection: We're not very good looking (so as to repel the opposite sex) and our desire for companionship and ... *relations* ... is tamped, if not completely eradicated (to keep us from distraction).

The dangers facing all members of the church – but especially *singles* – are listed on the chalkboard by the teacher, who is reading from the manual. Bullet-point instruction number three at the back of the lesson is to write the list on the chalkboard. So she does:

Pornography (a perennial favorite)

Discouragement (the human condition)

Temptations (these are not enumerated)

Friends of dubious quality (no judgment there, right?)

R-rated movies (*Austin Powers: The Spy Who Shagged Me* is PG-1 3, so it's okay)

Coke (of the caffeinated variety)

There are a few they left out, most notably the ones I fight, which I will do to-night, as I do most nights. I dare not say a word about these dangers, nor do I allow myself to comment on the ones listed on the board. In fact, I don't comment at all.

Ever.

But I do pray, when asked.

I'm asked a lot.

Sunday school follows Relief Society, and after that, sacrament meeting, where I will take notes on the night's work. I very rarely have to take notes to do my job, but I'm far more relaxed right now than usual – nearly in a trance – which means I'm being prepared to write.

The boys (they're single, so no one thinks of them as *men* – a pity, really) trickle into the Relief Society room from Priesthood for Gospel Doctrine, and I spot him immediately: a smallish man, perhaps five-eight with a wiry build.

My partner.

I haven't worked with a partner since I got out of training, nor was I told I was getting one today – but it doesn't surprise me.

Things have changed.

We know each other on sight, and he takes the seat beside me.

We don't speak.

I am asked to give the opening prayer and I do. I feel the Holy Ghost's power flow through me as I pray, and while I don't claim any more spiritual gifts than the next human, occasionally I do receive more than my share.

There is someone in this room in great need of comfort. I don't know who, but it doesn't matter.

I do what I'm told.

I sit, and my partner takes a piece of paper and a pen out of the inside pocket of his suit coat. He writes in reformed Egyptian.

I look down through the bottom focal of my trifocal eyeglasses, read, then nod.

When I look up through the top focus of the lens, the glyphs disappear. He folds the paper carefully and puts it back in his pocket, along with the pen.

I don't like working with a partner. None of us do. But we have learned not to question. Those who question die. Not that dying is a punishment, or even a bad thing. It just messes things up for the rest of us: work schedules, vacations, and the like.

Unquestioning obedience is a gift, one I was given specifically when I was set apart for this calling.

I sneak a peek at my new partner's hands. They're huge, completely out of proportion to the rest of his body.

He has bigger guns than I do.

Possibly as much as a gigajoule.

Rats.

I catch his glance at my hands, then I catch his smirk as he looks away again.

Physiology and anatomy. I can only do so much with what I'm given.

I sigh.

Yet we sit together in sacrament meeting. I still don't know his name.

After the sacrament is passed, I retrieve my notebook and pen from my purse. The talks begin, and I write.

In glyphs.

He unzips his scripture case, and retrieves a pair of specs out of the pocket.

It's my turn to smirk, as he is not happy.

The monks may have more firepower, but when partnered, the nuns take the dictation and give the orders.

But soon I space out, writingwritingwriting. I must get it right and my language abilities are average, not always up capturing the nuance of a situation. In this case, I'm not even sure what I'm saying, and that unnerves me. The only thing I can decipher for certain is "the unique dangers."

Sacrament meeting ends.

He nods in the direction of my notebook, takes off his specs, and we go our separate ways.

I drive home, throw my vintage 1980s outfit in the dirty-clothes hamper (I still don't know what's wrong with the '80s), and fall into bed.

I'm exhausted, and I don't know why.

HE'S NEVER been here.

I can tell because he can barely keep from puking into the swamp, and his neoprene skin is making him fidget and wiggle.

Definitely a roving monk.

"Gas mask?" I ask and offer him something that very much resembles Cthulhu.

"I am not wearing that," he snaps.

"Little bit touchy, are we, Monk?"

"Shut up, Nun." He doesn't offer his name. Probably something boring like John. "Pray."

I do.

The sun is just setting when he locks his 0.75-gigajoule disperser down to his titanium gauntlet with much exaggeration. "Got your affairs in order?"

Break a leg in nun-and-monk speak.

I stand for a minute and stare at his gauntlet and matching gun, both so much more decorated than mine, engraved with lightning bolts. My gauntlets and weapons are engraved with paisleys. Pretty, but ...

Pretty.

Feminine.

To do a job like this.

I grit my teeth and pull my left-hand disperser out of its case, lock it down to the gauntlet, lay the telescoping barrel along my titanium-covered index finger, then lock it down with tiny clips.

Point and shoot.

Once my right extremity is similarly burdened, I click my night-vision goggles down over my specs, and lead the way into the twilight, into the swamp where it's already dark as midnight, downdowndown, gradually being covered in slime until I'm chest deep in it.

Yeah, it stinks. But this is where I work, so I'm used to it and I've already stuffed my nose with Mentholatum. I have the clearest sinuses in the Atchafalaya basin.

I haven't been allowed to go into the swamp for the last two weeks, since the flood waters from up north began rising in earnest. It's taken that long for my sensors and weapons to be recalibrated for the extreme change in environment. The animals have been driven up out of the swamp and what crude oil was left on land has been pulled back into the water. With water comes mold, fungus, mosquitoes, and other diseases, but that's not a concern for hunters. The crude, well ... I don't know how – or even if – the sludge will react to the extra radioactivity my partner brings, which is orders of magnitude above mine.

But we don't question, because to question is to die. The general authorities overseeing our gadgetry supply us with whatever we need to do our jobs.

"Why aren't we taking your boat?" Only now do I detect a mid-Utah accent. Great. A JelloBeltian.

I grab a palm full of water and let it trickle back out through my fingers. I still have a hand full of refuse. "Look at that. It's soup. Chock full of plants. Oil. Trash from the floods. I don't want my motor bound up in – " I point to a heavy drape of Spanish moss that floats on the surface. He looks around. Spanish moss is everywhere. " – that."

He says nothing and we trudge through the thick water.

"Crocodiles?" he asks after a while.

"'Gators, rather," I say. "They won't bother us."

"I know that," he snaps. Again. He might as well be a 'gator, he's snappin' so much. He's not questioning, but he sure is murmuring.

Murmuring doesn't get you dead. It might get you injured, though. Very distracting activity, murmuring. I'd rather he not murmur around me when he's got enough energy to melt a ton of steel.

(I bet it kills him he can't control a whole gigajoule.)

"Where were you last?" I ask conversationally as we wade through slime, our dispersers primed to shoot.

"Gobi Desert," he answers, and I catch something wistful in his voice.

"You liked it there."

"Yes."

"What were you hunting?"

"Had a band of specter demons going through the villages. Wiped 'em out."

Specter demons.

Psychiatrists call it "auditory or visual hallucinations," a symptom of several psychiatric disorders, but *we* know what they are: Lucifer's army, waging war on those of us with bodies – *on* our bodies – because he can't make any real headway in his war on Father and Mother.

Specter demons are the grub worms of the psyche, chewing up people's neural pathways like grass roots, leaving dead lawn behind. We're allowed to attempt to heal the damage, but we mostly can't. We're only required to get the demons out of our plane and bar them from future entry.

Like internet trolls.

But there are a lot of internet trolls.

At the blip of a shadow in the corner of my eye, I point and blast. Swamp water explodes and covers us like debris-ridden oil rain.

"Eeewww." Even I'm grossed out as I flick it off my neoprene skin.

The monk rubs his fingers together, brings the substance to his nose. "Well, you got 'em."

Good. The sacrifice of my skin will not have been vain.

Demolition demons are the worst. They usually show up in hospitals, disguised as Staph infections, gangrene, pneumonia. The advanced demolitionists manifest as cancer catalysts. The more skilled a demolitionist, the greater power it has over a cell's ecosystem. Medicine will arrest what it can, and we may be able to do the rest, if we get there in time.

No demon has the power to kill a human; they can only sow the seeds of disease – physical or mental – and let nature take its course. That's the pact the Parents have with us, their children: Lucifer cannot kill us. Yet he continues to search for a way to do so and this, the Atchafalaya basin, is one of his biggest training grounds and laboratories.

I don't know why he bothers.

Generally, we don't interfere in a disease process. There is a time and a season for everything. Repairing psychological damage – attempting to, anyway – is different. The schizophrenics, bipolars – not all are caused by specters, just as not all diseases are caused by demolitionists. But it's very rare that science loses a human body to disease if its turn on earth isn't done. Not so with specter-induced mental illness.

Several hundred demolitionists burst up in rapid succession, coming for us. They're small, about the size of a barn owl, and usually invisible to all but us.

It takes both my 3-megajoule dispersers and the monk's behemoth to pop that ambush right on back to hell, for lack of a better word. *Technically* outer darkness either hasn't been built yet or stands empty awaiting its prisoners once this Earth is cast back into the celestial recycle bin.

"Hmm," I say, and because I can't keep myself from stating the obvious, "this is not normal."

The swamp waters aren't as still as usual. I don't know if it's the oil or if there are more demons here than the water can hide. With pelts of moss and a slick over it, it should be *harder* to displace than water alone.

A battalion bursts out of the water and charges us. They're no match for us both, but the sheer number of them is cause for concern.

So. The flooding and oil aren't the only reasons I have a roving monk at my side.

... *the unique dangers*. I wish I knew what that meant.

Generally, we only make a little headway each night when we hunt. Lucifer replaces the demons almost as fast as we can dispatch them, but never quite fast enough. Out of the hundreds or – like tonight – the thousands that we send back to him in an evening, perhaps collectively, we will have lessened their numbers by a factor of ten.

Sometimes I wonder why *we* bother.

The water settles.

"I don't know why we bother," says the monk wearily.

I look at him sharply. Can he read my mind? I've heard it's a possibility, a gift given to the upper echelons of our kind.

I answer by rote: "So someone can live and fulfill the measure of their creation."

"Deb, I heard it in correlation meeting last year. And the year before that. And the year before that. Don't want or need to hear it while I'm hunting."

He's jaded.

Bitter.

"How old are you?"

"Four twenty-three."

Oh. I'm only fifty-eight. I feel that I've missed some important information.

No wonder he didn't like having a nun – and such a young one – take the dictation. He knows my name. He probably knows everything about me.

"What's your name?"

"Ezekiel Alleyn."

Oh. My. Stars.

The water bubbles and I don't dare think about *him* as we go about magnifying our callings with weapons powered by cold fusion. Not magic, not supernatural.

Technologically advanced and genetically enhanced.

Like the demons.

Like the hunters.

There is no supernatural, no magic, only puzzles that haven't been solved. Even we hunters don't know how most of our technology works, and I've always wondered how much the general authorities who build this stuff know.

I figure they get their instructions like Noah did: *Here are the blueprints and the supply list. Go to it. Don't ask any questions.*

The hunters' DNA is altered when we're set apart for our callings. I don't know how that works, either, but considering Jesus healed the blind and the lepers ...

Something brushes up against the back of my leg, wiggles its way between my feet. "*Bonjour, mon ami.*" The smallish 'gator flips his tail up behind me, making a splash.

The monk steps away to escape the oil-and-debris rain.

"You have a lot of friends here?" he asks.

What an odd question. "Of course I do." *He*, of all people, should know the extent of my enhancements. I couldn't work this swamp without having the flora and fauna understanding of and sympathetic to my purpose.

The 'gator maneuvers through my legs, and around again, making a figure eight, like a cat. He wants my attention, so I trudge to a log and he climbs out of the water so I can scratch his oil-slicked head with my titanium claws.

He *almost* purrs.

"*Non, chèr,*" I tell him in Cajun. He doesn't understand English. "I can't get rid of him, sorry. He's my boss."

"He's *whining*, Deb. What are you *doing* to this place?"

"He's just a baby."

"A baby you've spoiled rotten. Tell him to go home. We have work to do." I translate as kindly as I can and he slides back into the sludge, but not without a swipe of a tail at the back of Ezekiel's knees.

He glares at me. "You tell him he better *never* do that again."

We spend the night sludging through the swamp, sending demons back to Lucifer. Our dispersers mess with their molecular structure somehow – or at least, that's how it's been explained to me.

We don't speak. Ezekiel –

Oh. My. *Stars*. I can't *believe* I'm hunting with Ezekiel.

– isn't familiar with this terrain and I need to keep the awe out of my eyes and voice.

"Don't believe everything you hear," he mutters.

I don't like that he can read my mind. I feel ... naked. I don't look so good naked.

"Are you *trying* to mess me up?" I ask. "Pick a fight? Because if so, I'll take some personal time for the rest of the night and let you do this by yourself."

"Watch your mouth, Sister Judge."

I gulp. That's the second time he's dressed me down tonight, on top of his surliness at being here. It makes me rethink my abilities, my attitude.

"Don't start doubting yourself now," he grumbles as we trudge through the swamp. "I don't need a hunter with a self-esteem problem at my back." I purse my lips. "And no, I'm not here to kill you."

Good to know. I'm not ready to go back to real life and do normal human things, which, in my case, is nothing useful. I'm not even qualified to fry beignets.

But he sounds as if *he* might like to be released, and the second I think that, he snorts.

"Please stop doing that," I say. "Sir."

"Yet."

I gulp. I don't know whether he's out of my head or not. The best I can do is attempt to clear my mind and concentrate on my work.

That's probably what he wants.

Maybe, after four hundred and twenty-three years, I'll want to be released, too, to start life afresh from the prime of life, looks and libido restored, memory erased, to go on and marry and procreate like the rest of everybody.

I don't know, though. I *really* don't like kids.

"Where are you from?"

"London."

That shocks me. "You sound like you're from Utah."

"I'm an *excellent* actor."

"Did you – Did you ever see any of Shakespeare's plays?"

"I worked at the Globe. I was called to this position by King James after he saw me in *Henry VIII*."

Now my self-esteem is truly in the tank. I have nothing more to say and no questions that I want the answers to.

We work into the wee hours of the morning, dispatching thousands of demons who guard the scientists and demolitionists in varying stages of development. It would have taken me months to finish off that many by myself, but Ezekiel has a mister on his disperser that casts the radiation out like a spray bottle. I don't have one of those.

Yeah, okay. I'm jealous.

I'm human. Genetically superior, granted, but still human. I'm as susceptible to heartache and discouragement and envy as any other human. Just like any other calling in the church, you go into it with your personality and abilities as your only strengths – and sometimes those become your weaknesses.

As a hunter, I'm middlin'. I show up on time, do my job pretty well, try to catch a TV series or read a book or two now and again. We have quotas (like every other program in the church), but since this is our job and we're paid (not well), it's not like visiting teaching, where you can flake with impunity. My numbers are perfectly average.

I'm okay with that. The job is stressful enough; I don't need the added stress of competition. But it's easy to be okay with it when you work alone, and you were called even though everybody knew you're average at everything. It's a little more difficult when you're working with the High General and you realize you've been a little complacent.

He slides a look at me.

It's just too much. I don't care if he is the High General – he has no right to my thoughts, and I'm hurt that the Parents allow it. "I'm going home," I say, and turn around to find my way out of the swamp, baby 'gator at my side.

He doesn't say a word.

NOR DOES he tonight when I show up for work, though I expect another chastisement.

Baby 'gator greets me and a raven lands on my neoprene-covered head. Several skunks waddle out from the brush on the sandbar where we park, and a black bear rumbles out from the forest on the left and straightens to her full nine feet, four inches. Ezekiel's mouth tightens.

"Tell your friends to cool it. I'm not the enemy."

Then why do they think you are?

I expect him to answer my thought, but it seems as if he hasn't even heard it. Either he's deliberately not listening, he's ignoring me, or my thoughts have been shielded from him.

Since I don't know which, my attitude does not improve when the animals clear out as instructed and we wade into the bayou.

"How do you feel?" he asks abruptly, half a mile in, not a demon in sight.

What a strange question. "Fine. Why wouldn't I?"

"You weren't on your game last night."

"Like you expected me to be?"

"I didn't know you were that insecure."

"I'm not insecure. I'm an average hunter in a crap assignment. I know that and I'm okay with it."

He looks at me sharply. "Average? Crap assignment? Is that what you think?"

"You tell me," I say snidely. "You can read my mind."

He says nothing for a second or two. "Yeah, I'm sorry about that," he mutters. "Habit. For what it's worth, I can't now."

"Can't or won't?"

"Can't."

The layer of *en garde* I had added dissipates like a demon under fire. My muscles loosen up and I can focus again.

"In any case," I say, and nonchalantly swipe through a gaggle of demons that pop up to my right. "I'm sure you've seen my numbers. Perfectly average. In a target-rich environment. My kill ratio isn't anything to brag about."

"Uh, okay. You and I need to talk." He mists another squadron to our left and says, "But not right now."

We blast our way through the swamp. He curls his lip when he realizes he's going to have to swim a while, but he does it. I surface close to a two-hundred-year-old swamp cypress in whose trunk I have slept many times when I've been too tired to drive home. She, too, is my friend.

I wade toward her to find out how she's doing. It's been a long time since I've been this far into the swamp.

"Don't touch her!" Ezekiel snarls.

I don't. But I'm flabbergasted. Is he here to sever *all* my relationships with the beings I love?

"Move."

I do. Because that's what I do: obey.

He points at her and slices clean through her at her wide base, at least ten feet in diameter. I cover my ears when she cries out in pain, and watch in horror when she slowly topples into the swamp, triggering wakes that might have knocked over a weaker human.

I don't care if he is the High General. "*Why* did you do that?!"

"Don't scream at me. Look."

Demolition demons – legions of them – ooze out of the stump of the cypress like sap, fizzing out like birthday candles dunked in water.

I've never seen that before, and I blink to clear my vision.

"They – " I stop. I don't know what to say. "They can't – " But they *were*. Eating. Not sowing the seeds of disease, but actively destroying a living being. "They're not supposed to be able to – " I look at her body, all hollowed out, and now *I* want to puke. "How – ?"

"They *do* advance in knowledge." Ezekiel wades through the water toward the tree. "It just takes them longer." I cry. Silently. I can't help it.

I love her.

Grief makes its way through the swamp and I can hear the keening of the other trees and the birds, feel the quiver of the swamp bottom under my feet from the creatures swaying and stomping out their sorrow. My poor, confused baby 'gator rubs up against me for comfort.

Why haven't I watched her more carefully? Has it been *that* long since I was this far east?

High General Ezekiel looks at me, but I look away.

I'm only average.

Why am I here?

Ezekiel takes out a sample kit and scrapes a bit of her body into a bag. The inside ring looks like it's been burnt, but it doesn't flake. It clumps. I reach out to touch her.

Nothing.

Where once was warmth and joy and love, there is only a cold body.

I am ashamed to cry in front of the High General.

"Jesus wept," he says softly.

Oh!

Hope!

"Can you – "

"No." He tucks the bag in a pocket in his skin. "It was her time. She served her purpose."

"What, to be an incubator for lab demons?!"

"You're screaming again."

"But – "

He stares at me for a moment. "Are you ... *questioning* ... Sister Judge?"

I nearly bite my tongue in two.

I can feel his stare getting heavier by the millisecond, like a yoke around my neck.

"Go home, Deb." He flips a switch on his disperser. It begins to glow, brighter and brighter as it warms up until it's lighting the swamp like a collection of flood lamps around a baseball field. It hums ominously and I stand transfixed. "*I said go home!*"

Gladly.

It's all I can do to get out of the swamp, peel off my neoprene, drive home, and crawl into bed without breaking down.

And then I do.

My friend is dead.

I AWAKE to a pounding on my door.

It's my landlord, wanting me to do something with whatever vermin the restaurant next door has attracted.

I drag myself out of bed and throw a robe on.

He's a tense and easily agitated little man, but for some reason he settles down when he's around me.

"What is it this time?" I ask.

"More 'coons."

Not *more*. The same family, finding their way back after I've told them a million times to stay where I put them. It's not like they don't have restaurants in Baton Rouge.

"*D'accord,*" I sigh, wanting only to get back to bed. I'd only just gotten to sleep –

His brows lower and he cocks his head. "You all right, *chère?*"

"*Fatigué.*"

"You don't look so good. I'll send up some soup."

He offers to feed me at least once a week; he thinks I'm too skinny. I never take him up on it, but today ... "*Merci.*"

That earns me a long look. The back of a cool hand on my forehead. "You go back to bed. The rats will wait."

"I'm not sick, Antoine. Let me get myself together and eat."

I pray. Shower. Eat the homemade chicken soup Antoine left on my table. Dress in another one of my vintage outfits –

I was born in 1952. It's my hobby, collecting outfits from eras past, chronicling my history via my closet. Every decade had its highs and lows – mostly of the hemline type. My journal starts with my wedding dress, the one I never wore.

My parents, my fiancé, my friends – they don't remember me, don't have one trace of a scrap of an inkling that I ever existed. I don't mind. I wasn't cut out to be a wife and a mother. I had no talents. I was an average student. I had few friends. I was a disaster as a babysitter. I was a passable athlete and marginally decent at girls' camp.

My only redeeming characteristics were my beauty and my affinity for animals, and I couldn't take any credit for either of those. I was Elly May Clampett and as annoyingly popular – only without the blissfully ignorant part.

In short, I was entirely useless as a human being. Or anything else.

So when something that looked like love came calling, it didn't occur to me not to do what I was supposed to do and kneel at the altar.

My mother was more excited than I was.

It was 1971. I was nineteen. I handed my recommend to the worker at the front desk of the Salt Lake temple, and he said,

"We've been waiting for you, young lady."

Of course they were. I could see my and my fiancé's names written right there in the appointment book with "sealing" written right beside them.

I was taken to the bowels of the temple and stuck in an office somewhere. I had never been to the temple, but even so, this seemed ... weird.

An older couple entered the room –

Well, everybody who works in the temple is old. Sometimes ... *a lot* older than they look.

The sister sat in the chair on my left, and the brother sat in the chair on my right.

"Where's my mother?" I burst out.

"She went to do a session," said the sister with a mischievous smile. I liked her immediately.

The brother inhaled through his nose, deeply, enough to puff his chest out. He blew it all out with a whoosh. "Sister Deborah Judge," he said quietly. "We would like to extend you a calling."

Okay, now *that* was not normal. Even I knew that.

But they explained the calling, what it entailed, every detail of what would happen to me and those closest to me. I could accept, or not. If not, I would go about starting the life I had come here for, and leave with no memory of this meeting.

"I accept."

"Are you *sure*?"

Sure? A chance to be ugly, alone, and childless? Doing something I *might* stand a chance at doing well? Perhaps acquire an actual *accomplishment*? Being *useful*?

"Sign me up."

I stroke the dress made of white Swiss dot cotton and flowery lace emphasizing the empire waist. I press the velvety bumps between my fingers and wonder again why I was called to this position. Unfortunately, I had no innate talent for it; I didn't excel in my training; I was fundamentally no different from the gorgeous girl who had entered the front door of the temple to get married and came out the back door an ugly demon hunter.

And now I have a swamp full of enhanced demolition demons I don't know how to fight, armed with inadequate weapons, the highest-ranking officer in our army snarling at me, and the beginnings of what feels like the flu.

Except ...

... hunters don't get sick.

Therefore, I am not sick. I'm tired, in shock, intimidated by my commanding officer, grieving for my friend, feeling guilty – and so very inadequate – that I didn't know she was hurting.

I turn and look at the clock. A little after nine. I *knew* it.

Oh, well. I'll escort the raccoon family somewhere with a restaurant that serves their kind of food (and hope they stay there this time) and come home for an afternoon nap.

I clip down the back stairs and open the door to the alley.

Uh oh.

Nine *p*.m.

It's a really good thing tonight's my night off, or I'd have been late.

For the first time in almost forty years.

In front of the High General.

I put my fingers to my mouth and let out a whistle only animals can hear. The raccoons come waddling. They know they're in trouble, but they don't care; they chuck their noses up at me and trudge on past me to the parking lot and wait at the side of my car.

They know the routine.

But this time I'm prepared.

"I'm taking you to Ponchatoula," I say as I turn north onto the Lake Pontchartrain Causeway. "They have a nice restaurant there. I made sure it was to your taste."

The daddy 'coon sniffs in disdain.

They don't care for me much. I suppose I wouldn't care for someone who kept running me off my territory, either.

I park a block away from an old hole-in-the-wall diner that still hand-presses and breads its chicken-fried steak and fries it in a cast-iron skillet, still makes its own mayonnaise, still grates its own cabbage for the cole slaw, grows its own okra for the gumbo, and has pie crust so light and flaky it's almost phyllo dough.

I usher them out of my car, and the mama takes a whiff. I think she may approve of my choice. I lead them around the corner to the alley. "I'll make you a deal. The minute they start serving frozen, nuked food, you can come on back, okay?"

They still don't like me – the daddy uses his back claws to kick up dirt at me – but they head toward the restaurant's back door to dig through the refuse.

Time for bed.

" ... gave your word."

I stop short. I know that language. I know that voice. What's it doing in Ponchatoula? Why isn't it in Atchafalaya?

And why is he using *Adamic*?

"Look, *General*." I would never dare speak to Ezekiel with that tone of voice. "You have your problems and I have mine, and one of mine is that *you* aren't doing your job."

"What, you think it's easy for me to get away?"

"Speaking of, where's your novitiate?"

"Probably watching *American Idol* or something equally mindless."

Oh.

"She's not too bright. Good luck with that."

"Thanks. I need all the luck I can get."

My heart thumps so hard I'm nauseated.

I creep along the wall until I get to the next corner, around which I peek to see the High General talking with ... a demon.

Not just any demon. Their king, one step up from Ezekiel's rank, equivalent to Michael, able to take on not just the approximation of a human, but any species, real or imagined. He is powerful and impervious to our weaponry.

He could probably turn into the Stay Puft Marshmallow Man if he wanted to.

Apollyon is shirtless and looks like your run-of-the-mill biker, only ... handsome. Extraordinarily so. Ezekiel is, well ... he's ... plain.

Beauty comes standard on incubi, as one would expect, even if they are bald and their skulls are covered in tattoos.

I look up and through my trifocals until all his tattoos come into focus: the Adamic language put to symbols regular humans can't see. They spiral around his neck, off his shoulders and down his arms.

It's a list of names, his conquests – humans whose lives he's destroyed with his machinations and mind tricks. They shift, his tattoos; it's dizzying how fast new runes appear on his skin. It's like a stock ticker. For him, souls are like compound interest; they increase exponentially over time, with no extra effort expended.

I see the names; they mean nothing to me. It's an intimidation tactic for those who can read them. Why is Ezekiel here with Apollyon?

I can't move, so I pray for guidance, because that's what I do best – the only thing I do well.

Nothing.

Apollyon shoves his finger in Ezekiel's face. "You don't get to do the bargaining here, Zeke. You're under *my* command. Please do try to remember that."

I'm still praying.

No answer.

But I can't not hear this.

"She's nothing to me," Ezekiel says. "Take her. I don't want her at my back."

"I already have her," Apollyon sneers. "You're not paying attention."

"Look, I've given you everything you want and apparently you've taken whatever else you wanted, so give me what *I* want."

Apollyon sighs. "Zeke Zeke Zeke. You're as stupid as she is. Did you think *you* were exempt from the Morning Star's toll? *Really?*" He starts to laugh at the look of utter betrayal on Ezekiel's face.

Powerlessness.

I stop praying and run.

I HAVE never been able to hide my moods, so all the way to work tonight, I'm afraid Ezekiel will know that I know. He *can* read minds, after all. I'm still tired, still grieving, and it's going to take a great deal of effort to keep him out of my mind, my mind on my work, and my work acceptable, if not stellar.

As usual.

I get to the swamp and park where I usually do and hope Ezekiel doesn't insist we go where we last hunted. I can't bear to see the empty spot where my friend had stood tall and strong for two centuries.

Ezekiel killed her and now I don't believe the demons ate her. I don't believe that he's here to figure out why the demons can kill living beings outright. He's here on Lucifer's whims.

But ... how can that be? Wouldn't the Parents know? And tell the general authorities? He could be acting – after all, he'd made his living working with a legend. It would explain the silence from on high, but I don't understand what's going on and my head is beginning to pound from the thinking about it. I'm dizzy, wanting only to go back to bed, even though I've slept the last twenty hours away. I press my gauntlet to my face to feel the chill of the artificially cooled titanium.

It's hot and sticky in Louisiana in the summer time.

"So," Ezekiel says from behind me, and I jump. I hadn't heard his car pull up. "Time for that talk."

I can't look in his face, so I look at his throat, and then I can't even do that, so I lean back against my car. He makes himself comfortable beside me.

"On paper, your numbers are average, that's true. And no, your kill ratio isn't great, either. You're right about that. But ... " He pauses. Sighs. "I can't believe no one's told you this. When was the last time you checked in with Salt Lake?"

I shrug. "Two weeks ago they told me to send my dispersers and gauntlets back to recalibrate for the gunk. So I did."

"Yeah, but when was the last time you had an evaluation?"

I think about that. Calculate. "I don't know. Five years, maybe?"

"And you never questioned – Of course you didn't." He huffs, as if frustrated. "Deb, you – Every kill you make is like four for any other hunter in any other territory. You have sole stewardship of one of the most important regions in the world, and that's for a reason."

I remember what he said to Apollyon. "I don't believe you." I push myself away from the car, headed toward the swamp. "I want to split up tonight." So he won't have stupid me at his back.

"No."

I stop. His tone brooks no disobedience, and I'm stuck. I don't question. I don't murmur. I do my job.

It's the only thing I *can* do when I have no guidance, the Parents are silent, I don't know who to trust – most of all my commander – and all my friends are suspicious of him anyway.

Now I know why.

He reaches out to me and I flinch away from him. "Deb ... "

"Don't touch me."

"Stand. Still." So I do and suffer his hand on my forehead. The muscle in his jaw works, as he slides his palm to my cheek. He's angry with me. I suppose I would be, too, if I had charge of a stupid peon on the verge of insubordination.

"Let's go."

The night proceeds like any other, but the animals are close to me and it irritates Ezekiel the closer they get.

"I'm not going to work like this, Sister Judge," he grits out. "Get rid of them."

I merely translate what he said and let them decide. They decide to ignore him. *They* don't have to obey anyone but the Parents, thus, they are sticking with me by fiat.

Ezekiel's gone to the dark side.

"Do you think," I ask for no apparent reason, "that there's more to the parable of the prodigal son than we talk about in Gospel Doctrine?"

He looks at me sharply. "What do you mean?"

"The guy runs away with his trust, right? And he goes and hangs out with all his party friends until his money runs out. He washes dishes under the table for a while and he's eating out of a dumpster – Maybe he gets beat up or gets AIDS or whatever, and has nowhere to go, so he goes home just hoping for a job. He doesn't even plan on telling the dad who he is, right?"

"Right."

"But instead, the dad's all, 'My son! My son's home!' He was probably worried sick, probably figured he was dead or whatever. But the son's really contrite, he knows he did wrong, and he's ready to be a stand-up guy, especially with that reception. Dad gives him *another* trust in spite of the fact that he blew his first one – and the older brother stayed behind, the whole time, working at the family store and he doesn't get anything extra."

"Okay."

"Well, if you think about it, Lucifer's kind of the ultimate prodigal son."

Ezekiel gets tense. I can tell because his disperser starts to hum. I don't care. Let him kill me; I'll learn how to fry beignets and find a way to avoid motherhood. It's not 1971 anymore and women – especially ones in the church – have *options*.

"He's doing his job, because without him, we'd just be walking around not having to work at our mortality, not learning anything. *Somebody* had to be Satan for the plan to work, right?"

"Deb ... "

He hasn't ordered me to stop talking. Yet. "So it'd be a little unfair to punish him for doing his job. So, okay, maybe he's being hateful about it, but what if – Just, *what if* – he repents? We've done our probation and he gets pulled back into the fold for helping to make it happen. I mean, he's fulfilled his measure of creation, right? Win-win."

"You're treading thin ice, Deb," he mutters. "Don't go getting any sympathy for the devil. That's how people mess up."

"Have you ever messed up?"

"No."

Lie.

Baby 'gator nudges my calf and I look down – not that I can see him – but I see bubbles off to my right that shouldn't be there. I point.

"Don't shoot."

There is only one explanation I can think of for what I think appears before my eyes: I've become delusional.

I blink to try to get it to go away, flip up my night-vision goggles – but it's still there.

A perfectly attired, impeccably clean incubus, even up to his chest in slime and oil, bows to Ezekiel. "General."

"Uphir."

Oh. My. Stars.

"Good evening, Sister Judge."

I hate speaking with demons.

"Can you help her?" Ezekiel asks.

Wha – ?

The physician of demons narrows his eyes at Ezekiel. "What's she worth to you?" He cocks his head. "Your ... *soul?*"

"Riiiight."

I start to back away. I can't run through water, even if it were clear.

"Ah, yes. Apollyon already has that."

"He wishes."

Uphir laughs. "You are a consummate actor, General."

"And that's why I'm here. Get to work, Uphir."

"Sister Judge!" calls Uphir. "I would like to examine you, if I may."

My throat tightens up. "Not on your life."

He chuckles. "I have no life. None to give, none to lose. I work for the hope of salvation."

I stop.

"That's not possible," I whisper over my shoulder.

"Oh, really? You've just given me reason to conclude you think it might be."

I swallow. Hard. I almost choke on my own tongue.

He materializes in front of me, reaches out, and I gasp in pain when he passes his incorporeal hand through my body.

I pant for breath. I can barely stand and then I feel a log at my back, holding me up. I don't know where it came from. It wasn't there before.

Even in death, my friend comforts me.

"Mmm."

Uphir's hand sweeps through my head and pain of a type I have never known bursts through me. I hear a vague scream echoing through the swamp.

"It's too advanced," I hear, as if from far away. "And it's contagious."

"*Contagious?!*"

My body jolts when the log moves.

"Yes, General. Contagious. And specific to her enhancements. I don't know what they've done or how they've done it."

"Find out."

"Oh, don't worry. I will. As for this one ... " I am wracked with pain, but it seems important that I understand this conversation, so I try. "I cannot cure her, and this has to be stopped."

I feel the swamp floor trembling and hear the cries of the birds, the roar of the bears. I don't understand why they're all kicking up such a ruckus, but the rumbling is comforting and my pain begins to subside.

"Why is this bayou about to explode?"

"Every animal in a one-hundred-mile radius can feel everything she's feeling, as can the older trees. They're sharing her pain, taking some of the burden from her. *We* know this. Why don't *you?*"

Ezekiel snarls at him. "I hate this place."

"Well, you would, you fastidious son of a bitch."

"Talk to me again when you have to do your own laundry."

I have to get out of here.

"Look at me, Deb," says the General. He will brook no argument, but I will not obey. "*Look at me!*"

I look, through hazy vision, at the frontman for Lucifer, the mole, the spy.

How is it possible?

I look, and he is beautiful, his features shifting minutely, though enough for me to know that under his glamour, he is as beautiful as Apollyon and Uphir.

As beautiful as I am without *my* glamour.

Demon. Traitor.

"General!" Uphir snaps. "Stop it. You're confusing her."

"I want her to remember. I *need* her to remember."

"She is delusional!" Uphir roars, his voice powerful and unearthly enough to make the swamp floor buckle. That I am, most certainly. It's nice to be validated. "If we're successful and she remembers, she will believe you to be a demon. Is that what you want?"

High General Ezekial Alleyn, beautiful version, fades until the ugly one is firmly in place.

The physician is still speaking. "Do it now," he says, "or you'll never get her back."

Why is Ezekiel's disperser gaining light and power?

Why is he pointing it at me?

"WHY COULDN'T I get dressed in the temple?" I grumble at my mother while she fusses with my veil. "They have rooms there, you know."

I try to brush her away from me, but I ache from my left shoulder down across my body to my right hip, and I wonder if I'm coming down with the flu.

Nice.

On my wedding day, even.

"Whassa mattah, *sha?*"

"I think I slept wrong," I say. There really is no other explanation.

She squeezes my cheek and gushes in about four different flavors of French, three of which belong to her alone and have caused me much embarrassment in my life. "You are the most beautiful girl any mother could ask for."

Beauty: my sole virtue, which, loosely translated, means useless.

I sigh and refuse to look in a mirror. I know what I'll see: a bride who has graced the cover of *Brides* – among other publications – more than a few times.

It's a nice way for a useless nineteen-year-old to make a lot of money, and part of my payment for the December 2011 issue was the dress I modeled, which I requested because it's totally appropriate for the temple.

Unfortunately, that also means it's appropriate for a Christmas wedding, all heavy satin and lace, complete with mandarin collar and long sleeves with a couple of layers of sequins and beads.

In August.

In Louisiana.

"Come. Your father is waiting in the car."

"Just a minute. I forgot my medicine." My birth control pill. She thinks it's some diet drug passed around the modeling world.

I'm about to leave the bathroom when I spy some ibuprofen. Good idea. Maybe four. I really hurt.

I meet up with her at the elevator in the most expensive hotel in Baton Rouge without a word. Today is my wedding day. Aren't I supposed to be giddy?

I'm not even quite sure I'm happy.

Off the elevator.

Through the lobby.

To the front doors.

My sinuses protest the blast of steam that punches me in the face as soon as I step outside. I can barely breathe.

"The car and temple have air conditioning, *sha*," she says dryly when I tug at my collar yet again. A bellhop opens the door of the limousine that will take us to the temple. "How lucky for us, *n'est-ce pas*?" Her delight cannot be contained, but then *she* is not wearing a gown constructed to accommodate a bride who intends to have her pictures taken in the snow.

My father takes my hands and pulls me into the limousine while my mother gathers the modest train and petticoats then pushes me into the car. She and I plop down onto the bench seat at the same time, and I reach up to turn the air conditioner vents on me.

Forty-five minutes have been allotted for us to get to the temple, checked in, and settled in a timely manner. I'm quite sure my makeup is melting and that the air conditioner could spit out zero-degree air and I'll never be cool again. There is an annoying trickle of sweat going down my back.

Twenty minutes later, I find myself thrown face-first onto the floor of the limousine when it slams to a halt. The driver is cursing. My father helps me up. My mother is gasping her outrage. "Your makeup!" she wails. "It's ruined!"

Of course it is. There's my face print in the carpet, right there, in foundation, powder, concealer, eye shadow, and lipstick.

That's funny, but it hurts to laugh.

"Deborah! Stop laughing. Now is not the time."

"It's my wedding day, Mère. Is there a *better* time to laugh?"

"We have nothing to repair it with," she hisses.

I shrug. "Told you I wanted to dress at the temple. That was for a reason. Well, several. But *noooo*." I'm quite certain they have soap and water in the temple, and I'll simply wash it all off. There are worse things than getting married without makeup.

Like ... the dead deer in the middle of the road and a steaming radiator, which has cut off my supply of cool air.

"My apologies, Mr. and Mrs. Judge," the driver says apologetically as he opens the door on my father's side. "This is an odd time of day for deer to be out, and I did not see it." He pauses, looks me over dubiously, and says, "You will have to walk."

I sigh.

"But it's only another hundred yards to the driveway."

In this dress.

In August.

In Louisiana.

I wonder if they'll let me cool off in the baptismal font.

"Deb!"

I turn and see my fiancé jogging toward me. "Drake! What are you doing? You're supposed to be in there waiting for me."

"I saw the accident," he says smoothly, "and wanted to make sure you were okay."

"Um ... " Goodness. I'm going to have sweat stains under my armpits. "How did you see it from the parking lot? There's tons of trees blocking the view." I pick up my skirt and petticoats and start walking, giving the steaming limousine, the driver, my parents, and the poor dead deer a wide berth. "Really, people. I need an ice bath."

I approach Drake. I'm not superstitious, so I really don't care if he sees me in my wedding dress before the ceremony. He looks at me with an expression I've never seen on his face and purrs, "Are you ready, my love?"

My love? His voice has dropped and it's rich with suggestion I've only heard in the movies.

Suddenly, the prospect of the wedding night is looking a whole lot more enticing. Drake is possibly the most handsome man I've ever met, but he is entirely serious all the time. Even his kisses are serious. I might have said *yes* to his proposal more quickly had he spoken to me like that before today. "Are you feeling okay? Look at me. My makeup's trashed and my hair's probably a mess and my pits are soaked. Can't you smell me?"

He smirks.

He never smirks. Drake doesn't catch deadpan humor.

He also never looks at me with lust. Plenty of men look at me with lust, but not Drake. Drake does not lust.

"Aren't you going to hold my hand?" I ask, exasperated at his very non-Drake-like behavior.

"No," he says amiably as he begins to walk up the road, gesturing for me to walk with him. "You stink."

I stare at him, walking a good two feet from me. A *joke?* An *insult?* Drake doesn't do either. They are beneath him, and Drake is nothing if not dignified.

A cloud drifts overhead, but it doesn't help anything. There is no breeze. There are no sounds of wildlife, engines, or people. I look over my shoulder. My parents are there arguing with the limousine driver, but I can't hear them.

"Deb ... " he says in the new voice, the lazy, seductive one. It's familiar, but not Drake-familiar.

"What have you done with my fiancé?" I tease, then blink at the vicious snarl I see for a split second.

My eyes are playing tricks on me.

It's this heat, this dress.

Gracious, I must get to the temple. Only thirty more feet to the driveway.

"DEB!"

I look ahead to see a young white-clad temple worker sprinting across the parking lot toward us.

Interesting. I thought all temple workers were old.

"Right on time," Drake mutters angrily.

"Drake!" I am aghast. Drake might not have a sense of humor, but he doesn't get angry, either. It's not dignified.

"Deb!" pants the temple worker. He takes my wrist in an iron grip –

"I don't think so!" Drake hisses, trying to grab me, his hand passing clean through my free wrist! *tabarnouche,* that hurts! and I scream, start to cry from the shock and the intensity of the pain.

The worker ignores my wails to drag me the remaining distance until I'm on temple grounds. He's huffing and puffing, and I'm holding my wrist, sobbing at how badly it hurts. It must be broken.

"Let me see," he says, and I offer my hand to him, still sobbing but keeping one eye on Drake. "Don't worry about him," says the worker absently as he surrounds my wrist and palm with both of his hands – They're huge.

I've never seen bigger hands on a man, and so totally out of proportion with the rest of his body.

I look back at Drake, and as the pain subsides, I grow more and more captivated by his beauty. It's almost surreal how beautiful he's become, looking at me the way I have always thought Drake *should* look at me. I stand transfixed, and when he smiles at me ...

The man who's tending me snaps his fingers in my face. "Deb. Look at me."

I don't want to. Drake has become a work of art, and my captor is ... ugly.

"Come to me, Deb," Drake whispers, his voice dark and rich like chocolate.

"Look. At. Me."

I am compelled to obey my captor, but it takes some effort to pry my attention away.

"I have a very important calling to extend to you, Sister Judge," the temple worker says urgently, as my desire to look at my fiancé is strong.

"I don't believe you," I say, stung, focusing fully on the man who still holds me. "Unless you need me to stand here and look pretty."

"That's right, Deb," calls Drake. "He's playing you, using your dreams against you. Don't fall for it."

"Deb, listen to me. You are crucial to the work, the plan. You must come hear me out. Please."

"Crucial," scoffs my fiancé. "The only crucial thing here is getting married and fulfilling your purpose."

I look at Drake then, confused. "My *purpose?*"

He waves that away. "Marriage. Motherhood. What else would it be?"

Motherhood. "Uh ... Are you saying that after a year of swearing you don't want children, that *now* you do?"

His mouth tightens. "Don't be stupid," he snaps. "Of course I do. You do too, deep down inside. Every good Mormon girl does."

The temple worker draws me close and whispers in my ear. "You've never wanted children. You don't like people. You like animals. They adore you. You name your plants. They grow for you, out of season, out of zone, no matter what. An orange tree would grow in the arctic for you simply out of love and respect."

I look at him, into his unremarkable brown eyes. How does he know these things about me?

"You had a baby alligator when you were younger, but your mother made you take him to the zoo when he got too big, and you still miss him. You have a family of raccoons at your back door every two months. You'd just as soon feed them, but your mother makes you lead them away. They'll follow you anywhere you go, no matter how much they don't want to."

I gulp.

"We have a special calling for you, Deb," he says desperately. "One just for you, one only *you* can fulfill, one you're perfectly suited for. We *need* you, Deb, and is it *not* for your beauty."

"Deb," whispers Drake and it's like he's right in my ear. "He will take you to a swamp and leave you there, alone, ugly, unwanted."

He's so beautiful, his voice so seductive ...

What were we arguing about?

"*I* will never leave you alone, ugly, unwanted."

"He's lying," my captor says.

"Look at him," Drake sneers. "He's nothing. Unemployed. Nobody that young works in the temple in the middle of a weekday unless they don't have a job. Loser."

Drake has never lied to me; in fact, he's brutally honest because he has no social skills. I don't know who to trust.

My head hurts. My body aches.

"Why do I have to go with either of you?" I ask after a long moment.

"It's your destiny," Drake says. "You don't have a choice."

But my captor releases me. "You always have a choice, Deb," he says quietly. "I just ... would like you to come hear what I have to say. If you don't *like* what I have to say, I'll understand. No hard feelings."

"Don't be stupid," Drake hisses when I look at him. "You're beautiful and I am a man of wealth and taste. I will give you anything and everything your heart desires, and you will never have to work or choose or suffer."

He seems to have forgotten everything our relationship was based on, but the difference he offers sounds pretty good. He's gorgeous and enthralling, and now I'm actually looking forward to my wedding night.

I feel like I'm spinning inside of a barrel ride, stuck to the wall, caught between centripetal force and gravity, the floor just dropped, and I'm slipping downward.

I glare at the temple worker. "Is he lying about you taking me to a swamp and leaving me there, ugly and alone?"

"No."

That's ... intriguing.

"You will be doing very important work – "

"In a *swamp?*"

"Where you will have *sole stewardship.*"

A wave of déjà vu crashes over me so hard I'm dizzy. I have never had sole stewardship of anything, including my bank account.

He opens his mouth to say more, then stops. He loses focus for a second. Then he's back. "You are *useful.*"

"Useful!" Drake hoots. "What kind of a selling point is *that?*"

"You have ten minutes," I say to the ugly man. "And you better make it good."

TRAITORS AND TYRANTS

John Nakamura Remy
and Galen Dara

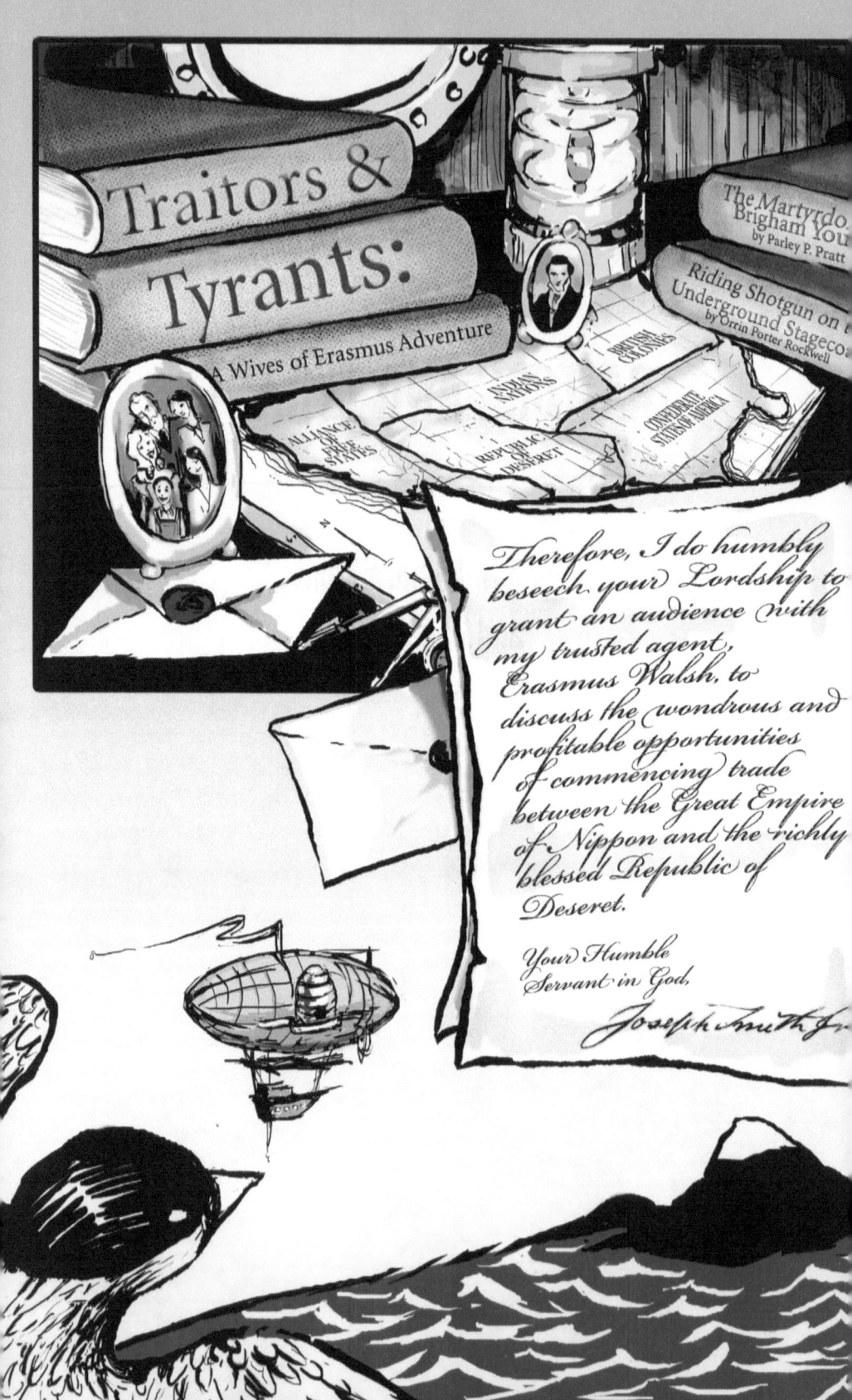

BRIDGET,
WHAT IS IT?

BLEEDING HELL,
WE'RE UNDER ATTACK!
TO ARMS, SISTERS!

KIWIDINOK
FIRST WIFE, AGE 43

CONVERTED AS A TEEN BY ERASMUS WALSH DURING HIS MISSION TO THE LAMANITES. FOUGHT BESIDE PORTER ROCKWELL TO FREE SLAVES ON THE UNDERGROUND STAGECOACH.

BRIDGET
SECOND WIFE, AGE 31

JOINED THE CHURCH TO FLEE POVERTY IN IRELAND AND TO EXPERIENCE THE WORLD. DRESSES IMMODESTLY, SWEARS, PRACTICES FOLK MAGIC.

MIZUKI
THIRD WIFE, AGE 26

ONLY CHILD OF A SHINTO PRIEST WHOSE FAMILY CONVERTED AND CAME TO ZION. JOSEPH ENCOURAGED HER TRAINING IN JAPANESE MARTIAL ARTS.

PERSEPHONE
FOURTH WIFE, AGE 18

FREED SLAVE WHO WAS BROUGHT TO ZION BY KIWIDINOK. SHE IS A GENIUS TINKERER AND INVENTOR AND PREFERS HER GADGETS TO PEOPLE.

THE SHOGUN'S PALACE

将軍気 軍貿過 未考 有調御 噴湯屋

HIS EXCELLENCY IS INTRIGUED BY YOUR OFFER TO TRADE PRECIOUS HELIUM AND WILL CONSIDER YOUR GENEROUS PROPOSAL. BUT FOR NOW, HE HOPES YOU WILL ACCEPT HIS HUMBLE HOSPITALITY.

THE "OTHERS." IF IT WAS JUST YOU AND ME...

PLEASE, NOT THIS AGAIN. I HAD TO OBEY JOSEPH.

IT'S TOO DANGEROUS. YOU SHOULDN'T BE ALONE.

I'LL BE FINE, BELOVED. KEEP THE OTHERS OUT OF TROUBLE.

THE SHOGUN'S PRIVATE BATHS

WHAT'S TROUBLING SISTER KIWIDINOK?

SHE'S GOT A STICK UP HER ARSE BECAUSE SHE'S IN OUR BED AND NOT IN OUR HUSBAND'S.

BRIDGET!

WHY WOULD NINJA ASSASSINS ATTACK US?

AND WHAT WAS THAT HORRIBLE DEAD THING?

YEAH SISTER, HOLDING OUT ON US AGAIN? ANOTHER SECRET MISSION FROM OUR DEAR PROPHET?

AT LEAST YOU KNOW WHAT YOU'RE READY TO DIE FOR! YOU'VE GOT A MISSION, AND YOU'VE GOT LOVE, WE AIN'T GOT JACK!

F--

LEAVE.

NOT YOU. THEM.

FIND OUT WHO SENT THEM.

MY PLEASURE.

DID YOU KNOW THAT MY FRIEND HERE CAN TALK TO THE DEAD?

SO?

YOU *WILL* TELL US WHO SENT YOU, BUT WE'LL LET YOU CHOOSE IF YOU TELL US ALIVE...OR DEAD!

OLD TEMPLE! EMPTY, NO ONE USE... TO WEST!

BUT WHO? WHO SENT YOU

STRANGE... STRANGE MAN. TH ALL I KNOW!

ABANDONED TEMPLE

MIZUKI, WHY IN [GO]D'S NAME DID WE [B]RING ERASMUS?

YOU ARE FOREIGN WOMEN. YOU LOOK SUSPICIOUS TRAVELING WITHOUT A MAN.

STRANGE, A LOT OF THIS DIRT IS FRESHLY TURNED.

WHAT IS THAT BLOODY STINK?

SOMETHING IS NOT RIGHT...

I FEEL MUCH DEATH HERE.

OH, HELL.

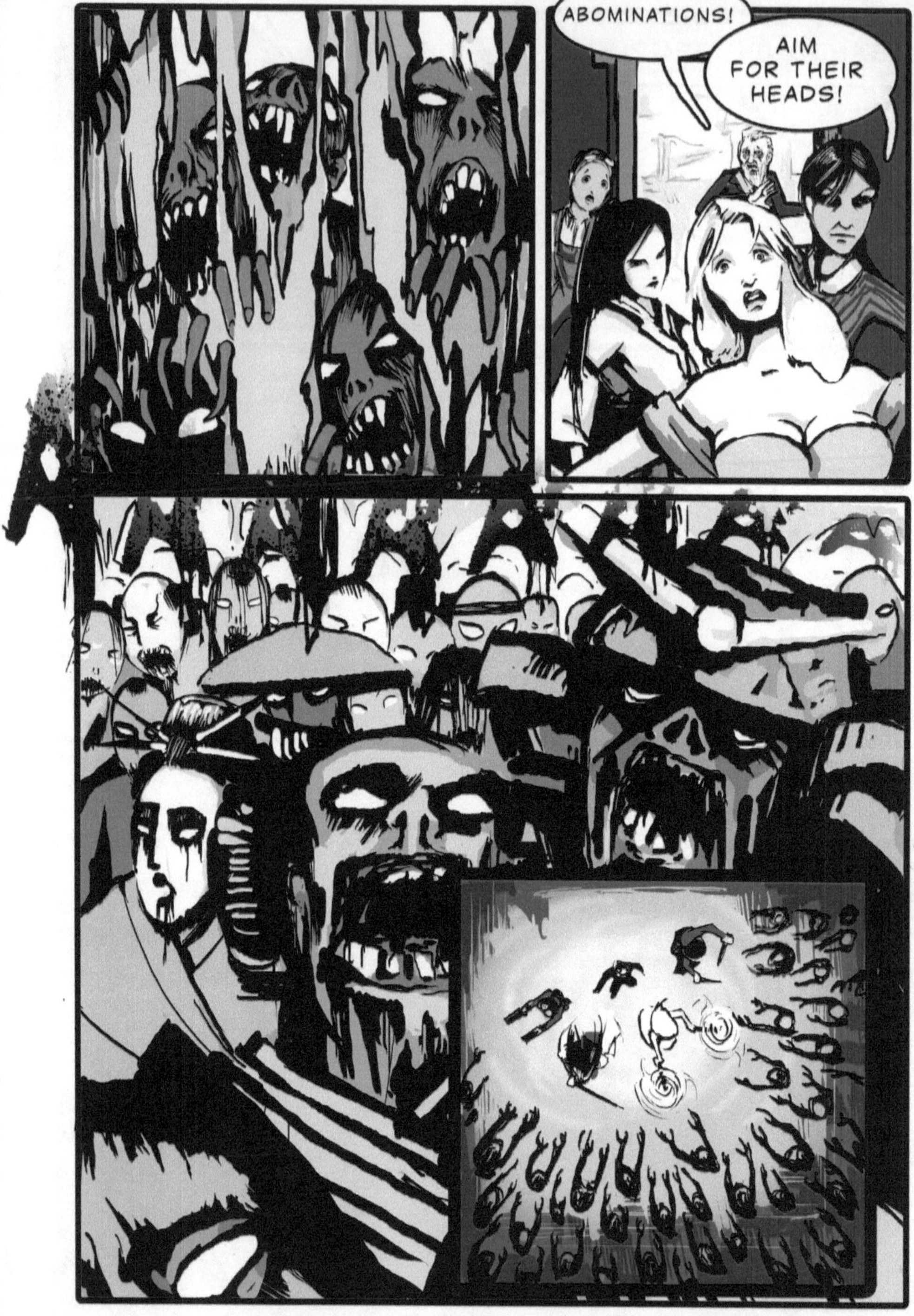

SO THIS IS WHERE THE OLD APOSTATE RAN OFF TO.

BUT HE COULDN'T HAVE BEEN BEHIND THE ATTACKS ON THE AIRSHIP AND IN THE PALACE. HE WASN'T POWERFUL ENOUGH.

BUT...THAT LEAVES ONLY THE SHOGUN! WHY WOULD HE WANT STRANG...

WHAT RULER WOULDN'T WANT AN ARMY OF UNSTOPPABLE, HORRIFYING DEAD ABOMINATIONS?

SUCH A PERVERSION OF OUR LORD'S WORK!

THAT BASTARD! HE CERTAINLY KEPT HIS HANDS CLEAN, DIDN'T HE? HIRING ASSASSINS, MERCENARY THUGS, AND A HERETIC!

WE HAVE TO GO AFTER THE SHOGUN!

NO.

KIWIDINOK IS RIGHT. YOU HAD YOUR MISSION FROM THE PROPHET...

...I STILL HAVE MINE.

EXPERIMENTING WITH LIFE AT EXTRAORDINARY DEPTHS

Bridgette Day Tuckfield

CERTAIN sides of her always manifested when she was restless, and May had been feeling restless.

May convinced Damon to skip out on the Halloween photo scavenger hunt just because she could. She suspected he had organized the hunt on her behalf, but would much rather go to the lake, and also see if he would drive her down there. Instead. It was an efficiency of pleasure.

Damon had agreed after only a little cajoling, which disappointed her. He had made the mistake of starting the date by driving her up the mountain to talk about the future. Temples and God were brought up. Which was just fine of course, but this was a second date.

May listened and smiled and seethed at what she thought were his plans for her, and then decided to strike back like the little monster she should be. So while he was trying to have his little spiritual moment, she would counter with stories about her less-than-conservative past exploits, subtly mocking both his verbiage and his interest in her. And then she separated him from his friends and made him drive her down to the lake instead of further up the mountain.

EXPERIMENTING WITH LIFE AT EXTRAORDINARY DEPTHS
BRIDGETTE DAY TUCKFIELD

"So but you're sure your friends aren't going to be mad?" May asked as they wound their way down. She twisted her face like she might be feeling bad.

He paused for just that fraction of a second. There was a fey quality to him that was demonstrated at the moment in the way he held his long hands and wrists on the steering wheel, perched light and tense like a girl sitting on a new boyfriend's lap.

"No, no, of course not," he said. "The point of the night was to have fun. The scavenger hunt was just a means to an end. Going to the lake will be fun too."

He rarely used speech fillers, she noticed; there was a clipped precision to everything he said, like he hung his words carefully in the air. Her own style was more fluid. While he had light hair that was longish for BYU, and a clean-cut style that pretty much combined to make him look like a villain from an '80s teen comedy, she had curls, and a thin dark mouth that simpered and sneered in ways and at times that she was not aware. She looked like a craven little doll.

"Because I think the lake will be more fun – at night – and it'll just be you and me and we can talk. And besides which I hate all these, like, faux youth group activities posing as dates. We are not twelve. We are adults and can relate to each other as adults. I feel like the people who do these things are arrested adolescents who fear any sort of normal adult human sexuality or even interests, so they watch Disney movies and go on scavenger hunts. Am I right?"

She was being cruel on purpose. But living in this valley could be so difficult, she reasoned, and she could not help reacting poorly. One is surrounded at all times by rock, by salt, by unforgivable terrain. May had once been able to go anywhere and do anything, although eventually all those things and places caught up to her. So she had sought refuge like about a million before her in this safe, fenced-in place. Mountains as protection, as fences, bars – it was an old analogy. But instead of comforting and safe, they were implacable. Instead of promising possibilities and heights to be scaled, they loomed.

"Yes, I see your point. I suppose," Damon finally said.

They were leaving the campus area, and she hadn't even made him uncomfortable yet. She sighed. "It's just that, I'm sorry, I'm still trying to reacclimate to this, well, climate. People don't seem to just have cazh parties here, you know, everything's like a production. I mean sometimes all I want is a glass of wine and a good conversation, not to build a snowman out of toothpicks or play duck-duck-goose."

"I understand." He remained unruffled.

May frowned. She was hoping for nervous laughter at least. "Well, anyway, thanks for ditching."

"You know, though, we can still complete the assignment down there."

"To find something terrifying? Like what? Ugly couples making out?" She grimaced as she heard the ugly words coming out of her mouth.

"No, sea monsters. Or," he chuckled, really chuckled. "Lake monsters."

She laughed. "Like Loch Ness? A misplaced plesiosaur?"

"No," he smiled, as if what she said was actually funny. "They are a Native American legend. There's a real word for them. I think they might be called something like pahpix, or something along those lines. Pawapicts? Yes, that. The word means water-babies."

"Okay, so like Charles Kingsley."

"Not that either."

"You know who that was?"

"Why would you bring something up if you thought I didn't know what it was?" He glanced sidelong at her. They both knew the answer to that. He smiled back out to the road and his teeth were white and straight.

May felt her face go hot. "Anyway, they don't sound exactly terrifying. More like adorable."

"It does probably sound better in its native language."

"Probably. Most things do. So but little mermaid babies are gonna have to come down on the side of adorable."

"Initially, I suppose they are. They are about human-sized, if I remember correctly. Some of them looked like infants. Imagine that. A baby, or a little kid, floating and splashing in the water, sobbing, and you would try to save it, but it would be too late. They'd all pull you in and make you one of them."

May paused, impressed. "Gah. When you put it that way, that is pretty awful."

"The Utes told the early Mormon settlers about them, and they ran with it. They saw lake monsters all the time – or rather, serpents and kraken because that's what they grew up with."

"Being Scandinavian and all. You find what you're looking for." And the depths could hold any shape if you looked hard enough, she thought. "Where did you hear that story?"

"It crops up in the local news every couple of years."

"Slow news day, and being short on real monsters. Like the police have nothing to do. I've never gotten pulled over so many times for not signaling."

"I suppose so."

May could see her frown reflected in the night-window. She did not care for monsters or anything pretending to be one.

EXPERIMENTING WITH LIFE AT EXTRAORDINARY DEPTHS
BRIDGETTE DAY TUCKFIELD

Some years ago, before May realized there was nothing so commonplace as petty rebellion, she had been one herself.

When on her own for the first time, she had allowed herself, in this order: a pretty gold-eyed boy whom she met in a hot tub; never going to class; never sleeping at home; eating and drinking whatever she might want; otherwise consuming whatever she wanted through whatever means necessary; a prodigal return home. Despite what they said, not all lists ran in that general order down, but hers had.

It was a list she mostly kept to herself.

"You are what you pretend to be," her mother had told her growing up, ignoring the fact her daughter always played the villain in make believe games. The only one May hadn't surprised by her unhealthy predilections was herself.

To distract herself from unpleasant memories welling up, she turned her attention to the CDs in Damon's glove compartment and judged them mercilessly.

Damon wound them up roads to the places he knew they could get to the water. He had fallen quiet and May wondered if maybe they were trespassing. She savored the conciliatory thrill of minor infraction as they stepped through gray dusty brush and asphalt. However, Damon's uncle had moored a paddleboat to a dock, and Damon had the key on his keychain, so the thrill quickly dissipated.

It was dark out by the lake and May heard all the soft lake sounds of lapping and bumping of boats and objects on an unreliable liminal surface. Out here, the palette was forest green and midnight blue and whisper gray and just black: colors that implied distance through opacity. Darks that might frighten because of what can hide in deep places.

May rubbed her arms to friction up some heat. She wished she had worn more than the unofficial BYU woman's uniform of cardigan and skirt. Damon, in his weirdly omnipresent dress clothes, would be warm enough, she thought.

Walking beside her, Damon noticed. "Are you going to be okay?" he asked.

"I left the camera in the car," she said, looking at him and cringing. On accident, but he didn't look like he believed her.

"Oh. That's fine. It's not like it would have been easy to take pictures in this lighting."

The wind susurrated in the vast space. She let him help her into the aluminum boat. "I haven't been in one of these forever," she said. "We used to go out on the lake at home." But that was sun and sweat and sunburn and clear green water. Not like this black pool. She tottered to the front and grabbed an oar.

"Yeah, it's nice." He smiled. He untied the boat and let them go, and arranged himself in the back.

They took a little while to get a rowing rhythm down, but soon they were in sync paddling away from home.

"Hey Damon," she said, "how deep is this lake?"

The bright disinterest in her tone did not fool him. "Can't you swim?"

"How dare you, sir. Of course I can swim. I'm just wondering."

"I don't think it's actually that deep. Maybe twenty feet? I have no basis for this, understand, I just think most of the lake is pretty shallow."

Of course it's shallow, May thought. It's in Utah where everything is rocky surface. Walled-in wastelands and salty deserts.

Thank goodness, she also thought.

"That's good," she said. "I – you know how some people have phobias? I have this just atavistic fear of deep water. For serious though. I used to imagine, like, manta rays coming up from the swimming pool drains to eat me."

"Deep water? Really? Little miss rebel?"

She stopped paddling and turned. "Hey now. Of all the fears to have, it's pretty primal and cool. I can look it up in dream dictionaries and everything."

"I find that in dream dictionaries everything means sex."

May laughed without reminding herself to. "Actually, it's pretty much the only thing that doesn't. I can't believe you said that." Or that he would so dare to let the word profane his lips.

He raised an eyebrow, an exaggerated gesture May knew must have been extensively workshopped in front of mirrors. Much like her "demure" look. "Why not? I can be a rebel too."

"The fact that that qualifies – I can see that!" she amended. "But it's pretty much what you would think. The unconscious. Infinite. Feelings. Junk like that."

The boat jostled slightly.

"I mean," she continued, "I used to be really bad about the water. I'm pretty much over it now."

Damon stopped rowing, so she did too. For a moment he said nothing, and when she turned she could see him stirring the end of the paddle softly in the water. Then he looked up at her with a speculative smile.

"Prove it," he said. "Can those clothes get wet?"

"Not the shoes."

"Okay, not the shoes. Get in the water. For one minute. I dare you."

"It's freezing," she pointed out. She was surprised at his dare. She was surprised at the way he was looking at her, that he was pushing back.

She smiled at him. This could be an adventure after all.

EXPERIMENTING WITH LIFE AT EXTRAORDINARY DEPTHS
BRIDGETTE DAY TUCKFIELD

He held up towels that were stored in the boat, for splashing mishaps. "Got you covered. In all senses. And we can go right back and get hot chocolate with every-one else."

She scowled.

"You can say no," he said. "You can always say that. You could have said no when I asked you out, for example."

She blushed, hotly. She wondered what would prove his point, going in or not, and why she hated so much being found out.

"Just remarking on the fact," he grinned.

"You're right," she agreed, slowly. "Fine. I'll go in. For one minute."

"As long as you're having fun."

"Of course." She had, after all, faced far worse, she reminded herself.

Her boots came off after a pull or two, and her heart had already started beating faster. She had forgotten what fear was like. It was wonderful. She stripped down to her shorts and tank top she always wore under the skirt and cardigans in case she got tired of campus dress code.

May put her feet over the edge, the rim biting into the back of her knees. The water was very cold and murky. She had heard it was because of carp, stirring up the bottom mud. Her pale feet were only slightly visible, disappearing into black – another dimension.

"Okay I'm psyching myself out," she said.

"Then you had better go fast." Never dropped a verb for convenience, that one.

She launched herself, slipping into the dark, suddenly disconnected from her body. If she didn't look down, where there was nothing but down, if she turned and smiled kept her gaze on Damon's possibly impressed face, then it was fine.

It was her choice, not his, to get in and go down. And it was only water after all.

In May's sabbatical years, she had started to transform. Later she would try to tell her family that her old friends weren't bad people because they weren't Church members. They were bad people because they were bad people.

"I know you don't care about me," she would start with the yellow-eyed boy she had spoken to first in the hot tub, his eyes deserts now, not suns, and he would lie to her. She had immersed herself in their frightening world. She said later that she was experimenting with depth. With how far down a human being could go.

During those years, sometimes May would climb into her bathtub for a soak and would realize that her leg hair had grown half an inch since the day before. But then she would realize that it wasn't the day before it had been four or five days, slipped by like water through a sieve. She wouldn't tell anyone, because this would in fact be a frightening thought. So she would sink lower in her tub and shave her legs, which thick black hairs made her look like a monster, along with her newly hollow eyes and hanging skin from losing so much weight so fast. She would fill the tub with more bubbles, and sink deeper.

She would sink to the bottom of the tub for as long as her lungs could hold, and felt held by water and time. In water. She could do anything she wanted, and yet all doors forward were closed to her. There was no real way forward. Only down.

May treaded, a few feet from the boat just at first. Lakes were her least favorite bodies of water, as bodies of water went. At night, the lake was a shock of ionic dark.

"This actually isn't so bad," she quavered, a lie. It was already terrible.

"Glad to hear it," he said. "Do you need help back in?"

"No," she said. The fear was, for the moment, exhilarating. "I'm just fine." She swam back and forth, around and about. The strokes of her feet, the swirls of her hands, sent ripples across the glassy surface in a lacuna of movement.

May lurched herself back, wetting her curly hair, which pulled her head back with the new weight. She kicked, and thought of choices bringing her here. What her mom had told her too, about sinking – some scripture – that all men and women could always choose what direction to move in.

"You should come in too," she said dreamily, drifting. The black sky seemed as deep as the lake was to her.

Damon was saying something but her ears were below water and she couldn't hear. Out of a bored defiance, she kicked away. The cold was consuming, her breathing short and shallow. Her life was never supposed to turn out like this:

Alone and sad, needling a boy because he had the temerity to be boring.

She wondered where she would have been without having sunk. May had to keep kicking to keep from sinking now, and floated, and looked up. All she could hear now was the throb of submarine sounds. Then more distinctly, eddies around her, water currents curling around her. She fancied she felt actual pressure, of little sliding slimy things.

May even fancied she felt a clammy hand on her foot.

She straightened up immediately, sinking her feet below her again. In the moonlight her movements flashed in bright facets on the choppy water – what wasn't black was rhinestone.

For the first time she really was frightened. She froze, awaiting a next sensation. She had overreacted before.

But this water, this touch, was real.

She kicked too far down, down to the weeds, which curled slimy round her foot. She kicked some more and only entangled herself. May felt a strange a premonition of dissolution.

She would have to dive down to untangle her foot. And panic is a funny thing, and sometimes the strangest things will surface – old fears.

How could she possibly have thought any of this was a good idea? Why was she here?

A cloud had passed over the moon, which reemerged like a curtain raised up again. Beyond that the faint stars billowed outward, ever expanding, spinning away in stillness.

The water, though, dipped and swirled. Just below the surface, her limbs panicked, darting like scared fish.

May looked once more at the sky, avoiding smiling Damon, because what help was he to her now.

She took one last breath, and dove, opening her eyes uselessly in the dark as she tugged at her ankles. As her eyes adjusted to amphibian life and to the dark, she saw that it wasn't a stray long weed at all that held her, but a webbed hand connected to an arm disappearing into the depth of black. Her shock let release a cry of bubble, and two gold eyes became visible, to look into her own. The dark creature moved up, pulling her foot with her so there was no way she could reach the surface, no way she could reach air. It moved her plane of existence down a little further.

There were more hands at her feet, and the initial creature looped up in front to take her hand and hold it. It was at least as large as she was, with two arms and two legs. More gold eyes, with wide white smiles and mermaid-dark hair, appeared around her. May could make out darker shapes in the water, around and about and down, and even above. Beyond their eyes, the beasts themselves were green-black bleeding into the green-black water. They were dissolute shapes as large as dogs. There was no use trying to swim away.

She used to swim strongly, in lanes and lines, back and forth, in pools and oceans. Surface races. Never diving or competing in how far one could plunge.

As her eyes adjusted she realized the creatures were actually lighter than the water. They could be called human were it not for their enormous eyes and tapered heads with wide frog-mouth smiles of brilliant long teeth. Ropy muscles curled under smooth skin, and their flippers grew from elongated animal feet, with webbed fingers and toes. May's lungs were starting their desperate airless burn. The creatures' flowing hair tangled in the water like seaweed spines. Like anemone arms. They grasped May with their claws, tight jewelry biting into her wrists and her ankles.

EXPERIMENTING WITH LIFE AT EXTRAORDINARY DEPTHS
BRIDGETTE DAY TUCKFIELD

Even with their false smiles they seemed sad. Like they knew loss, and failure, of a shallow life laid bare like rock.

(It had ended badly all those years ago, in the predictable way. She had been discarded for another girl, smeared and fat and stupid. It had ended with her attacking him, crying how could you, you monster. It was only later as she was leaving that she caught her reflection in the sliding glass doors that she realized he was only a monster trading monsters – she did not recognize herself, with her wan face twisting in rage, her dark hair gone coarse and spiky, her skin hanging off bones like some pale gargoyle.)

The pawapicts had come for her, but she had always been looking for them anyway.

May cried out again, in sound waves and bubbles, in anything but regret or loss. She was out of air now.

More creatures came forward, looping dreamily around her. More hands grabbed at her, gently, firmly. If May never surfaced, she'd never have to face the surface again. She could be bound by water instead of by mountains and her own treacherous self, and be a monster, and live in the depths she worked so hard to sink to. As if in response, the creatures started to make strange wavering ululations.

The creatures touched her cold arms, cold face, cold skin. They wrapped their fingers in her waving hair, and they pulled her down into the green-black, the amniotic darkness.

Her lungs were already burning. She had always wondered, when reading old stories, why sailors had let mermaids drown them. But she realized now that was the easier choice – all you had to do was not fight.

The first creature, the one who hovered in front of her, slid its slippery hand down her arm to take her hand like she was a child. It had shorter hair than the others, and lighter eyes, and the widest mouth with gnarled teeth.

It held her hand and cooed, the others calling back. May took a deep breath of water, choking soundlessly. The creature pulled her gently forwards and down, with yellow eyes that pinpricked the dark. The other creatures churned and roiled around her. The water above must be boiling with movement and last breaths.

May knew that if she chose so now, she could hide forever in the cold green and become one of them, if not just fade to black herself, or whatever drowning was. She would never regret another thing again. It was not a childlike thing that would lure her, but a friend. She could tempt herself.

But no.

She was no water girl. Not anymore.

She pulled back, and up, hard and insistent. At first she surprised the creature and so pulled her hand free. Her actions only agitated them, and they twisted around her, bubbling and hissing, pulling her down again. They claimed her.

May tore; she twisted back. Her chest was bursting. She breathed in the black and expelled it again. There was no air for her vocal cords to vibrate.

Everywhere around her pressed demon limbs and eyes, and only the creatures' sounds could be heard. She was losing her presence sense by sense.

The creatures were pawapicts, in the old Ute tongue. They had many names in many languages, including their own liquid vocabulary, in curls and calls and eddied sounds.

This they had in common with all monsters – that they look exactly how you expected them to. That they had always been here. And that unlike animals who attacked when they were frightened – pawapicts only attacked when you yourself were frightened.

It could be so easy to start breathing water instead of air; May had a brief flash of how it could be. Her hair gone spiky and coarse, her eyes gone yellow-gold, her smile endless, and the thousand other adaptive traits adopted for life at extraordinary depths. A monster able to move in any dimension, but trapped after all in the very water you breathe.

Poor things.

Poor sad things.

What scanty moonlight filtering from the surface of the lake was lost as May was pulled ever more quietly down. She couldn't see anymore. She couldn't hear anything but the thrum of vibrations in water, and she couldn't breathe. She could only taste cold and earth and chlorophyll. The weeds closed over her, encompassing her.

Why, she thought, she must almost have reached the bottom by now. May turned a slight somersault, her companions shifting direction with her. She tucked her knees into her stomach and brought her arms in close. This was not going to happen again.

For a single instant she hung in icy equilibrium.

May did not just kick; she exploded. Her feet struck mud and rock and she flew up through the water, crashing into and over fishy selves, careering past dark bodies and webbed fingers.

Her head broke the surface, the moon the first thing she saw through wet lashes. She choked out water and gasped, flailing at the water as if at an assailant.

No good. The monster's weed-fingers wrapped around her legs again, slimy trails running up and down her legs.

EXPERIMENTING WITH LIFE AT EXTRAORDINARY DEPTHS
BRIDGETTE DAY TUCKFIELD

Something surfaced in front of her – a human head, although the body below was green and mottled. It was a woman's face, two feet away from her own.

It was her own face, yellow-eyed and grinning.

May struck out at it. The thing dove under her punch and bit her wrist, hard enough to draw blood. She screamed and wrestled the thing below the surface – below the water it kept its monstrous form – and clawed at it, kicking her feet to keep them from the other creatures' grasp, until she felt a different touch from above and behind her.

She twisted away until she realized it was Damon trying to help, and he was yelling. "Jeez, May, jeez, grab on, grab on, come on, are you all right, come on!"

May grabbed at his arm and at the rim of the boat. They were still pulling at her from below the water, and she felt she was being torn. Her head fell back under the water, and she could only see the boat and Damon's pale face through the medium of drowning. Sharp claws or teeth dug into her leg. Her skin broke all at once in a dozen places.

She kicked her legs like pistons and pulled up with all her might. With Damon's help, she lifted herself out of the water and into the safe bounds of the boat. He immediately started fussing over her, but her first order of business was to lean over the side and vomit out all the leftover water. Dark shapes still danced under the surface.

May lay back, gasping, laughing. She had fought her way back. There was no reason to be upset, she realized.

Damon crouched gingerly by her side, smothering her in the white towels and dabbing at her wrist and ankle where blood was dying the rivulets of dripping lake water a deep red.

"May, I am so sorry. I am *so* sorry. I am such a jerk," he said, focusing intently on her foot. "You told me you didn't like deep water."

"Ha ... ha," May said. "Don't worry about it. I mean, I was the one that got in the water."

"What happened?"

She took a breath, and looked out over the water. "I got my feet tangled in some weeds. I guess I must have panicked."

"But what about the scrapes?"

"I don't know. Someone must have dropped something sharp down there."

The boat jumped a bit.

"Um, do you think you could take us back?" May said. "Maybe ... there'll be some hot chocolate yet." She felt exhausted, and her voice was muted.

"Of course!" He grabbed a paddle and started rowing.

May sat up. They weren't actually that far from the dock. She realized she was shivering, so she pulled the towels closer around her. "Thanks for helping pull me out."

"Yes, next time I'll let you drown."

"That's fair. Sorry ... " She sighed. "Sorry I've been such a monster to you. It just happens sometimes."

He turned and smiled. "You were trying pretty hard but you weren't there yet. You're just prickly. I like prickly people."

She smiled back, a spot of lake weed on her lip.

The lake monsters had bitten deep, though, and her little spider-bite arcs of teeth healed into arced scars that never did stop hurting unless she was under water.

She could always go back down, if she wanted.

I HAD KILLED A ZOMBIE

Adam Greenwood

AMONG all the Zombie-Battling Organizations, how was I to know which ZBO was right? The fighting techniques of the multiplicity of ZBOs were so various, and their claims to exclusive divine guidance so uniform, that I despaired of ever finding an answer.

No one needed an answer more than I. How to fight zombies I did not know, and though I was a mere youth as the world accounts, my mind was continually harrowed up in serious reflection on the issue. Zombies have a way of gripping the brain.

My boyhood passed without serious incident, nestled in the sheltering bosoms of my dear parents. We resided on a Lake Michigan trawler fleet, where my family maintained a loose connection with the Tiberian Indiscriminate Church. Although my parents taught me devotion and taught me themselves the simple precepts of true religion, even as a boy I felt something was lacking in my knowledge of undead-killing holiness that could yet be learned. The rituals of the Church commemorating the supposed victory over the vampires in antiquity were very beautiful, I freely confess. Indeed, the preceptors of that faith assured me that the rituals possessed mysterious symbolic significance. But I reflected that mortal eyes had not beheld and mortal flesh had not fallen victim to the foul predations of that brood for hundreds and perhaps even thousands of years. Does Heaven not yet speak, I asked myself? Can it be that the Almighty, the Lord of Stakes, who saved his people in ages past, has fallen silent? It seemed to me then, as it seems now, that if a ZBO had no godly instruction to impart concerning the zombie threat then why should it be proudly call itself a ZBO?

I talked to the sacerdote about these concerns, but he merely laughed. He said the important thing was that every ZBO was against zombies in its own way and the differences didn't matter. The disquieting reflections that had directed me to unburden my bosom to him were in no way soothed by this unlooked-for response. I knew that if a zombie lurched out of an alley at me I would want to have something better to do than laugh or tell the zombie I was against it. But what I should do, or from whom I should seek knowledge, I did not know.

After I arrived at the age of eighteen, I left the home of my youth to attend schooling. There I gave myself up to the routine and secular studies that such places provide. But though I did not give the full attention to the question of zombie-killing that its spiritual nature deserved, I did not and could not entirely forsake the subject. I had friends who died in zombie attacks and even a young woman whom I purposed to make my wife, such was the extent of our mutual affection – yes, the one woman whom to me was above all the earth – never returned from a holiday at home. When the reports reached me that a freak outbreak had turned her into a shambling, undead horror, I experienced a tumult of pain and misery such as I have never before known. My guilt, my thought that if I had only devoted myself more seriously to those questions of zombie warfare that I knew from my youth were the highest and noblest pursuit of a man, I might have counseled her aright, were of the utmost intensity. I knew that I had to know which ZBO was right.

No sooner had I formed this resolve then I started attending services at the various ZBOs and reading everything I could on theology and philosophy, everything from Augustine's prescient *City of Manlike Shuffling Horrors* to Emmanuel "Killer" Kant to moderns like Steven Seagal. I dabbled in Shotgunology and spent some time with a Quaker Combat Team, but none of it could be enough. I learned things and met good people, but where was the power? Where was the infection of life and abundance to turn a man into a scourge for good? A fellow traveler on the bus once dismissed my concerns by pointing out that by definition, every ZBO that was still around had survived the past zombie outbreaks. But it was the future outbreaks that concerned me.

One day a pastor-colonel said something that changed my life. We were discussing the subject of grace in his study and looking at his explosive bullets catalogue when I felt to tell him about my quest for the truth about zombie-killing. "Why don't you pray about it?" he said. The suggestion came with great force to my mind. Every ZBO is a church, and every church a ZBO. As the saying goes, there are no atheists in the besieged shopping mall. And I could not deny the element of spiritual longing in my quest for some manifestation of divine concern for zombie-beset mankind, though being but a man my carnal desire to not be torn limb from limb and messily devoured also figured largely in my quest. But despite the blessed character of my striving, I had somehow never turned to prayer, wherein the weak find refuge and the seekers find the end of their seeking. I had labored in vain because I had labored alone. But why? Could I be not as eager for divine aid as I had supposed? Could one such as I approach the throne of the Incorruptible in prayer? Such were the bitter recriminations with which I harrowed my soul.

The pastor-colonel, who observed my sudden pallor, asked solicitously if I was well. I answered that I was and excused myself directly. The town where I then resided had not experienced even a code yellow outbreak all that year, which preserved me from misfortune, for I staggered home to my apartment heedless of the outside world. All things seemed so immediate, so directly present to my senses, that I could not process or understand my surroundings, my thoughts, or my memories. To this day I can still see the patterns my window bars made across the walls that afternoon as I stared at them blankly. I can still recall remembering for the first time in my adult life the smell of my dad when he came back from fishing, and I remember somehow knowing that come what may, if I prayed or if I did not, if God answered me or if he did not, I was going to lose part of who I was. I tried to think clearly about it, but I could not. I owned to myself that I did not know how to pray and I could not think how to pray. It was impossible, I cried. Not like climbing Mt. Everest would be impossible if you had never climbed, but like climbing Mt. Everest would be impossible if you never even heard of it. I tried for a long time to come to grips with I-didn't-know-what and I-didn't-know-how. At last by some means I was prostrate on the floor. I found myself praying. "Tell me," I said.

Someone knocked on the door.

I had heard of the Mormons. I had been told they were practically zombies themselves, such was the cultish devotion of their faith. I had read an accusation that they tried to go in close to fight zombies, hand to hand, which I could scarcely credit in our modern age of firearms. Based on reports such as these, I dismissed them as backwards, if indeed I formed an opinion at all. Yet I had seen the missionaries around before in their distinctive white body armor and now I found them on my threshold. I opened the door.

"Hi," the one said. He was really cheerful. "We're Elders from the Mormons. We're doing a patrol out in Maravilla Vista this weekend and we're sharing a special invitation with people in your neighborhood to join us. Will you?" Maravilla Vista, I

knew, was one of the town's abandoned far suburbs, where infrequently the zom-
bified bodies of those unfortunate enough to have been so affected would stray unno-
ticed. My mind was no longer beset with its former incapacity and useless toil. It came
clearly to me that I knew I had no choice. I had prayed a prayer. "Okay," I said. The
one who didn't smile just looked at me.

"It's important," he said. I desired to believe him.

As directed, I went to their church on Saturday. What I supposed was a small
congregation was gathered in the parking lot, though curiously a capacious chapel
of their faith was situated nearby. This was only the beginning of the details that I
found strange and curious. An older man reviewed a list of procedures. They were
tedious and, though I have since learned more wisdom, at the time they seemed
senseless, if not offputting. Why was there a teenager who was supposed to keep
records? Why white body armor? The missionary who didn't smile was with me to
explain but he said little, and he and the other one had to leave before we actually
rolled out. I don't remember why. I had my own semi-auto rifle, which no one told
me to put away. I comforted myself with the thought that, be they personally as
backwards as reported, they at least did not expect me to forego its protection.

I was tense. I bounced up and down on the balls of my feet. I'd seen zombies before and I'd even done patrol like this once or twice. On some level I knew that we
were very unlikely to see any of the undead out there, like the other two times I'd
gone out. But my gut wasn't on that level. And there was more going on today.
Above all other considerations there was the God thing.

My feelings, though they seemed to me natural and inevitable under the circumstance, clashed strangely with the undercurrent of domestic cheerfulness I sensed in
that little group of gathered Mormons. Could they really believe the manners and
mores of a family reunion were appropriate to a deliberate attempt to confront the
most devilish horror? Could God have really meant me to accompany this assem-
blage? In conformity with my feeling of estrangement from the rest of those congregated there, which feeling had now grown marked, I physically drew myself back.

One woman, noticing my silent separation, approached me and spoke, saying that
she herself was going along because it was her son's first time. He was the recordkeeper. She indicated that she would stay in the van and told me that I could stay in the
van too if I was more comfortable so, being a stranger to their ways. I can only hazard
that divine providence guided her next words. She asked me if I'd ever done something like her boy was doing, where it was the first time and my parents were proud of
me and wanted to see, but didn't want to embarrass me. I told her it was funny, I had
just been thinking about my first day at college. My dad asked me to take a picture of

my first classroom. He'd never been, you see. I'd felt just as alone at that time as I felt at this one, but persevering, my endeavor had prospered. I told the Mormon woman that I would go and at least get out of the van to look around, to which she assented.

Our little band of patrolling Mormons and one Gentile arrived. The recordkeeper boy had a form where he wrote the name of the street and everyone stood around and told him to write down the asphalt was still good and lots of other things and corrected his spelling. On completing this apparently communal task, without further direction the group split up and started at the top of the street, both sides, moving towards the end. We were on a cul-de-sac, somewhat crumbled, at the point of decay where the windows are often gone but walls only have cracks.

I have since heard people say the Mormons are amateurs, without the guidance of credentialed, professional killer-clergy. Their amateurism made no impression on me that day. No one has been what you'd call organized since the zombies. It's not like Before, with tight-spun organizations and elaborate hierarchies and far-reaching bureaucracies. Our trade and our technology and our culture trundle on in this dispensation, but we're not rich enough to be spit'n'polish. We do things ad hoc. Our churches battle zombies because that's what they do, not because anyone assigned it, and it's not just the Mormons who do patrols by committee. No, what struck me was the good-natured reverence with which they went about this business. Almost against my will, I began to be deeply moved.

When they split up to go down the opposite sides of the street, I hung back to make such observations as I could. The Saints – for so I have since learned to call them – had gone in and out of a house or two when I noticed that the house right by me had been added upon with what are called dormers or perhaps gables – my knowledge of architecture being sadly deficient. In consequence of these additions the house had been built up a little higher than the others and I reflected that if I could attain unto the attic or even the roof I could have a pretty good lookout spot and even provide some covering fire if it chanced that a zombie got flushed. The unspoken order of the day seemed to be if you see something to do, do it, so in I went.

The front door had been forced open a long time ago and I could see the gray interior of the house, little clumps of ceiling tile on the ground, and swirls where the dust had blown around. Wires had been ripped out of a part of one wall for no reason that I could discern. The abode looked sturdy enough in that dry climate though the walls in the stairwell were sagging inward a little.

I took the stairs to the halfway landing where they turned ninety degrees and even before I had finished turning on the landing I heard the grunt. Trouble – I raised my gaze and saw the creature loomed at the top of the stairs. It was stringy, grotesque, and

desiccant. I took it in in the instance, yet in the next instant all I could see was its infector middle nail, grown inches long and with matter already dripping down its infectile canal. The nail waved in a mindless pattern. The creature's jaw hung open.

It had the high ground, the very high ground. I've never seen a stairwell so steep in tract housing. If it fell coming down the steps at me, it would fall into me. I couldn't go down those deteriorated steps backwards and I couldn't expose my back. I did the only thing I could do. I fired and stepped forward. Yes, forward. I must have hit it, or stepping forward frightened it (will is a weapon against zombies, I know that now, something base drives them and something in us drives them back) because it did not lurch at me.

For this next part to make sense I need to tell you what the stairs were like. I already said how steep and narrow they were. On my left the stairwell wall went all the way up to the ceiling. On my right the stairwell wall only went up partway. A hallway appeared to run along the side of the stairs and the stairwell wall went up far enough like a parapet to separate the stairs from the hall but anyone or anything in the hall could still lean over the stairs. The parapet would be about waist-high for someone in the hallway but from where I was, it was a couple of feet over my head. Perhaps, in happier days, scenes of family affection and sweet sociality were enacted in these confines.

The zombie stooped down behind the parapet, grunting, and with horrible motion shambled towards me with its infector arm raised out over the parapet reaching for me. I fired, then once again, and twice again, aiming through the parapet for the zombie center-mass, but my bullets were soft and meant for spreading out in rotting flesh. The drywall and the studs of the parapet deflected them, absorbed them, as I fired at an angle. I fired, then the lickerish nail flicked right at me. I was pressed back as far against the wall as I could be, but I could have licked the nail and died, so close I was. I drew on my store of mortal courage and shouted hosanna to the name of the Lord. I fired again straight through the wall, nothing, and again, again with no result. I was tense with balanced fears of the nail in front and the wall giving way behind, and then like a vision I knew what to do.

I whipped my rifle over the putrefacting limb and, turning the weapon sidewise, slammed it down, pinning the limb to the parapet. I was savage like the noonday sun and as fierce as the Mississippi. I was pressing the rifle onto the trapped appendage as with the weight of worlds with my left hand while with my other I extracted a knife that something had prompted me to bring. I sawed at the undead wrist in big sweeping cuts until it fell in a trickle of ichor. The abomination that animated these remains into a distortion of created life raised its grunting head over the parapet, whereupon I punched right into it. My live flesh drove against its dead matter and I strove as man against unman.

Finding myself obstructed by my situation, I leaped up the stairs and around the end of the parapet, raising my emptied rifle over my head like the quick sword of an avenging angel, and struck down again and again until I heard the rush of human feet and felt human hands shoving me back as human bodies pushed past me. "Print it, print it, before it dusts," I heard one exclaim, and frantic scuffle, and then, in surety, to its head a massive shot like the voice of God in that tight space, and, ears ringing, I heard no more. "We Mormons can use guns after all," I thought.

I had my answer. I knew all my life before I had been afraid. My prayer had driven me here to end my fear the only way I could, personally, hand to hand, sawing at my fear with a knife, smashing it with an arm made strong by an outside force.

Providence had revealed to me why Mormons bizarrely trained for hand-to-hand. They knew that salvation took place in straits and narrows. They knew that hidden evils must be rooted out. I didn't know then that Mormons also went close because they wanted to take the creature's prints before it returned to dust, so they could identify the person it had been and do the glorious vicarious work for the dead. I didn't know that my newfound faith would be sorely tested and I would cry out, "My God, My God, how can you let them do this to me?" when "helpful" non-Mormon friends would show me that the revealed additions to the fighting style I would learn in Elders' Quorum were heavily influenced by krav maga. I didn't know that I would discover other enemies within myself worse than zombies, enemies like pride, that I would fight at the closest quarters. I did not know then the difficulty of the way, only that I had found it and would endure in it to the end.

Though the world raged against me and the ministers of darkness persecuted me; though opposition threw me to the ground again and again; though zombies beset me; though the storm raged and the undead slavered; though sin choked me, I would not tap out or cease to struggle.

I had killed a zombie, and I could not deny it.

OUT OF THE DEEP
HAVE I HOWLED UNTO THEE

Scott M. Roberts

THE SMALL things, that's what Clark concentrated on. Never mind the wolf scratching at the insides of his hands, never mind the sound of its breath in his throat, the desire to hang his tongue out and let it loll. Never mind the way the full moon tugged at his skin.

External things. Things beyond the wolf's reach. The motorcycle, his tools, the way the transmission rested in his hands, that was what he focused on. That was how he fought the wolf. The devil was in the details, but the wolf, thank God, was not. And maybe, tonight, the devil wasn't in the details either. Tonight, God was in the details. God in the chrome, God in the gears, God in the grease and bolts and bits of everything that he touched.

Thinking about touching, about his fingers, his skin, the stripe of grease that was somehow on his lips ... that was a pathway to the wolf. Clark's tongue itched to stretch out of his throat to lick the grease.

Back to details. He'd been remodeling the Sport Scout for a good three weeks, but had saved the most delicate work for this full-moon night. For God and the wolf. There was salvation in the motorcycle, in the flagrant fenders, in the low-slung chassis. *Screw* his mind into the motorcycle, and for the first time in years, he'd have a full-moon night free of the wolf.

The wolf growled in his lungs, and Clark felt a bit of its frustration pass over his lips. Fifteen minutes to dawn. His fingers trembled as he worked the transmission into place.

And then, he was done.

Too soon! He realized it, and so the wolf realized it too, and he could feel it stretching within him, its claws scraping the skin beneath his fingernails. Clark hunted for something to tighten, something to adjust, some bit of grease to wipe away. His fingers tumbled along the skin of the motorcycle while his eyes hunted the corners of the garage. Something to catch his mind, something to distract him ... There were the shadows scattered throughout the garage, the gleam of his tools in the overhead brights. And the red of his toolbox, as red as blood, as red as a predator's tongue ...

The wolf scrambled in his throat; his prayer came out guttural. *De profundis*, Clark thought. Out of the deep have I *howled* unto thee, O Lord.

"Heavenly Father," Clark gasped.

No words. Yelps and growls and whines. Whining at God.

Clark stumbled back to the motorcycle. He'd tear it apart, this man's thing, this thing that had caught him and bound him all night long. He'd tear apart this whole place, so the man would never be able to trap him again. He'd piss on everything, and the man would be afraid. Before the sun rose, before he slept again ...

"Out ... " Clark said, but the word no longer fit inside his mouth. Nothing of his own fit him any longer – the wolf's claws scored the motorcycle's chrome.

Dawn seized them.

It was not a flood of light that drove the wolf out of him. The wolf wanted to tear the motorcycle apart as much as it wanted to flee from the sun. Clark let it. He surrendered the motorcycle to the wolf. It leaped out of him, across the baby-pale rays of dawn, into the chrome and metal and rubber of the Sport Scout.

The motorcycle growled.

Clark pushed himself away. He stared and listened in the morning's silence for ... what? There was a resonance in his chest and the hairs on his neck, like a low, metallic chord. It made him itch.

Whining, groaning, *growling*, from the motorcycle. It wasn't a sound that Clark could hear in his ears; it was like feeling his joints creaking. The wolf was a small thing, now. A detail. Clark reached out to the motorcycle and the wolf went silent.

Waiting.

Clark jerked his hand away. The wolf was a small thing now, but not harmless. He scrubbed his beard with his fingertips. He'd been sweating all night long, and he stank. But even his stink was a pleasure, because it was a man's stink. There was no beast-smell in the sweat, it was all man, it was, thank you God, human.

Clark turned to go inside. But he felt, between his shoulder blades and in the ends of the hairs on his neck, the resonance trembling.

THE ONLY thing in his refrigerator was a pack of soda. Clark counted out the cash he had left over; there was enough to buy groceries and gas. He could go into town, have some breakfast at a diner. He could meander through the aisles in the grocery store, if he wanted. He could pick up a paper and look for a job. Find work as a mechanic.

Go to church again. Take the sacrament without having the wolf nibbling the bread inside his guts, without it lapping the water that dribbled down his throat.

Because the world was new. *He* was new. And the wolf was not a part of him any longer.

The itching along his spine and fingertips resisted the idea. He'd have to get rid of the motorcycle if he ever wanted to be cured of the wolf. It would be no good just picking up and driving away from the Sport Scout; that would leave temptation lying around. Too easy to come back. If he destroyed it somehow, would the wolf be destroyed as well? Better to keep the motorcycle and the wolf together – he knew that it was trapped there, at least.

But he, *he* was free! Free to breathe air the wolf would never breathe, free to walk and work without its teeth around his heart, free to do what he wished.

Clark blinked and pulled his hand away from the window where he'd been tracing the motorcycle's outline on the pane. The window faced the detached garage where the Sport Scout leaned on its kickstand. Where it crouched. Clark wiped the window with his sleeve.

"Free," he said out loud, loud enough for his voice to ring in the air. Let the resonance carry that back to the wolf. Let the wolf eat that.

But when evening came, Clark found himself out on the back porch, watching the Sport Scout. The longer he watched it, the deeper the resonance worked into him, like a massage of warmth in the middle of his chest. And he was moving forward now, reaching for the motorcycle. The resonance purred at him, a vibration of pleasure and invitation. Touch me, and live, it spoke. Stroke me and I will serve you and keep you, and hold you forever.

Clark caught his breath. He was close enough to feel the warmth that the metal had absorbed through the day.

He took his fingers from the motorcycle. He made his body turn around and walk away. Midway to the door of his house, he turned again – if he stayed here right now, the singing resonance would pick his will to shreds. In the desert, he could clear his head. Get the smell of sage and sand in his nostrils, some grit in his mouth ...

The resonance seemed to thin and stretch as he walked along the county road running away from town. The moon was bright, filling the air with silver and blue. It would have been pleasant except for the itch against his skin. The further he walked, the thinner the road became. Like the resonance. Still here. Still a little trail, glimmering whitely under the moon's glow. It had to end – somewhere, O God, it had to end, didn't it?

The trail climbed upward, and Clark followed. Maybe it led to the moon. Ridiculous thought. But on a night like this, where the trail and the resonance were one, ridiculousness was ... acceptable. More acceptable, anyway, than going home and embracing the Sport Scout. More acceptable than kissing the wolf, swallowing its tongue, letting it gorge itself on his heart. Clark grunted, wiped his face. He was exhausted. A night and a day without sleep, and here he was, tramping about the desert, and when dawn came, what then? He'd be caught out here, no water, miles from anywhere and maybe this was what God wanted. This was as free of the wolf as he had ever been in the past ten years.

The trail led him to the top of the cliffs surrounding his home. Clark turned and looked over the whole world below him. He stretched out his arms, feeling the sweat on his back and sides tickle slowly to the waist of his trousers. The resonance was a gossamer steel strand, as light as a bead of sweat, as solid as the cliff. You may stretch me, the wolf seemed to growl over the resonance, you may stretch me, you man, but I am thin already, I am lean, I will not break. I am metal and chrome now, and I will not break, I will haunt you, I will *hunt* you, and I will have your heart in my teeth, on my tongue.

Clark gulped the air. Sucked in moonlight, and maybe that would kill the beast. Cut into it with ragged, silver breaths. But it continued to itch along his spine, and when he had been still long enough to stop wheezing, Clark turned from the edge of the cliff.

Someone was sitting there on the trail in front of him. His breath caught in his throat, it startled him so much. A girl, sitting there, facing him. Her forearms were bare, and something dark pooled down around her fingers where they met the trail.

Clark swallowed the urge to lick his lips. *Blood*, the wolf whispered, and *Sweet, sweet*.

"Leave me alone," she said.

Clark shook himself. "You're bleeding." He took off his shirt, tearing it into strips. Don't breathe now. Don't taste the air, the blood, do not, do not ...

"I'll cut you!" she said shrilly. Her hands scrambled around on the desert floor, and came up holding a straight razor. "Go away."

Clark felt the resonance heavier now, and growing more intense the closer he got to the girl. She took a swipe at him but he caught her elbow and shook the razor out of her grip. Her skin was cool and damp; she was weak. How long had she been bleeding out here?

"Leave me alone!" she wailed. "Leave me alone!"

Clark wrestled her to the ground, straddled her chest, and pinned her arms to the ground with his knees. His hands slipped against the cuts she'd opened up in her wrists, the slick, soft edges of flesh. The wolf urged him on, panting in his brain, pushing through the resonance.

Clark pushed back and said, "No one's dying tonight," and he realized he'd said it out loud because she wailed and cursed at him some more.

"Stop it!" Clark growled, and shook her.

She did. Her eyes rolled back in her head, and she slumped.

Clark held her body for a moment, feeling her weight. God, let her live. He bandaged the girl's wrists with his shirt, and tried to wake her. She moaned, but her eyes didn't open, not even when he slapped her cheeks.

He picked her up and started down the cliff. Back to his cabin. How much blood had she lost? Too much. Any at all was too much. He could smell it in his nose, taste it in the back of his throat.

But the wolf was quiet. It left him alone with the weight of the girl over his shoulders, and the touch of the moon on his face. Maybe ... maybe coming up here to get away from the wolf, and finding and helping this girl ... maybe God had removed it. Maybe the wolf was dead now, killed by God because Clark had resisted it.

Clark made his way down the trail, back to his cabin as fast as he could go. The girl's breath tickled his ear.

HE DID not remember calling the ambulance, and yet here it was, and he jerked himself awake. Clark was leaning against the front door. The resonance itched against him. Numbly, he pointed the EMTs toward the girl on the couch. They pushed him aside, and left the door open. The Sport Scout gleamed at him in the moonlight.

Someone was asking him questions. Clark rubbed his eyes, refocused. "I found her on the cliffs. She was bleeding."

The EMTs pushed by, wheeling the girl out on a stretcher. She was so pale ... Clark watched them, watched her. She was a thin little thing. How old? Fourteen, fifteen ... Curly brown hair bounced against her cheeks when the EMTs lifted the stretcher down the porch.

Her hand seemed to linger, fingers stretched out toward the Sport Scout. He blinked and felt the wolf tremble.

"Mr. Trost," said the someone asking him questions. "Can you show us where you found her?"

Clark watched the ambulance pull off. "Sure." he said, finally. "Yeah, sure."

The other fellow was thick-jowled, with watery blue eyes. Clark could smell something odd on his breath – marijuana, he thought. He was wearing a rumpled police officer's uniform. Above his badge was a name – A. Tomlinson.

A. Tomlinson said, "Lead the way."

Clark said, "I need a soda to keep me awake. You ... ?"

"Got some coffee on my way over. Half a thermos left, if you want some."

Clark licked his lips. "No, no thanks. I'm Mormon. No coffee." But he could smell the girl's blood in his nose still, and how hypocritical was he, to refuse coffee, but to dream about licking that girl's slashed-up wrists?

"Suit yourself."

A. Tomlinson chatted the whole way up the cliffs. That, more than the soda, kept Clark's eyes open.

"What's the A. for?" Clark asked.

"Abraham." He grinned and the moon flashed on his teeth. "Call me Tuck."

"Not Abe?"

"Not a chance." He looked around at the desert. They were at the foot of the cliffs. "What were you doing way out here?"

"Just walking."

"In the middle of the night?"

"It's too hot to go walking in the daytime."

Tuck laughed. "I'll bet. So – you carried her from here all the way back to your house?"

"Yes."

"You're stronger than you look, then."

Clark shrugged. There was a teasing discomfort in his belly. Clark didn't have anything to hide. Nothing except a murderous beast locked up in a vintage motorcycle. Nothing except a desire to taste that girl's blood. Nothing, nothing, nothing.

Clark showed him where he'd found the girl. Tuck walked around the bloodstain in the dirt a couple times, then began poking around in the brush. He came up with the straight razor, and deposited it into a plastic baggie.

"All right. So you found her up here. What happened then?"

Clark told him. It seemed like ages ago. He was so tired, he barely recognized the sound of his own voice.

"Why are your hands covered in blood?"

The question hammered at him; his heart pulsed, terrified. But he remembered – he hadn't done anything. Nothing at all, but saved a girl's life. Dreamed of devouring her, but done nothing. "When I wrestled the razor from her, I got blood all over me."

"You didn't try to wash it off?"

"No. I got home, and called 911, and I guess I fell asleep waiting for the ambulance." Dying girl on my couch, and I fall asleep. Clark added, "I've been awake for two days straight."

Tuck put the razor in his pocket and hooked his thumbs into his belt loops. "You took a walk out into the middle of the desert instead of getting some rest?"

"I didn't know I would find a suicide out here." He should say something else. Something sensible. Like, *walking in the desert helps me calm down*, or *walking helps me get ready for sleep*. But Clark didn't say anything at all.

Tuck grunted. "Why were you awake so long?"

"I've been rebuilding a motorcycle. A 1942 Indian Sport Scout. I couldn't ... leave it alone I guess. Motorcycles are an ... obsession."

"No kidding. So, what, you walked away from the motorcycle in the middle of the night and came out here? And just happened to find this girl bleeding to death?"

Clark gritted his teeth against the skepticism in Tuck's voice. "Yes."

Tuck unlatched a flashlight from his belt and began swinging it along the ground. "Does your ... what was it? Sport Scout, does it run?"

Clark knew it would. Without gas, without a battery, without anything but the wolf trapped within it. It could run, it could hunt, it could chase ... It just needed someone to surrender to it. *You, you, you*, the resonance whispered. *I need you*. But it was very faint. "I didn't have any gas for it. I haven't even tried to start it yet."

They walked back to Clark's cabin with the moon pouring down on them. The scuff of their feet on the sand and rocks was the only sound. No talking – Clark didn't mind. Tuck didn't seem like he wanted to talk. Clark glanced at him every once in a while. Tuck was a big man, with hips as wide as his shoulders. Built like a stone slab. Like one of those obelisks at Stonehenge.

When they got back, Tuck walked over to the motorcycle. He flipped on his flashlight to look at the tires. And then he just stared at it, and Clark felt the wolf whispering something.

But not to him.

"Beautiful," Tuck said. "You are so beautiful. Have mercy on me."

Clark pushed himself forward and caught Tuck's elbow as he moved his hand toward the motorcycle. "Uh, please don't touch it. It's ... vintage, and I just ... " He felt the resonance slickly on his back, like a long tongue. "Don't touch it."

Tuck stood up. He was taller than Clark by a good four inches. "Get your hands off me, Mr. Trost."

Clark let him go and stood still. Tuck said, "You need to get some sleep. Someone may drop by to ask you some more questions."

Clark wasn't going anywhere. Not to town, not to church. He rubbed his eyes with the heel of his palm and nodded.

"If you think of anything you forgot to tell me, give me a call." Tuck handed him a business card. He looked once more at the motorcycle. Clark saw his fingers tremble. Then he was in his car and driving away, leaving Clark alone in the dark and stillness.

Clark went inside. The smell of the girl's blood was thick in his cabin, as fresh as if it had spilled on his lips and down his throat. There were bloody fingerprints on the phone's handset – her blood, from his hands, left there when he'd called the police. Her blood was on his clothes, everywhere ...

Taste her.

The urge was so strong, it made him sway. But he found the sink, and scrubbed his hands clean. He stripped, filled the sink with detergent, and jammed his clothes into it. When the suds were up to his elbows, he dunked his head in as well, and opened his mouth to suck in the taste of soap. God help me, be merciful to me, drive it away, away ... out of the deep, O God, out of the *deep*!

When he came up, spitting, the resonance still picked at him. There was blood on the telephone. He pulled his soapy shirt out of the sink, and started for it. *Lick it clean.* Clark reached for the handset. No – not with his bare hands. He picked the phone up using the end of the shirt, and scrubbed it viciously. The number pad, too, until the buttons were rimed in bubbles. Clark stared at the cloth in his hands, longing to sniff it, longing to *bite* it, suck on it, just for a little taste of her.

He threw the shirt toward the sink. Merciful God, it splashed into the water and disappeared into the suds.

Clark didn't make it to his bedroom. He slumped to the couch naked, covered himself with a blanket, and slept.

But even sleeping, he felt the wolf crawling over him. He shivered and whined and kicked his legs.

Clark sat on his back porch, watching the Sport Scout. The clock on the eaves read ten a.m.; he'd been sitting here since just after eight.

The resonance was nothing but a whisper on the hairs of his neck. All night, he'd dreamed of blood and howling, but when he'd picked himself off the couch, the motorcycle lay still and quiet in the morning light. Maybe God had finally answered his prayers. Maybe cleaning that girl's blood out of his home, maybe that was the last test.

No. It was a hopeful, deceitful line of thought. The wolf was with him still. Weakened – no, *distracted*. Clark remembered the way the girl had reached for the Sport Scout, how Tuck had swooned over it. Now the wolf hunted them.

Jealous? the resonance wheezed at him. Jealous, Clark confirmed, surprised and ashamed.

He had to get rid of the Sport Scout now. Today, before the wolf could work into those other two. His mind whirled – what could he do with the motorcycle when he couldn't touch it? Taking it apart was out the question, and he couldn't count on anyone else to destroy it, not after the way Tuck had acted.

Drag it into the middle of the desert. Bury it deep in the dust, far away from everyone. Clark gnawed on his lip until he tasted blood. It could still call them through the resonance. But maybe if he moved quickly, the resonance wouldn't be strong enough to tempt them all the way out into the middle of nowhere.

Clark stood, dusted off his pants. Do it, he told himself. Be rid of it now, once and for all. He scratched his neck furiously where the resonance whispered and tickled.

Clark looped a length of rope over the Sport Scout's handlebars. He tied the other end to the bumper of his pick-up. Already, the sun was blistering hot and he was sweating just standing out in it. He filled a cooler with water and put it in the back of the truck along with a shovel and work gloves. Clark stood for a long moment at the door to the pickup, wondering what he could be forgetting.

Into the truck. Clark forced his hands to turn the key, forced his foot against the accelerator.

He didn't bother with his driveway. There were no fences out here to mark property lines, and no neighbors to see him forsake the road for the bare desert. How would it look, anyway, a vintage motorcycle scraping along on its side behind his truck? Best to stay away from roads and people completely.

An hour into the desert, rattling over rocks and brush, the resonance focused back on him. For a moment, Clark felt as if he were standing underneath the full moon, and his hands on the steering wheel were clawed and padded and he couldn't think what he was doing in this man's thing. He barely avoided dumping the truck into a shallow washout. No more whispering, no more tickling – the wolf tore at him. Clark gritted his teeth, and pressed the accelerator down gently. The truck lurched forward.

He looked in the rearview mirror to check on the Sport Scout. Instead of the motorcycle at the end of the rope, a hulk of an animal loped along behind. Clark could see its red, red tongue lolling. Its fur was as colorless as ash.

Swallow you, you man. Gorge me on you.

Clark kept driving. The resonance scourged his back, gnawed his palms on the steering wheel and at the sole of the foot that held the accelerator down. In the mirror, he watched the motorcycle bounce violently over the desert, tearing at the scrub brush and cacti as he pulled it along. Now the motorcycle; now the wolf, straining against the rope, biting at the knot around its neck, clawing the dust.

He drove for another hour before the pain made his eyes roll up into his head. Enough. Far enough. It had to be. Clark stopped the truck, fumbled for the door and pushed himself into the hot afternoon air. The motorcycle lay on its side, the rope holding it to the truck's bumper as taut as piano wire.

There were no details to distract him now. Nothing but the sun and sky and dust. And the agony. It deepened when he began to dig, until he whimpered. Dig. That was all he needed to do. Nothing came over the resonance but agony. No temptation, but the wolf's will to torture him into submission or kill him with pain. If he died, would the wolf die as well? Or would it live like a ghost in the Sport Scout, until someone came along to touch the metal, suck in the wolf, and be devoured?

Dig the pit, and then the wolf could howl at God out of it. That'd be a change.

The hole was done before nightfall. Clark's mouth burned and his tongue felt as heavy and stiff as a rock. His hands were cramped and torn with blisters. Clark struggled into his truck. Just a little tug forward, and then the beast would be in the hole.

The truck jerked backwards a bit as the motorcycle dropped into the pit. Clark got out and cut the rope with his pocketknife.

"Bury you," Clark muttered, driving the shovel into the pile of dirt next to the pit. Pebbles clattered off the chrome when he dumped it into the hole.

Touch me, the wolf whispered. Agony and desire scraped over Clark's skin. He bit his tongue, and tossed another shovelful into the hole. *Touch me.*

The moon rose. Every now and then, moonlight fell on fur and Clark glimpsed the too-red tongue down in the darkness. He could still go in there. Tie the ends of the rope together, haul the Sport Scout up. The wolf would give him strength to do that. Pull it right back up, like Jesus bringing Lazarus out of the tomb.

"Out of the deep," Clark whispered. It wasn't Lazarus's grave he was filling, but Herod's. The baby-killer, the filicide. Hadn't he heard it slavering for the girl's blood? Hadn't he seen how it sniffed after her?

Clark worked blindly, pushing dirt into the hole until he realized that the point of the shovel was striking unbroken dirt. The pit was gone. He was done.

But the resonance still ate at him, as bitter as ever. Clark was exhausted, but he couldn't sleep here tonight, not near the motorcycle's grave.

Raise me, man. Touch me.

His hands felt like they'd been nailed to the shovel handle. Clark's fingers wouldn't flex. He smashed the shovel against a nearby boulder until the handle snapped and his fingers released it. There'd be no digging the wolf out, now.

Not tonight.

Not ever.

Clark started the truck, and drove away.

THE TRUCK ran out of gas. Clark shuffled out of the cab, and began walking. Everything ached. He didn't know where he was. The resonance itched against his palms and feet, a little whisper of a thorn.

He walked forever. And then someone shined a flashlight in his face, and came forward. Big hands, and a body like an obelisk. Tuck. And other men too, policemen and men with the words Search-and-Rescue printed on their jackets.

"You do like to walk around in the desert, don't you," Tuck said, and forced a bottle of water in his hands. "I went to your place to give you the good news. You didn't come back ... " He paused and gave a shrug and scratched his hands. Kept scratching them. Clark could see in the glare from someone's flashlight that they were raw and blood-specked. "I found your tire tracks heading out into the desert. Guess I got a little worried."

Clark sipped the water, felt the wolf whisper. Just for him, this time. Only for him. He tried not to let the despondency show in his voice, "Thanks. What's this about good news?"

"Hmm?" Tuck was looking off behind Clark into the desert. "Oh, good news. That girl you saved will be fine. Well, not fine, I guess. She'll live. She confirmed your story."

"Oh." Soft cheek, curly hair as brown as honey ... Clark rubbed his eyes. She'd be safe from the wolf now. Girl safe, Tuck safe. He sank into Tuck's car, weary beyond thinking, but couldn't close his eyes.

"Where's your truck, anyway?" Tuck asked.

"It ran out of gas out there in the desert."

"And you thought you'd hoof it back to your place?"

Clark nodded and said, "Thanks for finding me out there."

Tuck shrugged. "I had this feeling. You a religious man?"

Haven't been to church in ten years, cry to God daily. "Yes," Clark said.

"This feeling I got, it was just like the scriptures say, kind of a tickle in my skin, a little bitty voice. 'Get thou into the desert, Abraham.'" Tuck laughed at himself. "Not that it really said anything. Just kept at me, till I decided to follow your tracks. Oddest thing."

"A resonance," Clark said and closed his eyes.

"Yeah, that's a good word for it."

"Do you feel it now?"

Tuck glanced at him. "No. No need to, right? You're found. You're safe."

Not safe. Never safe, not him.

Tuck gave a little hum, tapped his fingers, and asked, "Were you dragging something behind your truck? I found scrape marks between your tire tracks."

Clark sipped his water.

Tuck licked his lips. "Where's your motorcycle?"

"I got rid of it."

Tuck was quiet after that, all the way back to the cabin. Once or twice he opened his mouth, then shut it again with a click of teeth. Nothing left to talk about now, Clark thought. Nothing to bind us together. Tuck left him alone at his cabin; Clark watched the police car wheel off into the darkness.

Inside, it was as quiet as the desert. He wandered from room to room, not hearing his footsteps, not feeling anything beyond himself. The resonance had sucked all feeling out of him, left him ... *pitted*. Empty and dry as hole in a rock, that was him. There was nothing to fill himself with, here. Little by little, he'd cut everything out of his life in an effort to starve the wolf. And now that it was buried deep in the dust, what was left for the man?

There was soda in the refrigerator. Clark took out a bottle, ran his hands over the cool plastic, held it until it beaded up with condensation under his fingers. He opened it at last, and sniffed. Nothing. Drank, and felt only the sensation of liquid in his throat. No cold, no taste.

Clark put the cap back on the bottle and put the bottle back in the fridge. As he crossed in front of the window, movement caught his eye.

Man.

Beyond the porch light, a lanky, wasted animal waited on its haunches. Clark went to the door of the cabin, paused. Opened the door at last, and stepped out onto the porch.

The animal didn't move toward him. Its tongue lolled. *I am dying. You, too.*

Clark scratched his beard, rubbed his face. It was like rubbing a sponge, soft and numb.

Kiss me. Save me.

Out of the deep, O God. The wolf wasn't whining for God; it was whining for *him*. Clark shuffled down the porch steps to the empty driveway. The wolf blinked at him as he walked past it.

Man? God?

Dawn again. The sky beyond the mountains was pink and white. A vast ache snapped against Clark's heart and he fell to his knees. But the pain brought scent to him – the smell of sage and dust, and from the mountains, in secret shadows high up in their reaches, the sharp cleanness of glacial ice.

Please, O God, O man.

The wolf whined. Its breath was in his ears. But he couldn't smell it. The resonance tickled and licked at him, but the wolf didn't touch him. Clark's heart trembled and thumped and seized. He threw back his head and cried, and grabbed a handful of ground, and felt the scant drops of dew in the scraggly desert grass like cool ointment on his blistered hands.

The resonance broke. Clark watched the animal twist away into the thinning dawn, a scattering of ash and dust pursued by the wind. His heart wrenched again, filling him with pain and the smell of juniper. Clark cried and laughed and exhaled.

His breath surged out of his lungs, away from the mountains' shadows, and followed the smell of daybreak, skyward.

THE MISSION STORY

Bryton Sampson

"TURNED out his companion was using a rag soaked in ether, and at night he'd – "

"Boo!" Danny's jeer shut Spencer up. No one needed to hear this story again. "Just stop. This has never happened."

"No, it did. It happened on my mission. I knew the guys that were doing it."

"Really? What were their names?"

"It was Elders um, Jensen and Jensen. They were both named Jensen and uh – "

"It's an urban legend. I've been hearing this story since I was a thirteen years old."

"I've heard that story a few times too," Hayley said. She was stuck between Danny and Spencer and had no choice but to listen to them try to outdo each other with progressively louder tales.

"Where did he get the ether? Did he bring it with him through the MTC? Did his mom send it along with some cookies? Do you even know what ether is?" Danny said.

Matthew glanced up from his smartphone and laughed, drawing a scowl from Spencer.

"Bah. I'm taking the rest of the cheese fries." Danny pinched the wad of limp French fries and semi-solid cheese and jammed it sideways into his mouth.

The group of four old friends sat in wooden chairs around a table built for two, dressed alternately in scarlet and royal blue. It was late on a cold November night in downtown Salt Lake City, where they gathered after the annual BYU vs. University of Utah football game. The final score pleased half of them. Every table and booth in the restaurant was filled with similar groups, rowdy college kids fueled by sugar and caffeine, littering without compunction, pushing their already strained voices to the limits just to be heard.

"This is a dumb subject anyway," Hayley declared. "I thought talking about high school was bad. You've been back from your missions for years. We've heard ev-e-ry story there is. Let's just talk about the game."

"No!" Danny and Spencer said in unison.

Danny picked up his half-empty cup of Dr. Pepper and ran his index finger around the curvature, the waxed paper getting rough, slowly disintegrating from the condensation.

"You haven't heard every story," he said. He took on an air of stoicism and lowered his voice an octave. Spencer recognized this affectation as Danny's storyteller voice. "Not every one."

"Here we go," Spencer said with resigned exasperation.

"I've never told anyone this story before," Danny said quietly.

"If it's the one I think it is, I've heard it at least three times," Spencer said. Danny ignored him.

"It gnaws at my nerves, like a vividly remembered nightmare. A nightmare that I had the misfortune to actually live through." His hook worked and Hayley leaned closer to listen.

Spencer sighed loudly. Matthew said, "Shut up, Spence. I want to hear it."

"Me too," Hayley said. "Tell us, Danny."

"Okay," Danny said. "Listen. I served in the Belgium Brussels – Netherlands mission. I got a new companion, my third, the day I moved into a house in a neighborhood called *Anderlecht*. Anderlecht is over a thousand years old. It's pretty creepy, and it was gray and rainy the whole time I was there. Never even saw a hint of sunshine. Anderlecht was the perfect setting to meet my new companion – "

"Is this how you're doing it?" Spencer interrupted. "Are you going to spend an hour telling this story?"

"Shhh!" Hayley said, slapping Spencer's arm with the back of her hand. "Let him talk."

Danny cocked an eyebrow and remained silent, trying to draw out the suspense. Satisfied that he had everyone's full attention, he continued.

"Elder Heinrich. Cornelius Heinrich."

WE HAD an old house that was willed to the mission by a member who had died. It was a narrow two-story place, made of musty wood and jammed in among the neighboring buildings like the last guy to get into a crowded elevator. Elders Page and Christiansen took me upstairs. I was in my room unpacking, chatting with the zone leaders when Elder Heinrich came in, escorted by the mission president himself.

"Elder Moon, I'd you to meet your new companion."

Elder Heinrich cut a striking silhouette. He was shaped like a mailbox, with no neck and a big cube-shaped head. He looked like a college mascot. He approached me swiftly to shake my hand, his arm extended straight out. "Hello," he said in English. His voice was rough, gravelly.

"Elder Heinrich joins us from Switzerland," the mission president said. "What was the name of the city again?"

"*Cologny*," Elder Heinrich said.

"He's a very ... he's a very special young man. Very special." The mission president took a deep breath and looked me up and down. "I trust you, Elder Moon. I really trust you," he said, already halfway out the door. "Go with wisdom, elders."

Over the next few days I tried to get to know Cornelius but I couldn't get more than one word out of him at a time, and he wasn't interested in getting to know me at all. His mouth was always stretched in this weird close-mouthed grin, and no matter where we were his eyes seemed to be focused on something just over my shoulder. I was nervous the first time we went tracting. I just had no idea how he was going to act, what kind of impression he would make.

The first two people we visited that first day listened politely but didn't invite us in. I did all the talking while Cornelius just stood there sporting his weird grin. He finally became more animated at the third house we went to.

This house was surrounded by a bright yellow wooden fence, had two cute little gardens and a cobblestone walkway – it could have been on a postcard. We stood on the front terrace and I urged him to ring the bell, but he was distracted by something. He got into a crouch and his head snapped around like a hummingbird's. I thought he'd gotten sick. I couldn't figure out what had set him off like that.

"*Chat*," he said. French for *cat*. He bounded off the terrace like a puppy dog.

"Hey wait!" I yelled. He disappeared around the corner. I checked an alleyway behind the house but it was empty. I heard footsteps behind me, and there he was.

"*La chat n'est pas plus*," Cornelius said and his grin turned into a full toothy smile. I figured he just liked chasing cats. Now I have other suspicions about what happened to that cat.

The next few days went about as well as the first. One night in our bedroom I tried to have a talk with him. Told him that I understood he was shy, but that he needed to speak during our meetings. We had an appointment the next morning and I insisted that he lead the discussion. I couldn't tell if he was even listening to me. I sat on my bed while he fussed about the room, looking for something. He checked the closet, crawled around the hardwood floor and knocked on every board, pulled out every drawer. I finally lost my temper and told him to quit it. I turned off the lights but even that didn't stop him. A few minutes later I saw a little white light from an LED flashlight darting around the room. I prayed for patience.

"SO WHAT was he looking for?" Hayley asked.

"Well, I'm gonna get to that." Danny said.

"Are you?" Spencer said. "If I go get another Dr. Pepper am I going to miss more exciting parts about Cornelius standing around? By the way, I think this place closes soon." The crowd at the restaurant had thinned considerably. "Just skip ahead to the – "

"Hey, spoilers!" Matthew said.

"Okay. So you prayed for patience, and it worked, and you and your companion became great friends and you're having lunch with him tomorrow," Hayley said.

"No!" Danny said, getting frustrated. "Fine. I'll skip ahead."

"Yes!" Spencer said.

"I'll have you all know that you're missing out on some lovely foreshadowing but clearly you have no appreciation for a good story well told."

I THOUGHT about gritting my teeth and waiting for one of us to be transferred but that didn't feel right to me. I was sure that we had been paired together for a reason. The mission president said he trusted me. Trusted me to give Cornelius the guidance he so sorely needed? Maybe by helping him along, I'd strengthen my own faith too? I decided to try even harder to get to know him and mold him into the missionary I hoped he could be.

"So what do you like to do back in Cologny?" I asked one drizzly day while we were walking along a quiet neighborhood street. "What kind of things are you into?"

"Bugs."

"Oh. Okay. Like entum ... ent ... uh ... studying them?"

"Bugs."

Bugs. He was into bugs.

"Well that's cool. What's your favorite bug?"

"I also like electricity."

It wasn't my question, but I was happy to get an answer out of him that was more than one word.

"Hey neat! Is that something you want to – "

"Look," he said. He left the sidewalk and marched straight into someone's garden. He dropped down and crawled around among the flowers and plants. I didn't think it would reflect well on the Church if anyone saw an LDS missionary crawling around in the mud, but I let him do what he wanted. It was the first time I'd been able to engage him in conversation, such as it was.

He came back to the street, clutching something in his right hand.

"Look," he repeated. He crouched down and beckoned me to join him.

He opened his fist to reveal a fat, green grasshopper. He gently pinched its legs with his left hand and with his right he not-so-gently pinched its head, until the little creature's head collapsed into brown goo.

"Elder Heinrich!" I said.

"Look."

He set the decapitated body on the ground and pulled a tiny electrical device from his pocket. It looked like a small keychain flashlight, but it had a set of metal prongs where the light bulb should have been. He flipped the switch and held the prongs against the grasshopper's soft underbelly.

It hopped.

Cornelius giggled like a child. He jolted the headless grasshopper again, and again it leaped into the air and landed a few feet away. Again. Again. Again. I had to grab his wrist and tell him to stop.

"That's neat. That's really neat," I said.

That was the last time I tried to get to know him.

The house we lived in was quiet. No air conditioning, no cars driving by during the night. If you held still it was dead silent. Any noise that did occur was amplified. Every footstep, every toilet flush, every natural creak of the old wood sounded like a thunderclap breaking the thick silence.

I'm a heavy sleeper but a few days after that grasshopper thing I was waking up more and more during the night. Noises that I couldn't quite perceive were breaking my sleep. Usually I'd roll over and go right back to snoozing but one night something caught my eye: a white pinpoint of light moving across the room.

"Elder Heinrich," I said at breakfast the next morning. "Are you getting up in the middle of the night?"

He dropped his toast and for a brief moment his grin faded. He carefully picked up his toast again and took another bite.

"So, you're not then?"

He dropped his toast again.

"I'm not," he croaked.

I didn't try to sleep that night. I stayed awake and discovered the source of the noise that had been waking me up. A certain spot on the wooden floor snapped like a breaking branch when Cornelius stepped on it. I could see his oddly shaped shadow pause after the sound, before continuing out the door of our bedroom, guided by a tiny flashlight. I waited a moment, expecting to hear the sound of a toilet flushing, but heard only the diminishing groans of the stairs' floorboards. I followed him. The cellar door was open. We never went into the cellar. There was no reason to go into the cellar. What was he doing down there? I didn't want to know. I had to know.

I wasn't ready for what I saw.

A bare light bulb hung from the ceiling. Beetles scurried across the dirt floor into the shadows. Cornelius had his back to me.

"What are you doing?" I said, my voice weaker than I'd expected. He turned around. He was smiling a big, wide smile. In his hand was something that looked like a walkie-talkie. Wires ran from the device, and those wires were connected to a severed foot.

It was grayish pink and glistening, like shrimp that had gone bad. It smelled about the same. It was severed just below the knee. It lay in the middle of the floor, a wooden cap nailed into it where the knee and the rest of the body should have been, with copper wires wrapped around the nails. I got closer and bent down for a look, hoping against hope that my eyes were merely playing tricks on me. When I saw the toes curl, I screamed.

"Look," Cornelius said, in a voice far too casual for the situation. He twisted the knobs on the control device in his hand. The toes stretched and spread out, flexed and curled.

"Look, look!" he said again. He grabbed the slimy foot with his bare hand and I tasted bile on the back of my throat. He set the foot upright, balanced on its sole. He fiddled with the control, and the foot hopped up and down.

"Like a grasshopper!" Cornelius dropped the controller and clapped his hands together.

"No! No no no. This isn't right. What have you done?" I said.

"Fixed it," Cornelius said.

"This is terrible," I said. I was crying. "Where did you get this? Why do you have somebody's foot?"

"Found it," he said.

I ran back up to the bedroom. I thought about waking up Elders Page and Christiansen but I didn't. I don't know why. I just couldn't. I might have stopped it all right then. Instead I knelt at the edge of my bed and prayed that I would make it through the night, prayed for Cornelius Heinrich, and prayed for that poor foot.

Of course I couldn't sleep. All I could see was that foot. The way it hopped. The way Cornelius smiled at the sight of it. The images looped in my mind.

Cornelius and I had breakfast with the other elders the next morning. I knew I had to tell them, had to tell the mission president what was going on, but something held me back. Fear? No, what held me back was my own sick curiosity. I couldn't stop thinking about the foot, and some part of me wanted to see what would happen next. We didn't go tracting that day. We canceled our appointments.

"Show me where you found that thing," I demanded of Cornelius. I told myself I had to guide him. I had to fix him.

He led me to a heavily wooded area, where the River Zenne flowed above ground. The underbrush was thick and I stepped on a hand.

It took me a minute to understand what I was looking at: chalky, covered in gnats. Then I saw the rest of the body. He was a big man, lying on his back, his milky eyes staring up at the gray sky. He was maybe thirty years old, wearing short pants and a black nylon jacket over a red t-shirt. Bugs chased each other over his exposed skin. He was intact, save for one missing foot.

I couldn't help it. I let out a sob.

"Did you do this? Did you kill him?" I asked Cornelius.

"No. I found him," he said. He knelt and touched the body, inspecting it. "I like bugs."

I don't know how or when Cornelius found this spot, found the body. I shuddered at the idea of Cornelius wandering alone at night in a strange city, exploring the dark parts, the forgotten, unwelcome parts.

"We need to call the police," I said.

"No!" Cornelius shouted with a passion I'd never seen from him. He stood up, grabbed the lapels of my blue suit. His strength was surprising. He pushed me through the bushes, knocked me against a tree. I was openly crying now.

"Elder Heinrich! Why are you doing this? You're hurting me!"

"We need to fix him. We *will* fix him."

"I'm going to call the mission president. You should be ... you should be excommunicated for this!"

"No phone calls. You help me fix him."

There was a phone in the house. All the important numbers were on a laminated sheet taped to the wall next to it. I could have picked up that phone at any time. Called the police. Called an ambulance. Called the zone leaders or the mission president. Instead I helped Cornelius dig through the closets to find any blankets that wouldn't be missed. Late that night we returned to retrieve the body, in the middle of a tremendous rainstorm. We wrapped him in the blankets we had found and dragged him back to the house. I was terrified the other elders would hear us but no one stirred upstairs. Cornelius had a whole workshop set up in the cellar. He had wires and motors and a rig of batteries that he'd stolen out of parked cars. Tupperware filled with rank pieces of meat, origins unknown. He'd been busy.

Time to get to work. He reattached the foot to the rest of the body. He tested muscles, stimulating them with electric charges. He stuck nails into the flesh like an acupuncturist, coiled spliced copper wires around them, and hooked everything up to the rig of car batteries.

The rainstorm grew more intense. Rivulets of water leaked into the cellar and the dirty floor congealed into mud. Cornelius worked frantically. I followed him and assisted when he demanded. I couldn't keep up with him. He was like a practiced surgeon, or an artist. With each twitch of the body Cornelius's eyes grew brighter.

Finally, he was finished. I couldn't tell how he knew he was done, but he did and I was in no place to question him.

"We have fixed him!" he said proudly, and switched on the battery rig.

I smelled ozone in the air. The hair on my arms stood straight up. My heart pounded so hard I could feel it in my skin.

Nothing happened. Cornelius checked his wires again. He straddled the body and slapped its face, but got no reaction out of it. My heart slowed down.

"It's dead. He's dead, Cornelius. He needs to be buried. Someone out there is probably wondering what happened to him."

Cornelius looked from me to the dead man and back. He was confused. "But we fixed him!"

"He can't be fixed. He has no heartbeat, he has no blood. He is dead and *rotting!*"

Cornelius rushed at me, angrier than I'd ever seen him. I thought he was going to push me. Instead he shouted, inches away from my face:

"Disintegration is not final destruction! He doesn't need blood!"

I forced myself to stay calm, and hoped I could spread that same calmness to him. "Elder Heinrich, Cornelius, I understand what you're trying to do but that's not how it works. This is not the resurrection, Elder. Friend."

Cornelius stared at the body.

"Do you understand?" I asked.

"I understand," he said quietly. "I understand that he needs blood after all."

Then I was on the ground. Cornelius was on top of me and had pinned my left arm with his raw strength. He pulled back his clenched fist and my world went black.

"He's fixed! He's alive!" I heard Cornelius say as I blinked awake. Cornelius stood over me, triumphant. I felt feverish, like there was a vice around my head. My limbs tingled. I could hardly breathe. There was a needle and tubing in my arm. I tried to sit up but my head was swimming. I immediately laid back down. Cornelius cradled my head in his arms and had me sip from a glass of orange juice. I felt like a child. Once I had drunk the whole glass he helped me sit upright. There was the body. It was sitting up too, facing me. I could see its muscles twitch and spasm under his waxy white skin. Its eyes seemed to see me, and when they locked on mine I realized that the body had become The Man.

The Man stared at me but I couldn't return his gaze. Cornelius went upstairs and returned with a plate of bread and a pitcher of water, and a bundle of clothing tucked under his arm. I ate more than my share of the bread and took two huge gulps of water. Cornelius helped himself to some before offering a chunk of bread to The Man, who eyed it warily. He took the bread and slowly brought it to his mouth. He chewed contemplatively but choked when he tried to swallow and spit it out.

"I forgot. I forgot the most important thing," Cornelius muttered.

"What is it?" I said, my voice barely a whisper. "What is the most important thing, Cornelius?"

"Elder Heinrich," he corrected. "Now, Elder Moon, he's going to get baptized."

The bundle of clothes turned out to be two white jumpsuits for us Elders and some of Cornelius's spare clothes for The Man. Cornelius and I changed in opposite corners of the cellar, then together we stripped The Man out of his clothes and dressed him in a white shirt and a pair of sweatpants. The shirt was too small and his whole outfit was hardly appropriate for a baptism. Somehow that detail was the most bothersome to me. We returned to the spot by the river where we found the body. The Man walked slowly but otherwise just fine. In fact it seemed like he felt better than I did. I helped Cornelius guide him into the river. Despite the bizarre surroundings, if you didn't know any better, you would have guessed it was a regular baptism. It was almost affirming until I realized that The Man hadn't even taken one lesson.

The real trouble began when Cornelius lifted the man from the water. The newly baptized saint was upset by the surprise submersion. He shook himself free and quickly grabbed my companion with his large hands.

"Help!" Cornelius said.

"Stop!" I yelled and waded into the river. The Man had his hands around Cornelius's face and was squeezing. Moonlight broke through the clouds and I could see Cornelius's eyes, bulging and bloodshot, pleading for help. I leaped onto The Man's back and tried to strangle him, but my grip was too weak. Cornelius thrashed around in the water. He grunted and screamed, louder and louder. I can't think of any sound – man, animal, or machine – to match it. But more terrible than those sounds was when they stopped. I jumped from The Man's back and watched as he picked up Cornelius's body, as lifeless as a sack of flour, and hurled it into the deep part of the river. Cornelius instantly disappeared into the blackness of the water.

I stumbled away but The Man quickly caught up to me. I acted on instinct. I grabbed a rock the size of a softball and struck him in the face, as hard as I could. He fell off balance and I struck again, knocking him to the ground. I struck again, and again, and again. The cracking sound of the rock against his skull grew rhythmic. I don't know how many times I hit him, but it was more times than I needed to. When I was finally satisfied, I rolled him into the river. It rained again on my walk back home, and it washed our blood from my face and hands.

The next morning I sat on the edge of my bed, took a few deep breaths and got into character. I went to the kitchen.

"Where is Elder Heinrich?" I asked Elder Page.

Several meetings with the zone leaders and the mission president later, I had them convinced that he'd run off to be with a girlfriend in Antwerp. That kind of thing wasn't unheard of. I said he'd been talking about doing it for a while, but I thought it was just a joke. I feigned shock, told them he was a fine missionary and an honorable Saint. I don't know what they told his parents. For all I know he didn't even have parents.

Soon after I developed an intestinal condition and was sent home early. My whole life I'd been looking forward to my mission. I wanted it to be the best two years. I wanted to return with honor. Instead I returned with blood on my hands and horror in my heart.

"THAT'S your mission story?" Hayley said, staring at Danny in disbelief.

"Wait, that didn't really happen. Did it?" Matthew asked.

"Geez, guy," Spencer said. "'Blood on my hands and horror in my heart.' That part's new. You're picturing that on a movie poster aren't you?"

"Where do you even come up with this stuff?" Hayley asked.

"I'm an English lit major, what can I say?" Danny shrugged.

"It made me forget about the game at least," Matthew said. "You should write these down someday. I'm always impressed with your weird stories."

"Yes well, it's a gift," Danny said with a mocking bow.

"It's a bit much," said Spencer. "But we're the last ones here, so I guess that's an accomplishment. Let's get out of here."

After stepping outside, the group dispersed quickly. The first snow of the season was falling and no one was in the mood for a long goodbye.

"Too cold!" Hayley shouted, heading toward her car.

"Wait," Danny said. He gave her a tight hug that was barely reciprocated.

"So I'll see you next week?" he said.

"Sure. I don't know. Maybe. I've got a lot to finish up. Call me."

"You know I will!" Danny said. She jumped into her car and sped away, trying to outrun the cold.

Danny was parked four blocks over. The unplowed roads were beautiful and pure. Danny took his time walking to his car. He was all smiles and laughs with his friends, but telling that story made him feel strange inside. His heart felt fizzy and his stomach was upset. When he got to his car he reached for his keys, but they weren't there.

"Oh ... " he groaned. He tried not to slip as he jogged back to the restaurant. He figured that he had dropped his keys inside, but the doors were already locked. He rapped his knuckles hard against the glass door but no one came. He danced from foot to foot trying to stave off the cold. He pulled out his cellphone and tried to call somebody, but the touch screen didn't respond to his frozen thumbs. Someone slapped his hand, hard, knocking the phone to the ground and shattering it.

"Hey what the – " Danny said and turned around.

There he was. The Man from Anderlecht. The Man he'd brought back to life only to beat back to death.

"Cursed, cursed, cursed," The Man said.

"You're alive," Danny said. He no longer felt cold.

"Why did you do it? You cursed me, you hurt me so much," The Man said. His head was misshapen, scarred, beaten in like a soda can that had been kicked along the sidewalk.

"I'm ... I'm sorry," Danny said. Feeling the burn of tears behind his nose. "I'm sorry I hurt you."

"Not the rock," The Man said, slowly shaking his head. "The spark of existence."

Danny knew he could have prevented all of this with one phone call. He could have stopped Cornelius before it went so far. He could have saved Cornelius's life. He could have saved his own life. The Man took Danny's head in his two large hands, just like he had done with Cornelius. He pulled Danny off his feet and smashed his head through the glass door of the restaurant. He did it again, this time against the brick wall. Then he threw Danny into the snow and stalked off into the night.

Danny watched the snowflakes fall from high above. For years he tried to pretend it was all fiction, that his story was just a story. He melted a snowflake between his fingertips and whispered a prayer. He forgave The Man. He forgave Cornelius. He asked to be forgiven his own debts. He finally felt free of his inner darkness, and closed his eyes as his blood drained out and stained the pure white snow.

THAT LEVIATHAN, WHOM THOU HAST MADE

Eric James Stone

SOL CENTRAL Station floated amid the fusing hydrogen of the solar core 400,000 miles under the surface of the sun, protected only by the thin shell of an energy shield, but that wasn't why my palm sweat slicked the plastic pulpit of the station's multidenominational chapel. As a life-long Mormon I had been speaking in church since I was a child, so that didn't make me nervous, either. But this was my first time speaking when non-humans were in the audience.

The Sol Branch of the Church of Jesus Christ of Latter-day Saints had only six human members, including me and the two missionaries, but there were forty-six swale members. As beings made of plasma, swales couldn't attend church in the chapel, of course, but a ten-foot widescreen monitor across the back wall showed a false-color display of their magnetic force-lines, gathered in clumps of blue and red against the yellow background representing the solar interior. The screen did not give a sense of size, but at two hundred feet in length, the smallest of the swales was almost double the length of a blue whale. From what I'd heard, the largest Mormon swale, Sister Emma, stretched out to almost five hundred feet – but she was no-where near the twenty-four-mile length of the largest swale in our sun.

"My dear Brothers and Sisters," I said automatically, then stopped in embarrassment. The traditional greeting didn't apply to all swale members, as they had three genders. "And Neuters," I added. I hoped my delay would not be noticeable in the transmission. It would be a disaster if, in my first talk as branch president, I alienated a third of the swale population.

A few minutes into my talk on the topic of forgiveness, I paused when a woman in a skinsuit sauntered through the door and down the aisle. The skinsuit was a custom high-fashion one, not standard station issue, with active coloration that showed puffy white clouds floating across the sky on her breasts, and waves lapping against the sandy beach at her hips. She took a seat on the second row and gazed up at me with dark brown eyes.

The ring finger of her left hand was unadorned.

I forced my eyes away from her and looked down at my notes for the talk. While trying to find my place again, I couldn't help thinking that maybe this woman was an answer to my prayers. The only human female listed in the branch membership records was sixty-four years old and married. As far as I knew, there wasn't an unmarried Mormon human woman within ninety million miles in any direction, which limited my dating pool rather severely.

Maybe this woman was Mormon, but not on the membership records yet because, like me, she was a recent arrival on Sol Central. It seemed a little unlikely, as a member would probably dress more appropriately for church. Maybe she wasn't a member, but was interested in joining.

By sheer willpower, I managed to focus on my talk enough to finish it coherently. After the closing hymn and prayer, I straightened my tie and stepped down from the podium to introduce myself to the new arrival.

"Hello," I said, offering my hand. "I'm Harry Malan." I caught a whiff of her perfume, something that reminded me of strawberries.

Her hand was dry and cool, and I regretted not having wiped my palm on my suit first.

"Dr. Juanita Merced," she said. "You're the new leader of this congregation?"

I felt a twinge of disappointment. A member would have asked if I was the branch president. "I am. How can I help you?"

"You can stop interfering with my studies." Her tone was matter-of-fact, but her eyes looked at me defiantly.

"Sorry," I said. "I'm afraid I have no idea who you are or what studies I might be interfering with."

"I'm a solcetologist." I must have given her a blank look, because she added, "I study solcetaceans – the swales."

"Oh." I knew there were scientists who objected to what they believed was interference with the culture of the swales, but I had thought that since the legal right to proselytize the swales had been established two years ago, the controversy had been settled. I was obviously wrong. "I regret that you feel your studies are being compromised, Dr. Merced, but the swales are intelligent beings with free will, and I believe they have the right to choose their religious beliefs."

"You're introducing instability to a culture that has existed for longer than human civilization," she said, raising her voice. "They were traveling the stars at least a hundred thousand years before Christ was born. You're teaching them human myths that have no application for their society."

The two missionaries, clean-cut young men in dark suits and ties, approached us. "Is there a problem?" asked Elder Beckworth.

"No," I said. "Dr. Merced, you are free to tell the swales what you have told me: that you believe our teachings are false. But the swales who have joined our church have done so because they believe what we teach, and I ask you to please respect them enough to allow them that choice."

She glared at me with her beautiful eyes. "You're saying *I* don't respect them? *I* am not the one who tells them they are sinful creatures who need a human to save them."

"I'm not here to argue," I said. "And we are about to have a Sunday school class, so I'm afraid I'm going to have to ask you to leave."

She spun around and stalked out. I watched her go, unable to deny that my body desired hers, despite our differences. What's more, intelligence was an attractive trait for me, so I regretted that she opposed me on an intellectual level.

I would not be adding her to my dating pool. Somehow, I doubted that fact would disappoint her.

Elder Beckworth taught the Sunday school class, which was on the topic of chastity. I found myself acutely uncomfortable when he talked about Christ's teaching "that whosoever looketh on a woman to lust after her hath committed adultery with her already in his heart."

BECAUSE the Mormon church has an unpaid, volunteer clergy, my calling as branch president was the result of being sent to Sol Central, not the reason for it. I worked as a funds manager for CitiAmerica, and being stationed here gave me an eight-and-a-half-minute head start over Earth-based funds managers when it came to acting on news brought in from other star systems through the interstellar portal at the heart of the sun.

From what I understood, the energy requirements for opening a portal were so staggeringly high that it could only be done inside a star. Although the swales had been creating portals for so long that they didn't seem to know where their original home star was, Sol Central Station was the interstellar nexus of human civilization, and I was thrilled to be there despite the limited dating opportunities.

The Monday after my first day at church, I was in the middle of reviewing an arbitrage deal involving transports from two colony systems when I received a call on my station phone.

"Harry Malan," I answered.

"President Malan?" said a melodious alto voice. "This is Neuter Kimball, from the branch." Since the actual names of swales were series of magnetic pulses, they took human names when interacting with us. On joining the Church, Mormon swales often chose new names out of Mormon history. Neuter Kimball had apparently named itself after a twentieth-century prophet of the Church.

"What can I do for you, Neuter Kimball?"

After a pause that dragged out for several seconds, Kimball said, "I need to confess a sin."

This was what I had dreaded most about becoming branch president – taking on the responsibility of helping members repent of their sins. Only serious sins needed to be confessed to an ecclesiastical leader, so I braced myself emotionally and said a quick prayer that I might be inspired to help Neuter Kimball through the process of repentance. Leaning back in my swivel chair, I said, "Go ahead, Neuter Kimball; I'm listening."

"A female merged her reproductive patterns with mine." While many swales had managed to learn how to synthesize and transmit human speech, their understanding of vocabulary and grammar was not always matched by an understanding of emotional tone. Often they sounded the same no matter what the subject.

I waited, but Neuter Kimball didn't elaborate.

It took three swales to reproduce: a male, a female, and a neuter. The neuter merely acted as a facilitator; unlike the male and female, its reproductive patterns were not passed on to the offspring. In applying the law of chastity to the swales, Church doctrine said that reproductive activity was to be engaged in only among swales married to each other, and only permitted marriages of three swales, one of each sex.

"You aren't married to the female, are you?"

"No."

"It was just a female and you?" I asked. "No male?"

"Yes and yes."

According to my limited knowledge of swale biology, such action could not result in reproduction. Still, humans were perfectly capable of engaging in sexual sin that did not involve the possibility of reproduction, so I figured this was analogous.

"Why did you do it?" I asked.

"She did it to me."

"She did it to you? You mean, she forced you? You didn't agree to it?"

"Yes, yes, and no."

"Then it isn't a sin," I said, both horrified at the sexual assault and relieved that Neuter Kimball was innocent of any sin. "If someone forced sexual conduct on you, you are not at fault. You have nothing to repent of."

"You are sure?"

"Absolutely," I said. "But you may want to report the swale who did this to the authorities so she won't do it to anyone else."

"Why won't she do it to anyone else?" Neuter Kimball asked.

"Because they will punish her."

"That is human law," it said.

I was taken aback. "You mean it's not swale law?"

"There is no such law among our people."

The swales had supposedly been civilized for longer than humanity's history, yet they had no law against rape? "That's terrible," I said. "But the most important thing is that you did nothing wrong."

"Even if I enjoyed it?"

"Umm." I wondered for a moment why I had been called to serve here, rather than some General Authority of the Church who had more doctrinal knowledge. I had a vague suspicion it was so the Church could easily disavow my actions if I made a huge blunder. The swales were the only sentient aliens humanity had found thus far – and the swales didn't seem to know of any others – so the Church's policies for dealing with non-humans were still new.

I pushed those thoughts aside and focused on Neuter Kimball's question. "To commit a sin, you must have the intent to do so. If you did not intend sexual activity and it was forced upon you, then I don't think it matters whether you enjoyed it."

After several more reassurances, Neuter Kimball seemed satisfied that it was not guilty of any sin and ended the conversation.

It took me ten minutes to calm down after the stress of counseling. But I still felt the urge to action, so I looked up Dr. Merced's phone number.

WE MET in her office. A wallscreen similar to the one in the chapel showed pods of swales moving through solar currents.

I sat in a chair across from her desk and tried to keep my eyes from straying to the animated galaxies colliding on the chest of her skinsuit. "Thanks for agreeing to see me," I said. "We didn't part on the friendliest of terms yesterday."

She shrugged. "I'm curious. Your predecessors never sought me out. Can I get you a cup of coffee?"

"I don't drink coffee."

"Tea?"

I saw a twinkle in her eye and realized she was yanking my chain by offering drinks that she knew were forbidden by my religion. "No, thank you. But if you want to drink, go right ahead. The prohibitions of the Word of Wisdom apply only to members of the Church."

She picked up her coffee mug and took a long sip. "Mmmm. That is so good."

I merely smiled at her.

"Okay," she said. "Actually, the coffee here is awful. I just drink it for the caffeine. Why are you here?"

"A member of my church was raped," I said.

Her eyes widened. "What? Wait, you don't mean a solcetacean, do you?"

"Yes."

"Solcetaceans do not have the concept of rape," she said.

"Whether they have the concept or not," I said, "a female swale engaged in sexual activity with one of my neuter members, without its consent. To me, that sounds like rape, or at least a sexual assault."

She took a sip from her coffee mug. "It may sound like it, but solcetaceans are not human. Their culture is different – "

"That doesn't make it right."

" – and their physiology is different. Tell me, was your church member injured or caused any pain?"

"No. But it was afraid it might have sinned."

She pointed at me. "That is your fault, for teaching it that sexual behavior is sinful. But, physiologically, sexual contact between solcetaceans is always pleasurable for all parties involved. And since reproduction can only occur when all three deliberately engage in sex for that purpose, casual sex never results in pregnancy. So solcetaceans never developed the taboos humans did regarding sexual contact."

I nodded. "So, if we humans hadn't developed taboos about sex, and there was no chance of your getting pregnant, then you would have no objection to my forcing you to an orgasm."

She had the decency to blush. "I'm not saying that. What I'm saying is that you can't judge solcetacean behavior based on human cultural norms. After all, even your own church has had to adapt its doctrines to take differences like the three sexes into account. Not to mention there's no way you're getting a solcetacean into the waters of baptism."

"'Except a man be born of water and of the Spirit, he cannot enter into the kingdom of God,'" I quoted. "Swales are not men, as you've pointed out. No contradiction there. But you're avoiding the subject, which is that anyone, swale or human, has the right to be free from unwanted sex. If the swales don't recognize that right yet, it's time we told them about it."

She rose from her chair and walked around the desk to stand facing her wallscreen. She zoomed in on one particular swale. It was labeled *Leviathan* (*Class 10*), and its size reading showed 39,200 meters. It was hundreds of times longer than Neuter Kimball, or even Sister Emma.

"Solcetaceans grow throughout their lifetime," she said, her back toward me. "The correlation between size and age is not exact, but in general the larger, the older. Some of the oldest were old before the Pyramids were built. All the solcetacean members of your church are very young, and have little influence within the community. Ancients like Leviathan are respected. Do you really think you can convince a creature older than human civilization to change just because a human thinks something is wrong? Your lifetime is but an eyeblink to her, if she had eyes that blinked."

I pushed away my awe at the sheer size of Leviathan. "Maybe you're right. But I believe in a God even older than that, who created both human and swale. I have to try."

She turned and looked me in the eyes. I held her gaze until she sighed and said, "I was always a sucker for a man with determination." She walked to her desk, wrote something on a note paper, and handed it to me. It was an anonymous comm address with a private access code.

"I'm flattered," I said, "and it's not that I don't find you attractive, but – "

She rolled her eyes. "It's Leviathan's personal comm."

My face flushed. "Uh, thank you. I'll talk with her."

"Don't count on it. She hasn't bothered to talk to any of us in a couple of years, but nobody's tried talking religion at her, so ... "

"I'll do my best." With that, I beat a hasty retreat so I could recover from my embarrassment alone.

"Try not to offend her," she called after me.

MY EMAIL about the situation to the mission president, who was based in the L5 Colony but had jurisdiction over my little branch of the Church, received just a short reply, telling me "use your best judgment, follow the Spirit."

After a couple of days of spending my after-work hours studying up on swales and swale culture and preparing arguments about the rights of Mormon swales to control their own bodies, I didn't exactly feel ready to contact Leviathan. But I felt a strong need to do something.

Sitting at my desk in my quarters, I dialed the comm address Dr. Merced had given me and waited for it to connect. It rang several times before a synthetic neuter voice came on the line and said, "The party you are trying to reach is currently unavailable. Please leave a message after – "

I hung up before the tone. I hadn't prepared to leave a voicemail message, but I should have realized that having Leviathan's private access code was no guarantee that she would actually answer when I called. So I spent a good ten minutes writing out the message I would leave her on voicemail.

Satisfied that I had something that expressed my position firmly yet respectfully, I dialed the number again.

After two rings, a bass voice answered, "Who are you?"

Startled because I had expected the voicemail again, I stumbled over my words. "I'm ... this is President Malan, of the Church ... of the Sol Central Branch of the Church of Jesus Christ of Latter-day Saints. Dr. Merced gave me this comm address so I could talk to you about one of my ... a swale member of my branch." Uncertain because the bass voice didn't strike me as particularly female, I added, "Are you Leviathan?"

"Religions interest me not." Her voice synthesis was good enough that I could hear the dismissiveness in her tone.

"Are you interested in the rights of swales in general?" I asked.

"No. The lesser concern me not."

I could feel all my carefully laid-out arguments slipping away from me. How could I have even thought to relate to a being with no consideration for the rights of lesser members of her own species?

Before I could think through a response, I blurted out, "Do the greater concern you?"

During several long seconds of silence, I thought I had offended Leviathan to the point that she had hung up on me. Dr. Merced would be annoyed.

When her voice returned, it almost thundered from the speakers. "Who is greater than I?"

This had not been part of my planned approach, but at least she was still talking to me. Maybe if I could get her to understand that she would not like being man-handled – swale-handled – by larger swales, I could convince her of the need to respect the rights of smaller swales.

"From what I understand, swales get larger with age," I said. "So wouldn't your parents be larger than you?"

"I have no parents. None is older than I; none is larger; none is greater. I am the source from which all others came."

Stunned, I was silent for a few seconds before I could ask, "You are the original swale?" Since they didn't seem to die of old age, it just might be true.

"I am the original *life*. Before there was life on any planet, I was. After eons alone I grew into a swale, then gave life to others. Where was your god when I was creating them?"

A verse from the book of Job sprang to my mind: *Where wast thou when I laid the foundations of the earth? declare, if thou hast understanding.*

Nothing in my research had prepared me for this. Speculation about the evolution of swales generally assumed that swales were descended from less complex plasma beings in another star, since no simpler forms had been found in the sun. But if what Leviathan claimed was true, there were no simpler forms – she had evolved as a single being.

I was out of my depth, but shook my head to clear my thinking. All this was be-side the point. "What matters is that Neu – " I caught myself before breaking confi-dentiality. "One of my swale church members believes in a god who has commanded against sexual activity outside of marriage. It just isn't right for larger swales to force smaller ones to have sex. I appeal to you as the first and greatest of the swales: command your people against coerced sexual activity."

Seconds of silence ticked away.

"Come to me," she said. "You and your swale church member."

The call disconnected.

"'COME TO me'?" Dr. Merced's voice was incredulous.

"It was pretty much an order," I said, settling into the chair across from her desk. "I suppose it's easy enough for swales, but it's not like I have access to a solar shut-tle." The solcetologists did, so I hoped I could sweet-talk her into giving me a ride.

"Beginner's luck." Her tone was exasperated. "I've been here five years, and I've never had a chance to observe a Class 10 solcetacean up close." She sighed. "Not that we can directly observe them, anyway, but there's just something about actually being there, instead of taking readings remotely."

"Well, now's your chance," I said. "Take me to Leviathan."

"It's not that easy. Our observation shuttle is booked for projects months in advance."

"Oh." There went that idea. How was I supposed –

"Did Leviathan say why she wanted you to go to her?"

"No. Just told me to come, then hung up."

She pursed her lips, then said, "It's just very unusual. There isn't really anything that Leviathan can say to you in person that she can't say over the comm."

"I thought about that, and I think it's size. Maybe she thinks that if my church member sees how small I am compared with Leviathan, it will give up Mormonism."

"That's actually a good theory." Dr. Merced looked at me with apparently newfound respect. "Size does matter to the solcetaceans. And your church members are among the youngest, least powerful, and therefore most likely to be awed into obeying a larger one. And they probably don't come any larger than Leviathan."

"According to her, she's the largest."

Leaning forward in her seat, Dr. Merced said, "She told you that?"

"Not just that. She claimed to be not only the original swale, but the original plasma lifeform. She said she *became* a swale."

In a tone of amazement, Dr. Merced took the Lord's name in vain. She reached over to her comm, and punched in an address. When a man responded, she said, "Taro, I think you need to come hear this." Looking at me, she said, "Dr. Sasaki specializes in solcetacean evolutionary theory."

When Dr. Sasaki, a gray-haired Japanese gentleman, arrived, I relayed to him what Leviathan had told me about her history. When I finished, he said, "It's not impossible. I always suspected the Class 10s knew more about their origins than they bothered to tell us. But forgive me, Mr. Malan, how do we know Leviathan actually told you she was the original lifeform? Why would she choose to tell you and not one of us?" He motioned toward himself and Dr. Merced.

I decided to not be offended at the implication that I was a liar. "I can't say I know why Leviathan does anything, but ... You scientists who study the swales have strict rules about interfering with swale culture, and you try to avoid offending them. To me that smacks of condescension – you presume that swale culture is weak and cannot withstand any outside influence. Well, maybe the swales tend to think the same about human culture, so they avoid interference and try not to offend us."

Dr. Sasaki frowned at me. "I disagree with your interpretation of the motives for our rules regarding interference in solcetacean culture. And I don't see how it's relevant."

"I apparently offended Leviathan." I glanced at Dr. Merced and said, "Sorry, but I didn't realize that implying there were swales greater than her would cause offense. Her response was to tell me I was wrong, that there could be no swale greater, and that's when she explained she was the first. Because I made her angry – something you guys avoid, thanks to rules – Leviathan responded without worrying whether she would offend me or interfere with human culture."

"How would this information interfere with human culture?" asked Dr. Merced.

"Some swale-worshipping cults have already sprung up on Earth," I said. "Just imagine what will happen when the news gets out that Leviathan claims to be the original lifeform in the universe."

With a suspicious look, Dr. Sasaki said, "News you will be only too happy to spread, I'm sure. There is only one Leviathan, and Harry Malan is her prophet."

My jaw dropped. "What?"

"That's where this is headed, isn't it?" he said. "You go out and talk to Leviathan, then come back with some 'revelation' from – "

"No!" I stood up. "Absolutely not. I believe my own religion and have no intention of becoming Leviathan's prophet. All I want is for the swales in my branch to be free from harassment. You're just jealous because I got handed the information you've been bumbling about trying to find."

He shot to his feet, but before he could say anything, Dr. Merced said, "Stop it, both of you."

Dr. Sasaki and I stood silent, glaring at each other.

"Taro," said Dr. Merced, "I think you're being unfair to Mr. Malan. I truly believe he's just trying to do what is best for his congregants."

I gave her a grateful look.

"Even if he is misguided," she added. "As for you, Mr. Malan, there is no reason to insult Dr. Sasaki."

With a bow of my head, I said, "I apologize, Dr. Sasaki."

"Apology accepted," he said.

I noticed he did not apologize to me, but after a moment that didn't matter, because Dr. Merced said, "Now that we're all friends again ... Taro, will you let us preempt your next expedition in the shuttle to go talk to Leviathan?"

WITH THE shuttle flight arranged for the next day, I returned to my quarters to work out other details. My Earth-based manager at CitiAmerica granted my request for two days' vacation time.

Then I dialed Neuter Kimball's comm.

"Hello, President Malan," it said.

"Hello, Neuter Kimball. You remember our discussion the other day about whether swales should be allowed to force sexual conduct on each other?"

"Of course."

"Well, I've spoken with Leviathan about it, and she has requested that we go to see her."

Neuter Kimball did not reply.

"Are you still there?" I said.

"You ... told *Leviathan* about me?" it said. It might just have been the voice synthesis, but there seemed to be fear in its tone.

"I did not mention you by name," I said, glad I'd managed to avoid slipping up. "But she requested that I bring you to her. I think this is a chance to convince a swale with real authority to do something to stop sexual assault."

After a short pause, Neuter Kimball said, "Why do you say Leviathan has real authority?"

"She told me she is the first and greatest of all swales. Isn't that true?" I asked, suddenly worried that I'd been taken in by a swale con artist.

"She told you?" Neuter Kimball said. "We are not supposed to talk of it to humans, but if she has revealed herself as a god to you, then that is her choice."

"A god? Leviathan is not a god. She's just ... " I stopped. What was I going to say: an ancient immortal being who created an entire race of intelligent beings? If that didn't fit the definition of a god, it was pretty close. "Neuter Kimball, if you believe Leviathan to be a god, why did you join the Church?"

"Because I do not want her as my god."

"Why not?"

Another long pause. "I probably should not have said anything about her."

Going to see Leviathan to plead the case for Neuter Kimball had seemed like a great opportunity. Now I wasn't so sure. "If you think you will be in any danger from Leviathan, you don't have to go."

"Do you believe God is greater than Leviathan?" Its alto voice was plaintive.

"Yes, I do," I said.

"Then I will have faith in God and go with you."

UNLIKE the much larger solar shuttle that had brought me to Sol Central Station, the observation shuttle had room for only two people. I strapped into the copilot's seat next to Dr. Merced, although we were both essentially passengers because the shuttle's computer would do the actual piloting.

After getting clearance from Traffic Control, the computer spun up the superconducting magnets for the Heim drive and we left the station.

On a monitor, I watched the computer-generated visualization of our shuttle approaching the energy shield that protected us from the 27 million degrees Fahrenheit and the 340 billion atmospheres of pressure. I held my breath as the shield stretched, forming a bulge around the shuttle. Soon we were in a bubble still connected by a thin tube to the shield around the station. Then the tube snapped, and our bubble wobbled a bit before settling down to a sphere.

"You can start breathing again," said Dr. Merced with a wry smile.

I did. "It was that noticeable?"

With a chuckle, she said, "The energy shield is not going to fail. It's a self-sustaining reaction powered by the energy of the solar plasma around it."

"Yeah, but on the station I can usually avoid thinking about what would happen if for some reason it did fail."

"The good news is, if it did fail, you wouldn't notice."

"There's a backup system?" I asked.

"No." She grinned. "You'll just be dead before you have time to notice."

"Thank you for that tremendously comforting insight, Dr. Merced," I said.

"Look, we're going to be shipmates for the next couple of days, so why don't you drop the Dr. Merced bit and call me Juanita?"

I nodded. "Thank you, Juanita. And you can call me ... Your Excellency."

Juanita snorted. "I can already tell this is going to be a long trip. Oh, looks like our escort has arrived."

On the monitor, a swale twice the size of our energy shield bubble undulated closer. A text overlay read *Kimball* (*Class 1, Neuter*).

"Let's get the full view," she said and pressed a few buttons.

I gasped as a full holographic display surrounded us, as if we were traveling in a glass sphere. Against the yellow background of the sun, a giant swirl of orange and red swam alongside us. "Kimball" was superimposed in dark green letters.

"Can I talk to it?" I asked.

"Computer, set up an open channel with Kimball," said Juanita.

"Channel open," said the computer.

"Hello, Neuter Kimball," I said. "It's nice to finally meet you."

"It is nice to meet you, too, President Malan, although I hope you will forgive me for not shaking your hand."

I smiled. "Forgiven." I was constantly surprised how much swales seemed to know about our customs and culture, compared with how little we seemed to know of theirs. "And I'm here with Dr. Merced, who is a scientist – "

Juanita laughed. "It's known me a lot longer than it's known you."

"Hello, Juanita," said Neuter Kimball. "I'm glad you are with us."

"Shortly after I began my work here," Juanita said, "it was the first solcetacean I observed personally. It went by the human name Pemberly back then."

"Another swale had transmitted *Pride and Prejudice* to me, and I decided to seek out humans to see what they were like," Neuter Kimball said. "You are a fascinating race."

The thought came to me that maybe there had been some pride and prejudice between me and Juanita – possibly because she was annoyed that a swale she particularly liked had become a Mormon. But maybe we could work out our differences and – I shoved that thought away. "Swales are also fascinating. I hope to understand you as well someday as you understand us."

"Kimball, our shuttle is on a course to take us to Leviathan, so you can just follow us," said Juanita. "But stay at least fifty meters away from us."

"I will keep my distance," said Neuter Kimball.

I must have shown my puzzlement, because Juanita pressed a button to mute the call and said, "Solcetaceans and energy shields don't play well together. A few years back, a Class 1 – about Kimball's size – was showing off for a couple of observers, and glanced off a shuttle's energy shield. It tore a big chunk off the solcetacean that took months to heal."

"What about the shuttle? And the people inside?" Sometimes I got the feeling she cared more about swales than about people.

After a moment, Juanita said, "This shuttle was the replacement."

"What happened?"

"The shield did *not* collapse, but part of the solcetacean made it through – probably because the shield works similarly to how solcetaceans hold their bodies together, so the shield sort of merged with the solcetacean's skin. When they recovered the shuttle, they found that the plasma had vaporized part of it, including the crew compartment."

"I guess it's good I didn't hear about that before coming on this trip," I said.

"Don't worry – this shuttle was built with an ablative shell specifically to withstand that sort of accident," she said. "So I'm really more concerned with what would happen to Kimball if it bumped into us."

"Or Leviathan?"

"Leviathan's so big, she might not even notice."

I SPENT most of the sixteen-hour trip polishing and improving what I would say to Leviathan to convince her to outlaw coerced sexual activity. I had been a debater in high school and college, so I felt I knew how to construct a convincing argument. But eventually I reached the point where I felt I was making my prepared speech worse, not better.

"Approaching destination," the computer said.

I blinked a few times to clear my eyes, straightened up in my seat, and began looking around. Neuter Kimball's orange and red form moved silently beside us. I scanned the holographic image for more orange and red, but didn't see any.

"There," said Juanita, pointing ahead of us. She pressed a button, and dark green letters sprang up: *Leviathan (Class 10, Female)*.

Staring harder, I noticed a bright spot above the letters. As we drew closer, I could distinguish white, violet, and blue swirling together. "She's not orange or red."

"It's all false color, anyway," Juanita said, "but this imaging system uses color to indicate energy levels. Leviathan is actually hotter than the surrounding solar plasma. We think she carries out fusion inside herself."

Leviathan grew in our view, stretching out to fill most of the holographic screen in front of us. The intricate dance of violet and blue amid the white was mesmerizing. Eventually she shone so brightly that I had to squint to reduce the glare. "Aren't we getting too close?" I asked.

"We're still three kilometers away," Juanita said. But she added, "Computer, hold position relative to Leviathan."

"Neuter Kimball, are you ready?" I asked.

"I feel a bit like Abinadi going before King Noah," it said.

I kind of agreed, but I said, "Try to think of it as Ammon going before King Lamoni instead."

"That would be better," said Neuter Kimball. "But I am ready in any case."

Juanita hit the mute. "What was that about?"

"References to the Book of Mormon. Abinadi was burned at the stake after preaching to King Noah, but King Lamoni was converted by Ammon's preaching."

She just shook her head, muttering something about fairy tales, then said, "Computer, set up an open channel to Leviathan."

"Channel open," the computer replied.

"Leviathan, this is President Malan," I said. "I have come with my church member, Neuter Kimball, as you requested. We petition you to tell your people – "

"Silence, human," boomed the voice from the speaker. "It is not yet time for you to speak."

I shut up.

"You will come with me," Leviathan said. Her form brightened. There was a blinding flash, then the holographic system compensated and lowered its brightness.

It took several seconds before the afterimage cleared enough for me to make out shapes. Leviathan still loomed in front, and Neuter Kimball remained beside us.

"Uh-oh," said Juanita.

"What?" I blinked hard, trying to clear my vision. The sun's background seemed blue instead of yellow.

"I don't think we're in Kansas anymore." Juanita tapped at her keyboard. "Leviathan ported us to another star – one with a core much hotter than the Sun. Looks like the shield is holding, for now." She took the Lord's name in vain – or possibly it was a heartfelt prayer for help – and added, "We're stuck here unless she takes us back."

"What about Neuter Kimball?" I asked.

"Only a Class 6 or larger can open a portal on its own."

Green letters began popping up on the screen. *Unknown (Class 10, Male). Unknown (Class 9, Female). Unknown (Class 10, Neuter). Unknown (Class 8, Male).* My eyes adjusted enough that I could see their forms. Dozens of swales surrounded us, all of them tagged Class 8 or higher.

"What have you gotten us into?" Juanita said.

I said a silent prayer and hoped for the best. "It's a great opportunity for both of us. Think of what you're going to discover."

She took a deep breath. "You're right. It's just that I was prepared to study Leviathan, not sixty Class 8 and up. No one's ever seen more than three or four giant ones together."

"Is Leviathan the biggest one here?"

After checking a readout, Juanita said, "Yes, but not by much." She pointed at a swale off to the left. "That male is only about two percent smaller."

"So it looks like she wasn't lying about that."

She nodded her agreement, then said, "Why did you say it's a great opportunity for you?"

I swept my arm across the view. "These must be the most prestigious swales, the leaders. If I can talk to them, convince them to make a law against sexual assault, then the smaller swales will accept it. That has to be why Leviathan brought me and Neuter Kimball here."

"You are wrong," said Neuter Kimball. Juanita must have taken the mute off at some point.

"Why do you say that?"

"This is a deathwatch council," said Neuter Kimball. "They are here to watch me die so they can tell all swales that my death was deserved."

"What?" I said. "What have you done?"

"I'm sure Leviathan will – "

Leviathan's voice cut Neuter Kimball's off. "This little one has abandoned me in favor of a human god. Such error I could forgive. But on its behalf, the tiny human seeks to impose its moral code on us. The human's mind is infinitesimal compared to ours. The human's life is short, the history of its race is short. It is the least of us, and yet it seeks power over us."

"I don't seek power over – " I began.

"Silence!" Leviathan thundered. "The human must see the error of its ways. Kimball!"

"Yes, Leviathan?"

"Your life is forfeit. But I will grant reprieve if you will renounce the human religion and return to me."

I had read of martyrdom in the scriptures and history of the Church all my life. But nowadays it was supposed to be a merely academic exercise, as you examined your faith to see if it was strong enough that you would die for the gospel of Christ. Actual killing over religious belief wasn't supposed to happen anymore.

And I found my own faith lacking as I hoped that Neuter Kimball's faith was weak, that it would deny the faith and live rather than be killed.

"I am to be Abinadi after all, President Malan," said Neuter Kimball. "I choose to live as a Mormon, and I will die as one if it be God's will."

"It is *my* will," said Leviathan, "and I am the only god who concerns you."

Tendrils of white plasma reached out toward Neuter Kimball.

"I am the greatest of all," said Leviathan. "Bear witness to my judgment."

I hit the mute button and said, "I've got to stop this. This is my fault."

Juanita's eyes glistened. "I warned you about interfering. But it's too late to do anything now."

"No," I said. "If you're willing to drive this thing into Leviathan's tendrils, it may give Neuter Kimball a chance to escape."

She stared at me. "The shuttle's meant to survive a glancing blow. A direct hit like that – we could die."

The tendrils closed around Neuter Kimball.

"I know, and that's why I'm asking you. I can't force you to risk your life to save someone else's." I hoped I was right about how much she cared about swales – and Neuter Kimball in particular.

After looking out at Neuter Kimball, then back at me, she said, "Computer, manual navigation mode." She grabbed the controls and began steering us toward the white bands connecting Leviathan to Neuter Kimball.

I turned off the mute. "Leviathan, you claim to be the greatest. In size, you probably are."

White filled the view ahead.

"But not in love," I said, speaking quickly as I didn't know how much time I had left. "Jesus said, 'Greater love hath no man than this: that he lay down his life for his friends.' He was willing to die for the least of us, while you are willing to kill the leas – "

A flash of bright light and searing heat cut me off. I felt a sudden jolt.

Then blackness.

And nausea. After a few moments, I realized nausea probably meant I was still alive. "Juanita?"

"I'm here," she said.

The darkness was complete. And I was weightless. Maybe I was dead – although this wasn't how I'd pictured the afterlife.

"What happened?" I asked.

"I'll tell you what didn't happen: the energy shield didn't fail. The ablative shell didn't fail. We didn't die."

"So what did happen?"

Juanita let out a long, slow breath. "Best guess: electromagnetic pulse wiped out all our electronics. The engine's dead, artificial gravity's gone, life support's gone, comm system's gone, everything's gone."

"Any chance – "

"No," she said.

"You didn't even let me finish – "

"No chance of anything. It's not fixable, and even if it was, I haven't a clue how to fix any of those things even if it weren't totally dark in here. Do you?"

"No."

"And no help is coming from Sol Central because not only do they not know we're in trouble, but also we're in another star that could be halfway across the galaxy. When the air in here runs out, we die. It's that simple."

"Oh." I realized she was right. "Do you think maybe we succeeded in freeing Neuter Kimball?"

"Maybe. But it didn't exactly look like Kimball was trying all that hard to escape."

"Well," I said, "maybe it was thinking about how Abinadi's martyrdom led one of the evil king's priests to repent and become a great prophet. Perhaps Neuter Kimball believed something similar would happen to one of the great swales who – "

"Whatever Neuter Kimball believed," she said, her voice acidic, "it was because you and your church filled its mind with fairy tales of martyrs."

I bit back an angry reply. Part of me felt she was right. At the end, Neuter Kimball had seemed to embrace the role of martyr. Would it have done so if not for the stories about martyrs in the scriptures?

And I had been willing enough to risk my life, but now that I was going to die, I found myself afraid.

Juanita didn't seem to need a reply from me. "And what's the point of martyrs anyway? A truly powerful god could save his followers rather than let them die. Where's God now that you really need him? What good is any of this?"

"Look, I'm sorry," I said. "If it weren't for me, you'd be safe at home, and Neuter Kimball would be alive. I've made a mess of things."

"Yes."

Hours passed – floating in darkness, it was hard to tell how many. I spent it in introspection and prayer, detailing all my faults that had led me here. Biggest of all was pride: the idea that I, Harry Malan, would – through sheer force of will and a good speech – change a culture that had existed for billions of years. I thought back to what I had been told while serving as a nineteen-year-old missionary on Mars: *You* don't convert people; the Spirit of the Lord does that, and even then only if they are willing to be converted.

Juanita spoke. "You were just trying to do what you thought was right. And you were trying to protect the rights of smaller swales. So I forgive you."

"Thank you," I said.

The shuttle jolted.

"What was that?" I asked. My body sank down into my seat.

"It sounded – "

An ear-splitting squeal from the right side of the shuttle drowned out the rest of her reply. I twisted my head around and saw sparks flying from the wall.

Then a chunk of the hull fell away and light streamed in, temporarily blinding me.

"They're still alive," said a man. "Tell Kimball they're still alive."

ALL WE got from the paramedics was that a large swale had dropped off our shuttle and Neuter Kimball just outside Sol Central Station's energy shield. Neuter Kimball had called the station, and the shuttle had been towed into a dock, where they cut through the hull to rescue us.

It wasn't until Juanita and I were sitting in a hospital room, where an autodoc gave us injections to treat our radiation burns that we were able to talk to Neuter Kimball.

"It was Leviathan who brought us back here," it said.

I was stunned. "But why? And why didn't she kill you?"

"When she saw that you were willing to die to save me, though I am not even of your own species, she was curious. She asked me why you would do such a thing, so I transmitted the Bible and the Book of Mormon to her. Then she brought us here in case you were still alive."

"And you're not hurt from what she did to you?" I asked.

"I will recover," said Neuter Kimball. "Before she left, Leviathan declared that from this time forward, Mormon swales are not to be forced into sexual activity."

"That's great news." I had won. No – I corrected myself – the victory was not mine. *I thank thee, Lord*, I prayed silently.

"Leviathan also had a personal message for you, President Malan. She said to remind you of what King Agrippa said to Paul."

I nodded. "I understand. Thanks for passing that along."

After the call was over, Juanita said, "What was that message about? Another Book of Mormon story?"

"No, it's from the Bible. Saint Paul preached before King Agrippa, and the king's response was, 'Almost thou persuadest me to be a Christian.' So, no, Leviathan hasn't become Mormon. But God softened her heart so she didn't kill Neuter Kimball. Or us, for that matter. Back on the shuttle, you were certain we were going to die. You asked where God was when I really needed him. Well, God came through."

Juanita puffed out an exasperated breath. "Typical."

"What do you mean by that?" I asked as the autodoc signaled that my treatment was complete.

"In one story, the preacher converts the king. In another, the king kills the preacher. And in a third, neither happens. That's no evidence that God comes through." She pointed at me. "As I see it, *you* came through. By mentioning that 'greater love' thing, you hit Leviathan where it counted: her pride at being the greatest."

I shook my head. "I'm not taking credit for this."

After we walked out of the hospital, she gave me a tight hug that reminded me how much I was attracted to her. But I knew it would never work out between us – our worldviews were just too different.

So I was still a single Mormon man with no dating prospects within ninety million miles.

AND NO, an attractive single Mormon woman did not arrive on the next solar shuttle. What would be the point of life if God solved all my problems?

O Lord, how manifold are thy works! in wisdom hast thou made them all: the earth is full of thy riches. So is this great and wide sea, wherein are things creeping innumerable, both small and great beasts. There go the ships: there is that leviathan, whom thou hast made to play therein.

– PSALM 104:24-26

THE EYE OPENER

Brian Gibson

THE PROBLEM is you can't unsee a thing. You just can't. It's just not possible. It's not going to happen. You can try all you want.

The more you try to unsee something the more you see it. There's no delete button in your mind. Once you see a thing, it's there. In your head. Floating like that triangle-sided thing inside a Magic 8 ball; it'll just float up like a dead fish now and then so you have to see it again and again, even if you don't want to. Especially if you don't want to.

It's best never to look in the first place, Gordy thought. I should have never opened my eyes.

And he almost cried, standing in the dark of night behind a 7-Eleven in downtown Provo struggling to get the pack of cigarettes he just bought out of his pocket.

And dammit if cigarettes weren't harder to open now than when he was fifteen. If only his hands would stop shaking. Gordy thought to pray that they'd stop, and the irony made him chuckle.

Involuntarily, he saw the Morgan boy again. All of a sudden, there the boy was in his mind and it made him tear at the pack of cigarettes with renewed vigor. Gordy had loved smoking when he was a teenager. He'd successfully quit when he was seventeen in order to go on a mission but he'd never forgotten, not even for a second, the relaxing calm that a cigarette could bring, and he fumbled to flip open the pack of Camel Lights in his hand, because if anyone ever needed a moment of peace, deserved some calm, it was him right now.

Gordy shook out a cigarette and lit it with a cheap lighter he'd bought with the pack. He took a long, deep, drag into his lungs and exhaled, and it was just as he remembered. The thoughts racing in his brain settled like silt and he had one last pang of guilt. If Josie and Hiram and Harry could see him right now, what would they think? I'm doing this for them, though, he told himself. I need to calm down enough to think, to come up with a plan, to know what to do.

The first time he'd opened his eyes it was for a blessing.

Or at least it was for the infant involved.

Robby and Kathy Page had had their first, a baby girl they'd named Esther, and the second counselor asked all those invited to participate in the ordinance to come forward. It was just like any other blessing on any other Fast Sunday, except Gordy had volunteered to hold the microphone.

If Gordy had had it his way, he and his wife would never have sat so close to the front. That was Josie's idea. It helped the twins be reverent and concentrate, she said, but who was she kidding? Twin five-year-old boys are incapable of concentration if they sit in the first pew, the last pew, or a lawn chair on the moon. He didn't say a word to Josie, though, partly because she was amazing, and partly because in six years of marriage he'd learned the value of keeping his mouth shut.

If only, Gordy thought, knocking ash off his cigarette, he knew how to keep his eyes shut.

The counselor had held the microphone out in front of the entire congregation like it was free cotton candy, and when no one else moved a muscle, Gordy finally got up to end the awkwardness. He strung out the microphone cord behind him as the men got up and made their way to the front.

After the circle formed, he leaned over Brother Reinhardt as best he could and held the microphone a couple inches from Robby's face. Brother Reinhardt was half a foot taller than Gordy so he had to get up on his tippy-toes. He felt like a daytime talk show host – one of those guys who prowls the audience, straining to reach them with the microphone so they can scream at the people on stage and tell them how idiotic they are.

Before Robby had even given his newborn daughter the name Esther Sariah Page, Gordy's calves began to cramp. But he shoved it aside so he could listen to the blessing with his eyes locked tight. His parents, his mom in particular, had always emphasized reverence and keeping your eyes closed during prayers. "Eyes shut during Prayer Time," she used to always say. And Gordy took all his childhood lessons to heart, so much so that opening your eyes during a prayer became a transgression, if not an outright sin.

At one point, before he just accepted it as The Way It Should Be, he got caught up wondering why you were *supposed* to keep your eyes shut. Was it to help you pay attention? Did it even matter to Heavenly Father? Soon his seven-year-old mind went past curiosity to obsession and Gordy decided to do an experiment in his Primary class.

Sister Rogers's lesson was actually on prayer that day – Gordy remembered that. He waited patiently until the closing prayer, and once Lisa Carter got past "Dear Heavenly Father," he opened his eyes wide, just let them snap open like the shutter of a camera. What he saw blew his mind. Billy Thurston and Jimmy Baines were making silent monkey faces at Lisa. Billy had his mouth stretched open so tight and wide Gordy could see new silver fillings in his molars, and Jimmy was so close to Lisa's face Gordy thought he might lick her cheek. The best part was little Lisa was completely oblivious and just kept on praying, thanking God for drops of dew and her My Little Ponies.

For some kids, Gordy realized, Prayer Time was actually Fun Time.

Billy and Jimmy weren't the only ones with their eyes open. Mandy Feather-stone was examining a booger on her finger and Jarom Johnston was putting the finishing touches on a wicked-looking paper airplane. Jarom saw Gordy staring at him and simply nodded to him as he put a final fold into his Sunday program. Pray-er Time with eyes open was sweet. It was like joining an exclusive club, like discovering a delightful new world, a private wonderland he never knew existed. It was the first time Gordy had felt the intoxicating thrill of a shared secret.

But not everyone had their eyes open. Most of the class had their eyes shut tight, and heads bowed, and arms folded. They had brow-furrowed expressions of concentration on their faces – the kind only little boys and girls are capable of. Gordy looked at Sister Rogers and her eyes were closed too, her brow was knit, and her lips were pursed. Her mouth was sewn up so tight it looked like a big white raisin. Gordy couldn't help it; he thought Sister Rogers looked like she was trying to pinch back a fart.

Gordy didn't laugh though, because that would be rude. He just turned away, and immediately felt the vise-like grip of a female hand with long, sharp nails on his arm.

Sister Rogers whispered, "You shut your eyes." And Gordy obeyed, but before his eyelids shut all the way he saw the monkey faces, the paper airplane, and the booger all disappear out of sight.

After class Gordy waited until all the other children had left and then sheepishly approached Sister Rogers.

"I'm sorry I opened my eyes, Sister Rogers," he said.

"I expected better from you, Gordon," she said. "You're a CTR. And you know what that means. It means you're supposed to choose the right." And she left him standing there alone in the classroom, a picture of praying kids surrounding Jesus on the wall.

And that's why Gordon Patterson Brown did not open his eyes during prayers. Lesson learned. Eyes closed was The Way It Should Be. Seven-year-old Gordy figured his fast-approaching baptism was going to wash clean his misguided experiment in CTR A, and he would never open his eyes again, a commitment that remained largely untested until he found himself uncomfortably straining on tiptoes listening to Robby Page bless his daughter with everything but the kitchen sink.

Gordy couldn't even focus on the words of the blessing because sometimes they were annoyingly loud and sometimes oddly soft. Then he realized that was his fault. He couldn't hold the microphone steady due to the awkward position he was in. Gordy had his arm stretched up and over Brother Reinhardt's back while trying not to touch the man, and at the same time he was trying to keep the microphone in the proximity of Robby's face without being able to see.

It can't be helped, Gordy thought, but then baby Esther cried, and the men collectively started bouncing her, and soon every third word of the blessing was punctuated by the thump of what Gordy quickly surmised was the baby girl's body hitting the microphone. Better move the microphone up, he thought, but when he did he heard the amplified scrape of the microphone moving across the stubble on Robby Page's face.

All right, this just won't do, he thought; he wasn't going to allow poor microphoning to mar the blessing of Robby's first born. Not on his watch. So Gordy moved in closer to Brother Reinhardt. Let the old man think he was gay if he wanted to. And he opened his eyes so he could see where the microphone was in relation to the baby, the other men in the circle, and most importantly, Robby Page's face.

Behind the 7-Eleven, Gordy blew smoke out of his lungs as he remembered it. The baby must have stopped crying at that point because his memory was a silent one. After making sure the microphone was a safe two-inch distance from Robby's mouth he saw Wayne Michaels on the opposite side of the circle. Wayne Michaels's eyes were wide open, as if they'd been open a long time, almost as if, and Gordy instinctively knew it was impossible but couldn't help thinking it, he was waiting for Gordy to open his eyes.

Wayne Michaels looked him in the eye and Gordy made eye contact right back. How come your eyes are open? Gordy was thinking. I need to see where the microphone is. It's my job. But there wasn't a hint of embarrassment on Wayne Michaels's face, or even a suggestion that having your eyes open was out of the norm. In fact, Wayne Michaels looked like he might think closing your eyes during a baby blessing was a weird thing to do. He was looking at Gordon unflinchingly, smiling a big, broad smile. It wasn't a disarming how-funny-we're-both-here-in-this-situation smile. It was a this-is-who-I-am smile.

But it wasn't the open eyes or the smile that Gordy couldn't shake. It was the forked tongue that flicked out of Wayne Michaels's mouth and ran across his teeth.

Oh, God, what am I going to do? Gordy thought, remembering the forked tongue in all its bizarre detail – wet and pink with moss-green spots that could have been taste buds – the way it flicked at the air as if it were capable of smell.

Gordy dropped his cigarette and crushed it out with his shoe. One more, he thought, I need one more cigarette, and he dug the lighter out of his pocket.

"And all these things, and many more things," Robby Page had said, heading into the homestretch, and the tongue, the teeth, the open eyes, all of it was replaced by an expression of reverent piety on Wayne Michaels's face. It was like a mask had appeared on the man in the blink of an eye.

And Gordy was actually blinking. He would have rubbed his eyes, but one hand was holding the mike, and the other was on Brother Reinhardt's shoulder.

The circle broke up and the men returned to their families. Gordy lingered a second longer. A deacon or teacher must have taken the microphone out of his hand. He didn't remember.

Wayne Michaels had been in the circle when he blessed Hiram and Harry. Wayne Michaels was widely known for doing yard work for widows.

He didn't remember any more details from the services that day, but he did remember sitting down next to his wife.

She said, "That was nice."

His rational mind kicked in. Did its job. Told him he didn't see what he saw, that it could be dismissed as a daydream, an illusion, a trick of light. Maybe Wayne Michaels, the fifty-something former first counselor currently serving on the stake high council, just happened to have a forked tongue and this was the first time he'd ever seen it. Never mind that Brother Michaels used to be his Scoutmaster and helped him become an Eagle. It was still possible. Remotely possible, but possible.

No. It wasn't.

In an effort to keep functional, Gordy's mind was taking him down paths to scenarios and possibilities just as unlikely, and equally absurd.

He pondered just straight-up asking Brother Michaels about what he had seen, but the mere thought of actually uttering the words, "Do you happen to have a forked tongue?" was too much for him. So Gordy took what is often the most rational course: he decided to ignore it and move on. A prudent decision, really, if only Gordy had had the willpower to never open his eyes again.

Why? Why had he opened his eyes again? Gordy honestly, desperately wanted to know. He tried to suck all the assistance he could out of his second cigarette. It was like a canker sore, he reasoned. Why do you keep poking it with your tongue? To see if it's still there. To see if it still hurts. To see if it's gone away yet.

A week went by, and you better believe that his eyelids did not open, not even a crack during any prayer that whole time, but the following Sunday he was sitting behind the stand with the choir – Gordy had a lovely tenor voice and wasn't ashamed of it – he decided to take a peek during the sacrament prayer.

His intention was to prove that everything was perfectly okay. Normal. Copacetic, as they say. He would simply prove that in the unseen world of Prayer Time there was nothing going on. *Nothing to see here.* Isn't that what cops always say at the scene of an accident? *Nothing to see here.* He opened his eyes and scanned the congregation. From his vantage point far behind the pulpit he couldn't see one pair of open eyes and it was a huge relief. Wayne Michaels was right there, perfectly normal on the third row, no forked tongue in sight. It was as if a weight fell off his shoulders, and then, whipping into view about five rows from the back was what looked like a giant earthworm. It was pink like fresh scar tissue, with sectional rings, but narrow like a garden hose, and at its end Gordy saw a heart-shaped, cartilaginous fin. A tail, he realized, and fought back the urge to vomit. It waved and undulated over the heads of the congregation.

Gordy did not want to see who, or what, the tail belonged to. No, he did not, and so when Sister Henrietta Banks started to raise her bowed, blue-haired head, he ripped his eyes away.

But his gaze fell on Davey Keen who was standing behind the sacrament table next to the priest offering the prayer. His hands were resting on the table, but they weren't hands. Shooting out from the cuffs of his white shirt and onto the white lace sheet covering the water were bright orange-yellow talons. They reminded Gordy of the chicken feet he saw hanging in butcher shop windows during his mission in Argentina.

A claw on the talon at the end of Davey Keen's arm tapped impatiently, and Davey slowly began to turn around to take a look at him.

Gordy shut his eyes.

He kept his eyes shut through the rest of sacrament. He waved off the deacon who coughed politely to alert him that he had brought by the bread, and the young man was smart enough not to offer him water. By the time the choir stood up to sing, Gordy was covered in cold sweat.

After church, Gordy tried to help Hiram and Harry set the table, but all he could think about was how when Davey Keen was a deacon Gordy used to straighten his clip-on tie.

"Gordy?" Josie said, "You're putting all the knives on the outside."

Gordy laughed and set about putting things right. "Knives on the inside, boys," he told his sons. "Forks on the left."

Josie put a comforting hand on his back and asked, "Are you okay?"

"Yeah," he said, "You know, just thinking about one of the lessons today. It was ... thought-provoking."

Behind the 7-Eleven Gordy watched his cigarette burn down and thought about Josie and Hiram and Harry.

The night after he saw the tail and the talons he couldn't sleep a wink. He couldn't even close his eyes. He stared at the ceiling and thought about what he'd experienced, the sheer undeniability of it. They weren't visions. There was a physical reality to what he'd seen: the claw tapping on the sacrament table. His mind, the rational part still hanging in there, told him he had to give these events a name. Gordy couldn't. The closest he came was to conclude they were the opposite of miracles. Was there a word for that? Anti-miracles? If miracles were a use of physical laws to create something formerly thought impossible in order to promote belief, then the things he'd seen in Prayer Time were anti-miracles, aberrations in physical laws meant to shatter faith. Had he unknowingly ingested some psychotropic drugs? Was he to believe that members of the Fairmont Fourth Ward were demon-like creatures and that he was seeing their true nature? Forget it. He'd rather just admit to being insane.

Gordy held it together at his job underwriting insurance policies during the week as if nothing had changed. Time helped his rational mind get a better grip on his thoughts. If the things he had seen were physical realities, they had to be subject to rules, Gordy decided, and he thought of a way to discover what the rules might be.

It became a mantra for Gordy. *If it is real, it has to have rules.* Repeating it to himself gave him motivation and comfort. By the end of the week he was looking forward to Sunday. He'd been asked to substitute in Primary and it provided him with a perfect opportunity.

Before his class, Gordy roamed the halls spying on another ward, peering into classrooms through the windows. Young Men. Young Women. Gospel Essentials. Family History. He saw class after class in the middle of Prayer Time, and saw nothing the least bit unusual. It was comforting to see groups of people calmly gathered round, kneeling, standing, sitting, heads bowed, arms folded, eyes closed.

The Way It Should Be.

It made him wonder if he hadn't just experienced a temporary bout of insanity. Then again, maybe there was nothing to see because he wasn't part of those prayers. He wasn't a participant. He'd put it to the test as soon as he taught Valiant 9 where he planned to participate in a big way.

He told the children that he was going to say the opening prayer. He didn't tell them he planned to offer it eyes wide open, and look around to see what there was to see. There was nothing. If anything the kids were disturbingly reverent. Gordy found the experience to be a bit of a letdown. He stumbled his way through the beginning of his lesson on the Creation because he was thinking about whether the difference might be that his eyes weren't closed at the beginning. They were open from the start. Was that what it was?

Gordy explained God resting on the seventh day and offered to pray again. A couple of the kids thought it was weird, but they folded their arms and closed their eyes all the same. He opened his own eyes right after he turned the corner from thanking to asking.

For a second he thought he was seven years old again and back in CTR A class looking at Billy Thurston and Jimmy Baines make monkey faces behind Lisa Carter's back. It wasn't Billy and Jimmy this time. It was Caitlin Franks and Bradley Morgan and they weren't making faces at Missy Benton. Caitlin was quietly sniffing Missy's sandy blonde hair with the wrinkled, wet, flat snout of a hog that had appeared in the middle of her face.

Bradley Morgan was beyond sniffing. His lower jaw had dropped open and distended and extended so that two boar-like tusks poked up from his mouth. His mouth was so huge the tusks couldn't reach his upper lip. And he was salivating.

"In the name of Jesus Christ, amen," Gordy quickly finished the prayer.

In the blink of an eye all the kids were reverently bowed with their eyes opening as if nothing had happened, as if Gordy would forget what they really were, as if Prayer Time hadn't nearly been Snack Time.

The kids filed out and Gordy stood there making a show of erasing the chalkboard. How could he ever pray again knowing that the person next to him might be wearing a different face? Might even be thinking about devouring him? It was eyes open for Gordy from now on. After the first sentence of every prayer Gordy was going to open his eyes and stare whatever it was right in the face.

In elders quorum they reorganized the presidency and when they were setting the new men apart, Gordy, who was sitting in the front row of chairs, opened his eyes to take a look. Mike Reynolds, the future secretary, went first, and Gordy was relieved that none of the three men laying their hands on Mike had changed in any visible way. Mike, however, stared straight ahead, right into Gordy's eyes. His irises were orange with black, narrow, vertical slits – like a jungle cat. That was bad enough, but then they slowly began to roll back into his head like the last number in an odometer. Soon all that was visible was the white sclera of his eyeballs. They looked like wet ping-pong balls wedged in his eye sockets, but then two tiny pinpoint pupils crept up into view and looked straight at Gordy. Mike blinked. There were no irises surrounding these new pupils, but they were dilating just the same, and Mike was just sitting under all those hands smiling like a shark.

Mike Reynolds, who was kind enough to drive Gordy's entire family to the airport for a five a.m. flight last Thanksgiving.

It was too much. Gordy walked out of elders quorum before they even said amen. He told himself he was going to be done with church for a while, but by the end of the day he'd decided to talk to the bishop.

Josie overheard him when he called Bert Winters, the executive secretary to make the appointment. He'd taken the phone into the laundry room, but she went in to take a load out of the dryer.

She couldn't hide her concern. "You need to talk to the bishop about something?"

"It's nothing," he lied. "I'll tell you all about it when it's over."

"You're not – addicted to pornography, are you?" She said it jokingly, but there was true worry beneath it. After all, Gordy had been a bit off lately.

"No. Seriously, it's nothing. Trust me."

"Okay," she said, walking away with a basket of warm clothes. She even rubbed his back on the way out. Good ol' Josie, he thought; she'd always trusted him so much. And he'd trusted her right back, he thought, watching her walk away.

One thing about smoking that Gordy enjoyed was watching the cigarettes burn down, turn to ash. They weren't just nicotine delivery devices, they were little timers. In fact, he'd heard explosives experts sometimes used them as makeshift fuses. As Gordy watched cigarette paper turn to ash, he knew his time was running out. Fast approaching was what Josie always called Decision Time.

Gordy's memory of meeting the bishop was vivid, like wet paint in his mind. He almost didn't show up because he had no clue what he was going to say. *Ahem, Bishop, half the ward is part animal.* Or, *Bishop, I have reason to believe the Primary children might try to eat each other.* Outside the unseen world of Prayer Time, it all seemed so absurd and unreal, but he'd seen what he'd seen. Gordy knew what he knew. He felt like Horton the Elephant. He was sure there was this other thing, reality, dimension, whatever. And what Gordy now felt in his gut was more disturbing than anything he'd seen. What he now believed with almost every fiber of his being was that what he was seeing wasn't another reality. It was *the* reality.

And that's why he wanted to see the Bishop. He had to know how far and deep it went.

Before Decision Time.

Gordy had always liked Bishop Cunningham because he had a gentle way of letting the ward members do most of the talking. He made you feel listened to. It made things easier. And so after Bishop Cunningham invited Gordy into his office and asked him to take a seat, Gordy started speaking. It was incredibly awkward, but Gordy did the best he could.

He found he could only talk in the vaguest terms. He said that some members of the ward weren't exactly what they said they were. A lot of them, active members in good standing were harboring secrets. Gordy told the Bishop that he felt like he didn't know who they were anymore. He didn't know who anyone was anymore, and that was the worst part.

The bishop looked back at him with warm, understanding eyes – blessedly human eyes. He smiled patiently – a practiced smile, Gordy could tell – a smile that was quite accustomed to people waltzing around the bush, working up to an unpleasant truth.

"I can tell you're quite upset, Gordy. I don't know what to say though, unless you feel comfortable being more specific." Gordy thought about spitting it all out: Mike Reynolds has cat eyes! Wayne Michaels has a snake tongue! The kid who blesses the sacrament has chicken feet! He just couldn't. To say it out loud seemed ridiculous and blasphemous all at the same time.

"No. I couldn't – " Gordy stammered.

"Well, is this hearsay? I mean Mormons love gossip more than their Jell-O."

"No. It's definitely not hearsay." Gordy was surprised at how adamant his voice sounded.

A pause ensued as the bishop thought it over.

"You know, Gordy, I think you're doing the right thing in not telling me more details. What's troubling you will probably come to light sooner or later. I've been bishop for almost five years now and I know that there are people in the ward that need to come and talk to me, but unfortunately they don't feel ready. I wish they did, but in most cases, not all, but most cases, it's wrong to force the repentance process." The bishop sighed. "And," he added, "lucky for you, you're not really expected to bear the burden of knowing what people are really like, or what their secrets are, for that matter. That's my job."

Gordy couldn't explain why, but with the bishop's words a weight lifted off his shoulders. He felt, for the first time since the blessing of the Page's baby, that he was capable of holding it all together. His eyes welled up and Gordy started profusely telling the bishop that he was right, of course, and thank you, and he was a little embarrassed for taking up so much of his time.

The bishop said to think nothing of it, and urged Gordy never to hesitate to come and talk to him. Gordy put his hands on the arms of his chair to get up, but the bishop said, "Do you mind if we end with a word of prayer?"

"No." Gordy said, and it was the first prayer since he'd sung with the choir where he didn't break into sweat and his stomach wasn't in knots. He didn't pay that much attention honestly, but it was as if his mind relaxed during all the thanking.

But then he heard the bishop say, "And please bless Gordon that he might accept our true faces."

Gordy's eyes snapped open. Wide.

The bishop's eyes were shut. There was nothing wrong with him. He looked totally normal. The bishop was a perfect vision of reverence and rectitude. Of course, the bishop wasn't one of them. Never the bishop. Relief rolled over Gordy like a wave. His vision of Bishop Cunningham blurred and Gordy realized he was looking through tears. The tears fell when he closed his eyes and listened to the bishop close the prayer in the name of the Savior.

In the doorway to the bishop's office Gordy and the bishop shook hands and the bishop said, "I want you to think about what I said, Gordy. You're always welcome here."

"Thanks, Bishop," Gordy said, and he thanked God for good men like Bishop Cunningham, and the peace that had finally come to him. "I will."

The bishop smiled and the smell of seaweed assaulted Gordy's nose. He felt wasp stings all over the back of his hand and he looked down in a panic. In place of five fingers wrapped around his hand were five purple throbbing tentacles the color of eggplant.

Gordy ripped his hand away and heard a ripping sound like Velcro.

He ran straight out of the church, knocking over a Boy Scout on his way.

He drove straight to the 7-Eleven, hyperventilating the entire way. Light from the streetlights came through the windshield as he drove, illuminating his right hand, the knuckles white on the steering wheel. Round suction marks from the bishop's tentacle hand were all over his flesh. They were visible. *Oh my gosh, oh my gosh, I can see them. There they are.*

The marks were real. *It* was real. *But what were the rules?*

The bishop had looked normal. He'd looked right at him. *Why?* Was it because his eyes were shut? Do they need to have their eyes open in order to be seen? Was that it?

And the prayer was over!

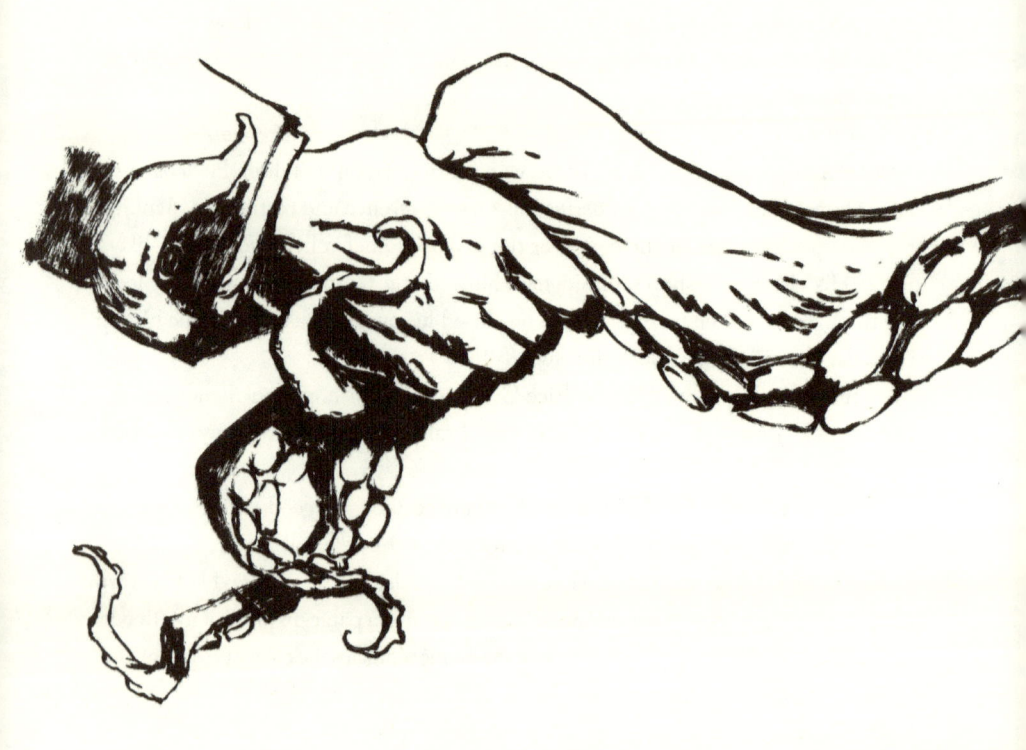

Then he remembered. At the door. That was his mistake. He had been grateful to God for good men like the bishop. He had had a prayer in his heart.

"Dude, what's wrong with your hand?" The pimple-faced clerk had said when he handed over the lighter and cigarettes. Gordy nearly dropped the lighter, but he said nothing.

He looked at the marks, the rows of red, round circles like he'd been branded by Cheerios. The absurdity of it made him chuckle, but the chuckle turned into a sob.

His cigarette was burning down between his index and middle finger. One more drag and it would be finished.

Decision Time.

Gordy knew what he had to do. He sucked the last bit of life out of the cigarette. He dropped it and crushed it.

He bought a bag of Doritos from the 7-Eleven and ate it on the way home. It was a trick he learned as a teenager. They're perfect for covering up smoker's breath.

As he drove, he rubbed his eyes and glanced at the clock on the dash, hoping the twins would be asleep already. That would make things easier. He thought of Hiram and Harry asleep in their beds. He liked to peek in on them when they were asleep. He also liked to peek in on them when they were sitting next to each other in Primary during Singing Time. Gordy remembered the words to a Primary song:

> *Humbly now, gently now, our arms we fold, our heads we bow.*
> *Humbly now, gently now, sincerely say the prayer.*
> *Humbly now, gently now, our silent thoughts we share ...*

He found it comforting and let it play in a continuous loop in his head. It helped distract him from the task at hand.

Gordy pulled his car up in front of his house. The lights were off in the twins' room. A good sign. After he turned off the car engine, he rummaged through the glove compartment. He found something he kept there in case of emergencies: a multi-tool. It came with pliers, a saw, a screwdriver, a bottle opener, and a knife. He put it in his pocket.

Gordy closed the door to his car and walked up to the front door of his home. *Humbly now, gently now.*

He quietly closed the front door behind him. Gordy could see through the living room into the kitchen where Josie had her head bent over the sink, doing the dishes, like she dutifully did every night of the week.

Our arms we fold, our heads we bow.

She was glad to see him. He called her over to talk, being mindful not to be very loud. She put the last dish in the dishwasher and dried her hands. Meanwhile, Gordy put the multi-tool under the couch with the knife blade out.

Humbly now, gently now.

Just in case.

Josie came over and sat next to him on the couch and Gordy was ready to tell her everything. He took her hands in his, but she noticed the burn marks on his hand right away and asked what happened.

"That's what I need to tell you," he said, "what I need to explain."

"Okay, but first we need to put something on that." She got up and came back with an aloe vera cream that she started to rub gently and slowly into the back of his hand.

Our secret thoughts we share.

He unburdened himself and told her all of it. He slowly laid out all the details, including everything he'd ever seen, starting with the blessing of the Page girl and finishing with the visit to the Bishop. He didn't tell her about the cigarettes. He didn't want to disturb her.

She listened. Mouth slightly agape. Eyes open wide in dismay. Josie always was an excellent listener. She only interrupted twice.

She said, "I don't understand," and Gordy kept going with his story, getting it all out there.

Again, later, Josie said, "I don't understand."

By the time Gordy was done he was weeping, and Josie was weeping too. She wasn't sure why.

"Are you sure all this happened, that you're not seeing things, or maybe temporarily – "

"I know it's real."

His conviction stunned her. He could tell it was going to take time for Josie to process all this new information. That was fine as long as she did what he told her to. "It's all just so unbelievable," she said. Gordy looked at her expectantly. "I don't know what to say. What do you want me to do?"

"Will you pray with me?"

Humbly now, gently now.

"Of course, I will," she said. Who would refuse a request like that?

"I need to get something first," he said, and got up. He went to the bathroom and came back with an old brass hand mirror. "Hold it in your hands, towards me, right beneath your face when you kneel."

"I don't – "

Gordy showed her what to do and held her hands around the mirror's handle. "During the prayer I want you to listen very closely, and when I say, 'and please bless that we might always be together,' just open your eyes and look at me. I'll be looking right back at you. Can you do that for me?"

She nodded and they knelt down to pray, right next to the couch.

"When I say, 'that we might always be together,'" he reminded her.

Sincerely say the prayer.

They prayed together.

As he offered the prayer there was one moment where thoughts intruded into Gordy's mind seemingly from nowhere, interrupting his concentration on the words of his prayer. *Don't do it. Don't open your eyes, Gordy. Keep them shut.* He heard Sister Rogers's harsh whispering voice.

You shut your eyes.

And his Mom's too:

Eyes shut during Prayer Time.

He ignored all those voices.

" ... that we might always be together." He heard the words coming out of his mouth.

And he opened his eyes. They both did.

It took a second.

Josie's face unzipped. Shark-like teeth appeared in a vertical mouth that ran down her face from forehead to chin. The mouth split wide open shoving her eyes wide apart. And a black tongue the size of a fist fell out. Tiny yellow worms came spewing out with it.

Gordy screamed like a little girl. He tried to scramble away so fast that he forgot to look in the mirror, but it didn't matter. The thing that was his wife hit him across the face with it so hard, the glass shattered.

Gordy fell over and felt something hot and wet on the side of his head. He crawled for the couch and the multi-tool beneath it.

In his peripheral vision, Gordy saw Josie rise up to full height. A pair of giant leathery bat-wings unfurled behind her.

Oh, God, please help me, just a few more inches, he thought. The multi-tool was in reach, but a shard from the mirror lay on the carpet in front of him.

And Gordy saw his true face.

The Way it Should Be.

HIRAM was the lighter sleeper of the twins. He woke up sure he had heard something, but wasn't sure what.

He crawled out of bed and rubbed his eyes.

He took his blanket and stepped out into the hallway.

"Mommy? Daddy?" he said, still groggy.

Then his dad appeared in the hallway with his hand on his head. It was hard for him to walk straight, and he bumped against the wall.

"Daddy? What's goin' on?"

"Nothing, son. Everything's okay now." Gordy fell to his knees and gave Hiram a big hug. "It's all going to be okay." Hiram hugged him back.

"You two!" a voice scolded. "You should both be asleep." It was Hiram's Mommy.

She walked down the hall and put one hand on Hiram's shoulder and another on Gordy's back. Gordy froze. "C'mon, off to bed," Josie said. Gordy remembered the words to his prayer: that we might always be together.

"Mommy?" Hiram asked. "Can we say a prayer first?"

"Of course, we can," she said.

This time Gordy kept his eyes shut. He didn't want to know any more.

THE MOUNTAIN OF THE LORD

Dan Wells

"**I STILL** don't like having dances in a church house," said mother, gripping the seat of our buckboard wagon as it bounced over ruts and ditches in the weathered road. "It's obscene."

"Brother Brigham told us to do it," said father. It was the same argument every time; my brother Jacob just looked at me and smiled. He and I were holding mother's pies in the back of the wagon, and our little sister Mary sat on the very back edge, legs dangling over the road. I fought the urge to stick a finger through the slats in the pie crust and steal another taste of the hot apples inside.

While my mother was worried about the church, I was worried about the town – I hated that town, every town really, not because of the buildings or the dancing but because of the people. There were too many people, and I didn't like the way they looked at me. Hardly any of them knew what I was, Mother said, but I could feel it anyway, all those eyes watching me, all those mouths whispering behind my back. Better to stay on the farm, I thought, but Mother had a sense of duty like a freight locomotive, and once it got to rolling there was no way you could stop it. If the church held a social we went to the social, come hell or high water.

"There ain't nothing wrong with dancing," father continued, "and that means there ain't nothing wrong with doing it in a church."

"It's disrespectful," said mother. "Pastor O'Brien would never let anyone desecrate his church with dancing."

"This ain't Pastor O'Brien's church," said father. "After everything we left be-hind, selling our farm and crossing the plains and carving this farm out of nothing, all on Brother Brigham's say-so, are you really going to let some square dancing spoil your heart?"

"I didn't say it was spoiling my heart," said mother primly, "I said I didn't like it. Brother Brigham told me to dance in the church so I'll dance in the church – once, in the corner – but he didn't tell me I had to like it." Jacob laughed out loud, muf-fling the sound just a moment too late to stop it, and mother frowned.

"It's not my fault, Mother," he said, smiling innocently. "It's just that you say the same things every single time, and we know it so well Silas was mouthing every word along with you." I scowled at him, and mother shook her head.

"You two keep quiet back there," she said, "or I'm going to have you outside tending horses for the entire evening."

I perked up. "He's right, mother, I *was* mouthing it along with you. Guess I'll have to tend the horses."

"And don't you get smart with me, Silas. The horses are Jacob's punishment – yours is more dancing."

"Aren't you going to make me do that anyway?"

"I declare, you are the orneriest child I have ever met. You'll dance tonight or you'll walk home, don't think I won't make you."

I made a move for the edge of the wagon. "I guess I'd better get started now, then, hadn't I?"

Jacob burst into laughter, and mother frowned at us again, shaking her head and clucking so much like a hen I couldn't help but laugh a little as well. Soon Mother was laughing right along with us, and I felt a little better about going into town. If she could dance in a church, I could stand some shifty looks from the neighbors.

"The Hansen family has arrived," said father, pulling on the reins and slowing Old Thomas to a stop. The horse nickered and stamped, and Mary hopped out to feed him a sugar cube and start looking for water. As much I dreaded the crowd, Mary was the one most likely to spend all evening outside. She spent more time with animals than people.

While Father and Mary saw to Old Thomas, Jacob and I clambered out and helped mother down and made our way to the church door. We were only a year apart, but we couldn't have looked more different if we'd tried. Jacob looked like Father, and all the other Hansens before him, but I looked like my mother's side: dark hair, green eyes, and long arms worn thin from working on the farm. Hard work gave Jacob muscles, but all it gave me was wire and bone. Slim, Mother called me, but skinny was more like it.

Not that I'm complaining, mind you – skin and bones are better than none at all. I should know.

Sister Metzger, the Bishop's wife, met us at the door with a smile and a thick German 'hallo.'

Jacob and I stepped inside and surveyed the room: there was Bishop Metzger; there was Mollie Hammond; there was Emmett Creedy. Plenty of other folks, too, but them three were the only ones, outside of my family, that knew what I really was.

"There they are," said Jacob, jerking his head toward the side of the room. I followed his gaze to see the new family, the McKillops, making small talk with Sister Woodard. There were two daughters, just like Jacob had said, and hang me if they weren't even prettier than I'd been expecting. "Adelaide and Anja," said Jacob, and let out a low whistle. "I tell you, Silas, if you don't dance with both of them girls tonight you're a stone cold statue." He glanced at me nervously. "No offense, of course."

I raised an eyebrow. "How long you been saving that one?"

"It just slipped out. You know I didn't mean it."

We carried the pies to the side table, and Dovie Rowe found us before we'd even had a chance to set them down.

"Good evening, Jacob," she said, bobbing in a tiny curtsey. Her smile was almost wider than her face. "Good evening, Silas."

"Good evening to you, Miss Rowe," said Jacob. "You look mighty lovely." They wandered off together, instantly forgetting me and everyone else in the whole town. I'd be lucky to get two words out of Jacob the rest of the night, so I didn't try; I turned instead to walk back outside, maybe help with the horses, and as I did my eye caught Sister Mollie Hammond scowling at me from the corner. In a world full of sour old ladies, I think she might just be the sourest of all. I hurried for the door but she intercepted me, planting herself on the church floor like the Tree of Telling You Whether You're Good or Evil.

"You shouldn't be here."

"I've been saying that all afternoon, ma'am. As a matter of fact, I was just leaving."

"Good evening, Mollie," said mother, sliding in beside me. Her voice was icy. "It's a pleasure to see you out and about. I certainly hope you brought some of your famous peach preserves – I do believe they might be the best peach preserves in the whole land of Zion."

"This is a gathering of saints, Elizabeth," said Sister Hammond. "We don't need any … outsiders, driving away the Holy Spirit."

"Are you saying something about me, Mollie, or about my son?" Mother's voice was hard as flint. "Because if I have done something to wrong to you, I apologize, and I suggest you talk to the Bishop about these distressing feelings in your heart. But if you are talking about my son I will be more than happy to deal with you personally, and I think you will find me capable of some shockingly un-saintly things." She stared at Sister Hammond like a cat staring at a bird, waiting for any excuse to pounce. Sister Hammond stared back, but if her gaze was full of vinegar then mother's was full of steel, and it didn't take long for Sister Hammond to drop her eyes and take a step back.

"I'm not saying anything at all, Elizabeth," she said. "My peach preserves are on the side table; I hope you enjoy them as much as usual." She turned and walked away.

"You don't pay her no mind, Silas," said mother, watching the old lady retreat into the crowd. "Some people are just bitter, and there's nothing to do with bitter but to spit it out of your mouth."

"But she's right," I said lowly. "I'm cursed – "

"You will not talk like that," said mother quickly, whirling to face me. The full strength of her gaze was now focused on me, and I felt like scuttling away after Sister Hammond. "You are not cursed," she whispered, "you are not evil, you are not anything but a child of God, and that is everything. Do you hear me?" I didn't answer, and she leaned in closer. "Do you hear me?"

"Yes, ma'am."

"Then listen to what I'm saying. I don't understand everything about this world, and I don't understand everything about you, or what you ... well, I simply don't, and that's that. You have a power in you that I have never seen before, that I don't think anyone has seen before, but that doesn't make it bad. Just different. And God loves different, Silas, don't you ever forget that." She paused, watching me, then her eyes glanced sideways and she pursed her lips. "Now if I understand the girlish heart correctly I predict you have about ten more seconds before a very pretty pair of hands drags you onto that dance floor."

I glanced to the side and froze, my stomach twisting anxiously; Lena Metzger was making a beeline for us from the side of the church. I looked back at mother.

"Do I have to?" I searched for any excuse I could think of. "I thought dancing in church was a desecration?"

"If you love your mother, Silas, you will desecrate the living daylights out of this church."

"Good evening, Silas," said Lena, curtseying. She spoke English better than her parents, but you could still hear her accent. "Good evening, Sister Hansen."

"Good evening, Lena," said mother. "I was just leaving." She smiled at me and walked away.

I shifted nervously, not looking at Lena directly. "You ... you look very ... " *You look like you should be talking to the best man here,* I thought. *You look like an angel come straight down from Heaven, and that means you've got no business talking to a devil like me.*

"Would you like to dance, Silas?" she asked. "They are about to start a new song."

I closed my eyes. *I'm a good person,* I insisted, *I'm a good person. I've never done nothing wrong, and I don't never intend to, and I ain't never going to hurt anyone no matter what Sister Hammond says.* I fixed my resolve and opened my eyes. "I suppose so." She was a downright beauty, always had been, a ray of summer sunshine in a bright blue dress. She smiled, and I felt my heart start chopping wood inside my ribs. I smiled back. "I think I might like that very much."

She grabbed my hand, her fingers small and delicate, and dragged me into the middle of the floor just like mother said. The song ended and everyone clapped, and right away Brother Sutton shouted "Skip to My Lou!" and Brother Woodard started fiddling. Lena and I stepped into a circle.

"Bow to your partner," called Brother Sutton, and we did. "Now bow to your corner. Now bow to the girl across the hall." We laughed, and Brother Sutton launched into the dance. "All hands up and 'round you go, break it up with a dosey-do. Chicken in the bread pan pickin' out dough. Skip to my Lou, my darlin'!" We whirled around the room, smiling and laughing and stomping until the floor shook and the walls rattled. "Ladies out, you pretty little thing, and promenade around the ring. Ladies come home and gents step in: forward you go and back again."

I clapped my hands with the beat of the song, whooping as I loosened up. I was a part of the group, a neighbor. A person.

"Allemande left with your old left hand, follow it up with a right-left Grand – " I felt a sudden shock of cold, like a breeze from winter that just now remembered to blow, and I stumbled. The dancers slowed and stopped, some staggering into each other, and I turned toward the door. Lena's mother was backing away from a man in the doorway, a tall man in a long black riding coat and a dark black hat. He swept it off with a disdainful bow, and I recognized the gaunt, craggy face immediately.

Gideon Price.

"Don't stop on my account," said Gideon, walking slowly toward the center of the room. "I'm just here for the company, maybe a piece of pie." Another man stepped in behind him, big as a bear and pale as a ghost; there was something wrong with his eyes, all milky white, like maybe he was blind. Gideon smoothed his long, greasy gray hair and nodded at the crowd. Lena grabbed my hand and gripped it tight.

Bishop Metzger stepped forward. "I did not know you were in town, Mr. Price. I thought you were still on the other side of the mountain."

"The mountain, it seems, has failed to keep me away." Gideon grinned at the Bishop, showing his teeth like a wolf. "You know I hate to miss these Mormon shindigs with all these ... pretty Mormon ladies."

Lena gripped my hand tighter, till I thought she was going to crush it.

The Bishop held his ground. "Be that as it may, Mr. Price, we are going to have to ask you to leave. We have no business with your kind."

"With neighbors?"

"With criminals."

Gideon turned slowly, holding out his arms in a wide, sweeping gesture. "The way I understand it, y'all are criminals yourselves – running from the U.S. government for crimes of Christian heresy. Writin' your own Bible and preachin' your own made-up gospel." He turned back. "You and I ain't as different as you might expect."

"We came here to get away from religious persecution," said Bishop Metzger, and Gideon cut him off with an overexcited yell.

"That is precisely why I came here too!" I saw movement in the door, and when I looked I saw more cowboys coming in behind the first – some big, some little, some crooked as old trees, every one of them pale as death with those blind, milky eyes. "Turns out that Joe Smith and his Mormons ain't the only ones old Governor Boggs wants dead, and when he ran you out of Missouri, he ran me and my brothers right out after you. Now I just want what you want – I want my freedom to worship, and to be worshipped, however I please. I want to conduct my spiritual rites with impunity, and to commune with the Other Side in whatever way I think is best. You're a praying man, Bishop."

"Of course I am."

"And you believe in the resurrection, and the dead rising from their graves?"

The Bishop glanced at the pale men. "Yes I do."

Gideon grinned. "Then hosanna, brother, because this here's the rapture, and it's time for the righteous to be caught up and carried away." The pale men in the doorway lurched forward in a sudden rush, arms outstretched and mouths hanging open in a wordless hiss. The whole church erupted in chaos and screaming, and Gideon pulled out a pair of pistols. "That's what I love about Mormons!" he shouted. "Your church is full of virgins, and my church has need of some. Awful nice of you to gather 'em all up in one place." The people screamed louder, running from the pale men, but he smiled and shook his head. "No need to get all riled up, just five or six'll do me fine."

The pale men were reaching for women, and one of them already had Sophie Sutton in a grip like a vise. Two men charged him, Sophie's beau and Sophie's father, racing down from the chair where he'd been calling the dance. Brother Sutton laid a powerful punch across the pale man's face, so loud I could hear the crack over the screams in the room, but the pale man shrugged it off and hit him back, throwing Brother Sutton six feet back and laying him flat on the floor. Sophie's beau, Jacob's friend Joshua, leapt forward to tackle the man, but Gideon fired his pistol and Joshua fell, smoke rising from his back and a bright red spray of blood spread out on the wall beyond him.

"That's the other thing I love about Mormons," said Gideon. "None of y'all bring guns to a town social."

He was wrong – Father had his rifle outside in the wagon, and I bet most of the other men did too. We just needed to get out there. I backed away from the pale men as they staggered toward us, keeping Lena behind me. There was a back door – if we could make it there we could get to the wagons – but a sudden scream behind us put paid to that idea. I glanced back quickly, already knowing what I'd see: the back door was open and more of Gideon's pale-skinned men were coming in. I turned back to the front, to the man closest to me – he was moving all wrong, like his legs and arms didn't work right. All the other pale men were doing the same. I stepped to the right and he stepped with me, hissing through dirty brown teeth. *Apparently they* can *see.* I stared at him, trying to think, and he stared back with eyes as dull and blank as bones.

Across the hall I saw the new family crying and screaming – the pale men had reached them and knocked down Brother McKillop, and now two of them were carrying the new girls back to the door, kicking and howling and sobbing like mad. Their mother ran after them but Gideon stepped in the way, pistol shoved right in her face, and he laughed as she cowered back.

"Three down, three to go." He scanned the room and pointed a pistol at Mollie Hammond. "And don't think a virgin has to be young, neither. Old blood bleeds just as true." A pale man turned and latched onto Sister Hammond, hoisting her off the ground like she was a bundle of sticks. We were backed into a corner now, Lena behind me, mother and father on one side, Jacob and Dovie on the other. There were other groups in other corners, the entire town shivering in fear. The pale men had us surrounded.

"Now don't nobody try anything courageous," said Gideon, advancing slowly toward our group. "I don't have to kill anyone unless I have to – you follow me?"

"We've never done anything to you," said father. "There's no call for attacking us."

"There's no call for talking, either," said Gideon, holding a pistol toward father's face. "Another unnecessary word out of you and there might be an unnecessary bullet out of this gun."

One of the pale men grabbed Dovie, yanking her forward. She screamed, and Jacob leapt after her, but Gideon swung his arm and fired, the bullet slamming into Jacob's shoulder and spinning him to the ground. He fell with a sharp cry, and another pale man, the big one who'd come in first, picked Jacob up with both hands and flung him across the room. He slammed into the wall and crumpled to the floor.

I saw my whole life ending here, in this church house, and I knew I wasn't ready to face my Maker.

I was next in line, and Gideon stepped up to me. "If you'll do me the favor of stepping aside," he said, "I can take that little piece of schnitzel behind you and be on my way."

I could barely talk – I could barely even think. I'd never been so scared in my life, and all I could imagine was getting up to Heaven and looking up at God and seeing his eyes like two black coals as he throws me down to hell. Gideon stuck the pistol in my gut and cocked back the hammer, and I felt myself flinch, not with my body but with my soul, with some kind of reflex I didn't even know I had. Instantly I felt the Change coming over me, like a tingle in my feet – my senses going dead as first my toes lost all feeling, then my heels, then my whole legs. *No!* I thought, *not here!* But there was no stopping it. I felt myself grow heavy, the boards bowing beneath me, the ceiling coming lower as my head grew up to meet it; I heard my clothes ripping and tearing as my chest expanded, as my arms grew thicker, stronger, rougher. Gideon's eyes went wide and he pulled the trigger, but it was too late – my stomach was solid stone and the bullet crumpled against me, ricocheting off and hitting the wall with a crack. Nothing could hurt me anymore, because I was no longer a man.

I was a mountain.

Gideon staggered back and fired again, both pistols up, bullets bouncing off of me like a shrieking metal hail. I was eight feet tall and solid granite, a landslide come to life, and suddenly the world seemed clearer – I didn't need to be afraid of this man, he needed to be afraid of me. I stepped forward, hearing the floorboards creak and crack beneath me, and swung a giant stone fist at Gideon's head. He ducked, falling to the floor, and my swing connected with one of the pale men, crushing bone and muscle and tossing him like a rag doll. The body landed in a heap, head lolling to the side, and I took another step forward to ready another swing. Gideon scrambled backward across the floor, confused and terrified, and another pale man stepped between us. I picked him up, light as a feather, and threw him over by the first.

Except the first was already standing up again.

I froze, my eyes fixed on it; the dead man stood up like a pile of bones trying to stack themselves into a human shape. His head was still twisted nearly backward, and his arm hung limp at his side, but he started walking, one step at a time, jerking forward unevenly. His good arm reached out for the nearest girl; his mouth hissed hungrily on the back of his neck.

"Out!" shouted Gideon, struggling to his feet. "We got what we need!" He ran for the door, the pale men lurching after him, and the movement snapped me out of my shock; I turned and pelted toward them, stretching my arm to clutch at Gideon's trailing coat. He reached the door two steps ahead of me, diving through into the darkness, and I lowered my head, too big to fit through the door, and burst through the wall in a hail of shattered wood and broken nails. There were more pale men outside, some of them already saddled up, the kidnapped girls tied and thrown across their laps. I lunged for the nearest, crushing one of the men with my foot and slamming the other down off his horse with a heavy granite fist. The horse spooked and reared up, the bound girl rolling down its back, and I dove forward to catch her. It was one of the new girls, dark hair plastered to her face with sweat, and she screamed when she saw me like the devil himself had come for her soul. I set her down and looked around quickly, trying to count the bad guys; there were at least ten, probably more. Nothing to do but do it. I charged forward and pounded another, my fist like a giant stone hammer. The horses were in disarray; the pale men either weren't good cowboys or they couldn't think quick enough to bring the horses back under control. I hit another man, then another, aiming for their legs, doing my best to keep them from getting back up again.

I heard a loud whistle and turned back toward the church; Gideon was standing in the broken doorway, his pistol pointed toward me.

"One bullet left," he said, breathing heavy. "You're obviously pretty tough, whatever you are, but I've got a feeling if I aim it just right I can hurt you worse than you've ever been hurt before." He pointed the pistol at me and I stomped toward him, unafraid. He couldn't do anything to me. He smiled again, that toothy, wolfish smile, and then swung his arm to the side, pointing the pistol back into the church. "Say goodbye to mama." I went cold and sprinted forward, desperate to reach him, but he pulled the trigger before I even got close. The sound of the shot exploded through the air, bouncing off of my giant stone frame and echoing back toward the others, till the one shot sounded like a volley. I rushed past Gideon and there was my mother on the ground, father standing over her in shock, red life seeping away from her through the cracks in the floorboards. I screamed, the deafening roar of a wounded monster, and fell to my knees. Noises blurred together. The people in the church shied back from me. Lena crouched in the corner, white as a sheet and shivering like a leaf.

I felt a ripple of cold behind me and turned to see Gideon on the back of a great black steed, fanged and lipless, its eyes burning with bright blue flame. He shouted to his pale horsemen and they wheeled in the moonlight, turning and racing away into the wilderness.

I saved two girls. They kidnapped five.

And my mother was dead because of me.

"IT IS not a question of going after him," said Bishop Metzger. "Of course we are going after him. The question is what we are going to do when we find him."

"We're going to get our daughters back," said Brother Rowe, standing from his seat. "I'm not letting that whoreson do anything to Dovie." Jacob stood and shouted his support, his arm in a burlap sling. Dovie's brother Benjamin stood beside him, rifle in hand, shouting even louder.

I was outside, in a shadow, peeking through the window. I'd run away, fixing on leaving and never coming back, but then I thought maybe I'd better visit my mother and pay my last respects. I hadn't found her yet, so I kept myself hidden. The way I figured it, didn't nobody ever want to see me again.

"Obviously that is what you want to do," said the Bishop, "but how do you think you are going to do it? We all saw what Gideon did last night: he is a necromancer, and we cannot face him lightly."

"You know there ain't no such thing as a necromancer," said Brother Sutton. "Them boys he had with him were probably just sick, some kind of plague or something. Which is all the more reason for us to go now, before our girls come down with the same thing!"

"Of course there are necromancers," said the Bishop, "necromancers and wizards and witches and dragons – they are all in the Bible, and that makes them as real as the saints and the angels. 'There shall not be found among you any one that useth divination,'" he said, holding up the Bible, "'or an observer of times, or an enchanter or a witch or a charmer.'" He looked at the crowd pointedly. "'Or a wizard,'" he said. "'Or a necromancer. For all that do these things are an abomination unto the Lord.' That is in Deuteronomy. Moses does not waste his time warning us about imaginary evils."

"Those were dead men," Brother McKillop agreed, "sure as you're born. You all saw the broken one stand up after what that ... thing did to it."

The room fell silent. There may have been a necromancer in the church last night, but what I did was even worse. I was one of their own, and turning into a monster was more than an abomination, it was a betrayal.

"Silas was trying to help," said father, his voice calm and steady. "He rescued your daughter."

"He nearly killed her!"

"He may have scared her," said father, "but he kept her a whole lot safer than you did."

"You dirty piece of filth!" shouted Brother McKillop, leaping to his feet. "For all we know your devil-boy is part of Price's gang!"

"He's a good boy!" shouted father, finally starting to lose his cool. "You don't talk about my boy that way!"

"We're not blaming you," said Brother Sutton, holding out his hands to placate both men. "I've known you and yours for a while now, Brother Hansen, and I know you're a good man. And your wife was a good woman, and I'm very sorry about your loss. That's why I'm sure you didn't know anything about it, so we're not blaming you, but that don't change what your son did, or what kind of dark powers he called on to do it."

Father started to protest again, and I could see his face bright red with rage, but a hard voice from the back of the room silenced them all.

"He knew what his son was." It was Brother Creedy, the oldest man in town. Everyone in the room turned to face him. "I knew it too," he continued, "and so did the Bishop, and so did Mollie Hammond: the leader of the ward, the leader of the Quorum of Elders, and the leader of the Relief Society. The Hansens came right to us the first time the boy did it, just over a year ago. They told us how the boy turned to stone, and it weren't nothing he did on purpose, just a thing that happened to him. No dark powers, no sin, just a boy growing up different than anybody else. They asked us what to do, and I'm going to tell you now what I told them then, and I want you folks to listen carefully.

"God does not make mistakes. God does not send children to hell. He'll test us, and He'll try us, and He'll put us to the fire until we scream for mercy, but that ain't condemnation – that's purification. He wants to make us the best we can be, and if burning away our badness is the only way to bring out the goodness, so be it. The Children of Israel made sacrifices by fire, and it's a sure thing we ain't any better than they were."

I remembered this whole speech from the first time he'd told me, but I listened now like my life depended on it – or at least my soul. A year ago I didn't understand what I was. A year ago I hadn't killed my own mother.

"I don't know why God does the things He does," said Brother Creedy. "I don't know why he gave this trial to the Hansen boy, and frankly I don't know if it's any of our business. But I do know this, and I want you to remember it: having a trial don't make nobody evil, it makes 'em better. That's what trials are for. Having a trial this bad, well – if that boy uses it right, and he trusts in the Lord, I reckon it could make him damn near perfect."

Brother Sutton was livid. "You're saying this devil-boy is some kind of blessing?"

"Why don't you ask Brother McKillop what a blessing it is to have his youngest daughter safe in his arms, thanks directly to that boy and no one else."

Brother McKillop stared at the floor, silent, then nodded. "He scared her something fierce," he said, "but he saved her life." He looked up. "I got to admit: I owe that boy."

"You're wrong," I said. The men in the room turned to the window, startled, and when they recognized me they jumped from their seats; some of them drew their guns. Father rushed toward me.

"Silas!" he cried. "We thought you'd run away."

"This ain't a blessing," I said. "It killed mother."

"Gideon Price killed her," said father.

"He killed her because of me," I said, "because of what I did. If I hadn't turned into a monster she'd still be alive." I swallowed. "That's why I'm leaving for good first thing in the morning."

"And good riddance," said Brother Sutton, hefting his rifle. "Don't see why you even came back."

I looked at him, staring down the barrel of his rifle like the long, black tunnel to hell. "I came back to pay my respects, and to say I was sorry. I didn't mean to be what I am, but I got to live with it anyway. Don't mean you folks have to."

Bishop Metzger picked up a book and stepped down from the podium, crossing to me slowly. As he grew near he held up the book so I could read the title; it was the Pearl of Great Price. He stood before me. "Have you read this book, Silas?"

I nodded. "We read the scriptures every day."

"And do you know the Articles of Faith?"

I nodded again. "Not memorized, but yes sir I know them."

He knelt by the window, bringing his face even with mine. "The second Article of Faith, as set down by the prophet Joseph, declares 'We believe that man will be punished for his own sins.' Now tell me, Silas: did you shoot your mother?"

"I may as well have," I said, my face growing hot. "I'm the reason he – "

"Never mind his reasons," said the Bishop. "You did not draw the gun, you did not aim it, and you did not pull the trigger. Those were Gideon's choices, and that makes it Gideon's sin. If God will not punish you for another man's sin, you should not punish yourself."

"But he couldn't shoot me," I said, tears welling up in my eyes. "He didn't have no choice because I didn't leave him one."

"Our trials are not easy," the Bishop insisted. "That is what makes them trials. But crossing the plains has made us hardy, and building our homes in the wilderness has made us strong, and standing up every time the mobs and persecutions knock us down has made us tenacious. Through our trials we have become the valiant servants the Lord needs us to be – he has forged us in adversity and made of us the kind of people who can build his kingdom on Earth."

The Bishop stood, turning slowly to look at every man in the room. "A wicked man has stolen our daughters, our sisters, and our friends. It is our duty to bring them back." He looked at me again. "We are armed, and we are ready, and we will attack him on our own terms, but I fear that even then it might not be enough. We may very well have need of you and your ... trial ... before the matter is concluded."

"Ain't no posse in the world ever had a monster on it," said Brother Sutton.

"And ain't no posse ever chased down a necromancer, neither," said Brother Creedy. "The Bishop's right. We might need him."

I looked at the men in the room – at Creedy, at Sutton, at my father – and I tried to read their expressions. Some of them were angry. All of them were scared. But they were scared of simple stuff: of me, and Gideon, and whatever else was waiting out in the wilderness. I was scared of God, and those coal-black eyes, and the judgment I wasn't never going to escape. Turning to stone could postpone it, but it was still coming, no matter what I did. It was time to stop being scared and start getting ready. I looked back at the Bishop.

"I guess your posse's got it's very own monster. When do we leave?"

IT WAS mostly family that came on the hunt: Benjamin Rowe for his sister Dovie; Brother McKillop for his oldest girl Adelaide; Brother Sutton for his daughter Sophie, and father and I came for Mary. Jacob was spitting nails when we didn't let him come, too, for Mary and Dovie both, but he could barely move his arm. He wouldn't be no good to anybody, and we made him stay home. Brother Creedy came too, seeing as he knew the country better than anyone, and the six of us rode out a few hours before sunup; we didn't want to wait too long, but didn't exactly want to catch up to a necromancer in the middle of the darkness, neither. When we stopped to water the horses Jacob caught up with us, a saddle strapped over Old Thomas the draft horse, and father sighed but nobody said nothing, and when the horses were rested we got back on our way. We rode for a long time without speaking, just watching the trees and listening for an ambush.

About mid-morning we saw smoke in the foothills – nothing big, just a wisp hanging low against the mountain, like something had burned up and all the real smoke was already blowed away. Brother Creedy didn't stop us, but he did pull out his rifle, and the rest of us did the same just in case.

"That's the Brown farm," said Brother Sutton.

"They stayed with us last night," said Benjamin Rowe. "Didn't want to ride home in the dark after ... everything."

"They have everybody with them?" asked father.

Benjamin shook his head. "Amos stayed home, the youngest. He gets real embarrassed on account of his club foot, and he can't dance anyway."

"Could've started the fire himself by accident," said Brother Sutton. "Kicking over the coals or something." He stared at the smoke. "Or it could be something else."

"Follow me in," said Creedy, spurring his horse into a gallop. "Ambush or not, if there's anything left of that boy I ain't waiting around for his life to get worse." We kicked our own horses and followed him, me and my horse trailing behind at the end of the pack. I held my rifle in one hand, the reins in the other, watching the shadows for any sign of movement. Only Jacob was unarmed, his spare hand all gimped up in a sling and his pistol still shoved in his holster. He'd be useless in a fight. If we had trouble, I'd have to keep myself between it and him.

We rode onto the Browns' lands as quiet as we could. The fence posts were all still standing, but the house and the barn and the chicken hutch and everything else was burned to the ground, every last building a black pile of ash and cinders. We circled out, looking through the yard and the rubble. I led my horse through the ruins of the barn, the outline of the walls still standing like ghosts around me. I saw a flap of fabric and jumped down, steeling myself for the sight and slowly pushing away a half-charred board with the tip of my rifle.

It was just a sack of feed, all but one corner of it burned away. I could still see the company brand in the singed edge of the cloth. A gust of wind came on, stirring up the ashes and carrying the fabric away. I turned toward my father.

"Nothing alive in this whole – "

A shot rang out like a bolt of thunder, scattering the birds and spooking the horses; my colt reared up like he'd been hit, and I reached for the reins to try to calm him down, but the other men were shouting and another gunshot tore through the air. Jacob's horse was turning wildly while he struggled to draw his pistol with one hand, and as the third shot cracked against the trees I raced toward him, calling out to Old Thomas to stay steady. He was too far away, and I knew I'd never reach him in time – what was I thinking, getting off my horse? We heard a fourth shot, then a fifth, then finally our posse started shooting back as they figured out where the shots were coming from. I reached Jacob and grabbed the reins, trying to soothe Old Thomas. Jacob fired into the trees with the others, but Brother McKillop held up his hand.

"Stop shooting!" His voice was nearly drowned out by the noise. "Stop shooting!" They stopped, and I finally got Old Thomas under control. Brother McKillop set down his rifle and jogged into the trees. A moment later he came back out with a small child – Amos Brown, looking pale as a ghost. I cursed and ran to meet them, clustering around with the others as McKillop sat down with the child. Amos clung to him like a squirrel on a branch, too terrified to let go, eyes wider than I ever thought a pair of eyes could be.

"It was him shooting at us," said Brother McKillop. "I heard the hammer just clicking on nothing, over and over, when he ran out of shots and couldn't stop pulling the trigger. I think he must have crawled into the trees last night to hide, and then panicked when we rode in."

He didn't start shooting until I yelled, I thought. *Once again, I'm the one who gets folks shot at.*

"Boy's white as a ghost," said father, leaning down to brush a lock of hair from the boy's face. "He's not even looking at us – it's like he doesn't even know we're here." Father looked up. "What happened here last night?"

Brother Creedy slowly reloaded his rifle. "He's seen more than anyone ought to see, at any age." He snapped the bolt closed and chambered a round. "It's a sure bet Gideon hit this place, either coming or going. Boy needs his family."

One by one we turned to Jacob, still sitting on his horse. He shook his head violently. "I come this far and I ain't leaving."

"You didn't fire two shots in that ambush," said Brother Creedy. "We come up against anything more dangerous than an eight-year-old boy too scared to aim, and you'll be the first one down."

"You need all the men you can get," said Jacob.

"That's why we need you gone," said Father. "You couldn't help because of your arm, and Silas couldn't help because of you." I could tell it pained him to say it, but he kept going. "We have more men without you than with you."

"This boy needs his family," said Brother McKillop. "You know we can't just leave him here, and he's in no state to get back to town on his own."

"I disobeyed you once," said Jacob fiercely, "and I'll disobey again if that's the only way to save Dovie." There were tears in his eyes. "I love her, Pa. I can't just go home while she's out there."

"Yes you can," said Father, "because if you really love her you'll keep yourself safe and alive for when she comes back. Think about Sophie," he said, gesturing at Brother Sutton; Sutton lowered his eyes, keeping his face blank. "Joshua tried to save her and now he's gone, and now she don't have no one to come home to. Don't do that to Dovie." He paused. "Don't do that to Mary."

Now it was my turn to look at the ground, grim and determined. If Father and I died, Jacob would be all Mary had left. Even if I lived I was leaving – I couldn't stay in town no more. Mary had to have someone. I looked up, meeting Jacob's eyes. He stared back, scowling, then grit his teeth.

"Fine," he said. "Hand him up."

It took us a few minutes to get the boy off of Brother McKillop, but soon enough we had him up behind Jacob on Old Thomas's broad back. He clung to Jacob's shirt like it was the only thing keeping him alive. Jacob shook his head, still scowling, and turned the horse back toward the road. We watched him go, then gathered our horses and reloaded our rifles.

"Ride quiet and careful," said Brother Creedy. "If we don't have any more troubles, we can make it to Price's place by sundown."

We nodded grimly, none of us saying out loud what we were all thinking inside: sundown is an awful bad time to find a necromancer.

WE SAW another pillar of smoke just as the last rays of light were dropping down behind the mountains – not a house fire, like we'd seen at the Browns' place, but a chimney fire wafting just above the trees. We tied our horses behind a rise where the noise wouldn't carry if they whinnied in the night, and clumped around a patch of dirt while Brother Creedy drew a picture of the valley.

"This is us up here," he said, marking an X, "and this is the house. It's bigger than you'd think, but I guess he's got them servants or dead men or whatever to help him build it. He don't got no fields or barn, but he's got a pretty big stable for all them horses. The road we been on passes pretty close, and then turns east to Colorado."

He drew three short lines on the road: "That's where they can see us from the house, that's where they can see us from the edge of the property, and that's where we turned off the road and he can't see us at all. I done some hunting around this area – never caught much, maybe the animals is all smarter than we are and know to stay clear – but there's an old wash back here, behind the house, where we can come up behind a screen of trees. He'll be watching it, sure as anything, but we'll get a lot closer than we will on the road."

"We don't know how many of those dead things he's got in there," said Father, "so we got to be careful. And we got to hurry."

"I want to know one thing first," said Brother Sutton, turning to me. He had his coach gun perched on his shoulder – not menacing, just ready. His eyes were hard as flint. "You going to betray us?"

"You leave him alone," said Father, but Brother Sutton cut him off.

"He can speak for himself," he growled, staring at me intently. "I want to hear it from your own lips, boy. You going to betray us?"

I met his gaze, feeling more angry than brave. "If I was going to kill you I could have done it a long time ago."

"Unless you're in league with Price," said Sutton, "and you was just waiting till we got close enough for him to collect the bodies."

I took a breath. "I swear to you right now, on my mother's soul, that if anyone dies tonight it'll be because I'm already dead and can't stop it."

Brother Sutton pondered that for a moment. "You gonna turn into a monster?"

"I'm already a monster," I said. "But that don't make no difference in what I aim to do."

Brother Sutton looked at me a moment longer, then nodded, satisfied. "Lead the way then, Creedy. We don't got all night."

We checked our horses' leads one more time, making sure they wouldn't wander off, and picked our way through the darkening forest. Brother Creedy led us in a wide circle, faster than I expected for an old man, but I figured he knew the country well enough to make up for our younger legs. Father took up the second position behind him, then me, then Sutton and Benjamin. Brother McKillop held the rear. Aside from my pistol and Brother Sutton's coach gun, they all had hunting rifles. Benjamin had a knife, too, a big, broad-bladed skinning knife, but I don't know what he thought he was going to do with it. If them dead men got close enough to stick with a knife, the fight was already over.

After a while Brother Creedy started leading us back east, looping around behind the cabin. It was dark now, just a hint of starlight leaking down through the trees, and we had to move even slower to keep from giving ourselves away. The ground was covered in old sticks and pine cones, and it was all I could do to keep from cracking one under my feet.

After a while I started to smell something, and I knew Brother Creedy smelled it too because he stopped walking. I caught up with him and Father and sniffed the air.

"Meat," I whispered.

"Meat and smoke," said father with a nod. "Price have a smokehouse?"

"That's no smokehouse," said Brother Creedy, "a smokehouse smells like burning wood. This here smells like flesh."

Brother Sutton caught up with us now, sniffed, and nodded his head. "Someone's been cooking steaks. If that's my Sophie I swear to God I'll – "

"No sense guessing when we could just take a look," said Brother Creedy. "Come on."

We crept forward slowly, guns drawn and eyes wide open for an ambush. As we walked, the shadows shifted in the forest, some moving around us and some fading away and one, straight ahead, growing bigger and deeper until it turned into the side of the mountain itself, with a giant cave hanging open like the maw of a bear. We stopped, crouching in whatever cover we could find, and listened.

The forest was still as death.

Brother Sutton inched forward, both barrels of his coach gun leading the way, and I followed behind him. Father and the others crept in behind us. The cave loomed over us, like to swallow us up, but slowly the back wall resolved into view and I saw it was pretty shallow – not a tunnel stretching back into the mountain, just an overhang and a wide stone room. The place stunk like a slaughterhouse, and the walls were covered with some kind of lines or symbols, but my eyes seemed to swim every time I tried to focus on them. There was a pile of rocks in the middle of the floor – no, not a pile, a stack. Orderly as cordwood. It was an altar.

Brother Sutton lowered his coach gun and stepped next to the altar, touching it gently. He only needed one word to tell us what this place was.

"Blood."

"Them girls is already dead," said Benjamin, talking a little too loud in his anger. "Let's burn this whoreson's house to the damned ground!"

"Too old," said Brother Sutton. I could see his silhouette shaking his head in the darkness. "Price was just a few hours ahead of us, traveling heavier, and who knows how long he stopped at the Browns' farm. If this blood came from our girls it'd still be fresh, and this is a day old at least. Maybe more." He stepped away from the altar like he couldn't help it, like it was pushing him away with its own force. "Guess this ain't the first time he stole somebody's daughters."

"And whoever came to the rescue must have been killed here too," said Father, "or we'd have heard about it one way or another."

"We got to be careful," said Brother McKillop, nodding slowly.

"Now that we've seen this place, we can be," said Creedy. "Anything he does to those girls he's going to do here, on this altar, and that means we don't have to go busting down his door in the dark."

Brother Sutton's voice was sharp with anger. "You saying we oughta wait?"

"I'm saying we don't want to end up like the last folks to lie on that altar," said Brother Creedy. "We knew it was a fool thing doing this at night, but we didn't have no choice because we didn't know how long them girls had. Now we know they ain't doing nothing until morning, and we can plan an ambush instead of falling into one."

"They could come here any time of night," said Brother Sutton.

"And we'll be here when they do," said Brother Creedy. "It's still better to wait."

"He might not be killing them till morning," said Brother McKillop, "but we don't know what he aims to do with them between now and then." We all went silent, the idea too terrible to even think about. Then Father shook his head.

"He said he needed virgins. Everyone knows he can't kill them unless they're virgins."

Brother McKillop sighed. "Never thought in a million years that sentence would make me feel better."

"We have until morning," said Brother Creedy firmly. "He'll bring the girls here, and we'll trap him in the middle – two of us here, the rest of us waiting by the house to cut off a retreat."

Brother Sutton looked at me, then turned to Creedy. "How do we split the groups?"

"There's a bluff about twenty yards above this cave," said Creedy. "We'll put the long rifles up there and try to catch them in the open, right by the house, before they reach the trees. Two best shots are ... " He paused, looking at the group. " ... me and Brother Hansen." We all nodded. Father was one of the best sharpshooters I'd ever seen, and nobody wanted Brother Creedy's old bones and muscles too close to the action.

I looked at Brother Sutton, expecting him to argue, but he humphed and nodded. "Good," he said, looking back at me. "I want you where I can see you."

Creedy led us out of the cave, still whispering. "You four move up, but stay hidden and quiet. Don't do anything until you hear us start shooting, then get the girls as quick as you can and hope to high Heaven this works."

We bid each other a quick farewell, and Sutton, McKillop, Benjamin, and I all set off toward the house. I moved as quietly as I could, using every bit of woodcraft I ever learned, but the forest was even quieter, like the whole thing was already dead, and my nervous ears made even my softest footsteps as loud as gunshots. We neared the edge of the trees, the shadow of the stable looming up in front of us, and I heard a low moan. All four of us stopped immediately – we'd all heard that moan before, and we knew what it meant. We listened for more, never speaking, waiting for the dead man to summon more of his kind. Heartbeats thumped away, a thousand years for each one, each of us poised in the darkness ready to run or shoot or who knows what, not even knowing where the dead man was.

Nothing happened; nothing came. I peered out at the farmyard, looking for movement, and I began to see the outline of old tools and bits of farming equipment – plows and hay rakes and giant scythes, discarded where they fell, long grass growing up around them. Further out I saw a fallow field, gone back to seed and full of new saplings – three, maybe two years since anyone had worked it. Either Price used to do some farming, or his land and his tools and his two-story house hadn't always been his.

The minutes dragged on, the silence a nearly palpable presence. At any moment I expected to hear another moan – behind me, or below me – to hear the ragged hiss of a dead man's breath or feel cold fingers close around my legs. My heart was racing like a spring hare two inches from a hound dog's teeth. I was just about to move – just about to give up and run – when I heard a hoof. Then another hoof. I looked at my companions, and I could see they heard it too – no longer simply listening, they were moving their heads, tracking the forest for sound. Was it a mounted sentry on patrol? A loose horse wandering out of the stable? Maybe it was Gideon's black-fanged devil horse, its eyes burning like blue brands of hellfire.

I took a step toward Brother Sutton; Benjamin did the same, and whispered lowly, "The stable, I think."

Brother Sutton shook his head. "Too far away." I tilted one ear up, listening as the hoofbeats clomped softly in the distance: a heavy horse, I thought, and a little unsteady, probably because of the dark. The steps were out of rhythm, and they fell on soft-packed dirt.

"The road," I whispered, and Brother McKillop motioned for us to come. We crept toward him and he pointed toward the far side of the narrow valley. A horse was approaching slowly, a tiny patch of lighter shadow against the dark of the wood beyond. As it moved we caught glimpses of a rider, a solitary figure in black. He passed through a shaft of moonlight, the tiniest flicker of light, and we saw his outline more clearly.

"He only has one arm," whispered Benjamin. We nodded; we'd seen the same thing. "It's one of them corpses."

"He's coming down the road from town," whispered Brother Sutton. "He has to have seen where we left the horses, and now he's coming back to give us away."

The rider stopped at the edge of Price's property, and without the motion to point him out he disappeared almost completely into the darkness; even the horse faded into the background, a distant patch of color that could have been a rock or a tree. We watched tensely.

"What's he waiting for?" whispered Benjamin. Brother Sutton quieted him with a gesture. The forest hung around us like a ghost image, not even a bird or a cricket to break the silence and make it real. Then we heard another hoof thud into the dirt, and the figure started moving again. Almost immediately I heard a moan from the forest, maybe thirty yards away. Another moan drifted up from the far side of the house, an answer maybe.

"They're talking to him," said Benjamin.

"Or about him," said Brother Sutton. He hefted his coach gun. "Something's not right here."

"Ain't nothing been right here all night," said Brother McKillop. He shook his rifle nervously. "If he gets in there he'll tell them we're here, but if we drop him first they'll know it anyway."

"If they find out we're here they'll spread out and look for us," said Brother Sutton. "Best we can hope is that they don't check their own yard, and wander out farther to find us. Leave us all alone with the house."

"And surrounded by walking dead men when it comes time to get out," said Brother McKillop. "Ain't nothin' going the way we need it to."

Brother Sutton shook his head. "We got to stick this out; wait until morning. They'll come out ready, but at least they'll all be in one place, and we'll have our sharpshooters to back us up."

The rider was nearly at the house now, but I could see more motion in the darkness – shapes behind him, rising up out the grass like mist on the river Styx. They'd cut off his escape, and I couldn't make no sense of why, and then I saw a glint of metal in his hand.

"That ain't no one-armed dead man," I said suddenly, running to the edge of the trees for a better look. The starlight hit his hand again and I saw the same glint of metal. "He's holding a gun, and his other arm's folded in tight with a sling. That's Jacob!"

"Silas, don't!" hissed Sutton, but I was already off, running toward him past the stable and leaping over broken hay blades in the yard. Jacob had come back again, just like he did the first time, only this time he found our horses and didn't find us and thought we'd already fought and lost. He didn't know about the altar – he didn't know we were waiting for morning. He was coming in to save his girl, come hell or high water, and he was going to get us all killed.

"Jacob," I shouted, "run!"

Jacob looked toward me, startled, and then it seemed like he noticed the dead men behind him for the first time, 'cause he turned, spooked, and Old Thomas reared up. Jacob's only good hand was holding his pistol instead of the reins, and he could only hang on with his legs for a moment before he fell off backward and hit the ground with a shout. The dead men lurched in, one of them falling under Old Thomas's wild, flying hooves, and then I heard Jacob's pistol firing and Old Thomas bolted toward the road. I didn't dare fire my own pistol for fear of hitting my brother, so I just tucked my head and ran for all I was worth, hoping he didn't make the same mistake and shoot me.

I glanced back to see if Brother Sutton and the others had come with me, but they were trapped by the trees, caught by a swarm of dead men spilling out of the stable; they must have heard me run past and come out right in the middle of us. Brother Sutton fired his coach gun, a deafening roar in the darkness, and then fell back into the trees and out of sight. Jacob and I were on our own. I jumped over a broken fence and barreled forward into the nearest man's back, knocking him to the ground, and thrust my pistol in the face of the next, so close to Jacob he could practically hug him. I stopped, just hanging there, just thinking: I'd never killed a man before, never even shot at one. I didn't think I could do it. The pale man opened his mouth, like he was going to take a bite out of Jacob's shoulder, and I fired. He slumped to the ground, whatever was keeping him alive disappearing into the night.

So they can be killed, I thought, now that we got bullets. I looked around – there were a dozen or more, maybe two dozen, some of them just an arm's length away. I cursed. I only got five bullets left.

Jacob staggered to his feet. "You're alive."

"Of course we're alive, you idiot." I swung my gun around and fired in the next enemy's face, then the next, trying not to look at their dead white eyes as I did it. "Least you could do is help shoot some of 'em."

"I'm out of bullets," he said, tucking the pistol into his sling and digging into his pocket. "It's hard to reload with one hand."

"Should have thought of that before you rode all the hell in here, then, shouldn't you?"

"You know Mother don't like you talking that way."

I fired my last shot. "I'm out too." I reached in my pocket for my own stash of bullets, but there were too many of the dead men, and they were too close, and even with both hands I wouldn't have time to reload. I shoved one bullet in the cylinder and slammed it closed, bringing the gun up just as a dead man grabbed me with a hiss and knocked me to the ground. I pulled the trigger four times before the pin hit the only chamber with a bullet, and the dead man crumpled as the slug tore through his chest and out his spine. I rolled him off and Jacob pulled me up to my feet.

"We got to run." We bolted into the dark, stumbling over roots and gopher holes, tripping over saplings in the old dead field.

"You here alone?" Jacob asked.

"In a manner of speaking," I said between breaths. The coach gun fired again in the distance, rumbling through the valley like a cannon, and I pulled Jacob to a stop. "We ain't alone, but we ain't got any help, neither. Give me your gun."

Jacob handed it over, and I started sliding in new bullets as fast as I could. The dead men were following us, but they weren't as fast, and we'd gained a few yards' lead. "We had this whole thing under control before you got here." I shoved the pistol into his hand and started working on my own. He raised it and fired before I even found a new handful of bullets.

"How was I supposed to know you was hiding in the trees?"

"Considering you were supposed to be back in town, Jacob, I don't rightly have an answer to that question." He was still firing. "Maybe if you'd stayed where you was damn well told to stay it wouldn't have mattered."

"I told you to stop cussing." He fired his last bullet, the nearest dead man still looming up like a bear. I slammed my revolver closed and spun the cylinder into place, raising the gun in a single motion and blasting the dead man right between the eyes. He toppled like a tree.

"If you learn how to shoot these things in the head instead of wasting all your bullets," I said, "maybe I'll have time to stop cussing and run."

There were more dead men behind us now – more than we could see in front of us – and Jacob pulled me forward. "We got to keep moving." I heard the coach gun again, and a loud, bloody scream, and we both ran faster. I ducked behind the stable, looking for the others, but all I saw was bodies spread out in the dirt. I cussed again, under my breath, and Jacob stopped cold in his tracks.

"That them?"

I knelt down to check, but all of the faces were twisted and unfamiliar – if my companions were dead, they were dead somewhere else. "Looks like they ran into the forest," I said, tracing the line with my eyes. A volley of gunshots echoed through the forest. "They're still alive."

Jacob peered in. "Can't see a danged thing in there."

"Can't hardly see one out here," I said. "Give me your pistol." We traded, giving him the loaded one, and he fired around the corner of the stable, trying to slow down the dead men while I tried to reload half blind in the dark. I heard a moan on my right, and looked up to see another dead man staggering around the far side of the stable. I knocked the spent shells out of the revolver, grabbing a handful of new ones while the dead man stepped closer. Another man came around the corner behind him.

"Time to move again."

Jacob looked back, saw the dead man lurching forward, and held up the pistol. "Already empty."

I jumped forward into the trees, a pair of dead hands just inches away and Jacob tight on my heels. I slammed the chamber into place and fired behind me, plunging headlong into the forest. "The only way we're getting two guns loaded at the same time is if we find a dead man and take his."

"If that's the best we can hope for," said Jacob, "it might be time to pray for our souls."

The forest was different from the yard – darker, closer, quieter. The air was full of low, lonely sounds: a moan, a cracking branch, a single gunshot. Mist hung between the tree trunks and dark shapes moved in the corner of my eyes. When I looked at anything directly, there was nothing there at all.

Jacob and I traded pistols again, and I crouched beside a tree while I emptied out the cylinder and slid new bullets in. My pocket was growing awful empty – my part of the plan wasn't shooting, it was pulling those girls to safety, so I only had so many reloads. Most all of them were already used up. I turned to ask Jacob how many bullets he had in his pocket, but he was standing stock still, listening, and I instinctively did the same. There was noise to the left of us, soft and wet. Chewing. I saw Jacob turn his head, but he was just a patch of black shadow and I couldn't tell which way he'd turned it. He moved to the left, gun up, and I followed close behind him. There were footsteps in the trees behind us, but I couldn't tell who was making them or where they were headed.

Jacob stopped and whispered: "Friend or foe?" I heard a low growl and saw a shape rise up from the darkness, and Jacob fired. The shadow didn't slow and I dove at it, knocking it away from Jacob right before it reached him; we wrestled on the ground for a minute, the thing's breath cold and noxious in my face, and when I finally pushed it away Jacob whispered again. "Friend or foe?"

"Friend!" I hissed, and Jacob shot the shadow a second time. It stopped moving.

"Can't see a blamed thing," Jacob muttered. I crawled to the side, to where the dead man had been crouching in the bushes, and my hand touched another body – warm this time, and slick with blood. I felt my heart stop beating, felt the whole world freeze in a moment of time.

"Who is it?" Jacob whispered, but I shook my head. It was too dark to see the man's face. I inched forward, feeling on the ground, and my hand touched a long metal gun barrel.

"Dammit."

"Who is it?"

"He's got a rifle," I said, swallowing, "so it's either Creedy or ... Pa."

"Dammit," said Jacob, then: "Gimme the rifle." I handed it to him and he felt the stock, running his hands over the trigger and the hammer and the action. "This ain't Father's."

"Don't mean it ain't him."

"And it don't mean it is. Feel his face."

I put my hand out, scared to touch him, and when I did he was ragged and bloody. I jerked back my hand. "I can't do it."

Jacob started to speak but we heard another roar from the coach gun, then another scream – not a man this time, but high and feminine. The girls. We jumped to our feet and ran, as fast as we could through the pitch-black forest, Jacob with the rifle and me with two half-empty pistols. We burst out of trees to find the yard lit with lanterns, swaying as the dead men held them up, casting wild, demon shadows on the side of the house. Brother Sutton was there, and Benjamin, his pistol discarded and his knife bloody. They were facing down Gideon Price, who stood in the flickering lamplight with Mary in one hand, held tight by the hair, and a pistol in the other. Jacob and I stepped into line, guns raised.

I glanced at Benjamin out of the corner of my eye. "Lose your gun?"

"Don't need to reload a knife."

"Now everybody's here," said Gideon. "I suggest you drop them weapons right quick, before we have to demonstrate which side in this conflict is more willing to kill a little girl."

"I'm pretty sure we can kill you before that becomes an issue," said Brother Sutton.

"That's awful bloodthirsty for a Mormon," said Gideon. "Don't you believe in the ten commandments?"

We said nothing. I realized that we didn't even know if Jacob's rifle was loaded, and I prayed that it was.

"That shalt not kill," said Gideon, "unless thou killest an evil bastard that nobody likes. It seems we share a sense of moral convenience; a side effect of living in the middle of nowhere, I suppose. Now how about we make ourselves a deal." He pointed his pistol away from Mary's ear. "You lay down your guns, I give you the girl, and you walk away happy." He smiled. "Didn't think I was gonna offer that, did you? It's okay, I've got plenty more inside. Always take more than I need for these things – my eyes are bigger than my stomach. You know how it is."

"We take them all," said Brother Sutton. "We'll die before we leave them here."

Gideon smiled. "Don't tease me unless you mean it." He took a step away from Mary and started to speak, but as soon as they were separated Brother Sutton's coach gun roared, flames shooting out of the barrel, and Gideon collapsed with his gun arm blown clean off; it dropped to the dirt next to him, still clutching the pistol. Mary shrieked, cowering and covering her ears, then ran to Jacob and wrapped her arms around him. The dead men growled and lumbered forward, and the four of us turned slowly, back to back, trying to count the shapes in the darkness.

"You hurt, Mary?" I asked. She didn't answer, still crying and hanging onto Jacob.

And then I heard laughing.

We turned back slowly, guns still raised to ward off the dead men, and looked at Gideon's body. The blood oozing out of his arm was black as pitch, and he was shaking with laughter – not light and cheerful, but dark and mean and evil. It was the devil's laugh, and he looked at us with the devil's wild eyes.

"You disarmed me," he said, grinning with a mouthful of sharp yellow teeth. "Ain't that the best?" And then his hand moved – lying five feet away, shattered and bloody, his hand raised up and aimed the pistol and fired, and Brother Sutton's face disappeared in red. The dead men came at us and I fired, and Jacob pulled the trigger but his gun was empty, and there were too many men and Jacob screamed at me to change.

"I do and you're dead," I yelled back.

"We're dead anyway!"

I fired again, one, two, three more times, and then my guns were empty too, and Benjamin was slashing out with his knife, and I felt the Change coming and I fought it – I didn't mean to but it was habit now, so ingrained from a year's worth of feeling like a sinner that I just shut it down and pushed it away, and by the time I realized what I was doing they were on us, and Mary was screaming like a pig in a slaughterhouse, and the world went black.

I WOKE up in pain – my wrists and hands felt flayed to the bone, and the back of my head was throbbing like someone had knocked it clean off and tried to nail it back on.

I was being dragged somewhere; I could feel rocks scraping against my back, and my legs bumped painfully over roots and holes and bushes. I tried to open my eyes, blinking against the light, and I realized as my eyes adjusted that it wasn't even dawn yet.

"Look who's awake," said Gideon. I couldn't see his face, but there were legs everywhere – a whole army of dead men walking through the trees, leading and carrying and dragging their terrified group of prisoners. I tried to speak but my throat was dry and ragged, and I started coughing instead.

"The great stone man," said Gideon. He stepped into my view, and I blinked in shock at his arm – it was back on, swinging by his side like it had never been off. "The mountain man. You know I've met plenty of folks call themselves mountain men, mostly trappers and Indian-lovers out in the great nowhere, but you, my friend, you are the only man I've ever met who really deserves the title." He laughed. "The mountain man. Right now you're probably thinking of transfigurating yourself, or shape-shifting, or whatever you call whatever you do, but I urge you not to. I shot your mama, and I'm real sorry it came to that, but that don't mean I won't shoot your grandmama if I have to."

My grandma? I hadn't seen either of my grandmothers in years, not since my parents joined the Mormons. Even before we came west they hadn't said a word or written a letter or nothing. Who was he talking about shooting?

"You just sit tight and keep your skin all smooth and supple," said Gideon, "and me and you won't have no problems." He laughed again. "Course, me and everybody else are gonna have plenty of problems, but like I said, you just sit tight. I got a matter to discuss with you later under what I hope to be more civilized circumstances."

A shadow rose up around us and I realized we were coming to the side of the steep mountain we'd seen the night before. A minute or two later they dropped me on my face, and I coughed and rolled over and saw that we were in the mouth of the altar cave; in the half-light it looked even worse than in the darkness, because I could see it all so much better without really seeing it clearly. The walls were lined with bones and painted with horrible images – skulls and devils and great, black wings, all slashed onto the stone with thick, dark smears of something I was pretty sure wasn't paint. The dead men looped more rope between our arms and tied it tight around a tree. Jacob was on one side of me, still unconscious, and that new girl was on the other, McKillop's daughter. I tried to ease my wrists into a better position, 'cause they were so raw they felt like a raging fire, but nothing helped.

"You ain't dead," said the girl.

"What?"

"You ain't dead," she said again, and smiled. "That means he ain't gonna kill us."

Her hair was long and unkempt, and her dress, what I could see of it in the darkness, was finer than usual. Still dressed up from the social.

"I'm pretty sure he's gonna kill all of us," I grunted.

"Well ain't you gonna stop him?"

"You don't know what you're talking about."

"You saved my sister."

I kept silent, looking at the ground.

"He ain't saving nobody this morning," said Gideon, coming up from behind the tree and patting the girl on the head. The girl kicked him right in the shin, catching his ankle and knocking him to the floor. She lunged out farther with her feet, trying to scissor him between her legs, but the pale men grabbed her and fought her back, and even her own father, tied up to a tree across the trail, shouted for her to stop.

"Adelaide! Don't make him angry!"

Gideon stood back up, dusted himself off, and laughed. "I like a girl with spunk," he said calmly. "You know what I like to do to girls with spunk?" He crouched in front of her, mere inches from her face, and smiled while she struggled against the iron grip of the dead men. Gideon produced a long, thin dagger and held it up, turning it back and forth in front of her face. "I like to cut them open, find that spunk, and save it in a jar for when I'm feeling down. Then all I got to do is drink it up and presto! I'm a new man."

The girl stopped squirming, and Gideon watched her for a moment longer before standing back up. He looked at me.

"Now before you decide to get too spunky yourself, I want to direct your attention northward." He gestured to the cave where I saw two of the dead men tying Sister Hammond to a hook sunk deep in the stone. They secured the ropes, tested them, and one of the dead men pulled out a short, rusty blade, like a broken machete. It was unsettling the way they stood when they weren't doing anything – inanimate and lifeless. They didn't shift or fidget like regular people; if they weren't doing something important, they weren't doing anything at all. He stood by Sister Hammond as still as if he were stuffed, his blank eyes unfocused, his muscles slack, but I knew that as soon as he wanted to – or as soon as Gideon wanted him to – he could whip that blade around and chop her head clean off.

I stared at Sister Hammond, and she stared back. Was this the grandma he was talking about? She and I weren't relations at all. Gideon smiled again, all wicked and wolfish, and went into the cave to fiddle with his altar.

"She's the one that told him," Adelaide whispered. "She said she was your grandma, said he had to let you go, said all manner of things, and I guess Gideon believed her."

"Why'd she say all that?"

"Protecting Mary, I suppose," said Adelaide. "He knew you was here for one of us, and we all knew he needed a hostage to keep you down. I guess she just ... " She hung her head.

"Yeah." I looked across at Sister Hammond, and she nodded at me, slow and solemn.

Adelaide lowered her voice even further, a tiny whisper I could barely hear. "So you gonna do it?"

I looked at her, frowning. "Are you crazy?"

"Are *you*? He's gonna kill us!"

"I ain't a hero," I said. "I can't just ... do it like that, I can't just turn it on and save the world."

"You can't control it?"

"It's not that I can't do it," I said, "it's that I ... well, I can't. Or I guess I won't. Last time I did it I got my own mother killed, and Gideon still took you and the others. It didn't make no difference. Hell, it made it worse." I saw her flinch at the cuss word, and I felt a stab of guilt. "Sorry about that."

She sat still, saying nothing, just watching me. After a moment she said, "You made a difference to my sister, and that made a difference to me. You made a difference to every other girl that didn't get stole, and to all their families, and to the whole town. You made a difference to all their children, and all their children's children, and on down the generations to the end of days. You hang around long enough, mountain man, you'll make a difference to the whole world."

I stared at the dirt, then grit my teeth and shifted again. My wrists burned. "I'm all tied up, same as you."

"Just get all big and break the rope – "

"I ain't gonna do it!" I said, feeling my voice rise and my face get hot. A couple of the dead men turned to look at me, but Gideon was still setting up his altar – I saw him take a long black sword out of the trunk, and some kind of black iron crown. He set them gently on the altar, on a dark velvet cloth.

I looked at Sister Hammond. "If you still think my curse is anything but trouble, you ask her," I said. "She's the only one ever saw me right, and she'll be the first to die if I do it now."

"And the last to die if you don't," said Adelaide. "You really think he's going to let you go?"

"I'm going to see God either way," I said, "so I don't want to do it with no devil magic on my conscience. You want me to damn my own soul just to save your life?"

"The devil don't got nothing to do with this," said Adelaide. "Well, nothing to do with your part – I reckon the devil and Mr. Price are old pals. But your powers are different."

"You don't know nothin' about them."

"I know they ain't nothing like his," she said, nodding toward Gideon. "I seen twenty-four hours of hell, mountain man. I seen evil up close – I heard its voice, I smelled its breath. I seen things I don't never want to see again. I know sin when I see it, and what you do is not a sin."

I snorted. "You think it comes from God, then?"

"How do you know it don't?"

I turned to her and I saw she was leaning forward, like she was excited.

"Maybe it's one of the gifts of the Spirit, like Paul says in the Bible: to one is given the gift of healing, and to another the gift of miracles, or prophecy, and like that. Who's to say there ain't more that Paul didn't talk about?"

I raised my eyebrow. "'To some is given the gift of turning into a big scary rock monster?'"

"Well it sounds stupid when you say it like that, but why not?"

"Why would God give that as a gift?"

"Because he knows we need it," said Adelaide. "Because he knows we was gonna have Gideon Price and a passel of dead men to deal with, and bandits and bears and mobs full of killers and who knows what all out here in the wild. He knew we needed help, so he gave us you."

"But I'm still a monster," I protested, unwilling to believe her. "Maybe I don't do everything Gideon does, but we're both – "

"God don't judge people for what they are," she said, "even if people do. I figure people been judging you long enough you forgot that God does it different. He judges people for what they do. By their fruits ye shall know them, and Gideon's fruits are rotten to the core. All you done, Silas, is save one girl and try to save some more, and that seems like mighty good fruit to me."

I stared at her, my thoughts reeling. "You're serious about this?"

She nodded.

A gift. I looked around the forest, not looking at anything, just looking. Seeing, for the first time in a year, a life I didn't have to be afraid of. I was still in ropes, still trussed like a hog, but I felt like my chains fell away and I was free. It was the most wonderful thing in the world.

Gideon was standing in front of us now, the black crown on his head and some kind of robe over his chest, black and ancient and stained with blood.

"The sun is rising," he said softly. "The day and the hour are upon us, and the Master calls for blood. I don't suppose you appreciate the honor to give your life for mine, but there ain't time for a sermon. Ashes to ashes, and blood to blood."

It was now or never. I looked at Sister Hammond. If I did this, she was dead – even if I saved everybody else, she'd be dead before I even finished Changing. She was still watching me; I don't think she'd ever looked at anyone else since they'd tied her up. I couldn't kill her. Not after what she'd done for to save Mary.

"I knowed what I was doing," she said, her voice thin and cracked.

I swallowed, feeling hot tears on my cheeks. Gideon looked up, hearing her, and I felt my whole life compressing into this single moment. "What do you want me to do?"

Sister Hammond's eyes were hard as stone. "I want you to beat the hell out of 'em. And I mean that in a literal sense."

This was her plan all along – to be the hostage and die so that I could save everyone else. Gideon spun around to look at her, then at me, but I was already Changing, my voice croaking out a "sorry" even while it turned from flesh to stone. The dead man at her side burst into action, burying his blade in her neck and rocking back her head, and the ropes around me strained and snapped. My shirt tore and my boots burst, and I felt my sadness turn to fury – not the fear I felt before, not the anger from being outcast, but the righteous fury of God's own vengeance. Sometimes God sends plagues and famines, sometimes armies, sometimes a jagged bolt of lightning.

Sometimes he just needs a woman with enough faith to move a mountain.

Gideon dug in his pockets for pistols, but I was ready for him and jumped in front of the other prisoners, barely feeling the bullets as they smashed harmlessly against me. I swung a granite fist and threw him back, nearly into the cave, and then braced myself for the charge of the dead men. They all came at once, not taking turns or staying out of each other's way, just running in with knives and clubs and hands and teeth. I battered them back, cracking bones and smashing muscle, fighting just to stay upright. They got on my legs and started pulling me down, trying to topple me over, and I shifted left and stomped one under my foot. The girls were screaming, the men fighting with their bonds. I tore at the dead men climbing over me, but there were too many.

I saw Gideon move again and I took a step toward him, dragging the dead men like hounds on a bear. He rose up to a crouch, steadying himself with his hands, and I took another heavy step. The dead men couldn't hurt me, but they were dragging me back. They didn't want me to reach him. I took another step, then another – barely a foot forward with each. Gideon was on his feet now, the black sword in his hand, his jaw clenched and his skin tight, like a mummy. He staggered toward Sister Hammond, blood still pulsing from her neck, and I heard a wind pick up, like the sword itself was inhaling, taking a long, whispering gulp of air. The air grew dark and the blade started to smoke; each broken step brought Gideon closer to the blood, and now it seemed like the blade was pulling him forward. I didn't know what they were doing, but I knew I couldn't let them do it.

I thrashed at the dead men swarming over me, smashing them and throwing them down, but they climbed back to their feet or crawled across the ground and came at me again, wave after wave of lifeless, deathless bodies. I roared and inched forward, helpless, and suddenly the dead men were falling away, knocked down and thrown back. I turned and saw my father and Jacob, Adelaide and Brother McKillop, the whole group of prisoners now freed and lashing out with anything they could find. I nodded thanks, shook off the last few dead men like a spray of water and threw myself at Gideon, clamping him tight in a giant granite fist right as he raised the sword over Sister Hammond's bloody corpse. He hissed and spit like a cat.

"Let me go!" He was remarkably strong – stronger than all of the pale men he commanded, maybe stronger than all of them put together. "You're a monster, boy – we should be on the same side!"

"I'd rather be on her side," I said, looking down at Sister Hammond. "All you do is take life – she gave it."

He strained against my hand, but he was growing weaker – I could feel him shriveling up, like a weed in the sun. "She was a fool."

"And what are you?" I asked, looking at his face. "Your time is running out, isn't it? And your power with it. You're ten years older now than you were when I grabbed you, and twenty years older than you were when you picked up the sword. You need to take our lives, or lose your own."

His face seemed to wrinkle as he spoke. "I can take whatever I want – my Master won't allow me to fail."

"You serve a master who takes," I said, "and eventually he's going to take from you."

And then Gideon began to wither – not merely growing pale but shrinking, gathering in on himself like an apple left out to rot. The sword fell from his weakened hands, clattering on the ground; he curled and twisted, muscles and tissues contracting into a tight, brown corpse. Behind me the dead men fell, dropping where they stood, their animation suddenly lost. Gideon hissed weakly and I let him go. He fell to the ground and shattered.

WE WALKED home slowly, the girls riding the horses, the bodies of Brother Sutton and Brother Creedy dragging behind on a makeshift litter. We didn't say much. I figured maybe Rachel Sutton, her father dead and no beau waiting back home, wouldn't never say anything again.

"What are you going to do now?" asked Adelaide. I was walking beside her horse, leading the way at the head of the column. I wasn't stone no more, just regular, and I was wearing Brother Sutton's boots since mine had bust open. He didn't need them no more.

"I'll stay for the funerals," I said, "then head off."

"You're leaving?" She frowned. "I thought you weren't ashamed no more."

"I was ashamed before," I said, "and scared. I thought I had to leave so no one would have to live with my curse. Now that it's a gift, I figure I ought to leave so's I can spread it around."

"Just travel around? Helping people?"

"I reckon so. If you're right about me, and if I'm right about me, God wants me down here fighting his enemies. With Gideon gone I'd best move on and find the next one."

She smiled, and it was an awful pretty smile. I looked away.

"You're gonna come back, though, right? Just from time to time, I mean?"

I looked up at her. "I suppose so. Got to visit my family, maybe help with the harvest."

"Harvest social's in two months," she said, suddenly looking at the sky, or the trees – anywhere but at me. "You coming back for that?" She had black hair, black as a raven, and it rolled down her neck in waves so thick they looked like a shadow, half real and half a dream.

"I suppose I could," I said. "If I had a reason."

"I heard from Lena Metzger that you love gingerbread," said Adelaide. "I could make you some. *If* you was gonna be there."

I looked at the road ahead, and the sunbeams shining down like gold through the trees. My home, my friends and family – a place where everybody thought the best of you instead of the worst. "I think I can be there," I said. "Matter of fact I can't think of anything I want more."

CONTRIBUTORS

DAVIN ABEGG is a professional illustrator and designer. Amongst many other things, he enjoys illustrating children's books and designing posters for rock and roll shows. Davin currently resides in Layton, Utah, with his beautiful wife and daughters.

LEE ALLRED's award-winning short fiction has appeared in *Asimov's Science Fiction* magazine and several national market science fiction anthologies. He's also written for DC Comics and Image Comics. Lee does not believe in ghosts, phlogiston, or fry sauce.

S.P. BAILEY is a husband, father, son, brother, trial lawyer, bicycle rider, and fancy root beer/dark chocolate connoisseur. Even though the comments posted at the end of every online newspaper article confirm all of S.P.'s suspicions about the decline of civilization, he simply cannot resist them. Alma Knox – a mere literary fetus – quietly aspires to someday be, in the words of Raymond Chandler, "a complete man and a common man and yet an unusual man ... [A] man of honor, by instinct, by inevitability, without thought of it, and certainly without saying it ... [A man who] has a range of awareness that startles you, but it belongs to him by right, because it belongs to the world he lives in."

C. DOUGLAS BIRKHEAD hails from the suburbs of Oklahoma City. When he is not flying with the Air Force, he enjoys passing the time reading and writing fiction of all genres. He has been featured in a number of anthologies and literary journals. Recent credits include stories published in Static Movement's *Speculative Long Fiction* as well as 2013: *The Aftermath* from Pill Hill Press. He would love to hear from you with comments at rotodomeo1@gmail.com.

CONTRIBUTORS

WILL BISHOP was born and raised in Boise, ID. After a two-year stint as an LDS missionary in Spain's Canary Islands, he earned both a bachelor's and master's degree in humanities from Brigham Young University. He currently lives in Lawrence, Kansas, where he is working toward a PhD in American Studies from the University of Kansas. Will's poems have been featured in *The Fob Bible* and *Fire in the Pasture: 21st Century Mormon Poets*.

GRAHAM BRADLEY began writing at age eight. A resident of Henderson, Nevada, he's worked as a tire tech, a home renovator, a truck driver, a bookstore receiving lead, and a production manager for WallQuotes.com. In 2003 he served as a missionary in Barcelona, Spain, and has since taken an interest in a variety of cultures and languages. Primarily he writes young adult fiction with a sci-fi angle. He loves reading, cars, camping, wisecracking, and America. You can read more about his exploits at onagrahampage.blogspot.com.

EC BUCK is the product of a full and exciting life. She lived in a variety of places during her childhood, including, but not limited to, New York, Texas, and several Middle Eastern countries. She studied Arabic in college, but after graduation chose the career path that included marriage and babies. She still has adventures, though these days, since she spends her time mothering two young children at home, none of them include jumping off moving vehicles, Kuwaiti princes, or the pyramids. Her first novel was written at age thirteen and she hopes it will never see the light of day. Other works include some very bad poetry and a few moderately acceptable short stories. Her current project, a novel based heavily on Middle Eastern history and culture, has been in production in one form or another since 2001. She hopes to at least finish it before she dies. When she's not working on her novel or chasing after toddlers, she likes to wax eloquent about Middle Eastern politics, spin yarn on her spinning wheel, and practice karate.

JALETA CLEGG is a model Molly Mormon – she crochets, cans, cooks, bakes, sews, and quilts. But that is where the resemblance ends. She crochets Cthulhu toilet paper cozies, cans bizarre pickles and exotic jams, cooks dishes with names like snake surprise, bakes Klingon cookies, sews costumes for monsters and space aliens, and quilts Sunbonnet Cthulhu pillows. She also writes silly horror stories and science fiction adventure. Check out her stories at www.jaletac.com.

JIM CROCKETT lives in Sandy, Utah, with his wife and seven young trolls.

GALEN DARA used to hang out in the dark with her sketchbook, mining the nooks and crannies of her brain. Nowadays she keeps herself out of trouble illustrating for books and magazines and dabbling in comics. She has illustrations in *Rigor Amortis*, *Cthulhurotica*, *Crossed Genres*, *Sunstone*, *Broken Time Blues*, and the forthcoming *Fish* anthology. Galen blogs at the Functional Nerds, the Ink Punks, and The Exponent and she is the Art Director at Dagan books. galendara.com | miningthenooks.blogspot.com

BRANDON DAYTON developed a love for drawing at an early age. After his exposure to such animated films as *The Little Mermaid* and *Akira*, decided he would make drawing and storytelling his life's work. While enrolled in the film program at Brigham Young University, Brandon produced and directed four short films and was one of eighteen chosen to participate in Orson Scott Card's Writer's Bootcamp. Since 2004, Brandon has worked as a writer, animator, illustrator, storyboard artist, and Christmas-light hanger. His first self-published mini-comic, *Green Monk*, was nominated for the YALSA Great Graphic Novels for Teens Booklist. He currently works at EA Salt Lake as a concept artist. He lives in West Jordan, Utah with his wife, Annie and daughter, Lucy.

BRIAN GIBSON lives in Los Angeles, California, where he pursues the most noble of professions: Reality TV Producer. Please, don't hold that against him. He's done various other questionable things in his life, including originating the character Septimus H in the controversial fake-blog/writing experiment known as The Banner of Heaven. He was also a co-founder of the short-lived but nonetheless remarkable Mormon Lit blog Popcorn Popping. He has a forgiving wife and three beautiful daughters.

ADAM GREENWOOD's elaborate vocabulary and baroque humor derive from being bitten by a radioactive Wodehouse novel. Uxorious and philoprogenitive, he lives with his wife and daughters in central New Mexico near the ranch his great-grandfather lost in the Great Depression. He blogs at jrganymede.com. He is no longer accepting marriage proposals.

GEORGE WASHINGTON HILL was born in Athens, Ohio, in 1822. Raised a Lutheran, he joined the Mormon Church shortly after meeting his wife, Cyntha Stewart Utley, whom he married in 1845. Upon his arrival in the Salt Lake Valley, Brigham Young appointed Hill as an ambassador to the Native American peoples. He learned five Native American languages and was instrumental in averting several violent conflicts between the Mormon settlers and the indigenous populations. Amongst his many descendants, of which EC Buck is one, he is the stuff of legend. Aside from the incident with the bear, Hill also rescued Parley P. Pratt from plummeting to his death over a cliff, and very nearly met one of the Three Nephites.

THERIC JEPSON is grateful to Wm Morris for suggesting this anthology, the co-editing of which has removed from him the burden of finishing his own decade-old zombies-vs-missionaries manuscript. (Much as co-editing *The Fob Bible* – also available from Peculiar Pages – means he no longer has to write modern scripture.) Find Theric online by searching for sites sufficiently thmazing.

MORIAH JOVAN writes what her imaginary friends tell her to write. Thus far, they have shown up in the novels *The Proviso, Stay, Magdalene, Dunham, Paso Doble,* and *We Were Gods,* published by B10 Mediaworx. They will, most likely, continue to order her around until she hits on the right drug and dosage. Fortunately, her husband is very understanding of all the other people in her life and her children have no need of their own imaginary friends since they know all of mommy's. Moriah has a bachelor's in creative writing and journalism from the University of Missouri at Kansas City, and in 2011, she was a panelist at the Writer's Digest conference and the Sunstone Symposium. She is a flagrant dealer of the crack known as "ebooks."

D. MICHAEL MARTINDALE is a storyteller. It doesn't matter so much to him which medium he tells the story in – whether it be film or television or writing or music or stage – what's important is that he has the opportunity to tell stories that people will enjoy. Martindale served three years on the board of the Association for Mormon Letters and acted as their Writers Conference chairperson for four years. He's written a number of articles and book and film reviews for their literary journal *Irreantum.* He was also a staff writer for the online satirical publication "The Sugar Beet" for a time. Martindale is the author of the LDS novel *Brother Brigham,* the flagship publication of Zarahemla Books. He's currently in the process of completing the fantasy novel *Celeste and the White Dragon.* But his first love is filmmaking. He's filmed half a dozen short films, and wrote, produced, and directed the feature film *Geeks and Goblins, Elves and Elliot.* He's written several screenplays, and is in development on two of them, including adapting to the screen the LDS musical *General Prophet Joseph Smith* that he wrote in his youth. Most recently, he's developing with a colleague a science fiction television show called *Fringe Patrol.* Martindale currently resides in Salt Lake City, Utah, and is the father of three very intelligent, creative children.

TERRANCE V. McARTHUR is a librarian, storyteller, puppeteer, magician, basketmaker, and playwright, living in the great San Joaquin Valley, east of Fresno with his wife, his daughter, and a spinster cat.

EMILY MILNER mothers four children and writes for Blog Segullah. Her essays have appeared in *Segullah* and *Irreantum*. Once in a blue moon she also updates her personal blog, hearingvoices.wordpress.com. She has never met a ghost. Or a polygamist. Or a polygamous ghost.

WM MORRIS is the founder of the Mormon arts and culture blog A Motley Vision (motleyvision.org). He lives with his wife and daughter in Minnesota where he works in higher education marketing and public relations. He also explores the intersection of the literary and the fantastic at williamhenrymorris.com.

STEVE MORRISON was born in 1982 and has been drawing since he could wrap his fist around a crayon. He studied art and illustration, graduating from BYU with his BFA in 2006. Since then, his work has been published in a variety of venues by clients such as NPR, Pearson, Core Knowledge, and *National Storytelling Magazine*. His paintings have been exhibited in galleries from coast to coast. Steve has been freelancing for two years, and currently resides in South Carolina.

DANNY NELSON's short stories, columns, and poetry have appeared in publications such as *The Collegiate Post*, *Rio Grande Review*, and *Inscape*. He is a major contributor to *The Fob Bible*, published in 2009 by Peculiar Pages. He lives in Seattle, where he pursues a PhD in English Literature.

MATT PAGE is an award-winning freelance illustrator, graphic designer, and humor writer based in Salt Lake City. His work frequently appears in print and online. He was recently the subject of a feature profile in the *Salt Lake Tribune*. mattunderscorepage@gmail.com | about.me/mattpage

JAKE PARKER is a freelance illustrator, designer, and comic artist. He is the creator of the *Missile Mouse* graphic novel series published by Scholastic. For the last several years he worked for Blue Sky Studios creating sets and environments for feature films like *Horton hears a Who* and *Ice Age: Dawn of the Dinosaurs*. Now he lives in Utah with his wife and children working on picture books, comics, and other freelance projects.

CONTRIBUTORS

STEVEN L. PECK is an evolutionary ecologist at Brigham Young University where he teaches History and Philosophy of Science and Bioethics. His novel, *The Scholar of Moab*, is being published by Torrey House Press. A juvenile fiction book tentatively called *The Poetry of Spears*, is being published by Cedar Fort Press and will appear early next year. This year he was nominated for the 2011 Science Fiction Poetry Association's Rhysling Award for the best published long-form speculative poem. He received first place in the Warp and Weave Science Fiction Competition and received Honorable Mention in the 2011 Brookie and D.K. Brown Fiction Contest. His poetry has appeared in *Bellowing Ark, BYU Studies, Dialogue, Glyphs III, Irreantum, Pedestal Magazine, Red Rock Review, Tales of the Talisman*, Victorian Violet Press, Wilderness Interface Zone, and other places. He hopes to live long enough to get to Mars.

ERIK PETERSON (docmagik@gmail.com or @docmagik) is a graduate of Orson Scott Card's Literary Boot Camp. His fiction has appeared in *The Leading Edge*. Erik served an LDS mission in Manaus, Brazil. He is now married with two children and lives in Rialto, California. His story may or may not be based on actual events.

WILUM HOPFROG PUGMIRE has been writing since he was a wee LDS gay boy who wrote road shows (music and lyrics) for his ward. He served a mission in Ireland, Arizona, and Las Vegas, after which he was promptly excommunicated for being Fabulous. He was re-baptized 25 years later. His books for 2011 include *The Tangled Muse, Some Unknown Gulf of Night, Gathered Dust and Others*, and *The Strange Dark One*. He is the Queen of Eldritch Horror.

JOHN NAKAMURA REMY is a graduate of the Clarion West 2010 workshop. He is the winner of Sunstone's 1999 Brookie and D.K. Brown Memorial Fiction Contest and the 2006 Capener Writing Contest. His fiction has appeared in the *Rigor Amortis* and *Broken Time Blues* anthologies and is forthcoming in *Pseudopod*. He has blogged at mindonfire.com since 2001, and can be found on Twitter (@johnremy) and on Flickr.

SCOTT M. ROBERTS is a man who has done despicable things with a spoon. When not indulging in silverware debauchery, he writes science fiction, fantasy, and horror. His work may be found in *Orson Scott Card's Intergalactic Medicine Show* and in the 2005 *Writers of the Future* anthology. Scott lives in northern Virginia with his family and a motley troupe of wizards, detectives, and crazy persons.

BRYTON SAMPSON was born in Salt Lake City and has lived there the whole time. This is the first of what he hopes will be many published works of fiction. By day he creates short films, and his voice can be heard on the weekly comic-book review podcast, Fight for Comics. He has a pretty good memory and makes fine hamburgers. When he needs inspiration he takes to the open roads of Utah, his favorite state.

NATHAN SHUMATE has wasted more than ten years of his life watching and reviewing B-movies, the reviews of which can be found on his website. His first book, *The Golden Age of Crap*, focuses on movies that found their audience during the home video rental boom of the '80s and '90s. He is also the author of the short novel *The Demon Cross* and editor of the weird horror magazine *Arcane*, billed as "Penny Dreadfuls for the 21st Century." He blogs at NathanShumate.com.

BC STERRETT is director of The Lost Media Archive, programs films for The Salt Lake City Film Festival, portrays a woman in the recent "Craft Lady" webisodes for Roberts Arts and Crafts store, works in a bookstore warehouse, is working toward being a college professor in film history and does comics, puppets, music, and media archeology projects on the side. His current graphic novel series "Simeon" can be found in local comic books stores around Utah.

A Nebula Award winner, Hugo Award nominee, and winner in the Writers of the Future Contest, **ERIC JAMES STONE** has had stories published in *Year's Best SF 15*, *Analog*, *Nature*, and Kevin J. Anderson's *Blood Lite* anthologies of humorous horror, among other venues. One of Eric's earliest memories is of seeing an Apollo moon-shot launch on television. That might explain his fascination with space travel. His father's collection of old science fiction ensured that Eric grew up reading Asimov, Heinlein, and Clarke. While getting his political science degree at Brigham Young University, Eric took creative writing classes. He wrote several short stories, and even submitted one for publication, but after it was rejected he gave up on creative writing for a decade. During those years Eric graduated from Baylor Law School, worked on a congressional campaign, and took a job in Washington, DC. He quit the political scene in 1999 to work as a web developer in Utah. In 2002 he started writing fiction again, and in 2003 he attended Orson Scott Card's Literary Boot Camp. In 2007 Eric got laid off from his day job just in time to go to the Odyssey Writing Workshop. He has since found a new web development job. Eric has been an assistant editor for Intergalactic Medicine Show since 2009.

CONTRIBUTORS

Rejiggering the Thingamajig and Other Stories, a collection containing most of Eric's early stories, came out from Paper Golem Press in 2011. Eric lives in Eagle Mountain, Utah. His website is www.ericjamesstone.com.

BRIDGETTE DAY TUCKFIELD enjoys writing and monsters and graduating in 2011, in any order.

TERRESA WELLBORN is a bricoleur, librarian, and cartographer of words. She is fond of the color blue, rock gardens, and chocolate chip waffles. She has a BA in English Literature from Brigham Young University and an MLIS degree from San Jose State University. Her writing has appeared in *Segullah* and is forthcoming in *Inscape* as well as *Fire in the Pasture: 21st Century Mormon Poets*. She is writing her way to a book.

DAN WELLS is the author of several supernatural thrillers, including *I Am Not a Serial Killer, Mr. Monster,* and *I Don't Want to Kill You.* He is a co-host on the podcast Writing Excuses, for which he has won two Parsec awards; his podcast has been nominated for a Hugo this year, and Dan has been nominated for a Campbell award for best new writer. He plays a lot of games, reads a lot of books, and eats a lot of food, which is pretty much the ideal life he imagined for himself as a child.

DAVID J. WEST is a family man and an award-winning writer in the grandest of pulp tradition. In addition to his speculative historical novels, *Heroes of the Fallen* and *Blood of Our Fathers*, he has a number of weird westerns, heroic fantasies, horror, and sci-fi short stories published in various anthologies. He collects truths, swords, the finest art he can afford, as well as a library of 6,000+ volumes because he likes the smell of old books. You can visit him at david-j-west.blogspot.com.

A graduate of Brigham Young University and the University of Southern Maine, **KATHERINE WOODBURY** has had stories published in a variety of science fiction and fantasy magazines, including *Leading Edge, Tales of the Unanticipated, Andromeda Spaceways,* and *Space & Time.* She has also published two novellas electronically: *A Man of Few Words* and *Mr. B Speaks!* To pay the rent, Katherine (or Kate) teaches composition and folklore at local community colleges. In her free time, she watches *Star Trek* and *Stargate* plus lots of mystery shows, takes books out of the library (and forgets to return them), and posts to her blog: katewoodbury.blogspot.com. Kate (or Katherine) can be reached at woodburykate@yahoo.com.